TIN OX GLOVE

A Draining Play

RANDY SANDERS

PRESS

For information contact :
randysandersbooks.com

Book and Cover design by Randy Sanders
Untouched cover photo provided by David Papillion, cc0 Unsplash.
Graphic pyramid designed by David Myers.
Dedication vectors provided by Kristy Pargeter and Xolo Piks, via Vecteezy
ISBN: 978-1-7345912-8-6

First Edition: April 2019

Printed before the formation of the Starnet Union

03 14 15 92 65 35 89 79 32 38

Dedicated to the Omni Rangers

This Psychic Song Is For You

Contents

Contents

CHAPTER 1

I awoke on the large circular bed with my head hammering. What the hell just happened? I was in my bedroom on *Tiger Mountain*. The circular bed was ridiculously large, think double king-size, and I was in the center of it. I scooted to the edge of the bed to get up.

To my left, a doorway revealed the large marble shower and bathroom. Directly in front of me were wardrobe drawers built into the wall, with a wide mirror hanging above. I walked over to the vertical window and looked across the landscape of *Tiger Mountain*. The window was very tall, a narrow three meters of glass. As I took in the view, I could see a hill not far from here, where a small gazebo stood. In the past, I used the gazebo as a meeting place for friends or visitors who lived "off mountain." Because this home was built into the side of a cliff, I could look down from this window and see the sudden drop-off realizing this house was perched very high on the cliffside.

I was still in a state of confusion over what just happened. Something did happen, but I wasn't sure what? I made a quick inspection of myself and noticed I was fully dressed. I wondered why I was here, at *Tiger Mountain*, when I should be aboard one of the starships where my wives serve? I felt like I was a different person in some new body or a new conscious overlay in an existing body. I began to doubt whether this place was real. It seemed a little cliché, but I wondered if I were awake in a dream?

A voice from the other room called out, "Hello?"

The bedroom doorway led to the open area between the sunken living room on the right and the modern kitchen on the left. A long curving counter was the divider between the kitchen and the walkway on the left that ended at the porch balcony. The counter was quite long and made of polished stone. High back stools lined one side, with a young African woman in her early twenties sitting at the end. In a second, I knew it was Candy. She looked at me and stood up as I entered, asking, "Is something wrong?"

"Did something just happen?"

I took in her expression as she speculated on the correct answer, giving me the impression that she might be deciding whether to lie. She looked off to the left, up, then back at me before saying, "I think so, but I don't know what."

"Whew. I thought it was just me. Do you know who I am?"

She cocked her head with a smile and said, "Yes. You're Sam. Have you been smokin' again?"

Without thinking, I tilted my head down to smell my clothes. I didn't smell any smoke on them, so I said, "I don't think so, but I don't really feel like myself. Something has changed."

"I feel it too," she said, and when I looked her in the eyes, I could see that she might be in the same boat I am.

"I wonder if a change to my identity has occurred?"

"So, who am I?"

A small smile came to my face as I realized how much I liked Candy, finally saying, "You're Candice."

"Yeah, but you always call me Candy, which I don't mind."

"What were we just doing?"

"I can't remember."

"I can't either."

Candy looked up to the ceiling and asked while shaking her head, "Ohm, what were Sam and I doing ten minutes ago?"

A pleasant synthetic voice seemed to ride on the air and stated, "You sat at the kitchen bar having a drink while Sam slept in the bedroom."

"Ohm, is it?" I queried the disembodied synthetic voice, "Can you verify the number of people in this room?"

"Yes, the number of people in this room is two. You and Candy," the synthetic voice stated.

"And who am I?" I asked sheepishly.

"You are Sam," Ohm replied with a brief pause, "my creator."

It was then that I finally identified how Ohm was communicating. The air around my head softly modulated to convey a voice. I noticed the slightest pressure drop as Ohm's last words faded.

"How can you know it's me?"

"Using voice recognition and transmitter detection," the voice went on.

"What transmitter?" I asked, slowly fearing the answer to that question.

"The one placed inside your brain," Ohm stated.

"I have a transmitter inside my brain? Who put it there?"

The voice answered, "Yes. Xanadu technicians installed your transmitter. Your first brain implant was installed three hundred and fifty-seven years, six months, and twenty-seven days ago. Splendor time, of course."

"Of course," I repeated, not exactly knowing what that meant.

"Several upgrades have occurred over time as new technology was discovered and deemed safe enough for use by you and the Guardians. Complete replacements swaps have occurred three times as the interface evolved. Most updates involve software running through the interface, but nineteen hardware modifications have been made, with the last update to the hardware taking place twenty-two months ago."

"What was the last modification to my interface?"

"The Blinn presented a revised bio fiber conduit that was stronger, smaller, and presented an increased cranial bandwidth compression rate of four point two percent, putting the improvement over the three percent threshold for new candidate considerations. This revised hardware was installed into your interface, and all Guardian interfaces," Ohm stated.

"You mentioned the Guardians before. Who are they?"

"The Guardians are *Tiger Mountain* citizens, your friends, that have pledged their lives and allegiance to the protection of *Tiger Mountain*. This commitment comes with an interface installed into the brain near the Broca area and the Temporal lobe. From there, a bio fiber conduit is woven outward onto the motor and sensory strips to allow the interface to relay information to the visual cortex. This information presents itself as an overlay to your normal vision. An invisible heads-up display, you once called it. The interface is probabilistically stable, so Guardians are not required to remain on *Tiger Mountain*. They may travel in various echoes and still receive updates through their invisihuds. The invisihud allows communication between the Guardians even if they are indifferent echoes," Ohm said.

Echoes, I thought. That was a Splendorite word. It was the word used to describe the result of chaos shining through the *Motif*. The *Motif* is an unchanging form that chaos constantly tries to erode. It is essentially the opposite of chaos. Instead of changing all the time, it never changes and is always the same. This interplay of chaos and the *Motif* makes up all the probabilities in every possible time and place. Imagine that chaos is a spotlight, and the *Motif* is a mask filtering the ever-changing input. The result of that masking is echo. As echoes ripple farther from the *Motif*, the form they take on blurs along the edges until the places farthest from the *Motif* have no bearing in shape or substance to the original form that generated them.

Candy looked at me, listening to Ohm's report, and gave a raised eyebrow. She was incredibly hot, but Candy was an all-girl player. Our relationship was not that of lovers, but it came close at times. Since then, we settled on remaining friends after being separated for some time, which caused me to wonder. Why was she here in the first place?

Once again, I was confused by the concept of I. Was I Sam or the overlay? I addressed Ohm as I walked around the long countertop to face Candy from the other side. This side was a service bar, laid out restaurant-style, and I asked, "Ohm, can you show me a condensed log of the sensor data for this location over the last four hours?"

"Certainly. Standard sensors, or are you looking for something specific?"

"Let's start with the standard sensor data."

A flood of kinetic data utterly shocked my cerebral senses. My vision overflowed with color, lights, and lines. There were blocks, spheres, and spheres within spheres surrounded by rings that thickened and thinned. Numbers and letters flowed out of them as the geometry jumped and bobbled into place. When the spheres settled, they left trails taking on lives of their own, changing to represent data over time. The letters formed headings that rotated every three to five seconds or traveled along the lines with the data paths they were attached to. This animation sprang to life in a one hundred and eighty-degree field of view in front of me. I was overwhelmed and staggered forward, catching myself on the edge of the bar.

"Turn it off!" I yelled, bent over, with my head facing down toward the sink.

The data streams faded from view, and the geometric shapes packaged themselves up, retreating out of view with a springboard-style effect.

"All right," Candy said, "I know something is goin' on here. You mean to tell me that this is normal? You're not actin' right, and I don't even know what just happened to you right now. Ohm, what is wrong with Sam?"

"Checking," Ohm replied.

"General health is normal, DNA match is exact, scans reveal no foreign or parasitic influence is taking place. His brain chemistry is a little off, indicating a slight state of anxiety."

"Slight," Candy said sarcastically. "Send me the sensor data that Sam requested."

"The requested sensor data contains packets requiring authorization," Ohm stated.

Candy gave me that look, nonverbally asking, "Well?"

"Remove the restricted data packets from the stream and send the rest to Candy," I said as I stood up and regained my composure.

What happened next was eerie. A glazed look came over Candy's face as she received the data. It was as if she looked past what was in front of her, focusing on unseen things. Her eyes moved, blinked, and darted here and there while sometimes drifting slowly. This trance went on for about a minute before a set of rapid blinks brought her back to a more normal expression.

"I don't see nuthin' in there," she stated as she held up both her hands, offering a small shrug before picking up her drink and sipping on the straw. "Whatever is going on is just you."

"But you just said something was up with you a few minutes ago."

"Somethin' is goin' on, but I just don't know what."

"So, you know that you are yourself and have always been yourself?"

"Yes, I am myself," she emphasized while going on. "I feel like myself, and I think like myself. But there was a moment where I was like, what just happened?"

"How did you get here?" I asked. "Where were you before you came to my house?"

She looked at me with a huff and a pout saying, "All right, I don't know."

"Don't know what?"

"I don't know how I got here. I was just here. The last place I remember was," Candy trailed off. "I feel like it is right on the tip of my tongue. But I can't put my finger on it. I feel like I was far away, then I was here, but no travel was involved. I guess I transported."

"Ohm, do I have a favorite or typical coffee drink?"

"Yes," said the synthetic voice.

"May I please have one?"

"Certainly."

A bright set of sparkles quickly appeared and faded on the counter. A white ceramic diner-style coffee mug with steaming hot liquid was left behind. I picked up the coffee mug and took a small sip of the hot drink. It was delicious, exactly how I liked my black coffee. I closed my eyes and took a moment to taste it. I could taste it. I was on *Tiger Mountain* drinking replicated coffee with Candy. I was still in awe that I was actually here as I opened up my eyes again.

"Looks like you needed that," Candy said. "Maybe you just woke up on the wrong side of the bed?"

"What side is the wrong side of a circular bed?" I asked, and she cracked a smile. "Ohm, what could cause an event, such as the one we are experiencing now? An event where there is no evidence a change has occurred, but a mental impression of change remains within the participants of the event?"

"Checking," Ohm replied before quickly stating. "The following could be possible causes of such events. Records have been tampered with, hallucination among participants of the event, living in an auragraphic environment and forgetting it is not real, self from future alters past self, participants do not realize they are dreaming, a psychic attack upon participants, confusing them."

I interrupted, "Stop," and Ohm stopped reporting.

"Future self alters past self," I said slowly and out loud as Candy met my eyes.

I took another sip of coffee and set the mug on the counter between Candy and myself. Putting both hands on the counter, I leaned in to look Candy directly in the face. "I do have memories of a probable future. That makes this the past. That other place I remember must be the time I came from."

Candy looked at me with her beautiful serious, brown eyes and said, "It feels right, Sam. So, who I was, is now in the future? But that doesn't sound right, either."

We both leaned back and took a breath considering the possibility.

"We're in the past. This moment is the past," I said softly.

"Yeah," Candy said under her breath, "What a trip. Where are our past selves?"

"Ohm, can you refresh us on Minekey's law?"

Ohm began. "Malardin Minekey was a Selurian physicist who postulated two models of time travel were possible. The physical model is where a body transports through time. In the other model, consciousness is transferred back in time to overlay upon its younger self. This mode would be a one-way direction, always from future to past. While this could limit certain temporal paradoxes, it could also enable..."

"Thank you, Ohm," I said before turning to Candy. "Maybe this confusion we are experiencing is a side effect of a future consciousness overlay to the past. We may be in our past selves' bodies. Which means we are our past selves. And if this is really true, then whoever sent our consciousness back must not be that far into the future. While I have a longer life span, you don't. I'm guessing thirty or forty years into the future, tops?"

"That is still a long time. And who would do such a thing anyway?" Candy asked.

"Probably us or me, I would guess."

"But why?"

"Because our future lives ended up in such bad shape that we decided to abandon them and try again. A type of do-over, hoping to avoid the mistakes. Which is the classic definition of the 'grandfather' temporal paradox taught at the Starnet Academy."

"But you said you remembered the future. Do you remember doing this to us?"

"No, that does not stand out in my future memories."

"If you don't remember doing it, then maybe someone else did this to us."

"Or we encountered some temporal anomaly together and experienced this shift. But I don't recall an accident either."

"So, what? An enemy took us by surprise and temporally transported here? And why here, why now?"

"I don't think it would be an enemy. Quite an elaborate way to get rid of someone. And we would not be guaranteed to be out of their life for good. I mean, we could just move forward through time and encounter the enemy again. I am leaning more toward the possibility we did this to ourselves for some reason."

"Ohm, did you do this to us?" Candy asked.

The synthetic voice replied, "No, I did not. I have no temporal-based technology at my disposal."

"But you might encounter the technology in the future," I said.

"Correct," Ohm replied.

"Can you check the sensor logs for any field variations that may have occurred in the last hour?"

"Checking," Ohm said. "Localized tachyon emissions were detected twenty-three minutes ago at this location."

"Ohm, analyze the tachyon emissions and look for any modulation patterns or technology signatures that might be present in the emission."

"Tachyon emissions contain overtones typically produced by a Scree Etch Ack Accelerator. This technology is known to be used by the Gilliux Hive," Ohm stated.

"Ugh, Gilliux," I said. "They might not care about sending people from other races back in time. We don't understand them that much. They are an overly large insect race that thrives in high-temperature environments. Starnet has a treaty with them but no real commerce or trade. They tightly guard their technology and have only shared it on rare occasions when attending inter-species galactic conferences."

"You mean, the Gilliux zapped our future selves into the past? What about our future bodies? Are we just laying somewhere in a vegetable state waiting to die?"

"I believe the rest of the Minekey theory states that consciousness forms the reality it perceives. The future, as we know it, no longer exists. Our bodies no longer exist to return to," I said with a frown.

"Ohm, I want to create a new rule. Please extend your current profile to include mentions of any type of time-travel discussions among *Tiger Mountain* citizens or off-mountain probable locations. Also, include if any tachyon emissions are detected. Notify me if this rule produces any hits."

"Me too," Candy added.

"New rule enabled and active," Ohm stated.

"I need some air," I said, and I made my way out to the wide balcony overlooking the vast virtual landscape of *Tiger Mountain*.

My house sits atop the highest mountain within the *Tiger Mountain* virtual landscape. It has a Frank Lloyd Wright feel to it with exposed stone inside and recessed floors. Made mostly of straight lines gives it a box-like rectangular appearance from the outside. The house is propped up on the cliffside by various beams conveying a precarious look. The only way for visitors to enter the house is via a stone bridge leading to the front door. This house is considered a protected area by *Tiger Mountain*, and teleportation into the home is not permitted. The home is continuously monitored, so even if unauthorized persons could find a way into the house, they would be immediately transported out. There is a large stone balcony where you can observe a breathtaking view of the valley floor below. This balcony is where I stood. Off in the distance, virtual city buildings can be seen while the gorge containing the water supply acts as a horizon line dotted by the evenly spaced hubs incasing and protecting the crystals powering the entire system.

From a distance, *Tiger Mountain* appears as an upsidedown teardrop or a right side up spinning top. The top surface area of *Tiger Mountain* covers several square kilometers surrounded by a trench containing the system's water supply. This production floor is where all the residents live. Below that is the necessary equipment to facilitate daily operations. Covering this surface is a dome of auragraphic emitters that project a virtual environment. Positioned at evenly spaced intervals around the outer edge are twelve gigantic crystals providing power for the entire system. And by gigantic, I mean each crystal is easily as large as a typical two-story house. Within the material making up the infrastructure of the crystal are microsized machines whose only task is to constantly repair the structure to keep it in ideal operational form.

The production floor continuously replicates any type of environment imaginable. There are many pre-programmed experiences where you can take a virtual vacation. You can visit historical or fictional places, live a life of luxury or poverty, be a hero from a story, or anything else you can imagine. Random generators are available that will mix and match from various cultures to make entirely new adventures for you. You can share an adventure with friends or venture out on your own.

I heard Candy walk up behind me and ask, "What do we do now?"

"The million-dollar question, eh?" I replied. "I don't know what else we can do other than just live forward from this point on."

"So, you remember the future where you just came from?"

I turned around to face her and said, "Yeah, I do. Don't you?"

Candy looked down at the ground and back up before saying, "No, I don't remember anything other than what has already happened."

She paused and asked sheepishly, "Am I in your future memories, Sam?"

"Yeah, and something wonderful has happened for you."

Her mood lifted at hearing this, and she put on a slight smile before asking, "For real? Like what?"

"I had better not say. A lot has to go right from this point on to end up in that boat."

"How long do I have to wait?"

"Who knows? I feel overwhelmed. I have to rebuild my life and try not to mess anything up to get back to where I was. It could take years."

"Years," Candy said as she rolled her eyes.

"Yes. So, I might as well get started," I replied. "Ohm, transport me to the vault."

The world around me collapsed in from the sides, placing me in darkness for an undetermined amount of time. While I waited, I wondered how any of this could actually be happening? Am I a conscious overlay? Am I still Sam, or could I simply fade from existence? A dim light flooded my vision as I materialized in a large cluttered room.

CHAPTER 2

The vault is a place inside *Tiger Mountain* where no one else was allowed. It was strictly off-limits to everyone on *Tiger Mountain*, including the Guardians. Like my house, it was also continuously scanned for intruders. If anyone is detected in the vault, they are placed in a cryogenic virtual reality sleep chamber, and Ohm notifies me. This event has never happened, so I feel about as confident as I can that no one visits this place except me. There are no doors or windows, and the only way in or out is through some method of technical transport or magical *Exspiravition*.

The vault is the size of a large gymnasium with a high ceiling. In the center is a large rectangular box table with different-sized drawers along all the sides. It is lit from above with several hanging area lights. The room contains various objects and shelves cluttered with items. In the corner stands a large armored mechanical suit. This human armored mechanical suit, or H.A.M. suit, is the very first technical item I managed to get to work throughout echo. It functions, even in Splendor, which is the most difficult of tasks because Splendor is not an echo but the generator of echo. To make an echo-based technology function to spec in a realm that generates echoes was a considerable accomplishment.

As I walked through the room, I saw various weapons, jewelry, artwork, books, and other items that were important to me at one time. While many were sentimental items, most of the things stored in this vault were here to keep them from falling into the hands of people who may misuse them. I found myself getting caught up in the history of the items on these shelves. Some were objects I put to good use while adventuring through this immortal life. Once the adventure was over, or the item was no longer of use, it was placed in the vault to keep it safe. There were also confiscated items I intended to return to individuals, but most of the owners of those confiscated items were probably dead by now.

I turned a corner and there, on a pedestal, was a lock of blonde hair suspended inside a glass bell jar. A small light illuminated Edna's hair from above. Edna was one of my true loves. I lived with her in a high mountain cottage hundreds and hundreds of years ago. I was with her most of her life, from her early twenties until the day she died in her late seventies. I spent all my time with her, hunting, fishing, farming, and maintaining the homestead while we grew old together. The problem was, I never grew old, but Edna did. One of the curses of being an immortal Splendorite is that fertility is not a strong point. I never had children with Edna or anyone for that matter.

With a deep breath, I gulped, trying not to get sucked into the nostalgia in this place. Moving past the bell jar, I saw an easel that was also one of those folding carrying cases for your paints. These were the first paints I infused with the *Motif*, a skill taught to me by my great aunt. Lexi taught me to create vignettes for people and places long, long ago. If she knew then, what I would do with that skill, she probably would have never gifted me with her craft. Behind the easel, another long shelf contained singles and packs of vignette cards. Some of these were obtained from family members I have tangled with over the years, but just as many were ones I created either by hand or later by automation once the blank probability canvas became functional. Yes, the secret to probable inter-dimensional transportation was the lowly or mighty vignette. This fact was a closely guarded secret, and I never told anyone exactly how *Tiger Mountain* worked. I rifled through the various cards and placed a few of them in several of the pockets of my shirt and pants. The pocket sizes seemed to be a perfect fit for these cards.

As I rummaged through the vignette selection, I came upon a drawstring bag near the center of the shelf. This bag is why I returned to the vault. I opened it up and pulled out the mechanism inside. It was a flat plate, about the size of a compact disc player with some flexible headgear plugged into the side. While looking around the room, I noticed a chair, a table, and a lamp. I guess, once, I actually spent some time sitting in here. I walked over and took a seat, placing the disc player on the table while I donned the headset and got comfortable in the chair. There was no indication the headset "locked" anything into place. It just sat on my head like a floppy hat.

I took a moment to think about what I was really doing. I still did not understand exactly what was going on. Was I some invader stealing Sam's consciousness? Candy thought I was Sam, and Ohm digitally verified my DNA record as the same as Sam's. Maybe I am Sam, and something has slipped or changed in my mind? The new memories I have would be from Sam's future. These memories seem to span two or more time loops. But how can information be transferred into a new time loop? By definition, when the time loop starts over, any information gained in the past loop would be lost. Typically, I would say that no one can be outside the time loop, but a probability traveler might be able to locate a reality that could satisfy that condition. Time, to a probability traveler, is not necessarily linear. I put my head in my right hand as I propped it up against the arm of the chair and thought, "How can I ever hope to get my life back to where it was?"

I faced hundreds of possible options and hundreds of areas where I could make a mistake. I knew of a few things I could do right away, but most of what I needed to accomplish required travel throughout echo. The only way to gain that ability was to engage the *Motif*. Ohm monitors all known *Motif* locations. There is Darwin's *Motif* and Grayson's *Motif*, which I nicknamed the rose *Motif* because of the shape. It is well known that only a Splendorite can engage the

Motif. Others have tried over the centuries, but all non-royal candidates ended up dead or dissolved in their attempt to engage the etheric line. That is what the *Motif* is, an unchanging etheric line fixed in its shape. It defies traditional Starnet scanning methods, so its true composition is unknown. While I was confident that past Sam could physically engage the *Motif,* as the present overlay personality, I was not so sure. I didn't want to bet this life that the *Motif* wouldn't reject me. That's what this device is for. It is a recording Sam made years ago while engaging the *Motif.*

This recording, when played back, once transferred the ability to travel through probability to the viewer of the recording. This device was invented over seven hundred and fifty years ago. I investigated a technology to improve log resolution, like an advanced sensory recording system. I considered the most grueling test of the recording system would be the harsh journey of engaging the *Motif.*

I chose Grayson's *Motif.* It felt a little less sharp and, in my opinion, was a slightly shorter experience. Once the *Motif* engagement was complete, I played the recording back to review the result. It looked like it worked. Later that evening, I shared the recording with my wife, Teela. There was a seedy feel to the tech. It stimulated the senses with data while mildly depositing tiny doses of a drug to enhance the experience. The drug expanded the spectrum of the senses to convince the brain the data was real.

"It's so real," Teela said as the playback began. "I can't believe I am actually doing this."

"I'm starting the strand. Oh god, it's in me. Damn, you have big feet. I can feel it, the rise in energy all around. I feel resistance to my steps. I mean, your steps," she spoke slowly.

"The resistance will increase as you slide along the strand. To continue, slide along it, push against it. But we can turn this off at any time," I let her know.

"I'm pushing, or you are pushing. It's working. I am understanding as I proceed. The strand itself is not just some design. It is the deposited knowledge of the creator of the *Motif.* Each step reveals and unpacks this knowledge. I can feel the transfer to my mind. I am becoming the *Motif,*" she said while breaking a sweat.

I remember being a little worried at this point. I imagined it would affect her like many of the other recordings we viewed. In those recordings, you were a sight-seeing tourist in a realistic environment. But something told me this was going a little too far.

"Why don't we turn it off?" I suggested.

"No, I'm okay, and I have almost made it to the end. It is all making sense to me, everything. I see how echo, chaos, and the *Motif* are all interwoven," she said in a forced manner.

Her face grimaced, and she leaned forward while opening her mouth, saying, "Ahhhhhh!"

I knew she pushed through the final penumbra before the end of the *Motif.* Right before my eyes, she vanished, and the headgear she wore plopped down on the couch. I was alone.

It hadn't occurred to me that a virtual experience of engaging the *Motif* was enough to grant the recipient of the experience the ability to travel through echo, to probability travel at will. But that seemed to be the case and later proved to be true. Teela could travel through echo after experiencing the recording, and the device made her immortal. The last time I checked, she was as old as I was, around eight hundred and thirty years old. It's hard to know for sure with the way time fluctuates from echo to echo. She could be much older than me by now.

This unexpected discovery was too big to keep to myself. At the time, I was still young, only eighty or ninety. I took this information to the King of Splendor, so he could know it was possible to "create" new probability travelers who held no allegiance to the throne.

Osric is the name of the King of Splendor that I pledged my allegiance to, as has every other probability traveler born from the line of Omer, son of Darwin. After completing my first engagement of the *Motif*, Osric and his wife Violet invited Teela and me to stay, supplying chambers in the castle for our lodging. We became close like family. This news was shocking to him, but he made no rash decisions. Teela and I both went before him together. I felt this was the best way to present this startling new information. On the spot, Teela took an oath and pledged her fealty to King Osric. I pledged to destroy the technology, and we both promised never to mention the incident again.

Well, we can see how that turned out. Instead of destroying the technology, I decided to create a place where the technology could be kept safe and unavailable to anyone. This safe place changed locations over the years, from hidden chambers to secret rooms and difficult-to-reach caves. Part of the reason for building *Tiger Mountain* was to provide a place where this device could be kept safe and out of reach. This vault is the final incarnation of the place that keeps the technology safe. I did keep my word about never mentioning it to anyone. I'm not sure if Teela did, however?

The recording worked once. Would it work again? Would it work for me? I cued up the recording and pressed play.

With a slight fritz and fizzle, my perception was janked around until it accepted a new input stream as the dominant signal. I felt the drug from the device coat my brain. It was like someone pouring a warm liquid over your head. I sat in the chair, but a larger part of my perception was driven by the data stream playback. I was outside. The air was crisp and very clear, with a light smell of pine in the breeze. I faced a large stone outcropping that looked like part of some ancient clam falling open. The bottom part was a flat stone shelf, while the top part of the open clam jutted up like coastal rock. Hovering above the stone shelf was the *Motif*. From this distance, it appeared as glowing purple neon with fine wisps rising.

On the left side of the rocky outcrop, there was a set of ramps and a railing. I chuckled to myself as the recording proceeded to move me along the ramp and up to the platform. I placed these ramps and rails here after the first time I engaged Grayson's *Motif*. It was such a bitch to climb up to the starting point. At the top of all the ramps that switch back and forth a couple of times was a relief plaque carved in the classic style of the U.S. Parks and Wildlife Department. It stated this was Grayson's *Motif*, and visitors should not approach the glowing line. A green metal trashcan and a small supply of faded pamphlets sat under a hinged glass lid below the plaque.

In the recording, it looks like I took a moment to really take in the majesty of the platform. From this position, it no longer looked like a clam at all. Grayson's *Motif* hovered above a completely flat surface with a glass-like look of polished stone. It was now more evident that the purple glow emitted from this single long strand occupying a large area, forming an intricate design whose entirety could only be viewed from above. The *Motif* cast a significant glow along the angled back wall. It, too, was polished and held a soft blurry reflection of the *Motif* within.

As I approached the *Motif*, I noticed I became a blurry reflection on the wall. There was a soft hum emanating from the glowing line, like the sound of a faulty transformer. Hovering above the floor at chest height, the purple strand was as thick as a small tube, about the size of half-inch PVC plumbing pipe. The strand was not perfectly round at any one point. It seemed to have a random-ness scattered along its length. Nowhere along the tube could you find a section similar to another part of the strand. It appeared as a series of distinct shapes stacked along the tube's length, with a master craftsman lofting a mystical sur-face between them.

The first shape of the strand was obvious. It took the form of a triangle. Being the first shape at the start of the strand, there was no other shape to loft to, so it collapsed to a point. I aligned my chest with the tip of the strand and took a step forward.

With the quickness of a striking snake, or a magnet jumping to a compan-ion, the tip of the strand dove into my heart, and a purple glow started expand-ing outward around the entry point. I pushed forward onto the strand, impaling myself, trying to force the etheric strand through my body. A plume of my blood flowed out, filling the interior of the strand as I mixed with the purple substance making up the *Motif*. Taking a step forward, I felt the tip slide out of my back. The tone of the *Motif* adjusted slightly, giving the impression I was integrating into some master equation, with the net result being the revised sound I heard.

As I looked down, taking the first step, I noticed that Teela was right. I do have big feet, or at least Sam does.

It is of the most critical importance to keep moving forward and not mis-step while engaging the *Motif*. You are basically acting as a conduit between the hovering etheric form and the solid world from which you originate. Each step deposits a blood copy of the etheric original on the floor behind you. Your footsteps must fall below the original hovering design, or gaps will appear in the deposited line of blood. It is important to keep the strand aligned with your heart. If you drift out of alignment, the magnetic attachment you experience upon entry will fail. In this case, you are repelled from the strand and left to bleed out through the hole in your heart. If you pause or stop for too long during the process, the purple ether expands, dissolving your body into the *Mo-tif*'s eternal glow.

The *Motif* will not allow everyone to engage it. Only members of the royal family hold that privilege. This detail is why people who were not of the Omer family line but wanted to engage the *Motif* ended up repelled or dissolved. In the Splendor library, there is a long list of cousins and distant relatives who wanted to test their "blood worthiness" by betting their lives they could become the first outside of the immediate family to claim the right to travel through probability. There is something in the family blood the glowing strand recognizes. If your lineage is too far removed, the *Motif* doesn't "know you," and the magnetic strand attraction fails somewhere during the process.

The *Motif* took a sharp turn to the left after a few steps, and I began the wide arc defining the outer section before it curves in on itself. The arc was not perfect. In fact, there were many minor variations where the line would briefly wander to the left then back to the right. This meandering process conveyed a sense that the person who drew the *Motif* was buffeted by winds as they attempted to create a straight line or a smooth curve.

It is about halfway through this wide arc when the engagee encounters the first penumbra. Until then, you are just traversing distance while depositing a blood trail behind you. A purple smoke starts to drift up from your heart as the continued exposure to the strand begins to cauterize the wound. At this time, you are too far along the path to think about stopping or turning back, so you push forward into the penumbra. Even the engagee does not directly "see" the penumbra. The penumbra makes itself known as a force against distance. There is also a psychological aspect that begins to trick the engagee. You start seeing things out of the corner of your eye, and auditory hallucinations come and go.

The next step felt like stepping into a large snowbank. Only there was no snow. There was only the invisible resistance against forward movement. The engagee is forced to adjust their gait and stance to lean in and push against the invisible force. The smoke around the entry point of my heart thickened as I took another forced step, sliding my body along the mystic strand. Doors to perception opened up, and a flood of images filled my mind. Images of countless lives passed through my perception, and not just the lives of people, but animals, insects, fish, and other creatures. The *Motif* presents the lifelong memories of everything ever born, in every probability, as a complex overlay to the conscious mind. All of a sudden, I didn't have just a single set of eyes for perception. Instead, I had the eyes of the creature, briefly presented, and all the images those eyes saw throughout its lifetime. An infinity of perspectives to choose from, and I felt lost for a moment, or was it longer? God, I can't stop, I thought, and I felt a panic rise inside me. Looking down, I noticed the area around my heart started to dissolve into the purple smoke. I mustered up what I could of my own perception and tried erasing the intruding perceptions by not focusing on the rising smoke. I turned my attention to the strand, which was becoming more and more obscured by the smoke. I put a conscious effort into pressing onward and managed several productive steps, keeping the smoke and invading perceptions at bay. The next step I planted seemed to sink into the floor. This step felt like contacting glue or tar. My feet doubled or tripled in weight as I began to sluggishly plod forward.

A sound rose with morbid moans and screams of all kinds, from birth to murder. A strong wind buffeted me, trying to blow me away. I felt a bit lucky that my feet were so heavy, but I was sinking, and hallucinations formed all around. Using both of my hands, I pulled my left leg up and moved it forward to take the next step. I did the same with my other leg, pulling it up and out of the muck, taking a large stride, stretching like the warrior yoga pose to cover more distance than a heel-to-toe approach. This process allowed me to slide along the strand quickly, but I felt highly unbalanced as the wind kicked up, which nearly knocked me out of alignment with the piercing strand.

After leaving the muck behind, it felt like an uphill battle. The smoke rose up to my neck, and I could feel the first penumbra vibrating and shaking, trying one last time to prevent my progress along the strand. As it shook, I shook, and the strand shook. Step after step, I pitted my will against the penumbra, and it gave way. I was through, and my stepping returned to normal. The smoke dropped back, and I could see the strand more clearly. At this point in the process, the engagee knows how to manipulate probability. The first penumbra has given up its secret. But the task is not complete, and the engagee knows his life is on the line at this point.

I took advantage of the decreased resistance and took the next few steps in bold strides. I traversed the entire outer arc and could see my starting point to the left before the *Motif* turned inward. My drying blood formed the tracing that I was still in the process of completing. It was so tempting to jump the line to return to the start of the *Motif* and step off, but I knew that would be suicide at this point. I began the inward spiral along the strand. The doors to perception remained open, and I freely hallucinated scenes taking place just beside the strand. The strand wove its way through war scenes, where fellow soldiers screamed and died, pleading for me to save them, reaching out and grabbing my pants to slow me down. Sailors in a storm called out for me to man the rigging so we all might survive. Swarms of oversized insects flooded over the strand and attempted to block my next footfall, crawling up my legs and getting into my shirt. They started biting me as I squished and punted as many as I could while keeping my balance and alignment with the strand. Storms washed them away, and a large herd of quadruped animals stampeded in my direction. I hastened my pace, but they were still closing on my position. A small ball appeared, rolling toward me along the strand from farther ahead. Pink rose petals peeled off and quickly settled around the strand, obscuring it from my vision. The ball struck me, and a blinding white light took my sight.

In my mind, I knew where the strand was, so I made the next step I took, the smallest step I took. While keeping my forward motion going, I looked down, trying to discover any hint of the strand. I hoped my next footfall maintained alignment. I almost came to a stop as the brightness faded, and I could see the hint of purple from the etheric strand. Good thing, too. My next footfall was leading me out of alignment with the strand. I quickly adjusted my down step and ended up with the strand only halfway through my heart. This alignment caused plumes to swiftly rise up, dissolving part of my chest as my vision cleared. Looking forward, trying to decide my next step, the *Motif* presented a three-way fork on the strand. This fork was the beginning of the second penumbra.

Pushing forward, I encountered resistance, much like the first penumbra, as

I chose the center path. I focused on realigning my heart with the strand as screams cried out, and the floor began to shake. Did I choose the wrong path? I was flooded with doubt and fear while the screaming rose to a higher pitch before taking another step, completing my commitment to the center path. The floor rocked more, and I saw the side paths turn to mist and float away. The floor gave way beneath me, and I found myself suspended in the darkness, balancing in the small area surrounding the last deposited blood footfall. I could hear the screams fading into the distance as they fell into the abyss. A deathly silence came over the darkness, and the only thing I could hear was my heartbeat in my ears. I heard a liquid thump, thump, followed by a squishy rushing sound of blood pumping through my body and outward along the strand.

The etheric strand illuminated the scene. There was a sound of electric arcing as I took step after step through the darkness while the air grew colder. I could see my breath in the air, and the smoke from my heart started climbing higher, past my neck again. Each step presented a diorama in my mind, with the mystic strand woven through it. In each demented room I passed through, the *Motif* presented a twisted version of actual events from my life. Individuals screamed at me, laughed at me, and threatened me. They tried anything to draw me away from the strand. They lured me with the smell of good food, not just good food, the most delicious of all foods. Women tempted me to stop for a moment. They invited me to watch them while they explored their own sexuality. The women spanned the range from slutty hookers to the ideal conservative wife standing next to children that were supposed to be mine. There were gatherings of good friends, making me feel most welcome while restricting my movement along the strand. I was on stage, and a crowd of adoring fans cheered while the spotlight tracked my movements through the theater stage in my mind. But the spotlight would not fade, and it changed positions to cast light in my eyes, blinding me from the next step. I kept turning my head from side to side to keep the light out of my eyes while trying to see the etheric strand I was sliding along. Each time I moved my head, the light realigned itself to blind me again. I felt the resistance building as the smoke rose into my face. Frantically, I tried to wave it away, to see where the next step should fall. And then, out of nowhere, a loud snap rang out. It reminded me of the sound of a large oak branch breaking in a frozen winter forest. I made two more steps forward, feeling like they were up a ramp, and I was through the second penumbra.

The raised rock platform returned to view, and I could see it was not that far until I reached the end of the cosmic design. I managed to get a few long strides in, but they were all uphill. The smoke around my heart was thickening as I stepped into the third and final penumbra. The third penumbra combined qualities from the other two penumbras with the intensity knob turned up. The strand no longer felt etheric, like it did at the beginning. It felt like raw energy coursed through the strand, with pain accompanying every step. I felt a cramp in my leg and staggered for a moment, coming to a stop along the strand. The smoke became frantic, whipped by an unfelt wind, as my chest began to dissolve. Smaller wisps jumped up even higher, momentarily blocking my vision. How long was I stopped? In a panic, I lurched forward, still in rough alignment with the strand, causing the dissolving to halt and begin to reverse. I struggled to bring my cramped leg forward and stretched my arms out to maintain balance and keep from falling over. This pose was a mistake because all manner of ghostly people and demons grabbed onto my arms and tried to pull me down.

A cacophony of sounds occurred, ranging from desperate whispers to evil guttural proclamations forecasting my demise. Drums, trumpets, acoustic, and synthesized instruments all played out of tune as I leaned forward, even more, dragging the weight of all those ghostly people behind me. The smoke rose up to my mouth, but I knew the end of the strand lay a few steps ahead. An expansion of time seemed to occur, and I felt like I moved in slow motion. I tucked my arms in closer to my side, trying to bring them forward as I took another step, feeling a little light-headed at having deposited a fair amount of blood on the floor. Thousands of dying people surrounded me, faceless tormented beings in dark rags latched onto me with their vise-like bone grips. The wind whipped into my face blowing cold, hard, ice needles into my skin, which turned hot on contact and burned my flesh. The smoke was in my face and nostrils, causing my breathing to labor as I made one last effort to push forward along the strand. I hit a wall, and there was no way forward. My arms continued forward to blindly push against this imaginary force while I followed through with another step, and an audible scream came out of my mouth, "Ahhhhhh."

Then I was through. I felt the end of the strand slide out of my back. The *Motif* dropped to the floor, consuming the deposited blood I left behind, leaving my ripped shirt but no mark on my chest to indicate that a puncture ever took place. I stood at the center of Grayson's *Motif*, bent over and drenched in sweat. I felt like dropping to one knee, but I shook off that notion and stood taller. I was a Lord of Splendor, and I fully understood that now. The *Motif* gifted me with the ability to travel through echo, and I felt my strength return. I pulled in power from the *Motif* to restore my fatigue. I now knew I could draw in personal power from the imagined image of the *Motif* itself. I also knew, like all others who engaged the *Motif* and reached its center, I could instantly transport to anywhere in echo from this spot. I made my choice, and in the blink of an eye, I was there standing in the grass. I maintained a dual perception for a moment, as part of me remained linked to the playback device on *Tiger Mountain*. It quickly faded as the virtual feed did a horizontal fizzle while the image of my previously recorded hand pressed stop on the recorder hanging from my belt.

CHAPTER 3

The Black Glass Building

Precita Park, San Francisco, circa 2369 A.D. The date was irrelevant, but the place was not. This city was the headquarters for the Starnet Union, not this park, but the San Francisco area. I remember, from future memories, living here and owning a tall building on the edge of the financial district. It was from this high-rise office building where I broadcast throughout the solar system and beyond. The building also held several apartments I offered to guests and friends who wished to live in this echo.

At this point, I felt like the separation between the overlay self and Sam started to blur. Engaging the *Motif,* even virtually, solidified my sense of Sam self. I held less doubt about who I was. I was more willing to accept that some temporal event happened, which cast me back in time. How far, I was not exactly sure? How Candy fit into this was still a mystery. As a probability traveler, I always thought of time as an aspect of probability. Such as this time period where I stood in the San Francisco park. I could have just as easily chosen San Francisco in the heyday of the gold rush, back in the 1820s. This choice did not mean I traveled through time, but instead, selected the features of a probability with time as an aspect to support those features. Sure, I could locate a probability where alien technology influenced the 1820s San Francisco, but that would be an aspect of chaos applied to the more "Splendorcentric" development line that San Francisco took in another probability.

The park was quite small. Some might consider it a patch of grass dividing the row of houses on either side. At one end of this park, there was a public offering of personal transportation devices. I made my way over to the corral. In other times there might have been bike racks here. Today there were a few lime-colored personal transport scooters here. Instead of having wheels, these devices used anti-gravity force fields to float above the ground.

I stepped onto one of the personal transports, and a small screen lit up with a map of the immediate area centered on the current location. Below the screen was a company logo made up of a swoosh and an oval saying, "Gravwave," but the locals just called them "Gravies." I used the touch screen to zoom out and target my office building. With a tap on the screen, a red line appeared between my current location and the target goal. An icon on the screen cycled through an animation, indicating I should grip the hand controls. Once I did this, the Gravwave rose about fifteen centimeters above the ground. It started making its way along the route. The Gravwave responded to my leaning and steering but also seemed to move on its own. This anti-gravity technology was a spin-off from the gravity plating used on starships to keep things from floating around in space. The Gravwave designers reversed it to work in a gravity-based environment.

While zipping along the streets and walkways, many of which seemed to be designed just for this type of transportation, I thought of the *Motif* in my mind. I held its shape before me, attempting to overlay it on the landscape I passed through. To actually own buildings, businesses, and property, requires permits, licenses, and contracts. This requirement is one of the easiest things for a Splendorite to alter in an environment. It became highly probable I was a real estate media mogul with physical interests held in buildings, production, apparel, and mining. There is a certain physical change in the environment when a Splendorite alters reality to conform it to his or her wishes. Often it takes the form of physical distortions or transformations of buildings, walls, roads, and terrain. Many times a glow or a halo accompanies these distortions. If they are paying attention, the inhabitants of the probability can see these temporary manifestations.

I continued along the street, and the sidewalk began to shimmer and shine in front of me. Behind me was a glowing trail of colors decaying into natural elements such as leaves and birds as they fell to the ground or took flight. I zoomed somewhat recklessly down the street. There was a certain exhilaration as I sunk into the moment and really started shaping the world around me. Words in window advertisements blurred and changed while I passed. Pedestrians gawked and rubber-necked as I flew by. I flew into a tunnel, one of those temporary construction sidewalks you find in big cities. The sound of rippling plastic stapled to particleboard walls rattled behind me as I emerged from the end of the tunnel. I flew out a little too fast and took a slight side route up a pile of lumber that conveniently formed a ramp. I momentarily had lift. The design of the Gravwave didn't support flight, and I bottomed out when I hit the ground, landing with a crunch and a scraping sound, sending sparks flying from the bottom of the unit. At the moment of impact, I solidified my choices in this probability, and all of the buildings around me tipped in, then back into place, as they took on their normal stance as buildings should. The Gravwave sputtered and stopped with a lurch as I tumbled forward from the unit. I stumbled a few steps and caught myself instead of falling down. With the Gravwave smoldering, I dragged it into a nearby corral containing other working Gravwave units, where I plopped it over on its side. A small boy holding his mother's hand looked over at me, and I shrugged, lifting my hands in the "what can you do?" gesture before walking off.

I came up a little short of my final destination, so I started walking toward a tall black glass building. It was a couple of blocks east. I zigzagged through sidestreets and eventually found myself in an alley leading to the street where the front entrance lies. As I walked past the loading dock, it hit me where I was, and I felt a rush of panic flood over me. In the second time loop from my future memories, I recalled a brutal attack happening in this exact spot. I used my technology to track and uncover form-altering aliens who call themselves Flexanites. They are focused on invading the Starnet Union by secretly killing world leaders and assuming their roles. I got good at this, finding them, too, good. In a temporary lapse of good judgment, a Starnet security officer, who was actually a Flexanite, tricked me. A message lured me to this very alley where I was nearly beaten to death by the Flexanite, who turned his arms into hammer-like pseudo-pods. If it weren't for Candy and her girlfriend showing up to save the day, I might have died that night.

I hurried quickly by and decided to sprint the rest of the way to the main street. After engaging the *Motif,* I felt more confident about my mental state, but having a panic attack in the alley unraveled some of that progress. One thing is for sure, though, I own a building in a probability where the Flexanites are in the process of infiltrating my homeworld. I walked up to the front door and placed my hand over a dark panel. A white line moved from top to bottom, and a red light turned green. The sound of efficient mechanical movement occurred, and the two front doors slid apart. After stepping into my building, the doors closed behind me with a soft "swish" sound.

"Ohm, are you there?" I asked out loud.

"Yes, Sam, I am here," Ohm replied.

"Let's get rid of the hand scanner on the front door. If someone wants in or tries to break in, let me know. Are there any life forms in this building?"

"Checking," Ohm said. "No life forms detected. All floors are vacant."

"Remove all prior office furniture and office items. Get rid of it all. Replace the ceiling tiles, and scan the conduits for any left-over espionage devices. You can keep the apartment floor plans intact, however."

"Renovation, in progress," Ohm replied.

I walked over and pressed the button to call the elevator. A soft ding sounded, and the doors slid apart. Stepping inside, I turned around and pressed the button for the twenty-third floor. A gentle upward motion and a steady acceleration took me up as a modern version of "The Girl From Ipanema" filtered through the speakers in the ceiling. A deceleration and a slow down to a stop took place. The doors opened up, and I stepped into the hallway. The twenty-third floor is where I created a series of apartments. I opened the door nearest the elevator and stepped inside.

This modern space was a luxury apartment with a view. The design was similar to my home on *Tiger Mountain*. There was a sunken living room, with rectangular angles dominant in the overall room design. Along the back glass wall, sliding glass doors revealed a deep balcony. This balcony offered a larger floor plan compared to the balcony from my home on *Tiger Mountain*. Opening the sliding glass doors, I walked to the walled railing to take in the view. The smell of the bay was on the air, and I could see the profile of Starnet headquarters from here.

"Ohm, I would like to secure this entire building using the same security methods I have in place for my home on *Tiger Mountain*."

"New rules in place," Ohm replied.

I returned to the apartment and headed for the bedroom. Damn, I was tired. The act of engaging the *Motif*, even virtually, exhausted me. I undressed, got into bed, and went right to sleep. When I awoke, I was solid as a rock, the morning wood. I couldn't help but think about my wives, Erin and Jorrie. In theory, they existed in this universe where the black glass building stood, but I had to locate them, get to know them, and hope I could do all the things right that caused us to fall in love in the first place. And I had to do that twice.

I heard some noise in the other room, followed by, "Are you up in there?"

It was Candy's voice. I put it to the side as I slipped on my pants and the shirt I wore the day before. I did a quick pat-down and felt the vignettes in my pockets. I carried my boots with me and walked into the living area. Candy stood behind the kitchen counter cooking something with cinnamon. I sat down on one of the high-back stools, on the other side of the counter, and put on my boots.

"So, where did you slip off to yesterday?" she asked while flipping what looked like French toast.

"Oh, you know, I had to figure some things out," I said vaguely.

She made a whatever kind of face and said, "Yeah right," before serving me a plate with two slices of French toast.

I looked at the plate and then looked up at her and said, "I have to wash my hands."

I walked through the bedroom to the bathroom, which was off to the side, and proceeded to turn on the water and wash my hands as I whispered, "Ohm, can you scan the food prepared by Candy for any poison contaminants or trackers?"

"Checking. It is safe. Your invisihud continuously scans your food and will alert you, but you can also manually view extended properties of many items in your environment," Ohm stated.

"I was sensitive to the invisihud data yesterday. Can you activate the properties of only a few items in this bathroom?"

"Certainly."

I looked down, and the water running from the faucet exhibited a slight glowing light blue outline. In the shower, similar outlines surrounded a bar of soap and a bottle of shampoo, but their outlines were a different color.

"Ohm, how do I work the invisihud?"

"Look to the left, and options will slide out. Look up and down to choose an option from the list. Blink to activate it. To disable the invisihud, close your eyes for a moment and look to the right."

"Got it, thanks."

"There are other follow-up lessons you can review under the help option at the bottom of the list on the left," Ohm continued.

After washing my face, I used the hand towel on the rack to dry off before making my way out to the counter. I sat down next to Candy, who fixed a plate of French toast for herself. There was a bowl of fresh chopped strawberries and some maple syrup here. I spooned some strawberries on top of my French toast and poured the maple syrup.

"Are you doing okay?" Candy asked as she poured two cups of coffee, one for herself, and handed the other one to me while looking me in the eye.

I finished chewing a delicious mouthful. The strawberries were perfect, and the maple syrup conveyed a smoky richness. I took a sip of coffee and said, "I don't think I'll be okay for a while, Candy."

Looking away, I quickly changed the subject and said, "This food is amazing. All the flavors taste pure and fresh. I guess that is what you get when a tech-savvy world eliminates chemical interference in its growing process and just goes all organic."

Candy shook her head in agreement while chewing a mouthful. A smile crossed her face, which brought joy to me. For a second, I felt normal. I think Candy felt the same way. We ate a few bites as we drank our coffee together.

"What about you? Are you doin' all right?"

"The last time I remember seeing you was when we arrived at Sinalta," Candy said while looking into her cup.

"The day you met Elowin."

"Yeah," she said sadly. "I just gave in when we met and fell in love with her. I followed her, I helped her, I cooked for her, and we made love all the time. Before I knew it, months passed by, and I realized I left you standing there."

"It's okay. I knew what you were about from the day we met. When we started foolin' around, it was just hot fun. It's my fault that I fell in love with you," I said into my coffee.

"I fell in love with you, too, but not in a wifey kind of way. You were my boo that I was chillin' with. And yes, those three ways we shared in all those probable realities were over the top hot. The last thing I remember was feeling sad and depressed. Elowin chose to return to her people, to help rebuild her community. I could dig all that, and I even offered to let one of her village men make a baby in me," she said with the last part in a staccato raised voice.

"I know."

"But Elowin's customs won't allow what we shared. In her community, a man owns a female, and that is where Candy draws the line," she emphasized the last part by moving her hand from left to right.

"No man will ever own me. Then I became aware I was in your apartment on *Tiger Mountain*, sitting at the bar. I felt odd. I could tell somethin' was wrong with you too. You moved differently and spoke in unsure phrases. I know you too well, Sam."

"If we each have been affected, but somewhat differently, we should check in on the other Guardians to see if they have experienced any discontinuity. I suddenly feel like I have a hundred things I need to do right now. And I feel that doing them in the right order is very important," I said.

"What do we do next?" Candy asked before she took another bite.

"I think the first step is to create some sympathetic auragraphic scenarios I can install into the Cryovirt's of both Lexi and Valentino. I am going to have to let them go."

"Oh," Candy said, slowly, "do you really think that is a wise thing to do?"

We finished breakfast and carried our coffee from the kitchen island to sit on the white sofa in the central, recessed floor area. I noticed a lot of the decor in this luxury apartment was bright, white-based materials with accents of tan, brown, and silver. There was a large glass top white box acting as a coffee table here, with empty open shelves where you could place knick-knacks or magazines below.

"I don't have memories of just one time-loop, Candy. I have memories of two. I guess I'll call them the first one and the last one. In the first one, much was the same as now. We stopped Lexi, Teela, and Valentino from accomplishing the dark magic they planned with my blood. I placed them into cryogenic virtualization pods or Cryovirts. They were still alive but mildly drugged and fed intravenously. The Cryovirts keep their minds active by presenting a convincing virtual reality to their memory centers and the frontal lobe. A mild drug-induced amnesia is introduced to keep them from remembering who they are."

"That's what you did with them?" Cand asked.

"So far, this has prevented them from escaping, and their life signs remain stable. There is always the possibility that they will remember they are Lords of Splendor and use their *Motif* or magic abilities to shift out of that probability and into one where they are no longer prisoners."

"Uh-huh," Candy said with a raised eyebrow.

"In the first time-loop, all was going well. We won. Our enemies were in prison, so why not go on a vacation, we thought? I always wanted to show you the woods of Rayleaf that lie to the southeast of Splendor."

"You took me to Splendor?" Candy asked.

I shook my head yes and continued, "Rayleaf is the first forest that all forests in every probability draw their source from. Even far-fetched creatures such as Centaurs, Pegasus, or Hippogryphs live there. As you approach Splendor, there is an increased perception of light. It is easy to look past it after a month or so, but newcomers are always in awe when they arrive in Splendor. Most describe it as a 'richer' perception of the world around them."

"In these woods?" Candy asked while holding her coffee.

I went on, "So, we made the trip together. We wandered deep into the woods, following footpaths, at first, finally abandoning them to explore on our own. I remember how you were really getting into it. You were the city girl out in the country. You spoke a little too loud and made comments about downed trees being in the way, but overall you enjoyed yourself and the perfect weather. It seemed like the afternoon went on forever. There is a timelessness that Splendor sits within. That is why no one grows old unless they move out of the area."

"Me tromping through the woods," Candy said. "What kind of shoes did I wear?"

"We took a rest by a fallen log. It was a big one, more or less concealing us from one side. I heard a sound, like an animal passing by, and motioned to you, silently, to peek over the top of the log. A short distance away, nibbling on the grass in a glade lit by a shaft of soft light, stood the shaggy Re'em."

"Wait a second," Candy said. "What is this Re'em again?"

"It's the creature that sponsored the creation of the multi-verse," I said.

"Oh, one of those," Candy said sarcastically.

"We sank back down so as not to spook it. When we looked up, the head of the Re'em loomed large over us. What seemed so peaceful seconds ago became absolutely terrifying at that moment. The Re'em blocked out the fading light of the afternoon, and its eyes shone gold with red streaks through them. It looked at me, and it looked at you. I turned my head to look over at you, and you froze in fear as I saw your eyes meet the gaze of the Re'em. You slumped to the ground, and the Re'em bounded off."

I picked up my coffee and took a sip, as Candy looked at me with an opened mouth expression for a minute.

"That all happened to me?" Candy asked.

"I shook you, but you wouldn't wake. I took you to the Blinn doctors at Xanadu, but they had no luck reviving you. I took you to Starnet doctors, consulted magicians, invited fairy tale princes and princesses to kiss you, while voodoo women told me you were cursed. I neared the end of my rope. After running out of ideas to break the spell, I received a note from the Splendor library assistant who located a book with a reference to a condition similar to yours."

"What was it? Sleeping Beauty?" Candy asked with a smile.

"The book 'Hamfeirg's Anger' was a short story about a hunter who drew the wrath of the shaggy Re'em by trying to capture it. Instead, the Re'em took the thing most treasured by the hunter, his wife. In the story, the Re'em looked into her eyes and she fell into a deep unwaking sleep. In the end, the King and a ceremony were needed to please the Re'em. The hunter offered up his bow, and he pledged to defend the Re'em instead of hunt it. The Re'em broke the spell, and the hunter's wife awoke unharmed."

"I see," Candy said.

"The similarities of our encounter with the Re'em and the hunter in the story were too close to ignore. I started to think, 'What can I return to the Re'em to break the spell?' It did not take long until I concluded the Re'em took your soul because I took two of its souls, Lexi and Valentino," I said.

"What does that have to do with anything?" Candy asked.

"All the Splendorites, Lexi, Valentino, and myself included, are born from the line of the Re'em. Although I am two more times removed from the source, compared to Lexi, and only one time removed, compared to Valentino. It occurred to me that my Cryovirt imprisonment of two of the Re'em's offspring might be what caused the Re'em to take your soul. I know it sounds like grasping at straws, but it was the only thing I could come up with. I gave it a try, and it worked. After releasing Lexi and Valentino, you woke up," I said to Candy.

"I don't know what to say to that," Candy said. "But, thank you."

"That is why I feel the need to release Lexi and Valentino before the Re'em retaliates."

"I guess that kind of makes sense," Candy said.

"Ohm, let's alter the progression of the virtual reality scenarios Lexi and Valentino are currently experiencing. We need to weave the results from my findings into their everyday life. Make the main focus on how they were not responsible for their actions due to the invisible chaos strands bound to their bodies," I requested.

"Working on possible scenarios. How soon do you want Lexi and Valentino to obtain full immersion?" Ohm asked.

"Take your time. Revise the current scenarios and conduct virtual tests to predict best possible outcomes when introducing new information."

"What is the best possible outcome, Sam?" Ohm asked.

"The best possible outcome is that they obtain some level of empathy or remorse for me and don't try to kill me when I set them free. Keep an eye on immersion factors for cerebral wakefulness. If imminent, notify me," I said.

Candy sat her coffee cup on the table and placed her hand on my shoulder before looking me directly in the eye and saying, "After all you did for me. I want to help."

"I know," I said. "I need to do some things on my own. It's easier that way."

"All right," she said before removing her hand from my shoulder and backing off. "I can dig, but you have friends. Let them help."

"But I did not actually do any of that yet. That is what is freaking me out. I am making decisions based upon memories of a future that no longer exists. Even the two time-loops I remember have significant differences. If this is the start of a new time-loop, does it make sense to try and cherry-pick the best outcomes from the other two future memories?"

Candy looked to the side while scratching gently at the back of her neck and said, "That might be one of those things you have to figure out on your own."

"Right," I said with a nod.

She stood up abruptly and said slyly, "Did you mention earlier that I could have one of these apartments?"

I smiled and said, "Sure, take your pick from any door on this floor. I have plans for the other floors."

"Great!" she said enthusiastically. "I'm gonna check em' out. Make sure you check-in. Don't make me come looking for you."

"Ohm, can you clean up the mess in the kitchen," I asked after Candy walked out the front door.

"Restoring kitchen to pre-cook state," Ohm replied, and our coffee cups vanished along with the plates and condiments on the counter.

I showered, shaved, and donned a fresh set of clothes that Ohm replicated for me. It was essentially the same thing I previously wore, a black shirt and black pants with a practical light boot for the foot. I transferred the vignettes from the old shirt to the new shirt and glanced at them briefly before placing them in my pockets. The collection of vignettes revealed pictures of a lighthouse, a man dressed in an orange and purple jesters outfit, a few more portraits of people, and a couple of vignettes leading to unknown places. The final card was an image of a technical archway. This card was the vignette to my hospital named Xanadu. I placed it in the zippered pocket over my heart, where I could have quick access to it if needed.

CHAPTER 4

Sound And Vision

The next part of my journey begins on the other side of the galaxy. Starnet has mapped out portions of space surrounding the member planets. Each species has contributed, providing an extended star map that all members of the Starnet Union share. Wide areas remain unexplored and are marked with general terms like Dili sector, Sini sector, and so on. The space I was interested in was the Gar sector. I only know of this because of my future memories. There is a lost Starnet ship in that sector named *Journey* that eventually encounters a low-tech space flotilla of human and cybernetic beings on the verge of extinction. One of my future wives lives somewhere on that flotilla. In the other time-loop, I led the space flotilla to a planet where they could start their lives again. It was a planet that could sustain the entire population. This planet was my next destination. To get there, I needed to visit the painting.

I mentioned earlier, when I virtually engaged the *Motif*, that there was a long list of relatives who made the attempt but did not succeed. My name could have easily been on that list. I was far enough removed, as far as the bloodline was concerned, that my odds for success were slim. But King Osric was convinced by his brother, Nicolas, to let me try. I was manually making my way through echo, via sailing ships and following tales of magical portals leading to strange lands, until I came upon the city of Amir where Nicolas ruled. Nicolas was the first Splendorite I met. I think it was the fact I looked so much like his brother, Grayson, that he listened to my story. Afterward, he gave me the chance to engage the *Motif* for the first time. This was the first *Motif*, Darwin's *Motif*. He believed my story that Grayson was my grandfather, and I got my chance to engage the *Motif*.

I still carried most of my travel gear with me when I approached the mystic strand for the first time. The initial stab and the thrill of sliding along the cosmic cable quickly turned to pain before I made it to the first penumbra. Yes, Darwin's *Motif* has penumbras too. The etheric strand started shaking, disturbing the alignment with my heart, and I felt myself begin to dissolve. In the distance, I could see from the looks on Osric's and Nicolas' faces that they saw this happen before, and I thought, "I'm not gonna make it."

During one of my uncontrolled movements, I brushed against the ornamental wand at my belt. When I started my quest through echo, it was nothing more than a quartz crystal glued to the end of a copper pipe I picked up at the hardware store. I helped a friend of mine replace the soft top on his Delta 88 convertible, and there was some leftover material. It was white on one side and black on the other. I cut two strips and made a spiral design of white and black, winding along the length of this pipe. Each time I traveled to a new probability, I noticed the wand would morph and change a little. In the probability where I constructed it, the wand did nothing, but as I moved through probabilities, it picked up some magic along the way. When I brushed against it, with my uncontrolled movement, the wand released an eddy of purple plasma that shot up to the ceiling. I felt the pain diminish and the vibration of the strand decrease as the plasma discharged. An epiphany occurred. I could use the wand to remove excess energy that would, otherwise, destabilize the strand.

Removing the wand from my belt, I held it firmly in my left hand and discharged another stream at the wall. The pain subsided again, and the dissolving started to reverse. I was on to something. If I could continually discharge enough plasma, I just might make it through this after all. As I entered the first penumbra, the smoke rose up, and raw discharges from the wand were no longer enough. I was losing the battle again. I decided, instead of destroying things, to try and create things. I started with plasma shapes, but the magic in the wand also added an organic element. Soon, I made things in the air as toy soldiers came to life to participate in hot ionized gaseous battles. I tried anything I could think of to keep the *Motif* busy and the strand stable.

When I reached the center of the *Motif*, I heard the sound of music. Looking to the back of the cave where this *Motif* hovers, I saw a harp guitar, upright in a stand, playing itself. It played beautiful music, the music of celebration and joy. Next to it, on an easel, was a painting with an ever-changing canvas. These two things did not disappear like all the other temporary creations I conjured along the way. I never really knew why, but I did know they were mine. I named them *Sound* and *Vision*.

Vision was the painting. On its own, it continually repaints itself with landscapes, people, and cities while presenting a mood and consciousness of its own. You can approach the painting with a place in mind, and *Vision* senses what you are thinking. It revises its own canvas to depict the location in your mind. Like a vignette, you can concentrate on the image and step into the painting to arrive at the location you have imagined. This feature makes it a portable center of the *Motif*. But there is a downside to it. When left alone, the images that *Vision* renders borderline on madness. An ever-shifting palette of gore and bloody nightmarish scenes parade across the canvas on any given day.

Originally, I gifted *Sound* and *Vision* to King Osric and his wife, Violet. I wanted to thank them for letting me engage the *Motif*. Violet loved the harp guitar *Sound*, and to this day, it still sits in her morning room in the castle. The images produced by *Vision* were so horrifying that the castle staff feared they would leap from the canvas and tear them apart. Osric asked the castle staff to place the painting in a closet, but even this did not bring ease to everyone because of the nightmares that soon followed. I offered to keep the painting safe, and it has remained in my possession ever since.

The *Deceptive* was my graduation project for starship design when I attended the Starnet Academy. It was the first working starship that managed to not fall apart when I shifted it through echo. I have taken the *Deceptive* across the entire spectrum of probability, from Splendor to nearly the Vectorless Vale, with most systems functioning as they should. I stored *Vision* on the *Deceptive*. It was at the end of a metal walkway, resting on its easel but covered with a cloth. Ohm transported me there, and I stood before the painting.

The painting was covered to avoid the stream of hellish images it seemed to produce, but this covering led to an unexpected side effect. When uncovering the painting, you would often see frightening large eyes pressed up against the canvas, as if they were most certainly going to burst through. Tentacles, worms, and gear-like teeth were also common themes. The trick was to have your ideal image mentally prepared and quickly remove the cloth while concentrating on your idea, not the one presented by the canvas. At least, that is how I did it.

I thought of the place I wanted to reach. The planet was named Zenith, the place where I met my wife, Erin. This first introduction happened in both memory loops, so I consider it one of those cherry-picked memories I mentioned to Candy earlier. I held the intention of my destination in mind and quickly removed the cloth covering the painting before dropping it on the floor. Large eyes surrounded by smaller eyes that were again surrounded by even smaller eyes formed a recursive fractal algorithm across the canvas. I hesitated, and the largest of the eyes turned to focus on me. The smaller eyes quickly followed suit, but there was a short delay. Mouths appeared, puking, and gnashing, trying to escape the canvas to devour me.

With the thoughts of green grass and the nebula-streaked sky of Zenith held firmly in my mind, the painting quickly rearranged itself to show me a pastoral setting. The painting, as with vignettes, took on an additional dimension, offering a metaphysical doorway into the rendered scene. While holding a conscious intent of arriving at Zenith in my mind, I stepped forward into the painting to magically arrive at the location.

Finding Erin was not going to be that easy. We do meet on this planet, but we meet in the future. Right now, there is no one living here, but it is an ideal candidate for humanoid life. This planet is where I eventually lead the Imperial Fleet of humans and Melogs to live in peace. For now, it's just me and the green field.

The plan is to send out probes from this launch point and scan in all directions, seeking any signals that a Starnet ship might generate. The probes look for trace elements used in Starnet ship construction. While scanning in all directions is the most logical course, I had a hunch and decided to use a focused cone approach to scan one area more densely rather than all areas more sparsely.

"Ohm, I want to create a single cloaked optical drone for launch in the valley below," I said.

"Constructing launch site for probe," Ohm replied

It took a few minutes for the Blinn replication factories, which exist in another echo, to construct the technical devices. After that, a series of sparkles materialized the probe and supporting launch mechanism into the scene.

The first probe needed to launch from the surface. Once it reached outer space, Ohm could spawn more companion probes. The cloaked optical drone was about the size of an airport shuttle van standing on its end. Imagine a tripod of landing gear supporting it. The probe presented the basic profile of a bishop chess piece with technical plating over its surface. I watched from a distance as it launched from the valley below. The tripod support contained chemical rocket boosters. The rockets did not have to be that large because part of the framework of the tripod leveraged anti-gravity plating. This modification reduced the effective payload the rockets needed to lift. Once the fuel was exhausted, the tripod launcher was discarded and fell back to the planet. The main bishop-shaped probe continued into space. It wasn't designed to land.

"Receiving data," Ohm announced, and my invisihud lit up.

I was getting used to the way the invisihud presented data to my optic nerve. Previously, I adjusted some of the options I found in the left side menu to tone down the brightness and tweaked the eye-tracking speed. The invisihud presented a simplified top-down layout, similar to seeing something projected on a wall. The first probe headed out of the solar system and into deep space.

"Commencing replication," Ohm continued.

Ohm replicated a new single probe, then replicated another, and so on. The newly replicated probes moved off with a conical expansion rate. The probes did not have an engine other than the small attitude adjustment thrusters. Their internal power supply was used for scanning, transporting, and remaining cloaked. They moved through space using a modified version of the *Vision* painting.

With the help of the Blinn, I was able to produce replicated copies of *Motif* infused blank probability canvases. The BPC offered a gateway to the echo optically projected upon them. Each probe contained two canvases and used the internal transporter to deploy a blank probability canvas in front of the probe.

The canvas was about the size of a large-screen television. It was transported into space in front of the probe. The probe used optical scan data from the direction it traveled to project a new destination, upon the blank canvas. This projection activated a magical emulsion which opened a doorway to the projected image. A short thruster burst caused the probe to move through the BPC hanging in space, conveying the entire probe to a new location. Using the transporter, Ohm would fetch the discarded canvas from the previous jump and deposit it in the storage area of the probe for reuse, while using the second canvas to plan the next jump. This leap-frog approach to travel was continuously repeated to allow movement through space, but the probes never really achieved a velocity much more than a few meters per hour.

The sensors on the probes were high resolution, which meant if a probe detected a planet or phenomena in the distance, it could use the scanner data, along with the optical telescope, to project a new destination onto the blank probability canvas. This projection allowed for an almost instantaneous jump from distant points in space to areas of interest.

"Ohm, let's leave a nine jump cloaked scanner trail for each probe. If they wander more than nine jumps from the original jump point, they will lose their way back. Also, drop down a terraforming module on the surface of this planet.

I'll need that later."

"Understood. Making adjustments. Deploying terraforming module."

"Ohm, notify me when we get a possible hit. Let's set the threshold to thirty-six percent."

"I will notify you when the threshold is crossed," Ohm said.

"Can you tell me the location of Jim Young?" I asked.

"Jim is in his house, in Twin Falls. He is alone," Ohm replied, adding the last part, anticipating my next question.

"Please transport me to the front sidewalk entrance of his house."

"Commencing transport," Ohm said, and the green field shot in from the sides of my vision, leaving me alone, in darkness.

This teleportation technology was based upon research obtained during the development of the blank probability canvas, the BPC. A small cloaked sphere houses a miniaturized version of the standard Starnet transportation technology. It was compact, low power, and worked at very close range. The transporter technology did not need to be any larger because its target, a miniature blank probability canvas, was only a few millimeters away. Ohm projected destination images onto the canvas to activate its probability connection. Once the connection was made, signals could be sent through. The most common signals I used were the transporter or communication signals. I have many of these spheres spread throughout echo, which allows me to transport from place to place without traveling through probability or painting a new vignette.

The cloaked spheres, which also contain scanning technology, move by manipulating magnetic fields and don't have a traditional engine. The technology was retrieved from what Starnet might call the twenty-seventh century. This makes them highly maneuverable on most planets but basically immobile in space. In space, I have dropped a few of them to act as relay buoys to get to planets much quicker. The space-based spheres that can transport entire ships are much larger than their walnut-sized atmospheric counterparts, but they are cloaked and emit energy only when in use. None of them have been detected as far as I know.

Cloaked scanners have a built-in protective artificial intelligence. They protect themselves and also defend any nearby Guardians. The smaller ones can combine together to form strong force fields, and the future memories reveal many situations where I used them to protect friends and save lives. They are so important to me that I requested Ohm to embed backups into the heels of my boots, two in each heel. They were constructed by Ohm using echo sturdy Blinn replication technology and can change their shape in a limited fashion. Four is an important number for the cloaked scanners because that is the minimum number required to form a basic Blinn replication aperture. A basic replication aperture makes hard-core survival much easier.

If you have never seen someone transported, it goes like this. The subject is there, sparkling lights appear, and then the subject is gone. If you are the subject, it goes like this. The world around you streaks in from the sides of your peripheral vision. There is a lot of high-frequency horizontal distortion when transporting through the cloaked scanners. The vibration breaks you apart, but you are not bleeding. You experience the realization that consciousness may not be bound to your body. The break apart is not just happening to you, but to the world around you. I guess that is what the senses relay to you when they are disintegrated. It all starts to dissolve. There is no spiral, no tunnel of light, nothing but a quiet, dark place. In the first days of human trials using the transporter technology, subjects reported the darkness and the silence lasted forever. The inventors eventually tracked this down to the refresh rate on the digital memory buffer. The slower the rate, the longer your perceived time in limbo. Only when this was identified and improved was the technology deemed safe for the public.

My awareness of the previous location was gone, and I remained in darkness and silence. There is nothing here, not even the beating of your own heart or the sound of your blood rushing through your veins. Even if you wanted to scream, you have no mouth to scream with. And just when I started to feel a build-up of panic inside, it all began to sparkle back together. The light shifted, compared to my departure point, and as the scene assembled, I was put back together.

I stood in front of a curved basalt walkway leading to an oversized single-story ranch home. There was a deck off to the side of the house. Tall pine trees stood here along with a few spruce. The house was of a modern design but constructed with traditional materials of wood and stone.

CHAPTER 5

Mist Door Friends

As I walked down the path to the front door, I thought about the first time I met Jim Young. It was in a green field on another planet. I traveled through echo with one theme in mind, to find friends. I hadn't had much luck and thought about giving up when I heard a strange sound, not too far away.

It sounded like muted mechanical horns accompanied by latches locking along with the sliding of stone on stone. I was on a small ridge overlooking a green meadow, hidden from view in a young wooded glen. I made my way out of the glen and down to the green grass floor of this mini valley. A short distance away, I saw a platform with a large archway standing upright on a stone mount. The stone platform it stood upon offered a set of steps leading up to the archway.

Presumably, people were expected to approach. Although the pillars supporting the arch were stone, the stacked elements making up the shaft of each pillar rotated in place. Symbols were spaced around the perimeter of each stacked segment, with some of the symbols glowing. It was fascinating, watching it move, wondering what it might do next?

As I approached closer, I noticed when the symbols on the segments between the two pillars matched, an illumination occurred, and a sound emanated. The illuminations stacked up from the bottom to the top. A new sound rang out as all the segments on both pillars illuminated. The keystone of the arch glowed last, and a thick teal mist filled the area of the archway, obscuring the scene behind it.

The mist churned and tumbled within the archway, filling it but not leaving it. I continued to walk closer but was cautious. I heard a sound similar to a backward piano note. Something appeared through the mist. A man emerged from the archway and stepped forward onto the platform. He was quickly followed by three more people, one at a time, who also stepped forward, making way for the next arrival. They were dressed in drab blue uniforms, carrying weapons and packs. At first, they did not notice me, and then one of the men tapped on the shoulder of another and pointed me out.

"Hello," he called out jovially.

"Afternoon," I said as I waved and proceeded to approach them.

They all descended the stairs and approached. He seemed to be the leader and pointed out his companions as he named them, "I'm Jim, this is David, Cooper, and that is Malik."

Jim was in his mid to late forties while David was younger. Cooper was a tall blonde woman in her early thirties. Malik was a dark-skinned muscular African fellow. That guy was buff. Malik was probably the most unusual of the bunch because he wore an elaborate silver wrist band based upon a nine-pointed star. The various tentacles were reminiscent of a starfish, wrapping around his arm, framing a large gemstone. The other three carried what looked like automatic rifles, and they each wore a pistol sidearm on their belts.

"I'm Sam. Nice to meet you," I stated as politely as possible.

Jim looked at me, took off his reflective sunglasses, and asked, "What cha doing here?"

I realized his military training forced him to evaluate unknowns, like myself, in such a manner. In olden times, knights I met on the road asked me similar questions in the form of, "Be ye friend or foe?" This question was a modern twist on the same old thing.

I was about to make up some story but thought about why I was actually in this field, to begin with, and said, "I am a probability traveler trying to make new friends."

"Oh really?" Jim asked while sliding his lower jaw back and forth, looking at the ground then back up again.

"I'm David Scott," David said as he stepped forward and shook my hand. "That is fascinating. Not the part about looking for friends, but the part about probability travel. But making friends is important to us too. What does that really mean, being a probability traveler? We're travelers as well. We travel through the archway."

"We call it a Mist Door," Cooper said, and she pointed at it just as the mist disappeared and the illumination ceased.

"Malik, have you ever heard of such things?" Jim asked his companion.

Malik spoke with a deep serious voice and said, "Never, Young."

"In its simplest terms, it means as I walk, I can reshape reality around me to best fit my desires, wants, or needs," I said.

Cooper chimed in with a challenging half-cocked smile, "Are you saying that you can change the physical world around you, just with your thoughts?"

"Well, as I mentioned, I need to be in motion or walking. But yes, and I don't often tell people that part about the requirement to be in motion to affect change," I said.

"Why are you telling us now?" Jim asked.

"My species is very long-lived. I am over eight hundred years old. A while back, I was tricked, imprisoned, and left to die a slow death. I recently escaped, only to discover many years passed, and all my previous friends were dead. I am out seeking new friends," I explained.

"Well, you don't look a day over thirty-five," Jim said, shaking his head in a comedic attempt.

"There are Ralla tales of long-lived old gods. But no one has ever met or seen one," Malik added.

Still the skeptic, Cooper asked, "If you can alter reality, why didn't you change the prison walls to paper and bust out?"

"The prison I was placed in, as well as all the members of the community I lived with, was a cryogenic chamber with a virtual reality overlay. The chamber sedated me and provided an alternate life via a virtual reality feed. Drugs suppressed my memories, and I thought the virtual reality presented was my own life. It was not until some years later, due to a mechanical failure, that I awoke emaciated and confused as to who I was, only to discover forty-four years passed by. Most of my friends died in the chambers they were placed in," I said.

"Who did this to you?" David asked with concern.

"It was my wife and some other family members. Ironically the chamber I was placed in, I designed myself, but not as a prison, as a recreational device. Unknown to me, the forces of evil and chaos influenced my wife and other family members in an attempt to usurp the technology I developed," I continued.

"Uh oh, here we go, chaos and evil. I don't like the sounds of that," Jim stated.

Cooper seemed a little less challenging and more sympathetic as she said, "Sorry to hear that."

"What kind of technology do you possess?" Malik asked.

Before I could answer, a long horn blast sounded out in the distance. I have heard that sound before, the sound of a blown animal horn.

Jim put his glasses on and said, "Let's move people. We'll talk later. We need to get undercover."

"Come with us," David said, gesturing, and we all moved off quickly to take cover in the glen where I previously emerged.

We hiked deeper into the wooded area and moved as quickly and silently as possible. During our trek, a few more horn blasts sounded out, indicating the trumpeter was in motion too. We were well into an hour or more of moving through woods and sprinting through clearings to avoid detection. Occasionally, Jim would call back, "Which way, Cooper?" and I saw Cooper check a map and a compass before silently pointing out the direction of our new heading.

Eventually, we came upon a structure in one of the clearings and took at the scene from a distance. We took cover behind some large rocks. It looked like a military compound, but I didn't recognize the architectural style. There were high walls, guard towers, and what looked like a spaceship sitting in a clearing outside the wall. The spaceship was larger than a shuttlecraft, probably a cargo vessel, or used for troop movements. I estimated that ship could deploy about fifty soldiers. Men in armor moved about. There were guards at the spaceship and the entrance gate.

I activated my invisihud and conducted a scan of the area, while the others viewed their objective using optical scopes. One thing I noticed right away was the guards wore the same wrist weapon as Malik. I mapped out all the living people in the compound, and my invisihud reported the guards as two living creatures. This species carried a symbiotic life form within a new organ that took the place of the appendix in their abdomen. The scan revealed a set of vertical gills located on the right side, below the rib cage. My invisihud marked four other people as human. They were in the basement of one of the buildings inside the compound. I took this time to scan the four people I traveled with and noticed that Malik was indeed carrying a symbiotic creature within his over-sized appendix. The other three checked out as human.

"Okay, here is the plan. We wait until nightfall, then sneak in and find our men," Jim said before he looked over at me, "And you'll stay here. It will be very dangerous."

"I have located a building where four humans are held in a basement. Are these your objective?" I asked.

"See, how can you know that," Jim said as he looked back from the compound he surveyed to meet my eyes.

"Don't be surprised, but I have an auragraphic map I can share with you. Is that all right?" I asked.

"Yes, that is all right. Do share," David added while looking over at Jim with a why not expression.

"Ohm, transfer my invisihud mapping data to an interactive auragraphic format that we can all see," I requested.

"Whoa," was all Jim said as he adjusted his military ball cap.

Auragraphics are light-based three-dimensional projections generated by emitters. The invisihud data appeared between us as an auragraphic map of the compound and the surrounding area. The map updated in real-time. It revealed guards walking the perimeter and making their way between buildings while conducting the business of the compound.

"It seems like the guards are of a different species, perhaps symbiotic. The humans stand out. I have located them here," I said while pointing at the map. "You can move the map and zoom in with gestures. This color of the individuals indicates their apparent health. It looks like a couple of your guys might be hurt, but they are still alive."

"This is so cool," Cooper said as she reached out and moved the map with her hand.

I made a gesture to her with my hands of placing them into the center and pulling outward, and she mimicked the move. The map zoomed into the area where the four humans were held. She repeated the gesture a couple more times, zooming in until she saw the faces of the humans.

"It's Vereddy and his team. MD-Gamma, sir," Cooper stated in a conformational tone.

David looked at me, pointing to the map, and said, "Is this your technology? It is impressive."

"Indeed," commented Malik.

"How does it work?" David asked.

"A small cloaked scanning device is hovering above the compound right now, relaying its current scan to another small cloaked device on the ground before us. It's projecting the auragram of the other device's data," I explained.

"You have invisible, flying scanners?" Cooper asked as she glanced up from the map with an incredulous look.

"Ya got anything in your bag of tricks to get those men out?" Jim asked in a flat tone.

"I can transport them out now if you like, but we better be prepared for first aid before I do that."

"We bought along first-aid supplies," David said.

"Ohm, can you materialize a standard Starnet medkit," I said out loud, and a white box with a red cross sparkled as it appeared on the ground.

"What is Starnet?" Cooper asked.

"I think we can talk about that later," Jim said, taking command. "Let's get our men and get out of here. Cooper, David, get out the medical supplies. Malik, keep an eye out in case something goes wrong. Sam, do your stuff if you can."

"Ohm, can you review Malik's physical makeup and prepare a sedative to temporarily render the aliens in the compound, like him, unconscious?" I asked.

"Your technology is voice-activated, isn't it?" Cooper asked.

"Compound prepared and ready for deployment," Ohm replied to me as a soft synthetic voice near my ear.

"Ohm, deploy the compound to knock out the guards and transport the four humans to this location," I said.

There was a slight rustle and crack to the forest floor twigs as the four humans transported in. They were seated before transport, so they appeared that way as they materialized before us with a sparkle.

David looked at them with his index finger held up to his mouth and said, "It's all right, Vereddy. It's us."

Malik watched the compound through field glasses and reported, "The guards are falling over."

Cooper said, "I see the same thing happening on the map."

"What just happened?" Vereddy asked.

"We're getting you out of here," Jim said as he moved up from the rock he used as cover to get closer to the wounded team. "This is Sam. He's gonna fix you up."

I opened the medkit and located the medical inspectrograph. It made a soft, whirring high pitched sound as I passed it quickly over each team member.

"Kyle's hurt pretty bad, sir," one of the men stated, and the medical inspectrograph concurred.

I focused on him as Cooper and David got out their medical supplies, handing out water to the men.

"How are we doing, Malik?" Jim asked nervously.

"I see no sign of movement. All the guards are down," Malik replied.

I located the medjector in the medkit and made some adjustments on the device before telling Kyle, who was still conscious but in obvious pain, "This will help with the pain. Then I'll work on that leg wound.

He nodded, and I pressed the medjector onto the right side of his neck. A moment later, I could see a bit of relief cross Kyle's face, and he slumped back into a more relaxed pose, almost falling over. Jim held him up from behind while Kyle's arms fell limp at his side.

The wound was a deep gash into the thigh. A blade might have caused this. The others stuffed remnants they ripped from their own uniforms into the wound and tied it off with a belt to act as a makeshift tourniquet. When I released the tourniquet, his blood started flowing. I was not getting an immediate spray, which was an indication there was no artery punctured. This discovery was a good thing.

Kyle slumped even more, and I realized my mistake in the dosage when I applied the sedative. I forgot to take into account the amount of blood lost. Jim gave me a serious concerning look, saying, "You gotta do something."

"Ohm, place a pressure-based local force field over the wound and disinfect the area," I said.

A blue see-through electric field appeared over the length of the wound, and clumps of dried blood and dirt started to vanish as Ohm began the sterilization process. The blood stopped flowing because of the field's backpressure and formed a bead along the length of the gash. While adjusting the skin sealer for deep cuts, Kyle conked out completely. I put down the skin sealer and picked up the medjector. After setting it for a mild stimulant, I pressed it onto his neck again. I waited and watched. Ten seconds, twenty seconds, and then Kyle moved his head up and experienced troubled breathing while kicking around. The blue field was locked in place and moved when his legs moved.

"Hold him still," I said to the crowd, and two of his teammates moved into position to help hold his legs in place while telling him it was going to be all right and to hang in there.

I retrieved the skin sealer and began slowly moving it over the entire length of the wound. The red ray formed a horizontal line on the skin as it passed through the blue force field. At first, nothing happened, and one of the team members said, "Nothing's happening."

After about a minute of continuous application, the skin started to grow together. "It's a slow and steady process," I said, remembering my bedside manner training. "You're doing great, Kyle."

At this point, I felt like everyone leaned over to get a look at the technology in action, but my focus was to keep the skin sealer moving. I stopped briefly to adjust the strength of the skin sealer several times. What started out as a fifteen to twenty-centimeter deep gash was reduced to four or five centimeters in length. My back and forth movements became shorter until I held it over a circular puncture that slowly filled in.

"Ohm, discontinue force field," I said, and the blue force field over Kyle's leg disappeared.

The entire process took about fifteen minutes, which is why this type of treatment is not very effective on deep wounds in a combat situation. That is one of the reasons why I wanted the compound guards knocked out because I did not know how long this field doctoring would take. Kyle looked better and started breathing easier. One of his buddies messed up his hair and smiled. I looked over at the other one who held Kyle's leg, and I noticed a nasty cut along his arm.

"Okay, you're up next," I said and proceeded to apply the skin sealer to his arm. This treatment was a much faster fix-up because the wound was not that deep.

With a little help from his teammates, Kyle attempted to stand, got up, and put his weight on his leg. Testing it gently at first, finally standing firmly on his own, Kyle said, "It feels okay. Thanks, thanks a lot."

"You're welcome. You may be a little light-headed. Your wound is repaired, but you still lost some blood," I replied.

"That's what I like to see, teamwork," Jim said excitedly. "Now, let's get out of here. Malik, what's the status?"

"They appear to be lifeless, Young."

Cooper moved over to the auragraphic map and said, "According to the map, they still have life signs."

"They should wake up in about an hour or so. I have not encountered this species before, so I was a little generous on the sedative. Ohm, discontinue the map," I said, and the map vanished from view.

"Well, that gives us a head start on getting back to the door," Jim said. "Gather up your gear, and let's move out."

"I don't mind the walk, but we can transport," I said. "Are we heading to the misty archway?"

Jim said, "Yeah," as he slipped on his pack and jostled it into place. "Transport us to the misty arch."

The members of the rescued team gave each other side looks, finally realizing for the first time that I was not part of the team, and I might even be an alien. David walked up to me while pushing his glasses up from his nose and said, "We call it the Mist Door, and thank you."

"Let's all gather close together," I said out loud, and everyone moved in, with Malik finally abandoning his watch over the compound to join us.

"Ohm, transport us all to the nearby structure known as the Mist Door," I said.

The scene collapsed in from the sides, and I was particalized through space and probability to be reconstructed atom by atom at the new location.

"Now that's different," Jim said as he shook his head and started walking toward the Mist Door. "Line it up, David."

David headed for a totem off to the side of the platform where the Mist Door stood. We all walked closer to the platform while David was busy rotating various segments on the totem. They lit up when he moved them. Each time he rotated a segment on the totem, the next segment of the pillar spun to match the companion symbol on the Mist Door. First clockwise, then counter-clockwise. Each spin issued a sound. These were the same sounds I heard earlier, leading me to this location. After several symbols lit up, David pressed a circular object at the top of the totem, and the Mist Door sprang into life. The keystone glowed, and the teal mist descended to fill the archway with swirling fog. The rescued team proceeded to walk into the mist, and the shape of their passing silhouettes disturbed the density as they disappeared from view. I heard the backward piano sound again as the archway consumed each one of the members of the team.

Jim looked at me and asked, "Coming?"

"Where are we going?" I replied.

"My place," he said. "It's easy. Just walk on through."

CHAPTER 6

Guardian Reunion

I rang the doorbell at Jim's Twin Falls ranch house and waited before hearing some footsteps approaching on the other side of the door. The door opened, and Jim said, "Sam," as he cracked a smile and leaned back with a beer bottle in one hand. "Come in, come in."

I stepped into the house and found myself with a hallway to my right, a sunken living room to my left, and the kitchen straight ahead. Jim walked into the kitchen and asked, "Can I get you one?" referring to the beer.

"Oh yes, please. A dark one if you have it," I said in a fake English accent.

He pulled a can out of the refrigerator and proceeded to get down a pint glass from the cupboard. He opened the can and started pouring it slowly down the side of the tilted pint glass.

"I know what you're thinking," he said while pouring the ale. "I can't believe I just traveled a million miles, and he's handing me a beer from a can. Well, this is a taste of Idaho's own local brewery, the best. It's called Toothy Knot, and it's the closest thing you're gonna get to a Scottish style ale, this side of the mountain."

"With a pitch like that, I gladly accept your offer," and I took a sip of the ale. Damn, it was good. It had a full-body with a mild nutty flavor. The only thing it was really missing was the creamy foam. I guess my face said it all.

"See, I told you you'd like it," Jim said as he motioned for us to move out of the kitchen and into the sunken living room.

We sat down in the cozy living room with a stacked stone fireplace at one end. Jim took what I assumed was his favorite chair, and I sat on the couch along the wall. There was a coffee table between us, and I sat my glass on a coaster while Jim held onto his bottle.

"So, what's new?" Jim asked as an ice breaker.

"About a week ago, I woke up kind of disoriented," I started to say.

Jim interrupted, "Happens to me all the time," as he took a sip from his bottle.

"I didn't know where I was, Jim. I was in my own home, but I felt like a stranger in my own skin," I said grimly.

"Have you thought about talking to a doctor?" Jim asked slowly.

"I should, or I want to, but I haven't had the time. I feel like there are hundreds of things to do, and I can barely make it through the day," I confessed before picking up my glass and taking another drink.

"What can I do to help?" Jim said, offering candidly.

"I was with Candy at the time, and she experienced some type of disorientation too. We were on *Tiger Mountain*. I am wondering if anything like that has happened to you?" I asked.

He propped up his elbow on the arm of the chair and leaned his head into his hand before speaking into it, "Now that you mention it, I was in my truck last week, and I did not know how I got across town. I was just there. You know it could happen to you. I mean, I do. That I could, at some point, lose the ability to be cognitive. What if this is one of the first signs?"

"I wouldn't worry about that, Jim. Your story sounds a lot like Candy's," I said. "She also described being in one place then all of a sudden was somewhere else. It may be some form of attack on the Guardian implant system."

"What!" he exclaimed as he leaned forward too quick in his chair, sprawling limbs in an outward gesture.

"I am just speculating. I have memories from the future. They're just there, reminding me of all the things I no longer have unless I do a hundred things right to get them back. Did anything like that happen with you?"

He switched arms on the chair and propped up his left arm this time and leaned his head into it and said sarcastically, "Ya know, I don't seem to have any memories from the FUTURE hanging around in my head."

"That's okay. I'm just trying to figure things out," I said.

"What do you remember about the future? Any lottery numbers or winning game scores you would care to share?" he asked.

"Sorry, nothing that useful, mostly interpersonal relationship stuff with people I have not even met yet," I said with a smile.

"If you have this list of things to do to get back to the future," and he mimed air quotes with both hands while still holding onto his bottle when he said the word, future, "what's next on the list?"

"I guess I'm just checking in with everybody. You're first on the list," I said.

"Aw, that's nice. What makes me first on the list?" he prodded.

"The fact that you had ale. I don't think any of the others would offer me this truly delicious Scottish ale replica," I said as I took another drink of the ale.

"Now that I can drink to," Jim said as he took another sip from his bottle.

The conversation turned toward more mundane things, and eventually, we ended up watching the last part of a televised sports event where young men tried to move a ball across a line on a large open playing field. It was players in red shirts vs. players in white shirts. The white shirts eventually won the day, which seemed to make Jim happy. Four ales later, I said goodbye and left Jim's house a little bit drunk.

I held out my hand and said, "Ohm can you materialize a marijuana joint and a lighter in my hand?"

"Certainly," Ohm replied.

My palm sparkled, and when the sparkles faded, I held a tightly rolled joint and a modern electric lighter. I lit up and smoked, putting the lighter in my pocket as I walked down the streets of Jim's neighborhood. I started shifting echo slightly as I strolled down the sidewalk. I cast the *Motif* over the bridge and around softly sloping streets until a cab approached, and I flagged it down.

It was a traditional yellow cab with a band of black and white checkers along the side. An Indian fellow wearing a turban was driving. As I opened the door and started to get in, he said while pointing at the joint, "Oh no, no, you can't bring that into my cab."

I tossed it aside and said, "No problem, sorry about that. Can you take me to the Takota mountain military base entrance?"

"Okay, it's about a thirty-minute drive," he said as he dropped the lever to start the meter running before slowly driving off.

Music came from the front seat where a hidden radio played some Indian raga, and the Sitar started jangling my stoned mind. I was actually quite enjoying it. A singer finally joined in, and it sounded a lot like Nusrat Fateh Ali Khan.

I must have nodded off because the next thing I remember was the driver lecturing me, "You can't sleep in my cab, no, no, please wake up," while looking back at me through the rearview mirror.

I said the same thing as before, "No problem, sorry about that," and I sat up and started shifting echo again.

I rolled the window down a little to add noise closer to my ears and block out the raga. I began shifting the driver and the car into probable versions of themselves until I was riding inside a jeep driven by a military officer. There was a folder on the seat next to me. I opened it and found a clip-on key card that I attached to one of the flaps on my shirt pocket.

"We're approaching the perimeter," the driver said.

"Thank you, sir," I said.

"Oh, you don't have to call me, sir. I am not an officer," he replied.

"Not yet, but keep up the good work, and you will be," I said, and he smiled back at me through the rearview mirror.

We pulled up to the gated entrance and came to a stop. Guards stepped out of a shack to inspect the vehicle. It was dark out, so they used flashlights. The driver provided papers. One of the gatekeepers shone a light on me and in my face a little too long. I averted my eyes and shielded them with my hand. The light moved away without an apology, and the gatekeepers stepped back. They raised the gate, and we drove on through.

After another couple of minutes in a tunnel, we approached the entrance to the mountain. Takota was a military base carved into the side of the mountain. The gigantic blast doors were thicker and taller than any vault door I ever saw. The doors themselves were a true monument to human engineering, let alone all the additional carving out of spaces inside and into the stone. The base offered many levels, and Mist Door Operations was at the bottom of the mountain.

When the jeep came to a stop, I exited the vehicle, grabbing the folder on my way out, saying, "Thank you, son."

The driver nodded and drove off, leaving me standing before those massive doors. The doors were only closed when the base was on lockdown. I approached the sentry at the entrance, and he stepped up with an electronic wand in his hand.

"State your name and business, sir," he said reluctantly, as he looked up and down my civilian clothes.

"Sam Richards. I'm here on official business," I said, nonchalantly.

"Place your arms outstretched and stand with a wide stance. I need to check for weapons," the sentry said, indicating that it was not optional.

As I assumed the position, I stepped slowly in place and reached into echo with the *Motif* in my mind to move this process along. He would find nothing. He swished his electronic wand over my appendages before pulling another device out of his jacket pocket to scan the key card hanging from my shirt. He looked at the device, looked at me, then tapped the device and put it back into his pocket.

"You'll find the deputy at the end of the lit hall over there," he said, pointing to a lit hall off to his right.

He was already walking away as I said, "Thank you," to his back.

Making my way over to the lit hall, I reached into echo, once more, to make this entrance to Mist Door Operations as favorably probable to me as possible. I proceeded down the hall, which divided at the end. On one half of the hallway, there was a bulletproof barrier with loopholes. The other side was an entrance with a scanning station.

I continued to shift echo as I walked up to the deputy and said, "Hello, Roger."

Roger looked up from watching a small black and white TV, leaned back suddenly, and then regained his balance on the chair before he stood up quickly after being caught slacking on the job.

"Hey, Sam, good to see you," he said while pulling a device out of his jacket and scanning my key card. It took a moment before he also tapped a device he held and put it back in his pocket.

I heard a buzzer, and a light changed from red to green. "Thanks, Roger," I said, and I walked to the end of the hall, where I pushed the button for the elevator door.

The sound of motors and pulleys whirred softly in the background, and a short time later, the elevator doors opened. I stepped inside and turned around to look at the controls for this elevator. There was a series of circular buttons with numbers and a few abbreviations. I pushed the button labeled LLMD and heard a double buzz sound. Realizing I needed the keycard, I slid it quickly down a slot next to the console then pressed the LLMD button again. This time a ding sounded and the doors closed before the elevator started moving. I attached the keycard to my front pants pocket using the little clip. The mountain was very deep, and this is probably one of the longest elevator rides I have ever experienced. There was a lit display above the doors changing as the lift passed by the numbered levels, descending farther into the mountain. Once I passed the numbered levels, the display above the door quit updating.

I thought about the way I used echo to manipulate people this evening. It does get creepy if you do it too much or all the time. Especially if it is someone you may have to work with or see again on a regular basis. The Indian cab driver still exists. He was just a mechanism to propel me through echo until I made the seamless transition to the jeep and alternate driver. This detail is why echo is the superior form of conveyance versus transporting. The caveat with echo is that you are physically bound deeply within the echo conveying you. The caveat with transportation is the dark empty space you are placed in every time you want to use it. But transportation, in general, is pretty damn convenient.

The manipulation of the guard and the deputy was really very minor. Who is to say I haven't met Roger before? The elevator continued down. I got a little panicked at one point and opened up the folder I picked up earlier from the seat of the jeep. It was full of blank pages, but that did give me an idea. When the doors open, I'll use the envelope as a distraction and seek out David's office instead. I began gathering up the *Motif* like it was some type of garland laying on the floor, and I was a Christmas tree decorated with it. I wanted the *Motif* wrapped all around me.

"Ohm, can you add a visual path to my invisihud that shows the way to David's office from my current location?"

"Certainly," Ohm said, and an optical overlay appeared with an orange line showing the map from where I was to the entrance of David's office. I could also see there was more than one person in the office. It looked like I needed to exit the elevator, move straight, then right, left, continue on past two junctions, left again, and I would find David's office on the right.

The elevator doors slid open to reveal Major Austin approaching, who said, "If you'll follow me, Sam."

He stood between me and my objective, with his arms spread wide and gesturing to a stairwell on the left. Two armed guards stood behind him with their weapons pointing up, holding them at their chest. It was time for a show.

I staggered out of the elevator and said, "I got here as fast as I could. It's all in there," as I handed Major Austin the folder of empty pages. During the handoff, I imagined the *Motif* garland flowing quickly down my arm and up along his arm, making it the most useful, probable information available. I also mentally pushed the *Motif* out in a general fashion to cover the guards behind Major Austin.

A frantic nature overtook Major Austin as he rapidly flipped from page to page and muttered under his breath, "Dear God." He tucked the folder under his arm and sprinted up the stairwell he previously gestured to.

I fell to my knees, stammering the last bit, and said to the floor loudly, "Don't just stand there, man. Make sure he gets there."

The two guards looked at each other and raced up the stairwell after Major Austin. I got up, dusted myself off, and followed the orange line inside the visual overlay of my invisihud. It led me through twisting hallways that I guessed were bored into the mountain using a very large circular drill. All the floors were a raised metal grate platform with cables and tubes you could see underneath.

The ceiling was similar. It was made of dropped metal grill panels with cables and tubing running above them. Lights were evenly spaced based upon the distance between the last and next intersection. I passed a few people in uniforms, but no one tried to stop me. I received the occasional nod but no salutes.

I let the *Motif* go as I locked in the non-threatening version of this reality. This echo adjustment meant Major Austin's recent epiphany never happened in this probability, and he and his guards were just fine. I took a left and then on the right. The door was open, but I knocked and leaned in, stepping into David's office.

"Sam," I heard David call from across the room.

Robin and Malik were here.

"It is good to see you, Sam," Malik said in his stoic way,

I walked over to shake his hand, Ralla style, which was like a typical handshake only instead of shaking at the wrist, you gripped the entire arm from the elbow down. Placing your arms together makes the bond stronger according to Ralla legend. I received a quick hug from Robin then shook David's hand before plopping down on a stool across from them.

"What brings you to our neck of the woods?" David asked.

Robin spoke up and said, "Something's wrong," while taking a seat at the table.

"Something has happened. I don't know if it is wrong yet," I said.

"What has happened, Sam?" Malik asked.

"It happened about a week ago. I was in my home on *Tiger Mountain*. When I woke up, I didn't feel right. I didn't know where I was. I felt like another person inside this body. But I have memories of future things I have done. And not only that, I feel the loss of being away from my future family," I said while looking at Malik as he walked over to join the discussion.

"Whoa," Robin said.

"Did you hit your head on something? I presume you checked, right?" David double asked.

"I did. I asked Ohm to scan me now and compare me to previous scans. There was no detectable evidence I have changed," I said to David. "Besides, it happened to Candy too."

"You were with Candy?" Robin asked.

"That's odd too because we were not together for quite a while, but then all of a sudden she was there the moment I have a lapse like this," I said accusingly. "But she did not know how she got there either, and I do believe her on that."

"Maybe," David began then, "never mind. Hmm."

"I checked with Jim, and he experienced a moment of loss last week. I thought I'd ask each of you if anything unusual happened to you last week?" I asked the room.

Everyone in the room looked at each other as they tried to recall. I went on, "Anything, you lost something, you found something, how did I get here? I thought..."

Malik interrupted, "I needed to do the same thing twice last week. Straighten up the gym. I thought I cleaned up after sparring, and when I came back, I discovered that I had not and needed to do it again."

"I was writing a paragraph over, now that you mention it. I thought I wrote a small blurb about a specific topic, but when I searched the document, I couldn't locate it. It was still fresh in my mind, so I typed it again. I mean, I rewrite things all the time, but it did happen last week," David said.

Robin put her chin between her thumb and index finger while shaking her head yes and said, "Me too, I ran some test. I was sure I logged the results, but when I checked the log, there were no entries. I conducted the test again."

"What does it mean?" Malik asked.

"I mentioned this to Jim, and he flipped. What happened to me may have happened to you in a lesser fashion, being relayed through the Guardian implant system. Do any of you have memories from the future?" I asked the group.

There was a unanimous head shaking no, and David asked, "What kind of memories from the future do you have?"

"There are so many years of daily activity," I said.

"Are we in your future memories?" Malik asked directly.

"You are, but we don't spend a lot of time together. We see each other at a few annual gatherings, and that is about it. My time is spent aboard starships with my two wives," I said.

"Two wives!" Robin blurted out.

"And a cat. In the future, I have a cat. And it's not just the memories of a single future, there are two sets of future memories on top of one another as if I am in a very long time loop, and I am just starting up again," I explained.

"How do you have two wives, Sam?" Robin asked.

I looked at her. Robin and I shared a brief relationship in the first time loop. After Candy dumped me for Elowin, I fell into Robin's arms, and we lived together in a small house here in Twin Falls. Things were going great but little did I know, Fabio's crazy son, Reziko, was out for revenge because I undid his murder of Isaac. In that time loop, I also learned Splendorites are not always in perfect health. We are eternal, as far as we know, but also mortal in the fact we can be physically killed. I learned Reziko was bipolar. One of the first steps I did in the second loop was to install a medical implant inside Reziko to balance out his bipolar madness. And I do mean madness.

He waited until Robin and I broke up. She took an off-world command then he sent a hoard of demons to slaughter her men. I got there just in time to save Robin, but everyone else was dead. I lost it that day and nearly murdered Reziko with a stone I found on the ground. But at the last moment, I couldn't do it. I placed him in a Cryovirt, with a virtual narrative making him believe he killed me instead. After months of monitoring, his bipolar condition was detected and corrected with a miniature echo-sturdy medicine dispenser implanted inside his body.

It looks like in this timeline, the span of time where I fell in love with Robin is the same time Candy skipped. She was with Elowin, then months later, instantly on *Tiger Mountain* with me. I don't remember having a relationship with Robin this time, but it happened during that time span.

"Their names are Erin and Jorrie," I said directly to Robin, "and I miss them a lot."

"I didn't mean to be insensitive," Robin said.

"To me, this is the past. In the first loop, I was married to Erin, and we had some problems. Somehow, she met Jorrie, and they fell in love. Eventually, I was invited into their relationship, and we married on Ursa Prime. The Ursonian people have a more complex marriage system. In this second loop, the relationships unfolded a little differently, but we still ended up all married to one another."

"Wait a second," David said, as he shook his head in disbelief, "you're from the future too?"

"That's the odd thing. My body is not from the future, but I feel like my mind might be. Last week I was with my family on a starship, and today I am living in the past," I said.

"Can't you just find them in echo?" Robin asked.

"I probably could, but then what? Hi there. You don't know me, but I am your future husband. I could locate them, but they won't remember me. And even if I just sit back and wait, the same series of events may not unfold. I may never meet them at all," I lamented.

"Your future memories are a map," Malik said in his simplistic way.

I looked over at him and said, "I think you're right, Malik. I need to use the future memories to navigate this time loop to find my future again."

"But if it's a time loop, won't it just happen again? What caused it?" Robin asked.

"I think I have to accept the possibility that I may have caused the loop somehow. A time travel experiment went wrong. Who knows? I do have a few memories from a loop even before the first loop. A zeroth loop," I said.

"Time loop zero?" Robin repeated. "What do you remember?"

"I remember receiving a message, from myself, with one command. Move *Tiger Mountain* back to Blinn space. I was on *Tiger Mountain* in my bedroom and sat up in the same exact spot where this future memory acquisition occurred last week. *Tiger Mountain* was currently in another echo, so I sent out the fifteen-minute warning to all citizens that *Tiger Mountain* would be leaving this area. If they wanted out, now was the time to do so. After that, I fired up the engines and cruised through space before shifting echo to bring *Tiger Mountain* into a protective stance near the Blinn homeworld. It remains there at this time," I said.

"Do you know why you gave such a command from yourself to yourself?" David asked.

"It puzzled me all through the first loop. I never did figure out any possible motivation as to why I should keep *Tiger Mountain* so close to Blinn. But in the second loop, it finally occurred to me. Construction stabilization. *Tiger Mountain*'s physical parts were constructed in the Blinn replication facilities. Then I reinforced each part's structural integrity with an image of the *Motif* itself. This infusion causes *Tiger Mountain* to keep its shape and not distort as it travels through echo. It allows all the systems to remain in spec, even if the concept of copper is fluidic in some given echo that *Tiger Mountain* might be visiting," I said.

"So, you were warning yourself about a possible disruption to structural stabilization," Robin said out of the blue. "If you were off in echo and some of the parts lost the protectivity of the *Motif*, the entire space station might be compromised or even destroyed."

"That was my guess too. And it would be nice to keep that information just in this group. If the parts lost their protectivity while *Tiger Mountain* was in Blinn space, there would be no distortion experienced at all. It would not break because it was in the echo where its parts originated. This conclusion led me to keep *Tiger Mountain* in the same echo all through the second time loop," I added.

"Therefore, the time loop prevents the destruction of *Tiger Mountain* in some possible future scenario," David said out loud.

"Indeed," Malik followed up.

"And the destruction of *Tiger Mountain* could be the catalyst that causes the time loop to begin with," Robin said.

"Oh god, I don't even want to think about that. I was supposed to fence with the Captain of the ship today. It was my turn to make dinner, so I was going to surprise everyone with Yama root stew," I said as the room fell silent.

"Well, I won't take up any more of your time. I just wanted to see if you happened to have a similar experience," I said.

"Wait a minute," David said hastily. "What do we do?"

"What can we do?" Robin injected.

"Major Cooper is correct. There is nothing we can do but wait," Malik said, looking directly at me. "I pledge my support to help you guide time as best possible. When you need my aid, call on me, and I will help."

"Thank you, Malik. I may take you up on that. For now, I am going to check in with the other Guardians to see if they have similar stories," I said.

"Oh yeah, there are others like us. I guess I hadn't thought about them in a while," David said.

"Well, until we meet again," I said to the group.

I stood up and said, "Ohm, transport me to Enki's Dale, the road at the base of Candy's house."

My world deconstructed as light streamed in from the side of my peripheral vision. The black silence commenced, leaving me in darkness. What did I learn? *Tiger Mountain*'s destruction could have caused the time loop? How long had this been going on, I wondered? Was there some way to break the loop? David's office was shortly replaced with a cool dark evening scene somewhere in the country as everything streamed in from the sides.

CHAPTER 7

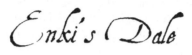

The insects must have detected my presence because the night was dead silent after my arrival. Then, as if unable to hold the breath of silence any longer, the crickets resumed their night choir.

The air was a bit chilly for me, so I closed my eyes and looked to the left. An invisihud menu revealed itself. I thought I saw some outdoor icon options when I reviewed the invisihud side menu. There was an optical cloak, life-enhance, deep space life support, and a few other options. I chose the life-enhance, which was essentially a personal shield and life support rolled into one. It wouldn't protect you in deep space, but on the surface of most worlds, you could survive. This menu option allows you to walk on or under the water. You can smoke inside the field and keep the smoke from escaping. It offered an adjustable radius to extend outward and encompass up to three people depending upon how many cloaked scanners you dedicated to the operation. The most important feature right now was it regulated body temperature, and I began to warm up.

I made my way up the incline of the road. There was a small cliff to my left, and I was at the bottom of it. Atop this cliff, and set back from the road, was Candy's house. I wanted to give her a gift, so we designed it together. Her best friend Alex and Alex's boyfriend Lucas lived in a house, a field or two down the road. Candy's immediate neighbors were Madison Griffin and Nick Baker. They were married now. A little bit down the road and across from them lived the Fosters, Ethan and Olivia. Olivia was also Nick's sister, so there was a family tie there. They had two children, Albert and Lulu, with Albert being the older one.

I came upon the official road entrance to Candy's house. In the first loop, when Candy and I designed the house, many magicians came to challenge me. They knew I lived with Candy, so we got three to nine challengers a month. To solve that dilemma, I constructed a gate along the main steps where Ohm scanned the would-be callers to see if they carried a wand. If Ohm detected a wand, it was swapped with a replica made in the off-world Blinn replication centers. The original was transported to a "safe place." If an intruding magician ventured off the path and tried to go around the door, Ohm transported them back to the bottom of the steps leading to the gate.

I took the steps up and reached a landing where an old white painted wooden door stood. The paint was aged, and it looked like it hadn't been painted in thirty years or more. To my right was a large metal drawer built into the stone wall. Above the drawer hung a sign reading, "Place your wand in the drawer." The paint on the sign also looked neglected for thirty years.

I opened the door and walked on through. It closed silently behind me. The stone walkway led up to a fairly modern-looking house. Its roof was an ill-placed trapezoid tilting toward the back of the home. When it rained, it all flowed to the back and left side of the house. But this tilt allowed for large vertical picture windows in the front, and you could see into the house from the outside. The lights were on, and I went to the side entrance near the kitchen to knock.

After a few moments, Candy rounded the corner, came to the door, and let me in. Her hair was wrapped in a towel. She wore pajama bottoms, and a light-colored cream covered her entire face.

"I don't want to hear a single word," she said while shaking her hand in front of me. "If it were anyone else, I wouldn't have even answered the door. What brings you around now?"

"Did you check with Alex and Lucas about what happened?"

"No, not yet, but I am going to, tonight. Ethan and Olivia are having a get-together over at their place. Were you invited?"

"Uh, no. I didn't get an invite."

"Well, you're coming with me. I have to finish getting ready," she said as she turned around and walked back to the room she emerged from.

"Do you have an extra wand I can borrow?" I asked as she walked away.

"Check the drawer."

"Thanks," I replied and headed into her kitchen. The "safe place" that the entrance door transported bad magician wands to was Candy's bakery drawer in her kitchen. I opened it up and saw several wands lying in the drawer, right next to the rolling pin and the cutting board. I removed them and spread them out on the marble countertop. I started rolling each one of them across the counter, similar to someone looking for the best drum stick from a bulk supply. I sat the ones that rolled the smoothest off to the side and put the more bent and twisted candidates back in the drawer. This selection left four wands on the counter.

I must have made a fair amount of noise because Candy called out, "Don't make a mess in there. I just cleaned up."

"I won't," I called back.

Each wand was of a different length and made from various types of wood. They all were thicker on one end and tapered thinner along their length. Above the grip dividing it in half, each wand offered some colorized band inlay. I don't know if this was part of wand construction or a signature of the wand-maker, but each inlay band was also unique. I looked down at the long thin zippered pocket near the bottom of my pant leg. When I awoke on *Tiger Mountain*, I remember wondering about the strange-sized pocket sewn into my pants, but I discovered a wand fit in the pocket beautifully. There were similar pockets along the outer sleeves of my shirt. I placed one wand in my leg pocket and another in the right-sleeve pocket before returning the other two wands to the drawer.

There was a bowl of fruit here, so I snacked on some grapes, cracked a few walnuts, and ate them while I waited for Candy to get ready. Sweeping the shell from the walnuts into my hand, I looked around for a trashcan. After opening and closing a few of the lower cabinets, I found it under the sink, of course.

"Ohm, can you scan the San Francisco marketplace for some wine stores? A single bottle of merlot and a white pinot grigio should do," I said out loud.

"Checking," Ohm replied, and a sparkle came and went leaving two bottles of wine on Candy's counter.

I felt a little bad about remotely shoplifting from the market, but eh, "I'll make it up to the vendor by buying something there someday," I told myself.

Candy walked in from the other room, fussing with an earring. Dressed and ready to go, she asked, "Well, whatcha think?"

I walked around the kitchen counter to the other side to get a full-length view of her. Her hair was a large, full afro framing her beautiful round face. She wore bright-colored eye makeup and a subtle lip gloss. Hints of a slight blush were on her cheeks, and she wore a top with a diving neckline revealing the top portions of her full bosom. The low cut of her top revealed her belly button, and she wore grey hip-hugger tight pants with some thin reflective thread woven into the fabric. Her open-toed platform shoes made her about four or five centimeters taller.

"Smokin'," I said while offering my best Jim Carey impersonation, which I thought Candy might recognize.

She smiled and performed her signature head tilt before grabbing a shawl from a hook by the door along with a small purse she slung over her shoulders. She buttoned the shawl at her neck as it draped over her shoulders like a small cape.

"You ready?" she asked while looking me over and commenting. "That's what you're wearing?"

"Candy, you know I don't do the dress-up thing," I replied as I grabbed the two bottles of wine from the counter and opened the door.

We stepped into the night, and Candy shivered a little as she walked carefully in her platform shoes, saying, "I thought we could Transfast there instead of mucking through the fields or heading down to the road."

Transfast was one of the icons available in the invisihud menu. It allowed you to look at something in the distance, and the cloaked scanners transported you there. It was great for fast trekking through open spaces or avoiding approaching calamities such as vehicles or attackers. Even though the night air was chilly, the night itself was beautiful and calm, and I said, "I was thinking more along the lines of an anti-gravity platform."

"All right," Candy said with a shrug.

"Ohm, one anti-gravity platform, please," I said out loud.

A wide sparkle appeared at our feet, leaving behind a large circular disc on the stone patio. I offered my arm to Candy, and we stepped onto the platform together, taking up a position in the center. An auragraphic light display zipped up from the floor with a map of the nearby area. Inside the auragraphic display, I tapped on Ethan and Olivia's place, and the platform gently lifted into the air and started moving across the field in the direction I chose on the map.

I noticed Candy was still a bit chilly, so I tapped on one of the environment control buttons inside the display. A visible force field surrounded the anti-gravity platform, which reduced the chill to make the ride much more comfortable. From a distance, and with the force field in place, we might have looked like a slowly moving oversized gumdrop.

"So, did you talk to anyone else yet?" Candy asked.

"I just returned from Mist Door Operations," I said. "Jim, Malik, Robin, and David all reported experiencing some form of 'do-over' sequence last week. They each thought they did something, only to discover that wasn't the case, and they needed to do it again. But none of them have any future memories as I do."

"This is nice," Candy said, "a lot better than trying to ride on a flying carpet. I always feel like I am going to fall off of those things. You have to hang on too much."

I nodded in agreement as the anti-gravity platform navigated around a few trees and made the slow approach to the Foster's home. It looked like there was a group of people on a patio, off to the right side of the house, so I tapped twice on the floor of the anti-gravity platform to bring up the map display. I targeted our approach for the patio before dismissing the auragram, which caused it to fall back to the floor and disappear.

We approached in a wide arc over the patio wall as the anti-gravity platform settled to the floor of the stone patio. A neatly stacked low wall surrounded the patio, keeping the more wild lawn at bay. The floor of the patio was made of well-placed locally sourced stones with a long rectangular fire pit in the center. A nice blaze burned there. The fire pit was walled and offered wide flat stones along the border so a person could take a seat close to the fire. There was a stack of wood at one end of the fire pit and a few iron tools for moving burning wood or poking the flames. Around the fire pit were several round metal tables with frosted glass tops. The chairs surrounding the tables were those plush high back springy lawn chairs you might find at an outdoor garden supply center. I took in the view of quite a few guests seated and standing around.

Candy and I stepped off the anti-gravity platform together, and I silently dismissed it by targeting it with my invisihud and using the recycle icon from the menu. A single person applauded our landing and quickly walked up to us, saying, "Bravo."

Ethan Foster was a thin guy who wore circular copper wire-rim glasses. He dressed casually, with dark pants and a sweater vest over a long-sleeve salmon-colored shirt. Ethan was a magician of great notoriety. Even at this young age, I would guess late-twenties, he faced and fought one of the darkest magicians of all time. Magical scholars were hard-pressed to find a more evil magician than the one Ethan defeated.

"I love bailiwick tech stuff," Ethan started off saying. "It's good to see you, Sam. It's been a while."

I stopped to talk with Ethan while Candy moved off to meet a couple approaching her.

"Yeah, it's fun. I hope it was not too over the top. I stopped by Candy's as she headed out the door, and she invited me along. I brought some wine," I said as I held up the bottles.

"Thanks, we can put them on the table," he said, and he took one of the bottles from my hand.

We walked together, across the patio, through the guests, to a long buffet-style table at the other end of the fire pit. While we walked, Ethan asked, "How have you been?"

His question hinted that he might have already heard about my condition from his neighbor Candy. Candy was close with all of her Enki's Dale neighbors. She called them her family and was especially close to Ethan and Olivia's children, who called her aunt Candy.

"Oh pretty well, all things considered," I started saying. "Something odd happened last week that I'm still trying to figure out."

"That's good to hear," Ethan said.

Hoping to change the subject, I immediately asked, "How are Lulu and Albert doing? I'll bet they're a foot taller than the last time I saw them."

Ethan beamed with a bit of pride, taking the bait, replying, "Oh, yeah, they are growing like weeds, but tonight they are off with their grandparents."

"Which means you can have an adult party."

We both put the bottles of wine on the table. There was soft music playing, but I did not see a radio.

He nodded with a smile, "Yeah," and his wife Olivia walked up.

She gave me a peck on the cheek and a light hug before saying, "So nice to see you, Sam. I'm glad you came."

"Thanks, it is nice to get out. The patio looks great."

"Thank you," she said as she took a slight bow. "Candy helped me set it up this afternoon."

"Would you like to be introduced to the guests?" she asked.

"Oh, that is not necessary. I can just mingle on my own."

Off to my left and behind, I heard a deep, bellowing voice call out, "Ethan, Ethan, my boy."

Olivia and I both turned to look, as Ethan said, "Excuse me," and he went off to meet a newly arrived guest.

Olivia looked at me and said, "Here's the who's who in our back yard. See the large plump man sprawling in the chair on the left? That is Garniel Find. He is in charge of granting permits when magic is involved in construction. He works in the same building as my dad and overheard my father mentioning we had a party. He showed up but was not invited."

"Kind of like me?"

"Not at all like you," she said, placing her hand on my folded arms and going on.

"The woman sitting with him at the table is Midely Handlecrock. She is one of the most famous psychic readers known across the land. But I hear you might be just as lucky flipping a coin to make a decision rather than following her advice. In the back there, that man gesturing, Filead Fanes, is one of the most boorish braggarts you will ever meet. He goes on endlessly about how amazing he is and has a hundred stories where he is the champion of some noble cause. And that woman over there," she gestured with her eyes, "is rumored to have been with half of Boffernon's staff."

"Olivia," I said with a slight head nod, "I'm surprised to hear you repeating such gossip."

A woman wearing an apron walked up and tapped Olivia on the shoulder from behind. She whispered something in Olivia's ear, and Olivia moved her head up and down, digesting the message.

"I'll be right back," she said, and she headed off the house to help with whatever emergency arose, leaving me alone at the table.

A moment later, I heard what sounded like raccoons rummaging through garbage. I heard a raspy voice say slowly with as little enthusiasm as possible, "May I offer you a drink, sir?"

I turned around, and there was a home gnome behind the table, standing on a couple of stacked boxes, struggling to maintain his balance. The gnome presented the appearance of a miniature person, not dwarf-like, more like an old child. He wore a charcoal vest and pants made of wool with a red shirt underneath. Upon the vest, over his heart, was a bright yellow pin in the shape of a flower. His hair was thick and grey, poking out of a plaid cap that reminded me of a beret.

"Certainly, how about the merlot there," I said, and I gestured to the wine I brought.

The following display could only be described as bizarrely comical. The home gnome leaned forward and grabbed the bottle, knocking another bottle over in the process. He fumbled with a wine service tool containing the corkscrew for a good thirty seconds. Holding the wine service in his hand, he unfolded all of the parts, eventually poking his hand with the pointy end. He cursed under his breath as he tried and tried to pull the pseudo-plastic blue foil covering from the top of the wine bottle. He used the knife end of the wine service tool to try and rip the foil open. It slipped several times. Sometimes he dropped the bottle, and other times the tool. Each time I thought for sure he was going to cut himself, but eventually, he pierced the wrapping, sticking his tongue out a little to the side of his mouth as he began peeling off the protective seal.

The gnome began the process of inserting the corkscrew into the top of the bottle. He sat the bottle on the table and gently spun the corkscrew worm over the top of the bottle. All it did was spin around without descending into the cork. He pushed a little harder, and the bottle fell over again. This time he held the bottle in his hand and tried twisting the bottle. The corkscrew started to go in, only to slip and fall off when he turned the bottle at too sharp of an angle. The bottle and the wine service tool fell to the table with a double bounce thump thud.

He looked over at me, conveying the intention that he was going to leap across the table at my throat. I made a gesture with both of my hands, indicating he should twist the wine bottle and the corkscrew together in opposite directions. His eyes narrowed, he pulled his tongue back in, and he slowly picked up the bottle in one hand and the corkscrew in the other, all the while keeping direct eye contact with me.

He lifted the wine bottle high above his head and placed the corkscrew into the indentation he already started, and firmly turned. His eyes moved from mine to the raised bottle in his hand, implying that holding it up to the light would make the task a little easier. He twisted the corkscrew again, and it went in a little farther. While looking over at me with a slight grin, I made the gesture again of twisting with both hands. He picked up on it and twisted both of them at once, and the corkscrew moved even deeper. In a quick frenzy, he twisted and twisted very fast, then came to a halt, still holding the bottle over his head. He eyed the gap through the glass between the bottom of the cork and the wine itself. Backing the corkscrew off slightly, he set it in the perfect position.

With the corkscrew inserted, the tugging began. This motion was probably the silliest of the movements so far. He struggled to pull the corkscrew out of the bottle in every which way. As a small, emaciated creature, he did not have the upper body strength to brutely force the cork out of the bottle. He tried with the bottle above his head, under his arm, and between his legs. He laid the bottle on its side, on the table, and lifted his oversized foot, which resembled a shoeless paw, on top of it. Glancing over at me, he must have read my expression because he quickly removed his foot from the table and brushed off the tablecloth with his hand.

Lying sideways on the table in front of him was the bottle with the corkscrew fully inserted. Once again, gesturing, I made a cup out of my right hand and plopped it on the table. I placed the index finger from my left hand, pointing down, and touching the outer rim of my right-hand cup. The thumb on my left hand played the role of the inserted corkscrew worm. I made a lever motion with my left hand, indicating a fulcrum-like move.

He sat the wine bottle upright, and the boot lever dropped down to slap gently against the side of the bottle. He watched it ever intently while an idea formed in his mind. As if carefully inserting a puzzle piece, he moved the handle and locked the boot lever into place on the lip of the wine bottle. He grabbed the neck of the bottle with his oversized hand, locking the boot lever in place before steadily pushing up on the wine service handle. He pushed with all his might and started turning a little red in the face before pivoting, adding his entire shoulder strength into the effort. He grimaced, puffed his cheeks, thumped his leg, and the cork began to move. It was an expression of utter delight that swam across his face as he continued, with all his might, to keep the cork moving. After shifting his position again, he centered on the wine bottle to give it one more try. With another heave, the cork pulled out with a "pop."

Setting the corkscrew down slowly, he wiped his brow and gathered his composure. The gnome slowly reached for one of the empty glasses on the table and poured a full cup. He lifted the glass to his lips and drank the entire thing down like someone chugging a beer. When he finished, he wiped his mouth with his hand. Looking at me, he realized he made a faux pas.

I placed an empty wine glass in front of him, and he poured me a full glass using both hands and not spilling a drop. He sat the bottle down on the table, and it looked like the wine went straight to his head. He lost his balance on the stack of boxes as they slipped out from under him, and he fell to the floor with a clatter and a thud. His hand reached up, feeling around, and finally located the bottle. With a quick snatch, he grabbed it from the table, spilling some as he did so, and scampered off with the bottled tilted up, drinking as he ran off.

I picked up my glass of wine and took a sip. Ah, California merlot. I know what you wine snobs are thinking. But this was a merlot made from organic grapes on a climate-controlled planet where pollution is nearly eliminated. It wasn't just a Napa Valley California merlot. It was a 2366 Napa Valley California merlot, and it tasted delicious.

Standing alone, I looked around the patio and zeroed in on Candy and her group of friends. I made my way over, sipping the wine a little while weaving through the guests. It looked like a few more guests arrived while I got my wine.

A man stepped forward smiling, with his hand out as I approached. I switched the wine glass to my other hand before shaking his and saying, "Lucas Morgan."

Lucas was a handsome Caucasian male in his early thirties with an average body build. His sandy brown hair was cut short, and he wore a two-day beard as he always did. Alex was his girlfriend. They were both Guardians of *Tiger Mountain*, but I transported them from Candy's original probability to Enki's Dale. I actually met Alex and Lucas before I met Candy. It was Alex that introduced me to Candy.

"So, how are things in your world?" Lucas asked.

"I done asked them," Candy blurted out from a distance, "and yes, it happened to them too."

"Oh, you know, trying to figure stuff out while not going crazy," I replied.

Lucas offered a smile and took a drink from the cup in his hand.

"There you are," said Alex, who was probably one of the most beautiful women I have ever met or seen.

Thick, dark curly hair bounced at shoulder length. Her beautiful eyes competed for your attention, as did her athletically toned, hourglass figure. The wine she drank darkened her full lips. Imagine all the exotic qualities from all the women in the world rolled into one, and you had a good starting place for the individual that was Alex. But it was not natural selection that brought her into being. It was genetic engineering. Alex was a test tube baby, probably the most expensive and most detailed test tube baby ever made. Amarok grew her as a special operations asset. That is until she and some of her fellow test tube babies escaped their cages. Eventually, she met up with Lucas, and they have been together ever since.

She approached me with one arm open while holding her wine glass to the side and came in for a hug, which I one arm reciprocated. She smelled of rose water.

"What's up with this future memory dealio that Candy told us about?" she asked before stepping back, so there was room between all of us.

"I guess I'm still trying to figure it out," I said. "I woke up one day with these memories of places where I will go and people I will meet. I feel like the next five years or so are already mapped out for me. I have an endless list of tasks to do. That is if I want to get back to where I was."

Lucas asked, "Do you think you are from the future?"

"It feels like I sent myself a message in the form of future memories."

"I see," Lucas said.

"I don't think I physically traveled from the future to now. I just remember people, places, and events from the future. As if my future self recorded memories in my past, self's mind," I replied.

"So, you're trying to reenact those events to get back?" Alex asked.

"When you say it like that, it makes me feel like I am just a performer following a script from some draining play. But yes, I am trying to use the future memories as a guide to decide what to do."

"What if it does not turn out as you remember?" Lucas asked.

"I guess that is when I'll improvise."

"Why is this so urgent?" Alex asked with an inquisitive look.

"Because the new future memories seem so real, like, they are mine. I was just in the future last week. To me, now is the past, but I want to be where I was, which is the future."

"And what's a person living in the present supposed to do?" Lucas joked, and we all laughed.

"I think we're all supposed to smoke this joint," I said before pulling one out of my hip joint pocket.

"We are not supposed to smoke that joint," Candy said flatly. "Put that away before someone notices."

We looked around the party, and about half the guests smoked something. There were pipes, cigars, and cigarettes attached to the end of long smoking sticks. I went ahead and lit up before taking a long hit. Damn, that is the green. It has the taste where you're like, ah, that's it. I handed Alex the joint.

"Chill out, Candy," Alex said, accepting the joint and taking a drag, "it's a party."

Alex offered it to Candy, who shook her head no. She passed it to Lucas, who accepted it, and he took his time as he pulled a couple of drags from the joint.

"See, if I hit that thing, you'll all walk off, and I'll be standin' here all high unable to move," Candy said.

"That tastes great," Lucas said before handing the joint back to me.

I took a few leisurely drags on it, tapping the ash before handing it back to Alex.

"This is tasty," Alex added, smoking and holding the joint like a fashion model before passing it back to Lucas.

Lucas puffed away and handed me the joint, saying, "I'd better level off before I smoke any more."

I nodded and put it out on the side of my heel before placing the roach in the same hip pocket where I pulled it from.

We stood in silence, for a moment or two, the conversation of the party rose to a more feverish pitch, when Candy said, "See, now you're all high."

Alex burst out laughing, putting her free hand on Candy's shoulder, and said, "You're right. I am high."

I coughed and cleared my throat as I laughed.

"You're a bad influence on my friends, Sam," Candy said to me.

There was a commotion over at the drinks table as food was brought out. It didn't take long for guests to queue.

"Oh, I am so hungry," Alex moaned before looking over at Candy, asking, "Will you come with me to the table?"

"Oh, now you got the munchies," she said to Alex. "Come on, boo," and they walked off together.

Lucas held up his empty cup and said, "I think I've got the munchies too," and he walked off toward the table.

I decided to walk around the patio and headed back to the wall where Candy and I arrived earlier. A voice called out from one of the tables, "Sam, come have a seat with us."

I walked over to the table and sat down. It was Madison Griffin and Nick Baker. Although, I guess she is Madison Baker now that they are married. But I didn't really know if she took his name. I received the lean-in peck on the cheek from Madison and a firm handshake from her husband, Nick. These two, as well as most of the guests here, were all magicians. Madison was probably the smartest of them all.

"It's so nice to see you," Madison said.

"It's good to see you two again. It has been too long. I apologize for being such a stranger," I said.

"It's no big deal," Nick said. "Say, if you have some time, could you pop over and look at the back wall? I think the rain has washed some of the bricks away."

"Nick," Madison raised her voice, "he just sat down, and you're asking the man to fix the garden wall."

"Don't worry, Madison. I'll gladly inspect the wall. It will give us some time for a proper visit," I said.

"See," Nick fired back, "the man loves the outdoors and working with his hands."

"And hanging out at parties," I said gregariously. "I just smoked a joint with Alex and Lucas, so I'm pretty high right now. Forgive me if I space out on you."

"Has Ethan already asked you?" Nick asked.

I turned and looked at him with my red glassy eyes and asked, "Ask me what?"

"Nicholas Baker!" Madison raised her voice again. "You weren't supposed to mention that. Please excuse me, Sam."

Madison got up and left the table, walking toward the house.

"Some people are so sensitive," Nick explained, with a baffled look.

"You better go and make it up to her somehow," I said, "it'll make things easier when you go to sleep tonight."

Nick looked at me and shook his head, saying, "I think you're right, thanks." He got up from the table and headed off in the direction that Madison took.

I sipped my wine and sat there for a moment, enjoying the night, feeling guilty that I was. I did feel guilty. I felt like I abandoned my family somehow. I thought of the promise that Erin, Jorrie, and I made to one another the day we married. The promise was to stay together as much as possible. As I sat here alone, I felt like I let them down. Did they still exist in the future? Was I missing in their time frame?

I waved as the Guardian crew made their way over to the table with plates in hand. Candy sat down next to me, and Lucas and Alex sat across from us.

"I made you a plate of food. Hot meatballs, some olives, and cheese," Candy said as she set a plate in front of me before taking her seat next to me.

I leaned over and put my head on her shoulder in thanks. I caught myself realizing that was something I did all the time with my wife, Erin. When she sat next to me, she rested her head on my shoulder. Sometimes, the roles would be flipped, and I would place my head on her shoulder just as I did with Candy. I snapped back into my chair quickly, presumably to take it back, and a tear came to my eye.

Candy looked over at me with a "What's your problem" type of look and noticed the tear rolling down my cheek before I wiped it away.

"If you don't want the food, you don't have to eat it?"

"Sorry. I mean, thanks. I like all these things," I said. "Fuck, I'm high."

Lucas and Alex gave a smile as she said, "I feel great. This is a good party," before she started munching on what looked like a barbecue chicken wing.

"So, why the tear, Sam," Candy asked, not looking at me while holding a piece of chicken in both hands and taking a bite.

"Well, if you must know, that move I just did, the head-tilt on your shoulder, I used to do that with my wife, Erin. It was a personal greeting for us. And now that she doesn't exist, I still did it out of habit, to say thank you, but with you instead of her. When I caught myself, it brought a tear to my eye because I don't know if I'll ever see her or know that kind of love again."

Candy stopped eating, but held her food in her hands, turned and looked at me, and said, "You really loved her, didn't you?"

"I love her so much that I feel like my world is empty now that she is not around," I said.

"See, why can't you say something like that to me, Lucas?" Alex said, jokingly, while kicking him playfully under the table.

"I'm working on a sonnet, or is it a bonnet? Would you wear a bonnet?" Lucas asked Alex, extending the play.

"Maybe," Alex said slowly, "you know, if it's cool enough," before returning to her munching as Lucas did too.

I leaned back into the chair and slumped a bit.

"You look tired, Sam. When was the last time you slept?" Lucas asked while still eating.

"I guess at the apartment in San Francisco," I said.

"Fool, that was three days ago. Where have you been?" Candy asked, once again, turning and looking while holding her food before her.

"I have trekked across the galaxy," I said, maybe a little too loudly while reaching for my wine glass.

"An apartment in San Francisco? When did that happen?" Alex asked.

"Recently, and yes, you and Lucas are welcome to one of the apartments if you like. I bought the whole damn building. It is a high rise. My new off-mountain apartments are there. I gave one to Candy too. Did you pick one out yet?"

"Mmm, hmm, yeah, the one in the northwest corner," Candy said.

"Ohm, add the high-rise apartment floor level as a new Transfast location in the invisihud for all Guardians," I said. "Check it out whenever you like. The time period is 2369 A.D. There are flying cars, personal spacecraft, tech weapons, and aliens living on Earth. Earth is part of a large Union made up of many planets."

"Plus, the marketplace is out of this world. I got bread, eggs, and fruit that were absolutely delicious," Candy said before turning to me. "You were right about the food that morning. It did taste great."

"Thanks, Sam. I am most certainly going to check that out," Lucas beamed while holding up his glass.

Let's toast to it, I said. "To the San Francisco high rise."

Everyone repeated it, and we clinked our glasses gently. I took another sip then started eating. The meatballs were all right, but the sliced parmesan and olives were easily twice as good. I started mentally measuring sips of wine with what was left on my plate, trying to balance what I was eating with what remained of the merlot in my glass. I took a bite of the cheese, let it melt and dissolve in my mouth, then cleansed the palate with a taste of merlot. I tried a green olive. These were the large kind with the pits. I quickly realized I sipped the wine way too fast, so I started doubling up on the food bites. I'd try half a meatball and a sliver of cheese, then a sip of wine. Yeah, I was pretty high at that table.

After finishing my food and wine, I sunk into the plush lawn furniture. I surveyed the scene. This party was like most parties, people who already knew each other tended to congregate together. I noticed many of the tables were like ours, with a few close friends hanging out together. From behind and off to my left, I could hear the blow-hard Olivia mentioned. He was going on about the time he did this or the time he did that. Did I ever tell you about the time when so and so asked me to do a great deed? I got sick of it. He was harshing my mellow.

I said, "Excuse me," to the table, and I got up to walk over to the open patio where Filead Fanes made exaggerated movements. He was a small man, shorter than me. Maybe that is why he felt the need for exaggerated movements, to take up the maximum amount of physical space he could? This act somehow made him feel larger. It is common in nature for creatures or animals to extend their extremities to fend off opponents or attract mates. This spectacle was the performance that Filead Fanes delivered to us this evening.

I placed myself between Filead and his audience, which was made up of two teenage girls, an older woman, and two middle-aged guys. I unzipped my hip pocket, pulled out the roach we smoked earlier, and lit it up. At first, I think Filed thought I would light up and move on, but when I remained between him and his audience, he repositioned himself with a bounding gesture, inviting them to congregate at his new location. I did too, and I blew smoke toward him while looking at him with my red bleary eyes.

"If you please, sir," Filead said, gesturing for me to move off to the side. "I am telling a story to my friends."

His voice reminded me of the cartoon cat from the movie Shrek. "Oh, do continue. I'm sure they can hear you," I replied. "Everyone on the patio can hear your stories."

It looked like he was weighing his options. Maybe he has been in this situation and was looking for the most elegant way to wriggle out of a confrontation? Some of his audience was already walking away when he said, looking past me, "Oh look, they are serving desserts."

Filead moved off to catch up with the teenage girls, who headed over to the table. He was silent for about the first twelve steps before I heard him chime in with, "Oh, now the desserts in Bruckel's bitter market, now those are worth making the journey for. Did I tell you about..."

I took another puff from the roach, which was nearly burnt, and Ethan Foster approached to say, "That was brilliant."

"I apologize for accosting your guests, but he was just asking for it. Did I tell you about the time I was at this party, when..." I trailed off, which drew a smile across Ethan's face.

I offered what was left of the joint to him, and he shook his head yes.

"Ohm, can you materialize a roach clip in my right hand," I said.

A quick sparkle occurred, and a long feather with an alligator clip appeared in my hand. I positioned the roach in the clip to maximize the remaining amount of joint but not burn your lips. I handed it to Ethan, who took a toke, and it went out. Reaching into my pocket, I pulled out the lighter to hand it to him. With a few spark-ups and a couple of quick inhales, the roach glowed orange, and Ethan got a nice hit. Maybe a little too nice. He coughed and sputtered, leaning over while handing the feather and the lighter back to me.

"They say if you don't cough, you didn't get a hit," I added.

Ethan cleared his throat a couple of times before regaining his composure.

"Sam, I hoped to ask a favor of you, so I'll just come out and say it. I have been thinking about this for a while, and I have talked with Olivia about it. Is there some way I can join up with this Starnet? Space travel has always fascinated me, and I wondered how I could learn more about it?" Ethan asked while straightening his glasses.

"Space travel is long and boring, Ethan. The technology is interesting, but you would be away from Olivia and your children a lot."

Olivia walked up and asked, "Did he finally ask you?"

I took a short puff on the roach to keep it from going out and gestured to Olivia, who accepted.

"He just did," I said, looking up at the sky and blowing smoke out.

"What do you think? He might be gone a lot and encounter dangerous situations?" I said seriously as smoke drifted up Olivia's round freckled youthful face.

"I know. I tried to talk him out of it, but he keeps reviewing spaceship specifications inside those electronic tablets you left for the kids. I swear he has spent more time playing with those gifts than Albert and Lulu combined," she said, handing the roach clip to Ethan.

He took another hit, killing the joint before handing the clip back to me. I targeted the roach clip with my invisihud, selected the recycle icon, and activated it. The dead roach and the feathered roach clip disappeared in a brief sparkle.

The gifts she referred to were a couple of Blinn tablets. They were lightweight, portable screens you could touch to activate various software features. I placed a special clothing designer application on the tablet for Lulu. It allowed her to make real clothes for her dolls. Ohm monitored the tablet and constructed garments from various prefab selections when Lulu touched them. The tablet for Albert was similar, but with more boy-centric applications making remote-controlled race cars, skateboards, trains, etcetera.

"The only way I'll do it is if you return to Enki's Dale, at least on weekends, to be with your family," I said to the both of them.

Ethan's face lit up and filled with joy as he smiled and looked over at Olivia, who also seemed pleased at this news. At least pleased to see her husband happy.

"I'll set up a site-to-site transport for you. It works a lot like a Peregrinate. It takes you between two places. I'll add them to the tablets. You'll be able to talk and see each other through the screens."

"You can do that?" Olivia asked.

"I just purchased a high-rise apartment building in San Francisco. The building is the same probability where Starnet headquarters resides. You can use one of the apartments as the target for the site-to-site transport. Then you'll have a local residence if you decide to attend the academy," I said.

"That is more than I expected," Ethan replied.

"Give me both of your hands," I said, taking their hands, the ones with their wedding rings. Their wedding bands were very nice. Olivia's was a well-set diamond in a gold ring, surrounded by other smaller stones. Ethan's offered the traditional male-style ring, which was a wide, gold band with a silver band in the center of the gold band. There was a small diamond as the feature stone and then two more stones on either side, each getting smaller in size the further it was from the central stone.

"Ohm, can you modify these rings to act as communication tracking devices between probabilities? If the wearer presses on the stone, open communication should occur," I said.

"Working," Ohm replied only to me, and the rings sparkled, disappeared, and then reappeared on their fingers all within ten seconds.

I let go of their hands and said, "This is so you will never be alone. Your rings are now communication devices. Touch the stone with your other hand and talk."

I gestured with my two hands to indicate the motion. They both looked down at their hands and pressed the center stone.

"Testing. 1,2,3," Ethan said, and Olivia smiled when she heard his voice.

"The voice will appear near your ear at low volumes, but if someone has their head near yours, they might be able to listen in on your conversation. It might work underwater, but I wouldn't rely on it. The voice is basically amplitude modulation in the air. Try stepping farther apart and give it a try," I said.

They moved farther apart, out of range of typical speech, and stood inconspicuously holding their rings while talking. I could tell by their facial expressions that it worked, and they were enjoying it. They rejoined me, and Olivia hugged me before saying, "Thank you."

"So, how do I get started?" Ethan asked.

"I'll have to integrate you into the target probability. Once you're there, you'll have to decide if you are going to tell people if you are a magician or not?" I said.

"What do you recommend?" Ethan asked.

"I say be yourself. Eventually, you will make friends, and if you hide the fact you are a magician, it might feel like you are lying to them all the time. But admitting you are a magician will, of course, invite all forms of skeptics to encourage you to perform tricks.

"Also, there will be a time differential between the probabilities you inhabit. A day in Ethan's world might be twenty-eight hours, and a day here might be twenty-four. It's a small thing, but it is worth being aware of. You each will age at a slightly different rate, as well as the children," I said.

"I see," Ethan said, finally realizing this new role might be more than just going to a school.

"I am working on a current project, trying to locate a starship lost in the Gar sector. It's a good opportunity to integrate you into that probability if you are still interested?"

"Count me in," Ethan said

"Right now, I have probes scanning a large area of space, trying to find traces of the starship or where it might have been. Once it is located, I'll probably just head right there and get to work," I said.

"How soon do you think that will happen?"

"I'm hoping, in the next few days, otherwise, I may have to retarget the search to redeploy the probes. You may want to pack a small bag and have it ready for standby departure," I said.

"I will. Should I bring my wand?" Ethan asked.

"Most certainly. The probability we are headed for is similar to this one, in the fact that magic does work there, but most of the species use technology. To them, magic is a myth. I have successfully cast *Meridiem* and *Remedium* in that environment. So I know some spells do work," I replied.

An older couple came up to us and said, "Please excuse the interruption, but Ethan, my boy, we are departing."

Ethan and Olivia turned to face their guests, and Olivia said, "I'm so glad you came to our first lawn party. May I show you out?"

"Thank you, my dear," the guest said, and they all walked toward the house engaged in conversation as Ethan looked back with a smile.

I think I started to feel the weight of not sleeping. I felt tired with the high mellowed by the effects of the wine. I wandered back over to the table where Candy, Lucas, and Alex sat and said, "I think I am going to head out. I need to get some rest."

"Bout time," Candy said as she stood up and hugged me goodbye. "We'll help you find her."

"Me too," Alex said, standing up and giving me a quick goodbye hug.

"I'm not gonna hug you," Lucas said, "but I'll see you soon."

I stepped back and said, "Ohm, please transport me to my bedroom in the new San Francisco building."

The evening party scene around me streamed into darkness. As I waited in the darkness, I thought, "I'm going to have to come up with some name for this new San Francisco apartment building." The black glass building was more than apartments, though. It offered office space and studios. My eyes stung just a little as tiny bright specks raced in from the sides, forming the apartment around me.

CHAPTER 8

Release

The sun was already up and shining in San Francisco, so I asked Ohm to install light-blocking curtains and pulled them shut. Ohm provided standard clean-up on all residences it monitored. This site was no different. The bed was remade automatically after the last time I slept here. Heading into the bathroom, I washed my hands and face. I brushed my teeth, returned to the bedroom, got undressed, and climbed under the blankets. It wasn't too long before I just drifted into a coma.

When I woke up, I took a shower, refreshed my clothes, and transferred things from my previous pockets to the pockets of my new clothes. Walking into the living area of my apartment, I looked out the window at the night sky. Lights were flying around, here and there. There were lights on the water and lights moving along the streets.

"Ohm, do you have a location on Reziko?" I asked.

"Yes, I do. The tracker is working as expected," Ohm replied.

"Is there a device in the Blinn database, or any other database, that can be placed inside the body for a slow medicine release?" I asked.

"Shall I transfer the results to your invisihud?" Ohm asked.

"Sure, let's see the results," I said, and quite a few three-dimensional models stacked up and floated around in the overlay view in front of me. "Can you filter the devices to show me only the ones that have all the requested features? Put outlines on those that have additional features," I asked Ohm.

My view updated, and many of the three-dimensional models fell out of scope leaving only three products with glowing outlines remaining.

"Remove all models that are not made by Blinn technicians," I said, and only one candidate remained. I reviewed the specifications. Not only could the unit deposit small doses directly into the bloodstream, it provided an onboard miniature replication function allowing it to be programmed for thousands of medicines, stimulants, or anesthesia. The unit also masked its presence in the body by emitting a bio-electrical field to make it appear as organic tissue to most scanners. "Let's go with the Blinn model. Can you evaluate Reziko's blood and come up with a basic regiment for bipolar disorder?" I asked Ohm.

"Checking," Ohm said. "For best possible dose match, a one-week sampling period is required."

"Let's get started. Install the device while he sleeps, and begin determining regiment. I want to place the same device into Lexi, Valentino, and Teela. Once you have a dose determination for them, you can activate their devices to begin treatment," I added.

I sat down on the white couch and asked Ohm to materialize some breakfast food and coffee. I ate in silence and wondered how long I could keep it up? How many days did I have before I settled for a compromised reality? Even in the memories, I recalled from the past two time loops, there were big differences between them. It seemed obvious to me that I used memories from the first time loop in the second time loop to try and avoid first-time loop mistakes. And now, I am trying to avoid first and second loop mistakes, to get back to where I was with my wives in the second loop. I guess that is the goal, the life I shared with my wives in the second loop. I looked inside, affirming that to myself, so I would know what I was doing, know what was important to do. I targeted my dishes with the invisihud and used the recycle icon to clean up. Heading into the bedroom, I put my boots on. I brushed my teeth, washed my face, and returned to the living room.

"Ohm, I'm going to release Lexi from her Cryovirt. If anything goes wrong, enforce the security protocols we have in place. Safeguard the mountain."

"Understood," Ohm replied. "Immersion factor from the previous request is holding at thirty-two percent at this time."

"Thank you. Can you materialize the vignettes Lexi carried with her when she was captured?"

There was a short sparkle on the table, and a small rectangular box appeared. The box contained vignettes, which were small paintings about the size of Tarot cards. These vignettes could be used as transportation devices to the location painted on the card. The ones with people could be used to communicate with the individual depicted. About half of them I recognized as various family members and the King. The others were bizarre, depicting Gothic castles, Gargoyles, and one was just a red mark on a white field. The only one that did not seem threatening was of a stone bridge leading to a small town. I removed all the bizarre ones, leaving the picture of the bridge in the pack. She had to go somewhere when I released her, so let it be there. I targeted the stack of bizarre vignettes with my invisihud and asked, "Ohm, can you place these vignettes back in the vault?"

"Certainly," Ohm said, and the small stack disappeared with a sparkle.

I returned the remaining vignettes to the box and put the box in one of the larger pockets in my pants.

"Ohm, transport me to the asteroid containment facility containing Lexi's Cryovirt," I said.

The world of my San Francisco high-rise apartment streamed in from the sides of my vision, and I was left in darkness again. I knew that releasing Lexi was risky, but I also truly believed that the Re'em might seek revenge for her imprisonment if I let it go on. My eyes materialized, and the new scene came into view.

I arrived at what I would call a small survival station on an asteroid floating in space. This single-floor facility was no bigger than a few hundred square meters. There was a Cryovirt, a bathroom, and a replicator. No doors could be found. Along one wall, there was a large window providing a view of the surface of the asteroid, revealing the stars beyond. I walked over to the replicator embedded in the wall and asked for a carafe filled with water and a glass. They materialized in the overly large indent in the wall. Picking them up, I carried them over to the Cryovirt, placing them at the head of the unit before pouring some water into the glass.

The Cryovirt was a long bed in a box with a transparent lid. The mechanisms keeping it operational were contained in the base and the head of the unit. This design made the Cryovirt portable, so it could be moved around. The power supply was part of the unit, allowing the unit to continue operation even if power within the facility was lost. It was space-worthy. A person could use it as an escape pod for suspended animation, but it offered no shielding at all.

I looked through the transparent lid at Lexi. She wore what she had on when we captured her, a green dress with black lace woven through it. Her hair was red, like her brother Hugo and deceased brother Fabio. She was Reziko's aunt as well as Valentino's aunt. And while she was pretty, she was certainly no ten.

"Ohm, start the revival process for Lexi's Cryovirt."

"Commencing revival process," Ohm repeated to me.

The entire cavity of the Cryovirt filled with a visible mist. It swirled and built up until I could barely see Lexi at all.

"Ohm, is that supposed to happen?"

"Yes, the revival process is proceeding as normal and expected. The mist contains nutrients and medicines to help ease the person back from cryogenic suspension."

As I watched, her body jerked slightly, and I saw her chest rise then fall. Again, rise, then fall. Mechanisms started activating on their own, and the side-wall dropped down, allowing the mist to roll out. The Cryovirt lid slid back so the person inside could sit up or get out.

A sudden streak of fear ran through me. I stepped back from the rolling mist and retreated to the other side of the Cryovirt, so at least the unit was between Lexi and me when she finally awoke. Her hand reached up, gripping the side of the Cryovirt, pulling herself up and swinging her legs over the edge, where the side dropped down. Her back faced me, and she still seemed groggy. It must have been a good minute of me standing in silence, watching her from behind, as she regained her composure. As a master witch, I was quite sure she might have some magic spell to kill me instantly, but I hoped she wouldn't. It was a gamble I needed to take. She slowly slid off the bed. When her feet reached the floor, she momentarily buckled at the knees while holding herself up by hanging on to the Cryovirt. She turned around and looked at me panicky, like a foe who knew they were at the mercy of another.

"Sam," she rasped out, turning that single word, my name, into the foulest possible curse anyone could utter.

"It's normal to be dehydrated after cryogenic revival. There is some water at the end of the bed there," I said as I gestured toward the carafe and glass.

She glanced at it then back at me, hesitating while I said, "It's not poison. I mean, why would I wake you up just to poison you? You were at my mercy inside the chamber you have just arisen from."

She thought about it and reached for the glass, taking a small sip at first before drinking the whole glass down and pouring another.

"Is this some kind of trick?" her voice crackled out as she gained her footing.

"No trick. I am setting you free, and I hope you don't kill me or my friends. I realize that this is a lot to ask, but I'm asking it anyway," I said matter of factly.

"You're afraid of my curse," she said with a grin, thinking she put it all together.

"Curses, get in line. Didn't the lords of the Vectorless Vale curse me already? It seems like you are just enforcing their decree by constantly conflicting with me. Besides, if I killed you in your sleep, you wouldn't have been able to utter your final curse."

She drank some water, and a bit more life returned to her face. My logic was sound enough. The "curse" is a Splendorite's last fuck you to the world of the living. As a Splendorite is dying, his or her last words can be used to curse enemies who have defeated him or her. This is what Lexi referred to.

"Why did you spare my life? Where are the others?" she asked while walking around the Cryovirt to approach closer. It was then I saw she wore pointed shoes, making her look more and more like the wicked witch from the west arisen from the dead.

"You and the others were under the influence of chaotic strands that were attached to your life force. I never figured out exactly who did that to you. I was able to detect them and eventually remove them. They were on nearly everyone in the family, but you, Valentino, and Teela were the most heavily affected. If I killed you all for your actions, that would play into the hands of the agents of chaos who are always trying to undermine the power of the *Motif*."

She digested these words while taking another drink from the glass.

I continued, "Valentino and Teela are still being held in facilities similar to this one. You are the first one I have awoken."

"What is this place?"

"I call it a survival station. It was built on an asteroid floating in space. There are no doors. All that is here is your bed, the replicator which can make food or clothes, and the shower," I said as I pointed out the named objects in the room.

"I want to be there when you wake up the others," she said demandingly.

I reached down to my pants pocket and pulled out the box of vignettes I selected for Lexi before handing them to her and saying, "These are the vignettes you carried with you when I placed you in stasis."

"I'll give Valentino your vignette when I awaken him. If he wants to talk to you, he can," I stated flatly.

"Not good enough," she said, smashing apart the glass and stepping up on me like a mugger with a knife in the park.

I repositioned myself next to the replicator and continued my sales pitch by saying, "You can replicate food and clothing here before you leave via a vignette. Just pretend the wall is a servant."

"Replicate two towels for showering," I said to the wall.

The wall unit sparkled, and two towels appeared.

She looked at them and then at me before saying, "Forgive my temper. My mood swings sometimes."

"Already forgotten. I don't want it to be like this," I said, looking straight at her. "I have done my best to remain civil for now. We can kill or curse each other later. Stay as long as you like, clean up, eat, shower. There are no exits to this place. You'll have to use the vignettes to leave."

I took a step back from her, and before she could say another word, I said, "Ohm, transport me home."

The sparse well lit survival station broke apart into thousands of specks as my eyes dissolved and the darkness took over. God, I hope I did not regret this move of freeing her. Seeing her initial contempt for me sent chills down my spine. I felt like I was freeing a wild animal and hoping it did not return to harm myself or my community. I did feel like she presented a change of heart, there for a moment. She was under the influence of the chaos strands for quite some time. It might take a little while for her to remember who she was or is, a Lord of Splendor. My San Francisco apartment crept in from the sides of my vision and fizzled my eyes back together. I stood in the living room I departed from a few minutes ago.

"Ohm, let's do the same thing for Valentino. Can you fetch the vignettes he carried on his person the day you placed him in cryogenic suspension?"

A small sparkle appeared, and another box materialized on the large white coffee table in the center of the sunken living room. I sat down on the white sofa and looked at this box. The box was about the same size as Lexi's, but its lid was a carved wood relief of some angry screaming demon. I was hesitant to touch it, but I quickly removed the lid, placing the demon facing down, before emptying the contents onto the table.

I sat the box aside and rifled through Valentino's vignettes. His set was similar to Lexi's. There were cards for most family members, Lexi included, and a card for Teela that I have never seen before. I removed Teela's vignette from his deck and set it back in the box. The other vignettes were painted in a different style than the rest, with a finer, more illustrative look. Several of them presented a hatched stroke style, which defines the inverted light in the scene, similar to an Escher woodcut. I separated the vignettes with the distinctive style from the traditional deck of cards and returned those to the demon box. I chose one for his escape card. It depicted a set of rolling hills with a tree in the foreground and a small cottage a short distance away. When I looked at it, I thought I might have been there before, but hundreds of years ago. As I stared at it, the image moved slightly, and the light direction changed. The hatch marks defining the light in the image faded away to be replaced by real light. The magical vignette conveyed a sense to me that I could step through the card and into the scene. I quickly sat the card on the table to dismiss the magic spell.

"Ohm, can you scan the area for nearby banks? I would like an empty cash envelope, please."

"Checking," Ohm replied.

I replaced the lid on the demon box and set it aside. A sparkle delivered a paper envelope as I straightened up the smaller stack of vignettes. It read, "Liberty Mutual," in large letters, and then in smaller type, "Integrity You Can Trust." I picked up the envelope and looked at both sides.

"This is close, Ohm. Can you replicate this but remove the address?" I asked, and the envelope sparkled out of my hand while a new one appeared on the table.

I placed the short stack of vignettes into the cash envelope and folded down the lip to seal it shut. I placed the cash envelope with the vignettes into the same pants pocket I put Lexi's set in earlier.

"Ohm, can you return the box of vignettes to the vault?"

A quick sparkle appeared on the table, and the box of vignettes disappeared. I was hesitant to return an artifact like the demon box to Valentino so quickly. He might be able to leverage some magic stored in the object that I can't detect.

"I might as well get this over with," I said out loud to no one. "Ohm, please transport me to the asteroid holding facility containing Valentino's Cryovirt."

The room collapsed in from the side, placing me in darkness. I felt nervous about this as I waited to materialize in an exact replica of Lexi's survival station. The view out the window was different, but this one was also on an asteroid in space. I placed each of my antagonists on an asteroid, in their own unique probability. I was so paranoid at the time I imprisoned them that I didn't want to take any chance of them breaking out and teaming up against me.

Once again, I walked over to the replicator and requested a carafe of water and a glass. I placed them on the head of the Cryovirt bed.

I looked through the transparent lid, into the Cryovirt's interior, to view its occupant. Valentino appeared to be about thirty-six years old. His hair was black, and he wore black clothes, similar to what I wore. A short beard grew while he was in the Cryovirt. I couldn't help but notice how similar my appearance was to Valentino.

When I successfully engaged Darwin's *Motif*, it was shocking news. I was the farthest removed along the royal bloodline to ever achieve such a thing. Setting aside the production of *Sound* and *Vision*, the fact I used a wand to deflect and redirect *Motif*-based energy during the process was also new and novel. This accomplishment earned me notoriety, and family members from all walks of echo returned to Splendor to visit me to offer their guidance and support. I was the new kid on the block, the baby.

Some of the older family members were fairly stand-offish and simply offered congratulations with an invitation to visit them in their own echo kingdoms. But Valentino and I hit it off rather nicely when we met some years later. He was a coder and a magician, inspiring me to blend technology and magic.

Tiger Mountain might not even exist if it were not for the many conversations Valentino and I shared about leveraging energy transfers between echoes.

There was a dark side to Valentino. He was Grayson's son, but his mother was one of the royal demon elite inside the Vectorless Vale. He was the first blending between these two opposite poles which create all of the reality we inhabit. Because the demons of chaos exist in an environment that is always changing, it is in their nature to change their form. This duplicity is how Valentino's mother tricked Grayson into having sex. Grayson probably wouldn't have just got it on with a demon woman, but a hot young lass from around the farm? No matter how it happened, she gave birth to Valentino and raised him in the Vectorless Vale.

Just as Splendor has the *Motif*, the Vectorless Vale has the *Vechnost*. The *Vechnost* is what empowers the demons of chaos. It gives them their mobility within echo. It is a set of twisting tentacles that invades your mind and presents endless variations to keep you within its ever-changing folds. Most creatures or people that pursue the *Vechnost* are simply lost and never heard from again. Some say the *Vechnost* is chaos and the Vectorless Vale is the first representation, much like Splendor is the first *Motif*-based representation of organized civilization. With the *Motif*, if you deviate from the path, you are destroyed. Inside the *Vechnost*, if you deviate from the path, you are lost forever. How do I know? I, like Valentino, have mediated the *Vechnost* and engaged the *Motif*. I carry both marks within me.

But what made us rivals and eventually enemies was the fact I called him out for entertaining evil. We disagreed at a moral level. When he revealed some of the more heinous aspects of his magical philosophy, I could no longer, in good-conscious, remain in his company. I don't know if the chaotic strands influenced him or he controlled them?

At one point, multiple family members simultaneously contacted me using my vignette to drag me through to Splendor. This mental attack was another aspect of the card. The person contacting ou could unwillingly pull you through the magical portal if their mental power exceeded yours. At the time, chaos strands were attached to all of the family members, and I was charged with crimes where the price of my disobedience was to be paid in blood. It was determined I would lose a finger.

Lexi used a spell to suppress my communications with *Tiger Mountain*, and I was alone in the King's den, surrounded by most of my family members. I still remember the strong arms of Garret man-handling me into position as Joshua approached with a huntsman's ax at his side. In one swift blow, he took off my right ring finger with the ax, and I started bleeding. The finger bounced to the floor. Joshua picked it up and handed it to Valentino, who put it in his shirt pocket. Valentino made a large circular motion with his hand, and a glowing light outline appeared across the room. Sparks gathered, shot off in all directions, and fell to the floor as a scene appeared and shimmered within the oval portal. Valentino crossed the room and stepped through the portal, followed by Lexi, who gave me a backward glance before disappearing into the collapsing ring.

A glazed look hung in Osric's eyes as I looked up at him with an accusing,

"How could you?"

With Lexi was gone, her spells no longer affected my communications. I used the invisihud to activate my personal shielding and quickly expanded its radius. This expansion threw Garret off guard for a moment, and I broke free of his massive grasp while we both tumbled onto the floor. My hand was still leaking blood, and I slipped on the bloody floor while trying to regain my balance before using the invisihud to return to *Tiger Mountain*.

I knew Valentino and Lexi concocted some kind of evil with my blood as a key element in whatever spell or scheme they planned. I sensed there might be a showdown on the horizon once I discovered how to detect the chaos strands attached to the royal family. I rallied my Guardians. They were Jim, Malik, David, Robin, Candy, Lucas, and Alex. They trained in one of the *Tiger Mountain* recreational vehicles that I modified for combat. The vehicle was a transparent flight cycle with heavy missiles installed. Jim was already a pilot. Robin and Malik were pretty good too. It was highly maneuverable and nearly invisible.

While Valentino made his way deeper into echo, heading for the Vectorless Vale, I took the attack to the front line. With the help of the Guardians, we dropped multiple tactical nukes on the Spectre Vorticle site, which completely obliterated Valentino's magical energy transport machine. In one of my future memories, I took Jorrie to the Spectre Vorticle site, where she discovered evidence of it trying to rebuild itself, but at an extremely slow rate.

In the end, it was a race between Valentino and me. He was probably in transit, inside one of his Vechnoport conduits heading for the Vectorless Vale. Time was a factor in this race. Time became exceedingly slower as you approached the Vectorless Vale but traveling from Splendor to the Vectorless Vale was the longest possible time compression one could experience. The location of the Spectre Vorticle was almost exactly between Splendor and the Vectorless Vale, in an echo right past the halfway point. I imagined his Vechnoport conduit simply collapsed when the Spectre Vorticle was destroyed, but I never found out for sure.

My first wife, Teela, whom Lexi corrupted when she attended a women's school for magic, waited at the arrival point in chaos. Being my wife and a citizen of *Tiger Mountain*, there was a tracking device implanted inside her long ago. She was my first Guardian but stripped of her rank. When Lexi and Valentino finally appeared at the location where Teela waited, I already targeted them using Teela's invisihud. Ohm to transported anesthesia directly into their bloodstreams. After that, I placed them all in their individual Cryovirt units and recovered my lost finger from Valentino's shirt pocket. This deadly, evil, black magic ritual stuff scared the shit out of me.

After imprisoning those three, I set off into echo with Candy, Alex, and Lucas. I looked for a magician that might be able to regrow my missing finger. This search is how I came to know the Baker's. It was Olivia's mother who prepared the potion that regrew my finger. In that echo, alchemy was an everyday practice, and there was even a cookbook with a recipe on how to regrow missing digits. Alex took an instant liking to that magic-based echo, and that is how the crew ended up with houses in Enki's Dale.

I thought about all of this history as I talked myself into saying, "Ohm, start the revival process for Valentino's Cryovirt."

"Commencing revival process," Ohm repeated to me.

The entire cavity of the Cryovirt, once again, filled with visible mist. It swirled and built up inside, obscuring Valentino from view. I didn't wait for the sidewall to drop this time. I immediately moved to the other side of the Cryovirt unit and cued up the personal shield icon inside my invisihud. The waking process was the same. A hand reached up, he sat up with his back facing me, and he finally stood up and turned around.

"You," he rasped out of his dry throat, then coughed a bit.

"There is a glass of water there," I gestured.

He looked over, thought about it for a second, picked up the glass, and took a sip. He downed the rest of the water and poured himself some more.

"It's been over four years since I placed you in that cryogenic chamber. I have removed the chaos strands affecting your judgment," I said as if I were offering a report.

"Oh, thank you," Valentino said sarcastically with a sneer while lumbering forward and leaning on the Cryovirt chamber. "You think you have it all figured out, don't you, Sammy?"

"I don't have anything figured out."

He stood there for a moment, drinking the remainder of the water, before setting the glass on the Cryovirt. Stepping forward, he asked, "So, why did you let me out? Has something gone wrong with your master plan?"

Reaching into my pants pocket, I pulled out the set of vignettes I placed in the banking envelope. I stepped up and handed him the package saying, "These were the vignettes you had on you when you were placed in stasis."

I noticed the dark bloodstain on his shirt pocket, where he placed my finger so long ago. Valentino accepted the package and noticed my finger was no longer missing. He looked at me, caught my eye, and asked, "You think this makes everything all right then?"

"I don't know that anything will make it 'alright,' Valentino. All I know is that this way, we both get to live," I said. "I just released Lexi about an hour ago. She was asking for you."

"You don't say," Valentino said. "I wonder what could possibly be on her mind?"

I stepped past him to the wall with the replicator and said, "Two shower towels."

The replicator produced two fluffy folded towels. Valentino stood with folded arms, unimpressed.

"You can replicate clothing and food with voice commands. There's a shower and a bathroom over there," I pointed as I walked and talked. "Stay as long as you like. The only exit is via vignettes."

He stood there, eying me with a slight hunch to his back, calculating what to do next.

"Ohm, recycle Valentino's shirt and transport me home," I said.

The bright room zoomed in from the sides of my peripheral vision, and I found myself in darkness. When I saw the bloodstain on Valentino's shirt, I shuddered inside. I have watched too many detective shows where the lawmen managed to catch the bad guys with only a drop of the victim's blood. I didn't want Valentino to have access to my blood, even if it was four years old and dried into his shirt. The transporter materialized me in my San Francisco high-rise apartment once again.

"Ohm, can you automatically manage the lighting for this apartment?"

"New rule in place," Ohm said, and the lamps around the room and in recessed cavities lit up.

"Thank you, Ohm. It gives the place a more cozy feeling rather than some dude hanging out in the dark."

One lit area I immediately noticed was the bar in the corner. I headed over to discover it was fairly well stocked. Checking the freezer of the mini-fridge, I discovered ice, which I added to one of the stainless steel shakers, the kind with the matching lid. I found a shot glass and measured two shots of bourbon, one shot of sweet vermouth, and a dash of bitters into the stainless steel shaker. I put the lid on and gave it a few shakes. There were rocks glasses here, and I emptied the contents of the shaker into one. With the ice, it filled the glass perfectly.

Taking a sip of my Manhattan, I sat down on the barstool, wondering if I did the right thing? I released known killers back into my life to prevent the possibility of the Re'em from lobotomizing Candy, which did happen in one of the future memories.

"Ohm, I want both Lexi and Valentino tracked at all times. If their trackers go off-line or their trackers appear in any of the probabilities where the Guardians are located, I want to be notified. If they attack me or any of the Guardians, return them to their Cryovirts," I said.

"Making adjustments to tracking rules," Ohm replied.

"While we are on the topic of tracking, Let's set up some new rules to help locate Flexanites who are taking over positions within Starnet and the local Earth government. This tracking involves deploying multiple cloaked scanning devices throughout the Starnet Union. We'll start here on Earth with key figures. Track them discreetly and match the modus operandi of the Flexanite species against the observed actions of world leaders. Look for extreme changes in world leader behavioral patterns. Review missing person reports that coincide with leaders taking unexpected actions.

"You can detect Flexanites by transporting part of their body to another location. If the sample materializes as a dark oozing substance, then that person is a Flexanite, and I should be notified. Take the transport sample from the subject's hair or nails, so it should not harm non Flexanite suspects. Place a cloaked scanner on as many ships as possible, as soon as possible. I know it is a long task, but I would like to have multiple cloaked scanners on every planet in the Starnet Union, including the outlying colonies and neighboring planets that might not have joined the Union. If you have the opportunity, extend the scanning to the Rulkan Alliance and the Bragorian Order," I said to Ohm.

"Considerable replication resources will be needed," Ohm said.

"Feel free to offload replication to the Blinn factories. Let's see how quickly they can make ten thousand cloaked scanners," I replied.

"Allocating project resources. I'll place updates inside your invisihud reports section," Ohm said.

I took a bigger sip from my drink this time. Liquor definitely works quicker than wine. The drink was a bit sweet but traditionally served with tart cherries. Before I knew it, my drink was gone, and I was sucking on ice.

Right about then, the loneliness kicked in. I was someone who could have anything I wanted, but what I wanted most was a relationship that did not exist yet. If I were back on the ship with Erin, we might be hanging out at Club Forward, the off-duty lounge. It was located at the bow of the ship where the top and bottom parts of the radial section come together, hence the name. The room offered stepped seating, rising to a rectangular window revealing the forward direction of the ship. Along one wall was a series of tall oval windows, one window for each level of stepped seating.

Often, Erin and I would meet there after her shift was over. Sometimes, duty shifts were assigned to me, but I was basically a tourist, the husband on the ship where my wife served as an able-bodied crewman. I'd walk in and see her sitting on the sill of the large oval window with the backdrop of stars framing her silhouette. It was wide enough for two. We sat together in the window and talked about our day. If the ship was in range of some space-based phenomena, we might have a good view. Sometimes, we hung out and kissed. Public kissing, for shame. But most of all, it was the togetherness making our relationship work. We were together, and we tried to remain together as much as possible, Jorrie included.

Another thing Erin and I would do for entertainment was to hang out and watch video-based political comedy from the past. I placed a cloaked scanner near a broadcast tower in an echo that most would consider the past compared to where we lived. But the signals were transferred using *Tiger Mountain* technology, so we could effectively peer into the past, in real-time, while eating popcorn and snuggling. Eventually, Spunky, our calico cat, climbed between us to start purring and acting cute.

My life with Jorrie was very similar. Erin served aboard the *Explorer*, which was Starnet's flagship, while Jorrie was the Captain of the *Concord*, a cruiser class vessel. I was the Captain's husband, so I was assigned no official duties on board, but I did help out in the galley, and my emergency assignment on the *Concord* was the same as *Explorer*, sickbay assistant. I split my time between the ships in one-week intervals, spending a week on the *Concord* then a week on the *Explorer*. Because Erin and Jorrie were future Guardians of *Tiger Mountain*, they could transport between the ships when they wanted. Most of the time, we would all get together no matter what ship I was on. I even constructed an inter-dimensional kitty door, so Spunky could hear us call to her from another probability, and she followed us from ship to ship.

I loved and married them both, and they loved and married each other as well. But being married to and pleasing two women was not all pie and roses. There were difficult times. We each struggled to adapt our previous selves to the new roles we each played in this complex relationship. I tried to make each of them feel special, and I often felt I was special to them. They loved each other openly and would often have sex, exclusively with each other. Many times, I watched them make love, and if I were lucky, they would invite me to join them. But we also made love together quite often, which was fine by me. One time, we were all going at it. When we settled down, Spunky jumped on my back and meowed loudly, indicating that she somehow wanted to join in. She cracked us up, and we burst out laughing while still naked in each other's arms.

While I find wallowing in nostalgia to be fairly pointless, it did bring one thing to the forefront for me, my duty as a sickbay assistant. In the future, I will learn a lot more about human and alien physiology, with a strong focus on healing and dealing with sudden trauma. In the first time loop, I learned of a substance called orgamorphic gel. In the second time loop, I managed to leverage the gel into an acceptable field-ready solution for deep cavity wounds.

When I treated Jim's team member, Kyle, on that field so many years ago, it could have gone a lot quicker if I knew about orgamorphic gel. The skin sealer deposits new tissue cells into the wound to accelerate the healing process. In deep wounds, many layers of deposits are needed to build up the missing tissue. Also, tissue cells change as the layers change, so a constant recalibration is taking place within the skin sealer when it is used on deep wounds.

My invention, the cellepulator, integrates a medical inspectrograph and a modified skin sealer. The skin sealer is heavily modified into a one-shot transporter replicator to deposit the gel in a single burst. The device functions like this. It scans the wound and creates a three-dimensional representation of the cavity it needs to fill before depositing the orgamorphic gel in the exact shape of the cavity. The only problem is, in this time loop, I have never encountered orgamorphic gel, so its replication profile is unknown. But my second loop self made friends with a doctor on a remote space station, who eventually gave up the recipe.

"Ohm, can you create a variation on my current clothes using some of the colors and stylizations found in the current Starnet uniform? I am heading to a Starnet space station, and I would like to blend in as much as possible."

"Certainly," Ohm stated, and my invisihud filled with a few variations ranging from downright ugly to over-the-top flamboyant. I flipped through the selections by moving my eyes left and right to choose a garment that was fairly close to my current clothing but with some slight angle stylization added to the blue Starnet shirt yolk.

"Let's go with this one," I said, and I blinked to activate it. "Place it on the bed in my bedroom."

I went into the bedroom, and there was a set of clothes lying on the bed. I went right to work, transferring my wands and vignettes from my current clothes to my new outfit. I kept the same boots. The garment was uniform-like but more casual. I wasn't trying to impersonate an officer or crewman.

"Ohm, transport me to the catwalk on the *Deceptive* where *Vision* resides."

My bedroom crammed in from the side, and I found myself in darkness. I psyched myself up, like an athlete before a game, with a little pep talk about how this felt good. I was on the right track. While the development of the gel depositing technology did not play a critical role in either of the future memories, the act of pursuing it did allow me to meet Brent Stevens, who would become one of Jorrie's close friends. I had to be careful, though, not to bump into Jorrie.

In the memories of both future loops, I always met Erin first. I would like to keep it that way. This action made me think of those temporal paradox classes I took at the Starnet Academy. I attended the academy hundreds of years ago, but only sixty years have passed compared to my departure time from this probability. One of the types of paradoxes discussed in the temporal mechanics class was a loop, where you could not change your actions. When I thought about preserving the condition of meeting Erin first, I wondered if I might be consciously enforcing that paradox? But the closer I stayed to the script, the better chance I might have of reaching my goal. The low lit tech insides of the *Deceptive* fizzled into view, and I stood on the catwalk with a covered easel at the end.

CHAPTER 9

Orgamorphic Gel

~

While walking to the end of the catwalk, I prepared the image in my mind. I was traveling to a space station called *Oasis Seven*. This place was the same space station where Jorrie lived and worked. I visited many times in both future memories, so I thought about a place I knew on the station with low pedestrian traffic and boldly removed the cloth covering from the canvas known as *Vision*. In a shocking first, the canvas was blank, and as I hesitated at this, a flock of flying eyeballs approached at high speed from an unknown distance. They approached fast and slammed into the canvas surface, striking the barrier that keeps them contained. Some of them burst on contact, and little writhing snakes emerged from the broken ones, seeking out living ones and burrowing into their sides.

The startling image caused me to instinctively jump back, and I dropped the cloth on the floor.

I focused on the space station, the time, the probability, Brent Stevens, and framed my thought for the canvas. The gory eyeballs faded, and a technical corridor scene appeared across the painting. With a single step forward, I was there.

I started walking immediately, in case someone noticed my appearance. Vignette travel does produce a light rainbow lensing effect around the traveler when someone enters or leaves an echo. I continued down the corridor, emptying onto the circular concourse. The entire station was basically a torus with a thin cylinder in the middle. Struts connected the center to the torus. The Bragorians designed the station, but it was managed by the Starnet Union. There was a planet nearby called Vasco. A stable radionic tile was nearby with a corridor between this Dili sector and the far away Ussu sector. You could take a ship through the radionic tile to travel over one hundred light-years in minutes. This radionic tile was also used by the Flexanites, who originated in the Ussu sector. This passage is how they entered Starnet space.

I walked down the concourse and stopped by one of the oversized oval windows revealing the stars beyond. Bragorian architecture was a mix of Grandiose and mundane functional. In this public space, the station was Grandiose, but as you headed into personal spaces or work areas, it became more mundane.

"Ohm, there is a Flexanite on board this space station. He is the head of public investigation. His name is Mod. He is one of the good guys and should not be bothered or tested. You can conduct limited scans on him to gain a base set of what to expect when you encounter a Flexanite."

"Understood," Ohm replied softly in my ear.

"Let's use this space station as a jumping-off point for the cloaked scanner deployment. Place cloaked scanners on as many ships as possible to accelerate the distribution of cloaked scanners to other regions of space. If cloaked scanners end up in the Ussu sector, keep expanding into ships and populated planets found in that region."

"Adjusting rules," Ohm replied.

I dove into my invisihud and located one of the cloaked scanner devices. I generally have four cloaked scanners following me around. Their artificial intelligence is smart enough to land on my clothing when it becomes obvious I am about to transport or pass through a vignette. Once I arrive at the new location, they redeploy automatically. I also carry a set of backup units, stored in my boots, two inside each heel.

The overlay was similar to flying a drone through a remote video device. I could see through the lens of the cloaked scanner, and it presented a series of detected candidates using the same technology as the invisihud. I directed it using my invisihud to take over the cloaked scanner's interface. This direction took the form of zooming the relayed video forward inside the optical overlay to present a "pilot's" view of the cloaked scanner's location.

"Quite a view," a voice said from behind.

I knew that voice too, or at least I had a future memory of that voice from the first time loop. I turned around to see a Bragorian male. His clothes were fine leathers of grey and blue with a vest, an undershirt, and an overcoat. His pants were well hemmed and covered a wide black boot. The Bragorian people are a little larger than the average human. Bulk them up about seven to eight percent in your mind. Their skin is rough and slightly scaly, with large ridges rising from their shoulders. The ridges run along each side of the neck, up the back of the head, and finally frame the eyes. If I were to describe them, I would call them dragon people. They have lizard-like skin with human facial features.

"I have to agree," I said as I offered my hand to him. "I'm Sam, Sam Richards."

He seemed utterly delighted when I offered my hand to him, like a kid receiving candy or a con artist zeroing in on a new mark. From what my future memories told me about him, he was a little of both, which I did not mind at all.

He took my hand slowly and said with a smile, "I'm Marcus, plain Marcus."

Letting go of my hand, he said, "I couldn't help but notice your garment. I find the construction and colors quite interesting."

"Well, this is the first time I am wearing it out. I designed it today," I said proudly.

"Really? I am a tailor myself," Marcus replied.

"I designed it so I would not stand out here on *Oasis Seven*. But I guess I failed that test rather quickly."

"Oh, not at all. I'm sure most people would not notice it."

"So, what is wrong with it?"

"It's not that anything is wrong with it," Marcus said. "It fits you quite well, and it is not outlandish. It might be that I was noticing the person inside the outfit more than the clothes themselves."

I walked over to the other side of this suspended walkway that we stood upon, offering a view of the shops and people making their way below.

Continuing, as he followed me to the railed overlook, "I think that is it," as if answering a question that he asked himself. "The cut of the garment helps emphasize your favorable qualities. It makes your stance and posture seem more confident."

"Thanks for the constructive criticism."

"Oh, not a problem at all. If you would like to talk more about garments or view the selection in my shop, it is right below," he said, gesturing to a shop on the concourse below.

"I'll keep that in mind, Marcus."

"Enjoy your visit to *Oasis Seven*," he said before walking away.

I headed along the walkway in a direction opposite Marcus. I took a lift down one level and started touring the outer ring of shops and service providers. I looked for Brent's sickbay. On ships, sickbay is an integrated part of the vessel. On this station, sickbay was considered a service and thus resided on the concourse.

I passed several stands selling Vascon goods, an open food court with replicator service for the general public, and a Warnock restaurant. Lepton's was the station's bar and casino, which appeared to be hopping. Across from Lepton's was Brent's medical offices. I guess the location made sense. If you got hurt in a bar fight, the doctor was just across the street.

I walked inside and found a receptionist sitting at a desk behind a wall of frosted glass. I knew Brent's offices were just behind that wall, but I had to do this right as I said, "I'd like to make an appointment to see the doctor."

The receptionist was a beautiful Vascon woman. The Vascon species were about the same height as humans, with additional sculpted features, on their noses, eyebrows, and ears. Most Vascons, this receptionist included, wore elaborate earrings on their left ear connecting to the side of their noses. The drape of the connecting silver chain and the various shapes of the jewelry offered insight into an individual's family and heritage. I never really learned how to read them, however.

"Certainly. I'll need you to fill out these forms for me," she said as she placed a tech tablet on the counter.

"I'm not really sick. I just want to talk to him."

She frowned, picked up the tablet, and placed it behind the frosted glass wall before saying, "I'll check if he is available."

"Thank you."

I turned around and looked out the windows of this medical office, watching the people walk by, and there she was. It was Jorrie. She walked with her friend Mia, and it looked like they were heading into Lepton's. I targeted Lepton's entrance with my invisihud and connected a cloaked scanner to that location. If you don't give a cloaked scanner a target, it goes into a roaming mode to scan what areas it can. I could see a blur of action through the cloaked scanner's zoomed back video feed as it rushed to the location I targeted. It was there in less than a minute.

Diving into the cloaked scanner's video feed, I took over its invisihud to search the room while trying to find her. I saw them in the back of the bar, on the spiral staircase leading to the upper level. I quickly targeted Jorrie and chose the observe and protect icon from the list. This option was one of the preset modes you could assign to individual cloaked scanners.

I was visibly startled when a hand tapped me on the shoulder from behind. I leaned forward with a start. While I was bent over, I closed my eyes and looked to the right to shut down the invisihud. When I turned around, I saw Brent Stevens. He was in a startling position himself, with wide eyes and his hands lowered to his side, saying, "Oh, I'm sorry. I did not mean to startle you."

"My fault. I was lost in thought," I said as I extended my hand. "I'm Sam, Sam Richards."

Brent took my hand and said, "Brent Stevens, Doctor," with a slight lift to his voice when he said the word doctor.

I forgot Brent was like this. It's not really his fault. Scientists manipulated his genome while in utero. His parents broke the law when they hired doctors to modify the DNA of their unborn child. It was not something Brent requested or was even aware of until later in life. But these modifications gave him advantages, such as a high degree of dexterity and an increased intellect. It also gave him an increased ego, putting people off initially, at least until you got to know him.

I used his title to appeal to his ego, "Doctor, I am working on an invention to help with the treatment of deep gash wounds encountered in combat or any dangerous situation."

"I'm not sure I can help you with that."

"I have a basic working prototype, but I don't have a way to replicate the orgamorphic gel. I am looking for a supplier or a recipe."

"A recipe? It's not a cake. Orgamorphic gel is a controlled substance, so it is not available to the general public," he stated sternly.

"Can you tell me who it is available to?"

"I don't think I like the direction this conversation is taking," Brent said while stepping back a bit and eying me up and down.

I quickly added, "I only ask because I am not the general public. I am a probability traveler."

Brent met my eyes, trying to determine if I was lying, and said, "Even if that is true, I don't think that alone qualifies you to receive access."

We stood in silence for a moment before he said, "Listen, good luck on your invention. It sounds useful. I have to return to my work now."

"Yeah, okay," I said with a diminished spirit, and I watched Brent walk behind the frosted glass divider.

I left through the front door. The next establishment to the left was a Vascon church. There was a bench out front, so I walked over and sat down. The bar, the hospital, and the church are all right next to each other. You can't fault Bragorians for their practicality.

I thought about revisiting the cloaked scanner's invisihud to see Jorrie again, but I did not want to become that creepy guy that spies on women from a distance. I thought about what Brent said. About not qualifying. I guess it brought me down rather quickly because his words rang true. Why did I believe I deserved special privileges? The Splendorite in me should consider that a ridiculous question not worth entertaining. These were echo creatures. Just walk in there and use the *Motif* to alter echo until it meets your needs. That is what a true Splendorite would do. But I realized I was caught in a web of my own making, trying to work my way to the center. If I tugged too hard on any one strand, the whole thing might unravel. I sat there on the bench, waiting. But I did not know what I waited for.

As I sat, looking at the ground, my field of view filled with a set of olive green pants with grey boots. I looked up to see Mod.

A sharp streak of fear passed through me as he loomed above me. Mod was the only known Flexanite in the Dili sector, and he was the head of investigation on this space station. He did not know that his people made their way through the radionic tile, murdering civilians and taking up the lives of those they kill while advancing themselves into positions of power. In the first loop, I clashed with Mod. He nearly killed me by altering his form into liquid and jumping down my throat to solidify inside me. It was Ohm that saved me that day, with an emergency medical evacuation to Xanadu. For him to be this close to me was quite unnerving.

"We have a no loitering policy on the concourse. You'll have to move along."

Mod spoke like that too. He would tell you why he asked you to do something and expected you to do it now. I guess in his mind, that was polite and made sense, but in practice, it made him seem cold and calculated all the time.

"Come ye all to my house and lay down your burdens, for your rest is eternal in the eyes of the Oracle," I quoted a Vascon scripture to him.

"That's all nice and fine, but you'll have to move along now," he said to me, dismissing my reply.

"According to the Vascon parochial government, all religious properties, no matter where they stand, are to be considered of the soil on Vasco. This church is the same as a church on the planet's surface. And on the planet's surface, I am allowed to rest eternally on a bench," I said, finally looking up at him as I spoke.

He moved from side to side, adjusting his folded arms, and said, "Oh really?"

Mod was probably the worst Flexanite I ever encountered. While he could change into various forms and hold them for long lengths of time, he never really got faces or ears right. Even his hair looked fake. His overall face contained the detail of a child's drawing. Oh, the features were there. He had a mouth, eyes, and a nose, but it all looked like a rubber mask.

"Technically, the church has overstated its boundary by placing these benches so far out from the entrance. If I were to pull up the space station schematics, I'm quite sure these benches currently reside under Starnet jurisdiction, which has a rule of no loitering," Mod smugly stated.

"Fine," I said as I stood up. I tried to pick up the red bench to move it closer to the church, but it was bolted to the floor of the concourse.

Mod chuckled as I struggled, making a soft, "He, he, he."

"Ohm, will you remove the bolts that are holding this bench in place and repair the floor, so it looks like the bolts and brackets were never there?" I said out loud.

"Whaa," Mod said, but I don't think he noticed the transport occurring on the bolts and brackets under the bench.

I looked over my shoulder at Mod and picked up the bench, moving it right up against the wall of the church. Turning around, I sat back down and said, "Are you happy now? The bench is on Vascon soil."

"How did you do that?" he said, taking a full stride closer to me. "Damaging station property is strictly forbidden."

"The eyes of the Oracle reveal no damage," I said as I gestured to the repaired floor.

He looked at the floor and realized there was no evidence, saying, "I've got my eye on you," before turning around and walking away in full strides.

I waited to see if Jorrie would ever exit the bar. She might have when I was not looking, so I asked, "Ohm, is Jorrie still in Lepton's?"

"Jorrie left Lepton's approximately forty-three minutes ago using an upper-level rear exit," Ohm reported.

Probably just as well. I didn't come this far just to fuck things up now with a chance meeting. If Jorrie was not in the bar, there was no reason I couldn't go in and enjoy a drink. I got up from the bench and headed over to the always open double-wide entrance of Lepton's.

It was full of aliens. Most of them were at tables, off into the room. There was an upper-level walkway surrounding the room, with smaller tables positioned, so you could look down into the lower level if you were seated above. There were a few empty stools at the bar, and as I sat down on one, I could feel it adjust to my height automatically.

A Drologo alien that could be best described as a short, hairless troll with overly large ears walked up to me from the other side of the bar and asked in a slightly tinny voice, "What can I get you?"

I have seen my share of creatures and bizarre humans in my time, but it still seemed weird to me when completely alien races interacted with me in a casual human manner.

"Do you have human scotch this far out?"

He looked at me with his bulbous eyes and said, "Yeah, it's the chief's favorite."

He rummaged on a lower shelf, pulled out a bottle, and read the label, "Lagavulin 16 year Single Malt."

"Oh yes, please, straight up, no ice or water," I said while nodding my head, yes.

"Name's Lepton," he said as he opened the bottle and located a glass before filling it halfway. "You just arrive?"

While still shaking my head, yes, I replied, "Yes, I arrived today."

"Business or pleasure?" he asked, saying the word pleasure, slyly.

"Sadly, just business this time."

He sat the glass in front of me, and while still holding it, he said, "Thirty-two credits. Can I get your chip?"

I was already reaching for the glass of scotch when I realized I did not set up any financial considerations before entering this echo. I changed my hand movement from going to the glass to placing my elbow on the bar and stroking my chin. Lepton sensed, immediately, that I might not have a credit chip and began removing the scotch from my reach.

"Will you take quaybit?"

"For a drink?" he said unbelievably.

"Ohm, materialize a strip of quaybit."

There was a quick sparkle, and as the glow faded, a single strip of diamond-stamped quaybit remained. I made a viola gesture with my hands over the quaybit strip.

"Oh, no. I don't deal in replicated currency. That is illegal," he said, the last part with a hushed voice.

"Let me assure you. This is not replicated. It is merely transported. I can't just carry this around. I'm one person, so I am vulnerable," I said while trying to convince him with puppy dog eyes.

He picked up the strip and inspected it on all sides, lightly tossing it in his free hand, attempting to guess its weight.

"I can't make change for this," he said, still holding the strip of quaybit and the scotch.

"What if you just keep the strip and let me know when I run out of credit with you?" I suggested.

He smiled and set the glass of scotch down in front of me and said, "You've got a deal."

I sipped the Lagavulin slowly, tasting the mellow smoky peat flavor dug from the bogs of Scotland.

Someone called out Lepton's name, and he walked away to greet and serve other customers. The place was not full, but there was a nice crowd. The noise level seemed to have risen five to ten decibels since I arrived. It all seemed louder, the patrons, the laughter, the spinning of the Nuna wheel. Then it occurred to me. There was no music. What kind of bar has no music? I thought.

I must have said that last part out loud. When Lepton returned, he chimed in with a reply, "We do have music on Tuesdays. It's Vascon. They insisted."

"Do they draw a good crowd?"

"The crowd is good, but they don't buy anything," Lepton complained as he washed a few glasses.

"Maybe you need a warm-up act, you know, something to get the people dancing so they get thirsty," I suggested.

He was bent over the sink, and he looked up as a slight grin came across his rodent face before saying. "You're right. Get them dancing, and they'll get thirsty. I need fast dance music."

"Have some of the Nuna girls positioned in the crowd to start dancing when the music begins. Dancing is contagious, so having them placed in the crowd will help relieve the inhibitions of the other guests."

He put down his towel, transfixed. He saw a new horizon of opportunity that he had never considered before, an opportunity filled with profit. Something changed his mind, and he shrugged a bit and said, "But Vascon music is so boring. It's not fast at all. You don't dance to it. You listen to it."

"Two words, my friend. Opening act," I said, going on. "Make the show longer and add an opening act. People will gather and wait for the Vascon music. While they're waiting, the opening act will play the dance music."

The faraway look returned to his eyes once again as he glimmered a possibility out of leveraging profit from this thing called music.

A familiar voice next to me asked, "Lepton, can I get an ale?"

"Sure, Doctor," he said, and Lepton headed off to get the drink.

I looked over at Brent Stevens and said, "Hello again, Doctor."

Brent looked down and said, "Oh, hello, Sam is it?"

"Yeah, Sam. Have a seat if you're not joining others," as I motioned to the stool next to mine, which was empty.

He hesitated for a moment, then sat down next to me as Lepton returned with Brent's ale. A voice called out Lepton's name, and he headed off in that direction to serve another patron.

"What are you drinking?" Brent asked to get the conversation going then took a drink from his ale.

"Ah, the rare jewel that is Lagavulin. Scotch whiskey."

"My friend Ernie loves that drink too. And he often talks about it the way you did. As if it were a delicate flower or some special treat," Brent said with a smile.

"Well, I am about halfway through my half-glass, and it feels like a nice treat to me. I want to apologize if I made you uncomfortable earlier today. I didn't mean to imply or coerce you into breaking rules. I am just trying to find a supply so I can complete my project."

Brent took another sip from his ale, and we sat in silence for a moment or two before he said, "It was puzzling me all day, what you said about being a probability traveler. What did you mean by that?"

"It's a characteristic of my species, Splendorites."

"I've never heard of your species before."

"That makes sense. There are not a lot of us, and we are not native to this probability. I am listed in the Starnet database as a unique entity. They gave me a number. I am entity four-five-seven," I said before taking a small sip from my glass.

"That's fascinating," Brent said, finally turning to face me. "But what do you mean by probability?"

"A probability is where we are now," I said plainly. "To you, this world is governed by a set of rules. Those rules might be the number of rotations on a planet, gravity, the fact that plants don't talk. But my species can change those rules and the world around themselves to locate a probability where plants do talk. And not only do they talk, but they also sing, gamble, and smoke."

Brent smiled before taking another drink of his ale and asking, "You're joking, right?"

"The thing is, everyone my species meets thinks their probability is the only probability. In a way, planets are a lot like probabilities. As a Starnet officer, you have visited different planets and immersed yourself in whatever society you have found yourself in," I said, and Brent agreed by shaking his head yes.

"To me, this probability is like visiting a planet. When I arrive, I have to accept all the rules of the planet while I am here. But my goal is to obtain goods only available on this planet. Then I will travel to another planet where the goods are sorely needed," I explained.

"And the goods you need are the gel," Brent said.

"I have friends, in another probability, who are fighting a ground war against a foe with superior technology. In that probability, there are no laws against orgamorphic gel, because it does not exist there. Having access to the gel will help me build a medical device that can save lives in that probability," I said.

"That's why you asked for a recipe," Brent said.

"Exactly, I don't intend to make the gel in this probability, but another probability, so it can be used in whatever probability I find myself in," I said.

Brent finished his glass of ale in a long final drink, got up, and said, "That is an interesting story, but I still don't think I can help you with your request."

"No problem. I think it is highly probable someone else will," I said with a smile, which he returned before walking off.

Lepton returned to talk to me and said, "I couldn't help but overhear your dilemma. Trying to get goods to friends in need. That is a worthy cause."

I lifted my glass and swirled the scotch, inhaled it, and took another sip. I nearly finished the drink and said, "If you can locate a small supply, I can foresee more quaybit strips in your future."

He picked up Brent's empty glass and used a dish towel to wipe the area clean while asking, "What do you consider a small supply?"

"One liter is probably enough," I said while tipping my glass up and finishing the drink.

With the mention of such a small quantity, Lepton smiled and said, "I think I can probably arrange that," with an emphasis on the word probably. Then, in a more hushed tone, he said, "Bring eighteen strips to the cargo bay near docking port two on the outer ring. I'll be there at oh three-thirty hours."

I sat my glass on the bar, nodding yes to him, stood up, and said, "Thank you for your fine service. The drink was delicious."

"Not a problem. Any time," Lepton replied as he picked up my empty glass and walked away to clean it.

I made my way out of the bar, a little bit tipsy but not really drunk. There were a few hours to kill, so I took a corridor with a sign above it displaying "Visitor Ring" in multiple languages. While walking along the circular corridor, I reached out with the *Motif* to shift echo and add a currency card and a guest pass to my pocket. It wasn't too long until I came upon a door and slid my guest card into a slot. It opened to a large furnished suite with no one inside. After looking around to verify no one was in here, I said, "Ohm, place a level three force field across the door."

I went into the bathroom, took a crap, and a shower. There was a loofah in the shower, which my feet sorely needed. I dried off and headed into the room, where I plopped down on the bed with the towel wrapped around me. Seeing Jorrie was both uplifting and depressing. When I saw her through the cloaked scanner's lens, my heart skipped a beat. There she was, as beautiful as ever. The sound of her voice filtered through the scanner as she talked and laughed with Mia. I took in her mannerisms, the way she moved, her face. One of the last future memories I have of Jorrie was aboard *Explorer*. She left her ship, the *Concord*, a bit early and found me in our quarters. She came up close and simply said, "I'm ovulating." That was all it took for us to get naked and immediately have at it.

The depressing side of it was I had low confidence in myself. I didn't know if I could successfully court her and obtain the same type of relationship I remember having with her in my future memories. The future memories started feeling like a burden. I thought about courtship, in general. I wondered how many couples could actually do it again if they had to start over? Especially knowing what they know about the other person, rather than discovering them naturally over time. What if the first date happened in another setting? Would that throw things off?

"Ohm, if I drift off to sleep, wake me at oh two-thirty hours. I want to get there early," I said.

"Alarm set," Ohm replied.

I lay there enjoying the feeling of the scotch as I drifted off to sleep. I felt a small nudge to the entire left side of my body as Ohm applied a gentle force field, saying, "It is currently two-thirty hours aboard this space station."

"Thank you, Ohm," I replied as I groggily woke up, realizing the slightly damp towel was still wrapped around my waist.

I discarded the towel and got dressed, giving my shirt and pants a quick pat-down. Everything seemed to still be in the pockets. I pulled up a map of the station on my invisihud. The cloaked scanners more or less mapped out the entire station by this time. The area Lepton mentioned was a cargo storage area near docking port two. I set a target for one of the corners of that room, behind some stacked cargo.

"Ohm, can you replicate twenty strips of diamond-stamped quaybit in a carrying case?"

A black leather carrying case, about the size of a day planner, appeared with a sparkle on the bed. I unzipped it, unfolded it, and counted twenty strips of diamond-stamped quaybit inside. There were ten in the pockets on each side of the folding case. After zipping it up, I browsed to a food selection inside the environment designer to place it in the quick slot of the invisihud menu.

The case of quaybit was heavy like gold, and I said, "Ohm, drop the force field on the door and transport me to the targeted location inside the cargo bay."

The scene broke apart as my vision dimmed to black. I hoped the deal went off without a hitch. I would hate to see anyone get hurt over this. But I had a nagging suspicion that a double-cross was highly likely. The world reassembled, as was I, leaving me standing in a corner behind some technical shipping crates. I could hear voices from elsewhere in this room.

"No, it's over there," a demanding voice boomed.

I found a gap between some of the crates and peered across the room. I saw a short, stocky round creature, the one speaking and gesturing, and another taller thin creature who fetched a container from the top of a stack of crates. The short, stocky creature was a Mercanite. The tall, gangly creature I did not recognize. I watched them go about their business, and after a few minutes, the tall, gangly creature returned the shipping crate to the top of the stack. He picked up some smaller containers he removed from the larger one and carried them all in his hands and under his arms.

"Be careful. Don't drop those," the Mercanite berated his companion as the circular door rolled open into the wall with a mechanical gear sound. They left the room, and the door automatically rolled shut.

It wasn't too much longer until the door rolled open again, and a lean figure dressed in black quickly darted in to take up hiding among the crates, much like I did. I was glad he chose a hiding spot on the other side of the room. Using my invisihud, I scanned the creature. He was a Dolamite. They were more or less humanoid in shape and height. I did not know a lot about Dolamites other than the basic facts they were members of the Starnet Union. They possessed flux technology, art, music, and a thriving culture of their own. Their heads were hairless with reptilian skin, similar to Bragorians but without the large neck profile.

He wore a black backpack, and my invisihud reported a container inside with an unknown substance. Browsing through the invisihud environment designer menu, I located the quick slot food item. Targeting the container inside the Dolamite's backpack with my invisihud, I selected replicate replace from the invisihud menu. Before executing the command, I added the food selection that was standing by. The transport took place, swapping the container's content with the food selection. Ohm transported the contents to the Blinn research facility. The Dolamite spun around quickly. He must have imagined someone tugging on his pack or approaching from behind. I looked over at the entrance, and the door rolled open. Lepton stepped inside, and the door closed behind him. I stepped out, revealing myself, and Lepton headed toward me.

He walked up close and asked, "You got the strips?" while looking to his left and right, making sure no one observed us.

I unzipped the case and unfolded it to reveal the contents saying, "There's a tip in there for you."

His eyes lit up, and a big smile came across his face as he accepted the payment. He quickly pulled several strips out of the case and placed them in his pockets. After double-checking the count on the remaining strips, he closed the case and said, "It shouldn't be long."

The Dolamite trader revealed himself, from behind a stack of crates, and stepped forward, with the backpack in his hand, while saying, "Let's see it."

Lepton opened up the case of quaybit, revealing the strips to him. The Dolamite looked at it, doing a quick count, then said, "All right," and handed me the backpack.

Lepton zipped up the case and handed it to the Dolamite, who stuffed it into his vest. At that moment, a commotion happened above us. We looked up, a little shocked, to see a piece of conduit piping morph into a blob as it dropped to the floor blocking the exit of the room. It slowly coalesced into the form of Mod.

The Dolamite was quick to react, pointing a gloved finger at Lepton.

I raised my hands halfway up and said, "Wait, we have done nothing wrong."

It has been argued among us Splendorites, that the words of a Splendorite carry more weight than the words of an echo being. The power of the *Motif* is always with a Splendorite, and thus the Splendorite acts as localization for the *Motif* in any given echo. This relationship means, conscious acts by the Splendorite subtly alter the echo, even if the Splendorite is not walking or moving within the echo. It seemed to hold true in this case because everyone paused for a moment and looked at me.

"It's just cake, Mod," I said. "Here, let me show you," as I started to open the pack.

"Hold it," he said sternly. "Hand it over."

I stepped up to him, handed him the bag, and stepped back. I caught Lepton and the Dolamite's eyes darting around, looking for an escape option. Mod held the black backpack at arm's length in front of him and unzipped it. Reaching inside, he pulled out a medical shipping container. Dropping the backpack to the floor while holding the medical shipping container in his hand. He said sarcastically, "Oh, what have we here?"

"It's a slice of wedding cake from Opturi. It's a gift for a friend. These men are simply couriers who delivered it to me from a great distance," I said.

Lepton and the Dolamite were sheepishly shaking their heads in silent agreement.

"Why is a piece of cake being shipped in a restricted medical shipping container?" he staccotocly sang out with contempt.

"It's a refurbished unit. After a certain amount of time, the radiogenic containment properties of the shipping container walls fail. They are decommissioned. The stasis seal still functions, however, so they are ideal for fresh food transport," I explained as friendly as possible. "Please don't open the container. It will spoil before I can present it as a gift."

"Sorry, I have to take a look," he said flatly.

"Please, I have a considerable investment in that slice of cake," I said.

He looked at me, released the six latches, and lifted the lid. There was a slight spiff sound when the seal broke. We couldn't see the contents of the box from where we stood, but Mod looked at it for a good while. He closed the lid and returned the latches to their locked position. Handing the box to me, he said, "Sorry to have bothered you, gentleman," before leaving through the cargo bay door with his usual wide stride.

With my hands up in a friendly gesture, I said, "So, we're all good then, thank you."

The Dolamite bolted for the door and headed off in the opposite direction Mod took. I picked up the backpack and put the container inside. I zipped it up and put it over my shoulder.

"So, was it cake? Were we ripped off?" Lepton asked me.

"It was cake, and we were not ripped off. The deal went perfectly. Thanks for setting it up," I said before heading to the door as Lepton remained behind, still confused.

There was no one in the hallway, so I said, "Ohm, send me to the Blinn replication center, where you transported the orgamorphic gel."

The space station corridors streamed in from the sides of my vision, looking like a light pressing through a screen, and the darkness over came me once again. I hoped the Blinn technicians could replicate the orgamorphic gel, or I would have to do all of this again. The room reassembled, and all I could say to myself was, "slick."

CHAPTER 10

It was years since I visited the Blinn facilities. I mainly interacted with them via Ohm to process transportation and replication requests. I materialized in a room of shiny polished white with accents of gold and black. It was the modern replication facility located in Blinn space. Where the walls met the floor or ceiling was a curved surface.

I arrived in a large production area, standing on a raised platform in the center. There were wide windows in one of the walls revealing an even larger area with more industrial-looking technology. Beyond the windows, robotic automation revealed machines making machines.

The young Blinn fellow approaching me wore a long white overcoat with dark pants underneath. He stepped up to me and took both of my hands in his hands while gently shaking them and saying, "Let me be the first to welcome you personally to KahDaLun. My name is YonBaHaDaMaSeNe."

The Blinn species were my pet species. I guess there is no better way to say it. They were beautiful people with human-like qualities. There were small differences, such as the webbing between their fingers and toes as well as a fold in the eyelid with hints of Asian characteristics. Their ears came to a subtle point near the top, with elfish overtones, and their general frame was lean but tough.

Blinn names built up over generations. When a new child was born, it was given a single syllable for its first name. When an elder died, a syllable was removed from the end of the name. If the child was a girl, it would inherit the mother's name as a prefix. If it were a boy, it would inherit the father's name. Therefore, the full name of any Blinn individual is actually a brief history of their entire living family line. Those with the longest names are the youngest, and the shorter your name is, the older you are. There are various cultural rights that a Blinn passes through in order to shed syllables from the end of their name as they age.

Eventually, every Splendorite comes upon a race of people that he or she loves and rules over. Because of the power of the *Motif*, it is possible to locate a probability where you are a king or a lord. This is the relationship I have with the Blinn people. I sought out a probability where I am their living god. This worship means I can't have a meaningful personal relationship with any of them, but I do respect their intellect and technical prowess, which is easily as advanced as any Starnet technology.

"Yon, may I call you, Yon?" I asked.

"Yes, Yon is fine," he replied.

"Yon, did you receive the transport of the orgamorphic gel?" I asked.

"Yes, we have received the transport of the organic substance. Here are the findings from the initial scan," Yon said, and he gestured wide with both hands, which activated an auragraphic projection hovering over a nearby table.

We walked over, and he reached into the auragraphic display to highlight a section before saying, "These key areas are still being solved. Once we have a solution for those, we believe replication will be possible."

"That is great progress. Perhaps we can move on to the delivery system while those areas resolve?"

"Certainly, Sam," Yon said, then asked. "May I call you Sam?"

"Yep, that's my name," I said. "Ohm, can you transfer the proposed plans for the cellepulator to this display?"

"Transferring data," Ohm replied to the room, allowing Yon to hear the reply.

The display updated with Ohm's interpretation of my requested device. Three parts revolved in three-dimensional space, the medical scanner, a central housing unit, and the modified medjector.

Yon fussed with the interface, made a swipe move, and a completely new auragraphic display rotated into view. He picked up a flat tablet from the table, which lit up. As he tapped and swiped on the surface, changes took place inside the auragraphic display. What was originally three distinct components combined into a single unit. The shape kept changing as they rearranged themselves for the best fit. After a while, it stabilized and sat there revolving inside the auragraphic display.

"Can we make a physical version? I'd like to hold it in my hands?" I asked Yon.

He made a few more taps on the lit tablet, and a physical version of the rotating object appeared on the table with a sparkle. I smiled and picked it up. It was heavier than I expected.

"It's a little big, and the weight distribution is off. It's too heavy in the front. We need to balance it out in the same way a weapon is balanced in a soldier's hand," I said to Yon.

I put the device on the table, and Yon said, "That is good feedback. Let me see what I can do."

At hearing this, I went on saying, "It is most typically going to be used by a field-medic in a ground-based combat situation. It should be tough, weather-proof, and easy to use. No more than three buttons, but I do like the touch display you already have in place."

Yon shook his head yes and said, "Got it, setting up solvers to accommodate requests."

The auragraphic display continued updating. The virtual device would change shape. Panels lifted off, rearranged themselves to form a new part of the hull, or shrink out of existence. At first, the changes were rapid and extreme, but then they slowed down as the device took on more of a Y-shaped look, with the vertical part of the Y being the handle and the forked end being the scanning emitter.

"That's looking better," I said.

Yon tapped a few more times on his lit tablet, and a virtual person appeared inside the display. With a few more gestures, he shrunk the device into the hand of the avatar, indicating the actual size when in use. Yon made some twisting motions, and the avatar grasped the device. I blurted out, "Let's freeze it there for a moment."

Yon tapped on the lit tablet, and the auragraphic display froze in place. I reached into the display and made a spreading motion with my hand to zoom in on the model. It took a few gestures, but I managed to zoom in on the hand holding the device.

"Yon, we need to flip the device around. Currently, the avatar is pointing the device down with the activation buttons underneath, similar to a trigger on a weapon. Medical personnel hold their devices up as I made a toasting gesture. Let's move the buttons to the top so they can be activated by the thumb and bring the display more in line with that of a traditional medical inspectrograph."

"Disabling solvers. I can make these final tweaks manually," he said, and he started making more precise movements on his lit tablet.

With each new request, the medical device continued to revise itself on the auragraphic display. It wasn't too long before Yon said, "I think we are ready for a new prototype."

The previous device sparkled and disappeared to be replaced by the newer revised model. It was smaller and offered a nice feel in your hand.

"The weight distribution is a lot better, and having the buttons on top seems right. It works in either hand. I like that too. Can we put some fabric-based material on the housing? The smooth metal here on the bottom feels a little slippery," I said while holding the prototype.

I handed the device to him, and he put down the lit tablet, testing out the device in each hand while checking its weight and button distance based upon his finger's length. Yon flipped the device over, looked at the back, and said, "A soft, ribbed surface added to this side should make it more stable in your hand."

He sat the device on the table and picked up his tablet, which lit up. After making a few long, swipe and wait motions, he moved on to another tapping session. I was watching the auragraphic display update when Ohm chimed in, "Positive identification of the starship *Journey* detected in the Gar sector."

Yon looked up from his work. He heard Ohm's announcement too.

"Yon, I have to leave now, but this is looking great. Work with the other team members to get this operational as quickly as possible, assuming the remaining gel solvers finally converge. And, thank you for your work."

"You are welcome," Yon replied. "It was wonderful collaborating with you."

I stepped away from Yon and said, "Ohm, transport the shuttlecraft *Zanna* to the Gar sector location where the signal was detected. Give young Ethan

Foster his fifteen-minute warning. Once the *Zanna* materializes in the Gar sector, transport me aboard."

The transportation of a ship is no trivial matter, but it was the lowly cloaked scanner that accomplished this. Individually, a single cloaked scanner can transport a few people or like-sized cargo. This feature requires leaving a single cloaked scanner behind, however, to act as a transportation anchor for the source location.

To implement the transportation of the *Zanna*, several steps were needed. There was already a cloaked scanner following the optical drone that spotted *Journey*. Ohm used that transport anchor as a target location to transport in several more of the larger variety of cloaked scanners. The larger cloaked scanners combined to form a transportation aperture providing the extended bandwidth required for the massive transportation operation. I called this combination of large cloaked scanners a transport sphere.

Once the ship arrives at the target location, the units making up the transport sphere are unlinked. Each unlinked cloaked scanner is transported back to a storage area inside *Tiger Mountain* so it can be deployed for future operations. In the end, every transport operation leaves behind a single cloaked scanner. The deployment allows access to the same location if needed, but it does waste a device in the process. This limitation is why the Blinn replication facilities are needed. The Blinn replication factories replenish the supply of cloaked scanners.

The gold accents in the room made a brilliant flash before zooming in from the sides of my vision. I found myself in darkness. I was unsure how the next set of events were going to unfold. When you add too many additional variables into the mix, the ability to shape echo is reduced, but bold gestures can still be used, especially from a distance. It felt like the walls of the room were crushing in on me this time. I guess that is the side effect of transporting from a very large area into a smaller cramped space. Everything solidified around me as I materialized in the small cabin of the shuttlecraft *Zanna*.

CHAPTER 11

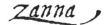

I made my way to the front of the shuttlecraft, took the seat on the left, and activated the virtual touch controls. The *Zanna* seemed smaller than I remembered. The virtualized control system allowed you to pass any control window from station to station. You did not need to be in one specific seat to control the shuttlecraft. There were four seats and four display consoles. Farther back were a couple of padded benches with a space below so you could store your gear under the bed. Beyond the benches were two transporter departure points. Past that was the engine area where the bathroom was located.

Touching the display, I brought up several system control windows. They worked a lot like the invisihud menu. There were lists and sub-lists with options you could activate along the way, but I haven't piloted this or any shuttlecraft in years. It all seemed foreign to me. I was able to activate the short-range scanners and conduct weapons and shield test. The systems all reported go. Everything worked.

The shuttlecraft was named the *Zanna*. That was also the name of the computer that managed the onboard operations.

"Zanna, can you overlay the position of *Journey* on top of the long-range scanners?" I asked.

"Working," Zanna replied, and a new window popped up on my display. I suddenly realized, "Oh, that is the icon for long-range scanners."

"Plot a course from here to *Journey*'s last known location."

The new window zoomed out, and a target marker appeared on the edge of the circular display.

"Zanna, overlay communication range."

The circular display tinted with a color radiating from the center. It looked like our ship's position was halfway from the edge of *Journey*'s communications range.

"Set course for *Journey*'s position, flux one."

There was a brief sense of forward movement. Another window popped up, indicating the velocity isolators activated to insulate passengers inside the ship from the speeds produced by the ship's motion. I thought I heard a faint sound and looked back to see the tail end of a transport sparkle, leaving Ethan Foster standing where I transported in a few minutes ago. He wore more rugged clothing compared to the last time I saw him at the party, and he carried a green backpack slung over his shoulder. I got up and greeted him by shaking his hand and patting his shoulder.

"Welcome aboard, Ethan. You can put your gear under the bunk there," I said while pointing to the long bench bed. "Just lift it up."

Ethan stowed his pack and came up front to join me. I sat down, but he stood, taking it all in. The stars look different when traveling at flux speeds compared to chemstream based travel. They appeared to streak by the ship and shift through a gradient of colors while passing. The stars are not really passing you by. It is an optical phenomenon of the flux field itself, which places the ship in the first layer of sub-space. This sub-space layer acts as a lens into normal space. The distortion of light passing through the sub-space lens causes an optical streaking.

"Have a seat," I said while gesturing to the one next to me, and Ethan sat down. "Sorry for the sudden departure, but we have a lock on *Journey*, and I did not want to delay."

"Oh, that's all right," Ethan said.

"How did the kids take it?"

"Lulu cried a bit, but Albert was extremely excited for me," he said.

"And Olivia?" I asked, prying a little too much.

"She said to stay safe and wished me well too."

"Well, here is a crash course on shuttlecraft operations," I said and started explaining the interface to him.

"This shuttlecraft has two sets of engines, chemstream, and flux. Chemstream is used for take-off, landing, and atmospheric flying. You can also travel short distances in space using chemstream. For long-distance travel, we use the second engine called the flux drive. It basically emits a field that creates a differential between sub-space and normal space. This differential pushes the emitters out of the way. The emitters are attached to the ship's hull, so the entire ship is moved in the process. By modulating the shape of the flux field, we can create forward movement through space. We are currently traveling at flux one, which is still kind of slow. Let's increase to flux two," I said.

"I see," Ethan said quite politely.

"You can make copies of windows and slide them around to share them with other team members at other stations," I said, leaning over to point at one of the windows on his display.

"Take that one and move it onto the icon representation of the work station in the lower left part of your display," I said while indicating to touch, drag, and release with his fingers.

Ethan tried it a couple of times, but it did not work. On the third try, he accomplished it, and a new window appeared on my screen. It was the communications controls. He leaned over to see the copy of his window appear on my display screen and said, "Wicked."

"Good, work. Now let me send you a window," I said as I dragged the flux engine controls onto the icon representation of Ethan's workstation.

"I see it," Ethan said with enthusiasm. "Now what?"

"That window controls the speed of the flux drive. Move the vertical slider up from the first position to the second position. It should snap into place," I said while watching his display.

Ethan tried a couple of times, but the slider snapped back to the first position. He finally managed to get it to stick in place, at the second position, and the ship made a soft groan as the sound of the engine took on a slightly higher pitch. He looked over and said, "You have to over-drag, and then it snaps back."

"Yeah, you'll get used to the feel of the console. Take a look at the top right portion of the display. Do you see a question mark?"

"Um, yeah, I see it."

"Go ahead and tap it. That is the ship's help system. You can flip through the pages or use the table of contents to find more detailed descriptions of the various ship's systems and the interface windows that control them."

"You can also talk directly to the ship's computer, which is named Zanna, like the ship itself," I said. "Zanna, how long until we are within communications range at our current speed?"

A synthesized female voice replied, "Seventeen hours and fifty-six minutes until this ship is within communications range of the last known location of *Journey*."

Ethan smiled at hearing the voice respond.

"Ethan, go ahead and bump us up to flux-four. This craft is a flux-five ship," I said.

I watched Ethan attempt the flux drive adjustment a couple of times before he got it, and the ship emitted an even lower groan as our speed increased.

"Now, you ask for the arrival time."

"Okay, just say it out loud, got it. Zanna, how long is it now that we are moving faster?"

"Referring to the last inquiry. The revised time is now four hours and twelve minutes," Zanna replied.

"When you are issuing voice commands, try to be as specific as possible," I said to Ethan. "Otherwise, the system may ask you to restate or clarify your request.

Ethan shook his head up and down, indicating he understood.

"Zanna, increase flux speed to four point six," I said, and the ship made a subtle groan as we increased speed again.

"What is our time to communication range with *Journey* now?" I asked.

"Two hours and twenty-six minutes," Zanna replied.

"When you're traveling near your maximum speed, it is always wise to keep an eye on the temperature," I said as I cloned the coolant system window and dropped it on Ethan's console.

Between the two front seats, there was a custom central display with an illustrated version of the shuttlecraft and its systems. I said to Ethan, "If anything goes wrong with the ship, the affected system will highlight on this central display. If you touch the affected system, a window for the control system will appear on your console."

I reviewed the engine temperature, and the coolant reported within a safe range. I said, "Let's head back to the engine room and take a look at the actual beast."

We spent the next couple of hours getting acquainted with the ship and its systems. When we reached the edge of the communication range, I sent a message to *Journey* but received no reply. This silence was bad news indeed. After another hour on course to *Journey*'s last known location, we picked up a garbled signal.

"This is the starship *Journey* to any passing ships. We are damaged and need assistance. Our coordinates are one three five nine macula seven," Zanna played the message, which repeated on an automated loop.

"Zanna, send this message as a repeating loop," I said. "Starship *Journey*, this is the shuttlecraft *Zanna* responding to your call for assistance."

"Message sent and looping," Zanna replied.

I felt a bit worried. There were no future memories of something like this happening. I remembered the reverse. The *Zanna* was damaged, and *Journey* offered to help.

Ethan was immersed in the displays, reading up on the help. He looked up when I said, "Ethan, I need to make some adjustments to this probability. It won't hurt, but it may seem strange. Reality might appear to change rapidly. Remain calm. It won't take long."

I got up from the chair and paced back and forth, walking the farthest distance I could inside the ship before turning around and repeating the same motion. I imagined the design of the *Motif* and tried to visualize it in front of me while overlaying it on top of everything and extending it into space. I reached into this reality and sought the best probable angle of approach for this incipient reality I was about to enter. The shuttlecraft shuttered, and its walls rippled while the sounds of metal stressing scraped against my ears. I pulled the *Motif* back into myself, reaffirming my immortality by accepting it as the ship returned to normal.

Warning sounds emitted from the front console, and Ethan said with concern, "Sam, I think something is wrong?"

I returned to my seat to see multiple alarms going off as we dropped out of flux. There were coolant leaks and proximity alarms. I quickly touched the shields up icon and then yelled, "Zanna, reduce our speed. Avoid this debris!"

It was too late. We encountered impacts, shaking the ship. The shields took some damage, deflecting what looked like ship debris floating in space. Zanna's autopilot took over to navigate us through the slow-moving larger pieces. We heard occasional small impacts, but the shields held as they dropped to seventy-two percent. The short-range sensors reported *Journey* on the display. I set up a navigational target, and Zanna moved us off in that direction while avoiding debris as she flew the ship.

It was the view from the cockpit that interested Ethan and me the most.

Looking through the front glass window, which was actually transparent graphene, revealed a great space battle must have taken place here. A large rectangular ship was adrift, split in half, and on fire. The debris Zanna avoided came from that ship. *Journey* was in view, but also adrift. It was obvious they lost their stabilizers because the ship slowly tumbled in space. It seemed intact, though. The was hull damage with breeches, but the nacelles were still attached, and it was not missing any major parts.

"What do we do?" Ethan asked.

"We'll have to try and dock and take it from there."

I sent another message, "Starship *Journey*, this is the shuttlecraft *Zanna*. We have arrived and are commencing rescue operations."

Ethan adjusted his glasses as he looked at me with concern.

"Zanna, scan for escape pods within the debris," I said.

The short-range sensor window refreshed, but there were no additional objects added to the display.

"No escape pods detected," Zanna reported.

Ethan interrupted as he pointed to his display and asked, "What does this mean?"

I reviewed the short-range scanner output and said, "It looks like those are life signs. Which is good."

The shuttlecraft maneuvered around to *Journey*'s shuttle bay entrance, typically sealed with a force field, but a power loss left this area open to space. Zanna matched the pitch angle of *Journey*, and we slowly descended into the bay. It looked like the gravity plating was off-line, a couple of shuttlecraft in the bay floated around with low inertia. Our shuttle landed with a thud, finally hitting a patch of active gravity plating, and a long scrape sounded as we skidded to a stop. We were finally aboard *Journey*.

"Zanna, seal off the coolant leaks and attempt repairs," I said as I moved back to the sleeping bench area. Lifting up the bench lid on my side, I said, "Let's get the medkits. We need to bring them along. Also, fetch your wand, but leave the backpack behind."

"Got it," Ethan said as he searched through his pack.

"Ohm, can you replicate a standard Starnet jacket with the science colors that fits Ethan?" I asked.

A folded jacket appeared on the floor with a sparkle. I picked it up, shook it out, and said, "Put this on. We need to look like Starnet members as much as possible."

Ethan put on the jacket with the Starnet blue color on the shoulders but sensed my concern about our current situation.

"Ohm, we need two Starnet communication brooches," I said while closing my bench and placing the medkit on top. I opened the medkit and quickly scanned its contents. Satisfied that it all was there, I closed it back up.

Two small trapezoid brooches appeared on the bench next to the medkit as I said, "The blue color indicates medical and science, the gold color indicates command discipline, and the red color indicates security or lower-ranking crew.

You'll encounter these colors on the uniforms of the people we are about to meet."

I attached one brooch to his jacket and the other to my shirt. They stayed in place because of magnets sewn into the garments we wore.

"This is called a communications brooch. You activate it by tapping on it and speaking into it like a phone or a two-way radio," I said as I touched mine. "Testing, testing."

I looked at him seriously and said, "When we encounter people, I'll do the talking. If we get separated, you must say you are with Starnet and that you are from the Dili sector."

He shook his head in agreement.

"And another thing. With that alien ship so close, there might be intruders on board. If they don't have Starnet colors and they look alien use, *Insipida* on them," I said.

He shook his head in agreement once more.

"Grab your medkit, and let's get in there. Ohm, transport us to the corridor beyond the shuttle bay doors."

I watched as Ethan dissolved in front of me while my own eyes dissolved into darkness. For some reason, my ears assembled before my eyes this time. I heard the distorted sound of the code-one before it all jammed backed together, leaving Ethan and me alone in the dimly lit corridor.

I touched my communication brooch and said, "To any crew. This is Sam Richards from the shuttlecraft *Zanna* responding to your distress call. Please respond."

It looked like emergency lighting was in place, but we still had gravity. We could go left or right, so I chose right, and we headed down the corridor. It was not long until we encountered damage and minor debris blocking our way. It looked like superficial supports or parts of wall paneling shook loose. We moved around it or over it as we tramped forward along the corridor.

"Ohm, send out cloaked scanners to locate the crew and map out the ship's damage," I said.

"Scanners deployed," Ohm replied.

My invisihud lit up momentarily as I watched multiple cloaked scanners spread out from our location and quickly travel away from us. I stood there for a moment, waiting for the scanners to provide some possible path to follow.

Our communications brooches crackled, and a thin-sounding voice asked, "Who is this?"

"This is Sam Richards of the Starnet shuttlecraft *Zanna*. We have arrived from the Dili sector. Who am I talking to?"

We waited for a moment before I motioned to Ethan that we should keep on moving. We continued down the corridor that ended in a T-style junction. Before reaching the intersection, Ethan pointed to a half-open door with some debris blocking it from fully closing. Inside was a fallen Starnet crewman.

Forcing the door open, we pushed it back into the wall. It was one of those sliding-type doors that retract under normal operations. We only saw legs sticking out from a panel that fell from the ceiling. Together, Ethan and I removed the panel, revealing a human male underneath. He wore gold colors, was barely conscious, and in obvious pain. Setting the medkit on the floor, I quickly opened it up to locate the medical inspectrograph. I scanned the wounded crewman, and the inspectrograph display revealed red highlights in several portions of the chest. I didn't need the device to see the cuts on his arm and face. It looked like he may have tried blocking the falling ceiling with his arm. There was a fracture along the ulna and his wrist on the left hand.

"Ethan, open your kit and follow along. Locate this device," I said while holding up the medjector.

"Twist this all the way to the left. That is the lowest dose. Twist all the way to the right for the maximum dose. This wheel allows you to quickly change the type of medicine. Move it all the way to the top for a sedative and to the bottom for a stimulant," I said.

Ethan clambered to open up his medkit and find the medjector. He twisted the knob and moved the wheel as he followed along with my instructions. I set the medjector to a mild sedative and administered the shot to the right side of his neck while saying, "Press the medjector into the skin to deliver the medicine. Use the right side of the neck for the best results on humans. This application will cause it to be pumped by the heart, through the entire body, before circulating back around through the brain."

The patient emitted a soft groan as I did this, and I asked, "What's your name, crewman?"

"Jenkins, Marvin Jenkins," he struggled to say.

"I'm Sam, and this is Ethan. You've got a few broken ribs and fractured your forearm and wrist. I know it hurts like hell, but hang in there. You're going to make it. I gave you a light sedative to help with the pain."

Our communication brooches crackled again, and the thin voice said, "This is the Auramedic. How did you get here?"

"Can you issue a site-to-site transport from your location? Marvin Jenkins is hurt, with several broken ribs and a fractured ulna?" I said, ignoring the Auramedic's question.

"The transporters are down. You'll have to treat him there," the Auramedic replied.

"I have some field training and have administered a level two sedative to relieve the pain, but I am not sure how to proceed with broken ribs. His breathing is labored," I said into my communication brooch.

"Can you bring him to sickbay?" the thin voice asked.

"I can probably rig a site-to-site transport using my shuttlecraft's transporter, but I don't have a way to target sickbay. I don't know this ship at all."

"Give me a moment," the voice said, then shortly replied. "I have detected your shuttlecraft in the shuttle bay, but I have no access to any of the systems. Can you release the lock-outs?"

"Zanna, are you there?" I asked.

"Affirmative," the synthetic voice said through the communication brooch.

"Zanna, coordinate with the Auramedic. Give him full access to the systems. We are going to use your transporter for site-to-site transport relays to sickbay aboard this ship."

"Understood," Zanna replied through the Starnet brooch.

"Auramedic, try again," I said.

It must have worked. A minute or two later, Marvin dissolved in a transport sparkle, leaving Ethan and me alone. A follow-up message from the Auramedic came through our communication brooches offering encouragement, "Good work. I have him. Try to locate more injured crew if you can? I'll check back with you shortly."

I packed up my medkit, and Ethan silently did the same with his. We returned to the T-junction and took the corridor to the left, which led us deeper into the ship. We came upon a map of a cross-section of the ship displayed on part of the wall. It revealed our current location. Tapping a location on the map marked engineering, I saw a red line appear indicating a route from where we were to our target destination. A set of repeating arrow-shaped lights traveled down the wall showing the direction we should follow. Ethan looked at me, and we headed off in the direction that the moving wall arrows indicated.

The wall arrows guided us through several twists and turns. We followed the moving arrows each time we encountered a junction until we came to a shaft leading down. Ladder rungs descended into the dimly lit tube. Next to the tube was a magnalift entrance where the wall arrows ended. I tried opening the magnalift doors, but they were off-line and would not budge.

"I guess we take the ladder, Ethan. I'll go first," I said, and I started climbing down into the tube.

As I climbed, I activated my invisihud and said, "Ohm, can you overlay a path to engineering from my current location?"

The resulting three-dimensional wire-frame overlay was confusing, so I said, "Let's view this as a cross-section," and my invisihud display rotated to present a better view of where we were and where we were heading.

We descended the first ladder and found ourselves at a four-way junction. Maintenance tubes headed off in all directions. A short distance down one tube, I saw a body sprawled out on its back.

"Watch your head, Ethan," I said as I made my way into the maintenance tube to the fallen crewman.

When I got there, he was unconscious but still breathing. He was Logican. I tapped my communication brooch and said, "Auramedic, we found another body in a maintenance tube. Can you lock on?"

"What's his status?" the tinny voice replied after a short silence.

"He is Logican. Unconscious but still breathing. I don't see any blood loss, probably head trauma, but I have not verified anything with the inspectrograph," I said while trying to be as detailed as possible.

"This makeshift site-to-site transport relay can't detect anyone inside the maintenance tubes. Can you move him out to a major corridor?" the Auramedic asked.

"We'll try. I'll let you know when we get there," I said before looking back to Ethan. "Can you levitate him out of this tube?"

Ethan replied, "I can try, but I'll need a clear view."

We both backed out of the maintenance tube, and Ethan pulled out his wand. He leaned into the tube, and with a flick of the wrist, said, "*Resurgemus.*"

The crewman's body rose up, unsteady at first, then became more stable. Ethan concentrated and stepped back while keeping his focus on the wand and the body. The Logican slowly moved down the maintenance tube toward us. He floated into the junction, where I nodded my head and prepared to catch the body. Ethan discontinued his wand treatment, and the crewman fell into my arms. That is when I saw that he, indeed, suffered a head injury and was leaking blue blood.

I lowered him to a sitting position under the open area of the tube leading up and asked Ethan, "Do you think you can levitate him up to the top of the ladder?"

Ethan looked at me, shook his head, yes, and said, "Yes, I think I can do it."

"I'm heading up the ladder. I'll grab him when he's near the top."

When I got to the top of the tube, I laid down on the floor and reached my hands into the tube as far as they would go, and called out, "I'm in place. Let's do it."

I heard the soft mutter of "*Resurgemus*" uttered one more time and watched as the limp body eerily rose up the tube. Realizing it might be better if I was actually on the ladder, I climbed back down a bit, hanging on with one hand while reaching out to grab the rising body.

The rise was slow and steady, and I talked to Ethan, not knowing if he could talk back while concentrating with a spell, "Getting close, Ethan. Just a little more."

The body rose up next to my shoulder, and I grabbed the Logican's arm to wrap it around my shoulder while holding onto his waist. He seemed to stir a bit. I took a step up, then quickly moved my free hand from one rung to another while trying not to drop this dead weight. I think I might have interrupted the spell when I touched the Logican. While carrying this heavy burden, I stepped up and quickly grabbed the next rung. I managed to climb to the top of the tube with the Logican in tow and pushed the body onto the floor. I climbed out and cleared the way as I heard Ethan ascending the rungs.

"Auramedic, we have him out of the tube. I verified a head injury, probably some form of concussion. Can you lock on?" I said into the communication brooch while sitting on the floor, catching my breath.

Ethan made his way out of the tube. He offered his hand to help me up. I took it and stood up, saying, "Whew."

The tinny voice replied, "Good work. I can lock on. Please stand by."

The body of the limp Logican sparkled away, leaving Ethan and me alone on the deck.

"The Auramedic is right. That was good work. I don't think I could have carried him out of there, on my own," I said to Ethan.

"I have never tried moving something that large before. At Nottingham, we practiced on small things like paper, feathers, and stones," Ethan said. "I haven't used that spell in years."

We stood there for a few minutes. I felt a bit overwhelmed at the task we faced, and I imagined Ethan felt that way too. I started pacing again and brought forth the *Motif* in my mind, projecting it outward over the entire ship. While seeking a more favorable situation for us and the crew, I ushered in lucky situations where systems were not as damaged as when we arrived, or the organic circuitry on the ship managed to repair itself much quicker than expected. The walls of the corridor rippled, much like the shuttlecraft when I shifted echo before. I drew the *Motif* inside myself to refresh my personal energies.

The tinny voice returned to our communication brooches, and the Auramedic said, "I have detected a downed crewman not far from your current location. Proceed to section five, corridor L."

I tapped my communication brooch and said, "We don't know the ship that well. Can you use the corridor mapping system to activate the wall arrows?"

"Good idea. Activating mapping," the Auramedic replied, and once again, we saw a set of arrows moving along the side of the wall.

I took off in a jog, and Ethan followed. I wanted to get there quickly. The echo shifting seemed to make the corridors less cluttered with debris, but there was still some obvious damage along the way. The arrows ended at a magnalift door, but this one was operational. We stepped inside, and it started moving automatically. I guess the arrow system included magnalifts in guiding guests. The time in the magnalift was only a minute, no more than two. We could feel it moving up and sideways, to finally slow down to a stop before the doors slid open. Stenciled on the wall, we saw a large number five.

We followed the arrows moving along the wall but did not have far to go. She lay on the floor in the middle of a three-way junction. I rushed up, sat my medkit down, and started looking for damage to her body. I could not find any until I rolled her over. That's when I saw the large black burn mark on her back.

Tapping the communication brooch again, I said, "Auramedic, we have intruders on board. We're at junction 5L, and this woman has a serious burn wound on her back, inflicted by an energy weapon."

Before the Auramedic could respond, I heard Ethan call out *Insipida*, and he pointed his wand at a target behind me.

Down the other corridor, behind Ethan, a Maylon invader stood with his weapon drawn. The Maylon are a warlike race, a little larger than humans. Their matted dreadlock hair flows at long lengths along their shoulders and down their backs as often as it is bound up to make their head seem larger. They wear tribal clothing and often have jewelry made from the bones of their fallen enemies. They are tech scavengers and seize any opportunity to obtain an advantage over rival tribes. When they are not fighting among themselves, they terrorize others. There was only a moment to reach up and shove Ethan out of the way before being hit by the blast. The last thing I heard was Union gleam-gun fire as I fell unconscious, inhaling the smell of my own burning flesh.

CHAPTER 12

Journey

I awoke to the view of a bald, middle-aged man looking down at me. I lie on a bed in some type of tech room while he slowly moved an instrument over my lower right abdomen. The Auramedic was a virtual doctor who took on the form of the species it was mending. This programming was a blatant psychological attempt to put the patient at ease while being treated. Why he appeared to me as a middle-aged, balding man was still a mystery?

"Hold still. I'm almost through. I am the Auramedic, and your friend Ethan here tells me you are Sam," he said as he finished the device movement and placed it on a medical tray.

I sat up and said, "Damn," as a sharp pain shot out from the area of my wound.

The Auramedic lifted an eyebrow at my exclamation and said, "It will probably smart for a day or two, but if the pain persists, come and see me."

As the Auramedic stepped away, I saw a group of three people approach the medical bed. Ethan Foster was farther back in the room, standing behind them. In the center of the group was a middle-aged, human woman. She was a bit stocky and wore the gold colors on her uniform. To her right was a larger human male with the body build of a boxer. His shoulders were wide, and he also wore gold on his uniform. The person to her left was taller and of a thinner build with brown-colored skin. He was a Logican. The colors on his uniform were red.

The woman stepped forward and said, "I'm Sara Mitchell, Captain of the starship *Journey*. Thank you for responding to our distress call."

"How long was I out? We need to put some distance between us and that other ship," I said slowly, easing my way off the bed to stand on my own. I looked down at my wounded area. There was a good-size hole in my clothing. It was burned and melted along the edges, but my skin underneath was healed.

"I am commander Tamakot. You were out for a day," the man on the right said.

"And I am commander Frelpok," the Logican said.

"Spoken like a commander. We are underway and have put some distance between us and the Maylon battleship," Sara said.

It was odd to get this far along and question why I came here in the first place. But getting shot does that to you. In my future memories, I was friends with these people. But now that they stood before my very eyes, I wondered if I could form friendships with them again? I guess this would be good enough practice. I would eventually have to do the same thing with Erin and Jorrie.

I called to the back of the room, "You okay, Ethan?"

Ethan replied, "Yeah, things have calmed down."

"Ethan has told us of his journey with you to reach us, but it has raised just as many questions as it did answers," Sara said to me.

Completing her thought, Frelpok said, "Foremost on our mind is how did you get here from the Dili sector?"

"Did Ethan tell you I am a probability traveler?" I asked Sara.

"He did, but I'm not quite sure what that really means," she replied with curiosity.

"When you walk across the room, it may never occur to you that the room you are approaching could be different than the room you are leaving behind. My people are called Splendorites. We can sense and select alternate realities as we move through space. For instance, I could see an apple on a table across the room. You could too. When I walk across the room and finally arrive at the table, I could find a banana. If you walk with me, you could find a banana too. If you stay behind, you might always see the apple."

Frelpok spoke again, enunciating every word, "Fascinating, you claim to be able to alter reality by simply moving through it? Can you prove it?"

"Yes, right before I was shot, I selected a better version of this reality, one where *Journey* was less damaged. The ability of the Splendorite is sometimes called luck. "I used that ability to make the damaged systems less damaged or more easily repaired," I said.

Tamakot said to Sara, "Those were almost the exact words some of the engineering team said to me. More than one person said we were lucky this or it was a good thing that didn't happen."

I continued, "Ethan and I took scans of *Journey* before we docked in the shuttle bay. You can review the shuttle logs and compare them to your logs to see if they match. My guess is these initial scans will reveal you suffered more damage than your current logs actually report."

Sara looked at me and asked directly, "Does your ability include taking control of other people?"

I shifted my weight and felt a little twinge of pain from my wound. Sara seemed to notice and looked down at it.

"Splendorite's don't have telepathic abilities or the ability to take over someone's mind. I can subtly influence people's actions by integrating myself into their narrative, however."

"Is that what you are doing here?" she asked flatly.

"When you say it like that, I guess I have to say yes," I replied to her, looking her in the eye.

Sara looked away, pacing, moving her hands as if trying to gather her thoughts before asking, "Why are you trying to influence us?"

"I'm stuck in a time loop, but this time around, I have memories from my future. In that future, I met a starship named *Journey* and became friends with that crew. Eventually, by knowing you, I meet a woman who will become my wife. I am not trying to influence you. I am trying to know you," I said softly.

"How can we be sure? Ethan demonstrated his ability to control the Maylon's mind," Frelpok chimed in.

"What happened to the Maylon?" I asked.

Tamakot replied, "We transported all intruders back to the Maylon battleship before we jumped to flux."

I looked at Frelpok and said, "Ethan is a magician. He is from another probability or dimension. In his reality, starships are things of fairy tales, just as his land of magic is a fairy tale to you. In his probability, most people are magicians. They all follow their magician rules and conduct themselves by those rules. What was not logical about Ethan's spell to control the Maylon's mind? It diffused a violent situation without causing damage to the victim."

"I agree that Ethan's actions were logical at that time. But what is to prevent him from using his power on others, on our crew?" Frelpok challenged.

"We all have some ability to lash out or hurt one another, and you don't need a special ability for that," I said while turning my head to look them all over. "I can personally vouch for Ethan's integrity. Even though he could turn you into a toad, I don't think he ever will. Will you, Ethan?"

Ethan replied with a strong British accent, "I'm not going to turn anyone into a toad."

Sara finally smiled, and I felt like I made it past one hurdle in actually getting to know her.

"What can you tell us about the Dili sector?" Sara asked, changing the subject to something practical.

"The sushi on Fisherman's wharf is delicious. There is this place called Yum Yum Sushi House that serves a great California roll, crisp veggies, and fresh tuna," I joked.

Sara tilted her head slightly with a "please spare me" look but willingly endured my bad humor all the while.

I continued, "My shuttlecraft is made of special materials that allow me to communicate between many probabilities. One of those probabilities is Starnet headquarters. I own a high rise there in San Francisco, across the bay."

Tamakot asked, "Are you telling me that you can transmit from the Gar sector to the Dili sector?"

I looked at him and said, "With my technology, every call is a local call. The Auramedic has full access to the shuttle systems. You can place calls through him."

The three looked at one another, and Sara asked the Auramedic, "Is this true?"

The Auramedic said, "I do have access to the shuttlecraft *Zanna*, but I have not accessed any system but the transporter."

"Try communications. I want to send a message right now," she said to the Auramedic.

"Checking, ah, there it is, and thank you, Zanna," the Auramedic said.

"What message would you like to send?" the Auramedic asked.

"Let's do this in your office, Auramedic," Sara said, and all of them moved to another room to send the message while leaving Ethan and me alone.

I walked over, and Ethan smiled as I said, "Let's go get something to eat."

We moved toward the door. Ethan and I glanced at the conversation taking place in the other room. Sara leaned over the desk speaking, and the Auramedic gestured while he spoke. They all took turns talking. I said to Ethan, "I think it is highly probable that they might be at that for a while."

He smiled and said, "Food sounds good," as we walked out of sickbay. Ethan walked at a normal speed, but as I tried to keep up with him, it hurt really bad, and I fell into the wall. He did not notice for a few steps but soon realized I was not next to him and turned around, asking, "Blimey, are you all right? I thought the Auramedic fixed you up?"

I stood up and said, "It still hurts. Can we walk slower?"

"Sure," he said, "how do we get there?"

I pointed over my shoulder and said, "Tap the map and talk to the wall."

He shook his head and said, "Ah, yeah," then moved over to the corridor wall and activated the map display for the ship. He thought for a second, then asked me, "What is the place called?"

"Mess hall," I said.

Ethan shook his head again and spoke to the wall, "Show us the way to the mess hall from here."

A red line appeared on the map, and the arrow strip lit up, pointing the way. While we walked down the corridor, following the moving arrows leading to a magnalift, Ethan said, "It's five decks down and to the right."

I took each step to the magnalift with slow deliberation. I knew I was still injured, but I demanded the *Motif* before me. I thought of it as a procession in my mind, with my body becoming reacquainted with the *Motif*. I envisioned being restored to my healthy self. With each step, I imagined the *Motif* coursing through the wounded area. The unchanging *Motif*, and myself being made whole by its static nature. I don't know if this visualization helped, but I did it anyway. By the time I stepped into the magnalift, I felt like I was more on the mend. Then again, the Auramedic said the pain would subside with time.

The magnalift produced a soft bump and started moving down. It smoothed out until the ride seemed motionless. It felt like falling silk. A display changed on the side-wall as we dropped, then we felt a slowing motion, another bump, and the doors split open from the center to empty us into a four-way corridor intersection. We stepped out and followed the arrows down one of the corridors. It was only a short way from the intersection where the arrows stopped at the mess hall doorway.

We stepped into the mess hall, which offered a nice setting for dining. I immediately thought that the ship's designer did a good job in this particular room. There was an informal cafeteria bar to the left and tables all along the right spaced between ceiling struts sloping at an angle. This room was obviously right up against the curved section of the outer hull. There were tall arcing box-nosed-shaped windows between the truss running from waist level to high above your head. Even from the doorway, I could tell the view of the stars was going to be great from one of those window seats. Below all the windows, and along that wall, ran a long cushioned bench. People were seated around the room, talking with each other and eating.

We must have lingered in the doorway too long, and a funny-looking fellow came out from behind the cafeteria counter and said, "Welcome, welcome, I am Nanook, Stexian, at your service."

Nanook was a Stexian and the first one I have ever met. He was humanoid in height and build, with standard bipedal features. His skin was a golden hue that transitioned to red in certain areas. He wore a chef's hat and a mutton chop beard with very thin hair. His face presented wide eyes with a grin.

"I'm Ethan, and this is Sam. We just arrived," Ethan said.

"And just in the nick of time too. Thank you for helping us. I, myself, have been on both receiving and giving end of help with or from *Journey*. And I have to say that these are truly good people," Nanook said.

"I'm a right might hungry. What cha got?" I asked with a western accent.

Ethan made a little chuckle as we walked up to the counter with food items already on display.

"Let me get you some of today's lunch special," Nanook said, and he disappeared behind a wall. I could hear some pans being knocked around and a muted voice calling out, "I'm okay."

Ethan and I looked at one another, and I said, "Well, we made it. What do you think?"

It looked like he thought about it for a few seconds and then said, "I like it. It feels creepy, weird, and exciting all at the same time. Like you're awake in someone else's dream. How can things be so different from home but so real at the same time?"

"I know that feeling," I said, then it occurred to me I was out for a day and asked. "Did you call Olivia?"

"I did, while you were out. Olivia called me, and it was a good thing too. After the Maylon shot you, they shot the Maylon. Frelpok deduced my wand was a weapon and took it from me. They led me to a room for questioning."

"Does Frelpok still have your wand?" I asked.

Ethan shook his head yes.

"We'll ask for it back. Go on," I said.

"So, I was in this room being questioned and telling them about you, me, and our journey in the *Zanna*. I told them about finding Marvin and helping the Auramedic. They were not really buying it when my ring started throbbing lightly. I knew it was a ring call from Olivia because we have used them a lot since you gave them to us. I answered the call in front of the group.

"Yeah, Olivia, we made it. We're in the Gar sector. I'm okay, but Sam's hurt. I think he will be all right. A doctor is operating on him right now. I don't know. I don't know. Go ahead and put her on."

Ethan stopped the recount of his first Gar sector ring call with Olivia to tell me they discovered if Olivia slid the ring onto Lulu's hand while the conversation was in progress, she could talk to Ethan without breaking the connection. This hand-off is what just happened in the call.

"Hi, Lulu. No, daddy can't come home tonight. What did you do in school today? A drawing, a drawing of what? The moon. No, daddy is not on the moon, but I want to see one someday. Slide the ring back on your mother's finger. Goodbye. I love you too. Yeah, Olivia? I'll call back later. I'm in a meeting. I love you too. Goodbye," Ethan said. "After that, the entire mood of the room shifted, and I was taken down to sickbay to watch the Auramedic treat your wound."

"Here we go, two lunch specials for two new special friends," Nanook said as he brought out two trays with the same set of food items on them.

Ethan picked up his tray, and I picked up mine, which caused my wound to ache. I must have winced because Nanook chimed in, "Oh, let me help you with that. You were just injured."

I accepted his help, and we followed him to a table near a window on the far side of the room. He sat my tray down on the table, patted the seat of my chair, and stood back, saying, "Some of the crew say this table is the best spot on the ship for viewing the stars. Enjoy. If you need anything, I'll be right over there."

Nanook walked away, and Ethan and I sat down. A napkin rolled up with silverware sat in a special indent of our multi-indented tray. Ethan and I both reluctantly picked at the offerings. The tastes were what I would call clashing. There was a rotten spinach goop, some small cut roots that were too fibrous to finish chewing, a white pudding that tasted like expired milk, and an orange mealy mush that was actually the best tasting of them all. It reminded me a bit of Dahl with mold in it. We both unanimously pushed our trays forward at the same time.

"Would you like to split a basket of fish and chips?" I asked Ethan.

He shook his head, smiling, and said, "Without a doubt."

I targeted the trays of food and used the recycle icon from my invisihud. The trays of food disappeared in a quick sparkle.

I said, "Ohm, can you locate one of the food vendors, along fisherman's wharf, in San Francisco? Place an order for two large baskets of fried fish, four servings of chips, tartar sauce, cocktail sauce, ketchup, and malt vinegar. And while we are waiting, can you get a six-pack of Toothy Knot from the Twin Falls brewery. Check the convenience stores near Jim Young's house."

"Working. I'll present items as they are acquired," Ohm replied as a soft voice near my ear.

A fellow sitting two tables over said, "Hi, I'm Brandon Palmer."

He stood up and walked over to our table, adding, "This is Tai Song," while his friend followed him over.

Brandon Palmer wore red colors on his uniform, and Tai Song wore gold colors on his uniform. As they walked up to us, a six-pack of ale in green and black cans sparkled into existence on our table.

Brandon said, "Wow, how did that get there?"

"Ohm, can I get four rocks glasses?" I said.

Immediately, four rocks glasses appeared on the table in a sparkle, and I handed a can of ale to each of my guests. I set the remaining two on the floor. Cracking a can open, I poured the dark Scottish ale slowly down the side of a tilted rocks glass, not really filling it up all the way, trying to keep the foam build-up to a minimum. As I did this, the others reached for a glass and did the same by opening their cans. Some ale ended up getting spilled, but after we each held a glass in hand, I raised mine and toasted "Salute, to success!"

Everyone said, "Salute," and then we tasted the ale.

"Mmm," said Brandon as he read the label on the can, "real Scottish ale."

"Now that is tasty," Tai Song said.

Ethan Foster said with his British accent, "It's almost as good as an English ale."

"We are tasting the finest replication of a Scottish ale that Twin Falls, Idaho can produce," I said as the center of the table sparkled, and the requested food appeared.

"Dig in, gentleman. Fried fish and chips from San Francisco's Fisherman's wharf," I said.

Brandon and Tai pulled up a couple of chairs and sat around our table as I passed the newly materialized paper plates around to everyone. The fish was fried to a golden perfection, as were the thick-sliced potatoes. The next few minutes were about tasting the food and dipping in the sauces, or in the case of the malt vinegar, shaking on way too much to get a visible flavor into the crust that seemed to absorb the malt vinegar on contact. It felt good to do something normal. Mucking around in dark, broken ships and finding injured bodies always left me a bit stressed out.

Brandon called out across the room, "Nanook, get over here. You have to try this."

As Nanook approached, I used a knife to cut a small tasting portion of fish and a half-slice of the chip before putting them on a paper plate. I handed it to Brandon, who passed it to Nanook as he approached and asked, "What's this?"

"This, Nanook, is real food. I want you to taste it, so the next time you serve us one of your 'creations,' you'll have a benchmark reference to compare it against," Brandon said.

Nanook took the plate and smelled it first, then took a small bite of the fish and smiled.

"Try one of the sauces," Tai said more politely to Nanook.

I said, "These three are traditionally applied to the fish, while this one, called ketchup, is mainly used on the potato."

"Oh, that is good," Nanook said as he grabbed another chair and crammed it into the table between Brandon Palmer and Ethan Foster. "Is there enough for me to have some more?"

Ethan Foster said, "Enjoy," and he gestured to the baskets of fish and the small boats of chips in the center of the table, which were rapidly depleting their supply.

We all munched a bit more, and Brandon asked, "So, how did you do this? Is this food really from the Dili sector?"

"Yep, this food is really from the Dili sector," I replied, then explained as simply as possible. "My technology inserts a probability relay between the transporter emitter and the target location. The transporter signal is not really traveling a long distance at all. It travels from the initiator to the relay, through the relay to the target emitter."

"But how is the subject reintegrated on the target side?" Tai Song asked.

"I keep a small cloaked device near me at all times. It contains the probability relay and the destination emitter," I said.

Brandon Palmer chimed in, "Wait a minute, you're telling me there is an invisible transporter emitter in this room right now?"

I shook my head, yes, as I tipped my glass, finishing the last of it and refilling it from the rest of the open can.

"Can we see it?" Brandon asked with a smile.

"This is very fascinating," Nanook said as he got up, grabbing another chip from the paper chip boat. "But duty calls," he said before walking over to greet a few more crewmen arriving at the entrance.

I usually did not reveal such details about the operations of my technology, but if these were to be my friends, I felt like this was probably a step I needed to take. Besides, I liked Brandon and Tai almost immediately. I activated my invisihud and looked down at the table while holding out my hand. After selecting one of my cloaked scanners, I set it to docking maintenance mode. It dropped its cloak and came to rest in my open hand. The cloaked scanner was a simple sphere with tiny panels across the surface, giving it an uneven displaced tech look.

Ethan Foster reached out and took the cloaked scanner from my hand, held it up to the light, and said with a smile, "It's an Orbreum."

"What's an Orbreum?" Tai Song asked.

Ethan Foster looked at Tai Song, saying, "On my world, there is a sport called Volantes. It is played on flying carpets. There are two sized balls, the Orbrefer and the Orbreum. The Orbreum is the smallest of them, about this size."

"May I?" Brandon asked, and Ethan gave the cloaked scanner to Brandon, who began inspecting it.

Tai Song asked, "Flying carpets?"

"Is that so far-fetched?" I asked. "Don't you dress up in costumes with emitters and toss energy around when playing Shaolin Angles? You could probably program an aurastage to emulate a Volantes match."

Ethan Foster asked, "What's an aurastage?"

Brandon Palmer handed the cloaked scanner to Tai Song, who began his inspection of the device and said, "An aurastage is a room on this ship where various scenarios can be simulated using force fields and teleported photons.

You program characters and environments, and then you can interact with them."

Ethan Foster said with a smile, "Wicked."

"I like that, wicked," Brandon Palmer said.

Tai Song handed the cloaked scanner back to me, and I placed it in my open hand before using the invisihud to reactivate it. It faded from view and resumed its duties.

Brandon said, "Wicked," then turned to Ethan Foster, asking, "Am I using that term correctly?"

Ethan Foster shook his head, yes, smiling while taking another drink of ale.

The voice of Captain Mitchell came over the intercom and said, "All senior officers report to the bridge."

Brandon said, "It looks like duty calls," as he chugged the remaining portion of his ale, then addressing Ethan and me, added, "It was nice to meet you both, and thank you for bringing real food back into my life."

Tai Song said, "Yes, thank you for the meal and the ale. Hope to see you around," and they walked off together, talking among themselves.

"Well, it looks like we demolished that," I said, referring to the baskets of food.

"Do you want anything else?" I asked Ethan.

"No, I'm full. That was really good fish and chips," he replied.

"I think I need to lie down and rest a bit," I said, and I picked up the remaining cans of ale from the floor while Ethan started stacking the remnants of the food baskets and empty cans into one pile.

"Let's talk to Nanook about quarters," I said, and I headed back to the kitchen counter with Ethan following, trying not to drop any of the piled trash.

As we approached, Nanook stepped out and said, "Oh, you don't have to do that. Let me take those," and he placed the trash into some bin hidden behind the counter, eying a few of the leftovers.

I asked, "Nanook, are there any quarters where I can get some rest?" I said while patting the hole in the burnt uniform I wore. "I was going to sleep in my shuttle, but it's a little cramped in there."

"Oh, right," he said. "I am sure I can find something," as he headed back behind a wall and returned with a tablet in his hand.

Nanook tapped some buttons on the tablet he held, waited, and said, "Yes, I think I'll put you right here."

"Follow me, gentleman," Nanook said as he walked out of the mess hall.

Ethan and I followed Nanook into the hall and watched while he tapped the ship's map and referenced the tablet in his hand, which set the arrow sequence in motion. Pointing at the map, he said, "Here you go. I have two singles right next to each other. Take whichever ones you want. They are both the same."

A teapot started whistling back in the kitchen, and Nanook rushed off, saying, "Oh, I've got to get that."

Ethan and I both said, "Thanks Nanook," and we followed the moving arrows back to the magnalift that brought us here.

The magnalift set off in motion, and we arrived very quickly at a new level with people passing through the corridor. Most of them walked at a brisk pace. Some were in small groups and talking as they walked. I would call this corridor, compared to the other corridors in the ship, a double-wide. It was like a mini concourse. There were no shops or inviting areas, only doors leading to living quarters. A few people said hello briefly or nodded while passing us by. We were obviously the tourists in their minds. The arrows came to a stop at two identical-looking doors with numbers.

"Alright, Ethan. I guess it's come down to this. I'm going to have to fight you over room number four one three," I said, joking.

"Ah, but I have taken over your mind with my magic powers. I wanted room four one five, to myself, all along," Ethan said, making a bad villain laughing sound.

We both started fussing with the door controls, trying to get them to open. Ethan's opened first before I realized that you needed to press the other circular button, and my door opened too.

I said, "Good night," to Ethan and walked into the suite Nanook provided.

The suite was classic crew quarters, thin but deep. At the far end was a small window looking out of the ship. The ceiling was curved, similar to the mess hall, but less extreme. These quarters must be located in the lower section of the ship, which was more tubular than the radial section. On the left was a desk molded into the wall panel. There was a screen on the desk and a mirror on the wall. To the right was a long bed, making me think this was a consideration for some of the taller species of the Starnet Union.

Heading to the rear of the room, I looked through the small square window. It had subtle rounded corners, and I could see we traveled at flux speed. There was a doorway to a bathroom, and the light came on automatically when I stepped inside. I noticed a cup by the sink, so I picked it up, walked over, and sat down on the bed. There was a night table here with a lamp, and it turned on automatically when I set down the two cans of ale. I opened one up and poured half of it down the side and into the cup. I kicked off my boots and leaned back on the bed, which offered a synthetic, neutral, musty scent.

I know I recently woke up, but the walk from sickbay to the mess hall and then to these quarters wore me out. I felt stupid for getting shot. I should have used my invisihud overlay as soon as we left the shuttlecraft *Zanna*. But maybe that was the *Motif*'s way of making sure things aligned to my requested intent. In the first future memories loop, I was injured, and *Journey* did help me. My echo manipulations made heavy modifications to this probability as Ethan and I entered into this echo. I needed to make sure the *Journey* we finally arrived on existed in the same time frame as the black glass building in San Francisco. I wanted the eventual two-way communication from Starnet headquarters and *Journey* to be in sync. When I stepped through the painting onto *Oasis Seven*, I made a similar adjustment to that time frame. With both of these distant locations synchronized to the black glass building in San Francisco, I felt like I removed some of the cobwebs hanging over the questions in my mind like, "How do I make sure everything lines up right?"

I took another sip of the Scottish ale, tasted it slowly then swallowed. A buzz at the door broke the moment of peace.

"Come in," I said a bit loudly, half expecting to see Ethan Foster at the door, but it was Captain Mitchell instead.

I started to stand up, but she motioned me to remain seated. She pulled up the seat from the desk and sat down. It was just then that a sharp pain radiated around the outer area of my wound. I began to think that the Auramedic might not be as good as he pretends to be.

Sara must have noticed this because she said, "You look like hell, so I'll make this brief. Your communications link works. I have spoken with Starnet Command on Earth. I have also reviewed your entry in the Starnet database, entity four five seven."

"Generally helpful but often found at the center of catastrophes," I finished her sentence for her.

"Our recent encounter with the Maylon certainly qualifies as a catastrophe," she said before standing up, pacing, and talking with her hands, which I saw her do in sickbay.

I took another sip of ale as she continued talking. This Starnet probability often leads to an exploration of unknown phenomena, which entails dangerous acts in itself. The fact that these "catastrophes" are often due to their own blundering seems to have been left out of my short one-line description.

"I have to ask. Did you stage the battle with the Maylon so you could arrive and help?" she said, looking at me seriously.

"I don't stage or lord over disasters. But in my travels, I sometimes find I can't avoid them. Do you think I have some form of probable Munchausen syndrome by proxy?" I asked.

She seemed taken by surprise and quickly retreated from the aggressive Starnet prosecutor to the simple farm girl who finally made captain routine, saying, "No, no. I did not mean to imply that."

"That is why I have developed some of my technologies. When I find myself in a bad situation, I can help myself and others rather than becoming victims," I said.

"You mentioned a time loop. Starnet and I are both concerned that we don't get dragged into that," she said.

"Too late," I said as I took another drink.

"And your wife?" she asked.

"You didn't mention that to Starnet, did you?" pausing my next drink to ask.

"I did. The Auramedic provided a full transcript of our conversation in sickbay," she said. "What's wrong with that?"

"I hate to break this to you, but in both of my time loops, the Starnet Union is under silent attack from a species of form-altering invaders that are murdering key political and business figures while assuming their roles unnoticed. The information about my wife was private, and now it could be that one of these imposters is gaining more information about me than I would like. I don't want to be on their radar. That's bad for us."

She looked at me incredulously, saying, "What? Do you mean an invasion?"

"In the first time loop, I made the discovery too late, and the Flexanites marched in with multiple armadas of attack ships. Manning these ships are genetically engineered slave warriors. An addictive substance known only as the key keeps them loyal. There were no defectors because if a soldier does not receive a supply of the key, he dies. This invasion generated massive casualties all across the Starnet Union. Centuria, Opturi, Ingvot, Ugawan, and Pinkton fell along with many other smaller out-lying planets in the frontier. Casualties totaled in the tens of millions. The battles destroyed entire fleets of Starnet vessels. In the end, it was me against the remaining Hatiss fleet."

"Hatiss?" Sara asked.

"The Hatiss fleet is controlled by the Flexanites who have grown weary of interactions with what they call us, the firmous. They feel they are a superior race. I used my cloaking technology to move in close to their ships, transport bombs aboard, and move away before they even knew what hit them. This strategy worked so well that I managed to destroy more than ninety percent of the Hatiss fleet in a relentless vigilante-style attack, which lasted for months. So, catastrophes, yeah, that one was of galactic proportions."

"That is unbelievable," Sarah said.

"In the second time loop, I had the memories of the first loop catastrophe and set to work almost immediately developing technologies to detect and detain Flexanites. It worked well. I was able to expose Flexanites and capture them. This approach prevented the Hatiss from gaining valuable intelligence about Starnet weaknesses. It created enough delays, and the invasion never came. While the Union was aware I captured and executed Flexanites without a trial, they never prosecuted me because of the heinous acts committed by the Flexanites.

"The modus operandi of the Flexanite is to detect a seat of power, observe the person holding power, practice emulating the person's traits, murder them, and take their place. They are very clever about how they hide their victim's bodies. That is what took me the longest time to figure out. Missing person's reports started appearing. By the time reports reached me, the Flexanite murdered someone else, in one case, the investigator to take on their role. But the way they hide their victims is in plain sight, often where the murder took place. I found one body unnaturally embedded in a wall. The Flexanite can meld with the wall while holding the body and deposit it inside the wall. I found another body behind a brick masonry support under a bridge. I was faced with three choices, kill them, imprison them or let them go. What would you do?" I asked.

"What about talking to them?" Sara asked while stating the obvious.

"We tried that. Captain La Salle was the Union liaison. We spent weeks in talks with captured prisoners who all told the same story. At first, they refused to admit they were Flexanites, but after about thirty-six to seventy-two hours, most Flexanites lose their ability to hold their imposter form. It is like their version of sleep. When they sleep, they revert to an organic gelatinous state. In retrospect, I can see that it was not the best solution to openly murder another species in such a methodical way. But I paid the price when a Flexanite infiltrated my inner circle and beat me to a pulp. If it were not for my friend Candy, I don't think I would have made it. The Flexanite shattered about seventy percent of the bones in my body before Candy rushed me to a medical facility," I said.

"This is so much to take in. How can I believe it? You're talking about future probable events that may or may not happen. And the way you describe the events, you are a villain and a hero at the same time," she said, once again gesturing with her hands.

"In this third version of the time loop, I have not murdered anyone. And those future memories where I remember the horrible things done on all sides has not yet happened. I can clearly see another option now. I can relocate Flexanites to another probability. I did not try that in any of the other time loops. Even though I have not yet committed any of those villainous future memory acts, I still feel the guilt and shame of those acts I remember committing, in the other loops," I offered as a defense.

"Where does that leave us?" she asked while looking up at the ceiling, stretching her neck, then looking back down, fatigued.

"No doubt you were instructed or may already be pursuing a way to push a teleportation signal through the communication channel I have provided. I can't allow that," I said. "I'll take the fall for that one. Let your superiors know that I said no, for now. It will prevent any immediate crew rotations, which is one way a Flexanite could get aboard your ship," I said.

She turned sharply and said, "My mission," in a glaring tone, "is to get this crew home. I have to explore all options to achieve that goal."

"And you are closer," I said. "Think of morale as the crew gets to talk to their families and friends? It is no different if *Journey* were in the Dili sector on a mission. They can talk and send messages but are still doing their jobs. And I am not saying no forever."

"The communications link it a good start," Sarah said.

"I currently have scanning devices deploying throughout the Starnet Union that are programmed to observe and detect Flexanite activity. Once I am convinced that Starnet command is not currently infiltrated, we might be able to arrange some type of shore leave schedule," I said.

"So, we are stuck in the loop already, as you mentioned," she said slowly, finally realizing.

"But we are stuck together, Sara. And we can help each other make better decisions this time," I said, trying to console her.

"By telling me this, you have placed me in the awkward position of deceiving my superiors. If I report all this, I could be reporting it to a Flexanite, who might use the information to accelerate an attack. If I withhold information, and it is discovered, I could end up court marshaled," she said to herself before sitting down on the chair.

"I believe there is an exception that states, somewhere in your code of conduct, that a captain is supposed to do the right thing, not the easy thing, even if that means disobeying orders," I said. "If you do end up on trial, I will be right there at your side presenting that rule and arguing on your behalf."

"I appreciate the support, but I don't want to end up on trial. I'm going to have to think about all of this," she said, and her face turned more friendly.

She got up, walked to the door, and said, "I think we both need some rest," before activating the door and leaving these quarters.

I think she was right. I put the rest of my drink on the nightstand and lie down on the bed. I was out cold, and before I knew it, I was asleep.

I awoke to the sound of the buzzer at the door. Sitting up slowly, I said dryly, "Come in."

The door opened, and commander Frelpok stepped in and said, "I am instructed to bring you to a meeting. Please accompany me."

I stood up and said, "I need to change first. I'm still wearing the clothes I was shot in."

"Do it quickly. I will wait in the hall," Frelpok said.

"Do it quickly," I said to myself, mimicking Frelpok's speech in my head as I made my way to the shower. Glancing out the window portal, I noticed we were traveling at flux speed. It took me a few minutes to figure out how to work the shower. As I waited for the water to warm up, I emptied out the contents of the pockets in my current clothes and asked Ohm for a new set of my basic black outfit. I transferred the vignettes, wand, and cards from *Oasis Seven* into my new clothes before jumping in the shower. As I washed up, I looked down at my wound and could not really see a mark anymore. I touched it, pushed on it, and it seemed okay.

I dried off, got dressed, and fixed my hair in the mirror with my hands. There was no time to shave, and I had a solid two-day beard going. Returning to the bed, I put on my boots and walked into the hallway where Ethan Foster and Frelpok waited.

"Good morning, Ethan," I said. "And good morning to you too, Frelpok."

"That remains to be seen," Frelpok replied with his Logican cynicism. "Please follow me."

Ethan and I looked at each other and followed Frelpok into the magnalift.

After stepping in, Frelpok said, "Deck six," and the magnalift started moving.

I noticed Ethan wore the same clothes he wore yesterday, and I asked, "You didn't fetch your pack from the shuttle yet, did you?"

Ethan shook his head and said, "No, I hoped to do that today. I wondered how these people wash their clothes?"

"There are laundry facilities aboard this ship. I can show them to you at a later time," Frelpok said.

The magnalift came to a stop, and the doors slid open. Frelpok exited first, and Ethan and I followed him. We passed a few crewmen on the way. They each acknowledged Frelpok's rank as they passed by us.

We came to our destination, and the doors parted as Frelpok entered first, then Ethan and I followed. It was a meeting room. Like the mess hall, with long curved arch supports along the ceiling and tall windows in between them. Several people sat around a long desk, the Captain, Tamakot, and two other crew women. One of the women had Warnock features, and the other woman clearly displayed robotic implants along her face and on her hands. Ethan and I sat down next to each other, and Frelpok took an empty seat across from us.

It looked like we walked into a call in progress. From what I could tell from Sara's appearance, she hadn't slept at all. She spoke into a box on the table, "Admiral, they have just arrived," before looking at me, saying, "This is Admiral Augustine, head of Starnet operations."

From my seat, I leaned toward the box and spoke louder than usual, "Hello Admiral, this is Sam. Can you hear me? Your signal is breaking up," as I located an icon for the *Zanna* inside my invisihud.

His signal came back loud and clear, "Hello? I can hear you fine. *Journey*, are you reading me?"

Once again, I said, "You're breaking up."

Underneath the icon for the *Zanna*, in my invisihud, several more icons represented the systems of the ship. With eye movements, I selected the communications system and disabled it. I also located the virtual shunt allowing the Auramedic to interact with the *Zanna* and terminated that connection. I placed the entire shuttlecraft into lock-down mode, and the communications link fell silent.

Sara asked, "Admiral, are you there?"

The woman with the mechanical implants picked up a tablet, sitting next to her on the table, touched it a few times before saying, "It appears we have lost the communications link."

The Warnock woman next to her said, "Let me see that. It worked fine when I conducted my test earlier," and the mech woman handed the tablet to the Warnock, who tapped some more.

Frelpok spoke up and asked me directly, "Why did you say that the message was breaking up? We all heard it clearly. Did you cut communications?"

"Yes, I did," I replied.

"Why would you do such a thing?" Frelpok asked in his methodical way.

"How would you feel if you discovered that I was tampering with your ship's systems while you slept?" I asked.

The Warnock woman spoke up, "It's only communications," she said.

"And what was the test you just mentioned?" I asked accusingly.

She got sheepish, looked at the Captain, then back at me, and said, "I checked to see if it were possible to send a transporter signal through the communications channel."

"What were the results of your test?" I asked.

"It looked like it might be possible," she replied, staring me down.

"My ship's systems weren't designed to be used or accessed that way. I gave the Auramedic permission, earlier, to use them because lives were at stake, and it was an emergency," I said. "My ship is very important to me, and I don't want to risk systems being damaged by curious individuals who don't even ask permission to modify them."

Tamakot spoke up, "I can relate to your point of view. Perhaps, in our excitement at the prospect of getting home, we took advantage of your generosity. You're right. We should have asked first. I apologize for all of us."

"Thank you. I accept your apology," I said. "I will work on a new communications device that is independent of my shuttlecraft. Something you can integrate into your own ship's systems."

"When can we expect the new device to be operational?" the mech woman asked.

"I don't know. I'll have to think about it," I said.

"Unacceptable," she replied strongly.

The room fell silent, and everyone looked at me, then Ethan's stomach rumbled loudly.

"What is unacceptable is having a meeting this early, without serving any food," I said.

"Meeting adjourned. Sam will think about how to get the relay up and running," Sara said before turning to me. "You'll keep me updated?"

"Certainly, Captain," I replied.

Sara stood up, as did the others. They made their way out of the room, but Tamakot stayed behind, seated as did Ethan and I, and said, "I have been placed in charge of making sure your needs are met while you visit *Journey*."

I selected the breakfast bagels, orange juice, and coffee icon from my invisi-hud food menu, and the table sparkled, leaving behind the requested food and drink. I poured a couple of cups of coffee and asked Tamakot, "Would you like some breakfast with us?"

He smiled and said, "Sure, if you don't mind me asking how you did that?"

I said, "These are sweet bagels, and those are savory. The cream cheese is neutral, the orange juice is fresh-squeezed, and the coffee is an Italian blend."

Ethan poured himself some orange juice and reached for a bagel as I handed Tamakot a cup of coffee.

"The materialization is using basic transporter technology you are familiar with. As I mentioned in sickbay yesterday, the call is local. The transportation is also local," I said. "This food came from a bakery in San Francisco."

"Could you transport a person back to San Francisco right now?" Tamakot asked as he reached for a sesame bagel and started spreading cream cheese on it.

"Yes, that is possible," I said as I started munching on a cinnamon crunch bagel.

Ethan reached for the coffee and poured himself a cup before asking Tamakot, "My wand was taken from me when I arrived. Is there any way I can get that back?"

Tamakot shook his head, yes, with his mouth full, and said, "Yes, I'll track it down. I think Frelpok might have it."

"A Logican with a magic wand. I can imagine him scanning it to figure out how it works or shaking it trying to get a spell out of it," I said with a smile.

I gestured with a comical arm movement, and they both laughed.

"How does it work, Ethan? How does magic work?" Tamakot asked.

"A wand is chosen from a branch of a young sapling. The wood type does not matter that much. What gives the wand its power is the magical element used in the wand inlay. All magic wands have some sort of inlay along the wand's surface. The pattern of the inlay is not important. It is the alchemical composition that gives the wand its power. My wand has a hippogryph feather as the alchemical base. You can get wands with phoenix dust, dragon eyelash, ghost gossamer, and other sorts of magical beast parts," Ethan said to Tamakot.

"So, magical creatures are killed to make magic wands?" Tamakot asked.

"Oh, no, they are not killed. They are merely convinced to give up their component. Often there is a quest involved, where a magician must provide a service to the creature to obtain the desired component," Ethan clarified.

"Is it a trade?" I asked.

"Yeah, at a basic level, it is a trade," Ethan replied to me.

"Another reason why I made this journey to your ship and brought Ethan along was to ask if it were possible for Ethan to learn about starship operations aboard *Journey*," I said. "Perhaps some kind of internship or something?"

Tamakot asked, "Ethan, do you know anything about starship operations?"

Ethan pushed his glasses up and said, "Sorry, I don't. I learned they were real after I met Sam. I mean, I have seen movies with spaceships in them."

Tamakot said, "I'll see what the Captain has to say about that. It is always good to have any member aboard to know at least basic operations to avoid misunderstandings and accidents," as he poured himself some orange juice. Tamakot sipped the orange juice and smiled, "Wow, that is delicious. I forgot what real orange juice tastes like."

Tamakot took on a more serious tone as he sat down the empty juice glass and said, "The Captain filled me in on your conversation last night, so I understand why you cut the communication line. But public displays of instant teleportation makes you come off a bit flamboyant or unconcerned. And your crude attempt at making a joke out of our morning meeting did not go over well with the other crew members at the table."

"I'm glad the Captain has filled you in, but the Flexanite threat is real. I don't appreciate being ambushed in the morning without warning and placed before the head of Starnet operations for interrogation. That is a probability that I don't care to experience," I said.

"And as a probability traveler, you are used to controlling the narrative and experiencing only the things you want. It makes you uncomfortable to have to adapt to our process. To remain on board, you are going to have to get used to following orders," Tamakot said to both of us. "Can you do that, Ethan?"

Ethan fell silent while we talked and worked on his third half of a bagel. He swallowed and said, "I think I can, sir."

"I know I can't, Tamakot. Taking orders from echo creatures is not something Splendorites do. It is against our basic nature and would be considered a form of madness. Letting the worlds we create and visit dictate terms to us is like letting the inmates run the Asylum. And for the sake of argument, let's say I follow the rules, and your society deems me guilty. How long should a punishment stand for an immortal being? Should I remain in prison for ten years, twenty? Your society could fall apart around me while I stood by honoring the judgment of dead men," I said.

Tamakot asked, "You're immortal? How old are you?"

"According to my record keeping, I am eight hundred and thirty-seven years old, and I am the youngest of all the Splendorites. My great grand uncle is rumored to be over ten thousand years old," I replied. "It is not my intention to become an undermining maverick, constantly going against the grain or your authority. I thrive on collaboration, and I hope you can find a way to make use of my offerings. But demanding that a carrot become celery will never make it so."

Ethan looked at me and asked, "You're eight hundred and thirty-seven years old?"

"Ethan, you were supposed to say, you don't look a day over three eleven," I said, trying to use humor to diffuse the situation and failing.

Tamakot chimed in, "There is my point. Even though I don't know Ethan that well, I can tell he is a bit shocked to learn something you obviously never told him, your age. A starship runs on discipline and order. Without that, we fall apart, especially in times of crisis."

I looked at Ethan and asked him directly, "Does it matter to you how old I am?"

Ethan took a moment and said, "No, but the mention of immortality brought up memories when I saw Lord Cadverus feeding on the blood of a slain Pegasus."

I looked at Tamakot and said, "Ethan is not just a magician, Tamakot. Ethan is the premiere magician of his land and slayer of the crimson lord, he who eats souls. An evil scourge so terrible that it terrorized multiple communities for forty years. Ethan sought out containers and freed those captured souls. He faced and defeated the crimson lord in open magician combat while an entire siege war raged around him. Sure, one more Starnet trained crewman might improve your performance rating, but a master combat-hardened magician is exactly what you want on your side in a time of crisis."

Without stopping, I turned to Ethan and asked, "Ethan can you make an asteroid appear between two ships?"

Ethan looked at me, and laughed saying, "No."

"What if Tamakot told you that the ship's sensors reported small particulate matter between the two ships. Could you make it grow?" I asked.

Ethan said with a smile, "Whoa, I might if I could visualize the original source."

Tamakot interrupted, "I get your point, and having additional options is always preferable. So, where do we go from here? Is this ship, this crew, to become your next set of people you manipulate for your entertainment? If I were to become your friend, would it really be because of friendship or your latent Splendorite power adjusting me to become what suits you best?"

"I guess we may never know. I can't remain aboard. I have other probabilities to visit," I said to Tamakot.

"Ethan, do you want to accompany me down to the *Zanna*? I believe your pack is still stowed away in the hold," I asked Ethan.

"Um, yeah," Ethan said as he stood up, wiping his face clean with his napkin.

"Do you want to join us?" I asked Tamakot.

"No, if you can find your way, proceed. I have other duties to attend to," Tamakot said.

Ethan and I walked out of the room and down the corridor to the magnalift entrance where we emerged with Frelpok. We stepped in, and I said, "Shuttle bay," which set the magnalift in motion.

Ethan turned to me and said, "It does not matter to me how old you are, Sam. I just never thought about it."

"It's okay. I don't really know how old you are either. I did not intend to conceal my age," I said.

"Twenty-nine, Sam. I'm twenty-nine years old. Olivia is twenty-seven. Albert is nine, and Lulu is seven," Ethan said.

The magnalift completed its downward drop and started moving with a horizontal motion.

"It's up to you now, Ethan. Do you want to stay with these people? I hoped for a longer get to know you period, but I can see my presence here is disruptive. Tamakot is right. They have to be very careful because they are the only Starnet ship and can't rely on backup," I said.

"After coming all this way, it seems like a waste to not try it out for a while," Ethan said.

"That's the spirit. The old college try," I said, and the magnalift doors split open.

The corridor was busy with a few people moving about their business. Ethan and I walked over to the large double door entrance to the shuttle bay. I tried the panel switch, and the doors opened. There were more people in the shuttle bay tending to their jobs. The force field that was down when we entered the ship was working and shimmered blue at the back of the shuttle bay. It looked like they returned one of the shuttles to its docked location while the other was still perched at an odd angle. A team of crewmen was busy trying to relocate it. There were several spot welders with face masks producing sparks.

We walked past the working crewmen, nodding as we passed, and headed over to the *Zanna*, which was docked at an odd angle. I could see the divots on the flight deck and felt a little sorry for the crew because our bad landing made more work for them. As I approached the shuttle, I located the *Zanna* icon in my invisihud and unlocked the ship. The back hatch entrance lowered, and Ethan and I walked up and into the shuttle.

Ethan went over to the hinged bench lid and fetched his pack from inside before he slung it over his shoulder.

"Ohm, I need two passage cards between two locations. They both should go to Ethan and Olivia's apartment in the San Francisco building. One should go to Enki's Dale and the other to the maintenance tube entrance, nearest to sickbay on this ship," I said.

"Working," Ohm said to me, then two vignette cards appeared with a sparkle on the bench beside me.

I picked them up and showed them to Ethan, saying, "They work like this," and I pressed the single button, which flipped between two pre-programmed images.

"It takes you between two places, like a Peregrinate. Press the button to pick the other location. This one goes from this starship to an apartment in San Francisco. The apartment is for you, Olivia, and the kids. There is a currency card there. It will allow you to buy things locally," I said.

"An apartment?" Ethan asked as he adjusted his glasses.

Then holding up the other vignette, I said, "This one goes from your home in Enki's Dale to the apartment building. This one is for Olivia, and the other one is for you. It will allow you two to meet up in San Francisco so you can remain in the same time frame as *Journey*. It requires some concentration. Pretend the image is real, and it becomes a doorway to that location. Then mentally, and physically take a step forward, and you will arrive there. To return, simply flip to the other picture and do the same thing. You can bring someone along when you step if they are touching you. Let Olivia know, through the communications ring, that the kids will need to hold her hands to come along."

I handed one card to Ethan and said, "Ohm, place this passage card on the dining room table of Ethan and Olivia's house in Enki's Dale."

The card sparkled in my hand and disappeared.

"I don't know what to say, Sam. Thanks, thank you," Ethan said as I walked him out of the shuttle.

"Oh, one last thing," I said as I bent down to fetch the second wand from my zippered leg pocket. "Take this spare wand. If Frelpok doesn't give you your wand back, try and *Insipida* him. It might be interesting to see if that spell actually works on a Logican? If the Captain asks, you can let her know that I am working on a new communications system, and it won't be too long before it is operational."

Ethan took the wand I offered, stepped off the shuttlecraft cargo ramp, and shook his head, yes. I returned to the shuttle and closed the cargo ramp that acts as the rear wall of the shuttle when in flight. He waved as I watched the back hatch of the *Zanna* close, removing him from my view.

Checking my pocket with vignettes, I found the one I was looking for. It was a vignette taking me directly to the catwalk aboard the *Deceptive*. This catwalk is where the *Vision* painting resides. I focused on the image on the card, and a shift occurred across the surface. That's when you know a connection exists between where you are and where the card will take you. I used my will and stepped into the place depicted on the card. This act was the same process I described to Ethan a few moments ago. I was on the catwalk, and I could see the painting sitting on the easel at the end. Ari managed the painting much like Ohm managed my homes. It was Ari's responsibility to return the cover over the painting after I stepped through it the last time. I walked up to the easel and thought about my new destination.

CHAPTER 13

Explorer

❧

I located the icon in my invisihud representing the environment suit and activated it. A snug, tight force field surrounded me. I could see through it, but there was an obvious energy field between me and my environment. This shield is what I should have had in place when Ethan and I were mucking about on *Journey*. It acted as a shield against external physical and energy-based attacks but provided a life support system for regulating oxygen flow and body temperature. You could survive in the arctic snow, underwater, or in the cold vacuum of space. This last option is what I activated.

"Ohm, can you verify the integrity of the personal force field I just activated? I am making a deep space dive."

"Checking," Ohm said, and my force field popped and tweaked as a pressure wave traveled from my head down to my toes.

It began again, moving from the left side of my body to the right when Ohm added, "The force field is fully operational and should protect you from deep space exposure."

"Thank you, Ohm."

I gathered up my thoughts and tried to frame my new destination. I knew the general area of space I was heading to, but there was a time differential involved compared to where *Journey* resided. This probable echo would be the past, compared to *Journey*. This time period was before the Starnet Union formed. I sought the first flux-five ship Earth sent out to explore the galaxy. It was named *Explorer*. Like *Journey*, I had future memories of being friends with the crew of the *Explorer*. Most notably, their doctor, whose name was Farouk. He was an Ursonian. In my future memories, I visited him many times to talk about how to manage my marriage with two women at the same time. On Ursa, each man could have three wives, and each wife could have three husbands. He, himself, married three times, so I sought his advice on how to navigate relational obstacles that inevitably arise from such a complicated arrangement.

With all of this in mind, I quickly whipped the cloth from the painting and dropped it on the floor. *Vision* waited for me and greeted me with a large gnawing mouth full of forked tongues with secondary forks at the end of the first forks. Floating eyeballs quickly popped open, revealing themselves as they darted around to observe me. I thought of the cold blackness of space. I thought of the time period. I thought of my friends, and the painting quickly faded to black. Stepping into the painting, I immediately felt myself weightless, floating in space.

If you have never been on a spacewalk or floated in space, it is one of the most terrifying experiences you can have. Surrounded by nothing but darkness fills you with a sense of insignificance. You are nothing to the universe. Barely a speck in the grand scheme of things. You have no control because there is nothing to grab on to. There is nothing to give you a size reference, especially if you don't happen to be near a planet or a star, which was my case. Your first instinct is to twist around, to look for a way back. In this situation, I knew there was nothing around me, not even a shuttlecraft, I could return to. No hose, line, or cable that I could tug on to feel a sense of destination. All around me were the distant shining stars like pinholes poked in a velvet drape.

I felt my breathing change as it became more labored. This difficulty is because we are so used to the force of gravity that we don't realize how much we rely on it for our everyday bodily functions. I tried to keep my cool, and I held my breath to slow down my breathing.

"Ohm, transport the *Zanna* to this location," I said, forcing out each word in between breaths.

The sparkle of the transporter was twice as brilliant in the deep darkness of space where there was no other light or atmosphere to diffuse the effect it generated. The sight of the ship in front of me brought a sharp perspective to the scene, helping reduce the anxiety and insignificance that quickly built up when I arrived. I had a goal.

"Ohm, establish a cabin force field inside the *Zanna* and open the back hatch," I said.

I used the invisihud to target the *Zanna*, whose rear hatch was opening, then located the jetpack sub-menu to activate the attract icon. It seemed like nothing happened at first, but in space, the sense of motion is nearly undetectable. The *Zanna* slowly grew in size as I approached. I was a little too late deactivating the attract icon and slammed hard into the outer hull. My shield crackled and sparked as I bounced off the ship, and started floating away again. Reactivating the attract sub-menu, I quickly turned it off as I slowly approached the *Zanna* from the top side. There were handles here, a ladder embedded into the hull of the ship. These handles were part of the shuttle's design, and you could find them on each side of the craft. I slowly pulled myself along the length of the shuttle, making my way to the open hatch at the rear. I felt a bit of an ache in my left bicep, which made hard contact with the hull. It would probably leave a bruise.

Climbing the rear of the shuttlecraft, I swung around in a space jump fashion. While still holding on to one of the handles embedded in the hull, I let go at the last second as I accelerated into the interior of the shuttlecraft. Directing my leap into the open cargo area at the back of the shuttle, I landed and bounced off the walls a couple of times, producing sparks when I came into contact with the interior. I had less velocity this time, but the entire maneuver was clumsy as I clattered to the floor.

Lying on the floor, I said, "Ohm, close the hatch and pressurize the cabin."

I saw the shuttle door close and lock into place. I lie there on the floor, catching my breath as the gravity plating helped ease my breathing distress.

"Shuttlecraft cabin is pressurized," Ohm said.

"Drop cabin force field," I said to Ohm, and I saw the visible energy field fade as I sat up.

I located the environment suit icon inside my invisihud menu system and deactivated it, dropping the force field around my body as I said, "Ohm, redeploy all of the Gar sector drones to this location. I want to begin a new search."

"Deploying drones. Specify search parameters." Ohm said.

"Review Starnet records of the first flux-five ship named *Explorer*. That is the ship we are looking for. Use the elements from the hull composition as a starting point. Feel free to add other criteria to the search if you come up with some unique identifier more suitable for detection."

"Deployment method?" Ohm asked.

"Let's use full spherical detection with the *Zanna's* current location as the center point. I don't have a general direction at this time."

"Search underway. I will update your invisihud when the target is detected," Ohm replied.

I made my way to the front of the shuttle and took the same seat when Ethan and I traveled together. I felt like I botched my visit to *Journey*, and I started to question whether telling people who I am and what I can do was really the best approach? But in my future memories, I did not lie about who I was to my close friends. I hoped I could smooth things over later when I returned with the communications device. I also thought about how Tamakot and Sara both zeroed in on the possibility that I may manipulate people around me to do my bidding. I knew I did not intentionally do that, but my latent Splendorite abilities could not be denied. If I looked at the origin of each of my Guardians, there was a clear pattern of offering a reward for helping me. I never thought of them as people I purchased with power, technology, and status, but an outsider could easily make that argument and be standing on firm ground. I wondered if I was blind to my selfish manipulations of others, and they were just calling it as they saw it. There was nothing I could do now other than try to not make the same mistake with this next crew I was about to meet.

"Ohm, can you make the cloaked probes available on the *Zanna* sensors?"

"Certainly," Ohm replied, and the sensors window appeared on the display.

I could see the spherical deployment evolve as each probe began its thrust journey through projected target points. The first few jumps were of a large distance. Each optical probe slowed its expansion rate as it considered more possible candidate options.

I figured this would probably take a while, so I headed back to the replicator and got a hot cup of black coffee. I checked the rations drawer and pulled out a cherry pie. It was more like an over-stuffed tart with a fruit flavor that sweetened my palate as I sipped the bitter coffee.

"Ohm, let's alter the expansion rate on some of the drones. Three groups of ten percent of the total count. Make each group have a random telescopic destination count between ten and sixty."

Telescopic travel for the cloaked optical drones was achieved by modifying the arrival mode. Typically when a drone arrives at the new projected destination, it starts to process a series of commands to scan the area. In telescopic mode, no commands are issued. Instead, another jump is made at the maximum optical distance along the same vector the probe arrived along. It's a faster way to get some of the probes farther out from the center. By using a few groups with random stop counts, I tried to fill in possible missing gaps that might occur with high telescopic counts. The uniform spherical expansion displayed by the sensor window altered as I watched the telescopic travel change the drone deployment. The outer edges of the sphere began to fray and no longer presented a uniform circular look on the display. A few extreme vectors jutted out, and one drone looked like it might be lost or backtracking for some reason. I decided to let the drones do their thing and went back to the bench bed to lie down.

Somewhere along the line, I must have nodded off because I awoke to the sound of a proximity alarm going off. I stumbled forward and into the pilot's seat, but I did not need to look at the sensors because there was a very large vessel outside the shuttlecraft. The *Zanna* was underneath the silver radial section of the front of the ship, and I looked at large symbols painted on the side reading, "*EX-01.*"

The communication panel popped up, and I could hear, "Unknown vessel. This is the starship *Explorer*. Please respond."

I couldn't believe my luck. The vessel I was searching for found me. I activated the communications channel and asked, "Jason, is that you?"

"Do I know you?" the voice asked.

"We did, or we will. My name is Sam Richards of the shuttlecraft *Zanna*. Requesting permission to dock," I said.

There was a long pause in the communication, more than a minute or two before I heard Jason's voice say, "Use the starboard side docking hatch. It's the one with the flashing blue lights."

"Understood," I replied, and activated the shuttle's navigational controls.

Using the navigation system of the *Zanna*, I activated the distance-based wire-frame tunnel overlay. I tapped on thruster ports while rotating and guiding the shuttlecraft to the midsection of the *Explorer*. I saw the flashing blue lights and maneuvered the *Zanna* around for a basic alignment with the ship before asking, "Zanna, can you initiate auto docking procedures with this ship?"

"Yes, predicting auto docking at ninety-eight percent," Zanna replied.

"Take your time. I want a nice, smooth dock. Don't hit their ship," I said.

"Understood. Doubling the length of docking procedure," Zanna said, and I felt the ship proceed under automatic movement.

I set the invisihud to grey mode, with the personal shield in the quick slot in case something goes wrong. Grabbing my coffee cup and the wrapper, I recycled them using the ship's replicator. While looking at my reflection in the window of the side door, I straightened out my clothes, brushed the crumbs from my shirt, and arranged my hair with my hands. I saw an expandable tube extending from the *Explorer* to the *Zanna*. The tiny window revealed people gathering around the other side of the *Explorer* door as the tube pressed firmly against my ship.

There was a soft bump and a thud accompanied by a strong hissing sound that eased to a stop. I watched as the pressure gauge by the side of my door moved to a safe position, which indicated there was a pressurized atmosphere on the other side. Activating the release, I opened the door and stepped into the walkway provided by the extended tube. I felt the weightlessness of space and held onto the handrail as I made the short crossing between the ships. As I approached the outer door to the *Explorer*, it opened, producing a slight hiss that quickly faded. Stepping inside the entry chamber, I closed the outer door. Another set of pressurizing sounds occurred, and the inner door latch became active. An *Explorer* crewman opened the inner door, and a small group of humans and one Logican greeted me.

The humans were all wearing olive drab jumpsuit uniforms, and the tall male in the front stepped forward with his hand extended, saying, "I am Jason Bowmen. Nice to meet you."

I shook his hand and said, "Sam Richards. Nice to meet you."

"This is my chief engineer Charles Tanner," Jason said.

Charles Tanner immediately interrupted his captain and said, "You can call me Chuck."

"My security officer Henry Lewis," Jason continued.

Henry said, "Nice to meet you," with a British accent.

"And my science officer Tenda," he finished.

I shook hands with Chuck and Henry and used the "Balance In All Things" hand gesture from a distance with Tenda. Logicans generally don't like to be touched.

"You mentioned something about already knowing me. How is that possible? I have never met you." Jason asked.

"I have never met you either, but I awoke a few days ago with memories of my future life, and the crew of the *Explorer* was in those memories. I have been trying to locate the people in those memories to see if they have been affected in any way. Has anything strange happened in the last week or so to any of you?" I asked.

They all looked at each other, and Tenda was the first to reply, "No."

"I can't recall anything odd," Henry said.

"Wait, I did drop a wrench last week. When I went to pick it up, I bent down, and I heard a strange sound. I distinctly recall thinking that was odd cause nothing was around to make the sound," Chuck said.

Jason shook his head, no, with a bit of a shrug and said, "Nothing out of the ordinary for me."

"Well, maybe I made this trip for nothing," I said with a sigh.

"How detailed are your future memories of us?" Chuck asked, revealing his southern accent.

"I don't have daily details of every single moment. There was too much time involved. The farther I get from the date when the future memories appeared, the vaguer they seem to be. Similar to the way a dream fades over the day," I said.

"How much time are we talking about?" Jason asked.

"There are different time ratios involved because I move around between probabilities, but I would guess at least five years or more," I said.

"You knew me for five years, in the future? Tell me one thing about myself that I would only tell a friend," Chuck asked.

"Okay, your favorite food is shrimp and grits, Cajun style," I said.

Chuck smiled slyly, saying, "That's pretty good."

Henry interjected, "But Chuck tells everyone what his favorite food is. It would be hard not to know that one."

Jason added, "What about me?"

"You have a dog named Patches, which is public record. What is not public record is that Patches came from a litter from your sister's dog, Sunshine," I said.

"That does not prove anything," Tenda said.

"You knew me well enough to tell me what happened to you on Rishar those long years ago," I said to Tenda.

Feeling left out, Henry asked, "And what about me, any revelations or dietary surprises?"

"You are a private man, but I do know one tidbit. You secretly yearn to be a writer, specifically mysteries that take place in the Victorian era," I said.

Chuck spoke up, "I agree with Tenda. A lot of that is public knowledge, but I do find it intriguing that you had something on all of us."

Jason asked, "What did you mean by time ratios and different probabilities?"

"I am a probability traveler, and while my ship may have some technology that could be considered from your future, the ship does not carry a temporal signature. It should not draw the attention of the temporal factions which are warring in this era," I said.

"Temporal factions," Henry said under his breath.

"Different probabilities can be thought of as gears in a watch mechanism. Some spin faster than others. That is what I have observed in my travels through probability. The way time relates to other probabilities does have a ratio compared to another. If I spend one week here, then go to another probability and check the calendar, I might have only been gone for three days. And that has nothing to do with the spinning of a planet or the way each probability might record their local time," I said.

"What do you know of temporal interventions?" Jason asked with a bit more serious tone.

"I know that it is a trait of this probability, so there is no avoiding or escaping it. The best you can do is learn how to surf with the changing tide. Maintain your stance to avoid complications with the temporal police."

"Who are the temporal police?" Chuck asked.

"In your probability, the temporal police are time travelers who visit this time from the future to change the past to stabilize their present. As soon as time travel was invented, a time loop was created as a simultaneous side effect. To preserve the time loop, the people in the future with time machines must go back and reinforce the past to ensure the time loop is created, or their future will cease to exist. They have little regard for deviation because their lives are literally hanging in the balance of the success of their actions."

"The Logican Science Academy has concluded that time travel is not possible," Tenda stated.

"What I have discovered as a probability traveler is that time is actually local to the probability it exists within. The future is no more dependent upon the past than the past is upon the present. There is infinite forking of all probabilities at every moment, and it is consciousness that determines what probabilities it finds itself within," I said, ignoring Tenda's statement.

"I don't know, Capn'. I think he might be pullin' our leg," Chuck said with an even more southern draw.

Jason asked, "We were drawn to this location by an energy signal. Do you know anything about that?"

"It might have been when I deployed my fleet of optical scanning probes. I transported in the ones from another probability to this probability to avoid replicating a new fleet. The transport of that many probes might have generated the signal you detected," I said.

"We didn't detect any probes on our scanners," Tenda said.

"That is good. It means their cloaking technology is working," I said.

"A cloaked fleet. How many probes are in this fleet?" Jason asked.

"I'm not sure when the original replication process halted, but I thought at least a few hundred. I didn't check the exact count," I said.

"Now I know you're pullin' my leg. You have a fleet of a few hundred probes, but we can't detect them because they are cloaked. That is mighty convenient," Chuck replied.

Jason, ever the investigator, asked, "What do these probes do if you don't mind me asking?"

"I deployed them to scan for *Explorer*. I knew you were in this part of space. One shuttlecraft is not able to scan a large area quickly. I transported the probes and set their exploration vector in a spherical expansion from my shuttle craft's location. The probes are basically rocket-based optical telescopes with shielding, cloak, and scanners. They have no weapons," I said.

"How did you know *Explorer* was going to be in this sector of space?" Tenda asked.

"In the probability I left, this moment is the past. Your mission is historic, and there are public records of *Explorer*'s missions. I reviewed them and chose this coordinate as my starting point. But this probability does not affect the probability I arrived from. That is to say, your past actions can't alter their present," I said

"If we're their past, then they are our future," Henry said.

"Not necessarily," I said. "That is what I meant by infinite forking. You can get up and put on red socks and go to work. You can get up and put on blue socks and go to work. That is two possible forked states of the same reality. What most people don't realize is that each one is valid. And that each one continues forward through infinity, continuously forking as it goes along. In this analogy, the place I just left is the red sock probability, and this place is the blue sock probability."

"Why, why would you make the distinction?" Jason asked.

"Because I have friends in both probabilities, red sock friends and blue sock friends. If I help blue sock friends, that could alter the future for red sock friends. I did not want to face that, so I try to make each probability I visit independent and non-influential on others," I replied.

"I guess it makes sense in an H.G. Wells sort of way," Chuck said.

"What are your plans now, Sam?" Jason asked.

"Well, I hoped to talk with Farouk if that's okay?" I said.

They all looked at each other again as I mentioned Farouk, and Jason asked, "You know Farouk?"

"Yes and not yet," I said with a smile.

"Can I offer you a drink, a refreshment perhaps?" Jason asked.

"Scotch would be great if you have any," I said.

Jason returned my smile and walked over to the wall where he pressed a button and spoke into the panel, "Doctor Farouk, will you report to the Captain's mess?"

A brief pause. A small voice emitted from the wall, "On my way, Captain."

Jason asked, "Would any of you care to join us?"

"I'll tag along," Chuck said with a smile.

"I'd like to return to my duties if you don't mind, Captain," Henry said to Jason before turning to me. "Nice to meet you, Sam."

"I, too, have duties on the bridge to return to," Tenda said.

"Have Trent resume course," Jason instructed Tenda.

"Aye, Captain," Tenda replied, and she walked off with Henry.

"This way," Jason said, and he gestured down the hallway opposite the way the other two took.

We walked through the corridors, which were similar to those on *Journey*, except these were certainly the first. There was no carpeting on the floor or flashing arrows embedded in the wall to show us the way. *Explorer EX-01* had more of a military battleship feel to it. We passed through mechanical bulkheads by spinning a large wheel, stepping through, then sealing it behind you, much like naval ships. We made our way to the interior of the radial section, meeting crewmen and women along the way. They offered minor salutes or acknowledgments of their ranking officer as we passed.

Chuck spoke up as we walked and asked with a smile, "So, if you have future memories, you wouldn't happen to know who is going to win the water polo match between Australia and Rio de Janeiro next week on Earth?"

I laughed a bit and said, "Sorry, I don't, but if you are just looking for a bar of gold, I'm sure it is highly probable that one is around here somewhere."

With that in mind, I reached out and brought forth the image of the *Motif* and imagined it projected over the walls and floors of the corridors we passed through. I sought a bar of gold, which was highly improbable, but the intention was there in my mind that gold could be found as we walked. Sure enough, as we rounded another corner, Jason nearly tripped and said, "What the?"

He bent down and picked up the bar of gold. He held it up with both hands and asked me, "Did you do this?"

I shook my head, yes, and said, "It's Chuck's gold."

Jason handed the Fort Knox style gold bar to Chuck and said, "Don't leave your gold lying around. Someone might trip over it."

Chuck took the gold bar from Jason, and it weighed heavy in his hand as we walked through an entrance to what looked like a cafeteria. There was seating, and one wall offered panels of frosted glass where you could see silhouettes of plated food. A few crewmen sat around the room eating and or checking readings on hand-held tablets. We made our way off to the right to another door with a small plaque reading, "Captain's Mess."

Jason touched a button, and the doors slid open automatically, similar to *Journey*'s door system. We followed him in, and Jason walked over to a cabinet to pull out a bottle of Johnny Walker Black label. He sat that on the table, along with four cups that were reminiscent of a red wine glass with the stems removed. The bottle was about three-quarters full, and Jason poured a good splash into each of the glasses.

The sliding doors parted, and in walked Farouk. Farouk was an Ursonian whose basic body build was a pear shape with legs. His wide forehead displayed an obvious split plate down the center, which reminded me of the Warnock forehead but was much less pronounced. Along the sides of the head and framing the eyes were small raised bumpy tubes that hinted at Bragorian features. His skin color was similar to humans with a peach tone. He wore combed-back hair.

"Ah, Doctor Farouk. Care to join us for a drink?" Jason asked.

"Certainly," Farouk said with a positive attitude in his tone.

Jason motioned for us to sit down around the table in the room. This room was smaller than the cafeteria area, and the table could probably seat eight people comfortably. We spread out as we each took a seat. Jason handed a glass to me and Farouk, while Chuck picked up the other one without being offered.

"Aren't you on duty, Chief?" Jason asked.

"I thought we were entertainin'?" Chuck complained.

"That will be one gold bar," Jason joked as he finally sat down.

"I just happen to have one," he said, and Chuck put the gold on the table.

Jason raised his glass and said, "A toast. To new friends."

We all echoed his words, "To new friends," before taking a sip.

I wasn't really a blended Scotch whiskey man, but the Johnny Walker Black label was not that bad.

"Mmm," I said. "Wow, this is smooth."

Farouk made a cheerful exclamation, saying, "I agree. Smoky and warming."

"Farouk, this is Sam Richards. He claims to know you and to know all of us," Jason started the conversation.

Farouk said, "I can't recall that we have ever met. Was it at a conference?"

"Not surprising, Farouk. Sam is from the future," Chuck added.

"I'm not really from the future," I clarified. "I awoke about a week ago with memories of future events. In those events, I spent time aboard *Explorer* and got to know many of the crew, you included."

"Intriguing. What was our relationship like?" Farouk asked as he swirled his whiskey and smelled the aroma.

"As a probability traveler, I have found myself aboard starships quite often. Some ships, I have even taken up residency on. My station was typically a medical assistant. And while I valued your medical input, I often came to you seeking advice about my marriage," I said.

"That is interesting, but why would you seek marriage advice from someone who is not of your species?" Farouk asked.

"I sought your advice because I married two women on the same day. We were married on Ursa Prime under the traditional Ursonian marriage ceremony. Each of my wives is of a species different from my own, and to remain together aboard starships, we chose a marriage recognized by the Union they served," I explained.

"Two wives?" Chuck exclaimed with a smile, then looked into his glass before taking another calculated sip.

I looked at Chuck and said, "I miss them both. Imagine you wake up tomorrow and find yourself in the past. Everyone you know or love no longer exists, but you still remember them as if they were just there. As I move forward from my new past starting point, I feel like my memories of those people are quickly fading away. That is why I am seeking out the people I remember before I forget who they were."

"Why don't you just seek out your wives directly?" Jason asked.

"Their names are Erin and Jorrie. I have located Jorrie and observed her from a distance, but in my future memories, I meet Erin first," I said.

"Now that's a tough call," Chuck said before taking another sip.

"I met Erin through a series of events, which I am trying to recreate, but there is no guarantee that it will work. Erin is a human clone built by robotic beings. While I could probably locate the clone ship which manufactured her, how would I know which one was truly her? Also, the relationship between Jorrie and Erin was special. They loved each other and married each other the same day they married me. What if I pick the wrong clone and my two wives don't fall in love again? What if I find the right ones, but they don't fall in love with me?" I explained and lamented.

"While it is rare for wives or husbands to marry each other on Ursa, it has happened. And I know the marriage complications of multiple wives all too well. I can sympathize with your position, but I am not sure what I can do to help," Farouk offered sympathetically.

"It sounds like the chicken and the egg problem," Chuck said.

"A human clone built by robotic beings. That paints a vivid picture," Jason said, raising his glass and taking a drink.

"And what species is Jorrie?" Farouk asked.

"You may not be aware of her planet yet, but her species is called the Vosip. Jorrie is special among her people because she is what they call a mingled Vosip. She is not unique, however. There are other mingled Vosip," I said.

"We haven't discovered that planet yet," Jason said.

"Evolution on her world produced two sentient beings, the humanoid Vosip and a slug-like being called the Limax. A Limax is medically placed within the body of a Vosip host, which produces a blended consciousness. Once blended, the host and Limax act as a single being. When the host dies, the Limax lives on and is placed in another body to continue its life."

"A vivid picture, indeed," Chuck said.

"This mingling can go on for multiple host lives. The Limax transfers the memories of the previous life into the current host body. Jorrie is the eighth host for the Limax, which is named Tusk. The hostname comes first and the Limax second. She is Jorrie Tusk. Her host is twenty-eight years old, but the Limax is about three hundred and eighty. She remembers being both male and female, and a parent of children that are long dead."

"If I weren't lookin' at this bar of gold, I'd still say he's pulling our leg," Chuck said.

"I have to say that is utterly fascinating. A symbiotic relationship that spans multiple lifetimes," Farouk said.

"What can we do to help you?" Jason asked.

"I'm not sure. I guess I am looking for something that does not exist yet. Talking and meeting with you has made me feel a little closer to my goal. I am trying not to fall into a pit of depression over the weight of this Herculean task of recreating my life. I don't even know if it is possible," I said.

Chuck asked, "So, Jorrie can remember what she learned in other lives?"

"Very much so. But it is Tusk, the Limax, that actually remembers. Jorrie is incredibly smart and holds multiple degrees in physics, flux field mechanics, and zoology. But Tusk has even more knowledge in other fields."

"And once Jorrie passes Tusk on, her life memories will be available to the new host?" Farouk asked.

"That is correct," I said.

"What about the clone?" Jason asked.

"Erin is incredibly smart. With those two in the room together, I feel like a dummy. The robotic beings who made Erin are called the Melogs. Her physical makeup is part of a series. Erin is considered a single revision or unit. They all have exceptional strength, intelligence, and recuperative abilities due to micro-machines placed in the bloodstream to facilitate more efficient cellular communications."

"Once again, that is astonishing," Farouk said before taking a sip.

I looked at Jason Bowmen and asked, "I guess I am asking if it is okay to pop in, from time to time, to talk with Farouk?"

"I think that would be up to him," Jason said while raising his eyebrows.

"Our travels lead us to many places, and we don't carry passengers. I am not sure how we could possibly meet again."

I turned to Farouk and asked, "Would you mind if I stopped by to talk from time to time?"

Farouk said indifferently, "As the Captain said, I'm not sure how that would be possible."

"I have a transportation technology that lets me revisit places I have been to at least once before. It works a lot like your transporter," I said.

"So, you have to physically visit the place the first time," Jason said, putting it all together and continuing, "and this visit is your first time visiting us."

"That is correct. That is why I mentioned the pop-in. I don't have to know where the ship is located to use my transportation device to return."

"What is the range of your transporter technology?" Chuck asked.

"Infinite for all practical purposes," I said.

Chuck slapped the bar of gold loudly and said, "I'd like to see the schematics for that."

I reached into my pocket and pulled out my business card with the words "Sam I Am" printed in red ink. I handed it to Jason and said, "I have to leave now, but you can get in touch with me by holding the card in your hand and pretending it is a radio. Just talk to it."

"I don't mind extending this relationship if you don't mind?" Farouk said.

"We'll give it a try under the condition that Farouk will report your conversations to me. Is that acceptable to you?" Jason asked.

"That sounds more than reasonable," I said as I stood up.

Jason stood up and activated a communications button on the back wall. He said, "Trent, drop out of flux. Our guest is leaving."

I heard a small voice reply, "Acknowledged," and I felt the motion of the ship change.

Chuck picked up his bar of gold, and Farouk stood up as we left the Captain's mess and began walking back to the docking port. Chuck and Farouk both said goodbye and excused themselves at some point during the short walk to the docking hatch. At the end of the walk, it was just me and Jason Bowmen standing at the door.

"Well, Sam, it has been interesting meeting you. I wish you luck on finding your way back to your wives," Jason said, shaking my hand one more time.

"Thanks, Jason. I am glad we met today too. Also, think of that card as your additional option if you find your back against the wall. I have technology that can change the tide of a battle," I said.

"I'll keep that in mind," he said, and he opened the hatch leading back to the *Zanna*.

I crossed the short walkway between ships to enter the shuttlecraft *Zanna*.

"Zanna, release docking clamps and move us to a safe distance away from *Explorer*," I said, and I heard the sound of the docking tube retract, leaving the *Zanna* free-floating in space. I watched as *Explorer EX-01* made the jump back to flux speed and was gone.

CHAPTER 14

The Teddy Bear Interface

I pulled out the vignette to the *Deceptive* catwalk, stared at it until the scene came to life, and I stepped through.

"Ohm, return the *Zanna* to the docking bay of the *Deceptive*," I said once I stood on the *Deceptive* catwalk.

"Understood. Returning the *Zanna* to the *Deceptive*," Ohm replied.

Once again, I walked down the catwalk to my demon painting *Vision* and removed the cloth covering to reveal fire burning flesh as mouths agonized in silent screams. Tentacles pressed hard against the canvas trying to reach out for me. I pushed it all away and thought of a much happier place, a world of nature and abundance, a world outside the reach of technology or magic, a world of outcasts. My prison world. A beautiful blue sky filled with clouds appeared on the canvas as the scene came to life. I stepped through the painting and found myself on a large flat grassy prairie. This planet is where I am going to dump all the Flexanites or other prisoners that get in my way.

I looked around at the beauty of this new world and said, "Ohm, leave behind a cloaked scanner, then transport me back to my apartment in San Francisco."

The scene streamed in from the sides to dissolve me into nothingness. I found myself in darkness again. I felt so much better about my first encounter with *Explorer* compared to *Journey*. I hoped Ethan was fitting in. Streaks of light shot in as my world reintegrated. It was daytime in San Francisco. I walked over to the sliding balcony doors and stepped outside. The fresh coastal air filled my lungs as I heard the horns of passing boats below.

"Ohm, I want to redeploy the cloaked optical scanning fleet back to the Gar sector. Let's deploy them in a cone-like fashion from the last known vector *Journey* traveled along. Widen the cone distribution by eighteen percent. We are scanning for the Imperial or the Melog fleet. These are pre-flux vessels running on chemical fuel. Look for fume trails or other characteristics that might match pre-flux engines. They use radio frequencies for communications. The fleet size should be around fifteen to twenty distinct vessels."

"Redeployment in progress. Applying new search parameters," Ohm replied.

I left *Explorer EX-01* abruptly because my invisihud reported a possible Flexanite detected at Starnet headquarters, which I was just across the bay.

"Ohm, has the Flexanite candidate failed the test?"

"This candidate has failed the separating hair from the body test. The hair strand reintegrated as a dark oozing substance," Ohm said.

"Ohm, establish a transporter lock. When the target is out of sight of others, transport it to a cell on asteroid containment center forty-seven."

"Transport in progress," Ohm said, then added after a short pause, "Transport complete."

"Ohm, I want to create a very small virtual character to act as my liaison for Flexanite communications. Install an auragraphic emitter outside the cell to project a stuffed animal-sized orange teddy bear beyond the transparent wall. Provide two-way audio communication, and link the character to my motions. When I walk and talk, the teddy bear should match my moves at the asteroid containment center."

"Working. Building character and interface," Ohm replied.

I took in a bit more of the fresh air and thought about Ethan Foster. "Ohm, what are Ethan Foster's vital statistics?"

"Ethan Foster's life signs are normal. He is in a low-stress state," Ohm replied. "Containment center forty-seven character interface is available for use."

"Ohm, let's make one more change to the interface. When I speak, I want my voice to sound like it is the voice of a teddy bear, not my voice."

"Making adjustments," Ohm said, and a short time later replied, "Adjustments complete. Character interface is ready for use."

"Ohm, can you drop an icon for the teddy bear interface into my invisihud menu?"

"Updating your invisihud with a new icon for the teddy bear interface."

I used eye movements to locate the teddy bear icon and activated it. Its visual feed appeared in my invisihud, much like a cloaked scanner. A video feed from the teddy bear's eyes appeared in the invisihud overlay system as a small glow off in the distance. Using eye movements, I selected the frame and zoomed in to look around the room from the teddy bears' perspective. Lifting up my stubby arms, I saw orange fur. I looked down, and I saw a round white belly. Looking up, I saw a glass wall. Behind the glass wall was a concrete rectangular room. Inside the room stood a man in a Starnet uniform with the colors red on his shoulders.

"Ohm, adjust the teddy bear's voice to be very loud compared to its size."

"Adjustments to speech volume complete," Ohm replied.

I returned my focus to the invisihud and looked at the trapped Flexanite.

"Flexanite, I am Mas," I said, thinking myself clever by reversing the spelling of my name.

At first, I don't think the Flexanite realized the teddy bear was doing the talking. He walked over to the window wall and knelt down to look at the bear.

"I am Field Marshal Jeremy Stewart. What is this place?" Jeremy asked.

THE TEDDY BEAR INTERFACE

"You can cut the act. I know you are a Flexanite," I said through the teddy bear interface.

"I have no idea what you are talking about. I am Field Marshal Jeremy Stewart," Jeremy insisted.

"Time will tell. I have not met a Flexanite yet who can hold their form for more than seventy-two hours," I said.

"I demand that you release me immediately, or there will be consequences. Starnet command will not stand for this," Jeremy raised his voice as he spoke.

"You are in another dimension in a prison built on an asteroid. A prison made to contain Flexanites. Even if you escape, there is nowhere to go," I said.

"You are making the biggest mistake of your life. When I get out, I'll make your life hell," Jeremy said, having totally lost his cool by now.

"There is only one way out, and I control that exit. Tell me where you hid the body of the real Jeremy Stewart, and that will go a long way to getting you moved to a nicer prison," I said as the teddy bear.

"Go to hell," Jeremy said.

"Actually, I'm going out for a drink, but I'll see you in a few days, and we'll try this talk again," I said before terminating the link in the invisihud.

"Ohm, what is the confidence rating on the Flexanite infiltration of Starnet?" I asked.

"One hundred percent of local Starnet personnel have been scanned. All but Jeremy Stewart passed the scissors test. This gives a high confidence rating that there are no other Flexanites on Earth posing as Starnet personnel at this time," Ohm reported.

"What is the saturation rate on deploying cloaked scanners throughout the entire Starnet Union?" I asked.

"Saturation rate is holding at eleven percent with a projected growth rate of zero point three seven percent per day," Ohm replied.

I walked inside, closed the sliding door, took a seat on the white sofa, and said, "Ohm, I want to construct a two-way communication module for *Journey*. Make the circuitry very limited. I only want communications signals to travel through this particular relay. No transporter data should be allowed. Place one receiver inside the statue in the courtyard of Ayeres Hall, on the Starnet Academy campus. Place another one on the white coffee table in front of me. The signals passing through these two devices should be encrypted and logged."

The coffee table sparkled, and a triangular device about the size of a paperback book appeared. There was a tapering cylinder embedded in the shape running from the tip to the base of the triangle.

"Ohm, can you create a two-way passage card between *Journey*'s sickbay and The San Francisco Opera House at the corner of Franklin and Grove street?"

There was a pause before a sparkle on the table left behind a vignette card with a single button. I picked it up and pressed the button to review the images. The button toggled which image was displayed. There was the image of *Journey*'s sickbay and the image of a daytime street scene outside the San Francisco Opera House. I returned it to the table.

"Ohm, can you gather up all the information we have on Flexanites and place it in a portable tablet?" I asked. Once again, the table sparkled, and a small rectangular Blinn tablet appeared.

"Ohm, create another tablet that can shop at the local produce vendors. It needs to be able to place orders remotely. Connect the payment to one of my local San Francisco accounts. After the order is placed, transport it to *Journey's* cargo bay three. Deploy a cloaked scanner to that bay for permanent transporter duty. It should always remain in 'hide and evade mode,'" I said. "Make this tablet's base a green color."

It was about a minute or more before the table sparkled again, and a Blinn tablet with a green base appeared on the coffee table. When I picked it up, it lit up. I tapped and slid my hand along the surface of the tablet to review the produce and shopping selections available. Seeing all the food made me hungry. I sat down the tablet, and its display dimmed.

"Ohm, can I get a soft folding wallet style carrying case for all these items, the kind that zips up?"

The table sparkled to reveal a black fabric case that was already open. It contained a few slots and pockets. I placed each item from the table into the case, a tablet on each side, the passage card in a pocket, with the communication module in the middle. Zipping up the case, I picked it up as I stood and asked, "Ohm, what is the location of Captain Mitchell aboard *Journey*?"

"Captain Mitchell is in her quarters on deck two," Ohm replied.

"Send a cloaked scanner to the hallway outside her room. Once it is there, transport me to that location."

The bright daylight of San Francisco crashed in from the sides of my vision as I dissolved into darkness. The darkness seemed exceptionally lonely this time. I felt like I was just going through the moves. How could I ever find Erin and Jorrie again? I hoped my meeting with Sara went better than my last meeting with Tamakot? A soft light crept in from the edges, and I found myself aboard *Journey* once again.

Walking down a corridor, I came to the doorway to her quarters. I reviewed the buttons by the door and pressed an icon with the expanding lines in the shape of a bell. I heard a stylized version of the doorbell sound and waited. It took a moment or two, and the door split open, retreating into each wall. There stood Sara Mitchell, in partial uniform, with a slightly surprised look on her face.

"Sam," she said, pausing. "Please come in."

Her quarters were spacious, compared to what Ethan and I were assigned, but it was still modest due to practical size requirements for shipboard living. She sat down on her couch, in front of her coffee table where a steaming cup of tea sat. It looked like she might have recently replicated it. I sat down in a stuffed chair at the end of the table, and Sara asked, "Can I get you something? A drink, food?"

"No, thank you. I have arrived here on business," I said as I unzipped the carrying case and unfolded it on the table.

Sara interrupted and said, "Before we begin, I would like to apologize if I or my crew offended you during our initial meeting. Even though you appear human, our meeting was a premiere encounter with a new species, and I fell short. It was not my intent to put you under such harsh scrutiny right when we met. When Ethan mentioned that you left, I couldn't help but feel a bit ashamed about how we treated you."

"How is Ethan?" I asked.

She smiled and said, "He is enthusiastically integrating into the crew well, and I must say that I find him to be a delightful person. His perspective on things is unique and friendly."

"That is good to hear, and I would like to apologize, myself, for being the brash asshole. I thought a lot about what you and Tamakot said. You challenged me to review my own conduct and to consider the possibility that my latent powers might have an unintended effect on you. But I assure you that it was never my intention to create tragedy to appear to be the hero."

"Well then, can we start again?" Sara asked as she sipped her tea.

"Certainly, and I am happy to report that as of this moment, after completing my scans of Earth, I only detected one Flexanite in the Starnet chain of command. It was Field Marshal Jeremy Stewart."

"Oh," Sara said.

"I have placed the Flexanite in an off-world holding cell, in another probability constructed on an asteroid in space."

"Jeremy Stewart," Sara said in a low voice. "He was an upperclassman when I attended the academy."

"I am sad to report that he has probably been murdered," I said. "My initial interrogation of the Flexanite revealed nothing. He refused to admit that he even is a Flexanite."

"How can you be sure that it is not him?" Sara asked.

I removed one of the tablets from the open carrying case and handed it to Sara, and said, "I've put all the information I have about Flexanites, their methods of infiltration, and ways to detect them on this tablet. You can review it before passing it on to the Auramedic. You may want to set him up to conduct screenings of new arrivals if crew rotations start to take place."

She said, "I will," and set the tablet down on the coffee table.

I removed the other tablet and handed it to her, saying, "This tablet has a green colored base so you can tell them apart. I made this one for Nanook. It is a food ordering system. This tablet is linked to a remote grocery service. You can place an order once a week, and supplies will be deposited in cargo bay three. I had to pick a fixed location. I hope that is all right?"

Her face lit up with a smile of genuine gratitude, and she said, "Thank you. Cargo bay three should be fine."

"Don't worry about the prices. That is just part of the shopping interface. I have this tablet linked to my personal finance accounts," I said as Sara made swiping gestures to move through some of the selections.

"I'm sure Nanook and the entire crew will thank you for this," Sara said as she placed it on the coffee table next to the other tablet.

I presented the communications device to her, which weighed about four kilograms. Her hand dropped a little as I handed it to her. She was not expecting the weight.

"This is the communication device. It connects to a fixed location in San Francisco. Do you recall the statue in the courtyard outside Ayeres Hall?" I asked.

She thought for a moment and said, "Yes, I believe it is a Logican."

"I have placed another one of these inside that statue to act as a target. Your signal to Starnet will appear to be local. They may track it down and locate it in the statue, but it will still function as a target if it is relocated, even on a ship in motion," I said.

Sara took in the information, nodding her head as I talked.

"I purposely constructed it as a low energy device. You can't pump a transporter signal through it. If you do, it will break. I suggest that when you reestablish communications, make it brief. Perhaps have the first time or two fail as you get better at dialing in the communications process. This could enforce my original narrative that the communications signal was cut," I said.

She sat the communications device on the coffee table, looked at me, and said, "It's something to think about."

"It meets the specs of an A7CM consumer-grade communications device, so your team should not have any trouble integrating it into your ship's system," I said before picking up the last object from the case.

"This is what I call a passage card. It takes you between the two places shown on the card," I said, and I pressed the button to toggle back and forth between the images to demonstrate how it worked before handing it to her.

"The target location is outside the San Francisco Opera House on the corner of Franklin and Grove. I wanted you to appear in a public space rather than a space controlled by Starnet. The return location is sickbay aboard *Journey*. This way, if you return with someone, the Auramedic can immediately screen them before further entry into the ship."

"Return with someone?" Sara asked, a bit puzzled.

"This passage card does not use transporter technology. It uses magic. It relies on consciousness to activate it. Try it. Look at the opera house and believe, playfully, for a moment that it would be wonderful to be there."

I watched Sara's face as she stared into the card. A surprise flooded over her expression as she said, "I can hear the traffic."

"To disengage from the scene, lower the card and focus on this room."

She did so, looked over at me, and asked, "I can travel to San Francisco right now?"

"You can, and you will. Let's test it. You might want to grab a jacket. You'll return via sickbay using the other image."

Sara stood up and located the jacket part of her uniform in another room, and walked back into this room while putting it on.

"You'll need the card to travel. It remains with you. If you lose the card or it is destroyed while you are at the target location, you can't get back," I said.

"Understood," she said as she picked up the card and asked, "What's next?"

"We hold hands," I said, and I walked over to her and took her hand.

It was warm. Even though I received a few hugs and shook a few hands here and there, the contact was quick and minimal. Her touch was the first prolonged skin-to-skin contact I shared with anyone since I awoke a month or so ago. It made me think of my wives. We touched constantly and made it a point to hold each other every day. It became a natural extension of our pact to remain together.

"The organic nature of magic is such that it will flow between people if the people are physically touching. This property means you can bring groups of people with you when you travel through the passage card. In a worst-case scenario, gather your crew in one place, hold hands and abandon ship back to the Dili sector. I suggest you keep it with you at all times. You may want to add a pocket to your uniform just for the passage card," I said.

"What's next?" she asked.

"Hold the card up, look at the target image, and reach out with your mind. Believe the place is real, that it is possible to be there," I said in an instructional tone.

"I see it move. I can hear the sound of traffic," she said.

"Keep that in mind and step forward. I will step with you," I said while watching Sara's feet.

She stepped forward, and I stepped forward with her. The ship was gone in a rainbow phase shift. We stood back from the street next to the San Francisco Opera House. Franklin Avenue was busy with traffic, and pedestrians made their way along the sidewalks. Sara continued, stepping forward, releasing my hand, and slowly lowering the passage card as she did so. She moved in slow motion, captured in awe at the sight of unexpected beauty.

All I saw was a city street. She turned and looked at me, wiping away a tear, and said, "I never thought I'd see Earth again. I mean, I had to try to get us home, but in my heart, I never actually believed I would achieve that goal."

I did not really know what to say to that, so I said, "The return journey is the reverse. Focus on the sickbay image, and you can return, bringing someone from this side back with you. This feature can allow for shore leave and crew rotations. But you may want to hold off on that initially."

"This is a lot to take in," Sarah said.

"You can always say, after talking with Ethan, you realized you can bring one person along and make initial journeys alone. Manage the device as you see fit. It can be used by anyone, so you could delegate a transportation liaison whose job is to manage passage card traffic."

Sara shook her head, affirmatively, as if agreeing on the recommendations, and said, "I want to hug you, but I don't know if I know you well enough for that."

I leaned in and patted her on the back, and said, "Well, how about the half-hug pat?"

She leaned in and patted me on the back, and said, "I'll take it."

"I want to see that you are properly returned to *Journey*. We can walk around if you like, but I do have some other pressing matters I need to attend to."

"Now that I know I can come back, I'll explore later," she said as she held the card up, conveying the impression of taking a selfie.

I faced her, but I could see she pressed the button with her thumb to toggle to the other image the passage card offered. I watched as she focused, paused, stepped forward, and was briefly outlined in a rainbow-colored light that quickly collapsed and disappeared along with Sara herself. I stood alone, surrounded by the bustle of a busy Franklin Avenue.

CHAPTER 15

Meadowland

∽

Landscapers tended to the plants in front of the Opera House. It looked like they were planting geraniums. The splash of red on the ground set off the white flowers of the short blooming trees. I made my way over to the busy street, flagged one down, and hopped in this floating cab. The cab driver leaned back and asked, "Where to buddy?"

"The spaceport," I said, but the destination was irrelevant because I took control of the cab as it moved along the street. I brought the image of the *Motif* forward in my mind and cast it over the passing vehicles. Some were rolling, and some floated. I was no longer a passenger in a cab. I was a dignitary being delivered by military escort to my destination. The cab interior deformed, and the interior space expanded as wings emerged from the sides. We took flight, becoming a small modern plane. The front of the cab morphed into a cockpit, and the driver became a pilot hidden behind a closed door separating the front of the plane from the passenger area. I reached out further with the *Motif* and dropped the military aspects of the aircraft. I devolved the modern design into a typical passenger jet one might have traveled upon in the late twentieth century. I sat in first-class with fellow passengers who talked quietly and read magazines. A flight attendant made her rounds and stopped by my seat to offer drinks from a cart.

"May I get you something, sir?" she asked.

"Do you have bourbon, straight, no ice?"

"Yes, we do. Would you like one?"

I shook my head, yes, and she located a flask from the lower area of the cart and poured some brown liquid into a plastic cup. She stopped the pour a little below half full and handed the cup to me. I said, "Thanks," and she moved the cart forward to service the next row up.

I sipped the bourbon and placed the drink inside the cup holder built into the armrest. Imagining the *Motif* before me, I made one last push with a strong intention for my final destination. This destination was temporally in the past compared to the San Francisco I just left. It was closer to Jim Young's time frame, but this probability does not have a Mist Door. I heard the engines groan an awful sound as I adjusted echo, which produced a visible rippling along the fuselage walls.

The Captain's voice came over the intercom and said, "We are experiencing some slight turbulence and are asking passengers to return to their seats and put on the safety belts. We are seventeen minutes out from our final destination."

Looking around for my seatbelt, I locked it into position as the flight attendants made their way down the aisle, checking passenger compliance and helping those who needed it. I downed the rest of my bourbon and sat the empty cup in the holder of the vacant aisle seat next to me.

The crew made their way down the aisle again, collecting trash as the Captain's voice came over the intercom one more time, saying, "We are making our final approach to Windsor Nova Scotia where the time is two-thirteen in the afternoon, and the temperature is a crisp eleven degrees Celsius, that is fifty-two degrees Fahrenheit. Make sure your tray tables are in their upright, locked position, and I hope you fly with Delta again sometime in the future."

I waited patiently and looked out the window as the airbus made its final descent, and the ground rushed up to greet us. There was a slight screech when the tires hit the pavement. You could feel the plane in contact with the ground as the sound of the wind amplified against the outer hull. We taxied, and passengers were busy fetching carry-on bags from the overhead compartments. I carried no luggage, so I stepped up to the door and was the first one off the plane. The jet bridge led me into the airport terminal where I used the *Motif* to locate some local currency. I walked by an open area with many empty seats. When I sat down to tie my boot, I leaned over to discover a wallet left behind. A quick search of the wallet provided me with some Canadian money, and I left the wallet lying where I found it. I continued through the terminal, past the food court and gift shops, until I made my way out to the street. Cabbies were already lined up and motioning to exiting travelers.

I walked up to the nearest yellow cab, opened the back door, and got in. The driver looked back and asked, "Where to buddy?"

"Meadowland mobile home park," I replied, and the cabbie pulled down a lever to start the meter running before we drove off.

We drove in silence for the first few miles. He kept glancing back at me through the mirror from time to time. I looked out the side window, taking in the view of a town that was both crumbling and growing at different rates. What most echo beings do not realize is that they too are traveling through probability, but at a much slower speed than a Splendorite. What I saw slowly taking place in one construction zone would happen in mere seconds if I passed through this area with the *Motif* in full force around me. To the natives of this echo, it might take weeks or months to complete. The drive was longer than I expected, and the neighborhood turned from okay to worse. We passed a gas station and a convenience store tagged by graffiti as the cab pulled up to a drive with a hand-painted sign reading, "Meadowland Mobile Home Park." The sign depicted a sun rising up from behind some hills while extending its rays in the background.

The driver came to a stop, switched off the meter, and said, "That will be twenty-seven dollars and fifty cents."

I pulled out the money I fetched from the found wallet and handed him two twenties while saying, "Keep the change."

He smiled, I exited the vehicle, and the cab slowly drove off. I made my way down the sloped road leading into the Meadowland trailer park. It was, as the name suggested, a park with mobile homes. Most of them were singles, on blocks with wooden lattice around their bases to keep animals from making homes underneath. There were also the occasional double-wides with nicer yards and cars in the driveway. I passed by a telephone pole with a flyer on it. There was a picture of two dudes wearing sunglasses, looking hard, with their arms folded in front of them. It read, "Let the mac pack rock your next event!"

I pulled down the flyer and held onto it while making my final push into echo. I wanted to locate the two individuals pictured in the flyer. I took a turn down a side loop, which was not yet paved, and a couple of kids on bikes zoomed past, throwing rocks at me as they sped by shouting, "Looser." One stone pegged me in the back, hard, those little assholes.

I checked the flyer, which offered an address, against the trailers in this small cul-de-sac. A light blue one matched what was printed on the flyer. I headed up the steps to a deck made out of pressure-treated lumber, walked up to the door, and knocked. There was loud music coming from inside the trailer, so I knocked again, this time against the beat of the song, hoping my knock stood out.

I heard a commotion, like someone stepping over something falling over and muttering, "Damn, dawg. I heard you the first time."

A young, thin Caucasian fellow came to the screen door, but he did not open it. He wore jeans, a t-shirt, and sunglasses propped up on his head. He was one of the guys from the flyer.

I held up the flyer and said, "Do you guys have an opening? I have an event that needs M.C.ed."

He held up his hand to his ear, indicating he might not have heard what I said. Stepping out on the deck, he asked, "What's up, dawg?"

Once again, I said, "I have an event, and I need a couple of M.C.s to rock it up and make it great."

I extended my hand to shake his, and he wound his entire arm back to deliver a handshake like an underhanded softball pitch, saying, "You came to the right place. My name's K-Mac, and I can make your event out of this world. Come on in and meet my partner, Byrone."

He held the door open, and I followed him into the trailer, which was an immediate hallway left or right. He headed right, which was where the music came from, and I followed him a short distance until we reached the living room. I was a bit shocked at the amount of crap piled into this small space. I thought about my spacious luxury apartment and how sparsely decorated it was. But this place had literally something piled on every horizontal space available. There were books, magazines, boxes for musical equipment, old food wrappers piled on dirty plates that were piled on more dirty plates. Soda and beer cans were discarded and left on their sides, empty on the floor, which was a dark blue shag carpeting that was probably never vacuumed or washed. A glass bong sat on the Colonial-style blonde wooden coffee table with burn marks and stickers on it. I noticed a tray with some marijuana on it, and the whole room smelled like weed.

K-Mac offered a wooden kitchen chair he placed in front of the coffee table before plopping down in an overstuffed Colonial recliner. The fabric of the chair contained images of horses pulling Conestoga wagons and said, "Byrone, this is," then he paused and asked, "What was your name again?"

A well-built African dude, which I also recognized from the flyer, sat on the couch with the same western Colonial design going on. He picked up a remote control from the coffee table and pressed some buttons a few times to turn down the music so we could talk. It still played softly in the background.

"I'm Sam, Sam Richards," I said, extending my hand out to shake his as I sat down, but Byrone ignored it.

Byrone looked at K-Mac and said, "Why are you lettin' unknown white dudes into our house? I mean, look at him. He looks like Mr. Pockets or something."

"Why you ridin' my jock so hard, Byrone," K-Mac said, "He's come to do business. He ain't white. I thought he was Arabian or middle eastern or some-thin'"

"And what if he's a cop?" Byrone asked.

"I am not a cop. I'm a client," I interjected while holding up the flyer. "I have an event, and I need M.C.s to rock it up a bit."

Byrone looked at me, still not feeling it, and asked, "What kind of event?"

"I'm looking to debut myself as a brand sometime soon and would like someone to be there with the mic to back me up, pump me up, or just set me straight like you did just now with Mr. Pockets. I didn't know that mattered. I use pockets all the time because I travel a lot," I said while reaching into my pocket and pulling out the lighter I replicated at Ethan and Olivia's patio party.

I handed the sleek lighter to Byrone, and he inspected it before passing it over to K-Mac, who said, "Ah ite, Ah ite. I'm startin' to feel ya. You're payin' to be part of the pack."

"That I can. I can pay," I said as I reached into another pocket and put the remaining cash from the airport wallet on the table. I didn't really count it, but from the bills I saw, I would guess three to five hundred dollars was on the table.

Byrone picked up the bills, straightened them up, and turned them around as he counted out the cash. He did not say the final amount but handed the bills to K-Mac, who also took to counting.

"Consider that today's consulting fee, you know, an offering to keep the conversation going," I said as I pulled a wand out of my zippered sleeve pocket to place it on the table.

Glancing at it but ignoring it, Byrone said, "You see that pocket there on the sleeve. I didn't notice that at first. That is what you want to try to do with all those other pockets on your clothes."

K-Mac chimed in, "Place the pockets on the side, boy. Byrone, that is not a bad idea. That or go on a pocket diet."

"K-Mac is right. You might want to rethink how many pockets you actually need in your outfit and get rid of a few," Byrone said in agreement.

"What did you put there on the table? Is that a smoking stick?" K-Mac asked as Byrone handed the wand to K-Mac, who began inspecting it.

"It's going to sound far-fetched, but I am laying it out there straight. You are holding a genuine magic wand," I said, which brought an uproar of sound and disbelief.

"Yeah, right, we all got a magic wand, right, Byrone?" K-Mac asked while slapping Byrone's hand.

Looking at K-Mac, Byrone asked, "Let me see that?" and K-Mac handed the wand over to him.

Byrone held up the wand, twisting it around while looking at the inlay, and said, "That is nice work. That is some tiny pearl inlay," before handing it back to me.

"That's my show. A magic act in the future," I said to dead-pan looks.

"I don't know. Aren't magic shows for kids? We do strictly adult-style entertainment," K-Mac said.

"K-Mac is right. Magic is kind of gay, and we don't swing that way," Byrone said. "Not that there is anything wrong with that. If a mofa wants to be that way, that's fine. It's not our way, though."

"What if I could show you a magic that is not gay?" I said a little too shucksterish.

"Come on. Magic isn't even real. That's why it is gay to believe in it," Byrone said frankly.

"This is good. This treatment is what I need, dealing with the heckler. But I can prove that this wand I am holding can duplicate any object you want to set there on the table," I said.

Byrone moved the stack of the money to the center of the table and said, "Duplicate that."

"Okay, there is a magic word, so hands out of the way and sit back," I said.

I waved the wand with a flick, pointed at the money, and said, "*Exemplum.*"

The stack of money jumped and reshuffled itself as the magic spell duplicated every Canadian bill on the table.

"Oh shit, I'm trippin'. Did you see that K-Mac?" Byrone said, raising his hands, signaling that he gave up.

"Word, Byrone. I saw it. Maybe we're both trippin', and we don't know it," K-Mac shot back.

"That's part of the show. Only it takes place in the future," I said, returning the wand to the zippered pocket along my forearm. I started to get a bad vibe out of them when they turned defensive, finally considering me a threat to their life.

"Look, you got to go," Byrone said as he stood up.

I stood up, and so did K-Mac, who said, "It's nothin' personal, dawg. We're just trippin' our asses off and don't even know if you are real."

"Ohm, transport us to the Black Glass Studio lounge in San Francisco," I said.

The room collapsed in on itself, and everything fell to black. I figured if Byrone and K-Mac were really tripping, then this should totally flip their wigs. Tripping affects a Splendorite a bit differently. You do start to trip, but because of the nature of the conscious link to the *Motif*, the *Motif* can start to fulfill your hallucinations and populate echo with real objects that match. Talk about when dreams become reality. At the end of the trip, the Splendorite is never in the same echo where the trip began. Hints of blue and purple overwhelmed the senses while our eyes were put back together, only to find ourselves standing in the center of a large modern lounge.

I finally found a name for the building. Or at least the top floor. Black Glass Studios was to be the name of the production company that broadcasts a unique set of programs with a lens from the past. I wanted K-Mac and Byrone to be that lens and busts all over the watered-down productions I have observed in this time period. I knew they could shake up and stretch the limits of what was truly acceptable to broadcast throughout the entire Union. Rattle the legal framework and challenge the very notion of free speech.

"This is the future part of the show," I said, walking forward and turning around with my arms spread wide, gesturing to the room. I walked over to the window and motioned them over, saying, "And this is our audience."

I pointed out the window at the futuristic city. The two joined me and looked out the window before Byrone finally said, "Kenny, I see flying cars."

"It looks like the set of Star Wars, Byrone," K-Mac replied.

"Yeah, I can see that," Byrone said.

K-Mac turned to me and asked, "Is this shit for real?"

"Not only is it real. It's yours. I'm askin' you both to be my voice in this future. This studio is on the top floor of a black glass high-rise building. I own the entire building. Black Glass Studios, our studio, is your voice in the world of the future. And yes, this is still Earth. We are living in San Francisco, California, in the year 2369. There are flying cars, there are ray guns, and there are alien hotties," I said, stretching out the mention of beautiful women.

This last part of my pitch seemed to have the most appeal for some reason because Byrone rubbed his beard and said to himself, "Alien hotties."

K-Mac made a similar motion and repeated the same thing, "Alien hotties."

"I'm thinking, Byrone," K-Mac said.

"I'm thinking we do it. I mean, fuck if we are trippin', this shit doesn't matter anyway," Byrone said.

"My thoughts exactly," K-Mac said. "What do we do now?"

"Let's return to the lounge," I said, and we walked away from the windows. We took seats on the modular black leather furniture framed in chrome. K-Mac and Byrone sat on the long couch, and I took the chair at the end of the low table sitting in front of them.

"Ohm, create a spherical interface on the table for all to see," I said.

A glowing tech sphere appeared, floating above the table. It slowly drifted and moved up and down, giving the impression that it was levitating. The panels on the surface were of various sizes, either raised or recessed from the sphere's surface.

"You can touch it and move it around," I said as I reached out to the sphere and gave it a quick spin.

K-Mac reached in and stopped it, saying, "Dope."

Byrone reached over and moved it back and forth.

"You can talk directly to it, but you have to say its name first," I said.

"Ohm, recognize K-Mac and Byrone for squire level access to *Tiger Mountain* interface offerings," I said.

"Try asking for a pitcher of water and cups for us all," I said to them both.

"Ah ite. Uhm, this is the kay to the em ay see, and I want a pitcher of cold water for all three," K-Mac said, in rhyme form.

"You said Uhm, instead of Ohm. But I like that," I said. "Ohm, accept input from K-Mac and Byrone using Uhm as an alias for Ohm."

The glowing sphere flashed as it spoke, "New rule in place. You may address me as Uhm."

Byrone spoke up and said, "Uhm, we would like a serving of cold water for three people."

The table sparkled, and three glasses of water appeared. I reached out for mine and took a drink. They hesitated for a moment before picking up their glasses and taking a sip.

"Ohm, create a link between here and K-Mac's trailer," I said.

The glowing orb flashed again, saying, "Link established."

"Byrone, I think the peak is over. I'm thinking this shit might be real," K-Mac said while sipping on his water.

"I'm feelin' that too," Byrone said. "How do we get back home?"

"Just like Dorothy in the Wizard of Oz, ask for it. Ask Ohm to send you back to your home. When you are there, you can ask to be sent here. Ohm will hear you even if you don't see a glowing sphere," I replied.

Byrone set his glass on the table and stood up, saying, "I think we should give it a try. Besides, I don't see any weed here, and I think I need a joint."

K-Mac set his glass down and said, "Let's blow this joint and smoke a joint!"

"Give it a try. Ask the orb," I said.

"Uhm, send us all back home," Byrone said, and once again, we disintegrated into nothing as the blackness crept in like an old friend.

I was not sure where this would lead. I did set up K-Mac and Byrone in a similar role in both future memories. I guess I was continuing to cherry-pick from the timeline again. I wondered if there was a syndrome name for that? The reconstructionist paradox, perhaps? I think my nose was actually assembled before my eyes this time because I could distinctly smell weed. The colors from the inside of K-Mac's trailer streamed in from the sides, and we were back.

Byrone walked around me and sat down on the couch in the same spot where I met him earlier this afternoon. K-Mac immediately went to the table and gathered up the cash before sitting down in the same large chair he plopped into earlier. This motion cleared the table and left space for Byrone to roll a joint. I held my glass of water and took another drink before sitting down on the wooden kitchen chair.

While K-Mac was busy counting, Byrone chopped up weed with a credit card before pulling out a cigarette rolling machine from a cigar box. He located a pack of rolling papers and placed a single sheet in the rolling machine. Placing a generous amount of chopped weed into the rolling machine, he packed it gently down and spread it evenly to distribute it from end to end. Licking one end of the paper and using both thumbs together, he rotated the rolling pins drawing the paper into the machine, wrapping it around the weed. He did this a couple more times until there were three joints on the tray.

"This is how we toast in this house," Byrone said, handing each one of us a joint and taking one for himself.

K-Mac produced a couple of lighters, handing one to me, while Byrone found one in the cigar box.

"To Black Glass," Byrone said.

K-Mac and I echoed him, saying, "To Black Glass," and we all lit up our joints at the same time.

I took a nice long puff and held it in. This weed was good. I finally exhaled and replied, "Damn, that is tasty."

"You know it," K-Mac said, following up. "Any time you need weed."

Byrone finished K-Mac's sentence by saying, "we can get it."

Down the hall, the screen door flapped as someone knocked, and K-Mac said, "Fuck, can't a person have some peace and quiet?"

K-Mac got up to answer the door. I noticed Byrone put his joint out, so I followed suit by dipping my joint into the glass of water. I put the joint into my hip joint pocket and stood up to leave.

K-Mac returned to the room with a couple of dudes and plopped back down in his chair. One said, "Hello," and the other one said, "Hey man."

"I gotta run, fellows," I said and headed off down the hallway, adding, "Black Glass."

I stepped onto the deck. When I walked past the trailer's window, I could hear Byrone say, "Yeah, how much you want?"

I descended the steps and headed to the unpaved road leading to the Meadowland loop. As I walked down the road, I saw a couple of guys heading my way. One was a stocky guy wearing all black. He held a drink in his hand, sipping on it while he walked. The other guy was a bit taller, with a pot-belly, and wore a bowling shirt that was a little too small for his size. It rode up, in the front, revealing his belly button in between steps.

I passed them by, and the taller guy called out to me, "Hey, pocket man, you got a smoke I could bum?"

"No, sorry man. I don't smoke," I said.

"I can smell the fuckin' weed on you from here. Don't tell me you don't smoke," the taller fellow said.

The stockier fellow grabbed his friend and said, "Ronnie, come on, we don't have time for this," and they both ignored me, walking off together, heading toward K-Mac's trailer.

I continued walking toward the park exit and thought about the next thing on my massive "to do" list. In the first time loop, the Flexanite menace was terrible. They flooded through the radionic tile and conquered the Dili sector. In the second time loop, my relentless search and destroy approach only delayed the Flexanite invasion. In that loop, I invented a new type of attack ship that was quite effective against the Hatiss warships.

The concept was a small swarm. Large ships, while effective in large ship to large ship combat rely on their armor and shields against smaller, less armored enemies. But at the heart of most large ships is still a biological crew reviewing the attack in progress and issuing offensive and defensive countermeasures. With my swarm approach, the concept was to overwhelm the large ship's capacity to respond to multiple simultaneous attacks and eventually transport a nuclear bomb on board. These swarm ships were unmanned, so there was no real consequence to me if I lost a few ships during the assault. The only catch was the swarm ships leveraged the Folded Space Link travel algorithms from the Imperial fleet, which has not been discovered yet. I did have the optical projection technique that the drones were leveraging for scanning, but the drones themselves offered no real speed or weapons.

"Ohm, let's create a new attack ship based upon the current design of the cloaked optical drones. I want to use the projection travel method of the drones in a close combat scenario against larger ships. The concept will be a swarm of smaller vessels against a larger opponent. Try to keep the ship size as small as possible. Make them no larger than twice the size of the current drones. They are completely unmanned, so all interior space is available to the designers. Life support is not required. They need to be flux capable with sensors and have an internal transporter system to deliver their payload while receiving new ordnance from Blinn replication facilities. Each drone should carry one nuclear device or more that can be delivered to a target using a transporter. There is no need for a launch mechanism. The ships will require shielding, and if possible, keep the cloaking mechanism intact."

"Preparing tasks for the Blinn engineers. Such a complex request will take time to create. I'll inform you when the proposal produces a timeline for an operational date," Ohm said.

"That sounds good to me. Thank you, Ohm."

I came to a playground inside the trailer park and took a seat at the picnic table. There were no kids around. An older woman walked her little, white-haired dog along the road. She waved at me as she passed by. I waved back and gave her a nod of acknowledgment. Fetching all the vignette cards from my pocket, I decided to take K-Mac's advice of going on a pocket diet. I laid out the vignettes I fetched from the vault over a month ago. In haste, I grabbed about twelve that day. As I reviewed them, I could see that I could get rid of a few. No need to carry them around. I would not want them to fall into the wrong hands anyway. I made two stacks. The ones I kept and the ones I was returning to the vault. The ones going back to the vault were mainly of Splendorite family members I thought I might contact. I realized I did not need to contact any of those people.

One of the vignettes I placed in the keep pile was a card to the medical facility I located in a fast time echo. I called it Xanadu. It was staffed by Blinn physicians with some of the most modern medical technology you could find. There were also living quarters there, and I kept a stable with horses too. I purposely located it in an echo that matched the technological similarities of the Starnet echo.

The time ratio from Xanadu to Splendor was eight to one. This difference meant if you got hurt in Splendor, and traveled to Xanadu to receive treatment, the time you experience in Xanadu would be eight times faster than the time passing in Splendor. In ten minutes of Splendor time, there were eighty minutes of Xanadu time. I set it up this way, so if you got hurt and needed medical attention, less time passed in the world you came from compared to where you were recovering.

The time ratio between Xanadu and various echoes was variable. I know, for a fact, that the current echo where I have the black glass building is running at one point seven-eight times compared to Splendor. That means a week in Xanadu is approximately a day of Starnet time.

Another vignette I placed in the keep pile was of the Lighthouse of Flynn. Flynn was one of the many lighthouses guiding ships along the coast of Splendor. It was a quick way to get close to Splendor without trudging through echo. I also placed an emergency technology cache behind some of the foundation stones at the base of the lighthouse. There was a medkit, a gleam gun, some rations, and a change of clothes, along with some vignettes stored in weatherproof cases This vignette was drafted by Darwin himself, the creator of the first *Motif*, and painted with a unique style.

The third and final card I placed in the keep pile led to the catwalk on the *Deceptive*. I used it the most in recent times and placed it on the top of the stack. I put the keep stack vignettes all in one pocket and said, "Ohm, return these other vignettes to the vault."

There was a sparkle on the table, and the stack of vignettes disappeared, which was exactly what I needed to do. I stood up and stretched for a moment. Inside my invisihud, I located one of the cloaked scanners left on *Oasis Seven*. The cloaked scanners could act as a relay for the transporter system used on *Tiger Mountain*. I flipped through a few of the video feeds and found a cloaked scanner in an unoccupied area before activating the Transfast feature of the invisihud. The sunny day at Meadowland streamed in from the sides, and a black silence enveloped me. I waited, and finally, my eyes perceived a dim lighting as my body reassembled on *Oasis Seven*.

CHAPTER 16

Mr. Pockets

A fter walking the corridors of *Oasis Seven* and checking some of the fixed map plaques I found along the way, I discovered I was in the upper section of the space station. I used the lifts and some stairs to make my way to the concourse. Because this space station was managed by the Starnet Union, it used Earth time for its operations. It was considered late afternoon on board. There was a nearby planet, Vasco, with its own day-night rotation cycle, which was often out of sync with Starnet time.

Making my way around the circular concourse loop, I reviewed the shops I passed by on my first visit. It was a busy spaceport, so quite a few people mingled, looking at wares and purchasing goods. The smell of food was in the air, and my stomach started to growl. It took a couple of loops around the concourse before I finally located the shop Marcus pointed out to me from the upper level. I walked into the tailor's shop and found no one inside. There were garments, both men and women, in various sizes and styles. The selection mainly focused on Vascon styles, but there were other offerings, such as Terran, Adnexo, and Warnock, to name a few. I must have been browsing very quietly because when Marcus emerged from the back room, he looked a bit startled. He quickly offered a smile, as he said, "Ah, my new friend," then paused as if he did not remember my name before finally pulling it out of a hat by completing his sentence, "Sam."

"Marcus, I found myself in need of a tailor, and I immediately thought of you," I said, knowing that Bragorians loved the art of conversation, the exchange, one sentence at a time, of information between two parties.

"How wonderful. What is it that I can do for you?" Marcus replied.

"First, let me apologize for the pungent odor. I was in a smoke-filled lounge an hour ago, and my shirt was made light fun of. I was called Mr. Pockets," I said.

"Oh dear," Marcus frowned.

"They suggested I go on a pocket diet. I considered their input and thought I'd give it a try. Can you alter this shirt to make the pockets less visible?" I asked Marcus, breaking the Bragorian rule of stopping between sentences.

"Can I ask you something?" Marcus asked, then went ahead and asked, now that we were breaking conversational sentence rules. "Is this an indoor and outdoor garment?"

"Yes, and it is a little too thin for outdoor sometimes. Some insulation placed between two layers would not be a bad addition, as well as, moving some pockets to the inside. I do want to keep the two zippered pockets on the outside of the arms. My critics claimed they were less conspicuous, from a front view."

"I can agree with that, and I believe I can alter this garment to your described satisfaction."

I started transferring the vignettes from my shirt pocket to a pocket on my pants. I also moved the wand to the zippered pocket along my pant leg. After removing my shirt, I took a good look at it before handing it to Marcus. Damn, I was Mr. Pockets.

"Do you collect a deposit for the work now?" I asked.

Marcus walked back to the door he emerged from while folding the shirt in front of him. Glancing over he said, "No, three hundred credits will be due in three days. I have a small backlog of work that is in front of your alteration."

"That's fine," I replied a bit louder from across the room as he disappeared into the back area of the store with my shirt.

He emerged with a smile. As he walked toward me, his eyes shifted to something behind me, and I heard a familiar voice ask, "Well, Marcus, are you ready to head over to Lepton's?"

I turned around and saw that it was Brent Stevens asking.

"I'm sorry to cancel on you, Doctor, but I have acquired an amount of work that I must attend to. My friend Sam, here, has come to me for an alteration on his garment," Marcus replied to Brent.

Brent put it together in his head as he noticed I wore a blue sleeveless tank top.

I said, "Oh, sorry to interfere with your plans," looking back and forth at both of them. "Can I buy you a drink to make it up to you?" I asked Brent.

Brent straightened his back, a little put off, but was a fairly easy-going fellow, so he said, "Sure, Sam. That would be great," and then over his shoulder to Marcus as we left. "Let's try again next week."

"Sounds good, Doctor," Marcus replied with cheer.

Brent and I walked off together to locate Lepton's. It was not very far from the tailor shop, and I saw the sign after twenty or thirty meters. To get the conversation going, I asked, "How was your week?"

Brent walked in silence, looking at the floor. He gave off the vibe that he wished he wasn't walking next to an orgamorphic gel scoundrel, then he looked up and said, "Oh, kind of quiet. I have been using the time to catch up on reading some new papers, you know, continuing research kind of stuff."

"Yeah, there is always something else to learn," I said.

"And how about you? What have you been up to since we last shared a round," Brent asked as we walked into Lepton's.

Before I could answer, I was greeted by Lepton, himself, as he walked around from the bar quickly, while looking around nervously and said with a quiver in his voice, "Sam, there you are."

"Lepton, I hope I still have some credit here? I'm looking to order some food and drink for myself and Brent. Put it all on my tab," I said.

He patted me on the back, escorting Brent and myself quickly away from the entrance while saying, "Of course, of course. Let me show you to your table."

He led us to the back of the bar, where a metal spiral staircase led to an upper level. He guided us along the balcony to a two-top table overlooking the first level.

Brent asked, "Is there something wrong, Lepton?"

"Oh no, no, just surprised to see new faces again," he said to Brent, then turned to me and whispered, "I'll catch up with you later."

"I'll send a waiter over immediately," Lepton said, and he quickly headed off and down the spiral stairs.

"Boy is he an odd one," Brent said, and I shook my head in agreement as I picked up one of the menus on the table.

Most of the items on the menu were for other species. I wasn't really sure what a lot of the ingredients were or if humans could actually eat them. I put the food menu down and took a look at the drinks menu. I was in a similar quandary. Most of the drinks were named after planets or space phenomena. There was the Adnexo Ale, Rishar Rush, Vasconian Volcano, Mercanite Sludge, and so many more that I put the menu down. Our young Drologo waiter arrived and asked, "What can I get ya?"

Brent went first and addressed the waiter personally, "Oh, hello, Bat. Can I have an English ale and a chicken Cesar salad?"

Bat tapped on a small tablet in his hand as Brent spoke, then he looked at me and asked, "And, what can I get for you?"

"How about a New York Ruben on rye toast with a crisp pickle on the side and a double-order of small-batch potato chips. I'll have a Scottish ale if you've got one."

"Got it," Bat said before walking off while tapping the device a few more times.

I repeated the question Brent asked as we walked in, saying, "What have I been up to this past week?"

"I finally did find a viable gel sample, so my invention is now in the design slash production phase. I am hoping to try one out soon," I said.

"I don't really feel comfortable talking about that subject," Brent said.

"Oh, sorry. I also hired some agents to help me with self-promotion. They suggested that I reduce the pocket count on my shirt. That is why I went to Marcus, to get it altered," I said, trying to change the subject.

"Why didn't you just buy another shirt? That would probably be cheaper." Brent said.

"Probably so. I typically make my own clothes, but how often do you meet a tailor who happens to come up to you to say hello?" I said. "And the very next week, you are seriously thinking about altering your clothes? I thought I'd give it a try. Let someone else make a clothing design choice for me."

Before Brent could reply, an all too familiar voice walked up from behind and said, "Hi, Brent. Who's your friend?"

"Oh, hello, Jorrie. This is Sam," Brent said, before turning to me, gesturing to each of them, "and Sam, this is Jorrie Tusk and Mia Nasal."

I looked up into the eyes of Jorrie Tusk. They were a clear sea-blue-green with light mascara around them. There were colors, in her Vosip eyes, that human women would never have. Her eyebrows were tucked and well-trimmed. Her lashes were naturally long, as are most Vosip. I pushed my chair back and slowly stood up to face her, keeping my eyes locked to hers as I rose. I noticed her long black hair was pulled back, as she often wore it while working. When it was let down, it flowed over her shoulders and down her back. Along a Vosip's hairline and down the sides of the neck are markings similar to a leopard's spots. They are unique to each individual ranging from blotches to intricate vine-looking structures reminiscent of ivy. The markings travel all along the body, down to the groin area, and frame the sex organ before descending down the legs to end at the ankle. Erin and I would often kiss Jorrie's markings and even came up with playful names for some of the shapes. Jorrie's markings, which Vosips call "appeal," were quite beautiful and intricate.

I held out my hand with my heart beating heavy in my ears as time seemed to slow down for a moment and said, "I'm Sam. Sam Richards."

She took my hand and politely shook it, but I saw that look more than once cross her face. It was the look of intrigue and uncertainty.

"I'm Jorrie, and this is Mia," she said, breaking my gaze and looking over at her friend.

I extended my hand to Mia and said, "Nice to meet you," before sitting down and trying not to look up at her.

Mia spoke to Brent, "Jorrie finally talked me into trying out one of the aurasuite games, so we're heading down there now. What are we playing?"

"Handball," Jorrie replied.

"Sounds like fun. Enjoy your time," Brent said.

The two women walked off, and I watched Jorrie for a moment or two. She and Mia talked fast and hushed, reminding me of schoolgirls gossiping. Jorrie glanced back at me just before descending the stairway. I let out a soft, "Whoa."

Brent smiled and said, "Yes, Jorrie. That's the woman for me."

"What a beauty. Talk about knock your socks off," I said playfully.

Bat returned with our drinks and sat them down in front of us on the table. Brent sipped his ale, and I tried mine. It was awful. It tasted more like a pilsner than a Scottish ale.

"Brent, do you remember when I told you I was a probability traveler?" I asked.

"I do, but I still don't really know exactly what you mean by that," he replied.

"Can I give you a small demonstration? You don't have to do anything but observe." I asked.

"Sure, show me how it works," Brent said, leaning back on the two legs of his chair.

"Ohm, replace our drinks on the table with two new drinks. Make Brent's an English ale from the Talbot's pub location and make mine a Scottish ale from the Shiftman's location," I said.

Sparkles replaced our two drinks with two new drinks of different sizes and colors. These were pint glasses. Brent flailed his arms to catch his balance, as he almost fell over backward when the two ales sparkled out of and back into existence.

"You can't issue site-to-site transports on this station," Brent said.

"It's not even detectable, other than the visible sparkle, so calm down," I said before picking up my ale and slurping the foam from the top of the pint. I nodded my head that Brent should do the same, and he picked up his pint and took a sip of the foam. His expression changed to a happier mood, and I said, "Yours is called Boddington, and mine is called Belhaven."

"Wow, that is some of the creamiest foam I have ever tasted," Brent said. "But I still don't see how a site-to-site transport makes you a probability traveler?"

"Well, your ale actually came from an English pub on Earth, circa nineteen eighty-five. While mine came from a Scottish pub on Earth, circa nineteen ninety-six. I have placed cloaked transport enhancers at the probable locations to target the pubs. Right now, a server in the past is probably bugging the bartender for another pint because she's come up one short on her order. You and I are effectively drinking stolen ale from the past," I said.

"So, now, you're a time traveler too?" Brent asked while sipping on his drink.

"As a probability traveler, time is just another location to me, similar to the way a planet is to you. You could go there and be there, but when you are there, it is just like any other place," I said vaguely.

"That does not really make it any clearer," Brent said.

"Okay, what about sub-space? There have been a few reports of sub-space ventures, most of them go wrong. When humans enter certain sub-space pockets, they encounter an environment that can be harsh to survival. Sometimes the change is not just to the physical body but to the psychological perception. Distortions in perception are cited in several of the reports. What causes that? Is it the mechanics of the physical universe? Is it sub-space itself? Is it the way each individual processes the experience?"

Brent shrugged and continued to sip the foam.

"There was Arould Chai, who made a solo journey into sub-space to return with a tale of enlightenment. Afterward, he could accelerate plant growth by simply touching them," I said.

Brent interrupted, "Yes, I believe I read something about that. It sounded unbelievable to me, but with an open mind, I guess these kinds of anomalies are bound to occur."

"What if sub-space is like Swiss cheese spinning? If you time your entry just right, you'll hit a hollow space and have a good time, like Arould. But if you miss the empty space," I said

And Brent completed my sentence, "you'll hit a wall."

"And have a bad time," I added.

Bat arrived with our food and put the plates on the table. It smelled delicious.

"Can I get you two anything else?" Bat asked.

"Nothing for me. Thank you, Bat," I said to Bat before looking over at Brent, saying, "I got a double order of chips. I thought we could share."

"Oh, thank you. I'll try them," Brent said as he tossed the Caesar salad to distribute the dressing a little better.

My Ruben was cut in half for me, which was great because this thing was stacked high with corned beef and melted Swiss. The bread was a little thin for the wetness factor of the steamy meat, melted Swiss, and sauerkraut. I had to be careful not to break the bread while I was eating it.

"So, you placed these transport enhancers in a pub just so you could steal ale with a site-to-site transport?" Brent asked.

"Precisely. I located the pubs by physically walking through probability. Once I arrived, I installed the transport enhancer and then returned to my home. That was hundreds of years ago, though. I walked all of the United Kingdom and Ireland locating the best ales and whiskey, installing transport enhancers at the best pubs," I said.

"Hundreds of years ago? How old are you, Sam?" Brent asked with his fork stopped in mid-air.

"I'm eight hundred and thirty-seven years old, Splendor time," I said.

"That's incredible, Sam," Brent said, and he resumed eating his chicken salad.

I finished up my first half of the sandwich and picked up the pickle to give it a taste. Not as crisp as I like, but still an acceptable New York sandwich accompaniment.

Brent took a sip of ale to clear his throat and asked, "How long-lived is your species?"

I took another sip and said, "My oldest sibling is over ten thousand years old. No one really knows how old Nicolas really is. At eight hundred and thirty-seven, I am the baby of our species."

"How many of you are there?" Brent asked while putting together another salad bite on his fork.

"There are so few of us that I don't really want to say," I said while reaching out and taking a small hand full of chips.

"Oh, sorry for getting too personal. I apologize," Brent said before reaching for some chips. Brent spoke, and sounded like Marcus in his phrasing mannerisms when he said, "I find our conversations fascinating, Sam. Even if I never experience your probability ability."

"Well, we could try a simple test. I'm having a small balcony party soon, and I would like to invite you. I have a site-to-site transport enhancer here and on

Earth. My place is in San Francisco, California. That's where the party is taking place."

"You're inviting me to San Francisco through a site-to-site transporter?" Brent asked, a little disbelieving.

"Yes, I'll send you a formal invitation. I'm still working on the guest list. I hope you have the time to attend. I realize service duties come first."

"I agree to your first test. If you can site-to-site transport me to San Francisco and back, I will come to your balcony party and enjoy the view," Brent said with a smile.

What I was about to say was interrupted by Brent's communication brooch, "Brent Stevens, please report to the infirmary."

He touched his brooch and said, "On my way."

Brent used a napkin to wipe off his mouth and said, "I have to go, duties, but I'll keep an eye out for your invitation," and he walked off from the table and back down the stairs.

I got up after Brent left and walked along this upper-balcony to the upper-level exit. There was a dogleg bend in the passage to some stairs leading up. This short hallway was empty, so I asked, "Ohm, transport me back home."

The corridor dissolved as my eyes disassembled again. I couldn't believe how quickly I went from being relaxed to being totally overwhelmed with anxiety upon meeting Jorrie. I almost froze in place. I felt paralyzed upon seeing her beauty. But it was like seeing something through a window. You could only see it was there, but you could not have it. Not yet, at least. My eyes reassembled to a beautiful pink and orange cloud-filled sunset as I looked out the glass balcony doors into the San Francisco bay.

CHAPTER 17

Broadcast One

I should have brought the rest of my drink with me, was my next thought. Dealing with the business of murder was not a task I looked forward to. In my future memories, I developed a profile for Flexanites and their modus operandi. With this first one, there was no previous data to draw upon. I knew Flexanites typically hid the remains of their victims near the crime scene, but that was all there was to go on.

"Ohm, can you scan public records for Jeremy Stewart and generate a possible map of movements over the last month or so?" I asked.

"Working," Ohm replied.

"Focus on his daily routines and his route from home to work. Feel free to hack into private databases or Starnet records but don't trigger alarms."

Data started flowing into my invisihud, and I took a seat on the couch. I was able to see the map of Starnet headquarters and the building where Jeremy worked. There was also a separate feed from another cloaked scanner locating his home residence somewhere in Arizona. I spent time guiding the cloaked scanners to places I thought were worth conducting detailed scans of, but none of them produced a hit. I got excited for a moment when remains were found in the back yard, but they turned out to be animal remains. I guess Jeremy buried his dog there.

Ohm couldn't find any evidence of a consistent route to work. It looked like, as a modern man, Jeremy did not travel by vehicles if he could avoid it. Instead, he seemed to favor site-to-site transports. His business led him all over the globe with transporter logs indicating visits to Kyoto, Helsinki, Vancouver, Rio de Janeiro, London, Cape Town, Mumbai, New Delhi, Orbital space platforms, and the moon base. These locations represented a lot of area to search.

"Ohm, let's examine any local reports on Jeremy's visits around the world. Look for clues. Check if he was late, missed an event, or some type of rescheduling occurred," I said.

The cloaked scanner I used to transport Flexanite Jeremy to the holding cell was still in place in his office. I reviewed the video feed and noticed his female assistant entered the office several times and used his terminal to pull up information before leaving the room to return to her workstation. I repositioned the cloaked scanner to target and track her. Her occupation was a desk job involving screen work and managing communication traffic coming into the office.

Realizing it could take days, weeks, or even months to comb through all the leads that Ohm quickly generated, I set it aside and shut down the invisihud for now.

The future memories I experienced so vividly from a month ago already started to fade as I feared they might. While I could remember the big details, it was more like a scrapbook of memories rather than a complete log of events. I managed to contact most of my close friends from the previous loops, but there were also some dear acquaintances that I had not met yet. It was weird, waiting for things to unfold, as well as stressful.

Heading to the bedroom, I said, "Ohm, populate my closet with clothing styles from this era."

I rifled through a series of shirts, long and short sleeves, but was most interested in the casual jackets with pockets. A black one caught my eye, and I put it on before walking out of the apartment and down the hall to the elevator. I pressed the button to open the doors and stepped into the lift. The button for the Black Glass Studios was at the top of a stack of other buttons on the panel offering numeric access to the various floors. The elevator began to rise, and it was not long until I found myself at the entrance to Black Glass Studios. I walked up to the doors, which were made of black glass framed by thick chrome. As I approached, they opened automatically to a waiting room with a stylized desk. The entire room design looked like an ocean wave, made out of blond wood and chrome. The desk was curved, and a prominent part of the wave flowed through the reception area.

There was a short hallway leading away from the reception area and past the restrooms to a curved stairway leading up. This stairway was double-wide, with a railing in the center and one attached to each wall. I hopped, skipped, and ran up the stairs until I came to the large open lounge where I met with K-Mac and Byrone a night or two ago.

Diving into my invisihud, I located the environment designer icon. In this mode, I could block out constructions inside the invisihud overlay and choose real objects to represent those blocks during the replication phase. This virtualization allowed me to quickly build a wall, make a bridge, or in this case, a stage. The seating area of the lounge offered a recessed floor. All around were small sets of steps leading up. In the back of the room, I projected a wide, deep platform hanging over the steps. This alignment provided a raised stage in the front. You could easily take the steps up, from either side, to get on stage. I replicated a Tama Swing Star drum kit on a raised platform, placing it in the center of the stage but far enough back to allow singers and musicians performance room in the front. I replicated a DJ workstation and placed a stack of speakers on either side of the stage.

I tried out the mic, "Testing one, two. Aw yeah."

I was in the middle of getting my kick pedal set up and adjusted when I heard, "Boyee, K-Mac's in the house. What up, dawg?"

I looked up, and Byrone and K-Mac returned to the Black Glass Studios. I stood up with the drum stick in my hand and asked, "What do you think? You ready to kick out some jams?"

They walked closer and looked up at me from the front of the stage before Byrone asked, "You play the drums?"

I said, "I practice the drums. It has been a while, so I thought I better get back to it. Do you guys feel like trying something out? You know, check out the gear and kick out a sound-check?"

"You know it, dawg?" K-Mac said, and he quickly made his way around to the side of the stage.

He took the steps up and jumped around in front of the drum riser. Byrone took the other side and found his way to the DJ podium. He flipped through a few albums and handed a mic to K-Mac before picking one up for himself.

"Byrone, you control the volume, there at your mixer. Turn it up louder if the drums are too much," I said.

"Got it," he said while putting a record on the turntable and dropping the needle.

Byrone spun us through several albums and songs, making good use of the cross-fade dual turntable system. He kept the beats going the entire time while switching out records. K-Mac free-form rapped over top the sound and often just sang along to the record if Byrone let the album drift into lyrics rather than beats. What is weird is that I did not take up playing the drums until a few years ago in my future memories. I did not know how to play the drums, but my future self did. I discovered I was able to pull in some of my previous training rather quickly. Leveraging the stick-in-hand exercises that I spent months, if not years on, was almost immediate. My hands were not used to drumming, so they started to hurt much sooner than I remembered from my future memories. This ache didn't bother me. I was able to keep a beat.

Afterward, K-Mac said, "Damn, dawg, you got right in there."

Byrone said, "Yeah, not bad for a first jam."

"I forgot how much fun it is to just rock out. My body feels so good after playing the drums, but I know I need to keep working at it," I said.

Byrone said, "We're still coming to terms with the fact that this place is real. We thought we'd come check it out again to make sure we weren't trippin'."

"That's right, and now that we are here, I'm flying through the roof. Talk about feelin' good. I am walking on sunshine," K-Mac said as he made his way over to the window to take another look.

"Come check this shit out in the day, Byrone," K-Mac said, and Byrone walked over to the windows too.

I put down my drum sticks and walked over to the window. "Somewhere out there is an alien hottie for us all. And this world is about to be flipped upside down with the new styling's coming from Black Glass Studios," I said.

"Word," said Byrone.

"We bout to hit em with styling's from the past so fast that they gonna wonder what was that?" K-Mac busted out in rhyme form.

"This place is yours, so don't hesitate to hang out as long as you want. You can bring guests, but they won't be able to leave this floor. You'll have to use Uhm to transport people back and forth. That means they are vulnerable and relying upon you to get back home when they are here. Ohm won't transfer guns or weapons. You can tell people that up-front. It's not your policy. It's mine."

"We don't have a problem with that. K-Mac and I don't do guns," Byrone said.

"That's right, and I can dig where you're comin' from as far as guests are concerned," K-Mac said.

"Follow me," I said, and I started walking while K-Mac and Byrone followed behind.

"Behind that kitchen area, off to my left, there are a set of suites. You can spend the night and so can your guests. I have an apartment downstairs on floor twenty-three. The suites have bathrooms, but there are also a set of public restrooms for guests in the hallway at the bottom of those steps. The kitchen is automatically stocked from local grocery stores in the San Francisco bay area, so check the news and ads to see what is available. You can alter what gets stocked by talking to Uhm," I said.

I continued walking past the newly constructed stage to some double-wide doors in the back. These doors were framed frosted glass and brightly illuminated because of the time of day. I walked up to the doors and said, "Recognize squire K-Mac and squire Byrone for doorway permission."

"So, why did you call us squires?" Byrone asked.

"It's just a title that represents a security level. If you bring guests, they will have the title of patron and won't be able to open these doors. But you and K-Mac will," I said as the doors slid open.

As we walked forward, the walls to either side sloped down to the floor, which became the roof of the high-rise building. Before the walls completed their final slope, there were doors on either side leading to small rooms that might be considered blinds if they were in the woods. I guess whoever owned this building before placed armed guards here to make sure the building was not invaded from the roof. We walked to the center of the roof, and I spoke loudly over the sound of the high winds saying, "There is nothing out here except this landing pad."

The winds were strong enough and unpredictable enough that I would not feel very safe standing near the edge of the roof even though there was a security railing around the perimeter. We headed back inside as the wind ruffled our clothing.

"Ohm, lock doors," I said, then looked at them, adding, "I didn't want you guys to wonder what was behind those doors. Hopefully, you can see why it is a good idea to keep them off-limits."

"Word, safety first," K-Mac said while Byrone nodded.

Walking over to the side of the room with the windows, I headed to a door at the other end of a short ramp.

"This is the broadcast booth. Come on in and check it out," I said as I opened and held the door for them while they walked in.

This room was a more personal space, like the client area of a control room if you have ever been in a recording studio. There were large screens forming a grid displaying the currently live broadcasts from thousands of networks in hundreds of languages. A network would appear, for a moment, in one of the grid slots before rotating to reveal another network. I pointed at the screen and said, "This is your window into the world of the Starnet Union of planets."

"You can go live from this spot, and it will broadcast to tons of worlds. The process also offers an automatic conversion feed to other languages, like closed caption TV," I said.

"This is sweet," Byrone said as he looked around at the gear.

Then K-Mac got ahead of me, asking, "What's in there, dawg?"

There was a door at the back of this small control room leading to a larger area with lights, rigging, and auraprojectors positioned around the room. We walked into the center of the room, and I said, "This is your stage. It is an aura-graphic projection area where you can create settings for whatever you want to do. You can visit another city or another planet without leaving Black Glass Studios."

"How does it work?" Byrone asked.

"This whole setup works by using your voice. Try something like this. Uhm, give me a beach scene," I said, and the tech guts of the room became obscured as the auraprojectors kicked into operation to present a believable beach scene. It was warm. You could smell the nearby water, and virtual people sunbathed on the beach having drinks.

"Whoa," Byrone said.

"Dang, dawg, is this shit for real?" K-Mac added.

"Actually, it's not, but you can touch it. The people aren't real, but you can interact with them as long as you stay in this room," I said. "Now you try? Ask for Meadowland to be recreated here."

K-Mac spoke up, "Ah ite. Uhm, make this room a copy of the Meadowland trailer park."

The beach scene faded and morphed into an exact copy of the Meadowland Mobile Home park. We stood on the dirt road leading to K-Mac's trailer.

"Fuck, this is blowin' my mind. We're in the future recreating the past," Byrone said.

"Now we just have to blow all their minds out there with flavor from the past," I said.

"Ohm, add the projection frame to the room," I said, and a large floating screen appeared, showing us standing within the aurastage environment.

"What's that?" Byrone asked while looking up at the screen.

"That is what the world sees when you broadcast. I call it the projection frame," I said.

K-Mac waved his hands and danced around a bit while trying to watch himself at the same time.

"That's too far away. Our show should be up-close and personal," Byrone said.

I looked at him with a shrug, and before I could answer, he said, "Use your voice."

"Use your voice," I repeated. "There are a lot of different camera presets you can check out. Have some fun. You can hang out and explore them. When you are ready to go live, let Ohm know, and you can begin broadcasting."

"Can we go live now?" K-Mac asked.

Byrone and K-Mac looked at one another, then at me, and I said, "Why not? Let's give it a try. I'll adjust the projection frame to zoom in closer."

I used my invisihud to target the projection frame, and it became a video plate inside my overlay. I zoomed in and moved it around until the boys took up most of the frame. I chose auto-target and zoomed out of the projection frame before dismissing the invisihud.

"Yeah, that is a lot better," Byrone said as he noticed the revised framing.

"What do you say, Byrone? Do you want to turn this mother out?" K-Mac asked.

"For sho," Byrone said. "Uhm, broadcast live on the count of three. One, Two, Three."

"Yo, this is Byrone and K-Mac here rapping to you future people live from Meadowland trailer park, the best trailer park in the world," K-Mac busts out.

"That's right, we're personally inviting you into our lives so you can see how real people live in the real world," Byrone said.

"This is our premiere broadcast. Where you can say, yo dawg, I saw it here first. I was there when K-Mac and Byrone busted onto the future scene. With a flavor that is so damn soft," K-Mac looked over at Byrone like he was handing off a mic.

"And sweet," said Byrone.

"Smokey," said K-Mac.

"Like hash," said Byrone.

"On the street," said K-Mac.

"We hide our cash," said Byrone.

They went back and forth like that as they walked up to K-Mac's trailer until, finally, one of them fell short. The rhyme broke down, and they both busted out laughing.

"Damn, dawg. I think we got like eleven bounces off that one," K-Mac said.

"It's like a tennis volley," Byrone replied.

Then with a big open arm, K-Mac invited the whole damn future into his trailer. I was monitoring the network feed on another smaller display, so I was off frame and not within the frustum of the projection screen. I pulled up the *Motif* before me and paced in a circle as I pushed all probable threads from other broadcasters to the side. This modification allowed our show to flow through to the farthest planets in the Starnet Union. Even some of the outer colonies and space stations picked us up. I fussed even more with the *Motif*, so people were actually engaged in the program. Grabbing the universe with my mind, I made the slightest nudge so when people saw the show, they wanted to see it again. K-Mac called out, "Yo, Sam, get over here. We about to light up his joint."

I entered the virtual trailer door and took a right as I did in the real world, but I was still outside the projection frame. I knocked on the wall as I stepped into view.

"Check it out, people. The man of the hour. The one that's makin' it happen, Saaymmm," K-Mac said, introducing me with a gesture from his hands while sitting in his favorite chair.

"Hey Union, what's up. I came over to hang out with my boys and check out their great new show," I said as I took the crappy uncomfortable wooden kitchen chair sitting in front of the coffee table.

Byrone spoke, as he used the machine to roll up the joint, "This here is Sam. He set us up with the gear to do the show, and we're bringin' it to you as often as we can. This show is our life for real. Nothing is staged or faked. We live like this."

"Damn straight, Byrone. I ain't seen a lot of the future, so I am hopin' to hook up with some future honey's out there. Ladies, we both single," K-Mac said with open arms.

"So don't come up to us frontin'. We don't play that. We like women that are real," Byrone said, popping the joint out of the rolling machine.

"Too boss women, for sure," I said as Byrone lit up the joint.

Byrone took a couple of puffs on it, passed it to K-Mac, and began speaking while he blew out smoke, "Sometimes the show is gonna be like this. Us, just chillin', but you're welcome to hang with us. We don't mind."

K-Mac handed the joint to me and said, "This is how we keep it real. We know you're alone out there. Hell, we're alone too. All we got is each other, and we ain't that way, but we're still looking to hook up with the ladies."

I took a long drag, handed the joint to Byrone, and said, "Damn, that tastes good. Thanks for doing this, fellows. I know it sounded far-fetched, a magic show in the future, but we made it to episode one."

Byrone passed the joint to K-Mac and said, "I had my doubts. I had my doubts for sure on this one. I didn't even believe the future existed. I mean, not like this where you can visit. But you pushed us on."

K-Mac handed the joint to me and said, "What did we pay for those flyers? Like two dollars and eighteen cents?" K-Mac said as he coughed.

"That's right. We were scrounging for coins on the floor to get enough money to print out twenty-four copies," Byrone added.

"And when I saw that flyer, I knew, I'll just say it. I knew that you two were the ones to make all this happen," I said, talking and holding the joint, which did not go unnoticed.

Byrone nodded, holding out his hand for the joint. He puffed a couple of times before reaching into the cigar box on the table and pulling out a roach clip. He attached the joint to the alligator clip, handed the clip to K-Mac before picking up a remote control device and leaning back into the couch.

Reggae music started playing, and the voice on the song sang out, "Get up, stand up."

K-Mac handed me the roach, which was about gone. I took a puff, then killed it, setting it in the ashtray on the table.

"Why do I love Reggae music so much? It is one of the most fun beats to play," I said.

"I heard some reggae kickin' out of that drum kit today," K-Mac said.

"For real, man. You're an all right drummer now, but if you practice up, you'll be out of sight," Byrone said.

"Do you mind if I leave them set up in the lounge out there?" I asked.

Byrone made a face like, what are you kidding. Then K-Mac said, "You can leave them set up as long as you like."

"Feel free to hit around on them. I feel musical instruments should be played, not looked at," I said.

K-Mac said, "Dang, dawg, Byrone, and I feel the same way. We got some gear we could hook into the speaker stacks."

Byrone said, "We got keyboards, compressors, and amps and shit."

"Feel free to modify the gear anyway you like. That was just my quick, get it up and running, setup. Some sound guys really know their stuff, though," I said.

K-Mac pointed to Byrone and said, "Freddie, am I right? Freddie is a friend, maybe just an acquaintance of ours, that has done some sound for our shows."

Byrone nodded his head when K-Mac spoke and said, "Freddie knows his stuff. I could always hear myself in the monitors when Freddie did our sound."

"Not like Barry and Noah, damn," K-Mac said.

Byrone laughed a bit and said, "Barry and Noah act like they know sound, but they can't mix worth a shit. And they don't understand power distribution either."

"I'm eager to take a look at the stats. Do you want to keep the show going or take a break?" I asked.

K-Mac said, "I could take a break."

Byrone said, "We have to sign out, though."

"Right," K-Mac agreed.

"This is Byrone," Byrone said.

"And this is K-Mac signing off," K-Mac said.

"The magic show in the future," I said.

"Black Glass," Byrone said.

"Peeace," K-Mac finally added.

I shut down the transmit of the feed using my invisihud, and we all gathered around the stats display to take a look. Byrone asked, "Are we off the air now?"

"Yeah, I hope you don't mind. I cut the feed when we got up," I replied.

"Dang, dawg, I don't know a lot about math, but we got numbers on a bunch of planets," K-Mac said.

"It does look surprisingly good for a first episode," I said as I started touching the display and moving some panels. I flipped a few pages and looked at a breakdown for Mars. There was good stream acceptance, and most streams presented a seventy to ninety percent retention span.

Byrone said, "Damn, that does look good. Does it really mean that people are watching our show?"

"I think it does. And not only are they tuning in to it, they like what they see enough to keep watching it," I said.

"Fuck, Byrone, we going straight to the top!" K-Mac said as he slapped Byrone's hand enthusiastically.

"I'm sorry to smoke and run, but I feel like I've gotta lie down for a while. I have been in a few different time zones, and it is finally catching up with me," I said.

"No problem, thanks for setting this gig up for us. I mean it," Byrone said.

"Get some rest, dawg. We'll broadcast again soon," K-Mac said as he slapped my hand, and we all bumped shoulders.

"You don't need me to broadcast. The broadcast button is right here," I said, pointing to the large red circular button on the wall.

"When it's lit, you are on the air, and when it's dim, you are off the air," I said, and I took my leave of the room as they began talking among themselves.

I made my way back through the lobby and down the hall to the elevator. I returned to the floor of my apartment. Heading inside, I lie down on the bed. Fuck I was high. Those two do have amazing weed. I needed to think about what I really should do next? Now that my future memories are starting to fade, I'm not sure what the next steps are? And somehow, I have this nagging feeling that I might have forgotten somebody?

CHAPTER 18

I must have drifted off. I awoke to another day of living in the past. The morning shower felt good. Yesterday's drum session left me with a mild case of the funk. Afterward, I freshened my clothes and fetched some breakfast through Ohm. While pulling up a few of the planetary news feeds inside my invishud, I saw the same headline across many networks. Starnet established two-way communication with the lost ship *Journey* in the Gar sector. An image of the crew gathered in the shuttle bay accompanied the story.

"Ohm, can I get a printed copy of the image of the crew, along with the headline?" I asked.

A sparkle appeared on the counter, leaving behind a color print and the news story about making contact with the ship. I was not mentioned once, which was great, as far as I was concerned. Looking over the faces in the photo, I saw him in the middle row on the left, standing next to Brandon Palmer. Ethan wore a smile on his face like many of the other crew members in the photo. I decided this would be my first task of the day.

After brushing my teeth, I headed back to the kitchen counter, where I picked up the photo article and said, "Ohm, transport me to Enki's Dale."

The bright San Francisco morning fizzled out of view to be replaced by darkness and silence. As I made these various acquaintances, I started to feel an obligation to follow up with them. I was highly reluctant when Ethan asked about starships at the party, but it did happen in each of my future memories, and it did not lead to catastrophe. Still, I knew a father separated from his family could have an adverse effect on the other members of his family. I wanted to check-in and see how they were doing. A grey mist crept into view as my eyes reassembled.

It was a foggy morning in Enki's Dale as I made my way down the dirt road past Candy's house on the left and Nick and Madison's off to the right. I thought the walk would do me good. The morning air carried the scent of pines, and I listened to the various creatures in the woods off to the left. There was a wide empty field off to the right, and through the fog, I could make out the silhouettes of tall trees beyond the field. That place was known as the Somber Woods, and some terrible things happened to Alex and Candy in those woods during the first time loop. It wasn't long until I came to the Foster's post box and headed up the walkway to Ethan and Olivia's house. I could hear the sounds of running and screaming from inside as I stepped up on the porch and knocked at the door. There was the sound of small feet running up to the door before it was swung wide open by a little girl. Her name was Lulu. She said, "Sam!"

"Mom! Sam is at the door," Lulu yelled back into the house before turning to me. "Albert has a newt, and it got loose in the house."

Just then, I heard a voice, "Close the door. I don't want him to get out."

Albert Foster was pretty much a spitting image of Ethan at that age. Although I never knew Ethan as a boy, the resemblance from family photos was striking, with the main difference being that Albert did not need to wear glasses. He noticed me standing there and said, "Sam, come in, quick. I don't want my newt to escape."

I stepped inside, checking the floor as I did so. I did not want to step on the newt or let it out. After I entered, Lulu used both hands to shut the door. Olivia walked out from the kitchen wearing an apron, asking, "What is going on with the door?"

When she saw me standing in the entryway, she said, "Sam."

"Hello, Olivia. I have some news about Ethan."

Olivia looked worried and asked, "Is he all right?"

"Oh, yes, yes. He's fine. In fact, he has made front-page news on some of Earth's broadcasts," I said, handing the article with the photo to Olivia.

She quickly read through the article while Lulu tugged at her apron, asking, "What does it say, Mommy?"

Ignoring her daughter for a moment, as she skimmed the article, she finally said, "It says Daddy's ship was able to send a message back to Earth."

"Like a pigeon?" Lulu asked.

"Yep, like a pigeon. Only Daddy's ship is so far away that even a pigeon can't fly that far," she told Lulu as she knelt to show her the photo.

It took Lulu a minute to find her father in the photo before pointing at him and saying, "I see him right there."

Albert moved around to look at the image, too, but became impatient and grabbed the article out of his mother's hand, saying, "Let me see that."

"Don't rip it, Albert," Lulu said to her brother as Olivia stood up.

"There he is," Albert said while looking at the photo before glancing over at me. "Is he really on a spaceship?"

"Yes, the ship he's aboard is called *Journey*."

"Oh, look, there's Marzipan!" Lulu pointed excitedly.

Albert handed the photo back to his mother, and the two children headed off into the other room in pursuit of the escaped newt, Marzipan.

"Thanks for bringing this by, Sam. Come on into the kitchen. I have some things I have to keep an eye on," Olivia said.

I followed Olivia into the kitchen and once again marveled at how magicians conducted their daily lives compared to non-magical folk. In the end, it was all the same, but what I used technology to accomplish, magicians used magic spells. The clock on the wall displayed only one hand, and it seemed to jump around. Instead of numbers, there were phrases rewriting themselves on the surface of the clock face. The hour hand pointed to the phrase baking for the Wand Girl's Society. An invisible force moved the rolling pin to flatten the dough. The home gnome from the party stamped out circular shapes with a cup and placed them inside a baking pan. A large wood-fired oven was in use. It heated the room up nicely.

"I wanted to check in and see if everything is working out with you and Ethan's new arrangement?" I asked while Olivia bent down to look through the glass of the oven door at some rising dough items, trying to determine their readiness.

She turned and looked at me while standing up and said, "Brilliantly. The rings you gave us are working great, and I did get the passage card you left on the table. Ethan told me how it works, and we were able to meet up in the apartment. The kids could not believe their eyes when they looked out the window at the city. It really means a lot to them to be able to see their father like that."

"That's good to hear," I said.

A small mechanical bird made of wooden parts gave off a gentle repeating cuckoo. Olivia touched the top of the bird to stop the sound. Grabbing a nearby oven mitt, she opened the oven, took out a pan of golden brown biscuits, and placed them on a cooling rack on the table filled with baking supplies.

While focusing on her work and using a pastry bag to drizzle white icing over the hot biscuits, she asked, "What about you? Are you doing okay? Ethan told me what you said to his Captain about searching for your wife who is missing in time."

I didn't mind that Ethan told Olivia about that part. I did not know Olivia as well as Ethan, but I wouldn't expect a husband and wife to keep secrets.

"Thanks for asking. I am doing my best to locate her. It's not that she is lost in time. It is simply that I have not met her yet," I said. "It's more like me that is lost in time."

"Well, please know that you are more than welcome here if you find yourself eating alone or just want the company," she said, with a smile that was in no way flirtatious. She placed a new pan of dough into the oven and picked up her wand from the kitchen table. Flicking it at the mechanical wooden bird, she started rocking with her spell by saying, "Saxum."

"I can see that you are busy, and I wanted to stop over and say hello to Nick and Madison too. I'll just let myself out," I said.

"Oh, it's not a problem," Olivia said as she walked me out of the kitchen and back to the front door. "And thanks for the article. I know the kids really like seeing their father on the ship with the rest of the crew."

"See you later," I said, and I headed out the door, making sure there was no rogue-newt around planning an escape before stepping outside.

The fog lifted quite a bit in the short time I was inside the Foster's home. I walked to the road and turned right toward the Baker's. It was shaping up to be a fine day. Their Tudor-style home is set back from the road. A wide patio was on the left and a walkway along the right led to the back of the house. I walked up to the front door and knocked. Stacked stones made up half of the Tudor's height. Cedar shingles, stained a forest green, covered the rest up to the sharply sloping roof. I waited a little while, then knocked again. After hanging out a little longer, I concluded they probably were not home. Taking the sidewalk to the back yard, I found a smaller patio off to my right. I could clearly see what Nick mentioned at the party. The far corner was in danger of falling into the ridge.

The Baker's house sat perched at the edge of a ridge that dropped off sharply to a grassy field below. The field extended for more than half a kilometer until it finally reached the edge of the Somber Woods. The corner wall on this small patio was in danger of falling into the ridge. Even now, it looked unsafe. I traced the root of the problem to a downspout on the house. It just emptied onto the patio and eventually found its way to the corner wall, where it eroded the foundation to the point of collapse.

"Ohm, can you transport the furniture from the patio to the yard, over there. I want an empty space to work in."

In a rather large sparkle, all the patio furniture disappeared then appeared a short distance away in the grass. I activated the environment designer inside the invisihud, and targeted the major features of the patio, such as the short walls, the floor, and the capstone of the walls. Each target was a different material, and I marked that in the replication section. I focused my attention inside the invisihud to the downspout and installed virtual underground piping from the house to the edge of the ridge. Checking the downspout on the other side of the house, I noticed the same thing. Erosion was taking place, but not yet causing damage. I installed a virtual underground drain pipe from the house to the ridge for this downspout. Where the edge dropped off, I added a wide white marble ledge. Deploying it across the width of their property, I extended the lip along the edge of the ridge as a slight barrier against erosion.

Once all the virtual construction blocking was in place, I activated the replication process, removing the previous patio. There was an odd clatter and groan as the replication process swapped out the old and installed the new. It took a moment for small crumblings to come to a stop. I walked over to the patio and jumped up and down on it, even in the corner. It felt solid as a rock. The replication results looked like flagstone, brick, and slate. If you were really looking for it, you might notice a distinct repetition in the tiling pattern. I returned to the house and inspected the downspouts. At the bottom of each one was a wide drain with a screen over it.

Returning to the patio, I said, "Ohm, return the furniture to the patio in the same arrangement as before the repair."

A distant sparkle followed by a close-up sparkle took place as the furniture transported to its original location. I walked up to the edge and admired my new lip addition. It was about a foot or so wide and curled up as a final warning that the next step could be your last. There really should be a fence here, I thought.

CHAPTER 19

Morodath

There were so many small tasks to accomplish, but the future memories were fading. I could no longer rely on them to tell me the order to do them in, so I decided upon one myself and set off walking into echo. The road just off the Baker's home led me North, past Alex and Lucas' house. As I walked, I reached out with my mind for the *Motif* and began shifting and shaping the world around me. It was a place that I only read about in the Splendor library. It was a place where Reziko imprisoned Valentino for a short time.

Reziko and Valentino were college buddies in a tech-based echo. This took place before Valentino even knew Reziko was Fabio's son. Valentino never met Reziko until he encountered him on campus, but Reziko knew Valentino was Grayson's son. Continuing with his mad theme of trying to murder all those who participated in his father's death, Valentino was fair game for Reziko.

The prison Reziko located was a cave carved entirely out of an echo canceling gem. If you were inside this gem cave, the *Motif* did not work. You couldn't shift echo to get out. It was highly effective at containing Valentino, and Reziko left him wasting away in that cave for weeks.

I wanted to locate that particular cave to obtain some samples of the gem material. I thought I might be able to leverage the properties in the construction of a portable vignette shield. In the second time loop, I invented a version of this shield, but there was never a chance to put it to use. The truth is, I could have used it in the first loop, where I was psychically attacked several times through the vignettes. I can't predict what might happen in this third loop, but investing time in developing a psychic defense against vignette attacks seemed practical to me.

I held the concept of this cave in my mind along with Valentino's brief description of the landscape he left in the Splendor library. In my mind, I searched for a place, that rocky landscape where the cave entrance lies beneath a tree. The light began to flash as days spun by, and night quickly came and went. Gusty winds blew, and animals howled to join in. I grew large as I stepped across this miniature landscape. I'm at the base of a rock cliff, reaching out with giant hands to pull myself up the side of a mountain. Holding the *Motif* in my mind,

I fixed on the location of Reziko's cave. One hand after another, I pulled myself up that rocky slope until I saw the top.

As I approach the crest of this cliff, the size of the rock started to shrink while I used the *Motif* to return to my native size. I made my way across a plateau revealing rolling hills in the distance. With a final mind wrench of the *Motif*, I grabbed onto the concept of Reziko's gem cave. With a mental slam of the *Motif* onto the landscape, the world visiby shuttered all around me. I caught my breath as I slowly crossed the last rise to see a tree growing out of a rock with a dark hole at it's base.

Using a series of eye movements, I navigated the invisihud menu to activate my personal cloak and shield. I needed to be careful. This place could still be booby-trapped. I did not want to fall victim or become stuck in a cave with no way out. I decided to use one of my cloaked scanners, in drilling mode, to create a narrow, hollow shaft leading into the cave. The shaft was only big enough for the ping pong ball-sized cloaked scanner to travel through. Once on the inside, transportation signals from the cloaked scanner could be relayed through the hollow space. Even if I did get stuck in the cave, my technology could offer a way out.

I sat on the ground and used the Transfood icon from the invisihud to materialize a bottle of water. All this trekking made me thirsty.

I thought about Olivia's offer of company. I must be projecting that lonely as hell kind of vibe. But I did feel that way. I did not realize how much my relationship with Jorrie and Erin changed the way I lived. Now that they were not here, I felt like I lived in a void where a part of me was missing every day. I held my breath, not free to breathe. Every step I took needed to be in the direction of finding them, or I would judge myself of being unworthy of their love. There was no clear path that sprung up before me with a sign pointing the way. And the worst fear was that I might give up and quit trying to find them at all. Seeing Jorrie for the first time did lift my spirits, so I gave myself a gold star for that. I didn't even try to find her, and she walked right up to ask who I was. That might be the Splendorite luck kicking in, and I could use all the luck I could get.

The invisihud flashed across my visual cortex to indicate the drilling of the passageway was complete. This should allow the cloaked scanner signals to pass into and out of the cave. My invisihud biological implant allowed me to mentally interact with the cloaked scanners. With the blink of an eye, I could see through the lens of the cloaked scanner inside the cave. My eyes directed its movements, and I quickly flew around the area. The cave was small, offering only a few spaces. There were some rags on the floor along with left-over food wrappers in one section, while the other looked like it was used as a toilet. In another area, there was a small spring rising up from the floor to supply water. I made another pass through the interior but switched the lens filter to locate the thickest part of these gem walls. It was on the other side of the toilet room. I used the cloaked scanner's object detection system to target the literal crap on the floor. It was all dried up at this time. With a series of eye movements, I transferred the list of targets to the invisihud recycle menu, and the cloaked scanner activated its disintegration ray to remove it from the room.

Walking up to the hole in the ground, I looked into the only way in or out of the cave. There was a large stone slab off to the side that Reziko used to slide over the hole and block the entrance. Activating my virtual anti-gravity boots generated by the cloaked scanner force fields, I took a step over the hole. The descent into the cave was slow. The walls were dark, with a purple tint. I wanted to be sure this was the cave that could block the power of the *Motif*. With the image of the etheric design in my mind, I tried to produce a change in the physical world while pacing around the floor of the cavern.

Once I entered this cave, my connection to the *Motif* was severed. It was such an important part of my life for many centuries. To have it gone, removed as a possible option, left me feeling diminished. Without my connection to the *Motif*, I felt as though I was missing an important sense or appendage. I was stuck in a single probability, unable to affect a change. I tried summoning the *Vechnost* and experienced a similar result. When I pulled out my wand to cast a simple light spell, there were no results.

"Ohm, can you record a detailed physical scan of me while I'm inside this cave?"

"Certainly," Ohm replied as a synthetic voice close to my ear.

I tried the same things again, manipulating echo, summoning the *Vechnost*, and producing a magic spell. I wondered if this muting of my personal powers was the result of the vibrational energy from the surrounding gem? After Ohm conducted test scans, I used the anti-gravity boots to rise up out of the hole. Covering the hole made sense, and with great effort, I managed to move the large cover stone over the opening of this natural oubliette.

"Ohm, can you calculate how much gem material I would need to collect to make a full suit of armor out of the gemstone?"

"Approximately twenty kilograms of mass would be needed to cover your entire body," Ohm replied.

"Let's go ahead and mine forty kilograms of the gem material located in the cave. Try to maintain large piece sizes. I have an idea for a new type of shielding that will require this material. Send the materials directly to the Blinn manufacturing facility. We'll talk about the design later. Once the mining is complete, leave the cloaked scanner here. We may need to mine more gemstone at a later date."

"Commencing mining process," Ohm said.

When I looked back at my immortal life, there were times before I pursued technological solutions, times when I was a dragon rider. I attended dragon training at a school that, in many ways, was very similar to the Starnet Academy. It was similar in that it focused on one goal exclusively, to prepare the students to achieve that goal. In this case, that goal was mastery of dragons. The school was called Morodath.

Morodath was located in an echo, far from Splendor, and time flowed faster there. It was several hundred years since I last walked those halls and listened eagerly to the words of the master riders, the dragon lords themselves. In the end, you either graduate or perish during the training. And the training was harsh and ruthless. If a dragon sensed your weakness, it would eat you. It was there that I met my dragon, Farrowbane. Many dragons and riders strike deals, a pact, so they can both escape.

For a dragon, life at Morodath was just as dangerous to them as it was to the rider applicants. If a dragon ate too many students, it was considered a rogue and hunted by other dragon riders to teach it a lesson. If the dragon was too lenient, it was taken advantage of and enslaved by the rider. So, a balance was sought, and the balance was the only thing that mattered to a dragon lord. That state was sought after so much that it became part of the credo of the academy, "Seek Balance to Achieve Freedom."

When I first arrived, I remember reading that statement on one of the banners flying high above the dragon-sized gates at the entrance to Morodath. Later, I found it carved in stone, wood, prominent in paintings, and various commercial products, such as clothing, baskets, and other wares. In locating this cave, I already traveled fairly deep into echo. I felt an urge to visit Morodath again. To reclaim my title as dragon lord and free a dragon from that torturous school.

With that goal held firmly in my imagination, I began reaching out to Morodath, forming it in my mind. And that was the point that Splendorites argued so many times before. The argument is that when you reach out with your mind, using the power of the *Motif*, you are creating the reality you desire to enter. But I believed what you are forming is an actual connection to the probability where the desired goal resides. All the realities already exist, even the ones you have never imagined. It is the power of the Splendorite to pick and choose freely from those offerings and physically immerse him or herself in that target destination. That is what I believed, and that is how I proceeded.

Diving into my invisihud, I located the Transfast icon which provided localized teleportation through an environment. This mode of transportation was similar to the way the cloaked drone probes projected themselves through outer space. Each cloaked scanner could act as a disintegrator or a depositor of matter. The concept is that you can transport to a nearby location that you can see. The molecules of your body are streamed through the cloaked scanner's blank probability canvas during this "fast transportation" process. You are disintegrated at one location and reintegrated at another. You need a minimum of two cloaked scanners to leverage this menu item. I typically carry four with me at all times. The farther you can see, the faster you can travel. In unobscured landscapes, you can traverse the terrain very quickly. It is less effective in crowded or close quarters but is still a useful escape mechanism in any case.

I started out walking but soon turned that into a light jog. Reaching out with my mind, I took hold of the landscape while mentally shaking it like a rug. In my mind, I shook loose all ties to where I was, compared to where I wanted to be. I morphed the land before me and used the Transfast menu item to quickly reach the other side, but the other side of what?

When I arrived at the target location, it offered a new view. The cloaked scanner providing the disintegrator functionality remained behind. It quickly flew across the distance to join me after my arrival. Repeating this process, I deployed the targeting cloaked scanner ahead of me to set up my next Transfast. I fell into a rhythm as I used the *Motif* to twist the environment around me to match the goal of reaching Morodath. I began oscillating through echo. I would

Transfast to the next location as soon as I arrived at my target. The world around me started to vibrate, becoming a faceted tube, with probabilities painted in action. Each face of the tube represented an exit point to a probable destination. Holding the goal of Morodath in my mind, I saw it flash by on one of the facets as I accelerated through the tube. Quickly changing the tube into a torus caused me to loop back around. I was still Transfasting forward to keep up the momentum, and Morodath appeared again. This time it appeared across multiple facets of the torus I traveled inside of. Another round through the torus and even more facets presented the Morodath narrative. I mentally grabbed onto the trailing ones, stretching them out even more and trying to slow myself down by holding on as I looped around once again. This time, large and clear, I saw a number of facets representing the Morodath probability. I changed my Transfast target to one of those facets instead of continuing my forward momentum. In a flash, I was there. It was night, and I tumbled like crazy, with my force field shield sparking against dirt and rock as I clung to the ground and finally came to a stop. I lay there for a moment, in silence, then the crickets and insects resumed their nighttime chirping.

Standing up and looking around, I found myself in a clearing of rock with trees and shrubs off to the sides. The place was dark, very dark. The only way I could make out any of my surroundings was by looking up where the sky met the tree line. There were so many stars filling the sky that they threatened to outshine one another. They shone with the brilliance of spilled glitter in a moonless sky.

As I looked around the entire tree line, I noticed a sharp point rising off in one direction. That mountain was my goal. Morodath was the mountain where the school resided. Moroloth lay below and was where the commoners lived, and commerce took place. That is where most students start their education. The first lesson after arriving at Moroloth is to figure out how to enter Morodath. There is a very thin set of stepping stones leading to Morodath from Moroloth. The staircase only allows a single person to travel the path at one time. Once you set foot on the path, there is no turning back. A very similar theme with the *Motif* here. But, I arrived from the high road, which brought a possible student to a cliff with a raised draw bridge. The students who take the high road often wait months before the draw bridge opens.

This time, however, I did not need to wait for the draw bridge. The cloaked scanners hovering around me provided additional tech support in the form of a personal energy shield and a virtualized jetpack. This allowed me to fly in the direction I faced. With these force field settings activated, I used eye movements inside my invisihud to direct their operation and increased my velocity in the real world.

Floating up, I cleared the tree line before targeting the mountain with the invisihud menu system. Within a few moments, I quickly sped toward the raised point in the distance. Above the tree line, the stars were even more beautiful, arcing down to the horizon line filling more of my perception. I had to look down, to stay focused. It seemed a bit brighter up in the air than down on the ground. Below, I saw a bending path meandering along the same direction I headed, peeking in and out from the tree cover. That was the high road. I was in flight, a good thirty minutes or more, and below, I noticed the road ended. I slowed my approach as I flew over the chasm looking down into the incredible depth which was easily twice as deep as the Grand Canyon. I could not see the bottom as I floated over the gap the drawbridge typically spanned. I targeted a ledge on the jutting mountainside and made the final journey to Morodath via a Transfast teleportation.

While Morodath is called a mountain, it might be better described as an extremely large stalagmite. It is riddled with tunnels of all sizes as dragons, for thousands of years, have been born here. Along its cone-like exterior can be found numerous turrets. Some of them were built by men, but many have been built by the dragons, themselves. You can tell the dragon architecture from the architecture of men by the lack of masonry work. Dragons pile stones and breathe fire or venom to shape the rock and create interior spaces. The architecture of men is clearly cut stacked stones with mortar. There are mash-ups where it is clear that a dragon's turret was partially destroyed, and men used it as a foundation to build upon. Some ruined works of men served as a base for seamless dragon melted rock-shaped structures.

The ledge was small, and even with my jetpack active, I felt uncomfortable hanging out on such a high perch. I used the invisihud night vision to locate a possible entrance from this ledge. Up above, I detected an entrance and used the virtual jetpack to slowly rise up. It was about the size of a large storm drain. I crawled in head-first. As I made my way through the passage, I realized this tube was definitely made by a dragon, probably a young one too. The passage twisted and turned but generally sloped downward and into the mountain.

It is not that uncommon for the parent dragon to be absent when the eggs hatch. This can happen if the dragon is tending multiple nests, is slain, or freed. When an egg hatches, the young dragon's first instinct is to fly. If the young dragon finds no parent or immediate way out of the cave nest, it uses its dragon breath to melt through the rock, leaving the inner walls of the tunnel to drip. Pulled down by gravity, they form what looks like strands of rock within the tube. That was my impression of this tube as I crawled through it, shielded, cloaked, and with night vision enabled.

The tube finally emptied into a large chamber with an accumulation of melted-rock forming crude steps down to the floor of the cave. As I looked around the chamber, I saw broken eggs. I walked over and counted them. It looked like four dragons may have been born here at one time. Looking around the walls and ceiling, I could see no way out. I counted three escape tubes, including the one I entered from. After further investigation, I found a skeleton of a small dragon. It may have become food for the others or had not developed its breath to a point where it could melt the rock. But the fact it did not take one of the other tubes indicated it was probably killed before the tubes were made. This did not leave me a lot of options.

"Ohm, please deploy all of the idle cloaked scanners to this location. Use as many scanners that are available to achieve the quickest possible mapping of Morodath. Can you give me an ETA?" I asked.

"Deploying scanners," Ohm said.

A continuous stream of random sparkles appeared above me in the cave as my virtual assistant, Ohm, transported a supply of cloaked scanners to this location. Even though the scanners were invisibly cloaked, I could tell something moved out through the tubes by the airflow in the room changed. I watched the light show above my head, which lasted more than two minutes. The sparkles were the byproduct of the requested cloaked scanners transporting to this location. After the sparkles stopped, Ohm said, "Five thousand six hundred and thirty-three cloaked assigned to mapping task."

"Are we still receiving new units from the Blinn replication center?" I asked.

"Affirmative. The previously placed, ten thousand unit order is being filled at a rate of twelve per day," Ohm reported.

Twelve per day seemed pretty low to me, considering the scope of the operation I set up in Blinn space. There were entire starship-sized factory replication centers at my command and multiple shipyard construction zones. I might have to show up and throw a little fear of god into these Blinn people to boost the production rates.

"Ohm, are there unmanned research stations placed on the asteroid belt near Blinn?"

"Affirmative," Ohm replied.

"I want to issue Blinn military orders to escort the heads of all replication departments and their top four staff personnel to these unmanned research stations. Assign each department head to its own research station. Treat this as a nine-month reassignment before rotating them back to the surface of Blinn. Promote the next staff members in line to become the new heads of each department."

"Issuing reassignment orders," Ohm said. "ETA coming in. Projected first draft mapping should be available in seventeen minutes."

Well, I had some time to kill, so I located something to eat from the Transfood invisihud menu. I chose skinless salmon with broccoli and carrots, stir-fried in a garlic hoisin sauce. I added steamed white rice and some oolong tea. Using the environment designer, I marked a virtual table that Ohm used as a template to transport in a physical table. Ohm transported my food request onto the new table, and I enjoyed my food using chopsticks while I waited for the deployed cloaked scanners to build a map of Morodath.

After I finished eating, I took a whiz over by the wall, and a notification icon popped up inside the overlay of my visual cortex. The map was nearly complete. Using eye movements, I activated the new notification inside my invisihud and saw the interior passageways of Morodath revealed to me. Because of the extensive amount of small passages, the map continued to fill in as I viewed it. The larger, more established passageways, were clearly mapped out. From what I could tell, this chamber was once an open area before a large rock face was moved into place to cover or hide the nest from other dragons. This manipulation of walls and doors was common, which is why no one held a complete map of Morodath. The dragons were constantly rearranging walls either by moving stones or melting rock to form or block passages.

Using the environment designer, I placed a virtual block through the rock face, capping off this area. Under the replication menu, I swapped the virtual block for a wide, rising staircase with a high ceiling. I adjusted the virtual blocking so it twisted and turned as I placed the stairway end in alignment with the main hallway. It snapped into place inside my invisihud. The replication of this new hallway took a few minutes to complete, and I slowly walked up the new steps as the rock face in front of me sparkled away, disintegrated by the cloaked scanners, to form an exit from this cavern.

My new passage emptied into a very wide and tall corridor. Adult dragons could easily walk side by side down this passage. Off in the distance, I could hear the sound of screeching and the mix of growling howls followed by low-frequency trumpeting noises. Located above was the dragon school, and man-made entrances were present along this large hallway. Most of them were small, and stacked stones blocked several entrances.

The role of the school's headmaster shifted as power struggles between men and dragons played themselves out on a daily basis. In Morodath, the number of passageways a person could provide or access determined their worth. When a person lost power, it was often due to their passages being blocked, either by men or dragons. It was not uncommon for Morodath to become your tomb if your escape routes were blocked off.

Continuing down this large hallway, I checked the virtual map overlay to make sure I headed in the right direction. The jetpack was more useful outside. For interior spaces, I used the virtual anti-gravity boots provided by the cloaked scanners. After increasing the collision radius, I created a cushion between myself and the floor. This adjustment allowed me to walk a little more silently as I made my way down the hall, sticking close to the wall.

The hallway abruptly dropped off as I reached the center of Morodath. This opening was called the central core and was simply a hole through the center of the enormous stalagmite that was Morodath. Looking up, I saw wooden planks about thirty meters above me, where the flooring extended over the ledge. This extension was one of the man-made entrances to the central core. Attached to these wooden planks were rigging. This approach was considered one of the fastest ways for a student to acquire a dragon. A student would repel down the side of the central core and locate a passage leading to one. But there were many perils to this, and the success rate was very low using this method. It was often used by older students who had not yet acquired a dragon through other methods. It was considered an honorable suicide. But there are also tales of students who took this route and managed to sneak up on a sleeping dragon and strike a deal.

After stepping off the ledge, I felt a quick falling sensation as the anti-gravity boots struggled to keep me afloat. The anti-gravity boots were not as effective when there was nothing to push against, such as this long empty hole. I pulled up the invisihud modifications menu and swapped the anti-gravity boots for a virtual anti-gravity platform. This force field preset was similar to the anti-gravity-platform, with the difference being that the AGP was a physical device.

I fell slowly, like descending on an escalator. Drifting past multiple dark openings, I smelled brimstone and ash. I could even see some fiery glow at the end of a few passages. But these were the younger dragons that inhabited the top. As dragons grew, they sought out larger caverns to inhabit. Many times dragons fought to the death over occupying a specific space. The farther you travel down the central core, the older the dragons typically become, with elder dragons occupying the base of Morodath. This is another reason why it was not practical to enter Morodath from the ground. You would be facing some of the oldest and most powerful dragons. But this was where I headed, the very bottom of Morodath, to face an elder dragon.

As I descended even further through the central core, entrances became fewer and farther between. The older dragons would often seal up passageways younger dragons may make to keep possible entry to their lairs to a minimum. The life support portion of my shielding kicked into operation as I dropped farther and farther down. At the bottom of the central core lies the Everflow, the lava river flowing through the base of Morodath. Its fumes and heat were affecting my shielding. I eventually dropped through the top of a cavern with an enormous ceiling. In certain places, the Everflow meandered through the stepped floor. A large passage led away from one of these areas, and I landed before it.I returned to the anti-gravity boots because they were more responsive than the platform. As I made my way along the passageway, the walls took on a carved relief. This was called the Pandrum. Literally translated as, "The Story of the Dragon." Each dragon's life was a Pandrum, but it was only the older dragons who took the time to carve their stories into the walls of their lairs. The younger dragons often had an elaborate seal, or emblem called the Panlol which was a brand they used to mark their territory. And the youngest created what was called the Panhote which simply meant the mark. Recognizing the relevance of these markings was one tool students used when deciding which passageway to venture into.

But this dragon was very old, and its Pandrum was quite beautiful. It seemed the farther I traveled down the large passage, the more detailed the Pandrum became. The dragon wrote its name into many of the panels. Homsoon was its name, and contrary to popular belief, knowing the name of a dragon does not automatically give you control over it. What it does give you, however, is some credibility with the dragon if you speak its name with honor during a conversation. That is, if you make it to a conversation, instead of being eaten. Many a student perished simply because they did not study the mealtime cycle of the dragon they approached. Approaching a dragon after it has feasted was more likely to produce a conversation than before.

"Ohm, stop mapping operations and deploy one hundred and twenty cloaked scanners to my location. Return the others to storage on *Tiger Mountain.*"

The passageway brightened briefly as the small fleet of cloaked scanners transported in behind me. I located them in my invisihud and set them all to one function, bind. I also set them up to auto-target and auto-combine in case things got too busy for me to manage all of them.

"Ohm, can you target three middle-aged cattle on the surface of Blinn? I want to transport them here on my signal."

"Cattle located and available for deployment," Ohm replied a moment or two later as an icon blinked ready inside my invisihud.

The end of the tunnel emptied into a large dome-like cavern with slanted horizontal slits along three sides. I imagined those large slits were where the dragon perched before crawling outside to launch itself into the air. The slits offered a wide ledge with a groove cut into it along a sloping ramp that ended at a small pool in the floor. The other two slits offered ramps feeding the same pool. When it rained, these must act as gutters to resupply the dragon's drinking water.

The walls of this interior lair were even more detailed with relief than the tunnel leading up to this chamber. There were clearly defined panels, and the artistry, itself, easily rivaled that of any contemporary or renaissance master. One panel depicted the elder dragon in majesty with wings spread wide as it rose up on its hind legs. Other panels showed a dragon in flight, destroying the structures of man. But most of the panels seemed to be about hatching eggs and raising young. I presumed these were portraits of her children. The dragon that I rode out of here, those hundreds of years ago, Farrowbane, was a male dragon. But I was guessing from this Pandrum that this dragon was a female.

Part of the Everflow was diverted into this chamber to act as an incubator, and on one side of the room were evenly spaced eggs sitting in dimpled impressions on the floor. Some eggs were closer to the Everflow than others, and several small, lanky dragons slinked around the eggs, sniffing and touching them with their wings while constantly moving from one egg to the next. Scattered about on the floor was a smattering of various bones. Most of the bones looked like domesticated livestock, but I saw the occasional human partial skeleton as a skull lying in a helmet along with discarded swords and shields.

Homsoon lie on her side, much the way a cat might lie down on a couch. She rested in a bed of small polished stones while several dragons groomed her in some way. One of the lanky dragons, an older one with a long thin beard, the type you might see in an old Chinese print, tended to Homsoon's scales. I noticed Homsoon embedded much of the classic dragon treasure right into her body. There were chipped scales repaired with gold plating, and almost every scale seemed to have at least four or more gems embedded along the edge, which reminded me of rhinestone embroidery.

With the invisihud, I targeted the small lanky dragons in preparation for binding them. Standing in the center of the open hallway where I arrived, I dropped the cloak and engaged the cattle transfer as I spoke using the amplified voice icon from the invisihud.

"Homsoon, old and wise, please accept my offering so we may speak," I said, as the cattle sparkled into view in front of the resting Homsoon.

The cavern was in an immediate uproar as all the beasts shouted out at once and leaped into action. The small lanky dragons spotted me and moved with incredible speed, like a deer bounding off in the woods. I activated the bind option, and visible force fields were cast around the moving beasts. Some managed to wiggle free and continue their way toward me only to be bound again as the cloaked scanner's auto-combine mode kicked in to create stronger force fields to hold them in place.

Homsoon rose up to her full height, spread her wings, and I realized why the panel of her in her majestic form was the first thing you saw when you entered the chamber. She mirrored the sculpted relief behind her in raised majesty as she reared back to spit fire above the cattle while targeting me. I could feel the heat as the force field shielding stressed under the strain of resisting the fire. With haste, I targeted Homsoon's mouth to direct some cloaked scanners to bind it. I scrambled to a new location, trying to escape the heat, and tumbled to the ground in the process.

Fear utterly streaked through my body as I barely executed these actions. While mentioned often that a dragon can strike fear into the hearts of men, what is left out is that fear is a psychic ability of the dragon. Slightly telepathic by nature, dragons can trick people and prey into doing things they normally might not consider. I felt Homsoon's glare as I tumbled and looked up in awe at the massive dragon before me. The sound of rushing blood sounded loud in my ears, amplifying the fear building up inside me.

With the muzzle binding in place, the room fell silent, and only the stamping of Homsoon's feet and wings against stone added noise to the room. The young dragons visibly continued their vocalizing, but the force fields contained the sounds they made while restricting their movements. I thought of the *Motif* and held it between myself and Homsoon as a protective shield.

Climbing back to my feet, I watched as Homsoon struggled to remove the force field muzzle from her snout. Like a dog with a cone around its neck, she tried to scrape it off using her claws and dragging her face along the walls.

"Homsoon, calm your struggle so I might extend your story," I boomed out while using the loud voice.

It was then that Homsoon slunk down to the floor and slithered over, bringing her car-sized head near my body. With her large eye, she cast her dragon spell upon me. It is well known that dragons are magical creatures, but most of them use what is called the Mothasol, meaning "Magic from Within," instead of casting spells as human magicians do. The quality of an individual dragon's Mothasol varies, but I could tell from the deep hypnotizing enchantment of Homsoon's eye that her Mothasol was strong. It was so strong that I forgot what I was doing, and before I knew it, she batted me from the floor to the wall with her tail. I hit hard. While the shielding protected me from much of the force, it really did hurt like hell. I slid down the wall to the floor in a slumped pile as Homsoon whipped around, lightning-fast, and attempted to eat me.

Fortunately, the mouth binding was still in place, and all she could do was knock me aside again. She moved me closer to the Everflow stream in this chamber. As my head cleared, I located the anesthesia icon inside the invisihud menu system and targeted Homsoon. I guess we do this the hard way instead of conversation. She made another lunge at me, and I rolled sideways to avoid her as the anesthesia kicked in, and she lost her footing. She struggled to stand and glanced over at me one last time giving me a look of betrayal.

I have not used the anesthesia icon on such a large creature before, relying on Ohm to determine the dosage. I acted quickly, realizing she may come around any time. Without pausing, I used the environment designer to block out a couple of large virtual tubes around the torso and neck. Ohm detected my virtual blocking inside the invisihud and swapped these two place-holder items with replicated versions of physical tack and harness. I took up the position of a dragon rider as I quickly climbed onto her back. Blocking out another virtual tube around her head, I focused on the eye area. Stories tell us that dragons have a weak spot. This weakness is often depicted as a missing scale or the soft underbelly of the beast, but the eyes are the real weak spot on a dragon. When dragons fight each other in close combat, it is often the eyes that each dragon goes for on their opponent. I replaced the virtual tube around her head with a light-blocking, form-fitting, tightly bound blindfold. And not a moment too soon. Homsoon stirred from the anesthesia slumber and groggily rose up on all fours.

Once again, I boomed in the large voice. "Homsoon, still your struggle, so I might extend your story," I said before releasing the mouth-binding, keeping it on standby inside the invisihud.

Homsoon belched a long stream of fire in the general direction she faced. I pulled hard on the reins to let her know I was on her back, and I saddled her, making her my property. She immediately rolled over on her side, trying to cast me off, and I found myself below the crushing weight of an elder dragon. I increased the radius of my shielding, pushing back against her massive frame. Using the invisihud, I directed the cloaked scanners to target the dragon's underside and repeatedly replicated stunning gleam-gun shots. This move caused her to roll over to protect her underside while she swiped blindly at the empty air trying to locate the assailant.

I activated the anesthesia icon, again, only this time half-strength. I felt her stagger a bit and calm down as she spoke, "Moolath drun dug at be line tam trail seck. Meeloo not ock can drum sigh."

One of the latent abilities of a Splendorite is to inherit the language of the probability where they reside. While it is possible to travel to an echo and block out that ability to become a stranger in a strange land, it is more practical to understand what people and even creatures are saying. This was the case now as I translated her syllables into meaning, "I have reached my story's end. My children shall perish."

"Mok toe ana mat Homsoon. Keelay mocka rise azure," I said, which roughly translated into "Meet your freedom, Homsoon. Let us rise to the sky together."

Targeting the blindfold with the invisihud, I used the recycle icon to remove it. The sparkle of the recycle transport around her eyes caused her to blink and squint as she shook her head from side to side, trying to shake it off. She bent her neck around to get a good look at me, the man who saddled her into slavery. She did not breathe fire on me or attempt to gobble me whole. Her eyes no longer held the mystical look, having put her Mothasol aside, for now.

"Nova locus azure. Samba net meeloo ahnk run," I spoke, translating as, "Move your location to the sky, and I will free your children."

She gazed over her children who were still trapped in the force fields and said, "Ush oo may," and the smaller dragons ceased their struggles and focused their attention on their mother.

Homsoon said, "Semla mot by tun drahk. Eeyoo aliso wyat. Sing car so long wove tale tree midden lay din un drak," translating as "With my heavy heart I leave you to the world. To tell the story of your life and write it upon your walls."

She went on to name each of her children and glanced at her panels as she did so. Then without glancing back, she leaped up to one of the ledge openings leading to the outside world. Her size was so large that she barely fit through the opening and tried in a last-ditch effort to unsaddle me by scraping her back against the ceiling as she made her way. I saw it coming and hung off to the side of the saddle as she lumbered ahead. We made it through the opening, where she sat perched on the outer ledge.

Even though we were near the bottom of the stalagmite mountain, we were a hundred meters above the floor of the flat grasslands surrounding the base of Morodath. There was a hint of a glow on the horizon as dawn was imminent. Homsoon stretched out her wings wide, stood up on her hind legs, and roared with her dragon voice.

Homsoon launched herself from the ledge but tucked her wings tightly to her body. And then we fell. The fear I felt in the cave was nothing compared to this free fall I experienced as the grassland floor rushed up. At the last moment, she extended her wings gaining lift as she arced back into the sky. The sound of repeated flapping took us higher and higher into the sky as the sunrise broke through quickly, as it tends to do in equatorial regions.

"Ohm, release the binding on the young dragons," I said while using the booming voice so Homsoon could hear.

I looked back and could see the base of Morodath rising from the grassland floor. Along the bottom, from the ledge where we emerged, I saw a small flock of young dragons take flight in direct pursuit. Homsoon took a sharp dive to the left and circled around to face the approaching dragons. I could hear their bleatings as they vocalized messages to their mother, but she ignored them, breathing soft fire at them and knocking some of them aside as she crashed through the center of the group displacing them in the air.

"Samba lol meeloo ahnk run. Cas sa el ray meech eck," I said to Homsoon, translating roughly as, "I have freed your children. Our journey begins."

Homsoon seemed to accept that I kept my end of the bargain. She turned around, heading away from Morodath, leaving her children behind as they called out to her. I brought the *Motif* forward in my mind and projected it over the landscape ahead of us. A storm of purple clouds quickly gathered, and we descended into the maelstrom as I shifted echo to reach my final goal. All atmospheric and ground-based representations fell away, as Homsoon and I were one, riding through this space between worlds, with only the sound of the wind and wings flapping.

There is a celestial nature to dragons making them timeless beings. Or at least they view time in the physical world as if it were a dream, knowing they are destined to return to AnuliSol, which loosely means, "Circle of Starting." I focused on my goal to befriend the elder dragon, or at least to agree with Homsoon that her physical form would rule over all other dragons in this space between worlds. I sang the contract to her in long-winded words of dragon song, which she revised and negotiated in a call and response form as we flew through this celestial space.

We came upon a large planetoid in this empty void, and Homsoon headed for a flat landing place. Reaching into echo, I brought forth a glowing light I held high in my right hand while managing the reins with my left. We landed with the brightness of a shooting star, and Homsoon let out a trumpet blast as dragons of all ages gathered around to rejoice at our arrival. Dragons of all sizes were here, and like the Blinn, these were my dragons and loyal to me under the authority of elder dragon Homsoon. That was the contract fulfilled.

I dismounted Homsoon, no longer fearing attack as my echo manipulations and dragon song bound us in contract. I targeted the harness and reins with the invisihud and used the recycle icon to remove them from Homsoon. Dragons gathered around the high cliff we landed upon, looking up at us.

Standing before the crowd of massive beasts, I said to them in dragon tongue, "Today is your day, a forever day, where you honor contracts of old. A day of celebration and victory as you live eternally within the celestial sphere. Homsoon will guide each of you to battle in due time. You will be called forth to battle mechanical beasts whose very hearts are pure energy, an energy that will feed your souls. Hold fast till the moment is upon you, and you too will know victory and spread fear amongst the dreaming."

While I held their attention, I started repeating, "Homsoon, Homsoon, Homsoon."

The other dragons growled and trumpeted in a frenzy, with their spouts of flames erupting into the air only to fall down and roll off the backs of the other dragons in the hoard. At that moment, I felt like a dragon lord once again.

CHAPTER 20

Xanadu

I pulled up the San Francisco transport apartment icon inside my invisihud, activated it, and the dragon scene fizzled into nothingness. While waiting in the black void, I pondered future options. Some far-fetched quests had useful outcomes in my future memories, but should I run around trying to complete goals without thinking about the bigger picture? I made contact with many of the people I remembered as future friends, but was that enough? In the future memories, these new friends became friends with each other. I guess Ethan Foster was the only one to attempt that in his current endeavor.

At first, I did not realize I materialized. I was in my bedroom. The light-blocking curtains were closed, and it was night. But as I started to move around, automatic lighting kicked in to dimly light the room. My shoulder hurt like hell, and I had a good-sized bump on my head. Carefully, I pulled off my shirt, trying not to lift my right arm as I wiggled out of it at the end. I hoped the shielding would protect me more than it did. Even with the force fields enabled, I overwhelmingly reeked of brimstone, which, in comparison to your basic campfire smoke, was about ten times stronger. I emptied my pockets of items, recycled my clothes, and took a soapy shower. I didn't shower long because even the softest shower head setting caused a painful throbbing across my right back torso. I dried off and lie down in my bed. Damn, I was tired.

"Ohm, wake me at eight A.M.," I said before I fell asleep.

I awoke to an arm on my chest and a slight shoving of my shoulder followed by, "Hey, wake up."

"Ow," I said as I sat up slowly, obviously favoring my left side.

"What's wrong?" Candy asked while sitting on the bed next to me.

"I got slammed around pretty good by a dragon's tail," I said as I twisted my back to show her the bruise.

"A dragon's tail," Candy exclaimed. "Oh my. You have to see a doctor, Sam."

Candy leaned over to look at my back and pressed her chest against me. She smelled wonderful, like a bouquet of flowers. I was immediately turned on and raised my knees up to hide my reaction. I held my knees, giving her a good view of my back. It has certainly been too long.

Candy stood up and said, with a direct, defiant look, implying I should not challenge her, "Get dressed. We're going to Xanadu."

I looked twice as she walked out of my bedroom. I dug her clothing style, tight pants wrapped around a fine frame. She had a boomin' body with a take no shit attitude.

I put on new clothes, transferred items between pockets, put on my boots. The shirt was the toughest, because my shoulder hurt so much. Making my way over to the counter, I thought I'd fix something to eat first, but Candy stood there saying, "No way. You get to eat after we visit the doctor."

"Fine."

Candy Smiled and said, "Ohm, transport us to Xanadu."

The bright and cheery San Francisco morning collapsed as my eyes dissolved into darkness. It seemed like I was just here a minute ago. Even though I had no stomach, I still felt hungry. While pondering that, a grey field tinted with blue filled my vision as I reassembled in a tech corridor at Xanadu.

This corridor ended at the general entrance. If a medical emergency occurs, Ohm is programmed to transport the distressed patient directly to the emergency room. The doors in front of us were transparent, revealing someone approaching. He was Blinn. He walked through the doors and said, "My name is, HorEl. How can I help you?"

Candy said, "Sam hurt his back. He has a bruise this big," gesturing the size with her two hands.

HorEl led us into a larger lab area with an egg-shaped bed rising from the center. He gestured for me to have a seat on the bed and walked over to a nearby control station. I sat on the edge of the bed, and I felt the foam mattress conform to my buttocks.

HorEl asked, "Can you tell me what happened?"

I said, "It might be easier if you just review the log. Ohm, can you forward the log from the Homsoon dragon fight to HorEl's workstation?"

"Certainly," Ohm replied.

A wide auragraphic projection arced across HorEl's terminal, and I saw the events of last night playing out on the display. Candy stepped around to watch the log playback.

"What the hell were you thinking? There are like," Candy started counting the smaller dragons on the screen and continued, "thirteen dragons in that cave."

"Please remove your clothes and lie down on the bed," HorEl said, looking up before returning to the log.

I really didn't think I needed a doctor, but I also knew my right side hurt, so I took my shirt off first. HorEl came over to help me remove my shirt once he noticed I struggled with it. I kicked off my boots and looked over at the display just in time to see the dragon tail slam me into the wall.

"Ohm, mark the log playback at that point," I said, then dropped my pants and stood there naked.

Candy looked up with a smile and said, "Got it," as she located the mark I placed in the log.

HorEl said, "Turn around. I see. Let's get you lying down. We'll do this in zero gravity," and he returned to the workstation.

I climbed onto the biobed and sunk into it. It was warm and felt like skin. I moved to the center, and I felt the bed begin to float. The edge of the bed was framed in metal bands that expanded and rotated away, docking into the ceiling or floor positions. The center of the bed gave way, and I fell into the fluidic interior. From inside, everything was tinted in a golden light.

I struggled to breathe while HorEl's voice broadcast into the fluidic pod bed, "Relax, breathe normally. In, hold, out, that's it. There is no rush."

Treachery flashed through my mind as I imagined Candy or HorEl taking advantage of my helpless state. I cued up the Transfast icon in case something were to happen, and I felt ashamed as I did so.

There was an audio component to the fluidic biobed that I did not notice until it altered. I heard low pulsing synthesizer music playing in a Morton Subotnick style. Lights followed, that either syncopated or tracked to the music. At the workstation, HorEl rotated the fluidic pod, with me inside. As he made changes at the workstation, the sounds and lights shifted playback, brightness, and location. There was something erotic about the whole process, leaving me aroused the entire time.

The music shifted as deep mid-tones slid along my backside. I could see small strands of bubbles gathering together. They appeared to be pushed by pressure through tubing, but no tubing was actually present inside the fluidic biobed. The tone scraped across the audible spectrum, brightness gathered around my head, and I felt a pinging sensation in my skull.

The viscosity changed, and I felt the fluid rub along my body. The pressure inside the fluidic biobed pressed on me with the strength of multiple soft hands. The fluidic hands simultaneously massaged all parts of my body, focusing on my right shoulder. The hands worked their way down my back, massaging my buttocks, arriving at the sex organ, and producing the expected result. They continued down the legs and to the feet, spending some delicate time on my soles. Meanwhile, the smallest fingers you could imagine massaged my face and ears. I felt hands running through my hair as the previously docked bed frame rings returned to support the unit. I was pushed up through the membrane to lie dripping in goo on the warm flesh bed.

Candy approached with a towel and said, "Dang, you looked like you needed that," while leaving her mouth open, eying my relieved naked junk.

"Did it work?" I asked, sitting up, not realizing I used my right arm while drying myself off to remove goop.

Candy walked around the bed, paused behind me, and said, "It looks better, way better."

HorEl walked up and asked the obvious, "How do you feel?"

I stretched out a bit and said, "It feels good, like the leftover ache from a workout. Thanks, HorEl."

This praise brought a slight smile to his otherwise completely professional face. I hopped off the bed and proceeded to get dressed. Candy walked around, picked up the towel I set aside, and shaped it into a point around her finger, using it to remove some final goo stragglers from my hair.

"HorEl, I have a product in the development phase on Blinn, in the off-world workshops. Can you give me an update on the progress?" I asked as I walked up to his workstation.

"Yes. Can you give me the working title or description?" HorEl asked.

"I don't have a title, but its main function is to deliver orgamorphic gel in the shape of a deep wound," I said. "Is that enough of a description?"

"Checking, let me see," HorEl said then, "Ah yes, it is still in development, but it has reached beta stage. Hmm, quite interesting for a field tool." Then looking up at me from his display, he said, "It appears that eighty percent of the milestones for the project have been met. The main hold-up is with live orgamorphic gel replication. Currently, you have to reload the beta with pre replicated charges of orgamorphic gel. They are also still working on making it smaller."

"Thank you for the update," I said, and my stomach rumbled.

"Now you can eat," Candy said, adding, "I know a nice place in our neighborhood."

"Ohm, transport Sam and I to Ferry park," Candy said.

The blue-white tech lighting retracted and dissolved as I disassembled, once again. I found myself in darkness, wondering if I could talk to Candy while we were disembodied? Candy, are you there I thought? But there was no reply. The darkness was always your own. I felt brightness and warmth again as we materialized in a grassy field in Ferry park.

Without hesitation, Candy said, "Come on. This way," and we quickly walked to a paved path heading for the park exit.

I did not see a reason to rush. I felt completely relaxed from the fluidic biobed experience and asked, "What's the rush? It's a nice day."

She looked at me with an "Are you stupid kind of look," and said, "I have to go to the bathroom."

"Oh," I said, and I picked up the pace.

We made our way out of the park and stopped at the corner for the light. While a lot of the traffic was airborne these days, there was still some traditional ground traffic here. After looking both ways, we crossed the street without waiting for the light. Ascending the short, round stairway leading up to the restaurant, we saw a sign above the door that read, "Florence's." Once we were inside, Stephanie, who seemed to know Candy, greeted Candy and me. Candy asked for a table by the window and immediately headed off to find the restroom. Stephanie guided me to the table and asked if she could start me off with a drink. I ordered Café au lait for two. She left two tablet menus on the table and headed off to fix the drinks. I looked over the menu and quickly decided on the Sunrise Smile, which consisted of two pieces of French toast, a side of bacon, and a glass of fresh-squeezed orange juice.

Candy took a seat at the table before Stephanie returned with our coffees.

"I ordered you one," I said to Candy.

"Thank you," Candy said to me, then turned to Stephanie and said with a smile, "Thank you, Stephanie."

"It's nice to see you again, Candy," Stephanie said.

"This is my neighbor, Sam," Candy said.

"Nice to meet you, Sam. Are you new to this area?"

"Kind of new. Newish. Within the last year."

"Look at me chatting you up when you're probably hungry. What can I get you?" Stephanie asked.

I handed her my tablet, with the Sunrise Smile selected, and said, "Sunrise Smile."

"I'll have the Good Morning Girl," Candy said, looking into Stephanie's eyes while returning the menu tablet.

"Got it. I'll get these orders into the kitchen," Stephanie said before walking off and glancing back at us.

"Did she just look back?" Candy asked.

"Yeah, she did. She looked right back at you," I said. "Hey, do you have any money to pay with?"

"Yes, I have money to pay."

"Good, cause I don't. God, I am feeling so nice right now. You should try one of those fluidic biobeds yourself. It's an orgasm machine."

"Maybe I will. After seeing you all excited like that, it kind of flushed me a bit," Candy said, flirting.

"Mmm. This is good coffee," I said as I sipped.

"Mine too," Candy said, pausing before asking. "So, what was all that dragon stuff about?"

"Backup. I now have an army of dragons that will fight for me," I said quietly.

Candy hushed her tone, too, and asked, "Who are you fighting?"

"Bad guys, Candy. You know shit happens sometimes. The next time, boom. Dragon in your face. How do you like them apples?"

"Bad guys. Whatever, don't tell me," Candy said as she rolled her eyes.

Stephanie returned with our plates of food, and we began eating. In the traditional California style, the amount of food provided was smaller than my appetite. When Stephanie checked back, I ordered a couple more eggs and another side of bacon.

From the window table, I looked across the street into Ferry park, the place where we arrived. I sat drinking my second cup of coffee in silence as Candy seemed to be occupied with her invisihud. Stephanie dropped off the check, and Candy produced a card for payment.

"So, whacha thinking about?" Candy asked as she returned her focus to the room instead of the invisihud.

"I'm thinking I have a lot of things to do, but some of them are dangerous undertakings."

"You mean like, fighting more dragons?"

"The dragon fight was tough because I tried to subdue it, not kill it. These next tasks might involve a more cutthroat approach."

"You were supposed to say 'Candy, why yes, I'd love to go shopping and pick out some better clothes. I have been wearing the same style since FOREV-ER,'" Candy sarcastically replied, not really liking my answer.

"I do need to look into some research."

"Do you want to get going?" she asked as she gathered up her purse and returned the payment card to it.

"Sure, let's head back to the black tower," I said, finally naming the building.

"The black tower? You aren't seriously calling the building that, are you?" We got up and headed for the door, with Candy adding, "Bye, Stephanie," in a sweet tone as we left the restaurant.

"You have a better name?" I asked.

"What about home? Or da crib?" Candy offered up alternates as we walked to a public transport access point.

While we stood waiting for the ground transport, I said to Candy, "You might as well find out now rather than later. This probability is under a silent siege by form-altering aliens. I caught one posing as a field marshal in Starnet headquarters recently. But the sad thing is when they steal someone's identity, they most likely have murdered that person and hidden the body. I need to find that body to expose the conspiracy."

"Damn, you go to all the trouble to find this nice place, and then you add that shit into the mix," Candy said, glancing down the street impatiently.

"This place is where Jorrie, Erin, and I live in the future. By stabilizing it now, I am laying the foundation for future events," I said.

"So, you really are trying to recreate the events that lead to your future wives?" Candy asked with a serious look.

Looking down at the ground, then back up at Candy, I replied, "Wouldn't you?"

"I guess so," Candy said, putting her hand on my shoulder as the transport arrived at our stop.

We boarded the transport, which was basically a ground bus. As with most public transportation systems, it mainly catered to the poor, yet to be successful, and the elderly. Looking around the interior of the bus, I viewed a median sampling from each of those groups as we took our seats and the bus resumed its route.

"If things turn weird and don't seem right, it could mean someone close to you was replaced by a Flexanite. I have come up with a test to reveal if a person is a Flexanite. I'm adding it to your invisihud now," I said as I located the scissors icon and used the share option.

"Got it," Candy said, "How does it work?"

"The test is simple. A Flexanite recreates the parts of the body they are imitating, including hair and nails. If you cut some hair from a Flexanite it reverts to a dark oozing substance. Presumably, consciousness is required for the Flexanite ooze to maintain its form."

"For real?" Candy asked with a frown.

"The icon is a way to conduct the test covertly. But if it comes right down to determining if someone around you is a Flexanite, the common scissor test does work."

"Shit. I don't want to think about that," Candy said with her expression going grim.

"And if you are conducting a test, you'd better be thinking about an escape or a target bind. Once exposed, they revert to a more animal-like approach to dealing with people and can deliver brutal blows in an instant."

"See, now, I wish you had just taken me up on my shopping offer," Candy said.

"My shirt. I had a new shirt made," I said, remembering and turning to Candy. "Do you want to come with me to pick it up? It's in a space station mall, so there are other shops to check out."

"Sure, I guess it's as close to shopping as I'll get out of you today," Candy said.

"Let's get off at this stop. We'll need to journey to somewhere else before we begin," I said enigmatically.

We moved to the front of the bus, holding onto the provided poles. The bus came to a stop before the driver flipped open the doors. We stepped off the bus, and Candy said, "Thank you," to the driver. The bus drove away, and we started walking down the sidewalk. I pulled out the vignette for the *Deceptive* catwalk, where *Vision* resides. While holding Candy's hand, I gazed at the vignette until the place seemed real. With my next step, we were there, back on the catwalk. I let go of Candy's hand and walked down to the end of the catwalk, where the easel stood.

"Wow, this old ship, Ari, are you still around?" Candy called out as she walked down the catwalk.

"Yes, Candy. It is good to hear your voice," Ari said in a synthetic voice similar to Ohm's.

What *Tiger Mountain* is now, the *Deceptive* once was. Ari is the precursor to Ohm. Both of their artificial intelligence networks were cloned from a single polytronic source. The *Deceptive* remains docked within *Tiger Mountain* as an added layer of security for the *Vision* painting. Even though the power of *Vision* is known to all the Splendorite family members, no one seemed to care I had a portable center of the *Motif* available. They were more concerned over my starship that could obliterate Splendor from space, helping feed the frenzy leading up to my first imprisonment. In my mind, *Vision* was a more powerful weapon because you could visualize your intended target remotely and launch a surprise attack. That is why I kept *Vision* hidden away under so much security. I did not want surprise attacks to be launched against me. And maybe that was why I feared the Spectre Vorticle's ability to transfer energy so much.

"Yours too, honey," Candy said to Ari as she came up next to me in front of the covered painting.

"Okay, look away or close your eyes," I said.

"Oh, that's right, I forgot about your gross creation. Wait a second. All right, my eyes are closed," Candy said.

I held the image of *Oasis Seven* in my mind as I whipped the cover from the painting to reveal maggots, large and up-close feeding upon dead flesh as flies arose banging at the painting surface trying to enter the room where we stood. Pushing back with my intention of *Oasis Seven*, it quickly appeared. If I am traveling through *Vision* to a place I have visited before, it seems to come into focus more quickly than if I am trying to reach an entirely new unvisited location.

"It's all right to look, Candy."

Candy turned around. I took her hand, and we stepped through the painting onto a deck of *Oasis Seven*, but I was not sure if we were detected. Some people turned the corner and nearly ran into us as we stepped forward.

"Oh, please excuse me," I said, stepping out of their way as they side glanced us both in passing.

Turning to Candy, I said, "There are a lot of aliens here, so don't freak out. The tailor we are visiting is an alien."

"I have seen aliens before," Candy said in a hushed tone as we took some steps down to enter the concourse.

I had a better sense of where Marcus's shop was this time, and I located it fairly quickly. Candy hung behind, eying a few things from the stalls as she passed by, but caught up with me as I came upon the entrance to Marcus' shop.

"I just want to go in, get my shirt, and get out. This guy can talk your ear off all day," I said. "If he goes on too long, make up some excuse to shop so we can politely leave."

Candy offered a pretty good impression of me as she lowered her voice and said, "Might involve a more cutthroat approach," then changed to her voice, "and here you are worried about being polite to a tailor."

"You have a seamstress, don't you?"

"I do. Her name is Melissa," Candy said, following up with, "and I am polite to her, so I guess I see your point."

"Ohm, can you replicate a folding wallet with six strips of diamond stamped quaybit?" I asked.

A sparkle appeared at my feet, and I picked up the wallet. I opened the folding case and saw three strips of quaybit on each side. We headed into Marcus' shop, and once again, the store was empty. I wondered how he made his living? Candy immediately started browsing and said, "Ooh," a couple of times as she looked through the clothes racks.

Marcus emerged from the back room and said, "Ah, arrived at last. I wondered if I was ever going to see you again?"

I haven't checked the calendar in a while, so I asked, "How long has it been?"

"Well, it has been about four weeks since we last spoke," Marcus said, eying Candy with a sideways glance.

"Wow, four weeks. I did not realize that much time had passed," I said apologetically.

Overhearing our conversation, Candy walked over to join us, saying, "Yes, you disappeared for four weeks. Why do you think I was there when you woke up? I asked Ohm to notify me of your arrival."

"I am Marcus, and you are?" Marcus asked.

"Genuine Candy, G.C.," she said, holding up her left and right hand shaping the letters with each of her hands.

"Uh-huh. Well, Candy, may I call you Candy?" Marcus asked, waiting for Candy's reply.

"Sure. That's fine," Candy said.

"Welcome to my shop, Candy. If you have any questions about the merchandise, feel free to ask," Marcus said before addressing me. "I'll fetch your garment from the back."

"Buy me stuff," Candy said as we headed back over, revisiting some of the racks of clothes.

I did like most of the clothes Candy picked out, even though they varied widely in style. Most were solid colored daily wear, but she picked out some large print summer dresses along with a few traditional Vascon religious garments. As she picked them out, I followed beside her while she held up clothes in front of herself and draped the ones she wanted to keep across my arms.

Marcus returned from the back room carrying my shirt, and I approached him with an arm full of Candy's selections.

"Oh, let me help you with that," he said as he put down the shirt and took the load of clothes from my arms. He placed them on a table and returned to fetch my shirt. Holding it up and unfolding it, he said, "Here is the revised garment. Let me know if anything is wrong."

I took off my current shirt in the shop and held up the new one. I liked the look. It was less of a fibrous surface and a bit sleeker. The shirt was a little heavier, as we discussed, with flexible insulation placed between the inside and outside layers. I unbuttoned the top few buttons and slipped it over my head, straightening out my hair after doing so.

Candy stepped up, almost immediately, and started straightening it out at the bottom and buttoning it up, saying, "Better. I like this better than the one you had on."

She looked over at Marcus said, "That's nice work," while continuing to inspect the seams.

I made a hands-off motion to Candy as I brushed her hands away and walked over to a full-length mirror.

"Oh, let me adjust that for you," Marcus said as he moved over and positioned the mirror at a less distorting angle.

I checked the pockets on the sleeves, and they were nearly invisible. The new zippers were a thinner, smoother style than I had before. I unbuttoned my shirt to test the access of the new interior pockets. Marcus slanted and expanded the top openings of the interior pockets to allow objects to move in and out in a much easier fashion.

"I like it, Marcus," I said, adding a a smile. "I feel like I am wearing quality."

"Yeah, you look good. Can we go now? I have that thing, and I can't be late," Candy said, playing her role perfectly.

"Sorry to rush out, Marcus, but we have to be going. How much do I owe you? Can you add Candy's garments to the same bill?" I asked.

"Certainly, let me prepare those for travel," he said while reaching below the counter and pulling out a white paper bag with twine handles. The bag was printed with the emblem of the *Oasis Seven* concourse cleverly hidden in the background, and the words, "Shopping Excitement" integrated into the design. Marcus went through each garment, removing the hanger and folding them up nicely before placing them in the bag one at a time. Each time he placed a garment in the bag, he entered a number on a tablet on the table. As Marcus tallied the garments, I transferred the items from my old shirt to this new one.

"Your alteration with the addition of Candy's garments comes to eight hundred and fifty-two credits," Marcus said.

"Do you take diamond-stamped quaybit?" I asked.

He thought about it for a moment and said, "I do, but I can't make change."

I knew a single strip of quaybit was worth one thousand credits, so I handed him two from the folding wallet and returned the wallet to my new inner right pocket, saying, "Keep the change."

"Oh, how generous. Thank you for your patronage," Marcus said, using both hands to give Candy the full shopping bag.

It was heavier than Candy anticipated, and she immediately handed it to me, saying, "Here, you carry this."

I grabbed my old shirt from the table and tossed it on top of the other clothes in the bag before saying, "Thank you for the great work. I'm sorry about the delay in the pickup."

"Oh, not to worry. I am flexible enough to serve the most demanding patrons, and you two are not demanding but endearing," Marcus said as we left.

"Thank you, Marcus," Candy said, and we walked onto the concourse.

"I'm heading back home. I have to catch up on some projects. If it really has been four weeks, I might have some clues," I said.

"That's fine with me too. I might have to invite Melissa over to help me with a fitting," Candy said slyly.

I handed Candy her bag and said, "Ohm, transport Candy to her apartment and me to mine."

The last thing I saw was Candy looking over at me as she dissolved away to the left. I wondered, from time to time, what caused the drifting effect of the transport dissolve? If velocity wasn't involved, it seemed consciousness was in motion and moving away. Or was it just the staggering delay processing of the memory buffer chopping through its units? A reverse build occurred as the new location assembled before my eyes.

CHAPTER 21

Drum Practice

Heading out to the balcony of my San Francisco apartment, I took in some fresh air. It was, once again, a wonderful day on climate-controlled future Earth. Inside my invisihud, I pulled up the teddy bear icon and activated it. The video feed appeared in the distance, and I zoomed in to look through the teddy bear's eyes.

"Jeremy, sorry I was gone so long. Some things came up. But I haven't forgotten about you, Jere. It's just that the people back home want closure, you know, something to bury. You're never going back there, so why not cooperate?" I monologued on, through the teddy bear's voice, and the heap that was Jeremy Stewart started to arise.

"Why not give up the location? Where did you hide the body, Jeremy? Somewhere a firmous would never look. Or maybe somewhere a firmous could not reach?" I said.

Flexanite Jeremy, rose up from the floor, resuming his human form, and feebly said, "Release me now."

"I know the limits of the human body, Jere. If you're wasting energy on keeping that form, I suggest you save yourself the trouble. What I don't know is the limits of a Flexanite. Do you get hungry? Do you get thirsty?" I asked as the teddy bear.

Jeremy gave the teddy bear one last look with human eyes before collapsing slowly into a puddle on the floor. I did not know if Flexanites could die from imprisonment, but I did not want my first prisoner to be a guinea pig.

I shut down the teddy bear icon and said, "Ohm, transport the Jeremy Stewart Flexanite to the Eden prison planet. Place him near water. Use a cloaked scanner to track him," I said.

A moment or two passed, and Ohm replied, "Transport complete. The subject is motionless."

"Moving on. I'd like to review the feed from Jeremy Stewart's assistant," I said to Ohm.

A new video plate appeared inside my invisihud overlay, and I dove inside. There was a lot here, so I said, "Ohm, filter the log to show only things done more than three times."

Her daily life was very routine, so that filter did not help much. I added, "Ohm, filter out any non-work related entries. Confine results to activities happening on the Starnet campus."

This filter reduced the data set, and I scrubbed through quite a few activities over those four weeks. But there was still too much to look through, so I said, "Ohm, filter out all activities with many people. Present the logs where the subject is alone but on campus."

This request resulted in many personal scenarios, so I added, "Ohm, remove restroom scenes."

Narrowing it down from the log, I determined she often took a walk around campus, either before or after lunch. I watched the playback over a few times before I saw it. She stopped in front of the Logican statue. The same statue where I placed the *Journey* transmitter unit. In the video log, she said something. I moved the log back and replayed her approach to the statue. I heard her say, "Oh, Jeremy," as she hung her head and walked off.

"Ohm, let's set up a random relocation for the *Journey* transmitter. Keep it on the campus but move it to a new location every eight days," I said.

"Moving transmitter. Applying new rule," Ohm said.

"Ohm, dispatch a cloaked scanner to the same location I have cued up in the log," I said.

"Dispatching cloaked scanner," Ohm replied.

I paced along the balcony, waiting for the cloaked scanner to come online. My invisihud flashed with a new location to view. Pulling up the sensors for that location, I issued a full spectral scan. The results were a bit shocking. There was an actual body inside the statue, placed in the exact pose that the statue held. Bizarrely artistic and maniacal at the same time. This corpse was probably poor Jeremy Stewart.

I didn't want to be involved with a murder, so I thought it best to defame the statue with graffiti. Inside the environment designer, I discovered auragraphic hooligans. I dropped in a few more cloaked scanners and used them as portable auraprojectors at the site. This way, any logging devices in this area will record the hooligans as the culprits. I scripted the hooligans to throw paint, to use iron bars to dent up the actual statue. One of the hooligans used acid to dissolve some of the mounting bolts. The staged event looked like the hooligans ran up and just had at it, leaving the supplies behind as they fled. The supplies were real, but the hooligans were not.

I did not know if this type of action was really the correct one to take, but I felt the sooner Starnet became aware of the imminent Flexanite threat, the better off we all would be. The discovery of Jeremy Stewart's body would certainly raise a lot of questions. Even now, it has been four weeks. That might be four weeks of non-reporting by Flexanite Jeremy. It would not surprise me if another Flexanite was dispatched to investigate or simply take on another role. Which would mean another murder.

"Ohm, any progress on the search for the Imperial fleet in the Gar sector?"

"The search continues, no matches have been found."

"Ohm, let's deploy the *Zanna* to a position near the radionic tile, by *Oasis Seven*. Keep it cloaked and send the *Zanna* through the tile. I want to establish a transport anchor in the Ussu sector," I said.

"Understood, deploying the *Zanna*," Ohm said.

I decided to head upstairs to the Black Glass Studios and jump on the drums. When I got to the main lounge area, the place was totally trashed. It looked like four weeks of daily parties going on here, and the build-up of left-over cans, bottles, and food was staggering. The music stage was still intact and I noticed some new gear added to Byrone's control booth. Checking out my drums, I discovered the heads were beaten to death. Some asshole left divots in all the drum heads. I never understood that. The hit your drum so hard it breaks the instrument mentality of some players. The drum can only get so loud in a room.

"Ohm, recycle all garbage in this room. Keep partially full liquor bottles, and place them on the table. Also, place any weed or other drugs on the table. Replace this drum kit with a brand new Tama Swing Star model, with new heads tuned to factory pitch."

There was a flurry of sparkles tidying up all around the room as items disappeared and reappeared. I couldn't help but think about how magicians used a spell for tasks such as these. I inspected the booze and weed remnants left on the table. There was enough here for another party, that was for sure. A mild scraping reverberation sounded as the new drum kit materialized. The cymbals echoed with a sheen, and the toms reverberated with a soft hollow boom. The entire room settled down as the sparkles faded and finally stopped.

"Ohm, can you place a lighter on the table?" I asked, and a lighter, similar to the one I replicated at Ethan's party, appeared nearby.

There were a few half-smoked joints in the collection, so I picked one, and lit up. I left the lighter on the table and headed over to the stage to take my seat behind the drums. There was a set of sticks with nylon tips resting across the snare. I puffed a few more times, holding it in, and used my invisihud to locate some pre-selected music from a list I set up before. These were songs I liked to play along with. I started the playback and began my drum practice. I was about halfway through the sixth song when someone walked out from the guest rooms area, asking, "Jesus fucking Christ, do you have to do that now?"

I came to a stop, turned off the music, and said, "No, I don't really have to play the drums right now," before standing up and walking over to the booze-weed table.

I picked up the lighter, lit up my roach, and the fellow joined me on the couch saying, "Thanks," while reaching for the joint I handed him.

"I'm Sam. I live in the building," I said.

"Right on," he said, smiling at me before handing the joint back. "I'm Ronnie. Soory aboot being a dick about the drums. I just have a wicked hangover."

"Ohm, replicate a medjector," I said, and a medjector appeared on the coffee table next to the booze.

I was not sure at first, but now I was certain. This was the guy who asked me for a smoke when I left K-Mac's trailer the last time I was there. As I looked

Ronnie over, I noticed he wore, from the first time I saw him, the same bowling shirt and blue track pants with a wide yellow stripe.

"Not a problem," I said as I picked up the medjector continuing, "I am a trained medical assistant, and I do have a cure for a hangover if you would like to try it?"

"Really?" Ronnie asked as he puffed on the joint, making a face. "What the fuck. Let's give it a try."

I dialed up the cure for hangovers on the medjector. It was essentially a mix of alcohol neutralizing agents with a mild sedative for the headache. It rebalances the blood and works fairly quickly. Ronnie handed me the joint, which was nearly gone, and I said, "It's like a shot in the neck, but there is no needle. Tilt your head sideways a little."

Ronnie tilted his head, and I applied the medjector to his neck, making a slight, "Shsss," sound.

"That's it? I don't have to drink anything or somethin'?" Ronnie asked.

"That's it," I said. "You should feel better soon."

Another person emerged from the backroom, and Ronnie said, "Hey Adrien, this guy, what was your name again?" he asked in mid-sentence.

"Sam," I replied.

"Sam here has a cure for hangovers," Ronnie completed his sentence.

I quickly remembered Adrien as the other guy with Ronnie that night. He wore all dark clothes and held a rocks glass in his hand about half full of a lemony liquid.

"I was about to roach this unless you want to get a couple of hits?" I said to Adrien, offering him the remainder of the joint as he approached the couch.

He walked up to the couch and reached over Ronnie to take the joint from me and said, "Move down, Ronnie."

We both moved down a place on the couch and Adrien took the seat at the end. He puffed on the joint a few times, before saying, "We have to head back home today. I have some things I have to check in with."

"Why do you want to go back to the park? We have everything here?" Ronnie asked as he reached for a bottle, holding it up to determine how much was left.

"This place isn't real Ronnie. It's an illusion or a game or something. I don't know," Adrien replied.

"It seems real enough to me," Ronnie said before taking a swig of Wild Turkey and then pointing at me. "Sam, here, is real."

"It doesn't matter. We have to go back right now, Ronnie," Adrien said.

"Right the fuck now. We can't just enjoy this place a little more," Ronnie pleaded with Adrien.

"We've worn out our welcome," Adrien said sipping from his glass.

"Please, don't think that. I just like to practice the drums. I didn't see anyone here so I thought I'd rock out a bit. It helps me clear my head," I said.

"See, Sam doesn't mind," Ronnie said.

"We've got to find K-Mac and Byrone to take us back," Adrien said.

"Oh, I can send you back," I said before standing up, and walking to the other side of the coffee table.

Adrien stood up and said, "Let's go, Ronnie," still holding on to his glass.

"All right, I don't know why we have to leave a perfectly good place to go chase down whatever the fuck it is you have to do," Ronnie said, standing up from the couch and walking around the table.

"Are you guys ready? Do you have everything you came with?" I asked.

Ronnie eyed the table, picked up a couple of bottles of booze, and a few of the joint remnants. Adrien looked at the table then grabbed the rest of an 1802 tequila bottle and said, "Yeah, we're ready."

"Ohm, return Ronnie and Adrien to the Meadowland Mobile Home park," I said, and their forms sparkled and disappeared. A minute or two later, I heard some rustling from the backroom, and K-Mac and Byrone appeared along with three women.

"Yo, dawg. I thought I heard some noise out here. What's up?" K-Mac said walking over and slapping my hand.

Then looking around he said, "I thought I heard Adrien and Ronnie out here."

"Yeah, I sent them back to Meadowland. Adrien said he had to catch up on some business," I replied.

Byrone walked up to me and greeted me with more of a forearm grip than a handshake and said, "I thought I heard some drums kickin' around out here."

"Yep, that was me. Sorry if it was too early. I just had the itch to bang around on them a bit," I said.

The women walked up with Byrone, and K-Mac said, "Come here, ladies. I want you to meet someone. This here is Sam. Sam, this is Tammy, Princess, and Tamika."

"Pleased to meet you," I said briefly, shaking each of their hands as they said, "Hello," in reply, and took a seat on the couch.

"Where you been? It's been a few weeks since we last saw you," Byrone asked.

"I know, sorry about that. I ended up in another dimension where time moved faster for you than for me. It's only been a few days from my point of view but it's been four weeks here," I said as I headed into the kitchen to make some coffee.

"Dang, dawg, I don't even know how that is possible. But I'm glad you're back. We've been broadcastin' through the roof," K-Mac said.

K-Mac and Byrone followed me over to the island separating the lounge from the kitchen, but the women remained on the couch talking amongst themselves. I asked across the room, "I'm making some coffee, are you ladies up for some?"

Tamika answered for all of them, "Sure, thanks for asking."

I checked the cupboard high and low and finally found a bag of coffee beans, some filters, and a grinder. I emptied the last batch of coffee grounds into the trash and got to work measuring out the right amount of coffee, and the right amount of water to match the richness I liked. After filling the water tank, I set the machine in motion.

"Are the ratings still looking good?" I asked during the process.

"We're hot," Byrone said before adding, "So hot that we are getting approached on the street like we're rock stars or somethin'."

I put my hand up for a high five and got one from each of them.

"It's ahite, but dang, some of those cats who approach us are such uptight white collars, and we can't dig that. But the fans are cool," K-Mac added.

"That's smart. The minute you sell out is the minute you lose your credibility," I said while both K-Mac and Byrone shook their heads in agreement.

"That's the way we feel too. I mean what the fuck do we need support from uptight corporate interests when we can just rock out here at Black Glass and tell it like it is," Byrone said while K-Mac nodded in agreement.

"Have you run into any legal hassles?" I asked.

"Dawg, there is always someone showin' up when we head out of the building, ridin' our jock about something we said," K-Mac said.

"We just tell them, hey, if you don't like it, don't watch it," Byrone said, and I shook my head in agreement.

"You might want to try some other exits from the building. As a matter of fact, why don't I just set you two up with a special exit to Yerba Buena Gardens? It's a little park, not far from here," I said.

"Dang, dawg, that would be awesome," K-Mac said.

"Ohm, provide a Transfast from here to Yerba Buena Gardens. Make it somewhere off the beaten path to minimize the transport sparkle," I said.

From behind me, I heard Ohm reply, "Transport site is now available for squire level access," and I turned around to notice the glowing sphere on top of the refrigerator.

"Yeah, we put the sphere out of the way. Once we had guests over, too many questions," Byrone replied.

The coffee machine finished its sputtering and heaved its final sigh of steam as I pulled down a few coffee cups from the cupboard and poured myself a half cup. I sat out cream for the others and said to the room, "Coffee's ready."

I walked into the lounge to make room for others to pour a cup. I sipped my coffee. Not bad. I think I needed to add a little more coffee or less water. It was rich-tasting, but I might not have added enough water. I always have trouble making larger pots than smaller ones. I have the simple four-cup recipe down pat, though, for most cases.

All of a sudden, I picked up a message through my invisihud audio system. I went ahead and transferred it to the room so everyone could hear it."

"Hello, hello does this even work? We are under attack. Heavy casualties. We need help," an unknown voice said.

"Ohm, where is that message coming from?" I asked.

"The message is being relayed through the business card you gave Jason Bowmen," Ohm replied.

"What the hell is that?" Byrone said.

"It's friends who need our help," I said. "Get into the broadcast booth. Were going live with this."

"Ohm, transfer my cloaked scanner output to K-Mac and Byrone's broadcast booth and transport me to the card's location," I said.

I looked down into my cup of coffee as the world disintegrated around me. I felt the cold black darkness envelop me. This turn of events was not good news, and I felt incredibly agitated waiting in limbo to appear. My ears must have materialized first. I could hear a repeating warning siren in the darkness as a field of red flashing low-lighting brought my senses back together.

CHAPTER 22

Rulkan Attack

I materialized in a small room of a starship with the arching ceiling conduits near my head. An impact rocked the ship, causing me to lose my balance, and I dropped my coffee cup as the ship took another hit. A woman was here, with her back to me, who screamed when she turned around, startled at my appearance. She was a young, Japanese woman wearing a drab olive jumpsuit uniform similar to the other *Explorer* crew members. I haven't met her yet, but I knew her name was Suki.

"I'm Sam. I got your message," I said to her startled face.

"We need help," she said and headed out a door that automatically opened onto the bridge of the *Explorer*.

It looks like I arrived in the Captain's office, off to the side of the bridge. Some crew were down, but I noticed Tenda, at her station, shouting orders to the navigator who performed an evasive maneuver. "Ohm, overlay the tactical situation to my invisihud," I yelled.

My invisihud populated with a representation of the battle taking place outside this ship. It looked like two Rulkan spider wings against this single ship, *Explorer*. I said, "Ohm place excessive explosive charges at the firing points on each attacking ship."

Henry, to my right, climbed up from the floor and back to his station while shouting, "Hull plating buckling on deck four."

"They're coming around for another run, Commander," I heard the navigator say to Tenda as he looked over at her with concern. I had not met him, but I knew his name was Trent.

"Seal off the affected decks," Tenda said to Henry and then to Trent. "Evasive maneuvers ensign."

I felt the ship tilt right with an audible groan as we watched the ships on the viewport bare down on our position in the classic Rulkan attack formation. In the next instance, the screen went white as the energy from a blast overwhelmed the sensor or camera, relaying the image. We felt a slight jolt as the explosions took place but not nearly as bad as the direct hits I felt upon arrival. Inside my invisihud, I noticed the attacking ship started to drift, and the second ship changed course, deciding to flee. I said, "Ohm, set off the charges on the second ship now."

The white overload on the screen subside, and the display revealed both attacking ships damaged and smoking, as I'm sure this ship was too. Suki ran over to the floor where Jason Bowmen was lying. One of the support beams from the ceiling collapsed, and it looked like he took a blow to the head. She tapped her communication brooch and said, "Medical emergency on the bridge!"

Henry reported, "The second ship is moving off, Commander."

"Should I disable it?" I asked Tenda.

The entire bridge crew looked at me, giving me the impression that I asked the stupidest question in the world. Commander Tenda said, "Disable the engines, but leave life support intact if you can."

"Ohm, disable flux engines on both attacking ships. Use known weaknesses for the vessels of this time and class," I said.

It took a moment, and the display reflected my request with staggered secondary explosions taking place on both of the ships on display. The first one, which was damaged when it fired its shot, took significantly more damage than the second one. Their starboard side nacelle was visibly askew and misaligned after the explosion.

Not commenting on the other ships, Tenda said, "Damage report."

I headed over to Jason's unconscious form and said, "I have some medical training. I can help until the medics arrive."

Suki reluctantly moved back, gently returning Jason's head to the floor, then returned to her communication station saying, "Yes, Commander. The magnalifts are down, and life support is critical."

"We're venting plasma from the port nacelle. Teams report deck four sealed, but we have multiple hull breaches," Henry reported.

"Ohm, I need a trauma medkit," I said as I made a visual inspection of Jason Bowmen. With a sparkle, the medkit appeared, and I quickly flipped it open.

"Ensign, move us out of the field of battle," I heard Tenda say, continuing to issue commands.

Using the medical inspectrograph, I made a quick scan of Jason's body. I was mainly concerned about his spinal column. I did not want to create complications by moving him if he suffered a spinal injury. The spinal scan checked out okay, so I moved him out of the contorted position he fell into and started a cranial scan.

"Reroute auxiliary power to life support," I heard Tenda say to Henry.

"Rerouting, but there is barely anything there," Henry said worriedly.

I felt I was in over my head in this situation. While I explored some basic field exercises with these devices, it was not until later, after I met Jorrie and Erin, that I took on a more regimented approach to my medical training. I searched my future memories, trying to recall anything that might help with cranial trauma. In a panic, I tapped Jason Bowmen's communication brooch and said, "Farouk, this is Sam. I am on the bridge, and Jason is down with a head injury. I have ruled out spinal column damage, but I'm looking for guidance to proceed."

I received no response. All of a sudden Suki said, "I'm seeing energy signatures. I think they are boarding us using transporters."

"Can we go to flux ensign?" Tenda asked.

"We can, but we only have one nacelle," Trent replied.

"Do it. A short burst of flux one to get us out of their transporter range," Tenda shouted.

"Aye, Commander," Trent said.

The whole ship started shaking, and more of the ceiling fell on my back as I shielded Jason from the falling debris. I took the first hit hard, collapsing onto him, then Ohm must have automatically kicked in my personal shield to deflect the other blows. I could hear large stressing metal sounds as the ship complained at moving so quickly with so much structural damage.

"Commander, we're going to break up!" Henry shouted.

The ship came to a stop. Tenda rushed over and cleared the debris off me and her captain and asked, "How is he?"

"Head trauma. I'm worried about the swelling," I replied.

I heard Farouk reply through Jason's communication brooch, "Who is this?"

Tenda answered for me, "It is Sam, the traveler we met a short while ago. He has a medkit and is attempting to treat Captain Bowmen."

"Sam, how are his vitals?" Farouk asked.

"His vitals are all right but with elevated blood pressure. I see bruising on the right eye socket and blood dripping out of the right ear," I said, trying hard not to lose my composure as tears formed in my eyes.

"Commander, I can't do any more here. If we're being boarded, I need to get somewhere I can help," Henry said.

"Go ahead," Tenda said to Henry as he headed over to fetch a gleam gun from the wall case and opened a side door revealing a ladder leading down.

"We need to slow the build-up of pressure on the brain. Does your medkit offer a way to administer tryaxanol?" Farouk said.

I riffled through the medkit and quickly pulled out the medjector to dial-up tryaxanol and said, "I have a medjector that can administer many drugs. It's set for tryaxanol. What dosage do I use?" I asked.

"Let's start with twelve milligrams," Farouk said, and I thought I heard noises in the background of his communication.

Tenda heard the noises too and said, "Do what you can for him," then, turning to Trent, said, "Mr. Fairline, you have the con until I return or the Captain revives."

"Aye, Commander," Trent said as Tenda grabbed a gleam gun and disappeared down the ladder.

"Farouk, are you there. Farouk!" I said to no response.

I applied the twelve-milligram dose to Jason.

"Ohm, what other drugs can be safely used in conjunction with tryaxanol?"

I asked, blinking the tears out of my eyes and regaining my composure.

Ohm began listing a series of drugs to safely use in combination with tryaxanol, and I yelled, "Stop. Ohm, I need a solution, not a list. What would a trained medical technician do after administering tryaxanol?"

"Monitor patient blood pressure looking for blood pressure reduction," Ohm said.

I activated the medical inspectrograph and reviewed the slowly sliding histogram for blood pressure on the display. I saw some reduction while the graph continued updating. Jason started to rasp as his breathing labored, and I saw the heart rate increase.

"Help me sit him up," I said to the room, and Suki came over to prop him up against his Captain's chair.

This position seemed to help his breathing, but his head fell forward. Suki held his head up as a little more blood flowed out of his ear. I knelt to pick up Jason Bowmen. Standing up, I could feel the blow to my back. Looking over at Suki and Trent, I said, "I am taking him to sickbay."

"Ohm, transport us to sickbay aboard this ship," I said, and the bridge dissolved around us.

I never liked transporting people who were seriously injured. It seemed odd to me they would reassemble in an injured state when it would be just as possible to materialize them in a healthy state. But transporter technology did not work like that. It was a one-to-one copy from the source location to the destination. I saw grey lights with green beams fizzle back into view as we materialized in sickbay.

Sickbay was under siege. There were some *Explorer* security guards in physical combat with Rulkan soldiers. Farouk was on the floor holding one-off with a metal tray, and I heard the sound of weapons fire as one of the Rulkans shot down an *Explorer* crewman.

I shouted, "Ohm, anesthetize the Rulkans!"

The Rulkan that shot the guard whirled around and aimed at me. His shot went wide, up to the ceiling as he continued to twirl while he fell to the floor unconscious.

Rushing over to one of the beds, I placed Jason upon it and said to Farouk, "I gave him twelve milligrams of tryaxanol, but I don't know what to do next."

I helped him up from the floor. Farouk was shocked for a moment but gathered his composure as he realized the seriousness of the situation. He straightened his clothes and said, "I'll take him from here."

Stepping back, I watched for a moment, then heard the groans of the wounded crewman. His buddy rushed over to help him.

"Ohm, materialize the beta prototype for the cellepulator," I said, and the unit appeared on the floor.

I picked up the device and moved over to the crewman, who looked like he was about to pass out from the pain. His wound was on his lower right side. The shot burned through his uniform near the spot where I took a hit on *Journey*. I knew he was in pain, but I decided to try the new cellepulator first, rather than materialize another medkit, find a medjector, and administer a pain killer. The cellepulator felt a little clunky in my hand. A cartridge attached to the back of the unit threw the weight off. I thumbed through the menus and located the scanner option before moving it across the wounded area. My hand was a little shaky, and the device could not get a good lock on the shape of the wound to produce a replicated bio patch.

The crewman's buddy said, "Hang in there, Karl."

I sat down on my knees in front of the crewman and held the device firmly in both hands, forming a tripod with my elbows as I steadied the device. This time, the detection mechanism relayed a wireframe image of the wound to the display. A few calibration lines rapidly appeared. They flashed, and a blue ray shot out of the device, depositing an orgamorphic gel patch over the entire surface of the wound. I felt the device heat up in my hand, and I dropped it to the floor as it made a large pop noise. The sound reminded me of an old-style flash photo bulb burning out.

I looked up at Karl and asked, "How is it?"

Karl shook his head yes as he showed a bit of relief.

"It's a special gel pack designed to quickly restore burned flesh. Try not to move for a few minutes. It takes a minute or two to set," I said.

Karl continued to shake his head, yes, and said, "Thanks," with a labored voice.

"Ohm, I need another medkit" I said.

A sparkle appeared on the floor next to me. As it faded, another medkit remained behind. I opened it and used the At-a-Glance feature of the medical inspectrograph. It wasn't sure what to make of the gel patch but recommended a dose of pain relief medicine. Tapping that suggestion, the medjector in the case vibrated and lit up. The medical inspectrograph automatically programmed the medjector. I pressed it against Karl's neck, saying, "This should help with the pain," and I opened a small bottle of water from the medkit before handing it to him.

Karl's crewmate secured the three Rulkans. He put their hands behind their backs and placed some type of plastic binding on their wrists. He did the same thing on their feet, then gathered up their weapons and moved them to a shelf on the other side of the room. Looking over, I saw Farouk was still busy working on Jason. I picked up the medkit and said, "I am heading down to engineering to see if anyone is hurt down there."

Walking out of the double-wide glass sickbay doors, I headed straight for a junction then took a left. In the second time loop, before we married Jorrie, Erin and I lived and served aboard this vessel. We shared one of the smallest quarters on the ship. It was closet-sized, and when we hung out there, it was like living in a small tent. The one nice thing about our quarters was a circular viewport that I enlarged so we could sit there. We were basically at the edge of the ship's hull and could feel the cold of space through the metal. We sat there holding each other, wrapped in blankets, enduring the cold so we could look at the stars together.

It didn't take long before I heard the sounds of weapons fire. My shield was set to auto, so I turned it on full and activated the cloak. I didn't want to get shot this time. The sounds of weapons fire led me down a few corridors to a dead end with a ladder down. I slid down the handrails, naval style, and leaped off at the bottom.

"Ohm, start scanning the ship for life forms. Add them to my hud, and mark them by species. Initiate a search from my current location," I said as I made my way along the corridor.

I was close, very close, when my invisihud populated with the nearby battle, but I didn't need the overlay to see the Rulkans at the end of this corridor. After targeting them, I used the sleep icon. The cloaked scanners implemented this feature with a Transfast of anesthesia directly to the target's bloodstream. The size of the candidate determined the dosage, and the anesthesia used was deter-mined by species. Dropping my cloak, I called out, "Sam, here. I have knocked out the Rulkans."

Henry and his men emerged from their points of cover. The guards turned around quickly and targeted me while I called out, "It's me, Henry. Don't shoot."

"Hold your fire and secure those prisoners," Henry ordered, and his men got to work.

I rushed up and said, "I took the Captain to sickbay. Farouk is working on him. We took out three Rulkans, who tried to take over the medical lab."

"Good work," Henry said with a smile, putting his hand on my shoulder for a moment.

I realized then that Henry was a good commander. Even though he was not my commander, I felt his sense of respect at the recognition of my accomplish-ments. I also noticed he treated those men around him with respect.

"I'm heading to engineering to see if anyone is hurt," I said.

"We're heading that way too. Let's move together," he said to me, and then back at two of his men, "Yoleti, Aronda, stay here and guard these prisoners."

"Aye, sir," they both replied, and Henry, myself, and one other man headed off in the direction of engineering.

We made our way, not meeting any resistance, as we headed down two decks and through corridors. As we approached engineering, weapons fire rang out. Each weapon produced a unique sound. We crept up to the entrance, and Hen-ry dashed across the doorway, taking up a stance on one side as his man took up a similar position on the other. Henry used a series of hand signals to synchro-nize the assault, and they executed it flawlessly. Two Rulkans stood on the upper deck of the engineering room, and one stood below. Henry shot the one below while his man took out the two up top, a single shot each. That is why Henry chose this man to stay with us. This guy was a sharpshooter. We entered engi-neering cautiously after a few people yelled out, "Clear."

Easing up on our stance, Henry called out, "Secure those two on the upper deck," as he moved over to secure the one on the floor that he took down.

As I moved through the room, I came upon Chuck slumped against a wall. He said, weakly, "Sam."

I moved over to his location quickly and opened up the medkit saying, "Hold on, Chuck. I've got you now."

I continued talking to him as I used the medical inspectrograph to scan his body for injury, saying, "We've taken out nine Rulkans that boarded us using their transporters. Trent moved us quickly out of transporter range, so I don't think many more could have possibly boarded."

As I gave Chuck the information, he shook his head, but I could see he was in a lot of pain since his face was pale.

"Ohm, replicate another cellepulator," I said.

Chuck looked down as the floor sparkled, and I could tell he may not have known if that was real. After the sparkle faded, I picked it up and quickly located the same burn preset I used on Karl up in sickbay. Chuck was shot more in the upper chest area. I ripped his uniform open as I propped him up, saying, "I just need to get a good picture of you."

Kneeling before him, I assumed the elbow triangle pose, pointing the cellepulator at his wound until it detected the burned area. I pressed the button and tried to hold the device steady, like a camera on a long exposure. The display scan lines moved, and the blue ray shot out of the unit into Chuck's chest, causing him to wince as it happened. I felt the cellepulator heat up, and I quickly put it down on the floor as it popped loud and fizzled a small stream of smoke. Using the medical inspectrograph, I scanned Chuck again. The wound registered less than before.

"Talk to me, Chuck. How are you feeling?" I asked.

"Better, a little better. It feels gooey," Chuck said.

"It's gonna feel a little gooey for a while. The medicine is called orgamorphic gel. It adapts to take on the surrounding cell type it comes in contact with. The initial surface patch is weak, at first, like a cake rising. Try to sit as still as possible until it hardens up. Do you want a drink of water?"

Chuck nodded and let out a labored breath. I retrieved another small water bottle from the medkit and opened it for him. He reached his hand out and took a small drink. I fetched the medjector and brought up a mild sedative for humans. I cut the dosage in half before applying it to Chuck's neck, saying, "This should help with the pain a bit, but not knock you out."

He nodded yes again. Much of the engineering staff gathered around to see how their commander was doing. Once Chuck became aware of everyone looking at him, he asked, "What are you standin' around for? We've got work to do. We have to contain that port nacelle plasma leak. Carson, get those relays up and running. "

I scanned him again with the medical inspectrograph, and even though his vitals were low, they were stable. I could see no other visible wound, but I asked, "Chuck, did you get hit anywhere else?"

Chuck shook his head no and said, "But this one's a bitch."

I smiled and said, "Your vital signs are good. Hang in there."

"You're not a very good liar, Sam," Chuck said, and he nodded off.

I picked him up and said, "Ohm, transport us to sickbay."

The room dissolved, and I hung in suspended dark silence, holding commander Tanner in my non-corporeal arms. It was the first time I almost felt a connection to the person I transported with. Even though I tried to mentally talk to Candy in this suspended state, there was no indication she was there. But while holding Chuck, I felt like a parent carrying a child, keeping it safe. The gold-white lights of sickbay flooded in from the sides as we materialized.

Looking around the room, I saw Karl felt good enough to move off the floor and sit in a chair. Farouk stood next to Jason Bowmen, who regained consciousness and sat upon a biobed relaying his life signs to a screen above him. The other security crewman rushed up to help me place Chuck on an empty biobed.

Farouk immediately walked over and began an inspection of Chuck, asking, "What is this?"

"It's the same thing I used on Karl over there. It is an orgamorphic gel patch. The gel is initially neutral but then takes on the cell structure of the surrounding cells to accelerate healing. I think the Rulkan weapons may have a secondary effect besides just burning. I gave him a half dose of a sedative as well," I said, filling him in as best possible.

Farouk scanned Chuck with a device, focusing on the gel patch, and asked, "Karl, can you come over here?"

Karl walked over to the bed and said, "I do feel better, and it seems to be shrinking," as Farouk moved the scanner over his gel patch, which was noticeably smaller.

Farouk returned to Chuck and used his medical injector, which brought Chuck around, asking, "What happened?"

"You're in sickbay. Lie still," Farouk said as he continued to work on him.

Jason gave me an inviting look, and I approached his bed. He said, "I guess you got the message."

"And in the nick of time, jeez," I said.

"Farouk filled me in a bit. As did Suki. You saved my ship," Jason said.

"We captured nine Rulkan intruders. We're still not sure how many transported onboard, though," I reported.

"I'm trying to say thank you, Sam."

"You're welcome," I said, paused, and continued, "Rulkan technology, of this era, is more advanced than your starship. Taking on two spider wings is tough, and we're not out of the woods yet. There are several hull breaches, and the port nacelle is leaking plasma. I feel like I should be there helping out those crewmen."

He shook his head, yes, and said, "Make it so."

I nodded to him and turned around, one more time, to head out of sickbay. Making my way to the port side of the ship, I located one of the maintenance tubes leading up the strut to the nacelle perched at the end. It was a quick climb. There were some gravity plates here and there but no full plating to hold you down. I pulled myself up the ladder, in a semi-weightless state, until I reached the top. Climbing out of the strut passageway, I made my way into the nacelle. There was gravity plating here, and I felt the rush of oxygen escaping through the hull breach. I checked my invisihud and could see there were two human engineers here. I moved to their location and announced myself as I approached, "Hello, friendly here. I'm Sam. I'm here to help with the plasma leak."

"I'm Jenkins, and this is Clark. We've found the leak, but the valve is too hot to shut off," Jenkins said.

Clark added, "And even if we could turn the valve, it might just melt or break under the torque."

"We need containment first to allow cooling. Can you show me the valve?" I asked over the noise produced by the escaping atmosphere.

Jenkins led the way along one side of the nacelle, then into some interior passageways where the walls were rows of pipes. Old school cooling, I thought. She paused at a junction to allow me to get in front of her. These passageways were only as wide as a single person.

"It's just up ahead," she said and pointed.

"You two head back. We'll stay in touch with coms," I said.

"Are you sure?" Jenkins asked.

"Yes, I need someone to relay stats from the monitors," I said. "Go, quickly."

Jenkins and Clark headed out of the winding-pipe service hallway, and I soon heard boots running against metal as they dashed back to the control station. I made my way forward and saw the leaking plasma escaping into space through a breach in the nacelle casing. We were inside that casing. As the hot plasma drifted toward the opening, it passed over the valve needed to shut off the flow. I followed the plasma trail back to the initial leak, and it was a large one. It looked like a perfect shot penetrated the plating and split the main plasma conduit causing an eruption down the pipe that grew into an open seam.

Activating the invisihud environment designer mode, I used a feature labeled extract from environment. This menu option sampled the world around me to generate a virtual copy inside my invisihud overlay. From there, I could add virtual additions to my world, which could be replicated into physical objects. Placing two thick virtual rings along either side of the rip in the conduit, I said, "Ohm, convert the two virtual rings into a ring-based shield generator on either side."

The rings materialized with a sparkle, and I waited to see if the additional weight of these new devices would cause any collapse. The tube stayed in place, so I called out, saying, "Activating shield containment for the plasma tube."

"Ohm, activate shielding and standby emergency transport for all members of this ship."

They jumped a little and made a scraping sound along the outer tube as they twisted and locked onto one another, forming a stable shield.

"That's it. We have plasma containment. Valve temperature is dropping," Jenkins called out.

Returning my attention to the environment designer, I placed a virtual tube over the length of the damaged section. With eye movements, I positioned the virtual tube over a non-damaged section of the conduit. The conform modifier forced the virtual representation to shrinkwrap to the shape of the actual plasma tube. Once they matched, I moved the prepared virtual tube over the damaged section and activated the replicate in place icon. There was a brief eruption of plasma when the new section materialized in place.

"Ohm, turn off the two shield generators and recycle them."

The shield rings disappeared in sparkles while the remaining plasma released by the shielding drifted out through the hull breach. I focused the environment designer on that location, created a large patch for the hull breach, and replicated it into a physical repair. The valve no longer needed to be tended to, so I left the maze of pipe walls and walked along the length of the nacelle to the monitoring area. Clark stepped up, approaching with both hands up, giving me double high fives as she said, "Yes, best possible outcome."

I returned a smile as I walked up to look at the monitors, and Jenkins said, "It looks good. The patch is holding. I think we could maintain flux now."

"If you don't need me anymore, I'm going to head down and check-in with engineering," I said.

"I think we can handle it from here," Jenkins said for the both of them. "Thanks, Sam."

Making my way to the strut passageway, I headed back to the interior of the ship. I had more of a rhythm this time. I pulled my weightless self along the ladder as I quickly made the return journey through the strut passage. I felt gravity start to kick in as I got close to the entrance, so I flipped around and used the ladder to make my final descent back into the ship.

I made my way to deck four and came upon a hatch sealing off that section. The door wouldn't open because there was no atmospheric pressure on the other side. Checking that my life support shield was enabled, I said, "Ohm, transport me past this door."

Once again, my world collapsed and dissolved into nothing. I waited in darkness, holding my breath before the low lighting crept into view as I reassembled on the other side of the hatch, sealing off deck four from the rest of the ship.

Deck four was non-officer and junior crew quarters and was laid out in a circular fashion around the radial section of the ship, with engineering at the center. This deck was where Erin and I were issued quarters when we served on this ship in the second time loop. I hoped all the crewmen were at their post during the attack because my invisihud readings indicated this section offered no life support and was exposed to space.

"Ohm, can you focus cloaked scanners on deck four? I am trying to locate the hull breach."

"Relocating scanners to your location," Ohm said, and a series of sparkles appeared and spread out to map deck four.

It was not too long before some of the scanners reported colder than others, and I took off in that direction toward junior officer quarters. These sets of quarters were along the outer hull of the radial section. I tracked the temperature drop to a group of three side-by-side crew quarters. When I peeked in through the doors, I saw a massive, single tear along the ceiling spanning across each room. Fortunately, there was no one here now, so I felt like I could implement a total section replacement.

"Ohm, can you gather up all the cloaked scanners and deploy them outside the *Explorer*, around this area? I want to use them as shields when we finally swap out the section."

"Redeploying cloaked scanners into space to act as shields," Ohm replied.

"Ohm, scan the ship for damage, reference any specifications for the ship available. I need a hull section replacement for the damaged area. Use the Blinn manufacturing facilities," I said.

"Cloaked scanners are in place. Working on generating a compatible hull section," Ohm replied.

I stood in the center room, looking around at the damage. Everything that wasn't secured was already gone, sucked into space. There was a white frost coating everything in the room. Up above, the frost coated the ripped-up metal to the point of the scorch marks. The entire room was an artist's study in frost, grey, and charcoal.

"Four sections identified for hull replacement. Three on deck four and one on deck two. Part replication is underway," Ohm reported.

I was not that far from our quarters in the previous time loop, so I walked down to the end of the corridor. Our quarters were more of an end cap, a left-over space the designers just put a door on. Before Erin and I first occupied them, it was used for storage. I pressed the wall button, and the door slid open, revealing a deep storage closet.

Everything was a mess. Boxes and supplies were scattered all over the floor. At the end of the room was a small circular window. In the other time loop, I shifted echo to the point of expanding the overall radial section diameter to get a larger space than the standard room offered. I stared into the clutter for a minute before pressing the button to close the door. I walked back to the quarters with the visible ceiling breach, and as I arrived, Ohm said, "Sections replicated and ready for transplacement."

"Ohm, are all areas clear of personnel?"

"Affirmative, no life forms present in the areas exposed to space," Ohm stated.

"Let's repair the smallest ones first and the largest one last. Establish external shielding using the cloaked scanners and proceed with hull section replacement."

"Proceeding," Ohm replied.

The swapping of the hull sections produced a series of tearing scrapes and groans. I felt like I could pinpoint which sections were being replaced just by where the sounds came from. Above me, in a barrage of sparkles, the ceiling vanished, and I stood in these quarters exposed to outer space. I felt like a character in a Kurt Vonnegut novel. Then, with just as many sparkles, the ceiling area lit up. The sparkles left behind the hull with a low boom.

"Ohm, review transplacement results. We have to be certain this repair is solid and stable."

"Checking," Ohm said. "Deck two hull patch is a one hundred percent match. Deck four patch one is a ninety-eight percent match. Deck four patch two is a ninety-nine percent match, and deck four patch three is a ninety-seven point five percent match."

"Explain discrepancies? Why are they all not a hundred percent match?"

"Subtle damage to the total ship structure prevents a hundred percent match, but all areas are one hundred percent sealed and ready for pressurization," Ohm replied.

"Ohm, attach the cloaked scanners, which are currently outside the ship, to the ship's hull. Place them in automatic shield mode around sensitive areas on the outer surface. Keep them cloaked. Protect communications, weapons, and engines first."

I walked back to the sealed hatchway I originally transported through and used the intercom on the wall to send a message to the bridge saying, "Bridge, this is Sam. I have repaired hull breaches on deck four and deck two. They should be ready for pressurization."

I waited with no response until I heard Suki ask, "Sam? Checking internal sensors now."

Another short delay then, "Pressurizing section. Standby," Suki said.

A long hissing sound tapered off to nothing. Some of the environment readings in my invisihud changed, and I heard a latch being thrown. The hatch sealing mechanism detected the pressure was balanced enough on either side of the door to allow entry or exit. I said into the wall communications panel, "Looks like it's holding down here. Opening the hatch to unseal deck four."

"Sam, the Captain requests you meet him in sickbay," Suki replied.

"On my way. Are the magnalifts operational?".

"Yes, Kirby got them up and running half-an-hour ago."

I opened the hatch, sealing deck four, releasing a small hiss. The pressure did seem to be holding. Heading down the corridor, I found the magnalift entrance. Stepping into the magnalift, I pressed the button for deck five and felt like I was falling. The ride was short, and the doors opened to reveal the corridors of deck five. It was the same circular pattern as on the deck above, but in the center was sickbay. Walking through the automatic double doors, I saw Chuck sitting up, and Jason was in his bed where I last saw him. He motioned me over, and I stood between the two beds.

"I am getting reports from my crew that you are doing exceptional work, extraordinary even," Jason said in his humble way, but also using it as a way to fish for information.

"As you probably heard, the plasma leak is sealed, and I replaced the damaged hull sections on deck four and deck two."

"Replaced entire hull sections? How large of a section?" Chuck asked slowly.

"Ohm, display a map of *Explorer*. Highlight the recent repairs," I said.

An auragraphic map floated in front of me, and I pushed it over to Chuck so he could review the highlighted sections, saying, "Just grab onto it like it is there, and you can move it around."

A smile came to Chuck's face as he grabbed onto the map of the ship and started zooming in to get a closer look at my repairs. Jason looked at me and asked, "I don't mean to sound ungrateful, but your actions are so extraordinary that I have to wonder what drives you to do this?"

"Ohm, playback Suki's initial card message for the room to hear," I said.

"Hello, hello, does this even work? We are under attack, heavy casualties. We need help," Suki said as the message played in the room, with the sound of the attack heard in the background.

"You mean why do I care?" I asked, shifting my weight as my back pain flared up.

My posture must have triggered some analysis mechanism inside Farouk as he stepped up and said, "You're injured."

He moved over to a table to fetch his medical scanning device, saying, "No fuss now, hop on the scanning bed."

I removed my new shirt that Marcus altered, which was now ripped in the back. I took off my undershirt to reveal my back, once again, to a doctor as Farouk asked, "How did this happen?"

"I arrived on the bridge when we were under heavy attack. When Suki and I returned from the Captain's room, Jason lie unconscious on the floor. The spider wings were hitting us hard. Tenda shouted orders, and I used a medkit to assess Jason's initial condition. Right then, we took another hit, and part of the ceiling collapsed on my back," I said as I retold my account of arriving on the ship.

"Let's move to the imaging chamber. I want to do a full-body scan," Farouk said.

He walked over to a control station. After pressing some buttons, a circular door embedded in the wall slid open to allow a composite-based bed frame to emerge.

"Go ahead and lie down on your belly. It does not hurt a bit," Farouk instructed, and I took up the face-down position he requested upon the scanning bed.

Farouk pressed some buttons, and the bed began to slide back into the wall as he said, "Try to hold as still as possible. It only takes a minute."

This bed was similar to a massage table. There was a hole for you to put your face into. As the bed slid into the wall, I located a special icon in my invisi-hud menu to activate deep sleep mode. In this mode, the invisihud hides itself by emitting biological signals instead of standard operational signals. While the signals emitted by the invisihud during normal operation are very covert and not likely to be detected, they would certainly stand out in a direct scan. The bed came to a stop, and I heard the circular door slide shut. Once again, thoughts of betrayal crossed my mind, and I tried to set them aside, reminding myself these people were supposed to be my friends.

A series of flashing lights began all around. They kept changing order, sometimes rotating in a circular fashion, other times hexaliptical, and finally in a runway order starting at the head moving in sync toward the toes. The lights stopped for a moment, and a mild hum repeated the same sequence as the lights, only with sound. When the hum finally fell silent, I heard the circular door slide open, and the bed started sliding out.

Farouk approached with a device in his and said, "Ah, ah, remain there, but lie on your right side."

He continued, "The damage is mainly soft tissue, no spinal column injury detected at all. This treatment is for the aches and a compound to prevent stiffness from setting in overnight. It will probably hurt in the morning so take it easy."

I felt Farouk dressing the small cuts along my back as he cleaned them out with a wet swab and applied bandages. I mentally counted six small gashes as Farouk tended to my wounds.

Jason walked over to examine the scan of my body projected on a display hanging above the workstation. He looked at the cuts on my back and said, "So, you are human."

"For the most part, yeah. Were you expecting gears and wires? Or maybe the scan reveals my hooves and horns?" I asked with the last statement getting a little smile out of him.

"I'm just trying to figure out what you are, Sam," Jason said with a poker face.

"These repairs look good, Capn'. I don't think space dock could have done a better job," Chuck said.

"Chuck, did you notice the associated deviations on some of the replacements?" I said over my shoulder while trying to sit up.

"Ah, ah, not yet. I am almost finished," Farouk said.

"I don't see it," Chuck replied.

"Touch the highlights and hold them for a moment. You'll get more detail about that repair," I said over my shoulder once again.

"Okay, trying that, and yep, oh, there is more info here," Chuck said.

Looking at Jason, I said, "There is a two-point seven five percent deviation in the ship's structural spec. It is not uncommon for a ship's framing to change throughout its life, especially if it experiences combat. The seals are all good, but when I made the parts to spec, the fit was not exact."

"I think I see what he's talkin' about, Capn'. Come have a look," Chuck said, and Jason walked over to review the report with Chuck.

"All done. You can put your clothes back on," Farouk said as he returned his supplies to a storage cabinet on the other side of the room.

"I think the repair is okay. It should certainly get us back to space dock. But now that I know about these deviations, I can make sure to compensate if needed," Chuck said to Jason.

I walked over to the two as I put Marcus' shirt back on, slowly feeling some of the pain from the cuts before Jason asked, "Is there anything else I should know about these repairs?"

"I left some cloaked shielding units on the surface of the outer hull. I used them for shielded containment while swapping out the replacement parts. Once the parts were in place, the units remained outside the ship."

"What do these units do, exactly?" Jason asked.

"They provide additional hull plating in a hemispherical area where they are placed. I docked them near the power supplies for communications, weapons, the engine, and along the length of both nacelles. They basically absorb energy hits until saturated. Additional hits after saturation will be taken by your standard hull plating. It can let you hang a little longer in a firefight, and protect systems from going down, even if the attackers land some direct hits."

"What are the side effects of these devices?" Jason asked.

"I'm not aware of any side effects on personnel. They are constructed using materials that might be considered from your future, so they could attract investigation by temporal police. But they only activate when they are attacked, so their energy emission profile is very low."

"How likely are these temporal police to discover these devices?" Jason asked, continuing with the grilling.

"I can't say. But if you feel uneasy about them, I can remove them when I leave," I said, adding, "and I think I should be on my way."

Jason took on a more friendly face and said, "Thanks again for saving my ship and the crew. And I think we'll keep those, what did you call them cloaked shields, for now."

"Good call. If you do run into trouble with temporal agents, use the card to contact me, and I'll do what I can to reason with them."

I shook Chuck's hand, and he said, "Thanks, Sam. I'm sure glad you came to our aid."

"No problem," I said.

Turning to Farouk, I said, "Thank you for tending to my back."

"It was my pleasure, and thank you for the work you did on the patients this day. Your actions mattered and saved lives."

I stepped away from the small group and said, "Ohm, discontinue map display, and transport me to the Black Glass Studios control booth."

The figures of my new friends fizzled and jumbled as I returned to darkness. Oddly enough, the only thing I thought about was how am I going to explain a new back injury to Candy? The soft light of the control room filled my eyes as I reassembled in the, muhaha, black tower.

I took a seat on the large, overstuffed leather couch and closed my eyes for a minute. I could really feel the back wound kicking in. Resting my head in my hand, I wondered what the hell I was doing, transporting from place to place? Is this how I live my life?

My thoughts were interrupted as Byrone and K-Mac came in from the broadcasting room with Byrone asking, "Dang, dude. Is your back all right?"

They both patted me on the shoulder, and K-Mac said, "We had to cut the feed after you beamed out of engineering, dawg, but that last line of Chuck's, 'But this one's a bitch,' sent ratings through the roof."

Byrone added, "Response calls flooded in, and it jammed up the system. What the hell happened after that?"

"Mainly a bunch of non-exciting repair work. I stopped the plasma leak and repaired the hull breaches, and Farouk fixed up my back in sickbay," I said.

"The system came back on by itself, but we were no longer broadcasting," Byrone said.

"That's right, dawg. We saw the whole conversation in sickbay," K-Mac said, asking, "What's up with that place? Are those people real?"

"They are real. They just live in another time," I said.

Byrone said, "That is some head trip, but it doesn't bother me that they live in another time. Hell, that's what we're doin'."

"That's right, we inter temporal now. I don't care if some mofo lives in the past or the future," K-Mac said.

"Me either. I don't care what time you're from. It's all about whether you're cool or not," Byrone said.

I interrupted their back and forth with an, "I've got it! We're making a movie. It's gonna be like what just happened. Consider that last broadcast an installment, a trailer for the film."

"Ah ite, Ah ite, I feel ya. An action movie," K-Mac said.

"Yes, action, for sure, because it will all be real," I said.

"And intrigue and suspense," Byrone added.

"I like it. The title is called, 'The Case of the Fake People,'" I said as I spread my hands apart while saying the title.

"I can dig. A case, a mystery to be solved," K-Mac said.

"An intergalactic case with romance, action, mystery, and all the special effects will be taken from real events," I said with a sparkle in my eye.

"With events like you just provided, we can promote the hell out of somethin' like that," Byrone said.

"The mac pack presents," K-Mac added.

I got up from the couch and said, "I think I need to lie down or something." They stood up, and K-Mac said, "We on it."

Byrone added, "Go get some rest."

"Oh, before I forget. The next time you are heading down to street level, stop off on floor twenty-three. There are some apartments on that floor, your neighbors. They are people like you, from other times and places. Not all of the apartments are occupied, so try knocking on a few doors. I'm not sure who took what apartment."

"Ah ite, not a problem. We like to know our neighbors," K-Mac said while slapping Byrone's hand.

"Ohm, transport me to my apartment on *Tiger Mountain*," I said, and the world dissolved around me while I was placed in the waiting room of darkness.

I felt like my parting with *Explorer* was a bit awkward. I could sense Jason Bowmen was not trying to look a gift horse in the mouth but also did not quite trust this stranger with even stranger powers. The room reassembled, and I found myself standing, once again, in my apartment on *Tiger Mountain*.

CHAPTER 23

Return To Tiger Mountain

This visit was the first time I returned to *Tiger Mountain* since I awoke confused several weeks ago. I went into the bedroom and took off my shirt before holding it up and looking it over. The back was completely ripped up, and the entire thing was dirty as hell. After checking the pockets, I discovered my cards and wand were still intact. I removed them from the shirt and said, "Ohm, scan the design of this shirt and recycle it. I would like to modify the material placed between the two layers. Check the Blinn database for suitable material replacement. Try to keep the weight about the same, but somehow increase the armor rating or protection level. Once you have a revised version available, please replicate a new one and leave it on the dresser."

"Revising garment," Ohm said.

I took off my undershirt and reached around my back to feel the bandages. The undershirt was trashed too, so I targeted it with my invisihud and used the recycle icon. I took off my pants, shoes, and socks and lay down in the middle of my big circular bed before grabbing one of the blankets and curling up.

In my dreams, I found myself in a stark landscape of jutting terrain which cut off my access and forced me along a single path. I could see people I sought and friends perched on high cliffs without any way to reach them. I was at the bottom of these cliffs while large beasts closed in on all sides. Leaping up on one of the jutting outcrops, I scrambled up with the beasts nipping at my heels. This move held them off as they could not make the climb, but their growls and yelps sounded angrily close. I looked around, and everyone started yelling at me from their faraway places, calling for help. The noise rose and rose, and I awoke in a sweat.

I shook off the dream and headed for the bathroom to take a shower. This shower was very large with marbled walls and brass hardware designed with four people in mind, but I can't recall ever using more than two shower heads at once. I peeled off the bandages Farouk applied and stretched my back as I soaped and cleaned the wounds. They were healing nicely, so I wasn't worried. My back was not that achy. I had to give Farouk some credit on whatever compound he added to the bandage. It did seem to work. I went ahead and shaved before washing my hair.

While drying off, I walked into the bedroom and said, "Ohm, please give me a fresh set of clothes."

There was a sparkle on the floor where I left my clothes last night, and a new sparkle appeared on the bed with a clean set of clothes. Looking at my blue undershirt, I said, "Ohm, let's swap this blue t-shirt with black. I have a feeling I may be seeping back blood all day."

The blue undershirt sparkled, vanished, and a black one appeared in its place. I got dressed, put on my boots, and headed into the living area with the long kitchen-bar divider. After walking around to the other side of the bar, I got to work making a pot of coffee.

"Ohm, can I get the reports on psychological suspects?" I asked.

"The psychological threat alert is minimal today, Sam," Ohm replied.

"Thank you, Ohm," I replied.

"Are there any outstanding dependencies within the general population?" I asked while grinding the coffee beans.

"Dependencies are as follows. Thirty-seven new cases have developed based upon programs derived from scenario Edison 7C. Hankey's journey recorded eighteen participant disbeliefs. Three hundred and eleven conflicts involving rights of passage through common space, eighty-nine distinct cases of Paxel's syndrome are developing, thirteen attempts to construct real weapons within the system occurred, one hundred and ten participants protesting virtual dominance, the Sahari tribe prays for more wood, ninety-eight cases of direct manipulation of another's experience," Ohm stated.

"Can you route all that to my invisihud?" I asked.

"Certainly," Ohm replied and my visual display updated to reflect the recent statistics.

"Let's scatter the one hundred and ten protesters across the spectrum of available real-world probable locations that are already established. Give them a taste of reality that they so eagerly crave. Also, send wood down the river for the Sahari," I instructed Ohm.

"Scheduling request," Ohm replied.

In the beginning, before there were any citizens on *Tiger Mountain*, I shifted the entire mountain through probability, visiting various worlds and inviting inhabitants to visit the mountain. Ohm explained they could stay if they wanted. Whenever I decided to move on to another planet, I would let the people of the current world know that if they remained, they would no longer be able to return to the world of their origin. This approach brought out the most adventuresome of any species and allowed curious individuals a chance to experience the world of their dreams before returning to their normal lives.

The Sahari, however, were a primitive tribe who considered the appearance of the mountain as a vessel of God and thought they were ascended to heaven when they arrived. They were drawn toward the outer edge of *Tiger Mountain* to the water supply and set up camps along the canyon where the water flowed. They have remained there ever since. They do not understand that the world is virtual and make no direct requests of the mountain whatsoever. They do continue their previous rituals, which involve prayers, dances, and singing to bring about change in their world. At first, I did not understand this and almost drove them to extinction due to my ignorance of their ways. It was Ohm who saw the messages in their rituals and suggested their rituals should be treated as requests. I agreed, and once Ohm began fulfilling their requests in that manner, they recovered and started to thrive near the water supply. They were the ones who dubbed the *Tiger Mountain* water supply, the River Of Dreams.

This process went on for several decades. I'd moved the mountain to a new planet and invited new people to visit. Some would stay, and some left as the mountain came and went. Through this process, I built up a diverse community of multi-species beings who were the first inhabitants of *Tiger Mountain*. For the most part, everyone got along fine. Sure, some races were problematic, and their nature did not allow for others, not like themselves, to coexist in harmony. Some occasional warlords thought they could leverage the mountain as a weapon to promote their power. But I handled those situations as special one-offs and tweaked Ohm's rules of daily operation to prevent the abuse of most systems.

What did arise, however, were several unexpected psychological syndromes. I studied some of the negative effects of living within a virtual environment while attending the Starnet academy. I took several classes in auragraphic programming, its benefits, and pitfalls. With *Tiger Mountain*, the believability rate was much higher because of the continuous replication of nearby objects. This enhanced rate led to some species or individuals developing obsessive symptoms ranging from depression to megalomania. It became necessary to monitor all individuals, not only for health and safety but psychological stability. If any group or individuals began exhibiting symptoms of concern to the safety of the population as a whole, Ohm removed them from *Tiger Mountain*, transporting them to the surface of the nearest planet to live out their life as they see fit.

I rarely concerned myself with giving individuals a second chance or notifying them if their behavior was not appropriate. The psychological profile of any individual can be thought of as a mental fingerprint and is fairly accurate in determining future behavioral trends. There were the occasional cases where I would bend the rules because I knew certain individuals personally and would let them know certain behaviors were not in the best interest of collaborative living. I also profiled Ohm and the system to make sure the rules I put in place were not the cause of increased trends in social disorder. New instructions were placed in the system in the form of billboards or messages through various media devices or outlets within the system.

Once the coffee was ready, I poured a cup and put the thermal carafe on the counter. I walked around to take a seat before ordering some breakfast from Ohm. I asked for eggs, sausage gravy, biscuits, and ham done southern style. The food recharged me, leaving me ready to face the world. But I still did not know what to do?

Deciding to do something fun, I headed out to the balcony and asked, "Ohm, can you provide an anti-gravity platform? I want to head down to the production floor."

"Fetching anti-gravity platform," Ohm replied, and an anti-gravity platform, similar to the one Candy and I took to Ethan's party, appeared with a sparkle.

Stepping on the platform, I tapped the floor to bring up the auragraphic controls for the unit. I activated virtual railings and set the anti-gravity platform in motion by targeting the production floor. The platform rose up and over the edge of the balcony wall as I drifted out across the vast open area. A rush of adrenalin flowed through me as I clung to the virtual railings, frightened of this great virtual height. Looking back at my house, it appeared so crappy and plain. It looked like a shoebox held up by chopsticks stuck into the side of the mountain.

Tiger Mountain provided a public arena program for musical events, so I asked, "Ohm, I want to create a new musical event program for drum practice. Include an exact copy of the drum kit I created in the Black Glass Studios."

"Creating new program. Awaiting further input," Ohm replied.

"Do you still have access to the music player from my prison virtual reality?" I asked Ohm.

"I do, the blue one and the brown one," Ohm replied.

"Replicate the brown one on the floor of this platform," I said, and a small sparkle appeared at my feet.

I bent down slowly to pick up the music player as the platform continued its descent. I quickly put together a playlist by thumbing through some of the selections of my favorite songs and said, "Ohm, take the playlist I created and generate an auragraphic representation of all band members for each song. I want to play the drums along with the songs while virtual band members accompany me."

"Generating auragraphic representations of band members," Ohm said.

"Include any historical references for the personalities of the various band members," I added.

The anti-gravity platform slowly headed down to the production floor. The production floor was where everything took place on *Tiger Mountain*. It was the most energy-efficient place on *Tiger Mountain* to recreate complex scenarios or events. Eventually, a village appeared here and grew into a town. Now it is a small city called Centropolis, complete with a park where musical events are hosted. That was my destination, the center of the park, dubbed Music Square.

The platform slowed as I approached the center of the park, performing a flawless, smooth landing. I stepped off the anti-gravity platform and put the brown music player in my pocket. Heading over to the stage area of this park, I said, "Ohm, swap out this stage setup with my rehearsal setup."

"Swap completed, but still constructing virtual band members. Only band members for the first four songs are available at this time," Ohm said.

"That's fine. I'll just play through the first four songs."

I proceeded to make adjustments to the song playback and the drum kit as I got comfortable with my new toy. I could now put on a live show of playing the drums along with my music player. What an achievement. If only I could play the drums better. I stopped playback from time to time to work on some basic exercises and paradiddles to try and get more comfortable holding the sticks. I worked on controlling stick bounce on both the drum head surface and the metallic surfaces of the cymbals. By the time I started playing through the list of songs, Ohm provided another set of band members ready to accompany me. As I fiddled around with hardware and drum tuning, I heard, "Hello, Sam."

It was David Scott. He walked across the stage, adjusting his glasses as I reached out my hand while sitting behind the drums, and said, "Hello, David."

"I hope I am not interrupting?"

"Oh no, not at all. I'm just setting up a new portable show, with me as the drummer."

"I knew you played other instruments, but I don't think I have ever seen you play the drums."

"It's the wildest thing. Apparently, I take it up in the future. Even though I have never really spent much time playing the drum kit, I have future memories of playing it quite a bit. The memories are so vivid I have been able to pick up where I left off. I mean, I still have a long way to go, but it doesn't hurt to practice."

"No, it does not hurt to practice. So, I am interrupting," David said in his talking to himself way of speaking he falls into now and again.

"Actually, it does hurt to practice as I held up my hands. I do have a blister going on each hand. Maybe, I should take a break."

"Great, I hoped to get some lunch and catch up. Are you free for lunch?"

"Sure, I think there is a cafe at the edge of the park," I said as I got up from the drums.

David and I left the stage and walked along one of the paths leading away from the park center to the rest of Centropolis. As we walked along, David said, "We were all a little concerned when you popped in the last time. You seemed so different and changed. It's nice to see you pursuing other interests."

"I decided to do something normal and fun today instead of obsessing over a future that may or may not manifest. Already, it feels like time is unfolding in a different way than my future memories recall," I said, walking around and enjoying the virtual outdoors.

"Maybe that is a sign that whatever happened to you is fading or less significant than you originally thought?" David suggested to me in a solution-like manner.

"I met her, you know?"

"Met who?" David asked as we continued walking.

"I met Jorrie, one of my future wives. I was on *Oasis Seven*, meeting with a Doctor named Brent Stevens, who helped me obtain orgamorphic gel in the last time loop. In this loop, he refused. While eating our lunch, Jorrie and her friend walked by our table. She asked Brent who his friend was, referring to me," I said to David.

David asked the obvious question, "What happened?"

"It was a rush of puppy love and near paralysis. I slowly stood up, looking into her eyes as I did so, and introduced myself to her and her friend Mia."

"That was it? You didn't ask her out or try to get to know her?" David asked as we approached the edge of the park.

"I was utterly speechless. My heart beat so fast, and what I remembered of her beauty was only a fraction of what I saw that day. Her eyes are crystal blue-green, and I forgot she liked to thread her eyebrows. She said if she didn't do it, they would turn into mops. She floored me with her beauty," I said, heading down the sidewalk to the left.

"And you just let her walk away?" David asked, a bit shocked?

"I did, and what a nice view," I said with a smile.

David smiled too as we came to a corner, and I pointed to the cafe across the street. I added, "She did look back with a smile, so I am hoping to talk to her again at some point."

"Yeah, talking to your wife is kind of an important part of any marital relationship," David said as we made our way into the restaurant and asked for an outdoor table.

Our waiter asked about drinks. David ordered a lemonade, and I got an iced tea. We sat down, and David asked, "Did you actually talk with the other Guardians yet?"

"Not directly, but Candy asked them, and they told her their stories were very similar to your own. They experienced some duplication where they did the same thing twice around the same time period."

"What do you think it means?" David asked, seriously.

"It could be because I am a probability traveler that time loops don't affect me the same way. As a Splendorite, I realize time is a location and that my future memories are simply an after effect or even normal operation for someone of my species," I offered up.

"But if you're in the loop, then we are too," David said as our drinks arrived.

We both glanced at the menu while the waiter stood by. David ordered the fish sandwich with coleslaw, and I ordered the potato soup and salad with raspberry vinaigrette. After taking a sip of tea, I set my glass down and said, "I'm sorry you're stuck in the loop with me. If I did not cause this on purpose or accident, then maybe it was done to me by an enemy."

"And by an enemy, you mean one of your family members," David said, adding some sugar to his lemonade.

"Perhaps, or simply a mechanism of echo they leveraged against me to deflect the fact that they were behind it. I have been over this in my head time and time again. It does no use to speculate. I may never be able to break the loop. Perhaps this is the curse of Na Gal Troth coming true."

"And who is Na Gal Troth again?" David asked, sipping his lemonade with more of a smile now that it was sweet.

"It happened on my venture with Candy to the Vectorless Vale. Na Gal Troth confronted me at the edge of the Pit of Eternity," I said dramatically.

"Oh, yes, yes, the Pit of Eternity. How could I forget? You know, when you've seen one Pit of Eternity, you've seen them all," David said, offering a pretty good imitation of Jim Young.

"Candy and I came to a stop near the edge of the pit as a massive demon lord emerged to challenge me. When he took his footing, the edge of the pit gave way under his massive weight. He lost his balance as the edge crumbled.

While tumbling backward and in a panic, he grabbed the reins of my fire horse which leaped into the pit with me on its back. I should have died that day, David. But I thought of the *Motif* and imagined it below my horse's hooves. Shaking the reins free, it galloped with all of its might along an invisible path that only it could see. As it galloped, fire from its hooves sparked against the *Motif* giving us lift, and I rode that horse out of the Pit of Eternity. It was, later, after returning to Splendor, when I learned the ruling party of the Vectorless Vale officially cursed me for killing one of their elders."

"Why would the King of Splendor honor a curse from his antithesis, the Vectorless Vale?" David asked as our food arrived at the table.

I used the grinder to add some black pepper to my soup, and we both started eating. I finally came back to his question and said, "My thoughts exactly. That was around the time when Robin's energy filter revealed the chaos strands attached to the members of the royal family."

"Which eventually led to the showdown with Lexi, Valentino, and the eventual destruction of the Spectre Vorticle," David said, indicating he did have an understanding of our history together.

"Who would want to screw me over? Take your pick," I said. "I am just sorry that you guys have been dragged into this."

"Sam, you have done so much to help Mist Door Operations and MD-Alpha personally that, as a planet, we owe our current existence to your contribution to our cause," David said in between bites of his fish sandwich.

"I am trying to help you out after you helped me," I said, munching on my salad.

"Yep, I think that is what friends do for each other, Sam. That is why we're so worried to see you in such a state the last time you stopped by," David said.

"Wait a second, did you guys draw straws to see who would visit me?" I asked with a smile.

David, being the diplomat, adjusted his glasses and said, "Yes, yes we did," before taking another bite.

"And you lost?"

"I won, Sam. I wanted to come and talk to you, to help you, to find out if there is anything we can do to get to the bottom of this. So did the others, but we thought a single person might be better than overwhelming you with a group," David said.

"I'm touched, David. But I don't know any way out of this other than to live through it again. I do feel a little better now that I have put a few things in place to help guide my present into the possible future I recall."

"Is that wise? What if those actions lead you back to another time loop?"

"As an immortal being, I don't care that much about the time loop. What I care about are my friends and my family. This time loop could be what hell looks like, David. Instead of Groundhog Day, we might be stuck in Groundhog Decade."

"What have you set in motion?"

"I aligned the time where Jorrie lives with the time where I know Erin resides, but I haven't met her yet. The black glass building in San Francisco is set up, so we would all have a place to hang out, meet, and live in the same time zone. I visited almost everyone I could remember, who was a close friend, to reintroduce myself for the first time. These meetings went from pleasant to awkward, but I feel like I have met some new friends from my future memories. I invented a new biomedical device to help with deep wounds in a combat situation. I'm working on a new attack ship design, and I have gone on a successful pocket diet with my shirt," I said as I pointed out my new shirt design to David.

"Wow, I guess you have been busy. I was going to comment on the shirt, but we went off in another direction," David said while eating the coleslaw after devouring his fish sandwich.

With a sparkle, a small glowing sphere popped up, and Ohm said, "Incoming transmission from Sara Mitchell."

"Ohm, go ahead and send her an invite to this location," I replied.

"Who is Sara Mitchell?" David asked.

"She is one of my new friends, the captain of the most advanced starship currently deployed by Starnet. The problem is, her ship is seventy thousand lightyears from Earth, so she and the crew are facing a lifetime journey to return, or at least they were."

"Let me guess," David said. "Until they met you."

"I recently installed a communication system that works across the long distance between her ship's location and Starnet headquarters," I said.

A sparkle appeared beside our table. When it faded, the form of Sara Mitchell dressed in a Starnet uniform stood looking around, asking, "Where are we?"

I stood up, approached her, and shook her hand, saying, "Welcome to *Tiger Mountain*, my home."

David wiped off his face with his napkin, got up, and approached too, saying, "Hello, I am David Scott. Pleased to meet you."

Sara shook David's hand. I offered her a seat at the table, but she declined, saying, "Sorry, I don't have time for pleasantries. I am up against a deadline. We have encountered a flotilla of primitive spacecraft, one of their shuttle vehicles is lost, and the pilot is running out of oxygen. They have exhausted their options on locating the crewman. I thought about your probability powers and your mention of 'luck.' Do you think you could apply it, in this case?"

"I would need a picture of the crewman and or the shuttle that is lost," I said seriously.

"I'm sure these people could provide that. I was just talking with their Admiral before arriving here. Can you send me back?" Sara asked.

"Sure, I'm ready right now," I said to Sara before looking over at David. "Sorry to cut out early."

"Wait, wait, can I come along?" David asked.

"This is no place for a tourist," Sara said to David.

I spoke for him, saying, "David's people travel from planet to planet using a Mist Door. He has probably traveled to as many planets as you have, if not more. He is a skilled negotiator and often seeks a peaceful solution to toxic problems."

"He can come, but he is your responsibility," Sara said, looking at both of us.

"I would not expect it any other way. And thank you, Sara," David said.

"Ohm, transport us to the location where you retrieved Sara from," I said.

The brightness of *Tiger Mountain* collapsed into the center of my vision, and darkness claimed my attention once again. Sara did not mention it, but she probably put it together that this might be the encounter with the people of my future wife, Erin. I mentioned it in our first meeting. Once again, I think my nose materialized first because it detected a musty smell of closed quarters mixed with a gym locker room.

CHAPTER 24

The Rescue

The room materialized around us as I heard the words, "Guards!" and the sound of rifle chambers loading a round.

"Hold your fire," a voice commanded loudly.

The room we arrived in was no bigger than an office meeting room. From the construction of the walls and doors, I would guess we were aboard some type of ship or military vessel. The armed guards at the door lowered their weapons. There were also two older men and two younger men in the room. While all the men wore similar colors, a dark blue, their uniforms bore a distinct cut leading me to believe three different ranks were involved in this group of men.

Sara spoke, "Admiral, this is the man I told you about. Sam, this is Admiral Danos Dmitri of the Imperial fleet."

"Sam, Sam Richards," I said, offering to shake his hand.

"I'm David Scott, Sam's research assistant," David said, shaking the Admiral's hand.

"Can you do what she says you can?" Admiral Dmitri asked directly.

"I can try. I'll need a picture of the pilot and a picture of the ship. Also, a general direction or star coordinates where I should begin the search and how much time we have left."

The Admiral said, "Lieutenant Nino, show him what we have."

One of the younger men stepped up with a folder and some stacks of photographic paper. He said, "The pilot's name is Sandra Gallo, and the ship type is known as a *Falcon*. She last jumped to this location, and her return is long overdue. We calculate she may have as little as thirty-six minutes of oxygen left."

As Lieutenant Nino spoke, he laid out photos and finally star charts for me to inspect. I picked up a photo. It was Erin or at least one of the revision nines she resembled. In the previous loops, this Sandra was not the one I eventually ended up marrying. I picked up the photo of the *Falcon* and remembered this ship well. It was more of a space bus that was barely spaceworthy. I moved to the star charts, which were telescopic photographs, presumably shot from this location.

"I will need to use some technology you may not be familiar with. It is not a weapon, but it will help me locate your crewman. Is it okay to proceed?" I asked the Admiral.

"What is the name of this technology?" the Admiral asked, skeptical, thinking this might be some Melog trick.

"It is a digital tablet with a camera and a projector. The projector produces an auragraphic image while the screen displays basic video," I said.

"Proceed," the Admiral said.

"Ohm, please replicate a standard Blinn auragraphic scanning tablet," I said.

Sparkles appeared, and there was a slight gasp in the room as the tablet materialized on the table. This device was similar to the tablet Yon used at the Blinn replication facility. I left the tablet on the table and explained how it worked.

"It senses when you are using it when you touch it. It lights up, presenting a series of lists with operations the tablet can perform. We want to use the camera tools. David, can you spread those photos out a bit?" I asked David, and he placed the photos in a row.

"Are these portions of a spherical projection?" I asked Lieutenant Nino.

"Yes, they are. Let me arrange those for you," Nino said.

Lieutenant Nino rearranged some of the photos, and I proceeded to photograph each one using the tablet. The others watched and saw that once I took the photo, it became an image on the tablet screen. I set the tablet on the table and asked, "Ohm, can you assemble these star charts into a three-dimensional auragraphic display? Place the result inside this tablet."

"Who are you talking to?" Admiral Dmitri asked.

"The tablet contains a microphone. I am talking to an off-site computer linked to that tablet. It can accept verbal commands," I said.

Nino looked at the tablet and said, "I think it might be ready."

I looked over his shoulder at the new icon Ohm added to the screen and said, "Yes, give it a try. Tap on the icon to activate the display."

He tapped the icon, and an orange glowing sphere emerged to float above the tablet.

"It's a map," the other older man said with astonishment.

"You're right, and we are at the center. What are those ship coordinates again?" I asked Nino.

"Three-four-seven strike eight-one-two, distance three-six-five-three-two-nine," Nino repeated while reading from one of the pages.

"Ohm, place a second sphere on the map at the location Lieutenant Nino provided," I said, and the map updated with a new glowing blue sphere some distance from the center.

Nino stepped away from the tablet as I stepped up to the glowing map hovering above the tablet. I adjusted the map and zoomed in closer on the blue sphere while saying, "I think I have what I need to locate your crewman. Once we are on location, you should be able to see through our cameras by looking at the screen."

I stepped back and looked over at David and asked, "Are you ready?"

David pushed his glasses up and said, "Yes, I am ready."

"Ohm, discontinue auragraphic map, and transport David and me to the catwalk on the *Deceptive*."

Once again, I dissolved into nothingness, and my dark empty friend was there to greet me, never judging or questioning my return. I preferred using the vignette card, but the entire group seemed edgy, and I did not want to introduce yet another piece of technology into their world. Besides, Sandra was running out of oxygen. There wasn't any time for explanation. The catwalk of the *Deceptive* materialized in front of me, and I said, "Follow me."

We walked to the end of the catwalk where *Vision* rested on the easel. I looked over at David and said, "This involves spacewalking. You don't have to come if you don't want to. I did this a short while back, and I experienced a high level of anxiety."

"Thank you for the warning, but I want to try. I can always transport out, right?" David asked.

"Right, you can. Remember, the anxiety is normal, and pay attention to your breathing. Go ahead and bring up your shield and the jetpack icons. We're not doing fancy flying, mainly traveling along a single vector," I said to David.

"Shield and jetpack. Got it," David said, and I could see a slight shimmer along the glancing angle where the shield curved to conform to his body.

"The next part is very important. I want you to look away from the painting until I tell you it is okay to look," I said.

"Oh yeah, the images of insanity," David said, and he closed his eyes before saying, "I'm ready."

I gathered my thoughts on the location from the map and thought about the crewman, not Erin. I also thought about the *Falcon*, its drift, the part of space I saw in the photos. While holding all that in my mind, I said, "Standby," and tossed the cloth cover to the floor.

The surface of the canvas flooded with hoards of hard-shelled octopus spiders. The mouths on their bellies revealed rows of sharp teeth. They pushed hard against the canvas, trying to get through, smashing apart their own exoskeleton and limbs as they did so. I regained my thought of the *Falcon*, the crewman, the part of space, and the canvas became a black sheet with finely focused glimmering stars. Looking deeply into the black field, I saw a slight reflective glint and detected the outline of the *Falcon* floating in space. I said to David, "You can open your eyes now."

"Whoa, that is so black and clean at the same time," David said.

"Take my hand. We step through together," I said.

David took my hand and the shields combined around our grasp. Stepping forward into the painting felt like falling as we entered the deep void of space. I held David's hand and said, "Bring up your radar, David."

"Trying, you are right, very disorienting. Ohm, can you activate radar on my invisihud?" David asked with his voice relaying through my invisihud communications channel

I brought up my radar of the surrounding area, and there was only one blip showing up. I said, "I have an idea. Let's hang on to one another, and I'll target the jetpacks for both of us."

"Sounds good to me, Sam," David said, struggling to speak.

"Ohm, begin broadcasting our feed to the tablet on the Admiral's ship."

"Broadcasting," Ohm replied.

We were spinning and not focused, floating in space. I decided to target the *Falcon*. Once I engaged the jetpacks, we swung around and started to approach the drifting spacecraft. Its tumbling silhouette blocked the stars while growing larger in our field of view.

"Ohm, can you manage our jetpack velocity? We don't want to slam into the ship."

"Managing velocities," Ohm replied, and inside the invisihud, I saw the vector angle and thrust adjust automatically, occasionally flipping around in reverse to reduce our speed as we approached the tumbling *Falcon*.

"How are you doing, David?" I asked.

"I'm good. I think you are right. The first minute is the most disorienting," David replied.

"When we get to the surface of the ship, we let go of hands and grab on. Got it?" I asked David.

"Yep, got it," David replied.

Ohm did a great job of controlling our velocities. We arrived with a small bump and grabbed onto a part of this small shuttle. This ship was not like a Starnet Union craft where, after years of space travel, the practicality of having ladders on the outside became part of the design specifications. Instead, this ship offered contours, ridges, and the outer frame of the glass canopy. David grabbed on directly in the center of the canopy and said, "I see movement. It's a woman. She appears to be the pilot."

"Is she wearing a helmet?" I asked.

"Yes, she is, gloves and boots too," David reported looking through the canopy glass at the crewman.

"If she is responsive, try to send her a hand signal to hold on to something," I said as I headed over to the side hatch.

"Trying," David replied.

I brought up the anti-gravity boots icon to lock my feet to the wing of the *Falcon*.

"I think she understands. She is buckling herself in," David said, giving the crewman a thumbs-up through the glass.

"Great, I'm opening the hatch. The released pressure will probably change the rotation of the ship, so hang on."

With my boots locked to the wing, I opened the hatch from the outside. A burst of gas emitted along the edge of the door, which immediately tried to open and push me away. Leaning into it, I tried to keep the door closed. I did not want our passenger to fly out. The anti-gravity boots helped a lot. Eventually, I no longer needed to resist the door. I opened it, exposing the interior to space. David made his way over to the hatch, and I reached out to take his hand. With a yank and a pull, I directed him into the interior of the *Falcon*. I followed behind and pulled the hatch shut.

"Ohm, pressurize and fill this cabin with a breathable atmosphere," I said as I made my way up front to the cockpit.

"Is she alive, Sam?"

"Checking," I said before tapping the pilot on the shoulder.

The pilot's chair spun around, revealing a Melog revision nine in a spacesuit. She looked just like my wife, Erin. I knew this moment was coming, but it was still a shock to see her. Even through the dim lighting of the helmet, her beauty drew me in. My invisihud readings brought me out of the trance I slipped into for a moment, indicating a pressurized atmosphere inside the craft.

"It looks good, David. I'm dropping my shield," I said, and I set my shield to automatic mode.

The shield sparkled as it dropped, and I could see the shock in Sandra's face. She may have thought we were some type of suffocation illusion she was experiencing as she died.

"It's okay. The atmosphere is restored," I said as I motioned for her to remove her helmet.

She seemed hesitant at first but may have decided if she was that close to dying of suffocation, taking her helmet off might not matter. She released the latch on the helmet, and I helped with removing it from her head. She hunched over, taking deep breaths, as she realized she was not dead, and asked, "Who the hell are you guys?"

David walked up and said, "I'm David, and he is Sam. Your leader..."

I corrected David in mid-sentence by saying, "Admiral."

"Yes, your Admiral Dmitri sent us to find you," David completed his introduction.

I sat in the empty pilot's seat and said, "Your fleet encountered a group of friendly aliens, who are mostly human. I happen to have met them a few months back."

"Actually, I just met them today. Well, at least one. We are talking about Sara, right?" David asked.

I shook my head, yes, and David continued, "The report of your disappearance happened to arrive when the humans were meeting with your Admiral.

"I think I can get this ship back to the area of the fleet. Do the thrusters still work?" I asked.

"Yeah, if the fleet were here, I could land this bird," she said.

"Ohm, transport us, and this *Falcon*, to the location of the Imperial fleet," I said.

I faced Sandra as she opened her mouth to say something, and we all dissolved into nothingness, along with the *Falcon*. Even though I knew this Melog was not my wife, I still felt an instant connection to her. Her mannerism and the way she spoke all reminded me of Erin. I knew I should keep my distance from all members of her revision if I were to end up with the correct one as my wife.

I met Erin the same way in both time loops, and this event put me on track for the same experience in this third loop. As we materialized, she asked, "What the faen are you talking about?"

The radio system crackled to life, and we heard, "*Arbrutus* actual to unknown ship. Please authenticate."

Sandra reached over to a panel on her right, flipped a switch, and replied, "*Arbrutus*, this is Hebe. Sending authentication."

A few moments passed as we waited for a reply.

"Welcome home, Hebe. We thought we lost you. You are cleared for landing," a female voice said over the radio.

"You and me both, Brie," Sandra replied, then turned to David and said, "Strap in. There is a fold-down seat in the back."

David took the seat in the back, and I remained in the second pilot's chair while Sandra went to work piloting the *Falcon*. Being lightweight, with an overpowered engine to mass ratio, the *Falcon* had a live thrust feeling to it, like riding a motorcycle. Each move she made caused the view through the canopy to change direction as she aligned the *Falcon* for her approach on the landing platform of the largest ship in the fleet, the *Arbrutus*. I knew this information from my future memories. I didn't learn much from Admiral Dmitri during our brief meeting. I was impressed with Sandra's piloting skills. She brought us in for a smooth landing, and a docking vehicle made its way out from the side of the deck to ferry us into an atmospheric environment.

While we sat there Sandra asked me, "How did you do that? How did you move the ship? That was not FSL."

"No, it is a form of transportation that I use. The new humans your fleet encountered have the same technology," I explained.

"Well, thanks. I don't know how you two did what you did, but I'll be glad to get out of this *Falcon* and get a shower," Sandra said.

David said, "I saw a large pointy ship move past the window while you were landing. It looked damaged."

"Yep, that is the Melog *Pentacraft*. Right now, there is a fragile truce between our two people. The *Pentacraft* took heavy damage in a conflict with our own people. The Melogs are at war with themselves and the humans. That ship is what is left of the Melog rebel fleet," Sandra said.

"One ship?" David asked.

"One ship," Sandra replied.

"So, you are a Melog?" David asked.

"Yeah, what of it?" Sandra asked defensively.

"Oh, nothing. I'm wondering why you are piloting an Imperial ship if you are a Melog?"

"It's a long faenin' story, okay?" Sandra said as she shook her head slowly.

"Sorry, I didn't mean to pry. I am just trying to understand," David said in his calming tone.

"At this point, it does not matter which side you're on. We're all faened, Melogs and humans if we don't find a habitable planet, and soon," Sandra said.

The sound of the external towing vehicle came to a halt. Sandra grabbed her helmet, moved to the side hatch, and opened it. The open hatch revealed quite a group of people gathered to greet us. At least twenty deck crew stood around in orange jumpsuits along with a few more people dressed in the dark blue uniforms we saw earlier. A voice called out from the center. It was Admiral Dmitri saying, "Welcome back, Hebe."

"Thank you, sir. Sorry about the late arrival. My FSL went down after the first jump," Sandra said as she made her way down the wing, which did have a few sculpted steps embedded into it.

"Take a rest, Lieutenant. I look forward to reading your report," the Admiral said to Sandra.

"Yes, sir. Thank you, sir," she said as she saluted. He dismissed her salute by returning it to her.

She walked off with her helmet under her arms as she shook the rest of her long hair out of her spacesuit, so it hung down her back. Walking past a few of the flight deck workers, she replied with a nod to them before passing out of view.

David and I climbed down the wing and approached Admiral Dmitri. Sara and Tamakot stood with him and the older man from the first meeting.

Admiral Dmitri extended his hand to David and me and said, "Thank you. It says a lot about a person's character when they go out of their way to help someone. To do what you say means a lot to me."

"We were glad we could help," David said for both of us.

"I am having a dinner tonight to celebrate our new friends from *Journey*, and I would be honored if you two would attend," Admiral Dmitri said to David and me.

"Thank you for the offer, but I don't think I could enjoy a meal at this time, knowing that the rest of the fleet is facing hunger and uncertainty," I said disappointingly.

There was a noticeable tension build up in the Admiral as I refused his offer. He replied, "While everyone in this fleet has suffered losses, I still have hope that we will prevail. Our new Union friends have generously provided relief in the form of supplies that are being distributed among the fleet. There is indeed a reason to celebrate, and the citizens of the fleet will be celebrating as well."

"I am happy to hear that, Admiral. The generosity of the Union is well known. Let me bring you one more reason to celebrate. In my recent attempts to locate *Journey*, I conducted multiple optical scans of this region of space. One of those scans revealed a planet with an environment suitable for human life. Green fields, blue sky, clear rivers, and a temperate environment for growing."

I held out my hand and said, "Ohm, materialize a card with the location to Zenith."

A small sparkle came and went while a card materialized in my hand. I handed the card to the Admiral. He took the card, looked at it, looked up at me, then looked over at Captain Mitchell and Tamakot before asking, "Will you accompany me to the center of operations? I would like to verify these coordinates."

"Certainly, I know all too well that the ship's business is never done. Lead the way," Sara said.

The group began walking off toward a door while David and I fell to the back of the group. David asked, "Is that true? Are those coordinates to a habitable planet?"

I shook my head, yes, as we continued along corridors heading out of the deck area and into one of the corridors along the outer hull. David looked out one of the small portals and touched my shoulder, asking, "That ship," pointing to the damaged Melog *Pentacraft*, "is the one I want to visit. Can we go there now?"

"And abandon the group?" I asked.

"Sure, why not?" he asked.

"Okay, turn on your cloak," I said.

David disappeared from view, and so did I as I asked, "Ohm, can you scan the damaged Melog *Pentacraft* in the fleet outside our current location? It is a large five-pronged ship. Transfer findings to my invisihud and David's too."

"Deploying cloaked scanners to generate a map," Ohm replied.

When two people are cloaked, by the cloaked scanners, they can still see each other inside the invisihud. Because the cloak is not one hundred percent perfect, you can see the outline of a cloaked person with the naked eye if you know where to look. The cloak also masks sounds within the field surrounding the cloak so no one could hear us talk. The field samples the noise we make and calculates the inverse phase to muffle the sound of our movement. This means when David and I talk to one another, our words are routed through the invisihud audio system as messages.

We waited and watched our invisihuds as a map of the Melog *Pentacraft* started to fill in. It looked like Ohm guided the cloaked scanners through the damaged area first and started wandering hallways to the center.

"Does any place stand out to you?" I asked David.

I could tell he was reviewing the map inside his invisihud by the way he looked past me and focused on some unknown subject. He finally shook his head, deciding upon a place by talking to himself, and said, "Let's go here."

A target appeared inside my invisihud as David shared his invisihud selection with my invisihud.

"Got it. Ohm, transport us to the location David has selected," I said.

The dim lighting of the *Arbrutus* hallway dissolved, and I returned to darkness. I wondered why David was so interested in the Melog *Pentacraft*? While it was a cool design, and an interesting fact that an artificial intelligence built the ship, I did not really see the value in visiting the craft. David was well known, among his team members, for being the constant explorer. He always wanted to see what was beyond the next horizon, and if visiting this ship is all it takes to empower David, I figure why not? A bright light filled my eyes as they materialized. The light faded to reveal a stark repeating hallway moving off in either direction.

David did not hesitate and took the corridor to his left. While I followed David, I set up a Transfast escape to my San Francisco apartment. I sent a copy of the icon over to David's invisihud. He said, "Oh, thanks."

The repeating corridors of the Melog *Pentacraft* were tall and oval-shaped. It made me wonder how big do Melogs get? The oval shape was fairly organic, and as I walked down the corridor, I felt like I was inside a ribbed tube. There were no eye-level windows, but up near the top of the corridor arch, were oval-shaped windows that repeated only so often, revealing the stars beyond. There were much fewer windows compared to ribs. It wasn't too long before we heard mechanical noises approaching us. We stopped moving and stepped off the walkway. It felt like standing on flesh. We stood up against the wall, inside one of the many indents formed by the ribbing, hoping the optical cloak would hide us.

The approaching Melogs were mechanical bipedal in shape and motion. They had two arms, two legs, a torso, and one head with a single blue light for an eye that pivoted on a stem. These body parts were all made of metal. They wore no clothing. Their size was much larger than a human. It looked like a human might be able to fit inside the armor, but the small waist prevented that in this situation. I remember Erin telling me the early Melogs conducted cloning experiment after cloning experiment to develop the Pilotoid and the Guardbot. These two main units managed the Melog ship operations. From her description, I would guess these were the Guardbot units passing by.

A third Guardbot followed behind the first two, in the center of the corridor. It passed us by, stopped, and quickly turned to face our position by rotating around head first, then torso. It took a backward step closer to us, dropping its arms into a right-angle, bent at the elbow. The pitch of the mechanical servos changed as the Melog made minute adjustments to its pose. It stared at our position with its mechanical eye swiveling freely as David and I stood as still as possible. I wasn't sure if the blue Melog scanning eye could see through a cloak? Suddenly, the Melog looked over its shoulder toward the other units, who already moved on. It twisted its head and torso to face the direction it walked and continued its march down the hallway to catch up with its companions.

"Well, that was close," David said.

"Uh-huh," I agreed.

We returned to the walkway and made our way quickly down the corridor to approach a four-way intersection with a large open area to the left. David took the left passage, and we stuck to the walls as we entered the large room. As with all the shapes I saw on the Melog *Pentacraft*, there were no right angles. The same was true with this large room, which seemed to be some hub entrance for this level. I was not sure how the Melogs generated gravity, but in the center of this ship there seemed to be none. We saw Guardbots and larger machines operated by Guardbots moving cargo around in low gravity.

"Wow, don't you find that fascinating? How they work together to move massive loads," David asked.

"Sure," I said. "But watching them work?"

"What do you think are in those containers?" David asked.

"Probably materials to aid in repair operations," I said.

"Could be," David said as he moved forward, trying to get a closer look.

I followed him to stay close while asking, "What are you looking for, David?"

"Just looking, observing," David said, slowly as if I were distracting him by talking to him. "I've never seen a race of robotic beings this close, let alone observed daily tasks or chores being performed."

It was a combination of the sound of the Melogs approaching, the look in David's eyes as he turned to face me, and the reflection I saw in his glasses. We were discovered. I said, "Ohm, Transfast David and I back home!"

There was a rattle of chain gun as the world around me dissolved into the void. I could not feel anything. I wondered how many times it takes before you embrace the void and forget about materializing? Maybe this is what it feels like to be scattered into space? My morose musings faded as the light of my San Francisco apartment flooded into my eyes. We heard a couple of ricochet sounds indicating a round or two of ammo transported with us.

"David, are you all right? Were you hit?" I asked, concerned.

"I think I'm okay," David said as he dropped his optical cloak.

I dropped my cloak and did a quick once over to see if I was hit before saying, "Damn, that was close."

"Yeah, you don't say. I guess we'll have to find a better way to cloak."

"Or try to keep out of their general field of view. If we were levitating, using anti-gravity boots, they may not have spotted us," I said.

"Good point. Use existing tools better. Making a note," David said with a smile.

"Would you like a drink?"

"Sure, sounds good. What have you got?" David asked.

"I'm going to make a Manhattan. Do you want one?" I asked while walking over to the bar in the corner of the living room.

"Ah, the classic. Yes, please," David replied as he took a seat on one of the stools in front of the bar.

I filled the shaker with ice and found the bourbon, bitters, and sweet vermouth. Mixing two parts bourbon and one part vermouth, I added a dash from the bitters. I gave the tumbler a couple of shakes before pouring the liquor into two rocks glasses and topping them off with the ice from the shaker.

"To not dying from robot death machines!" I said, offering a small toast.

"Hear, hear," David said with a smile and a sip, then raised his eyebrows, revealing he talked to himself again.

I took a seat behind the bar, and we sat there sipping for a minute or two before David asked, "I guess what I don't understand is how the Melogs evolved from those robots we just saw to the human Sandra type?"

"That has always been a grey area for me, too, even with future memories of being married to one. The clones of one revision can access memories accumulated by previous versions of the same revision. When a flesh version of the Melog dies, the consciousness travels along minute energy guides generated by the accumulator ship to retrieve its memories. The same is true for the biological creatures occupying the robotic bodies. If they die, they can revive and install the memories from their previous lives to carry on. Because of this shared memory, Erin inherited a lot of baggage that she preferred not to discuss. I did not blame her. I mean, who wants to talk about the time your child was stolen at birth. Or how about the time you were knifed in the hallway by one of the more xenophobic members of the crew."

"Wow," David said, "I did not know about that."

"The information I could gather was the Melogs stole a critical cloning experiment the Imperials performed on a secret asteroid base. They found out about it, arrived, and took the experiment, all while holding off an Imperial warship. It was believed they used the experiment to further their own cloning projects and produced the first Biodual. It was, more or less, a human female clone with biomechanical interfaces into the physical body. A ship was organically grown around the Biodual to form the *Pentacraft*, like the one we were just on. It was only after the Biodual was known to exist that these various revisions were created with no biomechanical implants. The machine portion was miniaturized in the form of bloodstream picamechs to help the body work more efficiently."

"See, now that is fascinating!" David said with a slight spill as he sloshed his drink.

"I was never able to confirm it, but I believe the Biodual directed the robotic Melogs in creating copies of itself while modifying its own structure in the process. Each set of modifications became what we refer to as a revision. Sandra and Erin are the ninth and last modification the Biodual made to itself," I continued.

"I guess I can see it. The Imperial story is like a rags to riches to rags story. Man creates machine, machine rebels, machine escapes, machine watches man, machine changes itself to become man, and machine destroys man," David went on, acting a bit too drunk from the modest drink I poured him.

"The Imperials have a saying. Where you might have 'Home Sweet Home' embroidered, they have 'What Came Before Will Come Again.'"

"Ah, it all leads back to the time loop," David said.

"Yeah, I guess I have been trying to set that aside for a while," I said.

"Today was a busy day," David said, slurring his speech.

"Now that you mention it, it was. From drumming to spacewalking to exploring alien space ships. That is a lot more than I usually put on my calendar," I said, then concerned added, "Ohm, scan David for wounds."

"David Scott is unharmed," Ohm replied.

"I'm right here, you know," David said, laying his head down on the bar.

"Ohm, how long has David been awake?" I asked

"David has been awake twenty-one hours and seventeen minutes," Ohm replied.

"Ohm, may I have a medkit?" I asked.

Sparkles appeared above the bar, and a medkit remained behind as they vanished. I got out the medjector, set it to hangover cure, and tapped David on the neck with it. Returning the medjector to the medkit, I stored it on a shelf behind the bar. I moved around the bar, lifted David, and lay him down on the floor. He resisted, but I said, "David, I am sending you home. I'll talk to you soon."

"Ohm, can you transport David back to his bedroom at Mist Door Operations?" I asked.

David's body sparkled and disappeared. I brought up my invisihud and checked in on the health status of all the Guardians. They were all alive and non-stressed, so I shut down the invisihud.

"Ohm, I want to activate the Zenith terraforming module. Let's create a classic town center with a meeting hall, a hospital, a well, small gardens with fruits or vegetables to harvest, and an ample supply of housing for up to one thousand people to start with. Weave the gardens in between the housing. Make sure service access points are available near the edges if colonists want to extend the terraforming themselves," I said.

"Are you expecting colonists on Zenith?" Ohm asked.

"Yes, they have been traveling for years, in small ship quarters, so make the housing spacious. The colonist are human, and there may be families with children, so throw in a park or two," I answered.

"Commencing terraforming operations using provided parameters with additional supplies for refugees," Ohm said.

"Ohm, when the colonists arrive, please notify me," I said.

"Certainly," Ohm replied.

"Ohm, can you transfer the transport memory buffer that contains the *Falcon* to the Blinn replication team? Ask them to rebuild the ship, with a focus on getting the FSL drive working. Also, have the team examine the Sandra subject cache, with a strong focus on creating real-world replicas of the micro machines in her blood," I requested.

"Transferring data and requests to specific Blinn teams. I'll notify you when progress is made," Ohm replied.

Taking the remainder of my drink with me, I walked over and sat down on the white sofa in the center of the living room. I looked out at the fading day as sunset crept into view while slowly sipping on the Manhattan and pondering my next task. Is this all there was left for me? A never-ending list of tasks to complete?

This next task is going to be a bunch of changes, all at once. The focus will be Vasco, with a minor in Union law adjustments and business expansion. In both loops, I owned property on Vasco and used Blinn terraforming technology to help rebuild hundreds of small neighborhoods destroyed or damaged during the Bragorian occupation. Jorrie's commander, Warren Turner, is considered to be a figure from their religious texts called "The Pharaoh Of The Oracle". The Oracle are non-temporal beings with a window into our dimension. The radionic tile is that window.

Vascon history is littered with sacred scrolls and artifacts exhibiting possible influence by the Oracle over the Vascon civilization spanning centuries. Taking advantage of this, I found it highly probable that a scroll was discovered detailing the actions of the Squire of the Pharaoh. The scroll hinted at a person or directed by the Pharaoh of the Oracle to aid in rebuilding Vasco. It was summed up with the phrase, "and the Squire of the Pharaoh shall rebuild and make Vasco whole."

The adjustments required to the Union law were very minor. K-Mac and Byrone were bound to end up legally challenged because of something they said. I wanted to have a few previous past rulings in place favoring their flavor of free speech. I also wanted to add an exclusion of action clause to the Starnet members agreement that clearly stated that a Starnet member could not be legally held responsible for an action they committed, witnessed, or participated in while under the influence of an entity.

The business adjustments were more focused and a bit far-reaching. In the first loop, the ship Jorrie commanded was called the *Kataru*, which meant "The Alliance" in the solar tongue. In the first time loop, Erin and I infiltrated the Shalimar Spaceworks starship construction yards and became laborers. This eventually led to a worker's revolt and a reshaping of the management, with Erin and I owning controlling interests in the entire facility. When Starnet offered Jorrie the captaincy of the *Kataru*, I was shocked to learn of the ship's existence. Typically, a flagship is always constructed at Shalimar Spaceworks. In that time loop, a third-party ship vendor produced the ship. In this current loop, I want to be that third-party vendor. I want to build the *Kataru*.

The back story is that I acquired a small Mercanite ship construction facility and overhauled the production for a more tourist-based approach to space travel. A new company was born, Replicraft. What made Replicraft such a success was the affordable Dream Song Five, which was basically an advanced shuttle with no high yield weapons and an expanded cargo area. It was useful, durable, and accepted Union replacement parts for maintenance. In reality, all new Replicraft products are produced at Blinn replication facilities.

I was down to sucking on ice and decided now was as good a time as any to get these changes in place. Putting the drink down on the coffee table, I stood up and pulled out the vignette for the *Deceptive* catwalk. Focusing on the location, I reached out with my mind as it seemed more real. With a step forward, I was on the catwalk once again. I made my way down to the end, where the covered easel stood. As I removed the cover from the painting, my thoughts were of Replicraft, the changes to the law, changes to Vascon history, my neighborhood, and my house.

The head of a giant three-eyed rat gnashed at the flat plane of the canvas, showing its tongue made of snakes whose forked tongues were made of electricity spreading across the surface of the canvas. I thought "Union Space" and the rat fought back while losing ground to my concept with blackness fading in from the sides. I thought "Vasco," and the rat face was obliterated and replaced with a cloud-covered planet revealing hues of green and umber surrounded by blue oceans. I thought "My Neighborhood," and I zoomed into the planet's equatorial region, quickly racing through clouds as the ground rushed up to reveal an overhead view of a series of houses along streets. I thought "My Home," and *Vision* presented the house I purchased in the first time loop.

Holding the intent of all I previously thoughts in my mind, I reinforced the probability as I took a step forward into my new "Squire of the Pharaoh," role who happens to own Replicraft. Pulling one last time on the threads of alignment, I passed the threshold of the painting frame, locking in my adjustments to the legal code.

CHAPTER 25

Vasco Residence

A wonderful scent reached my nose as I stood before my new home. The smell of blossoms was in the breeze. The property was once used as the Mayor's home, many decades ago, before the war. When war broke out, and the Bragorian occupation was established, old neighborhoods broke up, corraling people into concentrated areas. Only recently have neighborhoods begun to rebuild. My house certainly needed some love. The entire house was surrounded by a high wall and a double door entrance with one of the doors broken, hanging on by only one hinge. The wall was crumbling in various places, and it looked like this property once held off assailants because of the scorch marks from blaster fire and bullet holes. Stepping through the two doors at the gate, I walked up to the house proper. It occupied the area of a mini-mansion with an architectural profile looking like a stylish mix of colonial with southwestern hints. The front porch offered tall white columns chipped by weapons fire, and the roof was adobe clay with many broken tiles. I forced the front doors open. There were blast marks on them. Behind the door was a clutter of furniture used to barricade the entrance at one time. I made my way down the long hall leading to the back of the house where the kitchen resides. As I approached the kitchen, I heard multiple scrambling noises and the sound of feet running out the back. I picked up the pace and hurried to the back door to catch a glimpse of a few children who took turns hurriedly squeezing through a hole in the backyard wall.

"Ohm, put a cloaked tracker on those children. I want to know where they go," I said while looking through the kitchen door into the spacious back yard.

"Deploying tracker. Target obtained. Tracking targets," Ohm replied.

"Ohm, scan the house for any other life forms," I said.

"No other life forms detected in the house," Ohm replied.

I turned around to discover an open stairway leading up to some bedrooms. Below the stairway was an open dining area. Off to my left was a breakfast nook connecting to the entrance hallway. Where the hallway met the breakfast nook was a doorway leading into a large den. Rain made its way into this room, leaking through the ceiling to damage the furniture and floor. I considered the entire house a gut, so I stepped out back and asked, "Ohm, can you scan the current house and any Vascon references on architecture to restore this home to its original state?"

"Checking. Using references and scans, I can recreate this structure with a ninety-eight point two percent accuracy," Ohm replied.

"Okay, let's do that, but populate the interior with modern Starnet Union furniture and appliances. Install a copy of the virtual drum set from Centropolis park into the den area, treat that as a recording studio and populate it accordingly. Also, consider the height of the outer walls and the possibility of someone viewing the replication process. Try to use as few visible replication transports as possible," I said.

"Constructing temporary auraprojector to project the appearance of the old house while replication takes place," Ohm said.

"Ah, an even better idea, thank you," I said.

I walked into the walled back yard and turned around to watch the replication taking place. The auraprojector seemed to be doing the trick. The temporary projection was a little larger than the actual house. To the naked eye, the house looked the same. Inside my invisihud, I could see through the projection and observe the replication in action. This first stage was big, bold transports removing large chunks, starting with the roof and working its way down. The entire demolition took about twenty minutes until all that was left was the clean foundation that sparkled as Ohm repaired cracks. This house had no basement. Framing the house was the next phase, and I walked around to the front to see how the columns and roofing came together. I had the sneaking suspicion that I was being watched, and when I turned around, I glimpsed another child looking into the yard through the broken gate before darting away. I continued walking around the house as I watched the walls being built. They gave the impression of liquid pouring into a mold made of force fields. I continued around the house to the back yard and watched as the roofing tiles transplaced in, strip by strip, adding the final completion to the home rebuild.

"Ohm, can we match some of the weathering colorizations found in the original structure, so this new one looks less new?"

"Reviewing. Applying paint to emulate original aged hue of house," Ohm replied.

While the interior replication of furniture and appliances took place, I brought up the environment designer inside my invisihud. After extracting the property profile, I added virtual blocks to the outer wall surrounding my new home. I kept the wall height tall in the backyard area but lowered it to half-height in the front. Blocking out the two doors at the front gate, I marked them for removal so there was no barrier to my neighbors. The lower wall height was more in line with what I noticed in other walls separating homes in this neighborhood.

"Ohm, can you reference the blocking in my environment designer and apply it to the real-world wall? There is no need to mask the transport on this one. Let's simultaneously remove the old house projection when you replace the outer wall," I said.

"Working," I heard Ohm reply, and the outer wall shimmered with a moving line of sparkles making a complete circuit around the perimeter of my house compound. With the new wall in place, the restoration was complete. I stepped into my new home through the back door and watched as some of the last appliances and modifications took place. A few sparkles lingered, here and there. It had that smell of new construction, which I knew would fade over time, but overall, I really liked the place.

Jorrie, Erin, and I spent quite a bit of time here in previous time loops. Because it was on Vasco, it seemed less distant than having to travel to Earth to get together, but in my mind, I knew the distance did not matter. Still, in a practical sense, if anything happened to me, Jorrie could always catch a shuttle back to *Oasis Seven* from a Vascon ground port.

"Ohm, I would like to secure this house, similar to the apartments in San Francisco. If the children return, transport them to a nearby park with a supply of food and clothing," I said.

"Securing compound," Ohm stated.

I took the path out of my yard and walked up the cobblestone street until I came to a defunct well with boards placed over it. It looked like vehicles drove into the side of the walls, knocking many of the stones from the wall into the well. I removed the old boards and looked down the well. There was water down there, but it was certainly clogged and blocked. I set the boards off to the side, pulled out my wand, and said, "*Emergareformac.*" Nothing happened at first, and I thought about recasting the spell, but then a rumble and a grind emerged from the center of the well, as stones flew up from the bottom and started stacking themselves up, rebuilding the wall surrounding the well. Once the wall was restacked, I walked around the wall casting "*Mortusgamtite*" at the stones, which caused mortar to appear and harden in the area I targeted with the wand. This wand use was good practice for me. I always thought of the wand as a last resource device, but it offered some practical advantages. I made up both of these spells based upon some conversations I shared with Madison Baker about the practicality of magic. She insisted and referenced old books indicating spells leave a trail through the magical ether. Spells cast often can flow more freely, even if a caster is not that proficient. But the truth is, magic comes from the imagination of the spell caster, the intent of the spell, and the flair of the verbal component. A funny verbal component combined with a humorous intent cast by a competent prankster can lead to a very comedic spell result. But comedy can quickly lead to tragedy, and I find casting spells on people is one of the last things you really want to do.

After making my way around the well and testing the sturdiness of the wall, I took a seat on it and gazed down to the cleared-out well. There used to be a structure above the well, but that was removed or destroyed long ago. Using the invisihud, I imported the scan of the well into the environment designer. After placing a large virtual block over the well, I asked Ohm, "Can you locate a Vascon style well covering and replicate one for this spot?"

"Checking, please stand back, Sam," Ohm said.

I took a few steps away from the wall, and a large sparkle appeared over the well. When it faded, a Vascon-style wishing-well winch covered it. The roof tapered to a point, with a bucket hanging from a rope, ready to be lowered. I walked up to the new structure and tried operating it. It worked fine. There was a toothed gear on the winch with a spring-loaded auto-locking mechanism, similar to what you might find on a sailing ship. The new overhead structure came with sliding covers for the well. I looked into it and said, "Ohm, let's target all those additional stones and debris for removal. Go ahead and recycle them."

A series of several sparkles came and went at the bottom of the well as visible rubble sparkled away. I tried out the well by lowering the bucket down with a splash. The bucket also had a second thinner rope attached to it so you could tilt the bucket after it landed in the water below. Once the bucket filled with water, I cranked the winch to bring it up. The covers rotated. When the well was open, they offered a large flat space where you could move the bucket to or have collection containers ready to receive the contents of the bucket. I set the bucket down and said, "Ohm, can you replicate a medical inspectrograph at this location?"

A sparkle appeared next to the bucket. I picked up the medical inspectrograph and turned it on. After scanning the water, I found that it registered free of parasites and bacteria. It was at a seventy percent clean rating. You could drink it, but it could be better.

"Ohm, let's install a water purifier at the bottom of this well," I said as I dumped the water from the bucket back into the well.

"Placing purifier in well. At current well volume it will take eleven minutes to purify the water within five meters of the surface," Ohm said.

Stepping back, I walked around this circular well with a pointed roof. The ground leading up to the well contained special grooves flowing from the well out to the sides of the approaching streets. These grooved stone guides connected into a grooved curb on either side of the street. I guessed that this was originally a rain runoff system connecting gutters from houses to the street and then the street to the well. As I followed the path of the grooved guides, they ended in a clogged-up grass-filled drain feeding into the well. It looks like, without maintenance, these wells could end up in this state. Once again, I thought about using the wand first, and said, "*Repugnatone.*"

After flicking the wand directly at the clogged drain gate, the strangest thing happened. The plants clogging the drain became repulsed by it. In an animated fashion reminiscent of a David Lynch stop motion movie, the plants wriggled and moved, pulling up their roots and even dragging some of the soil with them as they settled into a new location beside the drain, scrunching out their neighboring plants with a bit of a rustle. I felt a streak of joy as I put some of Madison's advice to the test, inventing new magic spells. The well was originally constructed with four grates aligned along the cardinal points, and I applied the *Repugnatone* spell to them all.

"Well water tests report a ninety-eight point seven percent clean rating," Ohm said after some time passed.

Heading over to the well, I lowered the bucket, this time from the other side, to see if there was a difference. The main difference was the handedness of the crank on the winch. On this side, I used my left hand and on the other side, I used my right. The bucket dropped in with a splash, and I pulled the secondary rope to tilt the bucket and waited for it to fill with water as it sank farther into the well. I got to cranking on the winch and brought the bucket up to set it off to the side. Using the medical inspectrograph, I tested the water, and it came out one hundred percent clean. I pulled down a ladle I noticed hanging on a peg and tasted the water. It was good. It tasted clean with some of that well water mineral flavor that many people prefer.

A child's voice from behind asked, "Hey, Mister, did you just fix that well?"

The afternoon dropped into the early evening as I turned around and faced a single street urchin. The rule of thumb is if you see one, there are probably more watching and hiding. I sipped from the ladle and replied, "Yes, I fixed the well. Do you want to try a drink?"

"Nah, maybe later," the boy said.

"Well, that is what it's for. Now anyone can use it whenever they like. I'm, Sam," I said stepping up on the boy, which startled him for a moment as he jumped back.

He stared at my extended hand and finally took it, saying, "I'm Emeel. You're human, but not Starnet."

"That's right. I'm your neighbor now. I just bought the house down the street, the one with the big wall. I'm fixing it up. Where do you live?" I asked Emeel.

"Oh, you know here and there," Emeel said vaguely.

"I plan on fixing up more houses in the neighborhood," I said, a bit vague, myself.

I hung up the ladle, picked up my medical inspectrograph, and started heading off down one of the streets, saying, "Well, I guess I'll talk to you later."

I got about ten meters away, then Emeel shouted out, "There's one this way," as he pointed toward another street.

Emeel walked ahead of me, not really talking, and I followed him to the end of a cul-de-sac where a large manor-style home sat on a hill in disrepair. A few of the surrounding smaller homes were in a similar shape. Heading up to the house along the overgrown walkway, I asked, "Ohm, are there any life forms in this house?"

"Seven life forms detected, all children," Ohm reported.

"Emeel, I can fix this house today, but you have to ask your friends to leave for a short while. They can watch the repair from out here," I said, looking over at Emeel.

Emeel shook his head and walked up the broken front steps and into the open doorway. As I waited, I looked around at the various houses in this small area and brought up my invisihud. I targeted each of the roofs of the houses, blocked them out, and said, "Ohm, replace the blocks in my environment designer with brand new roofs. Add gutters and downspouts too."

There was a series of large sparkles as the damaged roofs were replaced with new ones. I must have been distracted because I felt a tug on my shirt and turned around to see a group of children looking up at me with Emeel holding a small one. Looking over the group of kids, I felt a bit sorry for the younger ones who were dirty and lanky. They all wore torn clothes, looked malnourished, and a couple of the older ones carried small knives at their belts.

I said, "I'm Sam. I'm here to fix up your home today. It won't take long."

I targeted the manor-style kid house with my invisihud and said, "Ohm, let's do a series of operations to this house. We are going to replace the roof, remove any broken glass, install a new kitchen and bathroom plumbing using Blinn water generators and recycle units. Add a basic food replicator to the kitchen. Replace the broken doors and repair the front and back porch."

"Who are you talking to?" one of the kids asked.

I said, "Okay, everyone, cover your eyes," as I lifted up my arm to block some of the brightness from the multiple sparkles generated from such a complex request. The sparkling lasted for well over eight minutes, and the kids quickly raised their arms up, blocking the brightness too.

"What is going on?" the same kid asked.

"New supplies are being transported into position. It will be a drier, warmer, nicer place. The pipes should work too," I said as the sparkles finally came to an end.

"Is it really ours?" one of the other children asked.

"For now, yes, but there may come a time where adults come and make a claim. If that happens, have Emeel come and find me. He knows where I live," I said as I walked up the stairs of the front porch and into the house, testing out the new front door.

The group of children followed me into the house as I reviewed the implemented changes. The place looked good. The walls and floors were still a mess, but the roof and ceilings were restored. Heading into the kitchen, I turned on the water faucet. It sputtered and then ran clear and steady. I said, "It has hot and cold water. Remember to turn it off, all right?"

I moved over to the replicator on the wall and said, "A plate of Goony fruit."

The replicator sparkled, and a plate of fruit appeared, sliced and ready to eat. I moved the plate over to the counter, where several of the children dove right in, helping themselves to the fresh fruit.

Emeel remained behind and asked me, "Can it make anything?"

"It can make only food and clothing," I said.

"A new pair of boots," Emeel said.

"For what species and what size?" a soft Vascon voice replied.

There was an uproar from behind me as the other children made fun of Emeel for talking to a female voice.

"Shut up," he said to the group, then turned to address the replicator wall saying, "My size, the size of a young Vascon male."

With a sparkle, a pair of boots appeared on the replication tray. Emeel revealed a smile in his eyes as he grabbed the boots with one hand and held them up. He said, "Bonba stick," and after the sparkling faded, he grabbed the sweet treat from the replicator tray before walking off to try on his boots.

At the mention of Bonba sticks, the other children said it out loud, and all ran over to the replicator. They yelled Bonba stick at the same time, and nothing happened.

"Please, children, one at a time. Ask for a Bonba stick, wait for the sparkles to fade, take it and move on."

The first one in line was an older girl who got it and ordered a Frazzle-flavored Bonba stick. The others waited their turn, and eventually, all the children were sucking away on their own Bonba stick. I felt like such a bad parent leaving these children with an all-you-can-eat ice cream buffet, but there were other things to attend to, and I headed out the door.

I made it as far as walking off the porch and down the hill to the front gate before hearing footsteps running up from behind. Turning around, I saw it was Emeel.

"Hey, Man. Thanks, thanks for everything. You're like the Squire," Emeel said with a smile.

"You're welcome. Make sure no one fights over the replicator, all right? If it happens, come and get me and we'll figure it out," I said.

Emeel shook his head, okay, and I walked off down the street, heading back to the well. Evening was setting in once I got back to the well. There was a small gathering of people inspecting it. I continued down the original street I chose before Emeel distracted me with his house. As I walked along the street, I activated my invisihud and asked, "Ohm, can you add structural integrity ratings to my invisihud?"

"Adding structural integrity, broken down by basic categories, walls, roofs, doors, and windows," Ohm said.

The invisihud updated, presenting a better understanding of what homes were damaged and what parts were the weakest. I wondered if there was a way to automate this, so I asked, "Ohm, can you take the provided structural integrity map and generate a repair plan for each structure? I'm looking for a ninety percent or better success rate before repairs are issued on occupied houses. Below that, automatic shielding supports should be used."

"Affirmative, safety measures are in place," Ohm said.

"How many structures can we repair at once?" I asked Ohm.

"Over ten thousand at once, making maximum use of replication facilities," Ohm replied.

"Let's not use the maximum. Use eighty-five percent. I want to conduct the first test on the ten highlighted units in my invisihud."

"Installing transplacements," Ohm said, and houses on both sides of the street sparkled and faded, leaving behind a newer building. I could hear a few starts and Ohs.

"Ohm, scan the transplaced houses on this street. Are the occupants okay?" I asked.

"No damage to occupants," Ohm reported.

"Ohm, I think we are ready for the big test. Let's replace as many structures as ninety percent Blinn capacity can produce in a single transplacement," I said.

"Scanning and building structural integrity maps," Ohm replied, falling silent. "Transferring candidate map to your invisihud."

My invisihud updated with an overhead view of the province where I stood. I was in the center of the map, and a selection set radiated out from me. It looked like approximately twelve thousand structures were expected to be modified in a single transplacement. I made a few selections inside the area of effect and said, "Ohm, these types of objects need to be more elaborate. Consult any references for the complexity of the water drainage systems. Parks should be more inviting and practical, bridges and roads should have more stability."

"Adding roads and sidewalks to restoration list, including historical references for all known Vascon architecture. This modification produces an eleven percent reduction in maximum area that a ninety percent load can produce in a single transplacement," Ohm replied.

With the new considerations in place, the proposed structure count dropped to nine thousand. I thought this was acceptable, so I said, "Ohm, let's try this. Transplace the currently proposed structures with the revised replicated ones from the Blinn replication factories. Oh, and don't forget to put water purifiers in places that make sense."

"Commencing transplacements," Ohm said, then fell silent. "Multiple failures from replication factory under ninety percent load."

"Are there any casualties?" I asked.

"No Vascon casualties. The transport was never issued on candidates without replication sources," Ohm replied.

"Did any of the transplacements work?" I asked.

"Thirty-six hundred structures were successfully replaced during the last transplacement attempt," Ohm replied.

"Great, shrink the total area so the new maximum structure count is thirty-six hundred. Issue a new transplacement for the new area," I said.

"Generating new structural integrity maps," Ohm replied, then added. "Transferring candidate map to your invisihud."

"The area looks good. Apply the same filter automatically for detecting special structures that may need more replication bandwidth," I said.

"Commencing transplacements," Ohm said, then fell silent.

"Multiple failures from replication factory under new load," Ohm said.

"How many transplacements did we get this time?" I asked Ohm.

"Twenty-four hundred successful transplacements," Ohm replied.

"Let's try the same thing again with the area reduced to match a twenty-four hundred structure count," I said.

"Commencing transplacements with a smaller radius," Ohm said.

This time Ohm reported, "No failures detected. Twenty-four hundred transplacements were requested, and twenty-four hundred transplacements were fulfilled."

"That is great. Let's continue the replication process in an automatic spiral radius around this original center until sunrise. If successful transplacement count drops below one thousand, cease operations," I said.

"Continuing with replication," Ohm said.

I made my way along the sloping streets to the compound of my new house.

As I approached, it looked nice. The entire neighborhood looked nicer, with basic repairs were done to the houses, sidewalks, and streets. Less of a "life during wartime" look and more of a classic old-world feel to it. I entered my new house and locked the front door, checking the back door too. Making my way upstairs, I reviewed the bedrooms. They were of a colonial design with modern influences such as electric lamps and view screens. I lie down on the bed and activated the viewscreen. The news was all about a series of sparkling effects. There was footage from ground sources and orbital satellites showcasing my handy work as it continued revising homes and issuing repairs. With tonight's massive transplacement event, I was shortcutting the romantic portion of being the wandering Squire in favor of a practical restoration in the safest, fastest way.

I must have drifted off to sleep because the next thing I hear is a repeated pounding on my front door. Heading downstairs while still wearing the same clothes I slept in, I looked through the peephole at a crowd of people gathered in front of my house.

I said, through the door, "Who is it?"

"Vascon security, open up," I heard a voice reply from the other side of the door.

I took a few soft steps back from the door and said, "Just a minute. I'm not dressed."

I brought the *Motif* forward in my mind and cast it into the world, projecting, penetrating, covering all aspects of this echo. I tried to make the scene behind the door more fluid, easier to change, or bend in my favor. I walked up to the door, and the *Motif* followed me, mentally bouncing off the door and walls causing it to congregate all around. I unlocked the door and flung it open, leaning back as I did so. Without as much as an introduction, the two armed guards reached into my house, grabbed me by my biceps, and dragged me out to the front porch. Leveraging the forward motion, I pulled the *Motif* behind me, casting it forward as a net over those near me. The guards did not stop there, they kicked me in the back of both knees, forcing me to the floor. Fortunately, the auto shielding kicked in, but I fell hard on my knee caps. In the faces of the crowd gathered in front of my house, I saw the reason for all of this. Pansa Nari stood in her robes, on my walk.

In the first time loop, when I purchased this house on Vasco, I knew nothing of the culture, so the work of the Squire was done slowly over time. While walking from town to town, I managed a Blinn terraforming module, restoring villages. I learned about the complex aqueduct structures of Vasco in the first time loop because of these personal wanderings. I also experienced the full wrath of Pansa Nari. She was like the Pope is to humans, the spiritual leader of the Vascon people. She was also one of the most vindictive, self-absorbed, selfish people I have ever met. In the first loop, she caused much strife in my personal life as I tried to understand Vascon religious beliefs. In the second loop, I came up with a simple role reversal for her. I altered echo so that she was no longer Pansa and all those terrible things did not happen in the second loop.

I mustered up the *Motif*, around me, and used what Splendorite's call, "The Imperial Voice," saying, "Unhand me. I have a right as a Union citizen to know what I am charged with!"

I felt the guard's grips loosen on my biceps, and I shook my arms free, straightening up my back, but not trying to stand.

"Enough!" cried Pansa Nari, adding, "Let him stand."

As I stood, I noticed Pansa Nari was already in motion, heading for the porch steps. It was part of her psychological nature to want to be on equal footing or above you when she lectures you. I immediately took quick steps forward to occupy the entrance to the porch forcing her to look up at me. This motion brought a swift response from the guards, and they moved in my direction. It was already too late, however, I mentally cast the full weight of the *Motif* upon Pansa Nari and continued forward, slowly stepping down the porch stairs toward her.

I shifted echo so that Lama Windsong became Pansa Windsong and Pansa Nari was just Lili Nari, an old Vascon woman who thought she was Pansa. I shifted the impression of the crowd in my favor, including the two guards approaching from behind. Continuing the concept that Emeel got the word out that I was the Squire of the Pharaoh, I embraced the role of rebuilding the land. By the time I walked past Pansa Nari, she was in rags, and the guards carried her from my property as she screamed and kicked at them.

I followed behind and said, "Thank you, officers. Make sure she gets something to eat."

I needed to face the crowd, so I headed to the end of my walk where it meets the street. As I approached, I used the *Motif* to reduce the crowd count. I drew closer an echo where the crowd was made up mainly of my immediate neighbors. I greeted them and said hello, one by one. Many of them thanked me for the repairs, and we talked about what repairs I applied to my house which, apparently, was the eyesore of the community. Some also mentioned the well. The crowd more or less dissipated when one final straggler approached from down the hill. She was an older Vascon woman and said her name was Marjoran. She ran a small restaurant called, "Aberithes'," which was just around the corner and halfway down the hill. She invited me into her restaurant, which was a short walk away.

"What brings you to Brecht province?" Marjoran asked with a smile, her long hair flowing over her shoulder.

I looked at Marjoran, who was hitting me with a serious, are you available vibe, and smiled back, saying, "The beauty, being by the sea. I love the landscape and the architecture."

"Thank you for the repairs on my restaurant, that is if you truly are the Squire of the Pharaoh?" Marjoran asked.

"You're welcome. I don't know if I am this mythical Squire of the Pharaoh. That name is just something one of the orphan boys called me yesterday," I replied.

"Some of the repairs I forgot about or got so used to that I did not see them as broken anymore, like my crooked steps out front. Last night, while serving evening meals, the entire restaurant sparkled all around me and the guests. We were frightened at first because there was a loud stressing sound, but when we looked around, nothing was wrong. As I looked around, I noticed more repairs. This morning, I checked the roof, and it looked wonderfully new. Previously, there were quite a few busted tiles and a few leaks," Marjoran said as we came upon the steps leading up to Aberithes'.

We headed up the steps and into the restaurant where Marjoran was greeted by her two children who were about nine and thirteen. The youngest was a boy named Dustan and the teenage girl was named Patrishor. Dustan rushed up, saying, "Is this him? Is this the Squire?" to his mother.

"Why don't you ask him yourself?" Marjoran said to Dustan.

"Are you really the Squire of the Pharaoh?" Dustan asked me.

"No, my name is Sam. I'm your new neighbor. I live in the big house at the top of the hill," I said to Dustan as I pointed in the direction of my house.

"Mom, he's not the Squire," Dustan complained.

"He's still a guest. Bring him some Gretull stew," Marjoran said to Dustan and then turning to Patrishor, said, "Some bread and tea for Sam."

The kids both headed to the back of the restaurant and disappeared through a doorway. Marjoran showed me to a table, and the bell on the door rang as some other customers came in. She greeted them, apparently knowing them very well, and led them to a table farther back in the restaurant before disappearing into the kitchen, herself. It wasn't too long before Patrishor returned with a small basket of bread, a teapot, and a cup with a saucer. She poured my first cup of tea before heading off to the other table to take their order.

The tea was hot and flavored like chai. The bread was flat and looked like it was cooked on a hot stone. It reminded me of Nan. Dustan arrived soon after I tasted the tea, bringing me a single bowl of warm stew. I said, "Thank you, Dustan," and he replied, "You're welcome," heading over to the other table, which was already calling him by name.

The stew was orange in color and smelled a lot like curry. It looked like Dahl with sweet potatoes. There was a large sliced hard-boiled egg spread across the center of the bowl and a sprinkle of green leaf, reminding me of parsley. I dipped the bread into the stew, and it tasted wonderful. The parsley ended up tasting a little bit like a ginger mint combination, which went well with this dish.

I took my time as I ate, and a few more customers came and went, but the restaurant was never packed full or had people waiting for a table. I was highly concerned that my massive replication factory failed when placed under a heavy load. I hoped to rely on that in the development of the *Kataru*. I tried to avoid another visit to the Blinn factories, but to get things running, I was going to have to review what happened and come up with some changes to improve performance. I finished my stew, and as I sat there sipping tea, I put my elbow on the table and leaned into my hand to mask the moving of my mouth as I asked softly, "Ohm, were there any casualties in the Blinn factories when the failures occurred last night?"

"Minor injuries were suffered by floor workers, but no fatalities. Most injuries were second and third-degree burns as conduits blew out," Ohm replied close to my ear so no one else could hear.

"What caused the conduits to fail? Was it the load or something else?" I asked.

"An investigation is underway to determine what caused the system to fail," Ohm replied.

"Make operational efficiency a priority and enforce stricter safety protocols. I want to perform another round of transplacements overnight," I said.

"Relaying information to Blinn teams," Ohm said.

I got up from my table and headed over to the check out counter of her restaurant, and said, "Marjoran, that was truly delicious, but I am afraid I did not bring any way to pay for the food,"

"Marjoran smiled sweetly and said, "Don't worry, it's my way of repaying you for the repairs. The first time is free."

"Thank you, I will certainly be back," I said, departing the restaurant and ringing the bell.

"Come again," I heard Marjoran say as I made my way down the newly aligned front steps. Deciding to find out what was at the bottom of the hill, I walked around the neighborhood, enjoying the pleasant weather.

As I walked, taking in the repairs, most of them were quite good. There were walls with finely restored embossed reliefs and planters built into walls and curbs, giving the overall impression of society, politely encroaching upon nature. I noticed the amount of green space woven into Vascon communities was fairly high. There were lots of small parks, glens, and patios that turned into yards.

I said, "Ohm, let the replication teams know that I am quite pleased with the results of the recent transplacements."

"Relaying appreciation to the team," Ohm said.

I must have walked for more than an hour before I came upon a ridge looking off toward the sea of Brenya. Below I could see a more sprawling community ending in docks and ports bustling with heavy boat traffic.

As I stood there taking in a hint of the sea air, Ohm interrupted with, "Multiple Imperial vessels approaching Zenith terraforming module."

"Ohm, halt current Zenith terraforming operations and track ships. When they land, transport me to their location," I said.

I reviewed my invisihud and set up a Transfast back to San Francisco in case anything goes sideways in this meeting. About ten minutes later, I felt the world dissolve, and I fell into darkness once more. In both time loops, there was very little participation in the daily happenings on Zenith. Once I met Erin, we split for the Dili sector, and I only returned now and then to fetch vegetables from the community gardens. This first meeting introduced the Imperials and the Melogs to the Blinn replication system. A beautiful band of solid green bars formed to either side of my peripheral vision and shot inward, dragging the blue sky in from the edge. My vision returned, and I stood before a small gathering of Imperial and Melog transport ships. The ships landed fairly close to the edge of the terraformed space. I stood in an open field with ships in front of me while replicated housing stood behind me. I could hear the sounds of ship hatches opening while some other people exited their vehicles and looked in my direction.

CHAPTER 26

I called out "Hello!" and waved my arms so as not to surprise them with my sudden appearance.

Soldiers brought their weapons to the ready, but the Admiral called out, "Hold your fire."

I walked up to him, and he wore a smile on his face as he said, "We meet again, Sam."

"We meet again, Admiral," I repeated his words as I shook his hand.

"Your coordinates worked. This planet looks promising," the Admiral said with hope.

"I set up this initial terraforming town center. It's just a short walk beyond those housing units," I said to the Admiral pointing in the direction of the town center.

"Lead the way," He said with a little gruff in his voice.

"This way, everyone. We're heading to the town center!" I said loudly to the group gathering around the Admiral and me.

We walked through the grassy field and entered the terraformed town by stepping onto the end of a road that stopped at the edge of town. We walked through the streets, passing empty houses, apartments, and finally to the town center where a kiosk stood. I waited for the group to arrive at the kiosk and said, "Gather around. I want to tell you what I know about this world and area of space."

"Oh," some of them said as they talked among themselves.

"Many predatory species occupy this same area of space. This planet is hidden from most of those species because it exists inside a gaseous cloud which is rarely visited or scanned. If you choose to settle here, I highly recommend you abandon space exploration until you rebuild your civilization. The fewer signals you emit from this gaseous cloud, the better off all citizens will be. Keep your ships in close orbit as a final escape option should you be discovered and have to flee."

I paused to let the crowd take in what I said, and they muttered among themselves. Finally, someone said, "Why should we trust you? Maybe those other species will help us even more?"

"There is your weakest link," I said. "If any one person leaves the group and talks to the hostile species, they will be exposing ALL OF YOU to possible slavery and exploitation," I said, raising my voice when saying all of you.

"That's neither here nor there. We have not decided yet," the Admiral said over his shoulder, then to me, "Continue."

"That was the bad news. The good news is this kiosk can replicate food, housing, schools, parks, farms, and many other things. It also acts as a local communication system. Take a look around you at these buildings," I said.

The crowd followed my guided gesture and took in their surroundings.

"They were constructed through a slow, low power replication process. The kiosk manages requests and replicates matter to fulfill the requests."

"So, this device grows buildings?" the Admiral asked.

"Yes, it can grow roads and bridges too," I said.

"Time for a demonstration, please stand back," I said, motioning for the crowd to spread out before continuing, "You direct the kiosk verbally, like so. Kiosk, replicate a folding table with a supply of coffee, tea, juice, water, and pastries, enough for forty people."

The kiosk behind me said, "Processing request," and the floor in the open space between us started unfolding itself, revealing that it was made of hinged little panels and not the stone it previously represented.

The panels continued to fold in and slid back revealing spinning mechanical workings that pushed out quickly, forming auraprojectors to transplace the table of food into place. The reverse panel folding process restored the floor to its original look, as the kiosk said, "Process complete."

"Some of you might be thinking, whoever controls the kiosk controls development or what gets replicated. This physical representation of the kiosk is just a prop. The kiosk exists anywhere there is a replicated component. This distribution means you can talk to the kiosk while you are in a house, over there, but not if you were in the field where the ships landed," I said while walking up to the newly replicated table and pouring a small cup of orange juice.

I held it up and took a drink. I thought it was not that bad as I shook my head yes to the group. And with that, the ice was broken as people gathered around the table, trying a drink and a pastry. The vultures, I dubbed those who skipped the pastry table, were circling, and the first one to land was Rose Harding, President of the Imperials.

Rose Harding was an older woman. She dressed like a frumpy school teacher but was probably quite fetching in her youth. She approached and said, "Sam, so nice to finally meet you," extending her hand.

"Likewise, Madame President," I said while shaking her hand.

"This is really a lot for us to take in. Your technology offers so much. I'm afraid it might be misused," Rose said, a little concerned.

"Well, that is something you have to work out as a people, don't you think?" I asked her.

"I agree, but maybe hold off granting access until some formal process is established," Rose suggested.

"Sounds like the same old story to me. The haves, controlling what the have nots get or see? This way it's all fair. Everyone is the same as everyone else in the Kiosk's eyes," I offered.

"I agree with that in principle, but sometimes, when people have the right to choose," she trailed off, and I finished her sentence for her saying, "they choose wrong?"

She offered a ho-hum face with a defeated look through her glasses as she said, looking up to me and repeating my words, "choose wrong."

"I did not offer the technology to lord over you. I offered it as a gift so that you might survive and rebuild. You may be surprised, that a worthless scoundrel that was dealt a bad hand in your previous culture may thrive and blossom, contributing greatly with this new land and opportunity," I suggested.

One of the revision four, Melogs approached and interrupted, saying "I want to thank you from the Melog coalition. This planet and gift of replication technology are very generous," she said.

"Well, I did not make the planet. It was already here," I said humorously, and we all laughed.

While the president stood there, I said to the blond female Melog, "You do realize that the mechanical versions of Melogs can not stay and live here? I suggest you give them the *Pentacraft*, and I'll relocate it in a favorable probability where they can continue their development."

This suggestion seemed to take her by surprise, and she said sheepishly, "I'll discuss that with the others."

"I don't mean to purposely exclude them, but they won't fit in with the new society. If you keep them around, they will eventually feel like outsiders, and you will feel like you betrayed them. It's best if you set them free now," I said.

A tall, muscular Imperial male approached, who said, "Hello, Sam. My name is Craig, Craig Anderton. You saved the life of my wife. She was the pilot in the *Falcon* that you and your friend rescued the other day. I just wanted to say thank you personally. It means a lot to me, and for my daughter, to have her mother back."

I shook his hand and said, "You're welcome, Craig. I'm glad we found her in time."

This meet and greet went on for more than a couple of hours. People came up to introduce themselves and thanked me for the replication and the planet. I spent a lot of time with the members of the press core, who seemed to be writing down many of the instructions I offered on how to activate and use the kiosk system to obtain personal items, such as clothing, food, and how to construct housing. I felt they would be the ones who were most likely to convey the fact that this planet and replication services were for everyone. By mid-afternoon, most members of the landing parties were already engaged with their interfaces to the kiosk and trying out some of the replication services offered. There were sounds of laughs and ohs as people began to discover joy again instead of just surviving.

After a few hours, I stood off by myself when I heard a voice I knew all too well, from behind, say, "Hey, Sam. We have agreed." It was one of the revision-nines speaking to me, Erin's revision. She was accompanied by three other Melogs, the revision-four blond, a revision-five woman, who was the last of her kind, and a revision-seven male who was also the last of his kind.

"We have decided to follow your advice in regards to the mechanical Melogs. How do we proceed?" the revision-nine asked.

"We will need to take a ship back to the *Pentacraft* and leave this area of space. One of the abilities of my species is to move people and objects through probability. That is what I will do with the *Pentacraft*," I said.

The male Melog asked, "You can do that? You can move a *Pentacraft* into another probability with your mind?"

"I can. I used that same ability to locate this planet which is safely hidden inside this nebula," I said.

The revision-five woman asked, "Well then, let's get going, shall we?" as she took my arm and we started walking back to the field where the ships landed.

It was nice to walk with a beautiful woman by my side. She acted a bit too familiar, touching my back as we walked, but I liked the attention. I kept staring at the revision-nine and thinking about Erin. Was that her?

Before we left the town center, the Admiral and the President of the Imperials approached, asking me, "May I ask where you are heading off to?"

"The Melogs have agreed to a separation from the mechanical variety. The human forms will be brought down to the planet, while the mechanical versions get to keep the *Pentacraft*. I will shift them into another probability. Even if they are discovered by alien races in the future, they will have no way to betray the location of this planet," I explained to the Admiral and the President.

"You have mentioned probability before. Can you explain what that means?" the Admiral asked with respect.

"It means, once I move the Melog *Pentacraft* to a new location, it can never jump back to here. It will reside in a parallel universe where this planet no longer exists. It also means the rebel Melogs can never locate that *Pentacraft* either," I said.

"Do you agree to this?" the Admiral asked the Melog coalition.

The revision-nine spoke for them all, "Yes, we do."

Then I said to Danos and Rose, "It also means you must fulfill your oaths and agreements as honorable men and women of the Imperial fleet. The Melogs will have no ships and will be relying upon you not to betray them."

The Admiral said, "I understand this and agree to keep our oaths and pledges we have previously made to our Melog allies. I also affirm to convey this understanding to the members of the Imperial fleet."

"Well then, I guess we are off to see the Wizard," I said, but no one got the reference, of course.

We continued walking back toward the field where the ships landed, and the revision-five turned to me as we walked arm in arm and said, "My name is Cassia."

"Nice to meet you, Cassia," I said.

The male offered his name by saying, "I am Leonard."

And the revision-four said, "My name is Kara."

We made our way to the assault craft the Melogs arrived in. The doors to the ship opened up automatically as we approached. I never explored how integrated human model Melogs were with their Melog based technology. When I knew Erin, she mainly wanted to forget about the whole Imperial war mess, but these Melogs seemed to communicate with the ship using their minds. The revision-nine led the way, and I activated my invisihud to take scans of the exterior and interior of the Melog assault craft. We all took seats with the revision-nine in the pilot's chair. Soon I felt the ship take off and rise up. I felt a significant thrust vector applied to my chests as we ascended from the planet, attempting to make orbit. The pressure eventually eased off, and a sense of weightlessness overcame me. I was still strapped into the seat, so I sat tight as the revision-nine did her job and brought the assault craft into one of the landing bays located at the center of the *Pentacraft*. My main thought was that I hoped the mechanical Melogs went along with the whole deal and did not shoot me on site for trespassing with David. I set the shield in my invisihud to auto.

Once we entered the landing bay area, I felt a certain amount of gravity return to the assault craft. By the time we landed, the hatch door was opening, and gravity was close to normal. I removed my safety harness and left the assault craft. We waited on the landing platform until everyone exited the ship. This particular landing area looked incredibly organic, even more, organic than the hallways David and I explored. This center area is more of a life form than the outer appendage hallways are.

"Your ship, this *Pentacraft*. It is a life form, isn't it?" I asked the revision-nine.

She turned around looking at me, leveling her face with mine, a trait that Erin exhibited all the time while saying, "Yeah, she is alive, and she is hurt."

We started walking along a path leading up to a set of double doors. The path formed a bridge over some organic tissue, and crawling along the surface of the flesh were stunted, gnome-like creatures. Their upper portion was that of a man, but the head was shrunken, and so was the waist having diminutive legs attached to it.

"Are those what Guardbots look like, without armor?" I asked the revision-nine.

"Yes, those are the bio units that operate the Guardbots," she said.

As we approached the double doors I said, "I may be able to help heal the ship when I transfer it to the parallel universe."

The revision-nine stopped and turned around, saying, "Really? That is good."

Leonard spoke up, "She's right. If we can help heal the ship, the bio units will be more cooperative."

Kara said, "And the Biodual will be more likely to agree."

Cassia asked, "That's great. How will you do that?"

"I'll need a diagram of the *Pentacraft*'s original design. I can replicate new scaffolding to match the damaged sections, filling in the missing pieces," I said.

"That still doesn't tell us how you're going to do it," Cassie said.

"Do you have any information on what would be the best material to construct this scaffolding out of?" I asked

Leonard spoke, "We need to consult with the Biodual. She may have specific materials in mind."

Kara said, "I agree. I think this can help us present our case."

"Let's get in there," the revision-nine said before leading us through the double doors to a central communication center.

My guess is we just used the V.I.P. entrance to the Melog *Pentacraft* bridge. The room was not that big, think a quadruple-sized office meeting room with a large rectangle area in the center. Above this rectangular area, and hanging from holes in the ceiling, was an array of multiple strands with drops of glistening fluid sliding down them, finally gathering in a small indent at the floor, which acted as a drain. There were several Guardbots posted around the room, and they eyed me while adjusting their servos as I walked in with the other Melogs. Leonard and the revision-nine moved directly to the center of the room and started touching several vertical fluid strands, which seemed to be a ship's interface for their Melog revisions. Tubes containing liquid with bubbles rose from the floor and disappeared into the ceiling.

"Displaying ship schematic. Can you see this, Sam?" the revision-nine asked me while she continued to manipulate the strand array.

I walked closer to the rectangle in the center of the room and saw the map displayed in a greyscale red hovering beside the fluid strands. I said, "Yes, I think that might work."

"Ohm, can you take scans of this ship, scans of the displayed original specifications, and create virtual scaffolding for the missing and damaged sections?"

"Working on generating virtual scaffolding," Ohm replied to me.

"Who were you just talking to?" the revision-nine asked.

I pointed at the hanging strands and said, "You touched the fluid strands and interfaced with your computer, right? I did the same thing with my computer using voice commands."

Cassia said, "That is fascinating, so where is your computer?"

The revision-nine made a joke and said, "Duh, in a parallel universe."

Cassia looked serious for a moment, she was slightly embarrassed by her fellow Melog, and then she burst out laughing as the tension level rose and finally broke. I laughed too but then said, "She is right, though, my computer is in another universe."

"No way," the revision-nine said in that friendly, challenging manner that reminded me of Erin.

Leonard spoke up, still manipulating the fluid strands with his hands replying, "The Biodual agrees and has specific material requirements."

"Leonard, can you try to overlay them on the displayed map?" I asked.

"I think so, give me a moment," Leonard said.

I watched the original display the revision nine brought up, and it started to fill in with complex molecule makeups and major material breakdowns. I said,

"Ohm, can you scan the display and start preparing the scaffolding based upon these requested materials?"

"Working, can you have the display repeat the results in a loop?" Ohm asked.

"Leonard, can you loop the information. I may have missed some of the initial data?" I asked.

"I think so. Let me try," Leonard said as he focused on the fluid strands.

The mechanical Guardbots, in the corners of the room, stepped closer, and I noticed that Kara stood in front of one, creating a stark contrast between a scantily dressed fragile female versus a highly polished massive machine. The Guardbot's scanning blue eye focused only on Kara and it appeared some unheard conversation took place between the two.

Ohm reported, "Processing new data, revising scaffolding."

Leonard said, "I think I have it repeating," he said, looking up and stepping back from the fluid strands, revealing that his interaction with it was a little bit draining.

Two of the five points of the *Pentacraft* were severely damaged, the tips were completely missing, making the ship look like a wounded amputee. These two tips were where the new scaffolding was to be installed. I checked my invisihud and predicted a nine-minute preparation estimate saying, "That worked, I have the data. Scaffolding for the two missing tips is being constructed off-site using the provided materials list."

Kara took a few steps back, then turned away from the Guardbot and said, "The Guardbots and Pilotoids are in agreement. They feel an end to the human pursuit is in their best interest."

Cassia said, "Well, that settles it. We are all in agreement. What's next?"

"You'll need to gather all the human model Melogs in one place. I'll issue a mass transportation to the surface where they can begin their new lives," I said.

Kara moved over to the fluid strands and "touched in" to presumably send messages to her fellow four revisions that an Exodus from the ship was about to take place. I noticed the revision-nine "touched in" with the fluid strands to ready her counterparts for the journey.

"How are you going to handle the transport?" Cassia asked as Leonard walked around to the same side where we stood.

Kara spoke, but not to anyone in general, while still using the fluid strands and said, "They are all gathering at the level six central hub."

"I have technology similar to the other Union humans you met. This technology allows the transport of living matter from one location to another. Once your fellow Melogs are gathered, I can target their location and issue the mass transport to the surface," I said.

"And what guarantee do we have that you won't betray us and simply destroy us all in one bold move?" Cassia asked.

Leonard said, "She has a point. We are placing a lot of trust in these unseen, unknown processes that reside in other dimensions."

"If you don't want to do this, then fine. I'll just leave, and you guys can all work it out with the Imperials," I said.

The revision nine and Kara gathered around me as Cassia asked one more question, "I guess I don't understand what's in this for you? Why are you doing this?"

"Why are you helping us?" the revision-nine added.

"Maybe it's not help at all. After you leave, we will be unguarded Melogs on the surface with no ships, weapons, or any way to escape," Cassia added.

Leonard said, "She has a point. What is to stop the Imperial soldiers from just slaughtering us once we are on the surface?"

"The thing about trust is that you can't prove that it exists until after you test it," I said, stepping back, opening my arms, and then to Cassia. "Here is a little exercise, you lean back, and I'll catch you and keep you from falling."

Cassia faced me and smiled, saying, "I get it," but refusing to turn her back and fall into my arms.

The revision nine stepped up and said, "I'll do it," turning her back then saying, "You ready."

"Ready, lean back," I said.

I couldn't see her face, but knowing Erin, I imagined the look on her face as she took a breath, closed her eyes, and leaned back. She wore a cream-colored corduroy jacket over a dark green oval neck shirt. When she leaned back, I watched her thick hair falling as I caught her in my arms, the scent of her Melog shampoo finally reaching my nose.

She turned around and smiled at me while sliding her lower jaw to the side as she opened her mouth a bit, in a flirtatious fashion, saying to the others, "See, trust exists. The revision nines are all in. Are you guys in or what?"

"Scaffolding replication complete, available for transport," Ohm said to me.

I interrupted, "The scaffolding is ready. And in another bold move demonstrating trust, I suggest we install it before moving the ship to the new probability. That way I can solidify the bond between the original ship and the repair when the transition takes place."

The revision-nine moved back to the fluid strands, saying, "Informing the Biodual," while Leonard headed over to the fluid strands again.

"Can the Guardbots help with the alignment? Can they exist in a non-atmosphere environment?" I asked.

Cassia seemed activated by this thought and headed over to the fluid strands. After a short time she said, "Yes, they can help."

The revision-nine broke in and said, "They can exist in a non-atmosphere environment a little bit longer than humans, but it is eventually fatal to them."

Kara came closer, with the Guardbot behind her, and looked at the diagram on the display as I pointed out the two main damaged sections and said, "Let's get Guardbot teams here and here. And these other damaged areas, it would be nice to have at least one if not two Guardbots there to verify when these smaller repairs are in place."

Cassia looked up at the map then focused back on the fluid strands saying, "Dispatching teams, but I'm not sure how close they can get to the damaged

"Ohm, erect force fields around all damaged areas. Try to establish atmospheric containment within damaged sections currently exposed to space," I said.

Referring to my latest Ohm request, Kara asked with a smile, "More fluid strand talk?"

"Yeah, I know it sounds weird," I replied.

Leonard spoke up, while focused on the fluid strands, "Confirmed. Guardbots are detecting a blue energy field around areas exposed to space."

"Ohm, let's do a transplacement on all the smaller damaged sections first. Take it slow on the replication side as needed, and give the floor manager a warning before you begin," I said.

"Issuing transplacement request and informing manager," Ohm replied.

The revision nine asked, "What is a transplacement?"

"Ah, glad you asked," I said in a friendly manner, "The transplacement is a word I recently coined. I got tired of saying transport the replication into place. That is basically all that is happening here. A scan is supplied to an off-site replication facility."

The revision-nine interrupted asking, "In another probable universe?"

I continued, "yes, in another probability, that generates the physical replacement part. Another scan is made of the damaged area to determine how much of the edge to remove. The area is prepared to receive the replicated part which is transported into place. The replacement part is designed to latch onto the new location's preparation slots after it materializes."

"Predicting a six-minute deployment session," Ohm stated.

"We have a few minutes before all the smaller repairs are finished. The larger ones we'll install after those are completed," I said, trying to kill time and keep the topic of betrayal to a minimum.

While looking over at me, Cassia said, "Guardbots near the large damaged sections are reporting atmosphere and environments are habitable. A large blue shield of energy is covering the opening."

The revision-nine, once again asked, "So, how does the shield work?"

I pointed to the display near the fluid strands and said, "Very similar to that display. The display is the result of emission. The shield is also a result of emission."

"Where are the emitters?" she continued with her curiosity.

"The emitters exist in this probability, but were transplaced to this location in a similar way the repair sections are being transplaced," I said, trying to explain.

Leonard broke in with another report, "Confirmation, damaged sections are becoming operational. The Biodual reports communications are working through the replacement parts."

"All right!" the revision nine said, enthusiastically as she flung herself into my arms, hugging me, then realizing that might have been too much as she backed off, gathering her composure but still looking into my eyes.

"Yes!" I said. "That is good news. I think the Biodual's material list helped a lot. This success gives me confidence that the larger sections can become fully integrated into the original ship."

Ohm sent me a follow-up message, "All smaller repairs have been deployed."

"Okay, I have confirmation that all the smaller repairs have been deployed and are in place. Do you have any further Biodual confirmations?" I asked Leonard.

"Checking, she is quite busy. I think these new repairs are taking some focus from her communication with me," Leonard said.

Cassia said, "Yes, maybe we should take a short break before introducing any more repairs to the Biodual."

"That's fine with me," I said, feeling the mood of the room turn darker again as the sound of the Guardbot servos adjusting became the only sound.

The revision-nine broke the silence by saying, "So, how do we defend ourselves once we are on the surface with the humans? We are bound to run into conflicts."

"You're right. It may be tough at first, but I think the best way is to hold them to their word is to leverage the kiosk. You could set up a broadcasting network so if you see a human doing something wrong, record it, broadcast it, expose the wrongdoer's action. Create social media networks that are outside any official political networks so you can follow what others are doing. In the end, the best way to get along is to help each other," I said.

"What do we do if they exclude us from their society?" Kara asked.

"The kiosk is a shared resource. If they build a society using the kiosk, they have the same building rights as you," I said.

"How does that help us?" Leonard asked.

"Let's say they build a wall around a settlement. You can build a door and enter. There may be some survivalists that just head for the hills and abandon the kiosk. Those are the ones I'd keep the most eye on. If you do wander and explore the world beyond the kiosk make sure you have replicated supplies and bring something extra to trade with if you encounter any survivalist," I said.

Kara said, "It sounds like a grim kind of life."

Cassia said, "You said it, Sister."

"I guess you're right, the glass is half empty," I said, then changing the subject, "I'll need to use drums to move this ship into another probable universe. Do you mind if I set up over here?"

"Why do you need drums?" Cassia asked.

"I'll be playing the drums along to the music with auragraphic musicians being displayed, is that okay?" I asked. "Ask the Guardbots to not freak out."

"You didn't answer my question," Cassia said.

"It's the mood of the music that will influence the attitudes that neighboring species will have to the Melogs once they arrive in the new probability. I'm going to play along with a song while I shift us to the new location," I said, figuring that this was as good an excuse as any to get in some drum practice today.

Besides, I have never tried shifting echo while playing the drums.

I walked over to the open area and addressed the two Guardbots in the corners, "I'm adding drums to this room and some auragraphic singers. You will see a large sparkle."

"Ohm, transplace my drum kit with virtual singers to this location," I said, and a large sparkle appeared and faded, leaving behind my Tama Swing Star drum kit and a set of sticks.

The Guardbots snapped to life, and what was once their clawed hands retracted into the forearm leaving behind a portable Gatling gun embedded into the forearm.

"Wait!" I shouted. "It's only drums."

Kara stepped up next to me while saying to the Guardbots, "It's all right. It's part of the process."

"Can you let them know that I am going to be playing the drums, and they might be a little loud?" I said to Kara as I headed over to the drum throne and took a seat.

I kicked out a few beats on the kick drum and stepped on the high hat as I got comfortable with the drum kit. I adjusted a few of the drum positions and used the drum key to tune up the mid tom before saying, "Ohm, activate musician playback of Led Zeppelin's 'When the Levee Breaks.'"

The music started to play, and auragraphic versions of the band members appeared in front of the drums as I jumped in on the mix and tried to lock in with that iconic drum beat. The volume level was a little loud and prevented conversation, but I thought it was just right for playing along with. I made it about halfway through the song, the singer said something like, "Prayin' won't do you no good," when I noticed Leonard making a cut-off signal with his hands. I stopped playing, cut the music, and asked, "What's up?"

"I think the Biodual is ready to accept more repairs," Leonard said.

"Great, let's do this. Ohm, transplace the two remaining ship sections," I said while sitting behind the drum kit.

Cassia returned to the fluid strands and touched in with the ship, so did the revision nine. After a few minutes, Ohm replied, "Transplacement completed on large section scaffolding."

"I have a confirmation on my side. The two sections are in place. What do the Guardbots report?" I asked from across the room.

"It looks like something was attached, but the blue energy shield is still in the way," Cassia said.

"Have the Guardbots lock on to something or fall back behind a hatch. I'll drop the shield, and we can see if the environment holds," I said.

"Okay, but wait before dropping the shield," Cassia said to me while focusing on the fluid strands, then saying, "The Guardbots have fallen back. You can remove the shield."

"Ohm, drop all shielding on the Melog *Pentacraft*," I said.

Leonard spoke, "I see it. The Guardbots are inspecting the repaired areas. The environment is holding."

"I see it too. They can travel to the portal tip," the revision-nine said.

"And what about the Biodual, is she all right?" I asked.

"She seems overwhelmed, again, but generally happy to be overwhelmed with new reports of systems coming back online," Cassia said.

"We're almost there. Let me know when you think she is ready to travel. It is very important the Biodual does not try to move the ship while I am shifting it into another probability. Try to relay that message to her when you can," I said.

Kara asked, "What will happen if she does?"

"I don't know. It's like a hatch while you're traveling through an atmosphere. You don't want to open it while you are in transit. Once we arrive, it will be safe to use FSL again," I said to the group, striking the snare a couple of times.

I began thinking about how to shift this ship into another probability and reached into my hip pocket to pull out one of the half-smoked joints that I picked up from K-Mac's coffee table the last time I cleaned up. I pulled out my lighter and lit up the joint. The Guardbots noticed it first, and I detected a shift in their servo noise emissions. I took a few puffs and offered it to Kara. She shook her head, no, so I puffed away on it a bit more. I was tapping my foot, thinking about the song I was going to use. This did not need to be a big production. I just needed to shift this *Pentacraft* and all members aboard into another echo.

I put the joint out on my cymbal then brushed the ash away before placing the remaining roach into my interior hip joint pocket.

Leonard said, "I think we are as ready as we are ever going to be."

"Great, are we all in agreement to do this?" I asked from behind the drums.

They all looked at me nodding their heads, yes, a couple of them said, "Yes," instead of nodding. I asked, "Ohm, can you transport the human Melogs gathered together in level six central hub to the surface of Zenith? Place them in the housing units and keep them together. Give them each a kiosk interface. Resume automatic terraforming operations with a priority on housing at a faster rate, more travelers are expected to land."

"Transport underway," Ohm replied.

"We need a vector into open space. No FSL, motion in a straight line," I said to the group.

The revision-nine said, "I'm on it," and walked over to the fluid strands to start, "touching in."

I decided on the song for this probability transfer. It was, "Don't Fear The Reaper" by Blue Oyster Cult. It was one of the songs I played along with a prominent cowbell part. It was a basic rock with a freakout part in the middle. Using my invisihud, I cued up the song and the musicians, under my new drum kit icon.

"We're accelerating along a vector. We're gaining speed," the-revision nine said, and I could feel the rumble of the massive Melog engines pushing us through space.

"I think that's good. You can cut the engine and we'll glide. It will save some fuel. Time for the shift, everyone. Hold on to your heads," I said and set the song in motion.

The guitar kicked in, and I pulled up the *Motif* all around me as I started playing along with the song. Maybe it was the weed, but the *Motif* was green this time. I managed to track along with the cowbell part by jumping back and forth from the hi-hat to the cowbell on the eighth notes. Because I sat in a room, I was not moving and the *Motif* just hung around me. I knew I needed to get the *Motif* into motion to make an effective change. With each drum hit, I imagined the drums pushing the *Motif* forward, telling the story of the singer. I tried to integrate some of the lyrics into the motion that the ship took, and I felt the echo around me modulate. Mentally pushing forward added speed as the song took a careening tone, and I struggled to keep up with the chaotic changes happening in the freakout section.

The revision-nine called out, but her voice was distorted, "Our speed is increasing."

The freak-out part of the song drops off to near silence then comes back with a drum roll build that breaks into a solid rock part. I kicked the *Motif* into shape and relaxed into this rock section of the song while making adjustments to echo, which brought this *Pentacraft* into a new probable universe. With an emphasis on the bond between the new parts and the original parts, I latched onto the words and used some of the elements of the story to install favor into this *Pentacraft*. Any aliens that the Melogs encounter should bend toward friendly if possible. The singer called out, "Love of two is one. "

I knew I could not do much more than this as far as shaping this echo from a drum kit, but it was interesting to see what mechanics were required to obtain any echo shift at all from a sitting position. I finished up the song, stepped away from the kit, turned off the display of the virtual singers, and said, "Ohm, return my drum kit to storage on *Tiger Mountain*."

A large sparkle appeared, removing my drum kit as the Guardbots adjusted their postures but remained calm and did not switch to weapons mode.

"What's next?" Cassia asked, stepping forward.

"Ohm, transport the four human Melogs to Zenith," I said, and the four different Melog revisions sparkled within the fading light, leaving nothing behind.

The Guardbots stepped out of their corners and moved in closer as I said, "Ohm, transport me back to my San Francisco apartment."

The sleek lighting of the Melog *Pentacraft* collapsed inward as I found myself surrounded by nothing. It felt exceptionally dark this time like being covered and hidden with a dark black cloth. I felt panic before the soft lighting drifted in from the sides leaving me looking out my window doors at the heavily illuminated late evening scene revealed beyond the balcony.

CHAPTER 27

A Fancy Dinner

✺

W hy did all of that seem so messed up to me? I headed over to the bar and made myself a Manhattan. David's glass sat there from the other night, and I placed it down below in the sink. That Cassia Melog was over the top controlling. Seeing them work in a group like that showcased some of the peculiarities of each revision. I knew each revision was a modification to the Biodual, but I wondered if other revisions had their say in the next revision's construction, creating an unwritten hierarchy based upon who was created first? Fuck I felt like I was way out in left field on this one. But seeing the revision-nine did remind me of Erin. Her overall vibe was basically the same. I started to wonder if it really mattered which one became my wife? Or if I could convince any of them to marry me. Is that what I looked for?

When I awoke, how many weeks ago was it, all I wanted was to return to my previous life. But now I wondered how I would ever integrate any kind of relationship into this jumble of experiences that I presently call my life.

I downed the rest of my drink and checked the time, it was seven fifty-two in the evening. I wondered if it were too late to just drop in on a neighbor, but I thought I'd give it a try. I stepped into the hallway and asked, "Ohm, which apartment did Alex and Lucas take? Are they there?"

"Alex and Lucas took apartment twenty-three eighteen, and they are at home," Ohm replied.

I made my way down the hallway, checking the apartment numbers until I came to twenty-three-eighteen. I knocked on the door and shortly heard someone approach from the other side. I thought I saw the light change behind the peephole, then I heard the door open, and Lucas Morgan stood there with a smile holding the door open, saying, "Sam, come in, come in."

I walked into their apartment, which was similar to mine, but it did have a slightly different layout. I noticed Alex approaching. She put on an earring as she walked up to greet me wearing a beautiful evening dress revealing her smokin' hot figure. But it was the smile on her face that was one of her most beautiful features. She leaned in and gave me a light kiss on the cheek and said, "What brings you out on a Saturday night?"

"Oh, is it Saturday night? I guess I lost track of the days," I said, noticing

Lucas was nicely dressed. "Oh, sorry. I'm interrupting date night, aren't I?"

Alex spoke, "Yes, I finally got Lucas to take me out on the town, but you are not interrupting. Why don't you join us," as she put on lipstick in front of the mirror in the hall.

"Are you sure?" I asked them both, feeling like a third wheel.

"Yeah," Alex said leaning over getting closer to the mirror and pressing her lips together, returning her lipstick to her small clutch and beaming with a sexy smile.

"We'd love to have you along," Lucas added, then checking some portable device he pulled from a pocket, said, "Oh look, our limo has arrived."

We all exited the apartment and headed down the hallway to the elevator entrance. I reached into echo and slightly altered my clothes to try and freshen them up and look a bit more dashing, less utilitarian.

"You're doing it, aren't you?" Alex asked.

"You mean shifting echo," I replied.

"Yeah, I can feel it somehow," she replied as we stepped into the elevator.

"Just freshening my clothes. How do I look?" I asked them both.

Alex reached into my revised outfit and adjusted my new white-collar, moving her hands through my hair to straighten it out, and said, "That's better. You clean up nice."

Alex gave off that sensual friend vibe, the same as Candy. They were always on the verge of turning me on, but I knew it was never going to go any further. It was some cruel revenge they both loved to leverage.

We descended in the elevator, and Lucas said, "We have reservations at Murray James."

The elevator doors opened before Lucas and Alex stepped out first, while I followed. We headed out through the building entrance to the street where a classic limousine town car waited with a Drologo attendant standing at the rear door. He opened the door, and Alex and Lucas climbed into the spacious rear seating as I joined them in the back. The Drologo closed the door and took on the role of the driver as he sat up front, looking back, asking, "Where to?"

Lucas replied, "Murray James, in the park."

"Ah, very good, Sir," and the vehicle started moving.

"What have you been doing that has you at such a loss for not knowing what day it is?" Lucas asked.

"Wow, a lot of stuff. I just acquired a new shipbuilding facility, it's called 'Replicraft'. I purchased a home on Vasco and started fixing up the neighborhood. I also introduced the Imperial fleet to their new possible home planet in the Gar sector. Now comes the hard part for them, Melogs and humans sharing the same world. Oh, and I programmed a few auragraphic musicians, so I had someone to play along with when I practice the drums," I said.

"I guess that might do it. I have been working on a thousand-piece puzzle of the bay area," Lucas said.

Alex added, "It's taking him forever. He spread out all the pieces on the dining room table."

"Have you seen Candy recently?" I asked.

"Yes, G.C. and I have been starting to get into this futuristic San Francisco lifestyle," Alex said, "But she mainly wants to meet new friends."

"So, Melissa, the seamstress is out?" I asked.

"Oh yeah, I don't know what happened, but for a week or so it was Mellisa this and Melissa that, and now she has moved on to someone new, who was it, Honey?" Alex asked Lucas.

"I think it might be Rachel?" Lucas guessed.

"No, not Rachel, something more alien-sounding, we talked about it the other day," Alex said to Lucas, then turning to me. "I swear, it is like guys somehow have this ability to sit there and pretend to listen, but everything I say just goes in one ear and out the other."

"Oh, right, right it was Clarashel," Lucas said, pulling the name out of a hat, defending the stereotype that men don't really listen.

"Yes, Clarashel, she is Opturi, I think," Alex added, looking out at something in the street catching her attention.

"We met the neighbors," Lucas said plainly.

"Oh, you mean K-Mac and Byrone?" I asked.

"Yep," was all Lucas could say.

I wondered how K-Mac and Byrone would be received. They were a bit rough around the edges, compared to Lucas who was raised as a rich boy from a wealthy family. Ethan and the Foster family were magicians, Alex was a genetically engineered killing machine, and Candy was Alex's roommate in their broken economy downtrodden world.

"Those two goofs? Why do you have them hangin' round?" Alex asked.

"They are my public relations guys. I thought this manicured future world needed a little taste of old-world realism. They are not afraid to say something politically incorrect. Besides, they have the best weed," I said.

"Ah, the truth comes out," Lucas said with a smile as the car rolled to a stop.

The driver put the car in park, turned off the engine, and headed over to the passenger side back door to open it for us. We emerged onto the circular brick driveway with a fountain in the center. The Murray James restaurant was located on the edge of Golden Gate Park, near Stanyan St., at the site of the old McLaren Lodge. The old lodge was torn down years ago, and this modest classic villa was built in its place. Later, it was turned into this restaurant and became a trendy destination for upscale diners. There were two curved staircases on either side, ascending to the front porch. We took the wide staircase on the right, and Alex took up a position between Lucas and myself as we ascended the staircase, looking as cool as possible. I pulled up the *Motif* slightly, giving my suit a final fashion tweak, and Alex squeezed my left bicep as we completed our ascent of the stairs.

We approached the doors, which were held open for us by uniformed staff, and walked through them, up another set of stairs to a greeting podium where an older Adnexian said, "Ah, Welcome to Murray James. May I have your name?"

Lucas spoke up, "Lucas Morgan, the Morgan party."

"Ah, the Morgan party," the Adnexian maitre d' said, slowly as he flipped through some screen, all the while eying me.

Lucas put a card on the podium and said, "We picked up a guest. Is there any way to extend our seating?"

While we waited, I noticed this thing Alex was doing. I guess I would call it posing. She used her physical appearance to passively change the world around her. I've seen her do this before, but it was only now that I put it together that she used it to get her way. I'm sure to her, it was just an Amarok training tool she leveraged to help her obtain her objective.

The Adnexian, whose eyes were fixed on Alex, quickly broke contact picking up Lucas' card, saying, "Not a problem at all, Sir."

The Adnexian maitre d' processed Lucas' card and returned it to him, then addressing another Adnexian, saying, "Arson, would you show the Morgan party to their table."

Arson said, "Certainly, this way, please," as he led us into a large terraced room filled with tables.

Imagine a church size worship area with all the pews removed. The terracing was modest, so there were no stark division between the levels. The ceiling was vaulted with stained glass, which was backlit to bring out the color in the panels. Off to one side, was a string quartet gathered around a grand piano. Music was softly playing. We sat at a four-top, with a white tablecloth. The waiter took our drink order and headed off to fulfill it.

"Now, this is what I call nice," Alex said, beaming as if this moment was the result of all the posing effort she put out at the entrance.

Nice? An opulent experience is what I would call it. There were quite a few aliens here, many of them I could not recognize their species. Some were non-native atmospheric breathers and wore devices hanging from their ears to their nose as some type of stylish oxygen mask. A slight mist emitted from the apparatus every so often. The groups of people at the tables were small, like the Morgan party. It felt like a room full of misfits to me.

"And you look lovely, my dear," Lucas said to Alex.

"Aw, thank you, Lucas," Alex said, and she leaned over to kiss him.

Our drinks arrived, and the Adnexo waiter set Alex's red wine down first. He then served Lucas some ale and finally placed my Lagavulin on a napkin in front of me before asking, "Are you ready to order?"

There were no menus at Murray James. The waiter offered a few specials for the evening, but you could order whatever you wanted. Alex spoke first and said, "I'll have the Peking duck you mentioned earlier."

Lucas said, "You sold me on the surf-n-turf on the first pass."

"Do you have something similar to the whitefish plate only with Adnexian fish instead?" I asked.

The waiter smiled and said, "Yes, certainly we can do that, and I'm sure you'll enjoy it very much. I'll place your orders now."

Alex lifted her glass of wine up and said, "To getting what you want."

I said, "I like that, getting what you want," as I toasted her and Lucas' cups.

"To getting what you want," Lucas said.

"Mmm, I like this wine, Lucas. We'll have to ask what kind it is," Alex said while sipping her drink.

"So, why Vasco?" Lucas asked.

"It is very Earth-like in its beauty and climate," I said.

"It's because his future wife Jorrie works on *Oasis Seven* which is just a shuttle ride away from Vasco," Alex said with a smug smile continuing, "but I do hear that it is a lovely place."

"They have conscious altering strands you can experience, Lucas," I said.

"What do you mean?" Lucas asked.

"Inside the radionic tile are aliens that live outside of time. They have ejected these filaments into the Vascon timeline. New ones are being discovered as recently as twelve years ago," I said.

"How do the filaments alter your consciousness?" Alex asked.

"You go sit in a church, and they open a box. The box contains a filament that glows and is forever changing. You look into the box, and you are transported to another place where you have an experience and then are returned to your body to think about it," I said.

"I don't know, church changing people's thoughts. I don't really like the sound of that," Alex said.

"I think I had to agree with Alex on that one. Sounds a bit cultish," Lucas said.

I gently twisted Alex's arm, saying, "What's wrong, Alex, are you scared? All the kids are doing it."

Alex played along, saying, "All right, all right, I'll do it. Let's change my mind," which brought a smile to Lucas' face.

"That sounds a little bit like what happened to you, with your memories and all," Lucas said.

"I guess, but using that model, what is happening to me now would be the experience from inside the filament. Once the experience is over, I would return to the future," I said.

"Have you ever had a filament experience?" Lucas asked.

"In the first time loop, I did. I shared a closer connection with Vasco, and so did Erin. In that loop, I even met the Oracles, the aliens living in the radionic tile. The filament experience is like dreaming while awake, but the dream is made up of symbols from your current belief system," I said as our waiter arrived with food on an anti-gravity cart. He served the lady first, then left to right, setting my plate of Adnexian fish and a salad down last.

We thanked the waiter and then dug into the food. It was truly delicious. At least mine was. In the first time loop, after Erin had graduated from Starnet Academy, we were married. This marriage allowed me to travel with her as a spouse on her first assignment aboard the Del Ray. The second captain of the Del Ray was Adnexian. One of my volunteer duties was kitchen help. To try and curry the favor of the Captain, I set up a Transfast location to one of the many Adnexian fish markets. The Captain was very pleased to receive her native food, and I also gained an appreciation for the fine seafood that frozen world has to offer.

"First time loop, second time loop, how do you keep it all straight in your head? You mentioned those Melogs. Was one of them Erin? Did you see your first wife?" Alex asked while eating.

"I talked to one of the revision-nines. She reminded me of Erin quite a bit, but I don't know how to be sure when they all act and look so similar," I said while trying my salad.

"I guess it would be a little strange to look at multiple copies of the same person and wonder which one is the one for me," Lucas said while eating a shrimp from the end of his fork.

Alex looked over, cutting into her duck a bit more, saying, "You mean, there was no one standing out? No twinkle in an eye or some familiar gesture?"

"That is what was odd. They all seemed just like her. It was very disturbing. All those little traits that I knew and observed from my wife were just character-istics of the revision nine itself," I said.

"Weird, I guess you know best on that," Alex said.

"How did you find her the first time?" Lucas asked.

"Well, both the first and second time, she was the first person to pass the test," I replied.

"A test?" Alex asked, "Why didn't you just give the test to the Melogs you just met?" Alex said, interrupting what Lucas was about to say.

"It was an ethics test, wasn't it?" Lucas asked.

"In a way, it was. When I provided the planet to the Imperial and Melog fleet, I also provided a terraforming replication system so everyone could make whatever they needed to survive or live. That is the meeting that I just returned from. I guided the Imperial and Melog fleet to the planet and presented the replication system. In the other two loops, I left the planet, and they proceeded to try and live together. When I checked in later, I learned that certain people prevented other people from using the replication technology and were basical-ly making slaves out of them while they replicated whatever they wanted. I was shocked and cut off everyone's replication privileges. I created a test, with Ohm, that each colonist had to pass to earn their replication rights. Erin was the first person to pass that test. And not only was she the first person, she was hours ahead of everyone else," I said, going on way too long, but they continued eat-ing as they listened.

"So, you're close," Alex said with a smile as she sat down her wine glass.

"Getting there," I said, smiling while eating an asparagus tip that came with the fish.

"You just have to wait for Imperial society to fall apart and the ugly hand of humanity to oppress their neighboring Melogs," Lucas said grimly.

"Yeah, but give them some credit, they were equal opportunity oppressors and enslaved humans too," I said while sipping on my scotch.

I went on, "I am kind of worried about how she will finally take it, if and when I finally find her, knowing that I treated her selection like some sort of elaborate Rube Goldberg contraption."

"What do you think Alex, how would you feel?" Lucas asked Alex.

"Well, I might be upset at first, but I would weigh the fact that you tried so hard to find me heavily in your favor. I'd get upset and storm off, but don't pursue me immediately, let me think about it. The next day I would accept your apology," Alex said.

"Thanks for the advice. I'll keep that in mind as the day draws near," I said.

The waiter came to clear the dishes and asked if we wanted dessert. Alex asked for Tira Misu. Lucas and I passed.

"Well enough about me, what have you two been up to?" I asked, changing the subject.

"Lucas has become a device addict. I am surprised he has made it through dinner without checking in on some news or statistic. And I have been teaching a young girls self-defense class down at the community center. I have girls from seven different species in my class," Alex said.

"It's true, I have become addicted to all the information that is out there. This futuristic San Francisco has at least one hundred unique internets, some entirely in alien languages. But there are also aggregate news platforms that try to pull it all together. I watched, about a week ago, and you were shown on the news aiding a Union starship that was in trouble. Ends up, that ship exists in the past," Lucas said.

Alex added while doing a pretty good impression of K-Mac with her arm movements, "And those two goofs from upstairs have superimposed themselves overtop your footage and acting like they're directing the whole thing."

"The news teams were confused at first then reported it as a hoax," Lucas added.

"See what I mean about K-Mac and Byrone? You just said there are literally hundreds of networks of hundreds of thousands of channels and who cuts through to prime time news. K-Mac and Byrone. Straight to the top," I said sipping my scotch.

Lucas smiled and finished his ale, as the Tira Misu was brought to Alex who said, "Thank you. It looks wonderful. Can I get a half glass?" while pointing to her empty wine glass.

The waiter took the empty wine glass and headed off.

"Have you thought about getting all the girls in the class a 'Girls Rock' workout shirt?" I asked Alex.

She was eating the Tira Misu, one fork full at a time, and pressing her lips together as she slid the fork out of her mouth to ensure that she got every bit of flavor out of the layered dessert before she shook her head, "Yep, I like that, something to make them a team."

Lucas got his hand playfully smacked away from Alex's dessert as he approached her plate with his fork. Then he dug in and took a bite. At that time, a warning activated in my invisihud. It was a Flexanite warning. Part of the Flexanite detection protocols I previously put in place caused any cloaked scanner to passively scan areas for Flexanites. Because a cloaked scanner follows me and any Guardians where ever we go, there is always one around. During our dinner, the cloaked scanners performed their Flexanite detection. Someone in this room was detected as being a Flexanite.

Alex noticed it first and said, "What? Something has happened?"

Lucas looked up, and I said quietly, "Don't panic, I'm sending you both the warning I just received," and I transferred the invisihud warning to their invisihuds as the waiter returned with Alex's half glass of wine.

"Flexanites," Lucas said quietly after the waiter walked off.

Alex got another fork full of dessert and leaned her head back and around as she enjoyed tasting the dessert, but was, once again, practicing her posing while scanning the room for the Flexanite. She finally faced us while pulling the fork out of her mouth, saying, "Two o clock, my facing," while darting her eyes in the direction of the suspect.

I was already facing the direction Alex indicated, and I zeroed in on the Flexanite. It looked like a female Amphibian who wore one of the atmospheric support systems. I targeted her with the invisihud and used the "Delayed Imprison" icon. This icon causes a cloaked scanner to follow the target around. When the target is alone or out of sight of any others, Ohm transports the target to a prison cell on one of the many asteroid confinement facilities the Blinn have constructed.

"What do we do?" Alex asked.

"I have targeted her for imprisonment as soon as she finds herself alone," I said, "There is not much we can do for the identity of the person she is impersonating."

"What do you mean?" Lucas asked.

"It's a Flexanite's modus operandi to kill the person they intend to impersonate. That Amphibian is already dead, and the body is typically cleverly hidden. Do you remember a news story about a body found inside of a statue?" I asked.

"I do," Alex said, "and I don't even watch a lot of news."

"I do, too. It was big news because the guy was considered a Starnet legend," Lucas said.

"He was replaced by a Flexanite who started making ship deployment decisions that generated temporary gaps in monitoring stations so more of his people could infiltrate deeper into Dili sector space. It's a slow invasion," I said, finishing off my scotch.

The waiter arrived, asking, if we needed any more service, and we all said, "No." Lucas gave him the credit card, and he walked off to process the order.

Still keeping his voice hushed, Lucas said, "If this is happening, shouldn't we alert someone?"

"Who? What would they do? Form committees and look into it? Committees that could be infiltrated by Flexanites? My detection methods are clearly in violation of citizen's rights. I would become a criminal overnight," I said.

"He's got a point," Alex said before she tried another bite.

"As a probability traveler, I could change the laws, so I was not a criminal, but then I would not be living where I should be. In both time loops, the Starnet Union was under invasion by the Flexanites from the Ussu sector. In the first loop, it was devastating, the invasion was undetected and unchecked. In the second loop, I set up detection and removal methods which slowed the invasion significantly. I am taking the same approach on this loop," I said.

"What can we do?" Lucas asked.

"Use your news junkie powers for good. Ask Ohm to help you analyze promising leads that might lead to more Flexanite detection and capture," I suggested.

"Now there's a thought, news junkie power for good. How are you detecting them?" Alex asked.

"A Flexanite can't pass the simplest of cut tests. Cut off part of their hair or nails, and if the cut part turns into a dark oozing substance, that person is a Flexanite. Once discovered, they become murderous bludgeoning animals, so beware when conducting the test," I said as the waiter returned with Lucas' card and a pen to sign for a tip.

Lucas signed the receipt, got out his device, and asked, "Should I call the Limo?"

Alex said, "Sure, let's bounce," as she took a sip of her wine.

Lucas said, "We have a few minutes while the car is approaching."

I continued watching the Flexanite and noticed her get up and move off to the restroom area. Flexanites did not actually eat or produce bodily waste, but they did need to drop off food and liquid that they hid in their body under the guise of eating. I dove into the cloaked scanner from my invisihud video feed and followed her into the bathroom. She went into a stall, and I saw the transformation as the food she ate as the Amphibian dropped into the toilet. Once she stood up and unlatched the stall door, Ohm transported her to the Flexanite holding facility.

I pulled out of the invisihud, and Alex asked, "Are you okay?"

I shook my head, yes, and Lucas stood up, saying, "I think our ride is here."

We walked out of the opulent restaurant and headed out to the front porch of the villa. We descended the staircase on the left and walked down the steps slowly, with Alex in the middle. Our driver pulled up and stood waiting with the rear door open as we took our turns getting into the back of the limousine. The driver closed the door and walked around, getting into the driver's seat. He looked back and asked, "Where to?"

Lucas said, "Take us back to the apartment building, please."

"Very good, Sir," the driver said, and the car started moving.

"What was that last little thing?" Alex asked.

I located the cloak menu and found a subset where you could specify a few of the components of the cloak. After activating the auditory mute, I sent Alex and Lucas an invitation for that icon.

"Oh, I see," Lucas said, and Alex soon joined in.

"I think we should take precautions like this when talking about the processing of Flexanites. At least until it becomes more common knowledge that they even exist. That last little thing in the restaurant was me observing the Amphibian Flexanite. She was dumping the undigested food from her body into the toilet. Ohm transported her to a holding facility constructed specifically for Flexanites," I said.

"That is disgusting," Alex said.

"You followed her into the bathroom?" Lucas asked.

"Yes, I followed the murderous monster who was posing as their victim into the bathroom. I wanted to be sure they were truly a Flexanite before processing her," I said.

"What happens to them now?" Lucas asks.

"They are placed in an off-world, off-probability, holding cell," I said.

"For how long?" Alex asked.

"I only captured one before. He would not budge from his cover story, even when he could no longer hold his form. It was the Flexanite who murdered Jeremy Stewart and placed his body inside the Logican statue. He lasted about four weeks without food and water before he looked pretty bad. I transported him to a special world I located just to house prisoners. It is an Eden-like planet. I plan on keeping this one for two weeks then releasing it into the wild on that world," I said.

"A planet of Eden filled with Flexanites," Alex said.

"And other scoundrels that get in the way," I added.

"Did you check on him to see if he survived?" Lucas asked.

"No, I did not, but I did place a cloaked scanner on him so you could ask Ohm for the logs and review them for yourself," I said to Lucas.

"It might be interesting to see if he did make it on that world," Lucas said as the car came to a stop.

We dropped the cloak, the driver opened the door for us, and we got out. Lucas said, "Thank you, Brach," and the driver said, "My pleasure, Mr. Morgan."

We walked into the black glass building through the front doors, which slid open at our approach. We pushed the button for the elevator and waited. While we waited, Alex asked, "What's going to happen now that the Flexanite is no longer occupying the Amphibian's life?"

"It should bubble up to a missing person's case," Lucas answered.

"Just like Jeremy. Once I discovered the body inside the statue, I had to find a way to reveal it to the local authorities without being associated with the discovery. I constructed auragraphic hooligans to vandalize the statue and draw a closer inspection upon it," I said as the elevator bell sounded and the doors split open.

We entered the elevator, and Alex pushed twenty-three. The elevator began to rise, and Lucas said, "I'll do some digging, keep an eye out for any Amphibian missing person reports."

"I'm sorry to drag you guys into this, but this is the world that I live in. If you want to return to Enki's Dale, I'll understand," I said, facing forward, talking to the closed door.

Lucas said, "That is a backup plan. I'm not ready to give up on this world yet. I kind of like it here."

Alex said, "Me too. At first, I thought all these aliens, I don't know. But after getting to know them and their kids, they just seem like people to me now."

The doors opened up, and I stepped out, saying, "That is a great way to look at it, Alex."

My door came first along the hallway, so Alex leaned in for a peck on the cheek and said, "Thanks for coming to dinner. That was fun."

I shook hands with Lucas and said, "Good night," and those two walked down the hallway, in love, as Alex placed her arm around his shoulder, and they began to laugh quietly together.

I turned to face the door, opened it, and entered my apartment. I did not bother turning on the lights, it was probably midnight, so I headed into the bedroom and got ready for bed.

"Ohm, how long have I been awake?" I asked.

"Eighteen hours and forty-seven minutes," Ohm replied.

"Goodnight, Ohm," I said and I went to sleep.

CHAPTER 28

Legal Issues

⟨~∽⟩

I woke to nothing out of the ordinary and asked Ohm to draw back the blackout curtains while I lay in bed thinking about what to do next. The production of the Vasco repair replication progress was up by more than fifty percent compared to the previous night's total unit replacement count. I reviewed the progress on Zenith and noticed the human count versus the Melog count grew.

"Ohm, can you send a message through the Zenith kiosk interface to all the Melogs? I want the message to read, 'Faster terraforming is possible if multiple users agree upon a single goal.'"

I figured one advantage the Melogs might have is that they cooperate with one another easier than humans can. I got up and took a shit, shower, and shave, then replicated new clothing from my virtual wardrobe before transferring my wand, vignettes, and lighter to my new pockets. I left the roach on my dresser and replicated a new, fresh joint to place in my hip joint pocket. Dark green was the color I chose for my pants and brown for the color of my shirt, but the basic design was the same as the standard black that I usually wear. In the kitchen, I started the coffee brewing and rifled around the cupboards looking for a pan to cook with. There were all these copper bottom stainless steel pots and pans, but I looked for a standard cast iron frying skillet.

"Ohm, can you replicate a basic, seasoned cast iron pan for cooking?" I asked.

A sparkle appeared on the counter and left behind an iron frying pan. I proceeded to get an egg and butter from the refrigerator before pulling a frozen hash brown patty out of the freezer. The timer on the microwave counted down the seconds required to thaw the frozen hash brown while I put butter in the pan and cracked an egg to start cooking. The glow of the toaster heated my slice of bread. I added salt and pepper to my eggs and transferred the thawed hash brown patty from the microwave to the iron pan for final heating and crisping up in the hot butter. In the cupboard, I found a plate before flipping the egg and the hash brown over. I took the egg out of the pan first and let the hash brown sizzle away in the butter as I turned off the flame and moved the pan with the hash brown to another part of the stovetop, flipping it one more time. The toast popped up, and I looked inside the refrigerator for some ketchup and jam. I found apricot jelly already opened. It must have been Candy, a few weeks ago, as I inspected the jam for any mold. It looked clean, so I spread some on my toast and put ketchup on my hash brown before pouring myself a cup of coffee and eating my breakfast alone.

What was my next task? Dare I take a day off from relentlessly trying to reestablish the life presented to me by my future memories? Was it possible to have two wives and live in happiness aboard starships? Were these memories to be trusted? Were they like advertisements, perhaps, only highlighting the best and most favorable aspects? I searched my future memories for bad times. I found quite a few in the first loop. My marriage with Erin fell apart on Vasco. She had an affair with one of the Lamas who exposed her to the Tempus Filament. It caused great strife within her and my life. It took me a year before I realized the Erin that divorced me was actually transposed with her future self. The woman I loved was transferred forty years into the future, and the copy of her that was in that future returned to the past, married to a man she no longer knew. This switch was an unknown ability of the Tempus Filament. Or was it? I often wondered if Lama Burial knew very well what he was doing when he exposed Erin to the Tempus Filament? Or was it just a side effect that the filament happened to have upon Melog physiology?

Erin's first venture to another probability happened soon after we got to know one another. She was so excited to experience the shift into another reality. In my haste, it did not occur to me that her bloodstream contained small micro machines made up of the elements of her native probability. As soon as I made the first echo shift to a new probability, Erin became ill, very ill. I quickly took her to Xanadu where the doctors detected her distorted micro machines and diagnosed her condition. I returned to Zenith and obtained fresh blood from one of the other revision nines. I used a special replication facility containing pre-*Motif*ed elemental sources for constructing replicated objects that can withstand the stress of traveling through echo without distorting or adapting to the echo. These same sources were used in the construction of the invisihud implants that I, and all the Guardians, have installed inside our heads. Also, medkits and other technical gadgets, like the cloaked scanners, are built from these pre-*Motif*ed material sources.

The pre-*Motif*ed material sources are probably one of my deepest, must-keep kind of a secret. I have never told anyone about this. I spent years, more than ten, researching in a small house laboratory I built at the edge of the Forest of Rayleaf, not far from Splendor. It was at the edge of this forest where I discovered certain materials change their atomic properties when moved through echo. I traveled into various echoes and gathered raw materials, making whatever scientific observations I could in the source echo. Then I would bring the materials back to my laboratory, at the edge of the forest, and conduct the same tests. In a log, I recorded the distortions in the various materials. I did this for years, reaching deeper and deeper into echo, fetching more exotic items, and measuring their distortions as they approached Splendor.

My initial goal was to try to construct some type of master material that could weather the changes as it passed through echo. I experienced small success with that approach, but there were too many variables to incorporate into a single material. It's like building a roof out of hardened sugar. The roof may work fine in a dry region, but as soon as it rains, it might melt. I flipped the idea on its head and wondered if there was a way to make an element or component maintain its original configuration? As soon as I asked that question, I revisited the memory of my younger days, when I was married to Teela, and we visited Lexi's woodland compound.

It was there, at her woodland compound, that Lexi taught me how to make vignettes. You couldn't use any old paint. You had to use *Motif*-infused paint when composing and rendering the final image on the card. That is what I ended up doing to objects I wanted to make, "echo sturdy." Eventually, I boiled it down to basic components. I discovered if I supplied raw elemental sources infused with the *Motif* to replication facilities, the replicated objects maintained their properties as I shifted them through echo. This discovery allowed me to build starships that could travel through echo. It also allowed me to replicate the micro machines inside of Melog blood, so that Erin could travel through echo without suffering ill effects. The Blinn doctors on Xanadu installed the *Motif* infused replicated micro machines into Erin's blood, and she got better. It wasn't until I scanned the temporal signature of those micro machines that I discovered that the Erin that divorced me was actually from the future.

"Your weekly report is available," Ohm said.

"Great, send it to my invisihud."

The invisihud switched to report mode allowing quick browsing of the documents. There was a large amount of data in these reports, but Ohm colorized much of it in a bright to dark fashion, so the most important items were the brightest. I shuffled through a few of the bright ones, and it did look like there were some legal issues against K-Mac and Byrone. Most of them were based on defamation of character. There were also a few larger complaints registered against the building because it housed K-Mac and Byrone's production.

I browsed through another section that was not as bright but entirely related to Replicraft matters. It seemed there were several outstanding complaints against the previous owner's product claims. Many users suffered failures deemed manufacturer defects. It looked like Replicraft was most popular in the outer colonies because that is where all the complaints came from.

"Ohm, can you put together a map of planets and planetside coordinates for all the complaints filed against Replicraft? I'd like to address them all."

"You can find the locations under your maps icon of your invisihud," Ohm replied.

I returned to browsing the reports and discovered that several previously requested projects were put on hold while the replication facility was being repaired or used for the Vascon restoration project. A few of the brighter pages were also Vascon related. It seems I was being personally blamed, by the Vascon government, for the unrequested restoration of the Vascon properties. Legal actions were filed against me under Union law. I also found a short news clip showing an interview with Emeel. Other residents were interviewed, and none of them complained about having their homes restored. The reporter seemed to be on the side of the people, featuring some of the neighborhod restorations of parks, green spaces, and the wells. The news reported a picture from an ancient stone rubbing depicting the Squire of the Pharaoh as a flute-playing minstrel, while Emeel said, "Yes, he is the Squire. We love him."

"Ohm, let's reduce the Vascon restoration project to use only twenty-five percent of the production capabilities. I want to get the cloaked swarm ship project back up and running. Are there any known hold-ups on this?"

"The main hold up is maintaining cloak capabilities at the current size," Ohm reported.

"Well, let's make them bigger. The final replicated ships will need to pass through the transportation systems for deployment, so make sure the design teams coordinate with the transportation teams on the largest practical size for the quickest transportation deployments. If we need to design larger transport services, set that in motion," I said to Ohm.

"Relaying instructions to the various departments," Ohm replied.

"Ohm, research any of the complaints against this black glass building. If the complaints are filed by a company, research buying the company. If possible, go ahead and make the purchase. If the complaints are made by individuals, conduct exhaustive background research. Look for any character flaws that might place them at odds against their current complaint filed against K-Mac and Byrone. Ask K-Mac and Byrone to start weaving the word 'allegedly' into their criticisms of people or corporations. If they forget, add it automatically to the broadcast. Explain the legal aspects of using the word 'allegedly' to them."

"Understood, conducting research," Ohm replied.

CHAPTER 29

Under Arrest

❧

From the kitchen, I looked across the room and through the window wall framing the balcony to notice the beautiful day. It was past noon, so I figured it was late enough to drop in on the boys upstairs. I headed out of my apartment and took the elevator up to the Black Glass Studios. The entry area was a mess but not too out of hand. One might say it had a "lived-in" look. When I reached the main lounge area, I would revise that phrase to being "trashed." The place was a wreck.

"Ohm, let's get a cleanup going in this area. You can make it a daily event after people have gone to sleep. Not a pristine clean. Try to keep the trash to a minimum and the floors and countertops clean," I said as I walked around the lounge past the sunken coffee table over to the kitchen area.

There were a couple of old pizza boxes here. I flipped open the top pizza box lid and took a whiff of the leftover pizza. I did not see any mold, and it did not smell bad, so I lifted a piece out and took a bite. Not bad, I liked the garlic in the sauce.

"K-Mac, is that you?" I heard a timid voice coming from the guest's rooms down the hallway.

"No, it's Sam. I'm eating some of your pizza. I hope you don't mind," I said to the unknown voice.

A human male emerged from the doorway, leaning from side to side as he walked. He wore a flannel shirt, grey pants with tan-colored boots. He sported short scruffy sandy blond hair and wore thick glasses kept on his head using a wide black elastic band. He stepped out and said, "Oh, hello there. Have you seen K-Mac or Byrone?"

"I just got here, so no, I have not. Did they leave you here?" I asked while chewing.

"Well, I guess so. I'm Frogs, by the way," he said as he stepped forward to shake my hand.

I put down the pizza, swallowed, and said, "I'm Sam, a downstairs neighbor," while shaking his hand.

Frogs looked around the room as sparkles appeared here and there while the low-profile tidy-up continued. He said, "I'm kind of worried about those two. It's not like them to be gone so long. I've been here a couple of times as a guest, but I don't know what to do?"

"Did K-Mac and Byrone ever show you how to talk to the sphere?" I asked.

"The sphere, no, I don't think so," Frogs replied.

"It's behind you on the fridge there," I said while pointing and grabbing another piece of pizza, a small corner piece.

"Uhm, where are K-Mac and Byrone?" I asked.

The sphere on the top of the fridge started glowing as it spoke, saying, "K-Mac and Byrone are in the custody of San Francisco police department on the corner of 3rd. Street and Mission Rock."

"They're in jail? What are we gonna do?" Frogs exclaimed at the news.

"I have some money. Do you want to go with me to bail them out?" I asked.

"Well, sure, let me get my jacket," Frogs said, and he headed back into the hallway to fetch his coat.

"Ohm, can you replicate a credit card for this location. I may have to pay a public fine. Also, can you bring up the playback of the incident where K-Mac and Byrone were arrested?" I asked.

A sparkle appeared on the kitchen counter, leaving behind a credit card. I placed the card in one of my shirt pockets and reviewed the incident projected above the pizza box.

Frogs returned and shook his coat into place, zipping it up when he noticed the display and said, "Wow, what is that?"

"This is the incident report from their arrest. This display works like video playback," I said as I demonstrated scrubbing to Frogs by swiping back and forth while manipulating the display.

Frogs stepped up and watched the scene as it looped a couple of times, then said, "I don't see what they did wrong?"

"I don't either, so I think this will be easier than I thought. Are you ready to roll?" I asked.

"Yeah, let's go," Frogs said, and we headed down the stairs leading to the entry room with the double doors leading out to the hallway. We headed down the hallway to the elevator, and I pushed the button.

Frogs said, "I tried that, it doesn't work."

"The button is coded for residents only. That is why it did not work for you," I replied.

"Oh, I guess that makes sense," Frogs replied as the elevator dinged, the doors opened up, and we stepped inside.

I pressed the first-floor button, and the elevator started dropping. I looked over and asked Frogs, "How did you meet K-Mac and Byrone?"

"Oh, those guys? They're like my family. We all grew up together in the Meadowland trailer park. I've known them all my life," Frogs replied as he pointed up with his index finger.

"That's nice when friends stick together," I said.

"Well, in the trailer park, you have to. When my gazebo burned down that one time, K-Mac rented me his popup trailer for a month or two. Living in this nice apartment building, you may not know what it is like to be homeless, but when I had no home, that popup was like a palace to me. It kept the rain out. I could sleep there, and I had a TV and everything," Frogs said as the elevator came to a stop and the doors slid open.

"I just recently met K-Mac and Byrone, but it does not surprise me one bit that they would go out of their way to help you out," I said, and we took the main doors out to the street level.

Looking both directions, I got my orientation. My building was at the corner of Bryant and Third. The police station was just down the street. I headed down Third street on foot, and Frogs kept up behind me as he said, "Oh wow, this is really a nice city. It even smells nice."

I came upon a public stand of Gravwaves and thought, what the heck saying, "Frogs, grab one. These scooters will get us there faster."

"Oh, I have never used one of these," He said as he looked over the instructions on the sticker, getting his face very close to read them.

"They're easy. They can even drive themselves. Think of it as a slow lumbering mini bike and get on," I said.

I was already standing on my Gravwave, which floated slightly above the ground, while Frogs pulled one of them out of its parking slot and stood upon it. He staggered, at first, regaining his balance, then grabbed onto the handles to stabilize himself.

"You've got it. Now drive it like a boat. Push forward and pull back to speed up and slow down. If you pull back while standing still, you can back up," I said as I idly maneuvered my Gravwave around.

Frogs started pushing, pulling, and turning the handle as he seemed to get the hang of it. He backed out of the parking area and pulled up beside me with a smile, saying, "Let's go."

Frogs' smile was such a genuine representation of happiness that it greatly lifted my mood. We sped off down the road with a slight breeze in our faces. Frogs kept up with me, and each time I looked over at him, he was overjoyed with the experience of guiding this Gravwave down the street. Reaching out with the *Motif*, I cast it forward, using the velocity of the Gravwave to propel it ahead of us as we took the wide curving bridge across the channel feeding McCovey Cove. I directed the *Motif* to saturate the police station and reached out with an intent for the best possible outcome for this meeting.

We pulled up to the corner of Mission Rock Street, and there was a parking area for Gravwaves in front of the Police Station. Frogs and I saddled ours up to an empty spot and headed to the front door.

"Do you mind if I do the talking?" I asked Frogs.

"I was just thinkin' about that. I don't mind at all. I'll just be there for support if you need it," Frogs said.

We headed up the final set of steps leading into the Police Station and approached a desk on an elevated platform. This elevation forced you to look up at the officer on duty. He did not acknowledge us, so I said, "I'm here to post bail."

A screen behind the desk held his attention. Without breaking contact with the screen or acknowledging us, he simply raised his arm and pointed to a door on our left.

We headed up some stairs and took the wooden doors to the left into a more bustling environment. Once again, there was a raised platform desk and an officer sitting behind it. He acknowledged us as we approached, and I said, "I want to post bail for two individuals."

The officer behind the desk called out, "Dael, you're needed upfront," then looked at us and said, "Detective Dael will be with you in a moment. Please take a seat."

He gestured to some wooden benches along the wall. Frogs and I headed over to the long wooden pew-style bench and sat down. The room was an odd mixture of low-tech nineteen seventies style police-station mixed with high-tech futuristic add ons. I could see gumshoe detectives wearing bad suits, sitting at classic wooden desks looking through auragraphic records while small floating drones dropped down to deliver messages to and from desks from above. It seemed highly inefficient but not really out of place when you consider that this is the product of California's design by committee approach to government.

I thought about how to present my case and asked, "Ohm, can you replicate a standard auragraphic tablet with the logs from K-Mac and Byrone's arrest?"

There was a small sparkle, and a Blinn tablet appeared between Frogs and me. The officer at the desk looked up, for a moment, before focusing on his desk work. It wasn't too long before a short, stubby Mercanite dressed in a cream-colored suit wandered out. He looked up at the platform desk where the officer pointed us out. After walking over, he said, "I am detective Dael. What can I do for you?"

I stood up, and said while shaking Dael's hand, "I am Sam, and this is Frogs."

Frogs experienced a serious freak-out-attack, and he froze up. I don't think he has ever seen an alien before, and he had a little difficulty coming to terms with this life form that appeared to be a person. Dael immediately noticed Frogs reaction and said, "What's the matter? You ain't ever seen a Mercanite before?"

Frogs swallowed and politely said, "No, forgive me for staring. I have never met a Mercanite before."

Dael looked up at the officer behind the platform desk and said sarcastically, "Thanks, Ed," then looked at us and added, "Follow me."

I decided that this might be a good thing to broadcast, so I activated the K-Mac and Byrone channel, using my invisihud, and started publicly documenting our police experience. We walked back through rows and columns of desks, all laid out in an open space. Dael finally picked one and sat down. Around us, other detectives worked with people. Some of them were idle or busy with auragraphic work. Frogs sat down in a chair across the desk from Dael while I took the other chair.

Dael asked, "What can I do for such fine citizens as yourselves?"

I placed the tablet on Dael's desk and said, "I have an auragraphic record of two citizens who were wrongly arrested, and I would like them released, please."

"Is that the record there?" Dael asked as he pointed at the tablet with his stylus while leaning back in his chair.

"Yes, can I play it back?" I asked.

"Sure, let's see what you got," Dael said.

I projected a gigantic version of the log, which expanded to cover several desks, and the playback volume loud. The entire room saw K-Mac saying, "Get off me dawg," and Byrone adding, "We didn't do anything wrong," while the police officers twisted their arms back using magnetic handcuffs. This log played and looped about three timesm causing everyone in the room to look up. I fussed frantically, trying to turn the display down, and finally reduced it to a soft audio playback with the log playing back about the size of a big-screen TV across Dael's desk.

"What is your problem? I should kick you out now," Dael said, staring me down.

Mercanites were like that. If any species were to be described as naturally argumentative, it would be the Mercanites. Arguing is to a Mercanite what conversation is to a Bragorian. I asked Dael, "What is their crime?"

Dael sat up, realizing he might want to pretend to do his job, leaned forward, and shuffled through the display log in front of him. After a couple of minutes of reviewing the log, he finally swiped it back to a frame and said, "Here, this is disturbing the peace and disrespecting an officer of the law."

I cued up the section that Dael highlighted and played back the conversation.

"We on top of the world, Byrone!" K-Mac said while stretching his arms wide and proudly stepping as they walked through the park.

"You know it, K-Mac," Byrone said as he made a boxing move to an air opponent while jumping to a new position in his imaginary ring.

Just then, a bright light shone on the two, and a voice said, "Stop what you are doing and drop down to the ground."

"What's this? Five-oh rollin' up on us while we taking a stroll in the park," K-Mac asked.

"Yeah, what gives with the light in the face. We haven't done anything wrong," Byrone complained while standing his ground.

"Drop to the ground as commanded, or we will take you down," said one of the officers in the background.

Dael reached into the display and paused it, saying, "Right there, they are resisting arrest."

Having overcome his fear of aliens, Frogs asked, "But what were they under arrest for, walking in the park?"

I came to Frogs support and said, "He's right. You can't resist arrest until you are under arrest. This log clearly shows they are not in a state of arrest yet."

"The log is the arrest," Dael said as if he were explaining it to idiots.

"I believe the officer codes states that conversation should be used before commands. There was no civil attempt by the officers to communicate before commands were issued," I said.

Dael sat there with an elbow on his desk. He rested his head in his hand while tapping the stylus on the desk, taking his time thinking about how to respond. He spun around in his swivel chair and wheeled over to a bookshelf, using his feet to move his chair as he scanned the shelf for a book. He searched from left to right, top to bottom, and then locked in on a thick, tall guide. Wheeling back over to the desk, he took his time while thumbing through the pages, humming to himself softly.

I scrubbed through the log and located the point where the officers forced K-Mac and Byrone to the ground with some kind of stunning light sticks, and I set up a loop point where K-Mac said, "That hurts mofo, that hurts mofo, hurtings mofo."

Dael was not amused and paused the playback saying, "I think I found it. It says right here, if suspects refuse commands," and flipped the book around, pointing to a passage. Frogs took the book to read the passage

out loud, "If suspects are engaged or conversed, and finally commands are disobeyed, consider suspects under arrest."

Dael raised his hands with a what can you do type of gesture as Frogs stopped and looked up, saying, "They were never engaged or conversed."

I took the book from Frogs' hand and handed it back to Dael, saying, "I have to agree. Your officers overreacted. Our friends should not have been arrested. Do the right thing and release K-Mac and Byrone."

Dael took his time as he wheeled over to the bookshelf and returned the guide book of codes to the shelf before saying, "Nobody bullies me in my office, at my desk."

"So, you're not going to let them go?" Frogs asked.

"I'm letting them go. But it's not because you bullied me. It's because your evidence is solid, and the code is clear," he said while bringing up an auragraphic Rolodex.

Flipping through it, he plucked out a couple of cards and punched them with a virtual tool. A small message drone dropped down from the ceiling, picked up the cards, and flew up to deposit them into a virtual suction tube.

"You can go meet your friends at the release door, third one over on the left. Now get out of here," Dael said.

"Thanks, Dael," I said, turning off the tablet and picking it up.

"Thanks, Dael," Frogs said, and we headed over to the release door.

It was a similar situation as the front area. Talk to the platform desk officer and wait on the bench. As we waited on the bench, I asked Frogs, "How are you doing? Sorry about not warning you there were aliens."

"I'm okay now. I'm sorry for reacting that way. I was shocked at first, but once he started talking, I thought he was just another person," Frogs said.

"That is a good way to look at it. Try to see them as people. It's an interesting world, alright," I said.

"I want to thank you for coming down here and getting them out. Who knows how long they might have remained locked up," Frogs said.

"I'm more concerned that the officers weren't trained very well. It really shows shabby quality control within the department," I said.

"Well, cops aren't always the sharpest tools in the shed," Frogs said. "But most of them are hard-working people just doing their jobs."

"I have to say that Dael was fair, not necessarily polite, but fair," I said.

"Yeah, I can agree with that. He listened and did the research right there in the codebook. He accepted the facts," Frogs said.

Off in the distance, we heard, "Boyeee," and Frogs, and I got up from the bench to see a smiling K-Mac and Byrone passing through the double door lockdown section leading to this lobby.

As I walked up to greet them, I said, "I just want you to know that we're live!"

"We're live, right here, right now?" K-Mac said.

"Hey Frogs, thanks for gettin' us out," Byrone said as they did a quick man shoulder bump.

"Not a problem. Sam did all the work," Frogs said, pointing at me.

K-Mac started jumping up and down, shouting, "World, we're free. World, we're free. World, we're free."

The officer at the platform desk yells over, "Take that shit outside!"

"I say let's take this outside," as I headed over to the doors with the exit sign above them, holding them open for the crew as we all moved outside.

"My people, my people," K-Mac started saying as he paraded forward along the exit walk with his arms held high.

"I thought we talked about that, K-Mac, it's our people," Byrone corrected him.

"Look, dawg, can we cut the live feed? We love our people, but we just got out of jail and need some decompress time," K-Mac said.

"Peace," Byrone said.

"Ohm, cut the broadcast," I said, then to those two, "Sorry about that. I didn't mean to put you on the spot."

"That's all right, dawg. I was glad to see you two mofos at the door, that's for sure. There's been some crazy shit happening, dawg," K-Mac said as we came to a stop before reaching the street.

"K-Mac's right. Suspicious characters are following us where ever we go. People on rooftops, I kid you not," Byrone said.

"Ohm, scan K-Mac, Frogs, and Byrone for any covert implant devices. Report so all can hear," I said.

"There are no implanted devices in any of the individuals," Ohm replied.

"You fellows want to go to another planet? It is very Earth-like. I want to put on a show tonight," I asked.

Frogs said, "Well, sure, I'm in."

"Tonight?" K-Mac asked with a pause and then said, "Ah ite."

Byrone said, "Sounds cool with me. Can we get something to eat, though?"

"Yeah, and you're gonna love the food. It's like Jamaican Indian," I said.

CHAPTER 30

The Concert

"Ohm, transport us to Brecht province on Vasco, the site of the old Selene Amphitheater," I said, and we all dissolved into nothing. It was a little concerning that covert agents watched K-Mac and Byrone because that also meant they were probably watching me and the other black glass building residents. I guess it does not take long if you keep a high profile before attracting some type of attention. I wonder what groups that attention represents? This turn of events swirled around in my mind as my eyes reassembled and we appeared on Vasco.

The Selene Amphitheater was renowned in Vascon history but stood as mostly rubble today. It looked like mid-afternoon, and I said, "Ohm, scan nearby towns for restaurants and transport enough food for four people to this location. Don't take all the food from one restaurant. We would like a sampling from around town."

"Scanning for restaurants," Ohm said in my ear.

"Well, fellows, you are officially on another planet. How does it feel?" I asked.

"Wow, look at the size of that moon," Frogs said as he gazed off into the horizon.

"It looks and feels about the same to me," Byrone said.

"Why we in this pile of rubble, though?" K-Mac asked.

The Selene Amphitheater was high, on a plateau, overlooking the small city below. We stood upon what might be considered the performance stage. There were stone seats carved into the rock in a semi-circular fashion, surrounding the stage, each row descending in a stepped-like fashion. Some additional seating curved around behind the main performance area.

"This is where we are doing the show tonight," I said.

"Who would want to come to this show? This place looks like an abandoned park or something," Byrone said.

"Alien hotties will want to come to this show. Think about it, a new venue this close to a modest town, with rebellious youth who have nothing better to do than rage against the system," I said.

"Ahite, I'm feelin' it, but it is still short notice," K-Mac said.

"I'm not expecting a sold-out show or anything. I just want to kick some ideas around but still have a live show. You know how it is when you're in front of a crowd. It makes it more real than just broadcasting from a studio," I said.

"I can help out if you like there, Sam," Frogs said.

"I have a new setup with some virtual singers. I can map them into your console, Byrone. Then you can mute them or effect them, but they'll look like real people," I said, trying to hype it up a bit.

"All right, all right, sounds good if you can give me the same setup. I can work with that," Byrone said.

"I'm going to run through a drum set, and if you guys want to jump in on a song, that's perfectly fine. You too, Frogs, the instruments are real, but the performers are virtual," I said as a set of sparkles appeared behind Frogs leaving a table and some chairs, with a few boxes on it.

"All right, boyee. Let's see what kinds of eats you brought up," K-Mac said.

The boys started unpacking the food and drinks as I stepped over to the center of the stage and brought up my environment designer. I blocked out some areas using a feature called 'extract from profile,' which extracted the current location and created a virtual version inside my invisihud based upon what it scanned around me. This feature worked out great in this situation because a lot of the original seating and walkways were still intact. I selected from the classic earth roman architecture styles then asked Ohm to revise the design for a more Vascocentric look based upon other known architectural styles and trends. I set the Blinn terraforming module into action by providing the final invisihud blocking to it as a target goal. The entrance included a long connecting road with extended park areas along the sides to meet up with the main road, revised seating, lighting for nighttime events, restroom facilities, and a modernized stage that could be raised and lowered with spaces underneath for actors. The sound of the Blinn terraforming module was like a mild ambient noise changing every so often when tasks completed and new ones began. I walked over to the food table, which the boys made a serious dent in, and I took a seat at the table while I poured myself a cup of tea.

"You were dead on, with the food description, Jamaican Indian," Byrone said.

"I'm really enjoying this food, and the tea too. I feel like I'm in a fancy restaurant or somethin'," Frogs said.

I grabbed a plate and started trying some of the various dishes saying, "Wow, this is like spicy smoked cashew raisin chicken."

"It's all damn good, Partner," K-Mac said, putting his hand up to be slapped.

I tapped him out to not leave him hanging, and Byrone said, "We really appreciate you getting us out of jail, man. Jail is no fun no matter what century you are in."

"Just to let you know, I broadcast the entire interview with the detective. I wanted the fans to see what it is really like when you have to deal with an establishment whose sole purpose is to process you as a number, not as a person," I said.

"Hey, Uhm, can I get a tablet? I want to check on our ratings," K-Mac said, and a sparkle appeared near him.

Frogs said to me, "These were kind of together, I think they are dipping sauces for these right here," as he motioned in circles with his hands over the food items.

"Mmm, I like this green one," I said as I dipped some deep-fried stalk into the green sauce.

"Byrone said to K-Mac "No, try the other one, yeah, right there."

I looked over, and K-Mac activated the Blinn tablet auragraphic projection. He reviewed some of today's police station replays circulating through the various media outlets.

"Damn, dog, this shit had some impact," K-Mac said.

"It looks like what you did in the police station shook up a lot of talking heads," Byrone said.

Then Frogs said, "That's me," as the display played back Frogs' statement, "Well cops, aren't always the sharpest tools in the shed."

Then in a concerned tone, he asked, "Can I get in trouble for that?"

"You can't get in trouble for speaking," I said, "and I think we are testing that theory with these statements."

The display showed my segment, where I said, "I'm more concerned that the officers weren't trained very well. It really shows shabby quality control within the department," then the display switched back to a bunch of talking heads arguing.

"How do you guys feel about all this?" I asked.

"We just want to get back to doing our thing," K-Mac said.

"Haters are gonna hate. We're above that, but we aren't gonna change up our style just to conform to bullies' demands," Byrone said.

"I hope none of this follows me back to the trailer park. I didn't mean to start a problem in the future," Frogs said.

"It ain't even your fault, Frogs," Byrone said.

"That's right. It was the officers that overreacted, and they bein' exposed by your honesty. You're just calling it as you see it, the Umpire," K-Mack said

"I like that, and on this segment of the 'Umpire,' we look into the poorly trained pretty boys that guard our parks and streets against loud hooligans who march to a different beat," I said.

K-Mac interrupted, "Converse before command. Dang, I like the sound of that," K-Mac said, then looked at me. "I wanna rap something about that tonight."

"That's the spirit, were puttin' on a show. And if them talkin' heads wanna know, they gonna have to grow," I said, trying to rap but not really pulling it off.

"Oh, this brown sauce is good. Try the brown one," Frogs said.

We finished eating and looked out from the stage as the Blinn terraforming process slowly converted the original rubble seating into modern undamaged comfortable weatherproof seats. We toured the left side of the amphitheater, which was completed down to the main entrance where the facilities resided.

Standing at the entrance to the amphitheater was nice. I could see the restored left side of the amphitheater while the right side was in progress. I asked Byrone, "What do you think about the look? I tried to match the old style with the new, so the residents are not too freaked out by the change."

"It looks good, man. You did a nice job of matching. The colors for sure. You made the seats nicer, which invites you in. I feel compelled to try one out from here," Byrone said with a smile.

K-Mac and Frogs rejoined us after trying out the restrooms, and K-Mac said, "Dang, I wish I had a joint."

"Me too, K-Mac," Byrone said.

I pulled out the joint from my inner pocket, handing it and the lighter to K-Mac, saying, "I found this on the table the last time I was in the Black Glass lounge. I set you up with an automatic cleanup. Uhm will lightly clean the rooms while you sleep."

"Now that is what I call service," K-Mac said as he took the two items and lit up the joint, handing the lighter back to me.

He passed to Byrone, who took a couple of long drags, and Frogs said to me, "Sam, this is all so amazing to me. I don't even know if it's real. I mean, I feel like I am going to wake up in my gazebo any minute now. If there is anything I can do to help out with the show, just let me know."

"It's real, Frogs," Byrone said as he finally exhaled his puff of smoke, handing the joint to me.

I took a few good puffs, and the joint burned nice and steady. It tasted good, too, like a bit of roasted chocolate with hints of strong herbal leaving a mint-like after-tone in your lungs but was not minty at all. It presented its own unique flavor. I held in the smoke and passed the joint to Frogs. When I finally exhaled, I said, "Will you look at that moon."

"That is one right fine moon, fo sure," K-Mac said as he took the joint from Frogs hand, taking a puff, looking up at the moon.

"I think I like this world. You're right, it is very Earth-like, but there is something peaceful about it," Byrone said, accepting the joint from K-Mac.

"Frogs, do you think you could handle some of the initial lighting? We want spotlights, like a Hollywood opening," I said.

"Well, sure, but I don't know how to do any of that," Frogs replied.

"K-Mac, hand Frogs that tablet. I think he can control lights from that," I said, and K-Mac gave Frogs the tablet.

"Ohm, can you place a list of possible arena lighting reinforcements into the Blinn tablet?" I asked.

"Placing list inside the tablet," Ohm replied to me.

"Ohm, let's create an app inside the tablet with an overhead map of the Selene Amphitheater. I want to be able to drop lighting options from the list onto the map and then have various controls for the lighting available to the user," I requested.

It only took a moment, and Ohm replied, "New app available inside the Blinn tablet."

Byrone handed the roach to me and said, "Sorry, man, I think it's out unless you want to risk lighting it up."

"I'll save that for later," I said with raised eyebrows and placed the roach in my hip pocket.

"Frogs, let me show you how to work the app inside the tablet," I said.

We both looked at the tablet, and I got Frogs into the mode of tapping to open things and sliding them away to dismiss them. The amphitheater map displayed the list of lighting reinforcements on the side of the screen, and I dragged one option into a spot on the map, and it locked into position. We looked up at the amphitheater, and the physical representation of the lighting unit transplaced to that location with a sparkle and became functional. I showed Frogs the long hold gesture on an icon to bring up more detailed options, and he started playing with some of the lighting controls of the newly replicated spotlight.

"Wow, this is really fun," Frogs said as he started moving around the area, thinking about where to place lighting.

I said, "Don't go too overboard. We don't want to blind anyone," I said as I headed into the restroom. That Vascon food ran right through me.

I washed up and returned to the amphitheater to find the boys all over the place, each standing on a different row, shouting to one another while the stage was in its final construction phase. The Sun dropped lower as evening approached, and the moon rose high in the sky but still did not lose any of its magnificent size. I headed up the left side of the amphitheater to the stage. As I got there, the Blinn module completed its task, and we all stood on the stage to shout something and listen to the acoustics.

"Not bad," K-Mac said, "I can dig the reverb."

"Not too much slap back. The descending slope helps a lot," Byrone said.

"Ohm, let's replicate a version of my portable drum kit show I used on the Melog *Pentacraft*. We're going to spread out on this stage because we have more room. Also, bring in a copy of Byrone's mix station from the Black Glass Studio lounge. Set up an interface so he can mute and affect the virtual singers from my playlist. Let's get a guitar rig for Frogs and a mic for K-Mac."

We turned around, and the stage was ablaze with a series of sparkles, large and small that dazzled the eyes for about a minute. When it was all over, we each inspected our rigs and started making some noise. I kicked around on the drums, Frogs tuned up on the guitar, and Byrone started playing around with turntables as K-Mac tested the mic.

"Frogs, let's get some lights moving. Have you picked out a place for the large spotlights?" I asked.

"Let me pull that up," he said, as he set his guitar in a nearby stand and started tapping on the tablet, "I think I have a few good places picked out."

We looked up behind us, and multiple spotlights waved back and forth above and behind the stage. There were particle streamers changing color as they moved inside the column of light generated by the spotlight. I said, "That looks great."

We took a break and gathered, stage right where I replicated a drinks table and fetched some weed remnants from Ohm's cleanup effort. Byrone got to work rolling another joint, and K-Mac started pouring drinks. He put together a batch of margaritas. When I saw what he made, I replicated a few limes and some salt to place on the rims of the glasses. Once we all had a drink in hand, K-Mac held his up and said, "I may not say it enough, but you guys are my family. I love you."

"To family," Byrone said, and Frogs and I echoed him as we clinked our glasses together and took a sip.

"I want to thank you all for helping make this happen. I have always dreamed about rocking out, in style, on an alien planet, and now it's about to happen," I said.

Byrone lit up another joint, and we passed it around, each of us taking hits. Once we smoked half of it, I said, "I'm ready to rock. Do you guys want to make some noise?"

"Let's do this," Frogs said, and Byrone killed the joint, placing it in his pocket as he climbed up to his mixing platform.

I sat down at my drums, pulled up the playlist for tonight, and started the music rolling. The first songs were mainly drumming warm-ups for me. We were a few songs into the list when Byrone started figuring things out, and I could hear his contribution to the mix. K-Mac and Frogs caught right on. Frogs locked into a lot of the guitar parts right away.

It was at this time when people started showing up at the amphitheater. K-Mac welcomed them over the mic while Byrone kept a beat going. I jumped in on occasion, fattening it up. Frogs cut in on the guitar in nice quick intervals, sometimes bold, sometimes timid, but his contribution fit in with the show.

We took a break after about forty minutes and headed over to the drinks table to pour a refill. Byrone lit up the rest of the joint, and we puffed away as we talked about how the show was going. When we looked back, the amphitheater was at least half full of people talking.

"I think this is it, fellows. Let's rock this planet," I said, and we headed back to our instruments.

I started the list with Nikka Costa's "Some kind of Beautiful" and played through a series of high-energy dance songs that K-Mac leveraged quite well. Once he got flowing, rap just came out of him. Byrone picked it up too. By song six, he sampled some of the virtual singers from the previous songs, adding samples from past songs into the present song. We played a good sixty or seventy minutes straight before wrapping it up with "Get up off of That Thing" by James Brown.

The crowd loved us, and it was nothing I did with the *Motif*. The audience was mostly younger Vascon people. Some of the older ones, I noticed, sat staring at our spectacle, but the young ones really loved the idea of a fun music show. The audience liked us so much that they called us back out for an encore, and I said, "This is your song, K-Mac, Converse Before Command," I said.

"Ahite, this is how it goes. Heavy and hard like you're in trouble or something. Some hard as fuck gangsta beats, Byrone," K-Mac said to us, and we returned to the stage with a resurgence of applause to start kicking out K-Mac's song about being arrested. It was a long final song because he had a lot to say, easily a twelve-minute piece. Afterward, we all took a bow in front of the stage as young alien hotties jumped up and down with bouncing breasts.

Once the show was over, I asked Frogs to shut off the lights, and people began to migrate out. K-Mac and Byrone struck up conversations with some of the ladies and offered them drinks at the table. There was a small harem surrounding them as Frogs, and I looked around. Frogs saw a man in uniform approaching and said, "I think I'm going to get another drink."

He wandered off to the table where he was immediately engaged in conversation by one of the young Vascon women. As the uniformed figure approached me, I noticed it was a Starnet uniform. I could tell he was a human male of African descent. He asked, "Are you, Sam Richards?"

I recognized him immediately, although I haven't met him in this time loop yet. He said, "I am Warren Turner, the Pharaoh of the Oracle."

"Nice to meet you," I said, extending my hand, "Sorry about being sweaty."

"Quite a performance and quite a venue. It was constructed so quickly," he said, angling as he looked around, spreading his hands out in admiration of the new space.

"I take it you don't approve?" I asked.

"Oh, I think it is wonderful for Vascons to have festive nights, although I'm not sure those daughter's parents are going to be too happy with this kind of consorting," he said, referencing the gathering of young women at the drinks table.

"Well, it looks like bad parenting to me. Where are their parents?" I asked.

He ignored my question and asked one of his own, "Are you responsible for the series of changes taking place across the surface of Vasco?"

"I recently bought a house here, and I thought I'd fix it up. Once I was done, I wanted to do the same thing for my neighbors. After fixing up their houses, I thought I'd extend repairs to others," I said.

"While I applaud your good intentions, it is not appropriate to change someone's property without permission. I'm asking you to stop the repairs," Warren said.

"But the Vascons love it. If I were to stop now, there would be a street where one side was repaired, and the other side was not. Wouldn't their religious beliefs lead them to the conclusion they were unworthy, in the eyes of the Oracle, to receive the restoration?"

Warren began, "It is against Starnet Union laws to use a transporter on," he hesitated for a moment, and I finished his sentence for him by saying, "on a lower species."

He glared at me for a moment.

"I am not a Union citizen. You have categorized me as an entity, which gives me certain rights under your laws. Rights that prevent you from applying your laws to the judgment of an entity's action. And what a folly your case would be, even if it were allowed? You're complaining that I am helping a people who begged the Starnet Union for years, Warren, seven years for someone to help them. While Starnet reviewed records and discussed options, the Bragorians plundered and raped Vasco of its resources and left communities in ruin. And now, when I pick up a hammer and help my fellow neighbors, you decide that you want to be involved, involved in the cessation of the restoration," I said, defending myself from his glare.

Taking another approach, Warren said, "I do believe Vasco deserves restoration. And your efforts have produced joy, hope, and no casualties. We see such power, progressing unchecked, as a concern."

"As an entity responding to Starnet commander Turner, I may oppose your requests, but as the Squire of the Pharaoh, I can be commanded by the Pharaoh of the Oracle. But the command must be made public. Give the command to the Squire to halt restoration so that all Vascons may know the will of the Oracle," I said.

Warren smiled and said, "Thank you for your cooperation. I will consult with the Oracle and get the public message out to the Squire."

"I await your command," I said

Warren tapped the communication brooch on his chest and said, "One to transport," and he disappeared in a sparkle.

"Ohm, recycle stage gear," I said, and a series of sparkles removed our instruments, leaving the amphitheater stage empty. There were a couple of oohs from the table as the sparkles faded.

I felt a certain "Hmph" overcome my mood, so I figured I might as well get a few things done and said, "Ohm, locate some of Vasco's most impoverished areas and re-target transplacement operations as an expanding circle using those sources as centers. I want to increase transplacement production to use up to seventy-five percent of replication bandwidth. Alert floor managers to expect the change."

"Alerting floor managers," Ohm replied.

"Also, once a center has expanded for a short while, relocate it to the next lowest poverty level, try to improve the most impoverished homes, in the shortest amount of time," I added.

"Relocating resources and generating repair profiles," Ohm said.

Frogs rejoined me and asked, "Sam, can you send me back to Meadowland? I really need to get back there to feed my puppies. I have been gone way longer than I planned. I'm kind of worried."

"Not a problem, but before I send you back, I want to offer you a promotion to the title of Page. You are now considered a page of the Squires," and I pointed to K-Mac and Byrone as I said squires. "This promotion means you can press the button on the elevator. The next time you return, the building will recognize you. Head over there and grab that tablet."

Frogs headed over to the drinks table, brought the tablet back, and handed it to me. I refused it and said, "That is yours now. You can use it as a phone to talk to K-Mac and Byrone when they are in the future."

"You mean I get to keep this?" Frogs said before he hugged me. "Thank you, Sam."

"You're welcome, and thank you for helping me rock this world. Are you ready to head back?" I asked, giving him a pat on the back.

"Yep, I'm ready," Frogs said.

"Ohm, transport Frogs back to his gazebo in Meadowland trailer park," I said, and a man-sized sparkle appeared before me.

When it faded, Frogs was gone. I headed over to the table, and Byrone asked, "Did Frogs just leave?"

"Yeah, he had to feed his puppies. He was a bit overdue," I replied. "Listen, I am heading out now. You guys can use Uhm to get home right?"

"What, dawg? We come all the way across the galaxy to play some tunes, to shake up some hotties, and now you're like I'm all out," K-Mac said.

"Who was that dude that you talked to?" Byrone asked.

"He was the Pharaoh of the Oracle," I said.

"What the hell does that mean?" Byrone asked.

One of the young Vascon women around the table spoke up and said, "The Pharaoh of the Oracle is the neutral mediator between Vasco and the Oracle. He is the living representation of communication with our gods."

"Whoa, what did he say to you?" Byrone asked.

"Can I tell you guys later? The conversation kind of dampened my mood, and I need to think about some things," I said to them both.

"No problem. Thanks for getting us out of jail. We still owe you and not just a stage show," Byrone said, and we shoulder bumped like men of that era.

I walked around to shoulder bump K-Mac as he said, "Yeah, we can use Uhm to get home. Put it up, dawg. You got us out of jail and rocked us up. But don't brood too much. You come and see myself and Byrone if you start feeling down."

I tapped his raised hand.

I walked off around a corner, so I was out of sight of the Vascon women before saying, "Ohm, return me to my home on *Tiger Mountain*."

The world around me collapsed, and I felt small but part of a larger whole. Were my thoughts the equivalent of a cricket's single rubbing against its hind leg? Am I nothing more than foliage for a larger consciousness that lives within the darkness? My world reassembled, and I found myself in my home on *Tiger Mountain*.

CHAPTER 31

The Cloak Puppets

～

I stood next to the long curved counter separating the kitchen area from the hall that connects the living room to the den area. I took a seat on one of the stools.

"Ohm, monitor Vascon media for messages from the Pharaoh of the Oracle. Also, monitor any *Oasis Seven* communications coming from the Pharaoh of the Oracle. If the message requests the Squire stop the reformation process, cease transplacements and return to other scheduled replication work."

"Monitoring communications," Ohm replied.

Feeling defeated at that moment, I wondered what was the point of trying? My original intention was to get K-Mac and Byrone to help me throw a party. I guess too much happened in one day. I felt a bit worn out, high, and drunk. Walking into the bedroom, I kicked off my boots and lay down in the center of the enormous circular bed in my *Tiger Mountain* bedroom.

In time loop zero, I remember lying in this bed with Erin. Somehow we started living together here on *Tiger Mountain*. As the time grows closer for me to meet Erin, I wonder what I should say or how I would convince her to become part of my life? If I don't tell her upfront, and too much time goes by, it will be an awkward reveal. That did not happen in any of the other time loops. If I tell her upfront, I'll be throwing a lot of pressure on her and she might not respond well to that. I do have a memory from the first loop when I met Erin. She wanted to send a message to *Journey*, so we took a shuttle ride away from Zenith before sending the signal. Maybe, that will be enough? I should have a shuttlecraft on-site, as I did in the first loop memory.

I must have fallen asleep because I woke up still in my clothes, in the middle of my bed. I got up, showered, and refreshed my clothing, transferring my belongings from one set of pockets to the pockets in the new clothes before recycling the old ones. Choosing a charcoal color for the pants, I kept the dark green color for my shirt. I headed out to the kitchen bar and made a pot of coffee before checking the Vascon news feed using my invisihud. Warren had not made any proclamations yet, so I inspected the results of last night's transplacement acceleration and was pleased to see we serviced over twelve thousand homes and structures using the higher capacity replication bandwidth.

"Ohm, we have previously been making transplacements on Vasco over-night. Let's make it a continuous restoration until I receive notice from the Pharaoh to stop," I said.

"Switching to continuous transplacement using previously established pa-rameters," Ohm said.

"Ohm, have there been any attempts, by non-authorized persons, to gain entry to the black glass building?" I asked.

"There have been forty-seven attempts by unknown persons to gain entrance through the front door or other various entrances. None of them have been successful," Ohm replied.

"K-Mac and Byrone mentioned they were being watched. Do we have any information on the people who are doing the watching?" I asked.

"There have been no requests to track or trace the origin of the observers. Currently, there are three known observation points established on the black glass building. Cloaked scanners have detected agents observing the black glass building," Ohm replied.

"And these observation points are located in high-rise buildings?" I asked.

"Vantage point one is located on the forty-fifth floor of the Cesar tower, vantage point two is on the twenty-fourth floor of the Marriott Imperial Hotel, and vantage point three is on the nineteenth floor of the Cassidy building," Ohm replied.

"Ohm, I want to construct a scenario similar to the auragraphic prank re-vealing Jeremy Stewart's remains. Instead of auragraphic hooligans, use a large flock of auragraphic sea birds. Stage three simultaneous flocks of seagulls con-verging on the windows of the observer's rooms. I want at least a minute or two of virtual seagulls attempting to fly into the windows only to bounce off the glass and try again. During the impact with the window, the birds should defe-cate, blocking the view. The birds will be virtual, but the feces should be real. Generate a large build-up of bird shit on all the various windows," I said.

"Preparing scenario. When would you like to deploy?" Ohm asked.

"Let's deploy as soon as you are ready and keep an eye on nearby floors and windows. I would like to know if the agents move to another location in the same building. Cross-reference any optical observations we already have of the agents in the observation rooms with the people who have made attempts to access the black glass building," I replied.

"I have matched seven agents with footage from the unauthorized building attempts," Ohm replied.

"Let's get to work on discovering who they are and where their families are located. Send their names to Lucas' invisihud. I want to know their dog's name, how many children they have, their career paths, psychological profiles, every-thing," I said.

"Conducting research," Ohm said.

"Ohm, I want to create a variation on the cloak. Instead of bending light to match the background, I want to bend light to create virtual representations of K-Mac and Byrone walking close together. Create a set of young human cadets wearing Starnet uniforms walking side by side. Use attributes from known psychological profiles to animate the attitude and walk of each individual. Use standard Starnet applicant profiles for the two cadets. The concept is that I can activate these alternate cloaks, and from a distance, I will appear as those two people," I said.

"Generating character profiles. Making adjustments to cloak technology," Ohm said.

I turned off the coffee maker, emptied the grounds, gave the pot a quick rinse before returning it to the hot plate of the coffee machine. Heading into the bathroom, I brushed my teeth and conducted a quick shave with the laser razor. I returned to the living area and walked out on the balcony of my *Tiger Mountain* home. This home sat high on the mountain and could see far into the artificial horizon where the River of Dreams circled *Tiger Mountain*.

Ohm finally replied, "Character profiles and cloak modifications are complete. You have new icons in your invisihud. Character believability factor should be high from six meters and beyond."

I flipped through the menu for the cloak and discovered two new icons. One icon depicted Byrone and K-Mac gesturing and striking a pose. The other icon was of a young man and woman standing at attention in Starnet uniforms. I activated them one at a time. While I obviously couldn't see what they looked like from outside the cloak, from inside the cloak it was pretty cool. The Starnet cadets were automatic walk and talkers. As I walked around the balcony, they appeared engaged in conversation. The K-Mac and Byrone cloak puppets were much more fun. They spun around, swivel back and forth, extended their arms with mine as they moved along, trying to keep up with my walk.

I returned the cloak to standard mode and walked over to the table on the balcony. After picking up one of the cup coasters, I said, "Thank you, Ohm. These modifications are great. Nice job. Can you transport me to the Yerba Buena Gardens transport location?"

"You are welcome. Commencing transport," Ohm said as my *Tiger Mountain* home dissolved away, leaving black and darkness. I realized I may need to put a little more effort into keeping this probability on track. Lucas voiced some concerns at dinner the other night, and he may have been right. I felt like the strong arm of Starnet was gripping just a little too tight. I wanted local security under intense public review, so they had less time to focus on or harass the tenants of the black tower, muhaha. Dark green colors rushed in, and the smell of pines filled my nose as I appeared at the park location.

I appeared in a hollowed-out blind behind some tall bushes. It was easy to step out and onto the walkway. Dropping the cloak, I said, "Okay, let's start broadcasting live."

"Broadcast active," Ohm replied.

"Hello, friends and neighbors on all worlds. I'm here today to conduct a test of Earth's security force profiling. We'll conduct our test using this lawn gadget," and held up the cup coaster I picked up from the table, "that you can purchase from Replicraft. It allows you to project an auragram from its base. The track your movements mode causes the auragrams to appear to be walking as I walk. This will be fun. Will the security forces be fooled? Let's find out. But to be fair to the security forces, I am letting them know this test is being conducted so they can be on their best behavior."

I activated the Starnet cadets auragram with my invisihud while pretending to press a button on the cup coaster. This action brought up the cloak puppets for the cadets. I said, "In this first test, we're just going for a walk as two Starnet cadets."

The cloaked scanners around me transmitted the nearby area to the broadcast station, so my viewers saw me as the cloak puppets. My cloak puppets were visible, but I was not. I began my walk through the park. The path eventually circled around, forming a loop through the park. The security forces were in the center of the park. I walked past the two security guards, which were about ten meters away from my location, and I received no reaction. I even changed my mind, turned around, and walked back past them again, eventually breaking into a run. They seemed unconcerned by my presence. I returned to the arrival blind where I transported in, dropped the cloak puppets, and said to the broadcast, "Well, there you have it. No reaction from the security forces when people wear Starnet uniforms. These aren't even official Starnet uniforms. They are just costume knock-offs. It looks like our fearless protectors have passed the first trial, but what will they do if presented with someone who does not look like Starnet? Let's find out."

I, once again, brought up the cup coaster and pretended to press a button while activating the K-Mac and Byrone cloak puppet. I quickly made my way from the bushes to the walking path, which was empty. Putting more of an attitude into my walk, the cloak puppets picked up on that. I took my time and shuffled down the path until I was within view of the security forces, who took notice of me. I got as close as twenty meters then I tapped myself on the shoulder. This self-tap translated into the Byrone cloak puppet tapping on the K-Mac cloak puppet's shoulder. From there, I pointed at a tree behind the security guards. That was all it took to set them into action, descending upon my position. I took off running back down the path as I previously did as the Starnet cadet couple.

Behind me, I heard, "Hey, stop!"

Running into the tree-covered area around the bend, I switched to the Starnet cadet cloak puppets, took a seat on the grass in the Sun, and pretended to make out with myself. This pose caused the two cloak puppets to start to kiss. When the security forces rumbled through the trees, they discovered a couple in the park making out.

"Did you see anyone run through here?" one of them asked.

I pointed to my left, and they took off in that direction. Once I was sure they were gone, I dropped the cloak puppets and returned to the broadcast as I walked down the path leading out of the park.

"And there you have it. That's one example of how security forces use profiling to enforce an agenda matching their own belief systems. In both cases, I walked down the path and ran away. But only when I appeared to look like non-Starnet personnel was running in the park an issue for the security guards. And even when they cornered me, they were easily tricked with an auragraphic switch," I said as I held up the cup coaster. "Get yours today at your local Replicraft center and start conducting some tests of your own."

"Ohm, end broadcast," I said.

"Broadcast terminated," Ohm replied.

At the end of the path, I dropped the cup coaster into a public trash bin and started down Third Street, heading back to the black glass building. As I walked, I pulled up the *Motif* and began subtly shifting this probability. I wanted more pressure on these observing groups, from inside and outside sources. With the slightest tug on the strings of probability, their projects became underfunded, and any past slip-ups made public. The citizens were upset with the establishment, placing the establishment on shaky ground. They needed to think twice before profiling and acting. In this echo, public settlements favored citizens who were done wrong by the system. I introduced these gaps to allow Lucas' research into missing person cases to yield better results. With the *Motif* in mind, I slowly burned these concepts into this echo as I made my way down Third Street to the black glass building. Once I arrived, I let the *Motif* go with a slight push on the nice weather. It was a beautiful day outside, but here I was going inside.

After exiting the elevator and heading into the apartment, I took a seat on the white leather sofa and brought up an Erykah Badu song, "Didn't Cha Know?" I listened to her sing about the woes of trying to find her way in the world as I racked my brain trying to figure out what to do next. Part of me just wanted to say fuck it all and wander through echo until I found myself again. That approach might mean I could lose the friends I already have. They could age greatly if I spend too long in certain echoes, and I won't know how long I am gone until I return to their time frame.

Erykah sang out, "So, many things I still don't know."

My thoughts returned to the concept of a party. What else do you do when you are feeling blue? The guest list would be all the people I have recently met.

After the song finished, I said, "Ohm, I want to fashion an invitation-based passage card. It should have an R.S.V.P. feature built into it so guests can respond by interacting with the card. The card should explain that it will offer transport to and from the event, along with any guests that are added to the invitation. The guests need not bring anything, and the attire is to be casual. Food and drinks will be provided as well as local entertainment."

"Sending prototype to your invisihud," Ohm replied in my ear.

I saw a new icon appear and flash slowly. I activated the menu option and that brought forward a series of envelopes and self-folding cards. I swiped through them marking a few here and there, and said, "Ohm, let's replicate one of each of the marked candidates from the virtual list."

A small series of sparkles appeared on the table and left behind three possible invitation options. The one on the left was a large gold envelope containing a traditional folded card. The penmanship was fancy and written in a gold ink that shined. The one in the middle was a self-folding card that opened up and presented the invitation audibly. The option on the right was the color red, which was right out.

"Ohm, the invitation needs to be small enough to fit in a pocket upon arrival at the event. I like the talking portion of the middle option, and I like the folded card of the gold option. Can we combine those to make a smaller folding invitation that presents the message when the card opens?" I asked.

"Revising design," Ohm said, and the three options sparkled away, leaving behind a single option. Imagine two business cards taped together along one edge so they could stand up when placed on a table. Printed on the front were two words, "You Are," in a fancy script font. When I picked up the card and opened it, the card started speaking the invitation printed on the inside. There was a small flashing print circle in red ink you could press to R.S.V.P., but closing the card did not press the button automatically.

"I like it, Ohm. Let's set the date for a month from now, a Friday afternoon from 1 p.m. until nightfall," I said, hoping such a wide time window allowed people to arrive at their convenience.

"Now for the guest list," I said. "Madison and Nick Baker, Ethan and Olivia Foster, Alex and Lucas, Candy, of course. Add K-Mac and Byrone with each having one additional guest. Include Frogs with two additional guests. Invite Captain Jason Bowman and six guests, Captain Sara Mitchell and six guests, Jim, David, Robin, and Malik with each having one additional guest. Also, Brent Stevens with one additional guest. How many guests is that?"

"If everyone invited brings along their maximum additional guests, expect thirty-eight guests," Ohm replied.

"Great, look into scheduling food and refreshments for that many people and think about a floor plan using the balcony as a reception area for the guests. Let's go ahead and send out the invitations to each guest. The captains should find their invitations in their ready rooms and place everybody else's invitations near where they sleep."

"Sending out invitations. Now you are committed," Ohm said.

While I was excited about the prospect of having a party, my mind turned to more grim matters as I considered a task I put off for a while now. Late in the first loop, I realized that the ancient magician school of Reloshief, where Lexi corrupted Teela, might be a seat of power for Lexi and Teela. When the second loop came around, one of the first things I did was reduce the school to rubble before releasing Valentino and Lexi. In this third loop, I have let the destruction of that school slide, and I wonder if that is a good thing?

When I was younger, Teela and I lived as man and wife. Lexi invited us to her ranch, where she taught me how to make vignettes. While I was learning vignette making, Lexi taught Teela some of the fundamentals of magic. Teela was from an echo where magic was commonplace, and she had an inherent talent for it. When we first met, our first journey was to visit a school of magic with maps of the surrounding area. I needed to review those maps to locate points-of-power across the land to construct a possible exit gate to another probability. This quest was before I engaged the *Motif*, so probability travel was limited to known portals or gates. Teela's echo contained no known gates, but I made my first trip from my echo of origin to her echo by constructing a portable gate and stepping through it. During my journey, from my original echo to Amir, I constructed three additional temporary gates, in three different probabilities, with Teela following me through them all.

It was soon after Teela and I departed Lexi's ranch when our marital diffi-
culties occurred. Teela already gained her mobility through echo by viewing the
recording I made of engaging the *Motif*. I thought it was just wanderlust making
Teela bored and mischievous. Nothing satisfied her anymore. It seemed that
Lexi filled Teela's mind with descriptions of wonder and greatness that could be
achieved simply by attending Reloshief. Lexi said that Teela was an ideal candidate for such a school and offered to submit her name for consideration at the
next convening council. I thought, why not join as a couple and we could learn
together. But Reloshief was a magic school for women only. This submission
was Lexi's first wedge between Teela and me.

Still, I went along with it, and soon Teela was initiated into the secret society
as I was excluded more and more from her life. I still loved Teela, however, and
I built a small gazebo on the outskirts of the school perimeter. I sang songs
outside of Teela's window so she would know I was still there, waiting for her.
At first, she loved the additional attention and the idea of breaking the rules to
meet her lover in a secret place. That soon turned sour, and even my songs no
longer tempted her outside of her new magical life.

At one point, after becoming worried and lonesome, I decided to sneak into
the school and find out if she was all right. Before things went silent between us,
she mentioned an important ritual she needed to focus on. This was before *Tiger
Mountain* existed, so I did not have an invisihud or a cloak. I used basic sneaking
skills and kept an escape vignette handy, in case I needed to flee the scene. As I
made my way through majestic halls, which were eerily empty, I wondered where
everyone was? I wandered through the school until I located a single student,
which I took up following. She held a crucible in her hand and located a secret
door along one of the hallways which I followed her into. Hanging back so as
not to be detected, I made my way down more carved stone passages that eventually turned into what I thought were lava tubes. It got hotter, and some fumes
built up as the single student carried the crucible into the depths of the school
to a large open chamber.

When my eyes fell upon the chamber, I realized this is where everyone was.
There were at least forty women in robes on either side of a stone bridge spanning an active bubbling pool of lava. The bridge crossed the pool and led to
steps rising up to a pedestal where a few other members stood, presumably the
leaders of this cult. While I did not see Lexi in the gathering, Teela was clearly
visible, dressed in thin white gossamer, holding a knife above some male youth
strapped to a stone altar. His mouth was gagged, but I could see from the fright
on his face that he was terrified. The student carrying the crucible continued
across the bridge. She brought the crucible to the head of the cult, who opened
it and sprinkled some of its content across the body of the nude male youth.

The group began chanting, "Hari, Kari Mari Jari."

They chanted it over and over, then a variation where everyone said, "Wan
Soom," at the end.

Teela seemed possessed, in my opinion. A frightful look of glee crossed her
face each time the words, "Wan Soom," were uttered. She faced the crowd like
a performer accepting the admiration of her fans. Then she turned and waited
for the next "Wan Soom" before bringing the sacrificial knife down into the

chest of the young man. It was freaky the way they all called out, in unison, "Halay!"

After stabbing him, she worked the knife around the wound trying to open it, to bring forth more blood. Even though the boy was gagged, I could hear the whimpers of muted screams, and I felt ashamed that I could do nothing to ease his agony. It was then that the cult leader brought forth a utensil from the crucible and ladled some of the boy's blood up and into the crucible. Additional attendants added powders and leaves, which each seemed to produce a small puff of smoke when dropped into the crucible. The leader, who was still anonymous because of a raised hood, set the crucible on a pedestal and brought forth a wand from inside her robes. She said loudly, "*Protegra Bondu*," and tapped the crucible with the wand, which caused the lid to jangle and vibrate as the entire group, once again, said, "Halay."

This vocalization seemed to seal some magical deal, and the lava beneath the bridge started to bubble more actively as wisps of smoke rose and took on ghost-like shapes wandering upward while a ghastly howling filled the room. As the lava bubbled and mist streams swirled, I noticed that the crucible was tilted to slowly fill a small silver cup. The wispy ghosts were attracted to this cup, and each one dove inside, disappearing as it did so. One of the attendants knelt before Teela, presenting her with the cup. Teela took the cup in both hands and once again grandstanded in front of her audience as they chanted, "Teela," over and over. She brought the cup to her lips and drank fully as the boy's body, behind her, burst into flames.

At this point, a latecomer to the event discovered me, descending the same path I used. She screeched a scream so loud that all the members of the entire chamber looked over in our direction. She wore a cloak, with the hood over her head, and from her scream pitch and height, I would guess she was about eleven to thirteen years old. I made a run for it, back up the passage I descended, barreling past the young girl, knocking her hard into the wall as I fled. I started rifling around my pockets to find my escape vignette and realized it was so dark in these passages that I didn't think I could see the vignette to activate it. It was one of the flaws of vignette travel, you needed light to see the image. I continued up the passage, hoping I would not meet any more latecomers, and I wondered what was the next step in the ritual?

Fortunately, I did not run into any more students or faculty along the way, and once I reached the main hallway, I located a window with enough moonlight that I could activate the vignette. Gazing upon the vignette to the Lighthouse of Flynn, I made my escape from that wretched place. After arriving at the seaside lighthouse, even over the sound of the surf, I still heard and felt my heart rapidly pounding in my chest. All I could think was how do people live like that, couched in mysticism? What type of power did Teela just gain? Did I interrupt the final step of the ceremony? What role did that latecomer play in the ritual? I never found out, and from that day forward, I lost my first wife to the grip of dark magic.

I stood and pulled out the catwalk vignette, thinking I might as well get this over with. Staring into the vignette, I stepped through the card onto the catwalk where the *Vision* painting sat. The cloth, once again, covered the canvas as I stepped up to the easel that held it.

I thought about the location of Reloshief and my small addition to its grounds. I thought of the gazebo I created where I sat and played my guitar for my wife so many hundreds of years ago. Wow, was I really that old? Will I look back on this memory, a thousand years from now, and think, "Oh, yeah, I was still a young pup back then."

I held the image of Reloshief in my mind as I whipped the cloth from the painting and cast it to the floor. I knew the painting could sense your thoughts, that is how it was able to target locations in echo. I never saw the preliminary image based upon any thought I had. But there it was, the face of the boy from the ritual with rags stuffed in his mouth. Tears flowed down his cheeks as his blood pooled up in the indent of his neck before bursting into flames. I was a bit shaken by this image, which was not at all the most grotesque image *Vision* produced. I was concerned because it came from my recent thoughts.

Pushing it aside, I brought forth the image of Reloshief from the vantage point of the gazebo and held it strong in my mind. I felt like *Vision* tried to bully me somehow, and I wanted it known my intent was clear, and I would not be stopped from finding the exact perfect location in echo that was my intended target. The painting gave way to a night scene with a cast of moonlight glow illuminating surrounding trees, with a large castle just beyond them. I stepped into the painting, and I was there.

The night air was a bit cool, so I brought up my shield to regulate my body temperature, and I said, "Ohm, deploy one hundred cloaked scanners to make a map out of the castle interior. I am most concerned with locating a large cavernous chamber in the center, probably below ground. There were secret passages behind walls leading to this chamber, so focus on that rather than detailing outer areas or turrets."

"Deploying cloaked scanners," Ohm replied.

I looked around, and I was indeed standing on a platform that once held the wooden frame of a gazebo, but the long years had dissolved it into nothing, and grasses encroached to cover the stone platform, so it merely appeared as a small hill. As I waited for the cloaked scanners to make the map, I beat myself up over what I should have done in the past to save Teela. I felt like, as a husband, I certainly let her down and did not protect her enough from the wicked things in the world. I thought I was setting her free after she gained the ability to move through echo. But in reality, I delivered a more powerful offering to the dark lords who eventually claimed her soul. Even though she was not considered "family" by the Re'em, I wondered how much longer I could keep her contained in the Cryovirt virtual prison. Now that Valentino and Lexi were out, they may come up with a way to wake her using spells or rituals.

I thought about lighting up a joint or ordering some wine, but then Ohm presented an icon in my invisihud, which I activated. Ohm presented a thirty percent completed map of the castle, but the main chamber I looked for was clearly marked.

"Ohm, stop the mapping process and recover all cloaked scanners except the one in the main lower chamber," I said.

"Mapping halted. Recovering cloaked scanners," Ohm replied.

"Ohm, what type of explosion would not only destroy the castle but also cause the underlying volcano to erupt?" I asked.

"Most volcanoes can be destabilized with low yield nuclear explosions to force some type of eruption," Ohm replied.

I pulled out the catwalk vignette and used it to return to the catwalk aboard the *Deceptive*. The cloth I cast to the floor was still there. I approached the painting, and it seemed to be displaying some sort of geometric repeating pattern, like a mystic screen saver. I wondered if the covering of the painting is what causes or amplifies the creepy factor when the cloth is removed? Stepping up to *Vision* once again, I focused on my previous location. The image of Reloshief castle quickly came into sharp focus.

"Ohm, transport two magnacite missiles, maximum yield, in a staggered vertical line formation into the cavern under the castle. Place the one deep inside the lava pool. Stagger detonation, so the lowest one explodes first, then the second one explodes last, in the chamber above the lava pool."

"Transport complete. Predicting the casing of the missiles embedded in the lava will become non-functional in forty-eight seconds," Ohm replied.

"Ohm, detonate the missiles," I said while watching the scene in the painting.

The view through the painting shuttered for a moment, and the explosion was way larger than I expected. The castle simply shot apart in all directions, made of the finest particles as the sky filled with a growing glow ten times brighter than daylight. In fear of being drawn into the catastrophic scene, I quickly changed my focus to the San Francisco apartment and stepped through the painting.

It took me a moment before believing I was one hundred percent safe. I carried with me the feeling that the explosion was going to track me through echo, somehow. If Valentino and Lexi manage to free Teela, she will have no source of power, at least not from Reloshief. Because of the *Motif* reinforced nature of the magnacite missiles and the fact that this was an act generated by a Lord of Splendor, I imagined this explosion rippled throughout surrounding echoes. I hoped it did not expand too far and catch the attention of other Lords of Splendor.

I lost most of the day to the preparations and execution of the Reloshief destruction plan. Heading out on the balcony, I started to block out some of the areas before night fell. I removed the current balcony furniture by targeting it with the invisihud and using the recycle icon. With the floor plan empty, I mapped out an arrival area for the guests, which would also act as their departure location. I placed this reception area a little to the right of center and further back on the balcony away from the glass doors leading into the apartment. Along the right side of the balcony, I added an area for food and drink. I included a small stage on the left side for playing some tunes or maybe even rocking out. The environment designer offered a wet bar that I moved closer to the glass doors and off to the left. Once I was happy with this setup, I saved the virtual layout as a preset so I could deploy the party set up when needed.

Headin inside, I ordered some food using a screen interface built into the refrigerator. This device was similar to the tablet I prepared for Nanook aboard *Journey*. I selected a pizza and some beer along with a few pastries for the morning. The items transported into the refrigerator, so I opened it up, got out the pizza, and put it in the oven for the final bake. The ale was okay, kind of watery for a true ale, but still refreshing. I reviewed the local news feed for the Starnet Union and San Francisco in general. It seemed there was a lot of talk about corruption and making people pay. High-profile individuals were caught doing bad things or caught doing stupid things. Lucas was right. There were so many channels to choose from. You could spend days, if not weeks, and never have a chance to view them all.

I turned on the oven light and watched the pizza cheese start to bubble as the pepperoni began to sizzle. Searching around the cupboards, I found a large cutting board but could not find a pizza cutting tool in my kitchen drawers.

Ohm interrupted with, "Flexanite detected in Tesson capital."

"What role has this Flexanite assumed?" I asked.

"The Flexanite is impersonating Handu Brine, an elder council member in the capital city of Draylopolis," Ohm replied.

I opened the oven door and placed the large wooden cutting board near the edge of the oven rack before sliding the hot pizza onto the board. I quickly moved the cutting board back to the counter while closing the oven door with my knee. It closed with a slight slam. I turned off the oven and pulled out the largest knife from the rack to slice the pizza into triangle pieces. After cleaning the knife in the sink, I located a dish towel to dry it off before returning it to the knife rack.

I heard a knock at my door and asked, "Ohm, who is at my door?"

"Lucas Morgan is at the door," Ohm replied.

I headed over to the front door of my apartment and opened it up. Lucas said, "Hi Sam, did you just get a report?"

"I did. Come in," I said as I headed back to the kitchen.

"I smell pizza," Lucas said as he followed me into the kitchen and took a seat on one of the stools on the other side of the counter.

"I just pulled it out of the oven. Are you hungry?" I asked.

"Sure, that looks good," Lucas said.

Opening up the fridge, I got out another bottle of ale. He twisted the cap off and took a swig. I pulled a couple of plates from the cupboards and fetched a couple of napkins too.

"Do you want a knife or fork?" I asked.

"For pizza?" Lucas asked as he reached for a slice. "Nah."

"Yeah, I wondered if you might have some ideas on how to process these detected Flexanites?" I said before I took a bite of the pizza.

"I did talk to the Amphibian you detected at the restaurant. I used the teddy bear interface, which is a little creepy, but it does offer a level of anonymity if they escape or report information," Lucas said.

"Any luck?" I asked after taking a drink of ale.

"I pretty much had the same experience you mentioned. Complete denial and utter contempt for the process," Lucas said, reaching for another piece of pizza.

"I thought of transferring this new one, on Tesson, to the holding facility. Can you think of any reason why I should delay that step and let their mischief play out in that society?" I asked as I fetched the rest of the ales from the fridge and set them on the counter.

"I thought about the 'observe them in the wild' approach too, but if murder is their modus operandi to take new forms, it seems negligent to let them roam free once detected," Lucas said.

"I agree with you on that. If one were considered a key element in a plot, it might be worth following it to uncover more. But for these single one-offs, I think it is best to just take them out of action," I replied.

"I wonder how long the Flexanite command will accept mysterious losses in the field before devising a new strategy?" Lucas asked.

"That is why I feel it is important to take the fight to the Ussu sector. I have a single cloaked ship hanging out at the opening of the radionic tile on the Ussu sector side. I would like to expand operations to scan each ship passing through the area. Give any crew members the scissors test before the ship reaches the Dili sector," I said.

"That sounds like a difficult task. How would you approach each ship? Or ask for permission?" Lucas asked.

"I don't think I would ask permission. Ohm, I want to create a variant on the current cloaked attack ship design," I said.

"Specify changes," Ohm replied to both of us.

"Let's change the weapon's transportation section into a Flexanite detection device. Use the transporter already in place to transport a series of cloaked scanners aboard a target ship. Locate all crew members and perform the scissors test to determine if they are Flexanites. Scan the cargo hold contents and perform the scissors test on inanimate cargo. Once the tests are complete, leave a single cloaked scanner onboard," I said to Ohm.

Lucas finished chewing, swallowed, then asked, "Wow, a cloaked attack ship and now a cloaked inspector?"

"I like that. Ohm, let's dub the working name for this variant to be 'The Inspector,'" I said before taking a drink.

"I do like the idea. Even if you don't detect any Flexanite activity, you'd have a tracker on every ship passing through the radionic tile," Lucas said.

"And if we keep getting one-offs, here and there, we might be able to make a map or expose some route they might be using," I said.

"So, we should place the Tesson Flexanite in the holding cell?" Lucas asked.

"I think so. In the other time loops, I kept Flexanites in separate cells, preventing them from knowing that others were caught. It might be interesting to just put them all in a single cell. Then, as they expire, transport them to the Eden world for final storage," I said.

"Interesting. The newly captured Flexanites will see what awaits them when older members simply disappear," Lucas said.

"Ohm, transport the Tesson Flexanite to the same holding cell where the Amphibian Flexanite resides. Bring up the display from the teddy bear's eyes so we can see what is going on in the cell."

A virtual viewport display appeared over the counter, and I walked around the counter so Lucas and I could see it from one side. I noticed the Amphibian dropped the breathing apparatus from her appearance. The Tessonian said nothing at first and merely observed the Amphibian while approaching the large glass wall, then turned and asked the Amphibian, "Where am I? What is this place?"

"I don't know. I arrived here a while ago. I don't really know how much time has passed," the Amphibian said.

"Who did this?" the Tessonian asked.

"I don't know. When I arrived, that little creature spoke," the Amphibian said as she pointed to the teddy bear on the other side of the glass wall.

Lucas and I continued eating and drinking while watching the Tessonian try to talk to the teddy bear. But it did not take too long for the Tessonian to get upset at the Amphibian. They went back and forth verbally until the Amphibian simply dropped her form and stood as a tall column of dark shiny liquid. The Tessonian gave up his form, and the two finally squished their way into one another.

"Whoa, they merged," Lucas said.

"At least putting them together is more entertaining than keeping them apart. They're worse than teenagers left alone in a room. Ten minutes and they are already at it," I said.

"What do you think they are doing?" Lucas asked.

"I remember learning in the first loop about the Flexanite culture. They combine their forms to share information. By dispensing with their shapes, they dispense with words. All that is left is direct mental communication. On their homeworld, there are vast oceans of them all mingled together. They call it 'The Final Form,'" I said.

"Wow, oceans. I wonder how much liquid makes a single person?" Lucas asked.

"I wondered that too? How do they maintain boundaries in a complete fluidic state? Is there just a single mind that works multiple bodies, or is 'The Final Form' filled with entire populations of conscious minds?"

The two Flexanites separated and took on humanoid forms, but neither chose to resume their prior stolen identity. They looked like aliens with dark slimy skin. One knelt before the teddy bear, and said, "Hello, I want to cooperate to gain my freedom."

Lucas looked over at me and I gestured with my hand that he should have the first turn in the teddy bear. Lucas' face took on that altered look one gets when using the invisihud, and I saw the teddy bear in the display spring to life. Lucas moved his hands back and forth and wobbled a bit which was not only comical in the kitchen, it looked pretty funny on the display.

"Please resume your original form. I want to know which Flexanite I am talking to," Lucas asked in the musical voice of the teddy bear.

The Flexanite approaching the glass wall resumed the Tessonian appearance.

"The first step to gaining freedom from this place is to reveal where you have hidden the body of the person you are impersonating," Lucas said, with the teddy bear voice.

"There is no body for this person. I assumed this form years ago," the Tessonian replied.

"You're asserting that you are the one and only, Handu Brine, elder council member, father of three?" Lucas asked as the teddy bear.

"Yes," the Tessonian replied stoicly.

"How can a Flexanite have children with a Tessonian wife? Is your wife a Flexanite too?" Lucas asked.

"My children are adopted, and my wife knows about my true form," the Tessonian said.

"I will talk with your wife then," Lucas said, and he exited the teddy bear interface.

"What do you think?" Lucas asked as he took another drink of ale.

"I think Flexanites lie and murder, but if he has been there for years or at least a couple of decades, he may be out of the loop on the invasion. I guess someone could track down his wife and talk to her," I said.

"You mean me?" Lucas said with a smile.

"Only if you're interested in it. Even if he is telling the truth, and we have captured an 'innocent' Flexanite, he has already linked with the Amphibian in the cell. This link means he would know all of her possible intel and whatever the master plan is. The only release any Flexanite will ever get from those cells is to the Eden planet," I said.

"I see you're point. Once they have linked, they could transfer knowledge," Lucas said.

"Ohm, discontinue display," I said, and the auragraphic display of the Flexanite prison cell faded from the room.

"I think we made a pretty good dent in this," Lucas said, referring to the pizza. We ate more than half of it.

There was a sound of the front door opening, and people entering was heard, followed by, "It's us."

"We're in the kitchen," Lucas called out as Candy and Alex walked in, taking a seat and placing bags on the counter.

"So, what's this about you throwin' a party?" Candy asked me.

"I figure it's about time. I wanted everyone I know to meet each other, so I invited all of you and the new people I have met," I said.

"You mean, future memory people?" Alex asked.

"That is just weird," Candy said.

"Yes, future memory people, and it does sound weird when you say it like that," I replied.

"I didn't get an invite," Lucas said sadly.

"Yes, we did, Hun, it was for both of us, on the nightstand," Alex said, draping her arm around Lucas as she passed by him, eying the leftover pizza.

"Oh, I stand corrected. When is this party taking place?" Lucas asked.

"In a month, right here. It is a balcony party," I said, pushing the cutting board with the remaining pizza to Alex, who smiled.

"So, what is the theme?" Candy asked.

"Theme?" I asked.

"Yes, every good party has to have a theme. How many people have you invited?" Candy asked.

"If everyone comes and brings their maximum additional guests, we are talking about thirty-eight people in this apartment or on the balcony," I said.

"That can work. Not too many but a bunch," Alex said, looking around the room with a slice of pizza in her hand.

"I want to help plan this, Sam?" Candy asked, reaching for an ale and the opener.

"Thank you, Candy. I appreciate any help I can get on this. I do have a basic layout for the balcony," I said, then located my saved environment designer layout and transferred it to Candy's invisihud.

"I wanna help too," Alex said.

I sent the same environment designer layout to Alex's invisihud, then said, "Ohm, transfer the guest list to Candy and Alex."

"Okay, got it," Alex said as they headed over to the glass doors leading to the balcony, talking about what to change or add.

"You're in trouble now that those two are on the case," Lucas said with a smile.

"I'm happy to have their help. Otherwise, the party offerings might end up as a folding card table with a bowl of chips," I said.

Lucas smiled while tipping his ale bottle high, drinking the last of it before asking, "What are you hoping to get out of this?"

"I wondered, too, what is the point of having people from different times and cultures meet, but when I look at the scatterbrained actions that appear to be my life, I wonder where I would be if I didn't have these acquaintances, like you, who make me feel normal and welcome. I guess I wanted everyone to meet so they could all share their experiences and get to know one another," I said.

"A mixer!" Lucas said with a smile.

Candy and Alex returned from the balcony, and Lucas said, "We have the theme. It's a mixer," a little too jovially.

"How many beers have you had?" Candy asked Lucas before she turned to me. "I have said it before, and I'll say it again. Sam, you're are a bad influence on my friends."

"Uhm, I guess it has been two," Lucas said as Alex wrapped her arms around him, giving him a half-chair hug from behind before taking her seat at the counter next to him.

"I like it, a social mixer. It fits the guest list," Alex said.

"All right, I can work with that as a theme," Candy said.

"Great, we're making progress. We have a guest list, a balcony floor plan, and a theme," I said with an arm raised in a faux cheer.

The R.S.V.P.s came in during the first week, so it looked like everyone planned on attending. Over the next few weeks, I lay low, stayed home, and helped out Candy and Alex, who seemed to enjoy the party planning. I monitored *Tiger Mountain*, adjusted Blinn replication projects, and practiced the drum kit. I created a couple of short playlists with only three or four songs on them in case the opportunity came up for a quick performance.

Warren issued a proclamation as the Pharaoh of the Oracle by stating, "Oh Squire, forget not yeah towns that were abandoned. Restore our rich heritage from times of old."

This proclamation was enough for me to take the hint and move the current restoration project from active dwellings to abandoned places. This change addressed the main concern by the Vascon government and Starnet that issuing unrequested repairs on occupied structures was both hazardous and reckless. I reduced the Vascon restoration initiative to a three percent replication bandwidth and created a list of abandoned yet important historical sites for processing. I set the Blinn terraforming modules to process these sites automatically and left it at that.

K-Mac and Byrone helped out with the left side of the balcony, coming up with a show to fulfill the entertainment promise of the invitation. Candy, Alex, and Lucas got to know them better after getting together a few times. I added a localized audio dampening field a short distance from the stage so even if the band got loud, you could back off to a comfortable listening distance. An additional benefit of the field was that it contained any smoking that might be going on.

We were tweaking the food list to the very last day. I asked Ethan to send along any Stexian recipes he could secret out of Nanook. Alex and Candy obtained some straight-up Ralla home cooking by trading technology with a village I helped locate in echo. We took a day trip to Ursa to obtain some traditional Ursonian party foods. Because of Logica's strong ties with Earth, there were a few local Logican establishments in San Francisco where I was able to obtain some broth and tea.

CHAPTER 32

Stolen Food

The day of the party finally arrived, and I woke up early, eager with anticipation as the long wait for the guests to arrive began. I passed the time idly and managed to make it through breakfast. I was in the process of scrubbing through the morning news when Candy came in saying, "We've got a problem."

"Oh, what is that?" I asked.

"Mulsad's says they can't fulfill our order that we placed two weeks ago. Seems that some Mercanite came in and bought the place out last night, and the late staff gave them our food," Candy said.

"They swiped our food?" I asked.

"Yes, they swiped our food," Candy said in a bad mood.

"I could try to locate it and swipe it back, but I don't like the idea of serving double swiped food to party guests," I said.

"Me either. Now we have to find someone who can fill this order, before three in the afternoon, on a Friday," Candy complained.

"I'm on it, don't worry. I'll take care of it," I reassured Candy.

"Ohm, can you locate a middle eastern family restaurant in Twin Falls, use Jim Young's residence as the center point for the search?" I asked.

"I have located eleven restaurants in a thirty-three-kilometer radius of Jim's house," Ohm replied.

"Can you give me the top two based upon community reviews?" I asked.

"Certainly, Fafiel's and Rashasha's," Ohm replied.

"Thank you so much for taking this off of my plate. That lets me focus on some other things I need to do. See you later," Candy said with a smile, and she left the apartment.

"Ohm, can you deploy a cloaked scanner to each of the two restaurants? I'll also need some money from that echo, three or four hundred in small bills."

"Deploying scanners and locating currency," Ohm replied.

A short stack of bills appeared with a sparkle. I picked them up and put them in my pocket, and said, "Ohm, transport me to the location of Fafiel's."

My apartment dissolved around me, and I found myself in the void of darkness again. It seemed kind of odd hanging out in limbo, wondering how I was going to obtain a plate of hummus and stuffed grape leaves? I needed some of those honey-based desserts, and not to forget the falafel and pita bread, too. Light poured in from the sides, and I heard the sound of a car horn honking as I materialized on the sidewalk in front of Fafiel's.

I immediately started walking, as I noticed a few looks from people passing in cars. I made my way up to the front door of Fafiel's only to discover they were closed. They did not open until 11:30 am. I started to feel Candy's panic as it was unrealistic for a restaurant to be able to prepare a large order in such a short time. That's when I realized I would need to use the *Motif* to get what I wanted in this case.

I headed around to the back of Fafiel's, gathering the *Motif* around me as I did so. I noticed a company van with the name, Fafiel's on the side in large letters. Looking around as I approached the van, I tried to dial in the best scenario for my situation. It was highly probable the back doors to the van were unlocked, so I climbed inside and pulled them closed behind me. Taking the seat up front in the delivery van, I rummaged around for some keys. I tried the console, the glove compartment, under the floor mats, then bingo, they dropped down into my lap as I checked the sun visor. There was a Fafiel's ball cap in the passenger's seat, so I put it on, started the van, and slowly drove out of the lot. It was a while since I drove any type of car or truck. This delivery van was a bit sluggish and bouncy. I took my time on the streets, obeying all red lights and stop signs. I used my turn signals and finally found an entrance ramp to the highway.

Once I was up to highway speed, I gathered the *Motif* around me and started shifting this probability ever so slightly. I shifted from the probability of driving an empty van to the probability of driving a van with a delivery full of fresh food. I noticed the daylight jump as the smell of delicious middle eastern food filled the interior. Merging into the right lane and finally over to the berm of the road, I brought the van to a stop. I took off the ball cap. Returning it to the passenger's seat, I placed the keys in the ball cap. I took the money from my pocket and stuffed it in the sleeve I found in the sun visor. Heading to the back of the van, I inspected my ill-gotten booty. There were quite a few of those soft pack insulated boxes strapped into racks built into the van. I removed the boxes from the racks and said, "Ohm, transport me and the food packages to the balcony of the San Francisco apartment."

The walls of the delivery van collapsed in on me, leaving me in the dark. I decided to count this time. I wanted to know how long I spent in this empty state. Did time pass external to my consciousness when I was suspended from my body? A bright light rushed in from the sides, bringing an afternoon cast to the scene. I was alive again and standing on the balcony, realizing I forgot to count.

Picking up a couple of the insulated food boxes, I headed over to the area that Alex and Candy designated as the buffet. The balcony looked great. In the center of the balcony, Alex and Candy set up a sign-in desk with virtual name tags for everyone and a guest book to sign. Behind the sign-in desk was a tall pillar of light with overly large virtual icons attached to it. The planet icon rotated slowly around the pillar of light. Below that was a timeline. The timeline and the planet both displayed curved red arrows pointing at them. The red arrow pointing to the timeline read, "This is Now," indicating today's date and the one pointing to the planet said, "You Are Here."

Candy and Alex added several plants to the balcony, a lot of plants, but it looked nice. There were benches between plants, and the plants near the balcony railings helped offset some of the height anxiety I experienced when getting too close to the edge. Candy and Alex also set up a shielding net around the perimeter in case of the unlikely event of someone falling off the balcony.

Several small standing tables dotted the balcony, offering places where people could gather or set their drinks. Each of these small tables provided a camera to invite guests to take photos at the party. K-Mac insisted on having a popcorn machine, so it was on the left side of the balcony near the small stage. Even though there was a bar inside the apartment, I added a straw tiki bar on the balcony, right when you step out through the glass doors. I replaced the sign reading, 'Tiki Bar,' with a black velvet painting of the classic dogs playing poker.

I dropped off the two insulated boxes behind the food table on the right side of the balcony and headed back to pick up two more. As I headed back to the food table on my second trip, I heard Candy yell, "Where have you been?"

"Getting food," I said, gesturing with a shrug at my full load as I set them down behind the food table.

I headed over and picked up the final two insulated food boxes while Candy walked with me, asking "What did you get?"

"I don't know. I haven't looked yet," I said.

"What? How can you not know what you ordered?" Candy asked

"It was too early. The restaurant wasn't even open. I had to improvise," I said.

"You stole the food!" Candy exclaimed.

"You know it is not stealing. I simply integrated myself into the possibility that I was delivering a bunch of delicious food to a high-class event. These packages are that food, and this party is the event," I explained as I set the two final food boxes on the floor.

Candy and I knelt before the boxes and unzipped them to see what was inside.

"This looks like stuffed grape leaves, two trays. Along with some olives and feta cheese," Candy said.

I opened the only silver fabric box and said, "Oh yeah, this one is desserts."

"Let me see that," Candy said as she slid the grape leaves box aside and dragged mine over to her crouched position for inspection.

I moved over to another box, opened it up and the smell of grilled chicken escaped. I quickly closed it to keep it warm and fresh. A sparkle flashed behind me, and I turned around to see Candy materialized another table where she busily transferred food from the packaging to nicer plates. I brought up the other boxes and said, "This one is chicken, this one has a few deep-fried variationsm and this final box has hummus, baba ganouj, and tabouli with pre-cut pita bread."

Alex and Byrone approached the table, and Byrone said, "Damn, that food smells good," while Alex asked, "What did we end up with?"

"Fafiel's, circa nineteen ninety-seven, Twin Falls, middle eastern," I said to Alex, who tried one of the stuffed grape leaves.

"Oh, these are good," Alex said while Byrone made a small plate of food by rummaging through the other boxes.

"Not from the plate, from the package," Candy said to Alex and then turned to Byrone, and said, "Will you please stop doing that. At least zipper the hot food back up."

"Oh, sorry," Alex said as she replaced the stuffed grape leaf she took from Candy's plate with one from the packaging provided by Fafiel's.

"Okay, it just hit me. I didn't have any breakfast," Byrone said, zipping up the hot food boxes and grabbing his plate before walking off.

Candy turned to me and said, "Are you going to wear that?"

I looked down, and I wore the delivery boy uniform that my clothes morphed into when I made the switch, in echo, to obtain the food.

"Oh yeah. I'm going to change," I said.

I headed into the bedroom, which I configured to be more of an overflow lounge. There was a door here, leading to the bathroom. I took a quick shower and shaved. My clothing options were pre-picked by both Alex and Candy more than a week ago. It was a charcoal suit with hints of old stylings and modern casualism. I insisted on having pockets for my wand and vignettes. I gave up my boots for this occasion, so I made sure the shoes I ended up with contained my emergency cloaked scanners hidden away in the heels.

On the balcony, I heard the stage mics being tested. I initiated the sound dampening cloak at a fifty percent reduction level inside my invisihud. I headed over to the food area, where Alex and Candy made final adjustments for the display. Walking up between them, I put an arm on each of their shoulders, squeezing them a bit with a half-hug, and saying, "Thank you both for helping with this party. I think it looks great."

Alex looked over at me and into my eyes, saying, "No problem. We love to help out."

Damn, there was something mental or psychic about Alex because, with only that look, I was incredibly turned on. Candy tilted her head down on my shoulder and said, "You deserve it."

She turned to face me, brushing something from my shoulder as she said, "You look good. Doesn't he look good?"

Alex stepped up, turning me on even more, as she felt my smoothly-shaven cheek, brushed imaginary lint from my lapel, and straightened my belt buckle stepping back, folding her arms, saying, "Yeah, he looks good."

Lucas arrived just as the two were tidying me up and said, "Ah, final inspection."

"I think I passed," I said to Lucas, who smiled.

"This does look, wonderful ladies. Now, all we need are guests," Lucas said.

"Oh, Lucas, I forgot that thing we want to bring over. Come help me," Alex said before she and Lucas exited the balcony, heading back into the apartment building.

Candy looked down at her clothes and said, "I need a quick change on these pants. I spilled some food on them. I'll be right back," before leaving the balcony.

CHAPTER 33

The Party

There was some time to kill, so I reviewed all the prepared areas I set up for the guest. I checked the bar inside the apartment. I checked the supplies in the tiki hut and placed some coverings over the food, instructing Ohm to remove them once the first guests arrived. I made sure the guest sign-in kiosk was functioning. Candy and Alex added this table to the balcony at the last moment, and I was not sure all the auragraphic features were properly enabled.

A large sparkle appeared on the balcony in the receiving area. Once the sparkle faded, a small trumpet burst announced the arrival with an invisible voice saying, "Jason Bowmen and party of six."

Jason brought Suki, Trent, Chuck, Henry, Tenda, and Farouk along. I gave everyone a moment to take in the location, then I stepped up and said, "Welcome to my San Francisco balcony party."

The group dressed casually, and they all meandered a bit forward with their Captain as he came upon the centerpiece and asked, "What's this?" while pointing at the sign-in table.

"It's basically an ice breaker, a place where you can sign the guest book and match names and faces to people at the party. When more people arrive, the display will add more faces," I said.

"I like your sign," Chuck said as he walked around and behind the guest book table before passing his hand through the auragraphic projection.

"Yo, dawgs, welcome to the mackest party this side of the baaayy. I'm K-Mac, and this is Byrone," K-Mac said.

"You need anything while you're here, you come talk to us. We got cha covered. We got food over there, for multiple species, and drinks over there," Byrone said to them.

"And don't forget the popcorn machine, Byrone," K-Mac said.

"These are my neighbors. They have an apartment on the top floor of this building," I said to the group who were introducing themselves, and I noticed Tenda walking the perimeter with a scanner.

Jason looked up after signing the guest book while Chuck and Farouk gathered around me. I asked, "Can I offer anyone a drink? We have a tiki hut."

"Sure," Jason said.

"Wonderful," Farouk replied.

"Sounds good to me," Chuck said.

Leading the way over to the tiki hut, I took a position behind the bar. Previously, I premixed a few different drink options and placed them in stasis last week. It was something I could chill down, give a shake and pour. I also made a few standing cards describing the drinks I offered and how much alcohol was in each one.

"These cards show what I have premixed, but I can make whatever drink you like," I said, then to Farouk, "But I don't actually have any Ursonian liquors, sorry."

"Not a problem at all. I lived here on Earth for more than three years, with a year and a half spent here in San Francisco. It does look an awful lot like our Earth," Farouk said wistfully.

Chuck looked at the cards and settled pretty quickly, saying, "I'll try the whiskey sour."

"Whiskey sour, coming up," I said, and I located my premix, which was basically bourbon and syrup. I sliced a lemon in half, juiced it, and added it to the shaker. A quick toss with a full pour, then adding the ice, I topped it off with a couple of cherries.

"Here you go. Those are Michigan cherries," I said before handing the drink to Chuck.

"I'll have the Sea Breeze," Jason Bowmen said, picking the drink with the lowest alcohol content.

"I'll try the margarita. Make mine a double, please," Farouk said.

The Sea Breeze was quick. I gave the premix a quick shake and poured it over ice with a lime wedge. The margarita was also a quick premix, and I asked Farouk, "Would you like salt along the rim?"

"Certainly, that's the part I like the most, mixing the salt and the drink in just the right amounts," Farouk said.

I used an extra-wide glass for Farouk's drink, so he had the most amount of salt to choose from. I handed the margarita to him and poured a little of the leftovers in a glass of my own, offering a toast. "To new friends."

"New friends," echoed the others as we all tasted our drinks.

"This is a nice place you have here," Jason said, sipping on his Sea Breeze.

"Thanks, it was acquired through probability travel," I said.

"How does that work?" Jason asked.

"I change the narrative of the probability to include the possibility that I might be heir or owner of certain properties or businesses," I said.

"And you do this mentally?" Farouk asked.

"Yes," I replied to Farouk.

"Is the world like a story to you?" Chuck asked.

I smiled and said, "I guess that could be one way to describe it. But not only do I live in the story. I also write the story."

"Which means there is no reason not to have a high-rise apartment building as part of your current life story," Jason said.

"Now you're thinking like a probability traveler," I said before downing the rest of my drink made from the margarita leftovers.

They smiled, and another trumpet blast sounded, followed by, "Frogs and party of two."

I excused myself from the tiki hut and walked over to the receiving area.

Frogs arrived, and beside him were Ronnie and Adrien, who already held a drink in his hand.

"Hello fellows, glad you could make it," I said to them all.

I gave Frogs a handshake while Ronnie and Adrien and I did the fist bump potato on top kind of a thing.

"Right on, this place looks fuckin' great," Ronnie said.

"Wow, this is nice. Is this your home?" Frogs asked.

"Yep, when I am in San Francisco, it is," I replied.

"Nice place. So, is this in the same building as K-Mac and Byrone's studio?" Adrien asked, looking around, taking the tiniest sip from his drink.

"This place is downstairs from Black Glass Studios," I said.

I motioned the group away from the receiving area and over to the food area, saying, "There is food and drink all around the balcony, and there are aliens here, but they are people."

"Far out, I can't wait to meet a fuckin' alien," Ronnie said.

"Keep it down, Ronnie," Adrien said.

"There is also a guest book at the center with pictures of everyone who has arrived. If you want to know someone's name or where they are from, you can look at the pictures before you talk to them," I said, gesturing to the kiosk then remembering, "Oh yeah, the bar is over there at the tiki hut."

Ronnie headed over to the tiki hut, and Frogs headed over to the guest book to sign in. This departure left me and Adrien, who said, "I know this might not be a good time to ask, but I'm kind of in a jam and could use a little loan."

"You take care of those guys, right?" I asked.

"I do. They are my family. K-Mac and Byrone too. What you have done for them is amazing," Adrien said.

"I think I can help you out, but it might have to be a little later in the evening. Don't head out without talking to me. Does that sound good?" I asked.

"Yeah, that sounds great," Adrien said.

"Enjoy the party, and have some food. I need to mingle around," I said, and he raised his glass as I headed over to say hello to Trent Fairline. Trent was a young African male, probably in his mid-twenties. He was Jason Bowmen's main navigator and the person at the helm when Suki used the communication card the last time I was on *Explorer*.

"Hello Trent, thank you for coming to my party," I said.

Trent greeted me with a warm smile and said, "A chance to get off the ship and catch some real fresh air. Thanks for inviting us. The last time we met, you transported Captain Bowmen to sickbay while the Rulkans continued to slam us."

"Whew, that was a close one, for sure. What was up with that? Was the attack just over territory?" I asked.

"We wondered the same thing. We think they might be watching us, using their cloaks to observe from a distance. But we can't confirm anything yet."

"Well, I'm glad that's over," I said.

"Me too. Say, your neighbors there, K-Mac and Byrone, they are certainly odd ones. But I like them," Trent said.

"I couldn't say it any better. That is a great way to describe them," I replied.

Suki walked up and said, "Thank you, Sam, for coming to our rescue that day and for inviting us to this wonderful party. It feels good to be back on Earth, something about the gravity. I don't know."

"You're welcome, and thank you for coming to my party. I know some of the guests might be a bit rough around the edges, but they are all nice enough once you get to know them," I said.

"I think I am going to welcome commander Tenda. If you'll excuse me," I said, and I headed over to the left side of the balcony where commander Tenda took scans of the cloaked sound-dampening field.

"Balance In All Things, Tenda," I said while making the hand gesture accompanying the saying.

Tenda closed the scanning device, placed it on her belt, and produced the gesture in return while replying, "Balance In All Things, Sam."

"I can remove the cloak if you would like to get a better scan. It is an auditory dampening field. I know Logicans are sensitive to loud noises, so I wanted my Logican guests to be able to move to a distance where the sound levels are not damaging," I replied.

"A sensible precaution for your guests," Tenda replied. "Your actions, the last time you were aboard *Explorer*, were extraordinary. You disabled the enemy and repaired our ship single-handedly."

"It seemed like teamwork to me. When I arrived on the bridge, the scene was desperate and chaotic. You commanded both Trent and Suki, guiding them to their duties at a time of crisis. It gave me peace of mind to focus on my patient knowing that you were in command," I said, trying to offer a compliment.

"How did you disable the Rulkan ship's weapons?" Tenda asked me, ignoring the compliment.

"I used technology that can transport through shielding to place explosive charges at the weapon's emitter points of the attacking ships. The next time they fired, they set off the charges, damaging themselves," I said directly to her calculating expression.

"Efficient, if one has such transport technology. How does it work?" Tenda asked.

"Instead of trying to predict the shield frequency, which can vary over time, I took the approach of going through another dimension to reach the other side of the shield. Optically, I can see through the shield, which allows me to construct a probable target on the other side. So, the transport ray does not go through the shield. The signal routes through an optical probable destination point on the other side of the shield, which causes the transporter ray to materialize at the optical location. Once inside the shield, all you have to worry about is armor plating," I said as I described the process to her.

Jason Bowmen walked up and said, "Commander, you can stop your scans. This is a party."

"Very well," Tenda said.

"I took the liberty of locating some local Logican broths and teas in the market. They are available over at the food buffet if you are hungry or thirsty," I said.

"Perhaps later, but not at this time," Tenda said.

Another trumpet blast sounded, and the voice called out, "Mist Door Operations and accompanying guests."

Everyone looked over as a large sparkle appeared. When it faded, there were eight more people at my party. I saw Jim Young, Robin Cooper, David Scott, Malik, who seemed to have brought a date, General Wagner, Eli Finch, and Doctor Marsha Bradley.

"If you'll excuse me," I said to Jason and Tenda, heading over to greet my newly arrived guests while they followed me, hanging back slightly.

"Jim, welcome," I said, extending my hand and shaking his, then to the others in the group. "Welcome to you all."

Robin stepped up and gave me a hug saying hello, and I briefly said hello to General Wagner, Marsha and Eli. I paused for a moment at Malik and said, "Win su row, Malik"

"Sam, I would like to present my heejumay, Kahr Men," Malik said, presenting the beautiful woman at his side who offered a slight bow mixed with a curtsy.

"Pleased to meet you, Kahr Men. What does heejumay mean?" I asked.

"It means, 'to live life with,'" Kahr Men replied.

David whispered in my ear as he passed by, saying, "It means girlfriend," and headed into the party to say hello to Lucas.

"Welcome, there is food and drink over here, and I have drinks over at the tiki bar," I said, gesturing to the guests to explore the balcony.

"Can I get you a drink, General, Eli?" I asked.

"Call me Sherman, and that would be great, Son," Sherman said as he followed me over to the tiki bar for a drink.

"Sure, thanks for the invite, Sam," Eli said.

While Eli and the other guests were members of Mist Door Operations, they were not actual Guardians of *Tiger Mountain*. And even though the General and I have had some disagreements in the past, I always knew he was just doing his job and looking out for all the people under his large command. Eli was like David's sidekick. He was an alien to Earth but human in all other aspects. He was exceptionally smart with a photographic memory.

While we walked over to the bar, Eli asked, "Robin tells me that this place is actually in the future. Is that right?"

"It's a future, but not your Earth's future. It's an alternate Earth's future, but many things are the same. Like the oceans, continents, plants, and food. Other things are different, like how past wars reshaped societal thinking producing alternate cultural growth," I replied.

"That is utterly fascinating, Sam. I love the way you explain things because I get it," Eli replied enthusiastically.

Eli was like that, he could get excited about possibilities. I guess with his exceptional intellect he was able to visualize possibilities without considering the morose first. I made my way around the bar and realized I really did like Eli. He was probably a way better candidate for a Squire position than K-Mac or Byrone.

"Step right up, Gentlemen. I have some pre-mixed classic cocktails, shown here on the cards, but I also have pilsners, lagers, ales, and darker," I said while gesturing at the mixed cocktail cards.

"The darker, the better for me," Sherman said.

"I'm going to go out on a limb here. I have a chocolate stout, which I originally thought, why? I tried it a short while back and fell in love with it. It is a dark ale with hints of chocolate and not too sweet," I said, trying to make a sale.

"Sure, I'll try a taste," Sherman said.

"Me too," Eli said.

I opened up the Samuel Smith's dark chocolate ale and poured the contents into three rocks glasses, handing one to Sherman, one to Eli, and taking the other one for myself.

"What should we toast too?" Sherman asked while waiting to take his first drink.

"The future," Eli said.

We held up our glasses and clinked them together, saying, "The future."

It didn't take long for Sherman to say, "Oh my. I see what you mean. This is good."

Shaking his head yes, Eli said, "I have to agree."

I took a sip and realized that I was truly an alcoholic. The taste of this delicious ale seemed to slow time, and the flavor occupied my entire palate. I took my time, finally swallowing and saying with a smile, "Yep, I still like it."

Jim Young walked up, saying, "Gents," then to me, "I really like this sign," while pointing at the dogs playing poker painting hanging on the front of the tiki hut.

"What do you got?" Jim asked.

"I have beers, ales, porters, juice, and liquor drinks," I said as K-Mac echoed my "liquor drinks," adding a "zing" to the end of his phrase while he walked by, heading over to the stage area.

"I'm looking for something kind of light, at first," Jim said, continuing his funny guy act, which he tries to fit into every situation.

"How about an Old Fort? It's light, like a beer, but has a nice flavor like an ale," I said before presenting the bottle.

"That'll do. No need for a glass, I'll just take the bottle," Jim said, and I handed him a cold bottle of Old Fort ale.

A line formed behind Jim, and I got busy, for a while, making drinks for the guests. This service gave me a chance to at least have a bit of conversation with each person. I made mixed drinks for Malik and Kahr Men. Marsha was a Seabreeze, Robin tried the old-fashioned, Frogs requested an ale, and I talked Ronnie into a pint of English ale, hoping to keep him away from hard liquor as long as possible. He was known to get falling-down wasted drunk. Suki asked for white wine, which I had, but forgot to offer to the others before her. Trent asked for a ginger ale.

At that moment, another trumpet sounded, and the voice called out, "Sara Mitchell and accompanying guests."

The line was gone, so I headed from the tiki hut over to the reception area. My newly arrived guests were Sara Mitchel, Tamakot, Frelpok, Tai Song, Brandon Palmer, Lyra, and Nanook. They were all dressed in modern casual clothing, not the daily uniforms I previously saw them in. I stepped up to Sara and said, "Thank you for coming to my balcony party," then to all the others, "Thank you all for coming as well. This way."

We migrated away from the reception area, and I pointed out the food and guest book sign-in area to the new arrivals.

Sara said to me, "This is an interesting gathering, Sam."

"Yes, it is. People from different times, places, and dimensions all getting together to have something to eat and drink," I said, taking a moment to admire the scene.

And it was only a moment because there was a loud mic falling sound followed by feedback starting to howl. It was quickly turned off, and I said, "Ah, the entertainment," using a distinguished accent, which brought a smile to Sara's face.

We stopped at the guest book sign-in while others wrote in the book ahead of us. I heard Robin come up and introduce herself to Tai and Brandon.

"Hello, I'm Robin Cooper," Robin said to Tai and Brandon.

"Nice to meet you. I'm Tai Song," Tai said.

"And I'm Brandon Palmer," Brandon said, shaking Robin's hand.

"I know it's strange to ask, but are you guys from the future?" Robin asked.

"No, I think we are actually from the present," Brandon said.

"Yes, but we are displaced seventy thousand lightyears in space," Tai added with a grin.

"That's incredible. You traveled seventy thousand lightyears to reach this party?" Robin asked incredulously.

"What about you? Are you from the future?" Tai Song asked.

"No, I think I am actually from your past, circa two thousand, the turn of the millennium," Robin said.

"Now that is wicked," Brandon Palmer said, caught borrowing Ethan Foster's phrase.

I continued walking around the party, eavesdropping on conversations as I made my way through the crowd.

I saw Henry Lewis talking to Adrien and overheard Henry ask, "So, you really have been in prison three times?"

"Yeah, mostly minor offenses," Adrien said to Henry while sipping on his dark drink.

I noticed that both Logicans, Tenda and Frelpok, located each other and spoke. I wondered how they reconciled the conclusion of the Logican Science Academy, which claimed time travel was not possible?

It seemed like Lyra was engaged in conversation with Malik and Kahr Men, and as I walked by, I heard Lyra ask, "Explain, what is a Gorgon?"

Trent and Frogs seemed to be having a lively conversation, and I overheard Frogs ask, "Do you really fly a giant spaceship through outer space."

"Yep, I was born on a spaceship. My parents hauled freight between worlds," Trent replied.

I noticed Alex and Suki talking. Alex acquired some red wine and changed into a hotter outfit than she wore before. Eli and Lucas hit it off, and I noticed Sherman Wagner in a deep conversation with Jason Bowmen about some previous event having them both trading story perspectives. Jim Young and Candy hung out at the tiki hut chatting while it looked like she got Jim another drink. It seemed the food was a hit as I noticed a good dent in the supply, and a few people were eating desserts at the pedestal tables while engaged in conversation.

At this time, Farouk approached me, saying, "Salutations, Sam. This is a delightful gathering," sipping on a new drink.

"Hello, Farouk," I said, shaking his hand. "I think this mixer is turning out okay."

"I have to agree. When the Captain approached me about the opportunity, I was excited, and to see San Francisco again is a real treat, even if it is displaced in time," Farouk said.

"I have a little feedback on the work you did on my back wounds. You were correct. Whatever you added to the compound eased the stiffness the next day," I said.

"That is wonderful. I love getting feedback from patients," Farouk said with a smile.

Marsha Bradley walked up and said, "I hope I am not interrupting. I just wanted to say hello, Sam."

"Thank you for coming. Have you met Farouk yet?" I asked Marsha.

"No, I am Doctor Marsha Bradley. I'm part of the Mist Door group," she said, extending her hand to Farouk.

"Doctor Farouk. I'm with the *Explorer* group," Farouk said, shaking her hand.

"Oh, you're a doctor too?" Marsha asked.

"Indeed, I studied here on Earth for several years in the multi-species medical initiative," Farouk explained.

"What is your species, if you don't mind me asking?" Marsha asked.

"I am an Ursonian. Our world is part of the Starnet Union of planets,"

Farouk said.

I listened as they talked when I noticed Candy waving me over from the tiki hut. I said, "If you'll excuse me."

I walked over to the tiki hut. Candy stood behind the bar, and Jim was on the other side with a half-empty beer bottle. He must have switched to another brand because the bottle was different from the one I gave him earlier.

"We need you to settle a bet," Candy said.

"Uh-oh, this sounds like trouble to me," I said to them both.

"Isn't it always," Jim said, tipping his bottle up for another drink.

"Jim said you can change your form. Is that true?" Candy asked.

I put my arm around Jim and said, "Sorry, Candy, you'll have to pay the man. Jim is right. I can change my form in a limited fashion."

"Pay up, Candy," Jim said.

"All I have is future credit. I don't carry cash," Candy replied.

"Well then, you owe me. We'll have to square up later," Jim said.

Looking around the balcony, he headed off in the direction of Sara Mitchell, which was probably the only female of Jim's age in the entire group.

"Trade me places and make me an Apple Martini, please," Candy said with a smile and a head tilt before walking around to the other side of the tiki bar as we exchanged places.

I started browsing through the screen which displayed standard drink recipes and located the Apple Martini recipe.

"Ohm, can you find a crisp green apple somewhere and transport it to this tiki hut?" I asked while locating the vodka, schnapps, and Cointreau.

A sparkle appeared under the counter as I mixed the liquors and juice. I washed the apple in the sink and sliced off a few thin slices, munching on one myself as I located a martini glass. This drink was pour-only, with no ice. I cut an apple slice to fit on the rim of the glass and set the Appletini before Candy, who seemed happy to receive such special attention.

A sparkle appeared in the receiving area, and another trumpet blast sounded, followed by "Brent Stevens and party of one."

As I looked over at the receiving area, I saw Brent Stevens and Jorrie Tusk arriving in a sparkle. Other guests stood around them, and they started introducing themselves to one another.

Candy looked over at the receiving area and then back at me, holding her Appletini high in her hand, asking, "What?" as she read the expression on my face.

"That's her, that's my future wife. She's not supposed to be here," I said in a panic as I felt my heart race.

Jorrie wore a long flowing blue dress reminiscent of Vascon styles. Her hair was gathered up on top with a few locks here and there hanging down across her shoulders and back. She wore a matching clutch hanging from her shoulder, and the dress was crafted so as she moved, it revealed her appeal running down her neck and along her sides.

"Damn, Sam, you sure know how to pick em'. That is one fine shawty,"

Candy said, smacking her lips at the sourness of her drink.

I had a serious panic attack as my heart continued to race, and asked, "What do I do?"

"What do you mean, what do you do? You go over and talk to her," Candy said.

"But in my future memories, I always met Erin before Jorrie," I said to Candy.

"Look, if you don't go over and talk to her, I certainly will. From what you say about her, she plays for both teams," Candy said slyly, grabbing her Appletini and heading over to Jorrie's position, who made her way from the receiving area to one of the plant-filled overlooks to take in the view.

I remained at the tiki bar as Candy approached and engaged Jorrie in conversation. I could hear every heartbeat in my chest as I watched those two converse. I noticed Brent Stevens struck up a conversation with Tamakot but then detected me across the balcony and caught my eye for a second. A couple of minutes passed, and Robin approached Candy and Jorrie. It only took a few back and forths between Robin and Jorrie before I noticed an upset look cross Jorrie's face. She abruptly left the area of Candy and Robin, rushing back over to Brent Stevens holding the skirt of her dress up so she could move faster. She tugged on Brent Stevens, rudely interrupting the conversation, and dragged him aside. Even from a distance, I could hear her say, "We're leaving, now."

Brent Stevens pleaded a few times but could not refuse her as she dragged him back to the receiving area where Brent Stevens pulled out his invitation, and the two disappeared in a sparkle.

I was shocked, wondering what was said, and quickly headed over to Candy, asking, "What did you say to her?"

"It wasn't me," Candy said.

"I'm sorry, Sam. I didn't know. When Candy said this was Jorrie, I thought you located her. I didn't know you hadn't met yet. I'm sorry," Robin said, genuinely apologetic for putting her foot in her mouth.

I put my hands on my head and paced in a circle for a moment, then said, "I have to go talk to her. Candy, can you see to the guests until I get back?"

"Sure thing," Candy said.

Tamakot walked up and asked, "Is something wrong? Those two left in a hurry."

"Yeah, I have to go patch things up, but please stay and enjoy the party," I said to Tamakot and then to Candy. "I'll be back as soon as possible."

CHAPTER 34

The Explanation

〜❦〜

Imade my way off the balcony and into the apartment. A few people hung
around inside, and I noticed Adrien and Ronnie over at the bar. They waved,
and I waved back quickly as I headed into the bathroom off of the bedroom. I
left the door partially open as I gathered myself together. I was still in a heightened state of anxiety, and I took a few deep breaths to calm myself down.

"Ohm, where did Brent Stevens and Jorrie return to?" I asked.

"Jorrie and Brent Stevens departed from Jorrie's quarters, so they returned
to that location as per standard operation of the invitation," Ohm said.

"Are they still together?" I asked.

"No, they quickly parted ways upon arrival with Brent Stevens leaving Jorrie's apartment in haste," Ohm replied.

"Ohm, transport me to the corridor in front of Jorrie's quarters as soon as
the corridor is empty. I don't want anyone to see me transport in," I said.

"Understood," Ohm said, and the small room around me collapsed inward
into darkness. I did not know what to say to Jorrie or how open she would be to
listen to me. I hoped I could smooth things over. The grey lighting of *Oasis
Seven* filled my view as I materialized in the corridor outside of Jorrie's quarters.

I knocked on the door, talking to it, saying, "Jorrie, it's Sam."

"Go away!" I heard Jorrie say in her upset voice.

"Please, Jorrie, let me explain," I said one more time, talking to the door.

"I said go away!" I heard Jorrie say again, and this time I heard something
thrown at the door.

I waited for a moment and thought, "Well, you certainly screwed this up,
Sam."

I decided to give up. What could I do, continue to accost her on the station
at her quarters? That was not my scene. I slowly walked away from her door,
heading down the corridor. I tried to find a hidden area and transport back to
the party when I heard Jorrie's door open from behind me.

Turning around, I looked at her as she stepped into the hallway and asked
me, "What did Robin mean when she said you found me?"

I faced her more directly and said from a distance, "That is a bit complicated, but I can explain."

She motioned for me to come in, and I watched her bend down and pick up a book from the floor, probably the one she threw at the door. Her quarters offered an entryway, then a few steps leading up. She stood on the top step, not inviting me any farther into the room.

The door closed automatically behind me, and Jorrie asked, looking down at me, "Why is the explanation complicated?"

"Okay, I'm just going to tell you the truth, as far-fetched as it seems. I hope you keep an open mind, being a scientist and a Starnet officer," I said.

Jorrie looked at me with a bit of skepticism.

"About a month or two ago, I awoke with memories from the future. You were in those memories. I reviewed medical logs before and after the memories appeared, and I detected no temporal anomalies or traces that I was physically transported through time. My past self, which is now my present self has memories from my future self," I said.

Jorrie was about to comment, but I continued, "Not only did I have memories from my future, but I also had memories from two such time loops. It appears I may be stuck in a time loop, and everyone I know is stuck with me. You appear in both time loops," I said.

"What role do I play in your memories?" Jorrie asked.

"In both time loops, you are one of my wives," I said.

"One?" Jorrie said with a bit of contempt, making me feel like I might only get to say one more thing before being booted out of this room.

Before I could say anything, she said, "If you have memories of me being your wife, then tell me one thing about myself that only a husband would know."

"Well, you snore, are a flailing sleeper, and get grumpy when you don't get enough food. I have memories of being slapped and kicked, in my sleep, more than once during our marriage. Your favorite thing to eat is steamed lansa beans," I said.

"Funny," Jorrie said, giving me an I'm not impressed look. "Those things could apply to anyone. And my food choices are public records."

"One time when you were young, your uncle Reshan took you to a restaurant to celebrate an accomplishment in winning a track meet. He ordered one of everything which stuck in your mind. But it was at that restaurant where you first acquired a taste for steamed lansa beans. You told me that was when you really started liking them. Oh, and your brother Kelren is a total asshole," I said, hoping to make a dent in her skeptic armor.

"So, how long were we married?" Jorrie asked.

"At least five years in the first loop but more like three to four in the second time loop," I said.

"You don't remember whether it was three or four years?" Jorrie asked.

"I don't. The memories are getting fuzzier the farther I travel in time from that day when I acquired those future memories. I don't even know what causes the loop to occur."

"Are you seeking me out to marry me again?" Jorrie asked.

"I'm seeking out all the people I can remember from the future memories before I forget who my friends are supposed to be. Most of those people at the party are future friends," I said.

"And why didn't I get an invitation?" Jorrie asked smartly.

"In both time loops, I meet my other wife, Erin, first. That has not happened yet. Meeting you first has caused this time loop to start to unfold differently," I said.

"I see," Jorrie said, and it looked like she might be reflecting on something before adding, "You want to unfold this timeline to match the previous loops. Why?"

I dropped my arms to my side, presenting a giving-up posture, and said, "Our love was real, Jorrie. Our marriage was important, not to just you and me, but to Erin and you. We were married on Ursa prime in a special ceremony. I married you and Erin, Erin married you and me, and you married Erin and me. When I awoke with the future memories, I lost all of that in an instant. Imagine yourself deeply in love, and then you are suddenly transplanted to a place where you have no access to that love. It no longer exists. But your heart doesn't know that. It still feels the lost love and longs for more."

Jorrie descended the two steps to face me and said, "I don't love you, Sam," pausing, "but I want to know more."

"I want to tell you more, but I have a balcony full of party guests. If you want to know more about me just ask them. Will you return to the party with me?"

Jorrie thought for a moment, then that wonderful smile of hers crossed her face, and she said, "Sure, let me get my clutch."

I followed her up the steps into the spacious officer's quarters. She fetched her small bag with a thin strap from the table and slung it over her shoulder. I held out my hand and said, "Ohm, I would like to construct a passage card from Jorrie's quarters to the hallway outside of my apartment in San Francisco."

"Who are you talking to?" Jorrie asked as her eyes lit up when the new passage card sparkled into my hand.

"I have a verbal interface that allows me to make requests for replication and transportation," I said.

"And that was a transportation?" Jorrie asked.

"Both, the card was generated through replication means, then transported to this location," I said while holding the card up to show her how it works.

"You press the button, and it toggles between two locations. To travel to a location, stare at the image, and accept the believability of the place. You'll perceive a change in the card," I said, setting the display for the apartment hallway and handing the card to her.

"Take my hand," I said, and we stood side by side holding hands while Jorrie held up the passage card, looking into it.

"I see what you mean. It does seem more real," Jorrie said after a moment of concentration.

"Step forward into the scene," I said, and I pulled her forward as she took a step on her own.

"Oh my goodness," Jorrie said as we crossed the threshold, stepping into the hallway outside of my San Francisco apartment.

"That was different from transportation, wasn't it?" Jorrie asked.

"Yes, it is. That is the way a probability traveler transports," I answered.

Jorrie handed me the card, and I said, "Keep it. You can flip it to the other picture to return home, any time you like."

"Thanks," she said shyly and placed it in her small purse.

I walked up and opened the door to the apartment, offering Jorrie to enter first, and the party was still going on strong. I felt like no more than thirty or forty minutes had passed. There were more people inside the apartment hanging out, and I could hear some music happening out on the balcony. We walked past the kitchen opening, and Candy said, "There they are!" loudly, revealing that she may have had a little too much to drink.

I was suddenly rushed by a few guests. Jorrie and I were quickly separated, but I heard Candy saying to her, "Come over here, girl."

"Nick, so nice to see you," I said as Nick Baker approached.

"Thanks for inviting us. This party is wicked," Nick replied with a drink in his hand.

"I know Madison would like to see you. She is out on the balcony with Olivia," Nick said, and he started leading me out of the apartment onto the balcony.

I noticed Ronnie and Adrien hung out at the corner bar talking with Malik and Kahr Men. A mix of the *Journey* and *Explorer* crew sat around the coffee table in the center of the living room. It looked like Alex, Suki, Henry, Marsha, and Sara shared some dessert and drinks around the large rectangular coffee table. They all seemed to be genuinely talking.

I made my way through the glass doors and noticed Brandon Palmer took up the role of bartender inside the tiki hut with Tai Song and Lyra as his customers.

Nick led me over to the food area, where Olivia and Madison had something to eat at one of the sit-down tables. It looked like Nanook was conversing with Albert and Lulu, helping them decide on a dessert to choose.

Madison stood up and gave me a one-arm hug, and Olivia did the same before they sat down to their plates. I pulled up a chair at the end of the table while Nick said, "I'm gonna head over and check out the band."

"Sorry I missed your arrival. There was an emergency guest situation to deal with. Thank you both for coming," I said to the two women.

"I was quite happy to receive your invitation in the mail. We have spells for talking invitations, but yours was different. I could not detect any magic upon it," Madison said.

"Yep, that was just old-fashioned bailiwick tech stuff. I have been playing around with trying to form new spells as we talked about a while ago," I said to Madison.

"Really," Olivia beamed. "Which ones?"

"I came upon a damaged well whose stacked stones fell in, and I wanted to rebuild it. I used '*Emergareformac*,' which caused the stones to fly up out of the well and re-stack themselves around it. The stone had no mortar, so I used '*Mortusgamtite*' to add mortar to the stonework. It took several castings as I walked around the outer wall of the well. Then when I discovered a clogged drain, I used '*Repugnatone*,' which caused the plants to repel from the opening, carrying their roots with them," I said kind of proudly.

"That is a significant advancement in magical ability, Sam," Madison replied.

"*Repugnatone*," Olivia said. "I'm going to have to try that one."

Tamakot approached the table with a small plate of food and asked, "Do you mind if I join you?"

"Please do. I'm Madison Baker, Nick Baker's wife," Madison said to Tamakot.

Tamakot sat down next to Madison as Lulu and Albert approached with way too many desserts on their plates. They sat down next to their mother, across from Tamakot, and Lulu said, "Tamakot!"

"Hello, Lulu, Albert. It looks like you two have full plates," Tamakot said to the kids.

It seemed obvious to me that Ethan introduced his family to at least some of the crew members on *Journey*.

Nanook was not far behind the kids as he took up a seat farther down, saying, "There you are, Sam. Thank you for inviting the crew to your balcony party. I can't believe that I am actually on Earth."

"I put together the Stexian food offerings myself, so I won't feel offended if I have missed the mark on taste or presentation," I said to Nanook as he sat down.

"I appreciate the effort. It does look truly delicious," Nanook said as he sat down.

"The chicken and hummus are very good. I can't remember the last time I ate tabouli," Tamakot said while eating.

"I have chocolate strawberries," Lulu said, placing one in her mouth.

"This is an amazing undertaking, Sam. I'm not sure how you pulled this off," Olivia said.

"I had a lot of help from Candy and Alex. They came up with the ideas of these areas. All I really had was the stage in mind," I said.

"Those two, K-Mac is it?" Tamakot asked.

"Yes, K-Mac and Byrone," said.

"They have a certain flair about them. They told me they were from nineteen ninety-seven," Tamakot said while taking a few more bites.

"That sounds about right. I never bothered to figure out what time offset you two ladies represent, however. Your echo is much more divergent from these others, so I don't know if any meaningful comparison could be made," I said to the group.

"I have to agree," Madison said, "Many a magician have attempted to integrate bailiwick-based time into our magical records, but it seems the land of bailiwicks can be reached from most historical magical contexts."

I noticed Tenda and Frelpok were sampling some of the Logican food offerings I supplied. I don't know why, but it made me very happy, which of course, would be illogical to them.

"There is that word again, echo. You used it when we first met. I wasn't sure what you really meant, but now I am guessing it means some type of fixed probability that you find yourself within," Tamakot said.

"Correct, we are all sitting in the same echo, right now, would be how to properly use it in a sentence," I replied.

"Oh, these are good, Sam. I think you have a knack for Stexian cooking," Nanook added to the conversation from down the table. "And might I add that green tablet you provided for ordering food aboard *Journey* has helped make my job so much easier."

"And we get better food because of it," Tamakot said with a smile.

Tenda and Frelpok adjourned to one of the standing tables with their soups and began eating them in silence.

Olivia reached over and tickled Lulu, causing her to giggle and slide slowly out of her chair and down to the floor, leaving streaks of chocolate on the table cloth from her sticky hands as she grabbed on to pull herself up. Albert made his way back to the food table for another round.

"There are still a couple of people that I have not said hello to. If you'll excuse me," I said, and I got up and headed over to the tiki hut.

"Tai, Brandon, Lyra, thank you for coming to my party. Sorry, I have been too busy to say hello sooner," I said to the group at the tiki hut as I approached.

Tai extended his hand. I shook it, and so did Lyra while Brandon asked, "Can I get you something to drink?"

"Check around down below. Do you see a green can of ale? Pass me one and a glass," I said.

"Ah, looking. Toothy Knot. This ale is what you served in the mess hall when you first arrived, isn't it?" he asked while handing me the can and a clean glass.

"Check out the can 'It's Like Sputnik,'" I said, and I showed the words printed on the can to the group before opening it up with a pop and then poured it down the side of the glass.

"First into space," Lyra said. "The meaning of the statement."

"I believe Sputnik carried no instruments and made no measurements," Tai said.

"Can you believe it was only this big," Brandon said while measuring with his hand spread out about one meter.

"In this case, I think it means 'Out of this world' delicious," I said. "Are you all enjoying the party?"

"I know I am. I can't believe all the beautiful women here, Sam. You're going to have to invite us over more often," Brandon said, taking a drink from his glass.

"I will, if your taskmasters will allow it," I said, making a whip sound with my mouth.

This sound brought a smile from Brandon and Tai but seemed to fly right over Lyra's head.

The Cyberton bioadapted Lyra when she was a small girl. She never knew any life other than being a brainwashed worker in the Cyberton assembly. The Auramedic managed to remove most of the Cyberton brainwashing dermatech mechanisms, but a few still remained around her eyes and hands. *Journey* freed her from the assembly and has been integrating her into their crew. She was at the original meeting where I disconnected the communication feed with Starnet.

"What about you, Lyra. What do you think of the party?" I asked.

"Your transportation technology is impressive. I find the surroundings inviting, even comfortable. This visit is my first time on Earth, so it is a pleasant experience," she said.

"I think that is as close to a gold star that you're gonna get from a former Cyberton," Tai Song said.

"Well, I'll take it. I'm glad the party is working out. I wondered how people from other times and probabilities would mingle or if they even would. But it looks like it is turning out fine," I said.

The afternoon drifted into early evening, and there did not seem to be a slow down on all the drinking. A few people walked past the tiki hut heading over to the stage, and then I noticed Frogs, who said, "There you are, Sam. We're really anxious to kick out some tunes. What do you think?"

Ronnie and Adrien were with Frogs, and Ronnie asked, "We're gonna light up this joint. You guys wanna get high?"

I looked at Brandon, Tai, and Lyra and asked, "Do you guys want to go smoke a joint with us?"

"I understand the words you said, but I don't even know what that means," Tai Song said with a smile.

"I think he is referring to illicit consumption of mind-altering drugs," Lyra surprised us with her brilliant understanding of our slang.

"Dead on Cyberton analysis. She is correct," I replied.

"Why not. It's a party. You coming Tai?" Brandon said.

"No, I'm not ready for illicit consumption yet," Tai replied.

"My Cyberton implants would treat such consumption as an invasion and quickly remove the drug. There is no reason to consume something that will immediately be removed," Lyra said.

We headed over to the stage, and Brandon said, "Hi, I'm Brandon Palmer," as he introduced himself to Ronnie and Adrien.

Over by the stage, I found Nick, Ethan, Eli, K-Mac, and Byrone talking. We walked up with our crew, and Ronnie said, "We're gonna light up this joint, you guys in?"

"You know it, dawg," K-Mac said.

"Sure," Ethan said.

"Okay," Nick replied.

"What's a joint?" Eli asked.

"How did the Cyberton say it, illicit consumption of drugs," I replied. "It's very mild and wears off in about an hour."

Ronnie lit it up, took a hit, held it, then said, "Just take a little hit," before passing the joint to Frogs.

"When it's your turn, you take a small inhale into your lungs. Hold it, then let go before you cough. But don't worry if you cough, everybody does," I said.

"That's right, Eli, don't worry, everybody coughs on the first time," and as if on cue, Nick coughs a sputter of smoke, saying, "I held it too long," handing it to K-Mac.

K-Mac took a puff, held it, and blew out the smoke handing the joint to Eli, who took the joint and almost dropped it before he put it up to his mouth. He got a weak puff, held it, then quickly blew the smoke out, saying, "It's got flavor."

The whole crew burst out laughing, and Frogs said, "Oh yeah, it's got flavor."

Eli gave me the joint. I took a hit then handed it to Brandon, who took a hit and managed to not cough. He passed the joint to Adrien, who took a couple of long puffs.

"Definitely flavor," Brandon said, and the group shook our heads yes.

The joint made it back around, and Eli passed on the second hit. Adrien ended up having to spark it up a couple of times before killing the joint.

"I don't know, fellows, but I think it's time to make some noise," Byrone said.

"Word up, dawg," K-Mac said, slapping Byrone's hand and heading up on stage.

"Come on, Sam. Get on the drums," Frogs said, and we all climbed on stage and took our place at our instruments. I kicked around on the kit, and moved the snare to make sure it was not crowding out my right knee. I pulled up the shortlist of songs I came up with for this party and told the fellows the names of them. K-Mac took some time talking up the event, which caused people to gather around. Byrone played some beats in the background as Frogs tuned up his guitar.

"Ohm, can you create a piece of paper with the names of all four songs in large letters? Transport one to the floor in front of Frogs, Byrone, and K-Mac," I asked.

Frogs looked back and gave me the thumbs-up as he picked up the paper and read the song names.

Once we got rocking, I started with, "London Calling," by the Clash. The words were all different, but Frogs locked in on the stacatto guitar track. Byrone played off K-Mac's vocal improv. We all sang, "We live by the River," together, and I thought it sounded pretty good. Byrone brought up an echo effect during the fall apart. The second song was "You and your Folks, Me and my Folks," by Funkadelic. This one got funky. Byrone jumped in on the piano, and we all ended up singing, "yeah, yeah, yeah," in the background at some point or another in the song. The mood mellowed as we played "Get up, Stand up" by Bob Marley. K-Mac switched to congas on this one, and we just let virtual Bob sing it for us. For the final song we played was a fast little rocker by the Romantics called "What I Like About You." Frogs nailed that old-fashioned tube sound and matched the strum on the guitar. K-Mac flavored it up with alternate things that he liked about his baby. We all yelled, "Hey!" in the middle of the song where the break happens. We finished it off with a series of "Hey, Hey, Hey!" and managed to all stop playing at the same time.

The guests inside the apartment wandered onto the balcony with the other guests, attracted by the performance. They all politely applauded after we finished. K-Mac introduced the band. After that, we all set aside the instruments and headed down from the stage to the balcony floor.

The General was the first to approach and shook my hand, "Thank you for a wonderful time. Duty calls, and I must get some rest before my next shift. How do we activate the return portion of the invitation?"

"Let's return to where you arrived. That is the departure point," I said, and I led the General and the rest of the Mist Door crew back to the arrival area of the balcony.

They fell into a loose formation in the arrival area, and Jim called out, "Next time, we'll have the party at my place. I mean that. Everybody's invited."

Robin was the manager of their card and used the invitation to initiate the return transport. She mouthed a "Sorry" before her face disappeared in a sparkle.

Jason Bowmen stepped up with his crew behind him and said, "I think it's time for us to shove off. It was a nice diversion to meet your friends and neighbors."

"Thank you for coming, all of you," I said, watching Jason pull out the invitation from his pocket, looking at me quizzically.

I gestured for him to tap it, and when he did, they all vanished in a large sparkle. Sara was next, and her crew fell into formation around her. She said, "Thank you for inviting us, Sam. It was wonderful to see your home and meet your friends."

Frelpok also added, "Indeed, an illuminating cast of characters."

Sara located her invitation, and her tapping brought forth another round of sparkles removing people from my balcony. I looked around, and Olivia headed over to me, with Lulu hanging from her. She said, "Sam, thanks for inviting us to your party, but I think I have to get these kids home and get them ready for bed."

Ethan Foster walked up and asked, "Are we leaving?"

"Yes, your daughter needs her father," Olivia said as she handed Lulu, who was a bit too big to be handed off, to Ethan.

"You smell like smoke, Papa," Lulu said.

"It's wizard's weed, dear," Ethan said, picking up Lulu then turning to me with a smile, "Thanks for inviting us. I had a great time."

"See you later. Thanks for coming," I said, and the Foster family walked off the balcony, heading for the front door. Lulu managed to take hold of an arm of each of her parents, and they swung her forward as they took more steps, exiting slowly, while Albert followed behind with a plate of food to go.

I found myself alone for a moment, and Jorrie approached. I asked her, "So, did you have a chance to talk to people?"

"I did. I managed to talk to most of the people here," Jorrie said.

"And?" I asked.

"I guess I am at the same place I was back in my quarters. I still want to know a little more," Jorrie said, taking slow steps to get closer to me and standing face to face.

The mood was abruptly interrupted as K-Mac, Byrone, Frogs, Ronnie, and Adrien passed by with K-Mac saying, "We takin' the party up to my crib, dawg. You all are welcome to join. Top floor bottom buzzer, you know."

Jorrie and I quickly stepped apart, both of us realizing something was slowly sizzling between us, and I think it was at that moment that I thought I might actually get her to spend the night. Adrien hung back from the group and said, "Sorry to interrupt, Sam, but that thing we talked about."

"Oh yeah," I said to Adrien, then turning to Jorrie. "Excuse me for a moment."

I headed over to the tiki hut and said softly while walking, "Ohm, can you place a small duffel bag full of Canadian cash from Adrien's echo on the lower shelf of the tiki hut. Make the cash amount thirty-six hundred in small bills."

Adrien followed me over to the tiki hut and stayed on the customer side while I headed around and fetched the duffel bag from the lower shelf. I put the duffel bag on the counter between us and unzipped the top. There were stacks of bills and some loose cash. I asked Adrien, "Does that look right? I'm not always sure what one location's money looks like."

Adrien pulled out a few bills, took a look, and said, "Yeah, that looks right," then stuffed them back into the bag, zipped it up, and slung it over his shoulder.

I walked around the tiki bar, and we fist-bumped as he said, "Good luck tonight," and made a gesture over my shoulder at Jorrie before, saying to her a bit more loudly, "So long, nice to meet you."

I headed over to Jorrie, who took a step or two toward me as I approached, and she asked, "So, what was that about?"

"Oh, just helping a friend out," I said kind of vaguely.

"Did that kind of reply fly when we were married?" Jorrie asked, not that happy with my dismissal of her interest in the Adrien transaction.

"No, I pretty much told you everything. We got to know each other over time, though. It takes a while to know someone," I said.

"I saw you give him a bag. What was in it?" Jorrie asked.

"It was cash that matches the echo where Adrien lives," I replied.

"How much money did you give him?" Jorrie asked, continuing her investigation.

"I gave him thirty-six hundred in cash, small bills," I said.

"Is that a lot?" Jorrie asked.

"I know how much a beautiful dress like that would cost in Marcus' shop on the concourse. I gave Adrien three and a half beautiful dresses," I said, trying to establish Earth's antiquated currency values to something she might relate to.

She smiled, making me feel like I might be wearing her stern resolve down, but then she asked, "Was it payment for something?"

"Not really a payment for something. More like aid to keep those guys out of trouble. They live in poverty, one of those percentage points that inevitably fall through the societal cracks. Ronnie, Adrien, Frogs, and K-Mac have all done time in the penitentiary. Society has no real use for their skill set, but Ronnie does grow amazing weed, which is illegal in their country. By giving them cash, it keeps them from having to come up with hair-brained schemes to earn money to survive," I said, hoping that was enough to dampen her curiosity.

"So, this weed is a cash crop for them," she said.

"When they can sell it. More often than not, the fields are discovered, or they end up in some kind of snafu that wrecks the whole thing. I support them so I can stop by on occasion and pick up some weed," I said.

Then Jorrie came to a realization and said, "You're addicted to it, aren't you?"

"Jorrie, I am both an alcoholic and a weed addict. Weed is only psychologically addicting, so I don't suffer withdrawal if I don't have it, but it is nice to have it around. It's one of the drugs compatible with my species," I said.

This admission of addiction was sparking another question in Jorrie's mind, but at that time, Candy, Alex, and Lucas walked up together, and Candy said, "We headin' out, boo. You two okay for the evening?"

"Yeah," I replied and looked over at Jorrie, who said, "It was nice to meet all of you. I enjoyed getting to know you."

"Same here," Alex said, "Feel free to stop by some time. We're just down the hall at twenty-three eighteen."

"Hey, do you mind if I put some of the leftovers in your fridge? I was going to transport them there," I asked.

"I don't mind at all, thanks," Lucas said.

"It's all right by me too," Candy said, then leaned forward and gave me a pat hug before they all turned around and walked off.

"What does it mean when you are the last one at the party?" Jorrie said after they left the balcony.

"It means you get to help clean up," I said with a smile, and I walked over to review the food supply.

Jorrie followed, and it looked like the food from Fafiel's was a hit. There was only half of it left.

"Human, Ursonian, Logican, and Stexian," I said as I pointed to each of the offerings.

"He was an interesting fellow. What was his name again?" Jorrie asked.

"Nanook," I replied, "He is the chef aboard *Journey*."

"Right, he told me how you gave him a food transportation device and that it has improved morale. Also, you provided a long-distance communication device that reaches the Dili sector. It was nice to meet another friendly species," Jorrie said.

"In my mind, the food transportation device I gave Nanook is the equivalent of the bag of cash I just gave Adrien. Each echo has its own needs," I said.

"I know everyone at Starnet is impressed with your contribution to communicating with *Journey*. And I am personally impressed with your recent restoration on Vasco. My friend Mia, that you met in Lepton's, tells me the Vasconian people are quite pleased with the Squire of the Pharaoh," Jorrie said, finally smiling at me, which was contagious.

"Ohm, package up the food for humans and place it into the refrigerators found in my apartment, Alex and Lucas' apartment, Candy's apartment, and Black Glass Studios. Recycle the remaining food items," I said.

A sparkle of transport activity removed the food from the balcony, leaving empty tables behind.

"What you just said. That was some verbal command, wasn't it?" Jorrie asked.

"The word, 'Ohm,' is the name of the central computer that processes my voice commands," I said as I walked over toward the stage area.

"Ohm, discontinue the auditory cloak and recycle the stage elements," I said, and there was a round of sparkle activity. When it faded, the stage was gone.

"Where is this, 'Ohm,' located?" Jorrie asked.

I looked at her and sighed at answering her questions, but I knew this was her way. We talked all the time in my future memories, so I said, "Ohm's location is in another dimension."

Sensing my frustration, she said, "Sorry to ask so many questions, Sam. It's just that you are such a mystery to me. And knowing you seems to mean knowing your technology. How does Ohm hear your requests if Ohm is in another dimension?"

"Where ever I go, cloaked sensors follow me around. They act as processors of requests and emitters for transportation services," I stated.

"That's remarkable," Jorrie said, "Are there sensors here, on this balcony, now?"

"Ohm, dock a cloaked scanner in my hand," I said, and I held out my right hand with the palm flat.

The cloaked scanner revealed itself and landed on my hand. I handed the small sphere covered with tech panels to Jorrie, who held it up and looked at it closely.

Anticipating her next question, I went ahead and offered, "It floats by creating a differential field against gravity. This limitation means it's not effective in open space. The miniaturized energy source and cloaking technology I obtained from an echo that you might call the twenty-seventh century."

"So, this is future tech," she stated, handing it back to me.

"Yes, but my species does not see time the same way other species do," I said.

"Ohm, reactivate cloaked scanner," I said, and the small tech sphere disappeared from view.

A cool breeze chilled Jorrie, and I said, "We can go inside. It will be warmer."

I placed my hand on her waist, and we walked together like a couple on our first date. She stepped into the apartment from the balcony first, and I followed. I closed the glass doors behind me, and we took seats on the white sofa with the large coffee table in the middle. Jorrie placed her small blue bag on the table and turned to me, saying, "This is nice, thanks."

Overall, the apartment was trashed. There were leftover food plates and drinks spread out all over the place. I decided to go for it and sat down next to her, opening my arms for a hug. She reciprocated by putting her arms around me. The angle of our seating was a little awkward at first, but then we adjusted our positions and found a way to get a full-on sitting hug going. It felt wonderful. I put my head to the side of hers and just held on. In truth, I never imagined I would ever hold Jorrie again. That day when I awoke with the future memories, I awoke with a broken heart after the realization that I was in the past. I held her close and moved my hands along her back. There were gaps in her dress, and I slid my hand between them to touch her skin. She moved her hands over my back and pulled away, sliding her hands down my neck and across my shoulders. She stopped with her hands resting on the end of my shoulders. We looked into each other's eyes, and both leaned in for a kiss, a short one at first. Then another one, much longer. We touched tongues, and I pulled her closer with my hands down by her waist. We kissed a few more times, getting pretty hot, then backed off.

"Do you want to get more comfortable?" I asked.

"Yeah, let's," she said, standing up.

We walked over to the bedroom entrance. It was still configured for guests. There were some chairs and tables, and it looked like a few people may have hung out in here. I asked, "Ohm, can you recycle everything in this room and restore my bedroom furniture?"

There was a set of dual sparkles, one removing the previous items and a new one to replace the bed and dresser. Once the sparkles died down, it was too dark, so I walked in and opened up the light-blocking curtains to allow the last of the evening light to shine in through the windows illuminating the bedroom.

I returned to Jorrie, who turned her back to me and asked, "Can you undo the buttons on my dress?"

There were only a few. I undid the lower buttons first and worked my way up the top, and the dress fell to the floor. She stepped out of it and wore a bikini bottom and a sports bra top which were also blue, to match her dress.

The bed was large, a California king. We made our way into the center and found our way back into each other's arms. I couldn't get enough of just holding her. It felt so good to be in her arms again. I stepped off the bed and undressed. Jorrie was busy taking her remaining top and bottom off, and we met each other in the center of the bed. From my future memories, I knew Jorrie liked my chest and shoulders. It was something that turned her on. She revealed this to me tonight as she ran her hands across my chest, ending up in my arms, feeling my biceps.

The content editor came in and removed the detailed first sexual encounter that Sam shared with his yet-to-be future wife, Jorrie. It was all rewritten as a one-liner reading, "We made love, and afterward, I wrapped my arms around her while lying in bed together."

"I can hear your heart," she said softly.

"God, feeling good. I mean really good," I said.

We pulled up some sheets, got underneath, and Jorrie wanted to talk while we lay in each other's arms.

"I do want to hear it, Sam, but thank you for not saying it. I don't know how to respond yet. This night. This encounter of lovemaking goes easily to my top ten list, and that spans multiple lives. I feel overwhelmed, fulfilled, and hungry for more which makes me feel reckless and out of control," Jorrie said.

"And being out of control invites danger. I get it. It's like being out on a limb. It's frightening, it's exciting, and you feel like you're this close to flying," I said as I made a size with my fingers.

"I do feel comfortable and familiar with you, Sam," Jorrie said, rolling sideways and looking into my eyes.

"I feel it too," I said, wanting to add more, but that would drift into future memory love as I kissed her.

Eventually, we ended up with me on my back again and her head on my chest. We must have drifted off to sleep because the next thing I remember was waking up to the sound of someone in the shower, with me alone in my bed. I saw her underclothes lying on the bed, so I assumed that it was Jorrie in the shower. The water stopped, and she emerged from the bathroom with her hair wrapped up in a towel and a towel wrapped around her body. There was something domestic about the whole scene, making me feel like I was home again. She smiled at me and said, "Good morning," as she gathered her underclothes from the bed.

"Good morning, baby," I said, feeling like if you have the right to call a woman, baby, it would certainly be the morning after.

"I have to get going, Sam. I have a shift in operations, and I'm busy the rest of the day," Jorrie said.

"Oh, okay. Do you want to get together later this week?" I asked while I put on yesterday's clothes.

She dropped the towel after putting on her underwear and leaned forward, offering a nice view of her breasts. She unwrapped her hair from the towel and slipped on her sports bra before flipping her long hair out as she said, "Sounds good."

She walked over to where she disrobed last night and pulled the dress back on. I stepped up behind her and buttoned her back up before she turned around to give me a short kiss. She put on her shoes and headed out of the bedroom. She was in search mode, then said, "Ah, there it is," and picked up her small blue clutch that went with her dress.

She walked over to me and slung the purse over her shoulder. It hung there for a moment, and the strap broke, sending it to the floor spilling its contents. I stooped down and gathered up the few items that spilled out, including the passage card, but then an alert went off in my invisihud. One of the items falling out of Jorrie's purse was a recording device.

I stood up slowly, handing the purse back to her, and she knew the jig was up, that I must have recognized the device. I said, "That's an Opturi empathic recording device."

"It is," she said with a serious look while reclaiming the purse and its contents.

It was so hard for me to believe at first, but once I said it, I knew it was true, "I was your mission, wasn't I?"

"Sam," Jorrie said as she read the emotional breakdown that must have flooded over my face.

And it was a breakdown. I felt myself fall apart inside. Everything I worked for, looking for, was lost or was never there, to begin with. I felt used, empty, and stupid all at the same time. I just wandered around and plopped down on the white leather sofa staring off into space.

"Sam," she said again.

"Oh, I'm okay. You got what you came for, I hope. It's my fault. I forgot that you are way smarter than I am," I said.

"Don't do this, Sam," Jorrie said.

"Do what? Feel stupid, feel used, I feel messed up inside, Jorrie. I think I need to be alone to figure this out. Thank you for coming to my party," I said as I put my head in my hands.

I felt her staring at me for a few moments, then she turned around and walked away with a slight slam on the door.

Maybe I should have handled that differently, but I was messed up inside. I have not felt like this in I don't know how long. I thought about everything I told her, how personal it was, and how gullible I was to reveal how all my technology worked. Now that information would go to Starnet. All the spies that have their claws in Starnet would have more data on me and my processes.

I must have sat there for an hour or more, trying not to think. I was out of ideas. The plans I set in motion were built on the foundation that Erin and Jorrie were not going to betray me. I did feel foolish. I was a fool to think I could recreate a massive timeline in my favor. Or maybe I was just arrogant. That is a quality of a Lord of Splendor. Part of me wanted to rage against echo to destroy something. I wanted to prove I was still alive, possessing some kind of power. Part of me wanted to hide away and dissolve with the rain. But the strongest feeling that arose was defensive. I felt like I needed to harden myself for the tougher times ahead.

I got up from the couch and looked through the glass doors leading out to the balcony. The sky was grey today, and a light rain fell. Despite this, sea birds landed on the balcony pecking away at the food leftovers from last night's party. I thought it odd to see them this high up, but maybe generations of sea birds have adapted to explore buildings as a possible source of food?

A knock at the door and I heard it open, "It's me, Candy. I hope you're decent?"

"In here," I said, turning around to face her. I was not in the mood for company.

"So, how did it go?" Candy asked merrily as she walked in from the entrance hall, and then she read my face. "Holy shit. What happened?"

"She was a spy, Candy," I said.

"What do you mean a spy? Jorrie?" Candy asked, concerned.

"I was her mission. Starnet sent her here to gain intel on me, us," I said, "I told her everything."

"Oh, I did too. I told her a lot of stuff," Candy said, feeling a bit tricked.

"I told her about my future memories, how my technology works," I went on.

"What do we do?" Candy asked.

"The best thing to do is to prepare for an attack. It could be my family members are manipulating this echo as a way of seeking information. From this point on, all things are secret," I said.

"Ohm, please add any attempted tampering with or blocking of cloaked scanner signals to my weekly reports. This new rule applies to all scanners in all echoes," I said.

"Making reporting adjustments," Ohm replied.

"You mean Jorrie might not have wanted to spy?" Candy asked.

"I'm sure she was under orders, and orders are one of the easiest things a Splendorite can manipulate within an echo," I said.

"Can we cancel those orders?" Candy asked.

"More like, can we cancel the report? I'd feel a lot better if that report were simply blank or non-existent," I said.

"Can you fix that with echo?" Candy asked.

I got stuck on that one. I guess it would be possible, but then I would be shifting this target reality even further from its original source. "What would be best, would be if Jorrie's commander, Warren Turner, were convinced that releasing the report would be a bad idea," I said.

Candy looked up at me and said with confidence, "I'm on it. I'll get Alex and Lucas to help too."

Candy left the apartment, and her visit did break the absolute betrayal mood I built up. There was nothing left to do but move on. Part of me wanted to just wander off into the wilderness and immerse myself in some training regiment. Another part wanted me to stay near tech. I didn't want to give up on this echo, not yet. In my future memories from the first loop, I also experienced heartbreak when Robin and I separated. Maybe, in some way, this heartbreak was just time's way of balancing some master equation? What I did in the first loop was to stow away aboard a starship and become part of the maintenance crew. I worked during the day and spent my off-hours with aurastage training programs.

"Ohm, how many Starnet vessels have cloaked scanners upon them?" I asked.

"There are eleven Starnet vessels with cloaked scanners onboard," Ohm replied.

"Send the list to my invisihud, please," I said.

A list of starships was displayed by my invisihud, and there were quite a few varieties. Science ships, medical vessels, battleships, and even the flagship appeared on the list.

"Ohm, can you scan the flagship crew? I need the same clothes that the ship's maintenance crew wear but with my extra pockets?" I asked.

A set of overalls appeared draped over the white leather sofa. I picked them up and headed back into the bedroom, then into the bathroom to take a shower. The bathroom was a bit of a mess as I would often find the shower area when I lived with Jorrie in the future. She also left behind her hair broach, which I moved into the medicine cabinet to put reminders of her out of sight. I showered and put on the ugly maintenance jumpsuit, transferring my vignettes and wand to my new pockets. I looked at myself in the mirror. My hair was too long to be considered within Starnet regulations, so I requested a virtual barber from *Tiger Mountain* to adjust my hairstyle to a more military cut. I located the cloaked scanner on the Starship *Explorer SSH-801*. This ship shared the same name as Jason Bowmen's ship and was a direct evolution of the *EX-01* spanning a couple of hundred years.

The cloaked scanner aboard the *Explorer SSH-801* completely mapped out the entire ship. I targeted the starboard nacelle, and the scanner started moving toward its goal. In every starship nacelle, even dating back to the *EX-01*, there was a small room at the farthest end of the nacelle. This space was called the "shed" or "shed view." There is typically a portal so a person can optically view what is happening directly behind the ship. Cameras and other sensors eventually replaced this manned station but the concept of the room remained within ship design specs because it offered a shielded area for a crewman to retreat to if some type of radiation or atmospheric leak were to occur within the nacelle.

The cloaked scanner reached the nacelle location I targeted, and there appeared to be no other crewmen in the nacelle at that time. I set my shield to mask life signs and said, "Ohm, transport me to the nacelle aboard the *Explorer SSH-801.*"

The room collapsed in from the sides, and darkness was my companion once again. I didn't blame Jorrie for doing her duty. It was just that I hoped for an outcome that was better than this. I still felt messed up inside. I put off the realization of what this heartbreak actually means to any future plans I may have had in favor of remaining busy in the moment. Light filtered in from the sides, and the sound of the nacelle in operation filled the room. My guess is we were traveling at flux speed.

CHAPTER 35

The Shed

I walked to the very end of the nacelle and noticed the door to the shed was not an automated one. It was an old-style hatch door, similar to what you might find on the *EX-01*. I opened the hatch and looked inside. This room was barely a storage closet. There were a few tools here and some parts in boxes on shelves. I stepped back about ten meters and brought up the environment designer to target the existing walls and door around the window portal, marking it for transplacement. I blocked out an area about eight meters deep and the width of the existing shed before choosing a compact quarters preset from the invisihud. Once everything was blocked out, I asked, "Ohm, can you relocate the existing shed to become the entry door to the compact quarters?"

"Adjusting design to accommodate the request," Ohm replied.

I activated the transplacement, and the existing shed moved forward while my new compact quarters were placed behind the back wall of the newly transplaced shed. I walked up to the new door and rotated the wheel-like handle to unseal the shed. Pushing on the back wall, it swung open into my new set of quarters. It was cramped but overall bigger than living in a shuttlecraft. I pulled the shed door closed and locked it by turning the wheel. I closed the secret back wall door with myself in the snug quarters. Walking to the very back of the room, I looked out the glass portal revealing streaks of stars trailing behind.

For the first few days on board, I moved around cloaked, getting the feel of the ship and the overall pace the crewmen took as they performed different tasks. I listened for any commands they used and observed how to operate some of the basic self-service technologies any crewman would be expected to know. I modified the port nacelle to have the extended compact quarters, so both nacelles looked the same if anyone bothered to investigate. On the fourth day, I fully integrated myself into the narrative of this crew by shifting echo. I was Sam Richards, assigned seven months ago. This echo shift means I altered the log and slightly the personalities of the members of the crew that I was expecting to work around. They were familiar with me being their crewmate, but no one was really my best friend. They saw me as the guy that barely made the cut. I showed up to work on time and did my job. A lot of the work was manual labor, such as cleaning and making inspections to determine if a part replacement was needed on key systems. Because I was assigned to this ship, I was also assigned quarters. Most of the time I slept in the compact living area behind the shed. I gained a better understanding of engine operations and asked lots of questions about how things worked, reinforcing the narrative I was still learning on the job, which was the case.

A few days into the first week on board, I received a visit from Candy, Alex, and Lucas in my compact quarters. They told me they visited Warren Turner on *Oasis Seven*, and he agreed to only report a portion of the log acquired by Jorrie under the premise that the recording device was damaged when it fell from Jorrie's purse. They told me the only way to convince him was to reveal the fact that there was a Flexanite invasion in progress. Warren considered that knowledge very important and disturbing. I appreciated their effort and thanked them, but it didn't change my adopted isolationist approach to dealing with this heartbreak. I just wanted to move on.

On week two, I received a report that the new larger cloaked attack ship design and the cloaked inspector were ready for service. I set a replication schedule and started deploying them in the Ussu sector.

At the end of week three, I got very emotional and wanted to reach out to Jorrie. I asked Ohm to package up the hair broach she left behind, and I sent a small card reading, "I'm sorry," on one side and "I miss you" on the other. Ohm mailed it to *Oasis Seven* through traditional space postal systems.

I spent my off-hours in the ship's aurastage as much as possible. I arranged my schedule, so I worked the late shift, which threw me out of sync with important crew members, like the Captain and the First Officer. I ran through most of the Starnet virtual reality training scenarios, which counted as official training credit on my made-up Starnet record. I also tried out many pure fantasy combat scenarios where you face creatures of different sizes using different styles of weapons. I also practiced horseback riding, fencing, then moved on to sword combat while mounted.

I was on board for almost three months, and life became fairly routine. I even made a few friends, and perhaps I became too cavalier in my appearances in the hallways. I tried to fit in another round of recently released official Starnet training. I traded shifts with Linus, who worked on the other shift, so his aurastage time was off my schedule. As I rounded the corner, I nearly bumped into Captain La Salle.

"Sorry, sir," I said, then proceeded to try to move away from the situation.

"Crewman, wait," Captain La Salle said behind me.

I turned around to look at him, and he asked, seriously, "You're Sam Richards. What are you doing aboard my ship?"

"Maintenance, sir. I was assigned seven months ago," I said, trying to wiggle out of this conversation.

"I think I would know if an entity were assigned to my ship. Follow me," he said, then looking back, "come on."

We entered a magnalift, and he said, "Deck five," starting the magnalift moving.

"How long have you been aboard my ship?" he asked, looking over at me.

"Almost three months, now, sir," I replied.

"Have you placed any devices or modified my ship in any way?" he asked.

"No devices, sir. I have modified the 'shed' in both nacelles. I expanded the area to contain secret quarters. I have liquor and a guitar stored in the starboard one," I said.

"You think this is a game, don't you?" he asked as the door opened.

"No, sir, I was just looking for a place to be of use," I said, trailing behind him as he headed down the corridor to a door.

I followed him inside what looked like an empty meeting room. There was a view of the stars, a large conference table, and some embedded view screens in the walls. Captain La Salle turned around and forcefully said, "My ship, my crew are not your playthings."

"Very well. I'll get my things and go," I said.

"Why would you choose to work on the maintenance shift of this ship?" Captain La Salle asked.

"It would sound stupid if I told you," I said.

"Oh, too stupid for me to understand, well, I guess I'll have to let that go then," He said sarcastically.

"I didn't mean that you are too stupid. I mean, I feel embarrassed about the reason," I clarified.

"Well, what could embarrass you so much that you would stoop to serving on the maintenance crew aboard my starship? I really am curious?" Captain La Salle asked with folded arms.

"A broken heart. There I said it. A woman broke my heart, and I am trying to forget about her by keeping busy doing maintenance, which I don't find too menial to do," I said.

"A broken heart, eh? Well, that is a serious condition," Captain La Salle said before raising his voice, "That does not give you the right to pose as an impostor aboard my ship modifying systems!" Then, as if not fully done reprimanding me, he asked, "And why this ship, why my ship?"

"Because this ship was my home, sir," I said, adding the sir hoping it might curry some sympathy from the agitated fellow.

"What do you mean was? You have never been aboard as far as I know," Captain La Salle said.

"In the future, it was my home. I have future memories of living aboard this ship with my wife. She was a commissioned officer assigned to *Explorer*," I said.

"Future memories? What officer?" Captain La Salle asked.

"It does not matter anymore because the future is unfolding differently this time around," I said.

"Are you saying that you are a time traveler?" Captain La Salle asked.

"Not in the Newtonian sense. I awoke with memories from the future, multiple futures. So, my body is not displaced in time, but I still remember things that will or can happen. But to me, they have already happened," I said, adding to the confusion.

"If you have memories of what is going to happen, why would you choose the woman who broke your heart?" Captain La Salle asked.

"In my memories of the other two timelines, she didn't do that. While this timeline started out similar to what I remembered, it has deviated, and I can't predict or know what the right thing is to do anymore. To pass the time, I have been fixing your ship and drinking myself to sleep," I said.

"If you don't know what the right thing is to do, I don't want you altering my systems. Is that clear?" Captain La Salle asked.

"Yes, sir, crystal. I will no longer alter systems," I said.

A message came over his communications brooch, "Approaching the Hacher Cluster."

He tapped the brooch pinned to his chest, then said, "Drop out of flux. I'm on my way."

He turned to me and said, "We're not finished. Consider yourself relieved of duty until further notice."

"Understood," I said, then added, "Captain," as he headed for the door.

"What is it now?" he asked fully annoyed.

"In my future memories, the Hacher Cluster was known for harboring Zitali attack ships. They strafe ships with attack runs designed to make you think you are in a combat situation, but in reality, they are transporting goods and crewmen from your ship to be sold at Zitali slave markets. Their attack is designed to disable your engines so you can't pursue them to regain your cargo," I said.

Captain La Salle paused for a moment to consider my information, then headed out the door, leaving me behind in an empty room.

"Ohm, can you transport nine cloaked scanners outside of this ship? Have them track the movement of *Explorer SSH-801*," I asked.

A few moments later, Ohm replied, "Cloaked scanners tracking along with *Explorer SSH-801*."

"Ohm, I expect there might be a three-ship Zitalis attack on this vessel. Divide the nine cloaked scanners, so there are three per ship when the attack arrives. The priority is to transplace explosive charges on the attacking ship's weapons launch tubes or energy emitters. The second priority is to disable flux engines using a graviton pulse. The final priority is to knock out the shield generators with transplaced explosives," I said.

"Waiting until ships are detected to deploy the plan," Ohm replied.

I left the meeting room and headed to my official crew quarters. There was no reason to remain hidden or secretive anymore now that the Captain knows I am on board. Waiting around for an attack that may or may not happen while being relieved of duty was a crappy way to spend your day. I changed out of my Starnet impostor uniform and into something more comfortable from my wardrobe. I asked Ohm to locate some Scottish ale from Jim's echo, and I sat there drinking and watching the wall.

I was well into my third pint when the code one sounded. The ship took damage, but it seemed like the shields held. I reviewed the output from the cloaked scanners in my invisihud to survey the scene. It was three vessels, two large ones, and a smaller cargo-style vessel. The ships took up attack formations and made a second strafing pass, one after another, at the *Explorer SSH-801*. When they fired their weapons, each attack ship suffered damage to itself as their weapons detonated the charges that Ohm deposited on their ship's surface. There was a series of secondary explosions on the Zitali based ships as their shield generators failed. Once the shields were down, I said, "Ohm, scan the cargo holds of the attacking ships. Transport any nonZitalis people from those cargo holds to cargo bay three of this vessel. Transport any remaining cargo items to the Eden-based prison world where I have placed the Flexanites."

"Transporting thirty-seven life forms from the Zitali ships to cargo bay three," Ohm said.

I left my quarters and rushed down to cargo bay three. There were other crewmen in a hurry, as we were still under the code one alert. I opened the double bay doors to the cargo area and stepped inside. There was a group of frightened aliens here, both young and old. Some took immediate cover behind the cargo boxes stored here.

"Ohm, can I get Starnet asylum request papers for thirty-seven people?"

There was a sparkle at my feet as a small stack of postcard-sized papers appeared on the floor. I picked them up and reached into echo to pull in the *Motif*. I used the *Motif* to lock in on their languages to speak to them in their native tongue.

"If you want to be released from slavery, please step forward and take one of these cards," I said, waving them high above my head. "These are asylum request forms that can grant you immunity from being considered Zitali cargo."

A fellow stepped forward. I guessed he was Opturi. He took the form and asked, "What do we do next?"

I continued through the group of broken-spirited aliens dressed in torn clothing and covered in dirt. I guess they were captured when their ships were heavily damaged or destroyed. I handed out all but two of the postcards.

One of the Pampu asked, "I thought Starnet was not getting involved in Zitali affairs? Why the sudden change of policy?"

"The policy is the same, which states that the Zitalis have no claim on asylum seekers located on Union soil. This ship and all aboard are considered Union soil," I said as I wandered the cargo bay looking for the two missing aliens.

I found them huddled in a corner, two Amphibian children. One was older than the other, but if I estimated their age in human terms, by their sizes, I would say the older one was six or seven, and the younger one was three or four. They were both having a hard time breathing.

"Ohm, can you replicate breathing devices for these two Amphibian children? Scan them and match the fit to their size," I said.

A moment later, a couple of small sparkles came and went, leaving two breathing apparatus on the floor. The Amphibians were water breathers by nature but could survive in a non-fluid environment. The Flexanite Amphibian that we discovered in the restaurant used such a device. Only at that device was part of the imitation of the form the Flexanite emulated at that time. I helped attach and activate the device on the older one, and a mist sprayed out, offering some respiratory relief. The smaller one just lay there a bit listless. I helped put the breathing apparatus on the small Amphibian and picked her up. At least I thought she was a girl because of the dress she wore. I tucked one of the cards into her hand and gave the last card to the older Amphibian before asking, "Is she your sister?"

"No, she traveled on the transport with my family when the Zitali attacked," the older Amphibian said.

While I tended to the Amphibian needs, I heard the cargo bay doors open and a few voices. When I stepped out from the hidden area with the smaller Amphibian in my arms, I noticed the large group of aliens encroaching upon a smaller group of Starnet officers and one large orange Zitali who stood at the door. Everyone talked at once, showing their cards and saying the word, "Asylum."

The Zitali grew impatient and said to Captain La Salle, "I demand you return our cargo at once."

The Captain said, "I see no cargo here, only people seeking asylum."

"It is against the agreements between the Zitalis and the Union to transport cargo from our ships," he said angrily.

One of the other officers, Commander Perry, said, "You have some nerve after attacking our ship to cite regulations."

"Calm down, Commander," Captain La Salle said.

I spoke up and to the Zitali, as I made my way through the crowd of aliens to face him, still holding the child Amphibian, "It was not the Union who transported your cargo. It was me. I am not a member of the Union, so that agreement does not apply."

"What kind of trick is this?" the Zitali asked, looking over at the Captain.

"It's true. I only recently discovered him aboard my ship posing as an impostor among my crew," Captain La Salle said, realizing he now had a legal ground to stand upon.

The child, in my arms, began to stir, and I asked in the Amphibian language, "What's your name, Little one?"

The child looked fearful at me and said, "I want my mommy."

I relayed the message to the Zitali, "She says she wants her mommy. Do you happen to know where her mommy would be?"

The Zitali's patience expired, and he reached out with his massive hands and found my neck. There was an immediate reaction by the *Explorer SSH-801* crew. My automatic shielding kicked in, but I still felt his massive grip tighten around and start to close off my breathing. The gleam gun fire from one of the security guards brought the Zitali down, although he was groggy. I used my free hand to check my neck for damage. Targeting the Zitali with my invisihud, I deployed a delayed poison dose. He would be dead in twenty-four hours.

The voice of the crowd rose again as everyone started talking at once, saying, "We want asylum. How can I get asylum?" as well as other variations of that same phrase.

The Captain raised his voice and said, "You will all be processed, but first, you must accompany my personnel to sickbay for evaluation. From there, you will be issued quarters."

Commander Perry said, "If you'll follow me, this way," gesturing with his arms into the corridor.

I walked with the crowd, and when I passed by Captain La Salle, he said, "Sam, please report to me once you have delivered the Amphibian to sickbay."

"Aye, sir," I said and headed into the corridor with the group.

From behind me, I heard the Captain say to his security officers, "Get this man off of my ship," indicating the Zitali.

We formed a line waiting for magnalifts to take us to the deck where sickbay was located. When it was our turn, I entered the magnalift, still holding the Amphibian and the older one at my side, along with a couple of other alien adults. One of the Opturi males said, "Thank you for helping us. Are you alright?"

"Yeah, those guards acted quickly. You're welcome. No one should be stolen or sold into slavery," I said.

The magnalift doors opened, and it was a short walk down the circular corridor to the doors of sickbay. When we entered, several nurses came up to us and guided us to sickbay evaluation stations where biobeds measured vital signs. I stepped away from the biobed and let the nurses do their thing. They brought out some juice and snack food for the Amphibians. My attention was drawn to the central evaluation area where more serious conditions were dealt with. There was a Davlonian female on the table being treated for several cuts and burns. The doctor administering the treatment was Madeline Enzo. She was a tall, fair-skinned woman with her long red hair pulled back. I met her before when I searched for a cure for Alex and Lucas. She looked up and caught my eye for a second, then returned her focus to her work.

I left the sickbay, heading to the magnalift, asking, "Ohm, where is Captain La Salle?"

"Captain La Salle is in his ready room, off the main bridge," Ohm replied.

I stepped into the magnalift and said, "Bridge."

While I waited, I thought about the fact that here I am at the center of another Starnet calamity. The magnalift finally came to a halt, and the doors slid open, revealing the bridge. It was incredibly modern looking. There were sloping polished panels. Some of them were made of wood and others of chrome. A few were made of shiny white plastic. The bridge was manned, and several people attended the stations. The Warnock security officer glanced over, and I decided I'd better get a move on. The Captain's ready room was down a short slope and to the left. When I walked by, I looked over to my right, and there sat my old academy roommate, Unimate, at the helm. I gave a side wave to him as I passed by, and he waved back, wondering why I was on board. I pressed the doorbell on the ready room, and I heard a muted, "Enter," and the doors opened. I was relieved to see that he was alone. I did not really want to talk to anymore Zitalis today.

He pointed to the chair and said, "Come in, sit down," adding, "What am I going to do with you, Sam?"

"Don't worry. I'm leaving. I just couldn't leave my ship when it was under attack," I said.

"I see. I looked over the logs, and I'm quite puzzled that all three Zitali ships suffered damage without *Explorer* firing a single shot. How do you explain that?" Captain La Salle asked me before turning a playing log around so I could see it.

I watched the segment that he cued up to loop, and I said, "My guess is those slave-driving Zitali privateers did not keep up on their maintenance. Once they fired upon us, it caused an overload that rippled along their power pathways, shutting down multiple systems."

"Quite convenient, for us, I mean," Captain La Salle replied.

"I watched the battle using my own sensor device," I said, adding, "Ohm, display the virtual log of the incident that Captain La Salle's log is referencing."

There was a sparkle, and an orange auragraphic sphere appeared over the Captain's desk and started looping through the same playback range. I touched the log and moved it around while demonstrating the zooming-in gesture. He was briefly interested in it, viewing the looping log from different angles as I said, "With all the system failures taking place aboard the Zitali vessels, I was concerned about the safety of the living cargo that they carried. I transported them aboard and knew that once they were here they could legally ask for asylum."

"But how they got here goes against an agreement that Starnet has with the Zitalis that prevents transportation," La Salle tried to explain to me.

"That's your agreement, not mine. You have classified me as an entity. I'll take the fall for it. Send any complaints that the Zitalis may have with this incident to my processing department in San Francisco," I said.

"Damn it, Sam! This is not a game," La Salle said.

"No, it's not a game. It's a sham. It's the same sham that the Union took while Bragoria raped Vasco. This 'don't ask and don't tell' agreement you have with the Zitalis is just a way to help yourselves sleep better at night because you know in every unscanned cargo hold there are people who have been brutally ripped from their lives and sold into slavery at auction," I said.

"Without that agreement, this sector could destabilize, resulting in war," Captain La Salle emphasized.

"Then I give you my probability traveler's promise that it is highly improbable that this incident will amount to any action by the Zitalis. The ships that attacked you are bottom feeders. Nobody likes them, and nobody cares what happens to them. My advice is to file your reports, as usual, and let it go."

"I don't like situations or solutions being forced upon me," Captain La Salle said.

"No one does. That's what this is all about. Do you think any of those people in sickbay wanted their situation forced upon them?" I replied.

"I want you off my ship, now," Captain La Salle said.

"Ohm, discontinue log display and transport me to Zenith, in the Gar sector," I said.

The lights of Captain La Salle's office fizzled and slid in from the side while I returned to take up my post in the darkness of nowhere. I guess I outgrew my welcome on that ship. In my future memories, *Explorer SSH-801* was my home with Erin. Walking those halls, knowing at the end of the day there was no one to return to made the place seem hollow. I guess that is why I spent so much time hanging out in the shed. The world reassembled around me, and I found myself at the center of the town on Zenith, where the kiosk stood.

CHAPTER 36

The Reset

It was nighttime, but the glow from the distant nebula softly lit up the sky. The place looked like a wreck. I did not get a good feeling about this. Spray-painted graffiti tagged the kiosk, and there were many smashed windows in the nearby apartments. Trash littered the street, and I noticed a few rats scurrying about. As I looked around, a few of the new buildings reminded me of project slums. I noticed some new colonial-style government buildings off to the North. I felt a little drunk and tired, so I asked the kiosk to provide a portable sleeping unit. The terraforming module responded to my commands, and the floor rolled back while a reconfiguration took place, providing a large, coffin-style bed with a glass lid. I climbed in and closed the lid. With the blankets pulled up, I tried to go to sleep.

The sound of someone tapping on the glass woke me in my coffin bed. I looked up yawning and saw two soldiers, one tapping the but of his automatic rifle against the glass. They wore full combat armor and motioned to me to get out. I waved and raised my index finger, indicating, "give me one moment," and they stepped back to wait for the coffin to open. I targeted them with my invisi-hud and located the sleep icon while fumbling with the internal controls to open the glass coffin.

The lid slid back, and one of the two soldiers said, "All right buddy, get out. You know the rules. No unauthorized replication without a permit. We're going to have to take you in for processing."

"Since when do I need a permit to replicate something? I thought replication was available for all to use?" I asked while climbing out of the coffin.

They immediately roughed me up, pushing me against the coffin and forcing me to lean over it while they searched me for weapons.

"That right was revoked after the replication riots. You know that," the other guard said while turning me around.

"Holy shit, it's him, the one," the other soldier said.

"Who?" his partner asked.

"The guy who brought us to this planet," the soldier said.

"I don't know. I thought he was taller," his partner replied.

"It is me, and I demand you unhand me," I said, shaking myself a little free from their manhandling.

"It doesn't matter. You'll have to explain yourself to the commander. Come with us," the soldier said.

I activated the sleep icon inside my invisihud, and the two soldiers collapsed. I grabbed them both to let them down gently before taking their rifles and handguns on their belts. Placing the weapons into the glass coffin, I said, "Kiosk, recycle glass coffin and weapons."

Sparkles appeared, and the glass coffin folded back into the floor, taking the weapons with it. I headed for a newly constructed street containing a marketplace. There were multiple shabby canopy stalls where people cooked food. At first, all I noticed were Imperial humans, then I saw a group of Melogs here or there, occasionally a group of people with a single Sandra or Kara revision mixed in. It wasn't hard to miss the soldiers patrolling this market area. I saw a few of them stop and talk to the stall owners to obtain some food.

I activated my personal shield and anti-gravity boots to rise into the air. I heard a few people gasp then talk until I was high enough that I was out of earshot of their voices. The replication looked very lopsided to me. There were large government-style buildings, and all around them were slums. I spun around to get a better view and saw a few terraformed offshoot areas. I wondered if the Melogs took my hint of terraforming fast by all agreeing on a single goal? It certainly looked like the humans fell back into recreating their broken society of old. The mention of replication riots was quite disturbing. How could people treat each other so poorly when resources were so abundant?

The good news was that it looked like it was turning out to be a wonderful morning. I located an open area and targeted the jetpack to take me there. I landed and said, "Ohm, I want you to reverse the terraforming the residents of this planet have put in place. Use transporters to remove people from the buildings before deconstructing them. Suspend all kiosk requests until each citizen passes the basic *Tiger Mountain* entry exam. Once they have successfully completed the exam, relay this location to them as a destination where they can finally become recognized to receive kiosk request privileges."

I was a good one or two kilometers away from any major constructions, but I could still hear the pandemonium of a light hum or buzz on the air. I watched portions of buildings brought down, the occasional glint of light as the sun reflected off the folding collapsing panels that previously made up the units. A few vehicles headed quickly away in multiple directions, some of them sparkled and were recovered by the terraforming unit, but other vehicles brought down from the ships continued fleeing the scene. I relocated the kiosk here, this time in the form of a fountain. My first request for the kiosk was to create a small park around the fountain. After that, I requested a folding table with some basic breakfast food, similar to what I provided the last time I was on this planet, when I revealed the technology to the Imperials and the Melogs for the first time. I ate my breakfast and drank coffee while waiting for the reeducated citizens to arrive.

"Ohm, can you replicate a Starnet shuttlecraft? Place it in that field over there," I said as I targeted an open grassy area. It took over twenty minutes before a large sparkle appeared in the grassy area, and when the sparkle faded, a class one shuttle was here on location.

The deconstruction took several hours to finally complete. The large buildings came down rather quickly, but all the other small detailed terraforming took the most time to reverse and remove. I knew it was selfish to judge these people undeserving of the technology I provided, but this was a total train wreck compared to what I envisioned. I guess this is the arrogance of the Splendorite in full form. I wanted things to be my way. I'm sure I'd get an earful from the supposed leaders and privileged citizens about how I had no right to disrupt their way of life, but I didn't care. I was tired of being accosted by soldiers who told me I could not sleep in my very own replicated coffin bed.

I waited for hours, and no one showed up. I took that time to inspect the shuttlecraft and verified that all systems seemed to be functioning. I smoked a joint and played the guitar for a while. Living in the shed aboard *Explorer SSH-801* gave me a renewed appreciation for the guitar. I played a classical guitar, not because I did not like the sound of an electric or acoustic, but mainly because I didn't use a pick. The guitar was an instrument for smaller spaces, not like the drums. I played through all the songs I could remember. When Teela imprisoned me inside a Cryovirt on *Tiger Mountain*, I spent a lot of time playing the guitar, and playing the guitar now brought back a mixed set of emotions. This association was the main reason I think I set the guitar aside for such a long time. While I enjoyed playing it, the songs I played reminded me of a past that I didn't want to revisit. I tried my best to discover some new tunes and even checked out a few instructional virtual tutorials while I waited.

I thought people would be so pissed that their world collapsed they would plow through the *Tiger Mountain* entrance examination and head straight here to reacquire their kiosk privileges. I waited at the location a few more hours, anticipating a wave of gleeful, responsible citizens to descend upon the park I set up as the receiving station for new users. But here I faced sundown, and still, no one showed up. Finally, along the crest of the hill, a single person appeared and descended the path leading to the speaking fountain at the center of the park. She was young, maybe nineteen or twenty, a beautiful woman with Asian features and long flowing dark hair. I recognized her immediately as one of the Melog revision nines.

"Is this the right place?" she asked.

"Yes. You're the first to arrive, congratulations," I said. "What is your name?"

"My name is Sandra Gallo," she replied.

"But isn't that the name of your revision?" I asked.

"We all have the same name," she replied.

"Don't you have a name just for yourself?" I asked.

"Not really. We're all the same," she said.

"If you were all the same, shouldn't all of you have arrived here at this location at the same time?" I asked.

"I see your point," she said.

"Do you have a middle name, Sandra?" I asked.

"I do," she said as she smiled, "Erin. Sandra Erin Gallo."

"Well, Erin," I said, playfully stressing her middle name. "As the first Melog to complete the *Tiger Mountain* entry exam, I think you have earned the right to claim your middle name as your own. Step up to the speaking fountain and state your name."

She approached the fountain, and a slightly synthetic voice said, "State your name, please."

"Erin Gallo," she replied.

"Welcome, Erin. You now have full voice rights for terraforming and replication operations," the voice said.

"Thank you," Erin replied, walking over to me and asking. "What do I do now?"

"Wow, that is the same question I ask myself all the time," I said which brought a smile to her wide face.

I took a more professional approach and tried again, asking, "What do you want to do?"

"I guess I need to build a shelter," Erin said.

"Everyone needs shelter," I said.

"Yeah, I guess it is a big deal to be the first one. I get to choose," Erin said.

"You get to choose until someone else decides to choose," I said.

"Yeah, and look how that turned out, eventually guns at your head with people telling you not to choose anything," Erin said as she wandered around pacing while she talked. I remember, from the future memories, her doing that a lot, especially when she was upset and feeling in a quandary.

"It seems the presence of weapons is throwing off my intended Utopian plan. My hope of people doing the right thing was foolish. I'm sorry," I said.

Even though we talked, it was my last statement that finally made me appear to Erin. She recognized me for the first time, saying, "At first, it was okay. We were all happy and making things. Not just for ourselves, for others. It lasted almost two months until the first murder occurred. It was between two Imperials, so as Melogs we were happy to steer clear, but soon after the arrest, the Admiral declared martial law, and 'kiosking' was considered a crime."

"What would you be doing right now if I had not returned and interrupted your day?" I asked.

"I guess I would be working on sending a message to *Journey*. During our brief encounter, I collaborated with the Cyberton woman in their astrophysics lab. I thought I could offer some of the Melog star charts to extend their maps. They're heading in a direction that we already explored. But sending a surface signal through this nebula cloud that we live in is proving more difficult than I thought," Erin said.

"I do have a shuttlecraft," I said, gesturing to the one sitting in the field. "We could transmit from outside the nebula."

"Transmit what?" she said defensively, "Your reformation of our society has taken all of my lab notes. I don't have my device anymore?"

"Kiosk, display an auragraphic map of the previous city layout," I said, and a glowing orange sphere hovered between us, providing an aerial view of the city.

"Wow, that's cool," Erin said.

"You can move and rotate it by grabbing and zooming in using gestures," I told her as I demonstrated the zoom gesture. "Can you locate, on the map, where your lab notes were yesterday?" I asked.

Erin played around with the map and zoomed in before saying, "Here, in this building, was my lab."

I moved the map to double tap on her target, and the map expanded, surrounding us with an auragraphic version of the lab where Erin worked. Erin said, "Holly molly, this is my lab," she exclaimed as she walked around the virtual room while still standing in the park.

"If you can locate your notes, we can extract them from the previous construction and replicate a physical copy," I said.

She looked over and asked, "You can do that?"

I shook my head, yes, as she turned and walked through the virtual representation of her previous lab. It was not a large room. She located a tablet on a table and said, "This is it. My notes are on this tablet."

"Ask the kiosk to target the tablet and replicate a copy," I said.

She returned to the fountain where she spoke to the kiosk and said, "Kiosk, locate the tablet on the desk in the virtual map and replicate a physical version."

A small sparkle appeared at her feet, and she bent down to pick up the tablet. She tapped it a few times and swiped around on it before looking over at me with a smile and saying, "I think it's all in there. We could send the data if we were out in space."

"Kiosk, modify greeting to mention the recovery of items from previous constructions is possible. Also, create multiple kiosk to process newcomers if lines start to form," I said.

"Modifications in place," the synthetic voice said.

"What do you think? Do you want to go for a ride?" I asked.

"Yeah," she said with a smile, and we headed over to the shuttlecraft.

I pressed the outer release button, and the side door dropped back, then slid into the hull, allowing us to enter near the front of the craft. I took the seat upfront on the left. Once Erin was inside the shuttlecraft, I said, "Computer, seal the door and prepare for launch."

Erin looked around at the interior gear and asked, "This is Starnet tech, isn't it?"

"Yes, it is. This model is a nice little shuttle design. It will reach flux four, has shields, particle weapons, long-distance communications, two light yield missiles, and a two-person transporter," I said while offering her the seat next to me.

I brought up the flight controls and mirrored my display onto the display in front of her saying, "I have matched your display to mine, so you can see what controls I use to operate the shuttlecraft."

As I made changes to the controls, the shuttle took flight, and I guided us in a large arc around the park I constructed. Erin and I could see several people approaching, but it looked like they were kids. "That should be interesting. I wonder what the kids will build before the adults get there?" I mused.

Erin caught on to this and playfully added, "Yeah, streets made of candy and ice cream cone stoplights."

"Why not?" I said as I guided the shuttlecraft to the sky as we made our way up and out of the atmosphere. I felt at ease with Erin, not all nervous as with Jorrie. I don't know if this is the exact woman I married in my future memories, but I liked this revision nine. I was not really sure how I was going to explain my future memories to her, but I felt in no rush to either.

Once we broke the atmosphere, she looked through her tablet, pulling up relevant data. On my control panel, I located one of the options to import local devices. I chose that window and sent it over to her display.

"The ship can detect and emulate devices like that tablet. I'm sending you a window that represents the tablet you are holding. It's a lot easier to drag data between systems by emulating the device," I said.

"Oh, I see it," she said and started tapping and sliding on the console in front of her. She eventually put the tablet on a shelf under the console and focused solely on the data in the emulation window.

"I'm ready. How do we transmit?" she asked.

"Well, *Journey* is out of range, even for the transmitters of this shuttle. We could set a course and wait until we are within range or use the local transmitter I set up on *Journey* the last time I was there," I said.

"What is the local transmitter?" Erin asked.

"It's like a tracker that I place somewhere. Once deployed, it can communicate, transport, or replicate from where I am to the tracker's location. I call this process transplacement," I said.

"You can communicate with *Journey* from here, across lightyears?" she asked.

"I did place a tracker on *Journey*, so, yes," I said to her. "Ohm, make the cloaked scanner aboard *Journey* available as a communication target from this shuttle."

"Ohm?" Erin asked. "The training mentioned that name."

"Ohm is my own personal kiosk. It processes verbal commands and manages transplacement requests," I said.

The connection to *Journey* appeared in the list of available communications options, and I sent the window over to Erin's console. I leaned over and pointed, "Right there, you can tap to activate it, then speak normally. Your voice will transmit to *Journey*. To transfer the data, drag it from the tablet emulation to the communications icon."

She shook her head in acknowledgment and tapped the communications icon before saying, "*Journey*, this is Erin Gallo of the Imperial Melog fleet. Is anyone receiving this message?"

We waited for a while then there was a reply. If my voice recognition skills were still intact, I would guess it was Tai Song who responded. "This is *Journey*.

We are receiving your message."

"While I was aboard your ship for a short time, I met with Lyra in astrophysics. I have some star chart data I wanted to share with her," Erin said.

There was another short delay, and Tai said, "Please stand by. Connecting you to astrophysics."

"This is Lyra. Who am I speaking with?" Lyra asked over the communications link.

"This is Erin Gallo. You may remember me as one of the Sandras. We discussed the possibilities of augmenting *Journey*'s star charts with some of the star charts the Melog's accumulated along our journey," Erin said.

"Ah, yes, I remember our conversation. How are you communicating with *Journey*?" Lyra asked.

"I am with the traveler Sam. He set up a communications link to reach you," Erin said.

"I see. You may proceed with transferring the star chart data," Lyra replied.

Erin looked over at me and tried dragging and dropping the data upon the communications link. It took her a couple of times as missed drops snapped back to their original location before she landed the data on target, causing the receiving icon to pulse. She said, "Transfer underway."

This talking back and forth was filled with short delays, so we waited for the data to transfer and Lyra to receive it. Erin looked over and said with a smile, "Thanks for doing this. It is fun and productive."

"Receiving data. Some of this fills in gaps in our star charts. Thank you for taking the time and making the effort to communicate this," Lyra replied.

"You're welcome. Signing off," Erin said.

We left the communication line open for a few minutes, but when there were no more replies, I went ahead and terminated the link and closed the console windows.

"I finally feel like I got something done. When our homes started collapsing today, I thought it was the end of the world. But now, I feel like none of that matters. I feel liberated being off that planet," Erin said.

"Does that mean you don't want to return to Zenith?" I asked.

"I guess not immediately. Can we go somewhere else, visit some other planet?" Erin asked.

"We could, but as a probability traveler, I can take you to places that this ship could never reach," I said.

"How is that possible?" Erin asked.

"It's the nature of my species to alter reality around me as I walk through it. Similar to the way water conforms and ripples around your hand when you drag it through the surface," I said.

"Can I see what it looks like?" Erin asked.

"The rippling effect can be dangerous to Melogs due to the micro machines in your blood that help regulate your conscious functions. Sometimes when I reach into echo, that's what my people call probability, I can pull forth an echo that might momentarily destabilize the concept of copper, for instance. Make it fluidic for a moment. And at that moment, the machines in your blood might fail to function, and you could become sick. There are a few Melog safe probabilities we could transport to, however, which removes the dangers of rippling through echo," I said, feeling like I was not doing a very good job of explaining it.

"Okay, let's try one. I assume it would be faster than just vectoring to a planet in this shuttlecraft," Erin said.

I sat there thinking about it for a moment. This Erin was different from the one in my future memories. In the first loop, we didn't even make it off the planet before we did it in the shuttlecraft. I didn't sense any of the hidden tension that was right up front with Jorrie. Erin seemed very young, she was beautiful, but I sensed no immediate attraction from her for me. In the first two loops, it was a tragedy that brought us closer together. In this time loop, I felt like I eliminated that, at least for now, and that seems to have cooled any romantic interest vibes from Erin.

"Hey, are you in there?" Erin asked.

"Oh, yeah, sorry, lost in thought. We should stand before we depart, or we might fall to the ground when we arrive," I said, and we walked back into the shuttle from the cockpit.

"All right, I'll explain the process. We are transporting to a probability where I have placed a target locater, similar to the one we just used for communications to *Journey*. This particular probability exists in what might be considered *Journey*'s past, so there are no aliens, and there are no spaceships. There are vehicles, aircraft, and it is on the cusp of computerization, so there is no artificial intelligence either," I said.

"Why do you go there?" Erin asked.

"I have some friends there. They grow a plant I smoke. It makes you high. Also, one of the fellows loves dogs. I think he has a few puppies this time of year. We can go pet them," I said.

She smiled and said, "All right, a mission through time and space to pet puppies, let's do it."

"The friends we are visiting are aware of other 'future' probabilities, but the general population is not. It might be best to avoid mentioning your Melog heritage, or you might have to explain it," I said.

"Got it. What's the name of this planet?" she asked.

"They call it Earth," I said.

"What? That is the planet we were looking for," Erin said.

"Ohm, can you transport Erin and me to the Meadowland Mobile Home park? Once we are there, place this ship in parked mode and transport it to *Journey*'s shuttle bay," I said.

The lights of the shuttle collapsed inward, and the last thing I saw was Erin's beautiful face before darkness replaced her. As I saw Erin's face fade, I realized I did love her or the memory of her. I loved her smile, her hair, and the way she moved. I wondered how long I could keep that a secret? The colors of a bright day zoomed in from the side, and we found ourselves under the shade of a young oak tree.

CHAPTER 37

Petting Puppies

W hoa, what the faen was that?" she said while looking all around, walking and twirling to see everything around her.

"That is how I transport from place to place. We are on Earth now," I said.

"How far did we transport?" Erin asked.

"There really isn't a measurement because we moved through probability but, scientifically, it might be around seventy thousand lightyears," I said.

"Seventy thousand lightyears, in the blink of an eye, faen," Erin said.

"Now that we are here, I can give you a small taste of the probability-changing rippling effect that won't affect your micro machines. Let's walk this way," I said, and we headed down the side of the road leading into Meadowland trailer park.

"While my friends do live here, I'm not one hundred percent sure that they are here now. It is highly probable that I can locate an echo where they are home. Also, they are all alcoholics, so showing up empty-handed, with no drink, would be considered a faux pas," I said as we walked.

"I see," Erin said as we walked along the road leading between run-down mobile homes that were there forty years or more.

"Here is an example of the probability ripple," I said, and I reached out with the *Motif* to change my clothing. I made it look less modern and fit more with the theme of this time period. My shirt changed from black to plaid, and my pants changed from black to jeans, but each garment still maintained my pockets and the items in them.

She half smiled, looking up at me, not really believing what just happened, "Wait, a second," she said, reaching out to touch my new shirt. It reminded me of the way Jorrie touched my chest.

There was plenty of garbage scattered around this place, so I shifted echo to fill one of the discarded plastic bags with liquor bottles. I jogged ahead briefly and picked it up, saying, "This is another example," as I held the bag open for her to inspect the liquor contents.

"So, you're trying to tell me that it was highly probable for you to locate a dirty bag full of booze left by the side of the road?" Erin asked, a bit skeptical.

"For my people, reality responds to what we seek, and I am not too proud to pick up a bag full of booze I found by the side of the road. Take a look, none of the bottles have even been opened. They still have their seals," I said.

"But that is just coincidence, isn't it?" Erin asked.

"I prefer to say that it is highly probable," I replied as we wandered through the trailer park.

The last time I was here, I only visited K-Mac and Byrone's place. I wasn't really sure where to find Frogs' gazebo. The park was not that large, so we continued wandering the main loop and side loops.

"Do you want me to change up your clothes? A new color, perhaps?" I asked.

Erin wore dark Melog leggings, which really showed off her fit ass, and a tight shirt with a short-cut jacket.

She didn't answer, but I reached into echo and adjusted her clothing to look more natural for this echo. I changed her pants to grey casual slacks, changed her shirt to maroon, and altered the jacket to a green corduroy while we walked. At first, she didn't notice, then she said, "What the faen?" as she glanced at the changes to her clothing.

I smelled food cooking, and when we came around the bend, there was a trailer with a gazebo next to it farther back into the lot. Ronnie was at the grill cooking with a spatula in one hand while tipping a bottle up with the other trying to keep the cigarette going, hanging from the side of his mouth.

"Hey, Ronnie. Is Frogs back there?" I asked as we approached the trailer's deck, shifting echo to add one more probable item to the dirty bag of liquor.

"Yeah, I think he is," he said, and the grill flared up, forcing him to tend to it.

"Did I hear someone say my name?" I heard from behind the gazebo door as it opened. "Sam!"

"Hey, Frogs. I want you to meet a new friend. This is Erin," I said.

"Hello, I'm Frogs," Frogs said as he looked down at her hands while he shook them.

"Nice to meet you," she said.

"I brought you something for your puppies," I said while reaching into the bag to hand him some Sani Dog wipes. "They let you give your puppies a bath while you pet them."

"Oh, these are nice. I have tried these before. Thanks, from my pups," Frogs said with a smile.

"I asked Sam if we could go somewhere, and he said he knew someone who might have puppies. We came to see them," Erin said.

"You are in luck. These puppies are at the perfect age for petting. Come on in," Frogs said, and we all crammed into his custom gazebo with walls.

Frogs put the Sani Dog wipes on the shelf, pulled down a large cardboard box from the top bunk, and placed it on the lower bunk so we could look inside. The box contained three young puppies, two brown ones and a smokey gray.

"Oh, these are so cute," Erin said as she leaned forward to look into the box while pulling her long hair back behind her ear. "Can I pick one up?"

"Sure. Move them slowly, support their bottoms, and they won't squirm too much," Frogs said.

"I try to spay and neuter all the dogs I take care of, but that can be a lot of money to cover veterinarian bills. Also, like these puppie's mother, I might find them already pregnant. Then what can you do? I couldn't just throw these little fellows away," Frogs said as we petted the dachshund pups.

"I like this grey one. He's a little feisty," I said as the little puppy gnawed on my finger.

Erin said, "I can't believe how cute these are, and this one is licking my face," holding the puppy up to her cheek for a moment.

A large dachshund jumped up on the bed, and Frogs said, "Oh, that's her mother. You can just put her puppy slowly back in the box. They're young enough that she still gets worried about them."

Erin returned the puppy to the box, and the mother dog looked at her for a moment. The mother walked over to inspect her puppies before leaning into the box and licking them.

"That is so sweet," Erin said.

"She is a good mother. I have found some dogs, mostly young ones that don't know a lot about mothering, but Roseanne here is a pretty good mother," Frogs said.

I stepped out of the gazebo, and Ronnie approached with his hand out, saying, "How are you, Sam? That was a wicked awesome party at your place."

"Yeah, I think it turned out all right," I said.

Adrien approached and said, "Hey, Sam," and we fist-bumped. "What brings you to this neck of the neighborhood?"

Erin stepped out of the gazebo, and Frogs followed. I said, "I met a new friend today. We were looking for somewhere to pet some puppies and get a drink. This lot was the first place that popped into my head."

"Hello, I'm Erin," Erin said, and she shook both of their hands.

There was an awkward silence. Did Ronnie and Adrien somehow detect she was a Melog? They didn't know what it meant, but something about her made them pause. Perhaps it was her beautiful, friendly nature?

I broke the silence when I picked up the bag of booze, and the bottles clanked. I said, "I brought booze. Do you have any ice?"

"Yeah, inside, follow me," Adrien said, and he headed up to the porch leading to his trailer.

We all walked up to the trailer, and Erin and I followed Adrien inside while Ronnie and Frogs talked about how long the meat should remain on the grill.

"Hey, I'm making margaritas. Do you guys want one?" I asked the porch crew.

"Sure," Ronnie said.

"Count me in," Frogs said.

"I have octopus rum for you, tequila, Curacao, and Roses lime for margaritas," I said, handing the rum to Adrien.

"Thanks, man. I have tried this before. It has a nice mellow spice," Adrien said.

"Do you mind if I rummage through your cupboards?" I asked Adrien while looking over my shoulder.

"Go ahead. Glasses are on the right, and there are ice trays in the freezer," Adrien said.

I found a shot glass in the cupboard with the other cups and pulled some ice trays out of the freezer. These were the plastic-type you twist, so I twisted the tray back and forth to loosen the cubes and added them to the glasses, three to a cup. I refilled the ice tray and put it back in the freezer. I could hear Erin and Adrien talking behind me as I made the drinks.

"So, how did you meet Sam?" Adrien asked.

"Actually, I just met him today. You guys know about other planets and stuff, right?" Erin asked.

"Yeah, we have been visiting Sam's future world, but I have never been to another planet," Adrien said.

I counted out the booze portions and the Roses sour mix for four drinks and used a makeshift shaker by fitting one plastic cup into another.

"Sam arrived at my planet today and changed things. I'm still discovering what that really means," Erin said.

I gave the makeshift shaker a couple of tosses over the sink, and it worked. There was a tiny bit lost to a leak but nothing to worry about. I poured out the four drinks and topped them off with the remaining ice.

"Yeah, I know what you mean. Things have smoothed out a bit for us since meeting Sam," Adrien said.

I said through the screen door, "Drinks are ready, fellows. Come and get it."

I handed one to Erin and then to Frogs and Ronnie as they came in the door. Picking one up, I said, "To Meadowland Party."

Everyone raised their cup and said, "To Meadowland Party," and we took a sip.

"Fuck, it's great to see you again, Sam," Ronnie said.

"It's nice to see you guys too," I said to them all.

"If anyone's hungry? The chicken is done," Ronnie said.

"I am starving," Erin said.

"What's the matter, Sam? Don't you feed this woman?" Adrien joked.

"That's why we came here. I know Ronnie is the grill master," I said.

We all filed outside, although Adrien stopped to get something from the refrigerator. He handed me some paper plates and napkins. Out on the deck, we each took a paper plate. Ronnie put some barbecue chicken on it. We headed down to the picnic table, carrying our paper plate and drinks, with Erin and I taking a seat on the same side, facing Frogs' gazebo. Frogs and Adrien sat on the other side. Ronnie joined us last, sitting next to me. Adrien brought out some potato salad and utensils that we passed around. I handed out the napkins. We got down to the business of eating, and Erin finally said, "This is really good, Ronnie."

"Yeah, this is good, Ronnie," Adrien said.

"No problem. I love to cook," Ronnie said.

"These drinks are nice, too, even if they are a little bit strong," Frogs said.

"I like making strong drinks so you can sip them slowly at first, then as the ice melts, you can drink them down a bit quicker," I replied.

"I think I'm going to make another one. Does anyone else want one?" Ronnie asked.

We all said no. We were still working on our first drink, but Adrien asked Ronnie, "Bring out the Octopus rum, will you?"

"I can't wait until we can get together and play again, Sam," Frogs said.

I explained to Erin, "Frogs and I did a couple of shows together, Frogs plays guitar, and I play drums."

"We have a couple of other guys in the band too, K-Mac and Byrone," Frogs added.

Adrien added, "They sounded pretty good at the party, mostly dance stuff but high energy."

"As a guitar player, I never really cared about dance music that much, but as a drummer, it is the most fun to play," I said.

"Do you play any other instruments?" Erin asked.

"I play the guitar, drums, piano, bass, and trumpet, but it has been a while since I played a horn," I said.

She smiled at me and said, "None of the people I grew up with played any instruments at all."

"Oh, that's too bad. I don't know what I had done without the guitar to help me through lonely times," Frogs said.

"That's interesting, a musical instrument relieving loneliness? If my people heard about that, I bet we all would have tried to learn one," Erin said.

Ronnie sat down and handed the Octopus rum to Adrien. His new drink was easily twice as tall as the one I poured.

"Gee, Ronnie, you got enough booze in the glass?" Adrien teased him as he poured some new rum into his empty rocks glass.

"What? I'm a big guy. I can handle more liquor than a properly other persons," Ronnie said while lighting up a cigarette, having finished eating.

"There's more up at the grill if you are still hungry, Erin," Frogs said.

"Yeah, help yourself," Ronnie said as he exhaled smoke.

"Thanks, this was the right amount. I just got to this planet, so I'm going to see how the food settles," Erin said.

"Oh, that's fuckin' right, you're an alien," Ronnie said as he looked over at her.

"That's not polite, Ronnie, calling someone an alien. She is just a person from a different place," Frogs chimed in.

"Yeah, shut the fuck up, Ronnie," Adrien said.

"I'm soory. Sometimes my thinkin' happenings don't properly word right out of my mouth. I do like you and I think you're cool, though," Ronnie said.

"Thanks, Ronnie. I try not to get offended over words too much. I like you guys too. You remind me of some of the flight crew I served with," Erin said.

"You served in the military?" Adrien asked.

"Yeah, I was a pilot. I shuttled personnel and cargo between ships," Erin said.

"You mean a spaceship pilot?" Frogs asked with interest.

"Yes. It was called a *Falcon*. It carried some attack ordinance, but my job was mainly reconnaissance and transport," Erin added.

"Fuckin' wicked. I'm sitting next to an alien space pilot. Well, I'm one seat down," Ronnie said.

I got up and cleared the plates, taking them to a large green trash can next to the grill on the porch asking, "Is it okay to put the bones in here?"

"Yeah, that's fine, Sam. Make sure the lid is on tight," Adrien said.

I returned to the picnic table and started sipping on my drink. I noticed Erin nearly finished hers. Adrien pulled out a joint and asked, "Ronnie, you got a light?"

Ronnie handed Adrien the lighter, and Adrien fired up the joint. He handed it to Frogs after taking a few puffs. Frogs passed it to Ronnie, who also double-puffed on the joint.

"What's this?" Erin asked, referring to the joint being passed around.

"If you remember, back in the shuttle, I mentioned these guys grew a plant. The buds of the plant are rolled up in that cigarette we're passing around," I said while looking at her.

"It's called weed, and it makes you high," Ronnie said while tapping me on the shoulder to pass the joint.

I took a puff, and it tasted nice. Releasing the smoke, I asked, "Do you want to try it? It is mild and goes away after about an hour, like a drink."

She smiled again at me and said, "Sure."

Erin took the joint from my hand, took a drag of the joint, and proceeded to cough, then took a slurp of the melted ice in her cup and said, "Oh wow, that is hot," as she handed the joint back to Adrien.

"I think the last time we were smokin', there were a couple of newbies," Adrien said.

"Newbies?" Erin asked.

"New to the process," I said, framing the reference for her as she shook her head in understanding.

"Yeah, I really liked the Eli fellow from the party. He was smart and friendly," Frogs said.

"Is this another flavor, Ronnie?" I asked, taking another puff, but Erin passed on the second hit.

"Glad you noticed. Yes, it is," Ronnie beamed proudly. "See, Adrien, I told you people would notice. It's a special high bird clone I have been working on."

Erin was a bit intrigued and asked, "So, you splice plants together to make this, 'weed?'"

"Yeah, the source clones are basically commercial products, but my blends produce different flavors," Ronnie explained.

Adrien added, "Ronnie's pretty good at growin' weed."

Erin put her head on the table, and while talking to the wood, she said, "I think I can feel my hair growing."

"That's completely normal," I said.

"Another phrase for the t-shirt gallery of getting high for the first time," Frogs said with a grin.

I put my arm around Erin, and she sat up, saying, "I feel so relaxed. I'm drunk, I'm high, I'm full, and I'm with friends."

"Mission accomplished, fellows," Adrien said, killing the joint and placing it in his pocket.

"You want another drink, Frogs? How bout you, Erin?" I asked, and they both said yes.

I took their cups and headed into the trailer to make a new round of margaritas. Walking into the living room, I targeted an empty spot on the floor at the end of the sofa and said, "Ohm, I'd like to set up a recurring transfast to this target. Reference the duffle bag of money I requested at my balcony party. Transport a new bag to this spot every month."

"New rule in place," Ohm replied inside my invisihud.

Heading to the kitchen, which was just a half-wall divider away from the living room, my thoughts returned to making drinks. It looked like Ronnie killed most of the bottle of tequila, but there was still enough there for three more drinks. I rinsed out the cups, located another tray of ice, and proceeded to mix up another round of margaritas.

Erin came inside the trailer and said, "Hey."

"Are you okay?" I asked.

"I am, but I feel like I'm dreaming a bit," Erin said.

"The weed will wear off soon. I do have a medical antidote if you want to come down right now," I said as she walked closer to me.

"It's not the weed, Sam. It's you," she said as she leaned in and kissed me.

I set the shaker down on the counter and put her head between my hands to kiss her again. I dropped my arms down and around her as I gave her a big hug. She held me, and we kissed again, more passionately. That's when my hands dropped to her waist. I pulled her closer to my hips so she could feel how turned on I was. She said, "Oh," with a sly smile, then kissed me again before stepping back.

"I just wanted you to know," Erin said.

"Thank you, I wondered? I like how you make things so clear to me," I said while pouring the margarita mix into the three cups and smiling back at her.

Handing her a cup, I asked, "Can you get the door?"

I took the other two cups, and we returned to the picnic table, where I gave Frogs the third drink.

"Thanks, Sam," Frogs said, and he raised the cup to me.

Erin leaned into me and said, "I just wish I could see what is happening on my planet?"

"Do you still have that tablet from Vasco?" I asked Frogs.

"I do. It's right in there. Should I get it?" Frogs asked.

"Yeah," I said to Frogs, and he got up and headed into his gazebo.

"We might be able to get an update on the display," I said, turning to Erin.

"Ohm, transfer the feed from the cloaked scanner on Zenith into Frog's tablet," I said.

"What the fuck are you saying?" Ronnie said to me.

"I'm connecting a video camera from Erin's planet to Frogs' tablet," I said.

"How? You're just talking?" Ronnie asked in wonder.

Frogs returned with the tablet, placed it on the picnic table, and slid it over to me. I tapped around and located the icon for Zenith that Ohm placed inside the tablet menu system. Once I activated it, the cloaked scanner relayed the feed from the greeting fountain. There were multiple lines of people waiting for their turn to regain their replication privileges.

I handed Erin the tablet and said, "The gesture system works a lot like the shuttle controls. You can spin the view around like this," I demonstrated.

"Whoa, it looks like a lot of people have made it by now," Erin said.

"What is that? Is that your planet?" Ronnie asked.

"Yes, it is the people on my planet," Erin said, setting the tablet down on the table so everyone could see.

"Why are they waiting in line like that?" Frogs asked.

"It's a long story," Erin said.

"There were some basic services I provided to the planet, and they weren't being shared. I reset the system this morning to remind everyone they needed to treat their neighbors better," I said.

"So, they are waiting in line to recover their services?" Adrien asked.

"More or less," I said.

"I'm not sure what good it will do. It might just turn out the same way," Erin said, wet blanketing the idea.

"Ohm, can you add the number of weapons that the kiosk reclaimed today?" I asked.

"Who the hell are you talking to?" Ronnie asked again.

"Ronnie, he's talking to his spaceship computer," Frogs said.

"What the fuck? Are you talking to a spaceship computer?" Ronnie asked me.

"Well, it's more of a space mall than a ship. It floats in space, but it is more like a miniature city," I said.

"A space station?" Frogs asked.

"Sure, it does have docking ports, but no one ever arrives by ship," I said.

"You have a space station?" Erin asked.

"Let's check the number on the kiosk there," I said, and I reached in to issue a long tap-hold on the tablet display. A rectangle popped up a details view reporting the count of reclaimed weapons.

"The kiosk will not replicate the weapons, so the weapons reclaimed are effectively removed from the society. Perhaps with fewer guns around, people will be more willing to work together," I said.

Erin picked up the tablet and scrolled through the list, saying, "I guess it's a start," then returned it to the table.

Adrien took a stab at issuing a few gesture commands on the tablet and located something odd. It looked like a small house on legs. Once he started panning around, he located a few more, and some were in motion. He asked, "What are those?"

Erin looked at the tablet and said, "I don't know what those are. They look like movable walking houses."

I thought for a moment and said, "Those kids. I bet that's what they replicated."

"And then fled the scene as more people approached, you might be right," Erin said with a smile.

"They look a lot like Baba Yaga's hut," Frogs added.

"What the fuck is Baba Yaga's hut?" Ronnie asked.

"I believe it is a Russian fairy tale about a witch who made her hut grow chicken legs to carry her around," I said.

"Thanks for bringing up that live feed. I feel better. This morning when I left, I wondered how my people would do? It looks like they might be all right after all," Erin said, handing the tablet back to Frogs.

"No problem," Frogs said as he returned the tablet to his gazebo.

"Hey, do you want to go for a walk?" Erin asked me.

"Sure, let's walk around," I replied, and we both got up from the picnic table.

"We're going to walk around. If we're not back later, take care, and we'll get together soon," I said.

"It was nice to meet all of you, and thank you, Frogs, for letting me pet your dogs and the weed. Not petting the weed, petting the dogs. Gods, I'm still high," Erin said.

"Right on. Nice to meet you too. I hope your people are all right," Ronnie said.

Frogs headed over and gave me a half hug, saying, "Think about it. We need to rock again. Nice meeting you, Erin."

We headed over to Adrien, and I said, "I left you something at the end of the sofa," while issuing a fist bump.

Adrien said, "Thanks a lot. It really helps."

Erin and I headed past Frogs' gazebo and exited via the back of the lot. There was a little path leading through the overbrush that we pushed through to reach a field with a path running through it. It wouldn't surprise me if this was used as a neighborhood bike path.

I took the path, and then after a few steps, turned around and asked, "Is this all right?"

"Yeah, I felt like I was going to pass out at the table, pounding drinks and smoking weed," Erin said with a cough.

She stepped up, faced me, and put her arms around my neck. She pressed against me and gave me a long, slow kiss.

"But I do like the flavor of it, the weed," she said while still standing close. "I like when I taste it on your lips."

I pulled her close, once again, and put my head next to hers, over her shoulder. I held on for a while, rubbing my hands up and down her back, finally finding their way to her hips, saying, "Your hugs feel like breaths. Like there is something extra besides touching happening."

"Yeah, I feel it too," she said, looking up at me. Erin was shorter than Jorrie, who could look me in the eye.

"So, how do I know you better?" I asked.

"It's like you read my mind. I was going to ask you that," Erin said.

"I'm a boring fellow. As you have just witnessed, I am an alcoholic and smoke too much weed. There are some things about my species that haunt me," I said.

"I know what you mean about species. Part of me feels like I should be back on the planet, trying to shape it into something useful for the future. But another part of me wants to escape, and here you are, offering me something new. I feel hooked, excited, worried, and maybe a little afraid, still wanting to experience just a moment more with you now," Erin said.

I kissed her again, and she kissed back, slow and gentle. Our tongues touched, and we took our time knowing each other with this tongue touching. We took a break to cool down, and I said, "I like this way of getting to know you. But I must let you know that I am falling for you, Erin."

A cool breeze blew by as the sun headed to the horizon. Erin buttoned up her green corduroy jacket while saying, "I like your choice of clothes for me. This outfit is something that I might pick out for myself."

"It's like Alex and Candy's style," I said. "Alex and Candy are my two neighbors in the future probability that Adrien mentioned visiting back in the trailer."

"So, do you have a girlfriend?" Erin asked, with her voice wavering.

"No, Alex is in love with Lucas. They live together. Candy doesn't go for guys, but we have palled around a bit," I replied.

"Oh, good. I felt like I was out on a limb there for a second," Erin sighed a relief.

"Your question from the shuttle is still relevant, however. What do we do now?" I asked her.

"Well, what are our options?" Erin asked.

"Shelter-wise, we have two planets to choose from. The luxury apartment in the Starnet shopping capital of the galaxy or the recently restored villa on the planet of Vasco. A planet rich in religious culture and new foods. Or we could get a motel room here," I said.

"Ooh, shopping, religious food or motel room. Dang, that is a hard choice,"

Erin said while sticking her tongue out slightly.

"We can, of course, choose one tonight and try another one later," I suggested.

"Part of my childhood memory implants included the mention of a villa by my uncle Stephan. I guess I romanticized the word in my mind. Let's go there, the villa on Vasco," Erin said.

"Ohm, transport Erin and me to the small park at the bottom of the hill leading to Aberithes'," I said, and the light of dusk collapsed inward, placing me in darkness. The vibe I got from Erin was very intense but still exploratory. I was surprised at how quickly I fell for her. I felt like a fool again. A fool for women who are supposed to be my wives? I don't know how this will all end up? I knew that I was already stuck on her. The soft afternoon light drifted in from the sides of my perception as I materialized by the large relief at the bottom of the hill where Aberithes' resided. I looked over at Erin standing beside me.

CHAPTER 38

Tentacle Attack

∽

This planet is called Vasco. On this planet, I am known as 'The Squire of the Pharaoh' because I have used my replication technology to repair some of the areas damaged by a hostile alien invasion force that occupied and extracted resources for more than a decade. They have moved on, but many homes were left destroyed or in disrepair. This neighborhood and these restored reliefs are some of the recent work I have done here," I said.

"It's beautiful," Erin said, heading over to the wall, touching the stone relief.

"The villa is just up this hill," I said, gesturing.

We walked through the sunny neighborhood, past Aberithes' and some of the other homes. A few older Vascons waved at me from their yards, and Erin and I waved back.

"It's so peaceful and beautiful here," Erin said.

"Now, yes, a few years ago, it was a war-torn state. There are still many areas that I have not restored. It became an issue with Starnet and the Vascon government. My methods, that is," I replied.

"What was it about your methods they disagreed with?" Erin asked.

"The Vascon people are highly religious and mostly an agrarian society. Modernization, including space travel and advanced weapons, was only developed in the last hundred years before the Bragorian invaders arrived. So, most of the population lived very simple lives with beliefs shrouded in mysticism built up over thousands of years. I did not ask permission from any of the residents to modify their damaged homes," I said.

"Well, that's a little rude, isn't it?" Erin asked.

"Ohm scanned their houses, came up with a replacement plan to transplace the solution into the occupied. It was completely safe, and no casualties were reported even after I repaired over a hundred thousand homes," I said.

"That's a pretty impressive track record," Erin said as we walked.

"But Starnet and the Provisional Vascon government asked me to stop unrequested modifications. I eventually did stop modifying occupied structures, which was their main concern, and have established a slower campaign to restore unoccupied parks and national monuments," I said.

"Sounds like you might be the hero of these people like you are on Zenith," Erin said.

"Really, is that how I am viewed on Zenith?" I asked as we reached the top of the hill and headed for my house.

"Well, yeah. It's not religious or anything, but everyone was glad to get out of those ships, breathe fresh air, and have real food again. And that was mostly due to your location of the planet and the replications terraforming technology. It got bad. Even on the Melog ships, clone production was limited due to food supplies being short," Erin said as we walked up the front steps.

"I did not get that impression. Thanks for telling me. This is it," I said, gesturing around the interior of the house we stepped into.

"Over here is the band-room slash smoke-room, a breakfast nook there, this is the kitchen, the dining room is over here, beyond the dining room is the front sunroom and up those stairs leads to bedrooms and bathrooms," I said.

"I like it," she said, draping her arm across my shoulder and guiding me to the stairs.

We walked up the stairs and headed into the bedroom. The last time I slept here, I awoke to the Vascon police banging on my front door. Ohm managed to tidy the place up while I was gone, and the bed was freshly made. Erin walked over to the double doors that opened to a balcony outside this master bedroom. She walked onto the elevated porch with railings and looked back at me, smiling through the doors she left open, saying, "This is nice, just how I imagined a villa might be."

I sat down on the end of the bed, and she walked back into the room, slowly straddled me, and sat on my lap, hugging me as she lay her head over my shoulder. I embraced her while she shifted and pressed a little closer to me. There was no hurry. There was no rush. We were just feeling the energy of each other. And that is what it felt like to me. Our proximity to each other balanced some emotional potential mismatch. I wondered if this detection was some side effect of the time loop? It felt so right that I was sure this must be the correct revision nine that becomes my wife. But how do I explain the time loop and other oddities about my life to her? This explanation was often the quandary any Splendorite faced when trying to form a relationship with echo-based people. I have gone the lying to my lover route many times in the past. And hundreds of years ago, I was even the scoundrel to love and leave them more times than I care to admit. But in my recent adventures in echo-based relationships with friends, lovers, and acquaintances, I have been trying to come clean. Which means often answering a lot of questions. I thought of this as I held Erin and felt her body.

"Erin, I have something I need to tell you before we go any further," I said.

"I knew it. I knew it was too good to be true," she said, getting off my lap and standing up, looking at me with a "What now?" expression.

"A few months ago, I awoke with memories from alternate futures. You were in those future memories. Over the last few months of my life, I have been on a mission locating people from my future memories to reintroduce myself," I said, and I could see her forming a question in her mind.

"How is that possible? How can you have memories from the future?" Erin asked.

"I don't know how the memories were placed in my mind. The working theory is there was some type of temporal accident in the distant future, and I received these future memories as a side effect from the accident," I said.

"A temporal accident," she said, and she started pacing and putting her hands on her head. This motion was something I saw her do in the past. I mean, in the future memories.

"I think I am in, we are in, a very long time loop. And because I am a probability traveler, I somehow, have access to memories from previous loops," I said, gesturing with my hands while still sitting on the bed.

"Loops? How many times has the temporal accident occurred?" she said, getting even more upset.

"I have clear memories for two loops and partial memories from a third. But, like a dream, they are fading as I travel forward from the time when I first obtained the new memories," I said.

"What do we do?" she said, a bit panicked.

I patted the bed and said, "There is nothing we can do, as far as I know. Please sit down."

She did sit down, but it was clear that I upset her with this new information. Then with a tear in her eye, she said, "What am I to you in this future memory?"

I looked her in the eye with tears welling up in mine, and I said, "In my future memories, you are one of my wives."

"One!" she said, standing back up, pacing, and blowing out long breaths.

"We were married on Ursa Prime, in a traditional ceremony. I married you and Jorrie, Jorrie married you and me, and you married Jorrie and me. In their society, a man may have three wives, and a woman may have three husbands. I know this is a huge bombshell, that's why I wanted to tell you upfront," I said.

"You don't say," she said, wiping a few more tears from her eyes.

"In both timelines, we were married the same way, on Ursa Prime. And in both timelines, we were all very much in love and shared a wonderful life. I know I don't have any right to demand love from you or Jorrie," I said.

Then she got angry and said, "So, you've met her, Jorrie, you've already fucked her?" Erin asked.

"I have, and I did, and the very next day she broke my heart. I was her mission. She was spying on me for Starnet to obtain more information on my operations and technology," I said.

"Oh great, so I was just the second one on the list then," she said, holding back a cry.

"No, you're not just someone on a list to me. You're important, and I have been trying to find you since the day I awoke and found myself in a world without you. Even though my future memories told me I meet you on Zenith, when I went there, nothing was to be found," I said, tearing up a bit more.

"You led us to that planet so you could meet me, didn't you?" Erin asked.

"Yes, but I still did not know which revision nine you were," I said.

Then, a light bulb went off in her head, and she said, "The terraforming reset was to find me."

"It happened that way in the other two memory loops. You were the first one to reach the fountain after the reset," I said.

"Oh, gods, I don't know what to think," she said with a sigh of relief, sitting down beside me.

I put my arm around her and said, "I know it's a lot to take in, and I'll understand if you want to return to Zenith."

She looked over at me, smiling with red eyes and an expression suggesting "you stupid dope" before saying, "Sam, I don't know what this all means, but I still want to know you. It's pretty heavy thinking about being your wife and the wife of someone else, so can we just keep things moving at this slow pace."

"You bet. In the first loop, we lived together for years before we married. In the second loop, it was a shorter time frame. And please tell me if you don't want to hear those kinds of extra time loop things. I'm not trying to recreate an exact match because even the two time loops I remember have discrepancies within them," I said clumsily.

"For now, let's drop the future memories additions unless it is super important. I want to get to know you in our own way. In our own time," Erin said, moving closer and taking a position on my lap once more.

I looked up at her and said, "Thank you for letting me be part of your life," as she kissed me.

There was a definite mood change, however. It wasn't about sex anymore. It was about hanging on, hanging on to whatever part of ourselves we still had left. We kicked off our shoes, moved to the middle of the bed, and lay together, holding on to each other.

"So, you did this same thing with what is her name?" Erin asked.

"Jorrie. Her species is called a Vosip. She is a blended symbiotic being whose host body is twenty-eight years old, but her Limax is three hundred and eighty-four years old. Her Limax has a name, Tusk. Her full name is Jorrie Tusk, host-name first, Limax second," I said.

"That's weird. She's an alien then," Erin said. "And she believed you?"

"She didn't believe me at first and quizzed me on things that a husband should know about a wife. Later she confessed that she felt a similar ambient attraction that we both are having for each other now. I fell in love with her that night, and the next day, by accident, her purse strap broke, and the contents spilled onto the floor," I said.

What did that matter?" Erin asked.

"Contained within the fallen items was an Opturi psychic recording device. She questioned all the guests at my party about me and obtained psychic impressions and references for her mission. When I picked up her purse, I saw the device, and my heart fell apart. I felt utterly betrayed. I couldn't even say goodbye. She walked out, and that was the last I have seen of her."

"You haven't spoken to her since then?" Erin asked.

"It messed me up a lot. I didn't know how to put myself back together again. And that's how I felt. I felt like part of me was missing, and I just had it yesterday. I ended up as a stowaway on a Starnet ship and worked my way onto the maintenance shift. It was the only way I could stop thinking about her, to stay busy," I said.

"Do you still love her now?" Erin asked softly, looking into my eyes while we lay there on the bed.

"I do. I still have hope that somehow, we can be a family again. I know it's just words to you, but we were so happy. We had each other, you and Jorrie had ship assignments, and we ate and laughed and loved," I said sadly with a tear rolling down my cheek.

Erin wiped my tear away and said, "I believe you believe your story, Sam. I don't know if I can be this second wife, but I am going to hold on to you. My mind is mad. My logic is mad because I don't want to be used or tricked or have my heart broken. It's telling me to get out of here, don't let him make you into his second wife. But my body feels your love. I feel your love, and I feel I am becoming lost in emotion," Erin said.

"I feel it too. I didn't realize how utterly lonely I became, living aboard that starship. The only thing of importance was the daily work. My goal has never been to trick you or trap you. I always wanted to empower you. That's why we were all married on the same day. So, no one would be the second wife," I said.

"My entire life was programmed for me. Machines created me to trick and lie. The revision-nines are really good at that, Sam," she said, frightened. "I just want you to know what I am too."

"I know, and in retrospect, it might not have been wise to have all the revision nines install the memories of the original Sandra. Her actions were superimposed memories which caused the entire line that acquired those memories to also acquired the guilt for performing acts that were not your own. You have to learn how to forgive yourself or logically suppress the weight of Sandra's emotional influence upon your decision-making," I said.

She looked at me with a less desperate look that turned more thoughtful and said, "So, is that from a future memory?"

"More of a paraphrase from future memories. We have talked about the relevance of memories lived by another person placed in your mind but you never told me any details about acquiring memories from a deceased revision nine. There was always a wall, where talking about your life aboard the Melog *Pentacraft* was off-limits. So, if I am prying too much, just hit me with the pillow," I said with a smile.

"You are dead on about that. We were the non-deployed, drones to the ship. The Biodual was our queen, and we lived to service her. We had sex with each other and other revision lines daily. We ate and bathed together and rarely wore clothes. It kept us in a heightened sensual state, much like I am feeling here with you. Servicing the ship was life. When our *Pentacraft* was damaged, the Biodual felt it, and we felt her pain too. Thank you for repairing the *Pentacraft*. Even though I'll never see her again, that Biodual was like my mother," Erin said.

"That's interesting. You never told me any of that before," I said.

"So, what do you think that means?" Erin asked,

"I think it means we are still in control of our own destinies. This time loop does not have to play out the same way as the previous loops. Even if we never get married, I'm still glad to know you," I said, pulling her close to me again.

"Me too," she said, and we fell even closer into each other's arms. It felt like one of those "I'm never gonna see you again" hugs where you hang on extra long. I looked into her eyes then we kissed again, slow with the lightest tongue touching.

We eventually fell asleep in each other's arms, but when I awoke, I was alone with my morning wood. I heard noises from the bathroom located off of this bedroom, and Erin came out with a towel wrapped around her hair and one around her torso. She carried a small bottle in her hand and a smile on her face saying, "Good morning. The shower felt good. I hope you don't mind?"

"Not at all," I said while sitting up.

The cruel content editor appeared and removed the hot and steamy morning sex scene, leaving the reader with a one-line reply from Erin, saying, "Faen, I needed that."

"Oh, me too," I said with a smile. "I like your good mornings."

She grabbed the towel on the bed and got up on her knees to wipe off, saying, "Wow, that was a lot."

She twirled the towel up and flicked me with it, saying with a very big smile, "Time to get moving, Mister!"

I headed into the bathroom, and she snapped me with the towel a couple more times. Picking up her clothes from last night, I tossed them out the door to her, then turned on the shower. I located a clean towel before stepping in and washed my hair, thinking, damn she was amazing. All I could think about was her saying, "Wow, that was a lot." I hope I didn't just knock her up? In both future memories, I did not impregnate either Erin or Jorrie even though we tried lots of times. Splendorites are not really known for being exceptionally fertile. We always assumed it was nature's way to keep from having too many people manipulating echo. That didn't mean I couldn't get her pregnant. Melogs also had a fertility issue. They could not impregnate each other, but they also tried with other Imperial humans. There was only one successful pregnancy carried to term by a revision nine. It was Hebe, the revision nine David, and I rescued from the damaged *Falcon*. I rinsed out the shampoo. I rarely use conditioner and finished up by shaving in the shower.

When I returned to the bedroom, she was gone, but I could hear her downstairs. I requested new clothes from Ohm, this time, green for the shirt and grey for the pants. After transferring my vignettes, lighter, and wand to the new clothing, I replicated a fresh joint for the hip joint pocket, and said, "Ohm, I would like to assign one of the cloaked scanners on *Oasis Seven* to follow and protect Jorrie. If she boards a vessel, stay with her."

"Behavior modification applied to the cloaked scanner on *Oasis Seven*. Protecting Jorrie is now the priority," Ohm replied.

I targeted the clothes and wet towels, with my invisihud to recycle them, and went downstairs to the kitchen where Erin made some food. She came over to hug me, saying, "You realize we're officially in love, now don't you?"

"I do. I feel it," I said before grabbing her hips.

Smiling, she hit me with a short kiss on the lips, then the teapot started to whistle, and she wriggled out of my arms, returning to the stovetop to turn off the flame. "Do you want some tea?" she asked.

"No, I'm going to make some coffee," I said and proceeded to get down a bag of coffee grounds and a paper filter for the basket.

I looked for the measuring spoons when I bumped into her and said, "This is one of a relationship's hardest tests. Can the couple both work in the kitchen at the same time?"

"Uh, oh, I think we are failing," Erin said, grabbing her toast and tea before heading for the breakfast nook.

I finally found the measuring spoons and got the coffee started. I found some butter, bacon, and eggs in the fridge and hash brown patties in the freezer. I proceeded to cook up breakfast for Erin and me, adding toast and jam at the end.

"Wow, he even cooks for me. Now I know I'm dreaming," Erin said light-heartedly as I put a plate of food in front of her.

"I don't mind cooking, but I also like picking up prepared food. Can I tell you something that is not so serious as last night but is highly practical?" I asked.

"Sure," she said, raising her eyebrows while taking a bite.

"I have my own version of the kiosk. You may have heard me address it. My kiosk's name is Ohm. I would like to extend you an invitation to use Ohm. With access to Ohm, you will always have food, shelter, clothing, defense, localized money credits, information, and transportation between worlds or on the surface of a world," I said.

"That sounds like a super kiosk to me. What do I have to do?" Erin asked.

"You don't have to do anything. The way it works is a cloaked scanner follows you around to relay signals between your current probability and other connected probabilities. It's unobtrusive. There is one following me right now," I said.

She glanced around, "So, you have had one on us the whole time?" she asked a bit sheepishly.

"I always have one around me. I fear attack from other Splendorites, and this technology gives me a measure of safety, some peace of mind," I said.

"Why do the other Splendorites want to attack you?" she asked cautiously.

"The short story is that I am cursed. The forces of chaos seduced my fellow Splendorites. I detected this. By the time I presented this information to my King, he was already taken over by the elements of chaos. I was seized, and they cut off my finger and gave it to a powerful magician named Valentino. Valentino, and the King's sister, Lexi, devised some magical ritual involving my blood."

"What do you mean, magic?" Erin asked.

"It was a photo finish, but I managed to stop Valentino and Lexi by placing them in suspended animation. I kept them in that state for years, but after receiving the future memories, I knew I needed to release them to try and prevent another tragedy from occurring."

"I don't like the sound of any of this, Sam," Erin said.

"There is also Reziko, who is Lexi's nephew. Reziko's father, Fabio, was slain by other family members for tearing a hole in reality and trying to redesign the way universal energy flows based upon his ideas," I said.

"Holy shit, you said this was not serious," Erin said, standing up and going into her panic pacing. "And now you're telling me about crazy chaotic magicians, holes in reality, and murderous revenge seekers. What the faen! Is there any more?"

"I am eight hundred and thirty-seven years old, Erin. I am steeped in history, and most of mine was spent trying to construct some type of defense against my family and against the forces of chaos," I said with my voice cracking when I said chaos.

"Whoa, I'm like five years old. My consciousness emerged into this fully grown body. I never knew childhood at all. What if I'm in over my head here? How would I know?" Erin said.

"We don't have to stay here. We can return to Zenith. It's not my intention to cut you off from your fellow Melogs or even human friends. If you accept the cloaked scanner, Zenith will become a travel point you can visit any time, as this place will be too," I said.

"When I felt like this on the *Pentacraft*, I would go to the central chamber to be with the Biodual and listen to her speak. Her vocalizations were often just reports or updates happening as she functioned, reading continuous log entries out loud. The Leonard's said that the divine spoke through her and that her consciousness was suspended between life and death, allowing her to see beyond mere sensors," Erin said, calming down.

"When I leave an area, via transport, the cloaked scanner gets left behind to act as a return anchor. After I shifted the repaired *Pentacraft* into the other probability, I transported out. This means you could travel back to the *Pentacraft* and sit with the Biodual if you like," I said.

She sat back down at the table in front of her plate and said, "Okay, I can always turn it off, right?"

"Yes, you can," I said. "Ohm, recognize Erin Gallo for Squire level access to all *Tiger Mountain* offerings."

"Welcome to the *Tiger Mountain* Squire program, Erin. I am Ohm. If there is anything you need, don't hesitate to ask," Ohm said in the low pressurized air modulation voice targeted near Erin's ear.

"I can hear a voice now," Erin said with a slight mood improvement.

"Try asking Ohm for a display of Zenith," I said.

"Just say it out loud? Okay, Ohm, show me a display of Zenith," Erin said, and an orange glowing sphere appeared between us.

I could see her smile through the auragraphic display between us. She reached in and started looking over the landscape around the fountain, and there were still a few lines of people who were obtaining their terraforming privileges. The landscape was highly populated, with the walking house concept. Erin said, "Wow, it looks like a lot of people went for making their own walking homes. That is so cool. If you don't like your neighbors, you can just pick up and move."

"I like it too. Ohm, have there been any fatalities related to yesterday's terraforming reset?" I asked.

"No detectable loss of life indicated on Zenith," Ohm said.

Erin said, "I could hear Ohm's reply to you."

"That's the way it works. Once you are granted a title, you can listen to non-private transmission to and from *Tiger Mountain*," I said.

"So, my title is Squire now?" Erin asked.

"For now, yes. You are a Squire of *Tiger Mountain*," I said proudly, and I got up from the table to walk over to hug her.

Before I arrived at her side of the table, a strong wind blew through the house, and I wondered if the front door was open. Before I could turn to look, the room grew dark, and the wind grew cold. I noticed tentacles crawling along the walls, floor, and ceiling. Some tentacles were large like bridge cables, and others were thin like vines or garden hoses. They constantly moved, damaging the room to the sound of cracking wood and breaking glass, with particle chips flying everywhere. There was a compression of time that slowed everything down. A series of cables wrapped around my waist and jerked me backward into a void from which the tentacles originated. There was only a moment to yell to Erin, "Find Candy!"

I fell. I could see the view of my kitchen collapsing as I was dragged further into the void, down a long tube. The tube curved, and darkness replaced the bright light from the kitchen scene. My invisihud fell back to local mode, which meant I couldn't communicate with *Tiger Mountain* or Ohm. From behind me, a terrible screeching noise could be heard. It grew louder as I struggled against the tentacles, trying to free myself, but they gripped tighter. I passed through a flock of black, winged creatures, their echolocation voices overwhelming my ears while the bats that impacted me left tiny claw marks on my exposed skin. The tube curved again as I was continually yanked through the passage. Small tentacles attached themselves to my wrist and ankles, positioning me away from the walls of the tube, which I almost slammed into more than once. Then it hit me, something that was said to me hundreds and hundreds of years ago when I was negotiating the *Vechnost*. An old man that I met on the mental journey through the winding ways of the *Vechnost* said, "The tentacles lead everywhere and nowhere."

The tentacles of the *Vechnost* are like passageways to echo destinations that are always in flux. I knew there was a *Vechnost* influence at work here, but I held no power over it. If the *Motif* and the *Vechnost* were instruments, I could play the *Motif* very well, while on the *Vechnost* I could barely carry a tune. After mediating the *Vechnost*, there was no bonus reward compared to when you reach the *Motif's* center. There was only the knowledge and sympathetic connection to the *Vechnost* that lingers within you. And like an instrument, how you leverage the *Vechnost* depends upon how often you play with or experiment with it. I did very little exploration of the *Vechnost*. If I had, I might be able to undo or command these tentacles.

As I passed through another turn in the tube, I felt acceleration, and then the tentacles spun me like I was the fan on some pinwheel. With an explosion of sound similar to stressing metal and someone rubbing a giant balloon, I was shaken to a stop, throwing up my breakfast and suffering from extreme dizziness.

Tentacles stretched my limbs out in all directions, like Davinci's Vitruvian Man, leaving me suspended in the air, in some Gothic high vaulted chamber. With my head hanging down, I could see the tentacles originated from a pool of liquid below me, and that familiar voice of Valentino said, "Ah, how nice of you to drop in, Sam."

I was only, now, regaining some of my orientation as I felt the tentacles convey me forward and toward him as he approached the open flooring around the pool. He seemed to command the tentacles with hand gestures, and there was an indication of mental concentration. He did not speak as he moved the *Vechnost* tentacles into a more convenient position with me bound in front of him. I started to speak, and tentacles tightened around my neck, constricting my breathing while Valentino said, "Only I get to speak here, Okay?"

I shook my head, yes, and Valentino smiled saying, "I'm glad we understand each other, Sam."

Valentino stepped up to me, patted me down, locating the vignettes in my shirt and the lighter in my pants pocket. He missed the wand in my lower pants pocket because the tentacles were wrapped around my legs at that point. He inspected my hand for rings, and that's when I noticed his. He wore rings on almost every finger. Stepping back, rifling through my vignettes, he said, "Three vignettes, the Lighthouse of Flynn, such a nice rendition by Darwin, don't you think?"

He showed me the card before continuing, "A tech doorway. I recognize this one. Too bad you won't be needing it anymore," and he tossed the vignette to Xanadu, into the pool where the tentacles sprouted.

"What's this, a dark metal catwalk. This one looks interesting," then he tucked the two remaining vignettes into his vest.

"And finally a lighter to see your escape vignette if you are caught in the dark. I admire the bare-bones essentials. I really do, Sam. There is a lot I admire about you, but then there is a lot about what you do that just pisses me off!" Valentino said, raising his voice at the end, causing winged creatures roosting in the rafters to take flight. I could feel his anger being transferred to the tentacles in the form of contraction as if they were a manifestation of his emotions.

As the tentacles tightened even more around my neck, another line from the old man I met inside the *Vechnost* came to mind, "All thoughts are tentacles."

"I thought it was rude, the way you dismissed me at our last meeting. Acting as though you were too important to just talk it out with an old family relative. I mean, there is so much to say, and yet you never seem to have the time," Valentino said as he paced back and forth, grandstanding in front of me.

I had difficulty breathing and experiencing mild convulsions as my body's muscle system was not used to supporting me in this awkward position.

"And I see the dilemma you face. What do you do with a problem relative? My father's eyes were burned out, did you know that?" Valentino asked as he reached the end of his pace distance and turned around, looking me in the eye with the question. "His brother Leif burned his eyes out and threw him in the dungeon, knowing that a blind man can not walk through echo. This act saved Grayson's life. By not killing his relative, only blinding him, they both could live. That's what you said to me, 'This way we can both live.' But you're blinding me, Sam!

You placed me in a candy-coated virtual world, driving me crazy with kindness. I still wake up with the sounds of inane pop tunes from your simulation in my head. What have you done to my mind?" he said, getting up in my face.

"Endless meaningless job scenarios and boys night out with Jerry at the bowling alley while I knew all along that my wife Jane was fucking Billy down at the gas station. Dipshit neighbors who couldn't think or talk about anything other than their lawns or the weather," he went on with a gleam in his eye as he tilted his head.

He must have sensed I was about to pass out because the tentacles loosened, and I could breathe again. He continued, "And when I travel to visit the site of my long-term project, I find it utterly destroyed, nothing left, completely bombed out! I wondered who would do such a thing? And I, of course, thought of you first. Did you destroy my Spectre Vorticle, Sam?" Valentino asked with a raised voice.

I shook my head, yes, and he raged, "I knew it!" as madness revealed itself across his face. He looked at me and gestured with his hands, causing more tentacles to emerge and surround my head. I feared they were going to poke my eyes out.

In a panic, my eyes shifted around, and my invisihud activated. There was a glowing option. It was the medical implant I installed inside Valentino and Lexi before I revived them. He didn't remove it. I located the sleep icon as tiny tentacles pried my closed eyelids open. I targeted Valentino's implant, and we all slumped to the floor at once. Valentino fell over first, and when he passed out, his control over the tentacles was released. They retreated into the pool, leaving me collapsed on the floor. I was heaving and trying to catch my breath as I pulled myself over to Valentino with my arms, unable to stand up yet. Reaching into his robes, I located my vignettes. I removed all of the rings from his hand. He was also wearing a necklace with a large jewel as the centerpiece. I took that too. I pulled off his boots, and on the left toe next to the little toe, there was another ring that I removed before stuffing them all into my pockets.

In the near distance, I heard the alarm sound. With the vignette to the catwalk on top, I focused my attention on it. I got up on all fours and crawled to enter the vignette as I saw grotesque armored beings approaching with spears and swords. In a rainbow lensing effect, I transported to the catwalk of the *Deceptive*. Crawling at first toward the easel before climbing to my feet, I made my way to the end of the catwalk and removed the cloth covering the painting. I was in no mood to entertain evil, demented images, and flying eyeballs fled the canvas sensing my anger. With Valentino's Gothic castle in mind, I requested an image of the *Vision* painting and said, barely able to speak, "Ohm, cloaked scanners."

"Deploying cloaked scanners into the painting location," Ohm replied.

CHAPTER 39

The image on the *Vision* painting shifted as I thought to locate Erin. With a total surprise to her, I stepped into the scene and fell on the floor in front of her.

Erin said, "Sam, oh my gods. Are you hurt?" and others in the room looked her way.

We were all in Nick and Madison's house in Enki's Dale. There was a rush of movement as Candy, Alex, Lucas, Nick, and Madison came over to help me up.

Alex said, "Ohm, medkit."

I could hear Erin weeping, and Nick said, "Blimey."

Candy asked Ohm about my medical condition while Lucas asked, "Sam, can you hear me? Are you all right?"

I shook my head okay to Lucas, who stood behind Alex. She used a skin sealer on some of my weeping scratch wounds and deeper gnashes cut into my wrist by the tentacles.

"Who did this to you?" Lucas asked.

I managed to whisper the name, "Valentino," and Candy, Lucas, and Alex all looked at each other.

Erin caught on in an instant and asked, "What does that mean?"

"Are we in danger, Sam?" Lucas asked.

I shook my head, yes, and used my invisihud to locate the cloaked scanner I deployed to Valentino's location before sharing it with the group. Alex leaned over me, tending to my wounds, and she paused for a moment and said, "Got it," before continuing with the skin sealer.

"He seems to still be down. Soldiers are carrying him away. What should I do?" Lucas asked.

Once again, I managed to say a single whispered word, "Nothing."

Candy flipped out, saying, "Nothing! He brutally attacks you, and you want to do nothing?"

I said with my raspy voice, "Payback for Spectre Vorticle."

"And you think this attack will make you even in Valentino's mind?" Lucas asked.

"No," I said, coughing. "Nothing will ever pay that debt."

Alex said, "Let me see that back."

Erin said, "Oh gods," as she helped me with my shirt, lifting it to reveal my back.

"It's not bad, Sam. Thanks for the basic medkit training. There are some deep cuts on your back, but the skin sealer will take care of them. Just give me some time," Alex said, practicing her bedside manner and giving a nasty look to Erin while she began applying the skin sealer to my back wounds.

I reached out to hold Erin's hand, and she gripped it tightly while the muscular convulsions started to subside. Madison asked, "Sam, can I make you some tea?"

"Yes, thank you," I rasped out, and Madison left the living room, heading off to the kitchen.

Lucas asked, "What kind of danger are we in?"

I was drained, and my eyes were weeping, but I managed to say, "Retaliation."

"Retaliation against us for destroying the Spectre Vorticle?" Lucas asked, trying to form my one word into a conversation.

"Yes, must research defense," I said.

"Defense against the tentacles?" Lucas asked, and I shook my head yes.

"We might have a lead on that," Nick said. "Madison found a description of the tentacle event in one of her magical tomes."

"Good work," I barely said.

"Sam, let's get your stomach and sides now," Alex said.

I sat on the floor of the living room in front of the unlit fireplace, leaning against a small raised platform of stonework that formed the fireplace hearth. I lifted myself up onto the hearth and sat up, revealing my chest and stomach. Alex got to work on it, saying, "These are healing up nicely, Sam. Don't worry."

I looked over at Erin, who sat next to me. Her red eyes, which recently cried tears, left clear paths on her dust-covered face. Splinters of wood were still in her hair. She moved up on the fireplace hearth, sitting next to me, and said, "Sam, I don't know if I can do this."

I rasped, "You don't have to."

"Yeah, but we do. We helped you destroy the Spectre Vorticle," Alex said.

"Alex is right. Valentino is going to come looking for us too, once he finds out we helped," Candy said.

"We'll worry about that later. It looks like the sleep dose was set for two hours, so we have some time to catch our breath," Lucas said.

"What's a Spectre Vorticle?" Nick asked.

It took me a few moments to respond. I paused between syllables, and said, "An inter-dimensional magical weapon."

Lucas picked up on the description, saying, "When the Spectre Vorticle was operational, it could transfer energy from one probability to another. You could dump a series of tornadoes in one spot or flash flood your enemies. It was not a precision instrument, more like a blunt device."

Alex finished up on me with the skin sealer and put it back in the medkit while saying to Nick, "But if you don't care about additional casualties you can just drop hot lava on an entire town."

"Geez, a massive elemental transport device," Nick said.

"Thanks, Alex," I rasped to her.

Alex razzed my hair with her hand and took a seat on the sofa across the room, putting the medkit on the floor at the end of the sofa.

Madison returned with tea for everyone but gave a special cup to me, setting it next to me on the fireplace hearth. She put the tray down on the coffee table in front of the sofa, saying, "That sounds like a description of Lillypool's Lament."

"What is that?" Erin asked, standing up slightly to accept a cup of tea from Madison.

I sipped from my cup, and Madison went on, saying, "It's mentioned inside of 'Saraphene's Sacrum of Unmentionables.' That was the book we were reviewing before Sam arrived."

Nick took the hint from Madison and left the room in search of the book just mentioned.

"It tastes like slippery elm," I said to Madison, feeling my voice returning.

"A closely related magical cousin, Jasper's talisman. Singers often use it to keep the voice in top shape," Madison said.

I put my arm slowly around Erin. It hurt like hell, and I said, "A rough first day together, huh?"

"Yeah, you could say that," Erin said with a hint of relief.

Nick returned with the book handing it to Madison, saying, "I marked where we were with the royal blue ribbon."

The hardback book was quite thick. The cover read, "Saraphene's Sacrum of Unmentionables," with a silhouetted picture of a pointed hat female magician in a robe, holding a triangle in one hand and a wand in the other. This book had ribbons sewn into the binding, allowing one to easily mark specific pages for quick reference. I could tell by the number of ribbons sticking out of the stacked pages that Madison marked quite a few of them.

Lucas and Candy took a seat on the sofa, helping themselves to some tea, while Madison knelt on the other side of the coffee table, flipping through the pages of the book. It took Madison a couple of times to finally locate the entry she mentioned and started reading, "Lillypool's Lament was of significant importance during the age of Ackmon the third, who ruled over the magical lands as a tyrant king. Earnest Lillypool located a magical device held within the hand of the mountain. It spoke and offered great power in exchange for cobalt offerings."

I interrupted Madison asking, "Cobalt? The story specifically mentions cobalt?"

She looked over at me and said, "Yes, the offering was cobalt ore," then continued reading. "While Earnest recorded transfers of winds, storms, and other natural phenomena from unknown locations to locations of his King's enemies, he was unable to save his true love from the broad stroke of the device's mighty power, forcing him to lament his actions."

"Interesting. I see the similarities. With a device as powerful as the Spectre Vorticle, it was bound to cast an echo of its own. Earnest's device might have been one such echo," I said as the tea helped my voice return.

"I agree," Madison said. "This Spectre Vorticle may have been the original source of Lillypool's Lament," flipping back to the page Nick marked with the royal blue ribbon.

"Here we go," Madison said, laying the book flat again and pulling a piece of paper out from the back of the book.

I stepped up and looked at both the sketched image in the book and the printed piece of paper, which looked like a video frame from the log of the event in the Vasco villa. Both pages depicted a cloud, and within the cloud were tentacles reaching out. The book contained a black and white sketch with some annotation of an arrow pointing to the outer ring of the phenomena connecting it with one word, "rainbow." When I looked at the color printout from the log, there was a definite red-blue shift along the outer edge.

Madison began to read, once more, "Taneth's Terrible Tendrils is one of the most gruesome and terribly horrible things one can witness from afar let alone to be the recipient of such an attack. Taneth was a young magician studying at Farolding's Emporium of Continuing Knowledge when he found a ring lying in a dirt pile in the courtyard. When he put on the ring, a wide hole opened before him with tendrils reaching out. He soon learned he could control the tendrils while wearing the ring. He used this power to murder his way to the top of the magician world only to lose it all when he slipped on a sheet of ice, causing the ring to slip off his finger and roll down a mountain slope. Victims were often found strangled and or dismembered due to the powerful gripping and yanking force of the terrible tendrils."

I reached into my pocket and pulled out the rings I took from Valentino's hands and toe. I put them on the coffee table and said, "When I arrived at Valentino's location, he thoroughly searched me while the tentacles bound me. I thought it odd that he spent so much time checking my hands. That's when I noticed he wore a ring on every finger. When I knocked him out, I took them all from him."

Alex started to lean forward to pick one up, and Madison quickly said, "No, don't touch them. A magician's rings should never be handled without a proper neutralization spell being cast first. They sometimes contain counterspells to ward off would-be thieves or as a last damaging vengeance upon a foe if they are slain in combat."

She closed the book, moved it aside, and used the printed piece of paper to arrange the rings into a line on the table without actually touching them herself. She pulled a wand from out of her sleeve, and one by one, pointed it at each ring, saying, "*Markielvayle*."

With each flick of her wand, a ring would jump and shudder for a moment, then settle back down, all except one. She used the paper to move the rings that reacted to her spell over to the side and left the unaffected ring in the center of the table. Using her wand again, she said, "*Sporayzee*," then, "*Alodunkinsworth*," but there was no visible effect on that ring.

The ring was gaudy, like costume jewelry. It looked like an ornate mood ring with the small central flattened dome containing a constantly swirling mist. Madison said. "I am convinced that this ring was important to the magician, perhaps granting him additional power."

"Thank you, Madison. I'm going to secure them all just in case," I said to her. "Ohm, place these rings in the vault."

The rings all sparkled, and when the sparkle faded, the rings were gone.

Lucas said, "So, that's good news, right?"

"Taking those rings was very risky, Sam, but you may have reduced his power in doing so," Madison said.

Erin drifted back into her pace, wander, stress mode, and said, "I need some air."

"Let me show you the way to the patio," Madison said, walking over to some glass doors off of this room, which visibly opened to an outside patio we could see from here.

"We got lucky today," Alex said.

"Yep," Lucas said.

"Nobody died," Candy said.

"Are you okay, Sam?" Nick asked.

"I think I will recover, and, yes, I feel lucky, but I can tell Erin is terrified," I said.

"Today gave us all a scare," Candy said.

"And today is not over yet. What will Valentino do when he wakes up is the real question?" Lucas said.

"Are you going to observe him?" Alex asked.

"I don't know if I can handle any more Valentino today. Can you guys do that?" I asked.

"Not a problem. I was planning on it anyway," Lucas said.

"Don't interact with him directly. His magic is powerful, and he may be able to reverse a spell back through the communications link," I said as Madison came back into the room.

"I'm going to check on Erin," I said and slowly left the room through the double glass French doors.

Outside, I walked up to her and touched her on the shoulder, saying, "Hey."

She looked up at me and put her head on my shoulder as I wrapped my sore arms around her. Wrapping her hands around me, she said, "Sam, I just want to go home, but I don't know where that is anymore."

"Home is where we are together, Erin," I said.

"I know," she said with a defeated voice.

I started picking debris from her hair and said, "I have another apartment, the shopping reality, remember? We can get cleaned up and relax a bit. I don't think there will be another attack any time soon."

Erin leaned back and looked up into my face asking, "Really? I thought we only had two hours?"

"Two hours until he wakes up defeated and defanged. I trust Madison's judgment. I think she may be right. The ring might have been amplifying his powers. Lucas is going to take the first watch. I feel like I need to lie down, but I'm not leaving your side," I said.

"I don't want to be away from you, either," Erin said with tears welling up for a moment while acting very clingy.

"Don't worry. Things will get better. This mess is what I call a really, really bad day. They're all not like this," I said, trying to reassure her.

"All right, let's go to the other apartment. I could use a bath," she said with her dusty face.

We walked back into the Baker's home together, and I closed the glass doors behind us.

"What's the scoop?" Alex said.

"We're heading back to San Francisco to get cleaned up. I am starting to feel the aches from all that tentacle stretching in my body. I think I need to lie down," I said to the room.

Candy got up from the couch, walked over, and put my head in both of her hands before saying, "If you need anything, don't hesitate to ask."

She gave me a light hug and looked over at Erin before saying, "You too, girl. I'm just down the hall."

I looked around the room and said with my eyes tearing up a bit, "Thank you all for being such good friends. I don't know what I would do without you."

Everyone echoed likewise sentiments, saying goodbye, and I asked, "Ohm, transport Erin and me to the San Francisco apartment."

The warm cozy living room of the Baker's home drifted in from the sides to be replaced by nothing. I wondered what all this really meant? Would Valentino back off? Did manhandling me with the *Vechnost* tentacles today count as enough payback for destroying his Spectre Vorticle? Would he seek to recover the ring? For now, I hoped to make it to tomorrow. The dim evening light of the San Francisco bay filled my vision as I reassembled in the living room of my apartment, looking out the glass windows to the balcony at the approaching evening.

CHAPTER 40

Home Again

 ✧

"This is it," I said to Erin. "Alex and Lucas have an apartment down the hall, and so does Candy."

I headed into the bedroom, and Erin followed.

"I think it's best if you cut my shirt off. My shoulders are getting sore," I said while slipping out of my pants.

"Where are the scissors?" Erin asked.

"Ask Ohm to replicate them," I said to her.

"Ohm, replicate scissors that I can use to cut the shirt on Sam's back," Erin said.

A small sparkle appeared on the bed leaving behind a large pair of tailor's scissors. Erin took her time and carefully cut the fabric of my shirt so she could slide the sleeves from my arms, and the rest of the shirt fell off.

"Now it's your turn to get naked. I want to rinse the grime of today off of you," I said before heading into the bathroom and starting the shower.

She undressed in the bedroom, walked into the bathroom, and got into the shower, rinsing her face and hair. I watched as the water turned brown then finally ran clean. I asked her to step out, and I did one last rinse of the tub before I stopped it up and started drawing our bath. There were some bath salts here that I added to the water while Erin watched me, dripping wet on the rug.

"It looks like Alex missed some areas. You still have several cuts. I want to learn what she did when she healed you," Erin said.

"Try saying what Alex said. Ask Ohm for a medkit," I replied.

"Ohm, medkit," Erin said, shortening it as Alex did.

A large sparkle appeared and left behind a white box with a red cross on it.

"Open it up. The skin sealer is typically placed on the left in a newly replicated kit," I said.

Erin opened the latches and lifted the lid of the medkit. Inside there were basic first aid items like gauze, medical tape, bandages, and creams for burns and fighting infection, but there were three main tech items present. The medical inspectrograph, the medjector, and the skin sealer.

Erin handed the skin sealer to me, and I showed her how to turn it on and choose a setting. Light, medium, and deep wounds were the settings. I instructed her on the basic principle of its functioning, such as the depositing of new cells to accelerate skin growth. She caught on pretty fast and was soon regenerating some areas around my waist and under my arms that Alex did not reach. Once our bath filled, I said, "Let's get in."

Erin stepped in first and sat with her back against the end of the tub before I got in and leaned back into her, asking, "Is this okay?"

"Yeah," she said with a smile as I looked back at her for confirmation.

Our bodies displaced the water, and the bath was close to overflowing. I opened the drain to let a little out and said, "I'm so sorry to involve you in my messed-up circumstances. I know it was selfish to pursue you and invite you into my broken life. Please forgive me."

"So, I take it that the tentacle attack did not happen in any of your other future memories?" Erin asked.

"No, it did not, but a rocket attack from space did happen on that same house in the first time loop. It was not Valentino, however, it was Hugo and Lexi," I said.

"I'm not going ask any more questions today. Is that okay, baby?" Erin said.

"Oops, that was a question," I said.

"I just want this, us, together, holding on. I want to reach tomorrow," Erin said.

"I do too, baby. And we will," I said, looking back at her.

She seemed to be in a diminished state. I wondered how long a Melog could live on their own, separated from their clone counterparts and the *Pentacraft*? When I came up with the plan to move the *Pentacraft* into another dimension, I did not realize how linked they were to it. This Erin has told me more about her Melog origins than either one did in the other time loops. She ran her hands through my hair, down my chest, and even stroked me a few times, but it was not about sex or arousal. It was just touching. In my future memories, I was always close with Erin. We spent our off time eating, hanging out, and holding each other. But it looks like this is part of their internal makeup, at least for the revision-nines. The water eventually turned cold, and we got out and dried off. She spent some time picking more splinters from her hair and finally got it to comb out. I returned to the bedroom and was lying back, taking in the events of the day.

My muscles hurt like hell, and I wanted a joint and drink, but I was too lazy to get up and make them. I started to cry. I tried to hold back man tears, but today was really close. I could have easily lost my eyes or been ripped apart by the demon tentacles. Erin came into the bedroom wearing a fluffy robe. She crawled in bed next to me, wiping the tears from my eyes, and said, "Don't worry. I'll protect you."

When I awoke the next day, I could barely move, or more accurately, it hurt when I moved. I felt like I unwillingly completed a triathlon. Erin was not in the bedroom, and I noticed her robe discarded on the bed, so I called out to her with my raspy, broken voice, "Erin?"

I heard no reply, so I asked, "Ohm, where is Erin?"

"Erin is down the hall in Candy's apartment," Ohm replied.

I sat on the edge of the bed and looked at my ripped and cut-up clothes. Fetching the two vignettes from the shreds of my shirt, I noticed the gold chain hanging out of the pocket of my pants. When I put the rings on Madison's coffee table, I forgot about the necklace I took. After hearing Madison's warning about taking a magician's jewelry, I was reluctant to touch it and shook it out of my pants pocket onto the floor. I targeted it with my invisihud and said, "Ohm, can you transport the targeted necklace to the vault. Place it near Valentino's rings."

I watched as the necklace sparkled and disappeared. I checked the pocket on my lower pants leg, and sure enough, my wand was broken in three places. I had to get another one somewhere.

"Ohm, can you inform me if any of Valentino's jewelry items end up missing from the vault?" I asked.

"Certainly, the vault is routinely scanned, and no items placed in the vault have gone missing since its creation," Ohm stated.

I targeted the clothes on the floor and used the recycle icon on them. Using the wardrobe menu of the environment designer inside my invisihud, I replicated some boxer briefs and a bathrobe. Out of habit, I placed the vignettes inside the pockets of the robe. I put on the briefs and robe before heading into the living area. Sitting down on the white leather couch in front of the large rectangular table, I thought about the last time I sat here. It was right after Jorrie broke my heart. I sat in this exact same spot all day. It seemed so far away from who I was now. I spent so much energy trying to remove what I felt for Jorrie from my inner self that I wondered how I would ever integrate both Erin and Jorrie into my life at the same time? I realized it was no longer a priority to me. All I wanted now was to continue to live with Erin at my side. This cohabitation was how it unfolded in both of the other time loops. I spent years with Erin before meeting Jorrie. Right now, I felt broken and hoped to make it through today. I used the food icon in my invisihud to replicate some coffee, eggs, bacon, and toast. I sat on the couch, alone, eating slowly. My neck was still messed up, and it hurt to swallow, so I took many small bites, trying to chew everything really good before swallowing.

It was not too much longer before I heard the front door open, and in walked Erin and Candy. Erin wore new clothing, and it looked like she was in a better mood. Candy looked great like she always did.

"Candy has been showing me how to use the offerings provided by *Tiger Mountain*," Erin said as she headed over to the couch where I sat and took up a seat next to me on my left.

Erin kissed me on the cheek and pulled my robe a little more closed, patting me on the chest while Candy took a seat on my right and reached over, taking a slice of bacon from my plate.

"What's the word?" I asked, looking at both of them.

Candy spoke up with half the bacon in her left hand, chewing, saying, "The word is that Valentino didn't do much of anything after he woke up."

"I watched the log too, using the virtual display. Besides an initial burst of screaming, yelling, and throwing things, he settled down into brooding," Erin said while keeping her hand on my chest.

"Girl's right. Lucas and Alex watched it too," Candy said, finally putting the other half of bacon into her mouth and licking her fingers.

"Did you have breakfast yet?" I asked Erin.

"Yeah, I did. Candy served me breakfast and showed me how to get clothes and food from Ohm," Erin said.

"How are you feeling today?" Candy asked.

"I feel like I have been beaten with a board all over, but especially in my joints," I replied. "I can barely move."

It looked like Candy was focused on her invisihud, and all of a sudden, said, "I've got to run. I'm meeting Clarashel for brunch at Florence's."

"Eating my bacon and going to brunch?" I quizzically asked Candy.

"Ha, ha, very funny. I'll see you both later," Candy said, and she headed out of the apartment.

As soon as the door slammed, Erin moved her hand inside my robe to touch my chest and leaned in for a good morning kiss. I kissed her back with my coffee breath, and she repositioned herself to gently straddle my lap while wrapping her arms around me for a full morning hug. She leaned back, and I put my hands on either side of her cheeks, drawing her head back down to kiss her again.

She got up from my lap, sat beside me, and said, "I have not had a proper good morning yet."

The content editor came in to remove several paragraphs describing Erin's morning greeting, leaving a single line that read, "Erin kissed Sam."

"Dang, baby, that was so great. Is it okay if I get you back when I can move a little better?" I asked.

"Yeah, doing that makes me so wet," she said, kissing me one more time before getting up from the couch and heading off to the bathroom.

I targeted the remains of my breakfast and used the recycle icon to clean up the area. Getting up, I walked around, forcing myself to do some stretching. I wondered how this was going to affect my drumming? I gave up on stretching and returned to the white sofa, locating the log from the cloaked scanner that I left behind to monitor Valentino. It looked like the soldiers I saw approaching before I escaped picked up his body and took him to a room, placing him on a stone table. They simply stood guard against the wall and did not attempt to render any type of first aid.

When Valentino awoke, he screamed at the guards, "Where is he? How could you let him escape!"

He took their spears and used them to smash things in the room. He hit the guards on their heads and eventually wore himself out. The tranquilizer has a grogginess effect when you just come out of it. I followed him along castle hallways, eventually reaching some inner sanctum with a fireplace, bed, wardrobe, and a small library. It was then when realized his rings and necklace were missing. He raged again, throwing a few books into the fire before quickly pulling them back out and dusting them off.

I felt sorry for Valentino as I virtually followed him around his Gothic castle. He didn't seem to have any friends, and he berated those that served him.

Erin returned to the living room and sat down beside me, asking, "You are using your internal hud device, aren't you?"

"Yes, facial muscles change, so if you're looking for it, you can detect when someone is using their invisihud because of their expression," I replied.

"That's it, that's what Candy called it, an invisihud," Erin said. "What were you doing with it?"

"I was reviewing Valentino's log. After watching it, I really feel sorry for the guy. He doesn't seem to have any friends at all. I mean, would he be as pissed off as he is if some beautiful woman gave him excellent head in the morning?" I asked.

Erin smiled and said, "Probably not, but we'll never know."

"I think he is exhibiting all the classic symptoms of someone with ADHD," I said.

"What is ADHD?" Erin asked.

"Attention deficit hyperactivity disorder. It happens to humans and possibly other species when the individuals experience a traumatic event, are exposed to toxic chemicals, or suffer brain damage," I said.

"Have those things happened to Valentino?" Erin asked.

"It's hard to say, but he is older than me, so at least one to two thousand years old, I'm guessing. That's a lot of time when he might encounter any one of those triggers. Considering Madison's mention that the Spectre Vorticle required cobalt might mean other dangerous chemicals were used in its construction. I toured it when it was operational, and the pools of liquid surrounding it were incredibly toxic," I said.

"How does knowing that help us?" Erin asked.

"Before I released Valentino and Lexi, I implanted a biochemical monitoring device that can administer medicine inside both of them. That was the only thing that saved me. He used very small tentacles wrapped all around my head and forced my eyelids open to poke my eyes out when I noticed the medical implant was still available in my invisihud menu. I chose the sleep option, which caused the biomedical implant to release a tranquilizer inside him. He quickly passed out, releasing his control on the tentacles. If that was not in place, I would not be here right now," I said.

"Wow, a medical device saved you," Erin said, reflecting on that.

"Ohm, the next time that Valentino goes to sleep, I want to start a regiment of medicine to treat ADHD. Monitor norepinephrine and epinephrine levels for sudden spikes," I said.

"Regiment will be implemented based upon currently known standards for treatment," Ohm replied, and Erin heard the reply.

"What now?" Erin asked.

I transferred the monitoring of Valentino to a cloaked scanner in the room.

The auragraphic display allowed Erin to see what I saw inside my invisihud. He was on a low balcony overlooking a forest, sitting at a table having tea while guards stood by.

"Ohm, I want to target the table where Valentino is currently sitting. Locate a set of generic military sunglasses that offer night vision and infrared options. Make the design generic. I don't want any branding on the final product. Deliver them, as a gift, along with a card. The card should say, 'Thank You,' on the front, and when you open it, it should say, 'For Not Killing Me,' on the inside. Make these two messages in an elegant font, then add this other message in a smaller handwritten script, 'Use these glasses when the world is about to blind you. They let you see in the dark,'" I said.

"Table targeted, and the gift is ready for deployment," Ohm replied.

I said, "Ohm, deploy the gift."

Through the virtual video feed from the cloaked scanner, I could make out two small sparkles when then the card and glasses were delivered to Valentino's table. He looked around quickly, trying to detect where they came from. Picking up the card, he read it, placed it back down on the table, and picked up the glasses. He examined them but did not put them on. He lifted his hand high in the air giving me the middle finger, and yelled, "This is not over, Sam!"

"Ohm, discontinue the display," I said, and the glowing orange sphere faded and vanished.

"Well, that's not a very nice thing to hear," Erin said.

"I didn't expect much, but maybe it will give me something to talk about the next time he tries to kill me," I said with a frown.

"So, what do we do now?" Erin asked.

"Are you up for visiting a starship? I know a doctor on the ship who might be able to give us a little more insight on how to treat Valentino," I asked.

She smiled and said, "Sure."

"Can you help me get dressed. I don't want to go like this?" I asked.

"I don't know. I kind of like you like this, you know, easy access and all," she said with a playful smile.

It was good to see her smile after yesterday's horrible experience. We headed into the bedroom, and I took off the robe, removing the vignettes from the robe pockets. She placed her arms around me from behind and hugged me, saying, "I can't stop touching you, Sam. It just feels good to have you in my life."

I turned around and looked her in the eye and said, "I feel the same way. Your touch makes me feel good. I guess that is too simple of an explanation. When you touch me, I feel at home. I feel like you are a part of me that I was missing for so long, and now that you are here, your touch makes it all seem real. Even just looking at you or your smile reaches inside me, but the inverse is true too. When I see you sad or frightened, I can't help but feel your sadness and fear. I don't want to disappoint you or let you down. I don't want to let you go either."

She stood on tiptoe to look me in the eye and wrapped her arms around my shoulders for a kiss. Dropping back down from her tiptoes, she put her beautiful head of hair on my nearly hairless chest. It was like holding some exotic creature the way her beauty affected me. I knew she was changing my emotions with her presence, but I didn't care. I liked it. Anyway, what could I do? She was my future wife.

We parted after a long hug, and I said, "Ohm, can you replicate a new set of clothes and two new passage cards to Xanadu?"

The bed sparkled, and my standard black clothing set appeared on the bed. Next to them, two new vignettes appeared. I put on my pants, and Erin asked, "What is this?" picking up one of the vignettes.

"That is what Splendorites traditionally use to transport to a specific location. You concentrate on the card, and the place seems more real. Once you have established a mental link with the location, you can step forward into the card, and you will find yourself transported to the location. That card leads to one location I call Xanadu.

"Xanadu is an advanced healing facility. If you get hurt, or a friend gets hurt, you can transport them through the vignette to the facility, and the doctors will help you. You can bring multiple people with you as long as they are all touching. Keep it with you at all times. I suggest you modify your clothing to accommodate the vignette," I said as I tucked my three vignettes into the inner pocket of my shirt.

Erin said, "Thanks, I will," in a more serious tone before placing the vignette in the back pocket of her pants.

I leaned over halfway, with my arms out, and asked, "Can you slide the shirt on?"

It was a bit comical, her helping me slide my shirt on, and it hurt like hell as it finally slid over my shoulders, but we managed to get me dressed. I went into the bathroom and brushed my teeth, then came back out and said, "I'm finally ready. Are you ready to go?"

"Yes, I'm ready," she said with a smile.

"Ohm, what is the location of Doctor Farouk?" I asked.

"Doctor Farouk is in sickbay aboard the *Explorer EX-01*," Ohm replied.

I said to Erin, "This ship is about two hundred years in the past compared to the *Journey* crew. Doctor Farouk is an Ursonian. He is an alien friend. I also told him about my future memories and you and Jorrie. I just wanted to give you a heads up before we go. Is that all right?"

Erin seemed to tense up for a second at the mention of Jorrie, then said, "Got it, today time travel and aliens. Yesterday was tentacles of chaos and evil magician."

"Ohm, transport Erin and me to the *Explorer EX-01*, outside of sickbay," I said.

The light of the room rushed in from the sides, collapsing into darkness as I waited for materialization. I actually did it. I managed to locate Erin, and it felt so good to be with her. I just hoped this Valentino crap worked out for the best. A grey silver light filtered in from the sides of my vision, leaving Erin and me standing outside the glass double doors leading to sickbay.

CHAPTER 41

Visit Farouk

Erin blew a breath of air out, saying, "Whew, that is so weird. Does it seem weird to you, Sam?"

"Every time. That is why I like traveling by vignette if I can. It is a more organic and natural way to travel," I said.

I gave Erin a head nod and motioned over to the doors. They opened automatically as we walked in slowly, and I said to an empty room, "Hello?"

There was a rustle from behind a partition, and Farouk came out saying, "Sam, welcome, so glad to see you," his extra-wide Ursonian smile giving him a cartoonish look for a moment. He walked up to Erin, offering his hand, and said, "I am Doctor Farouk."

"Nice to meet you. I am Erin," Erin said.

"Ah, the Erin?" Farouk asked, looking at me.

"Yes, we finally found each other," I replied, feeling a little awkward.

"If you'll excuse me for a moment, I have to fulfill a duty," Farouk said, and he walked over to the wall and pressed a button to activate the communications panel.

"Doctor Farouk to Captain Bowmen," he spoke into the wall unit.

"Bowmen here, what is it, Farouk?" Jason asked.

"Just reporting that Sam and his friend Erin have arrived in my sickbay," Farouk said.

"Understood, on my way. Bowmen out," Jason said.

Farouk turned back to us and said with a smile, "Now, where were we?"

"There is a family member of mine who is exhibiting uncontrollable outbursts of anger. I diagnosed him with attention deficit hyperactivity disorder, and I have begun a medicinal regimen starting today, but I am concerned that I might have missed something. I know he has worked in construction, using heavy earth elements, and I wonder if these elements may have passed through his skin and accumulated, causing his current condition," I said.

"I would love to help. Bring him in for an examination, and we'll come up with some treatment options," Farouk said.

"I can't really bring him in. Not only is he angry, he does not want to have anything to do with me," I said.

"Well, then, how are you administering the treatment?" Farouk asked.

"I have covertly placed a medical medicine dispenser inside his body and have configured it to dispense medicine for ADHD," I said.

"That is highly unethical, Sam," Farouk said with a frown, "The foundation of medical treatment is transparency and consent."

"What about emergency cases?" I postulated. "There is no consent there. You do what you think is best to restore the patient to health."

"I agree that, in emergencies, consent is a secondary consideration. But what you are talking about is a chronic illness," Farouk said.

Erin said passionately, "This is an emergency. Valentino is out of control."

"I'm not asking you to administer the treatment. I'm just looking for advice. He is immortal, probably over two thousand years old. I believe that heavy metals may have built up inside his body slowly, accumulating over centuries. It has made him mad, but he was not always like that," I said.

Farouk heaved a disapproving sigh and said, "Heavy element buildups can cause uncontrolled outbursts in many species. That is why safety protocols were established, but in cases where there were no protocols put in place or protocols were not enforced, there is not a lot that can be done to remove them from the body."

"So, there is no cleanup compound that can be constructed? Or some sponge that might soak them up, and then you could remove the sponge?" I asked.

"Theoretically, if some programmable blood cells were constructed that could target a specific compound, they may be able to deposit the compound into the urinary or digestive tract for removal. But as far as I know, no such technology exists," Farouk replied.

The doors opened behind us, and in walked Jason Bowmen, saying, "Hello, Sam, and who is your friend?"

"This is Erin Gallo. Erin, this is Jason Bowmen, captain of this ship," I said, introducing the two.

"Hello, nice to meet you, Erin," Jason said, offering his handshake to Erin.

They shook hands, and Erin said, "Pleased to meet you too."

"It was nice getting to know your friends at the party. Probably the strangest group of party guests to be gathered in one place," Jason said.

"Thanks for coming, to both of you. I am sorry I did not have a lot of time to spend talking with you. I think the guest count was too high for a one evening event," I said.

"I must admit it was a fascinating gathering, Sam. I was delighted to meet your friends from other probable universes," Farouk said.

"That's an understatement for me. I could not believe I talked with a starship captain from the future, and I must admit, you are pretty good on the drum kit," Jason said with a smile.

"I thought people might congregate with their arrival group, but overall, I saw some decent mingling taking place," I said with a little pride.

"I know I enjoyed my discussion with the Mist Door doctor. What was her name, Marion?" Farouk asked.

"Marsha, Marsha Bradley," I said, helping Farouk remember.

"Ah yes, that is right. Marsha is responsible for the health care of several teams that use a mist door to explore planets within their galaxy. Very exciting stuff," Farouk said merrily.

"So, what brings you to *Explorer*?" Jason asked.

"I hoped to get some advice from Farouk about treating a family member who has a rage sickness. We are at odds about the ethics of treating someone against their will, but my great uncle would never submit to experimental medical treatment," I said, hoping Farouk might continue this discussion.

"And that is another thing that I dislike about your approach, Sam. It is experimental. You have not confirmed your diagnosis, yet you have already begun a treatment regimen. That is not good medicine. And now you want to extend that even further with more exploratory experiments to search for heavy compounds within the body? You are conducting science backward. You don't construct treatment and hope to find the sickness along the way," Farouk said.

"That's why I am here, Farouk. I know I am out of my league on this, and I do appreciate your input and guidance, but his anger is starting to focus on me," I said.

Erin remained silent the whole time, listening to the conversation, and finally said, "What Sam isn't telling you is that Valentino almost killed him yesterday. Ohm, replay the log from the Vasco villa where the tentacles grabbed Sam."

"Valentino, as in King Edward's magician?" Jason asked.

Before I could answer, the glowing orange sphere that Erin requested appeared before the group and started the playback of yesterday's kitchen scene. I stretched it out and repositioned it with gestures so we could all see it better. As the playback commenced, there were a couple of ohs and awes as the tentacle ripped apart the kitchen and yanked me back into the void.

Erin spoke, once again, saying, "Ohm, playback the part where Sam arrives at Madison's house."

The log replayed, and Farouk and Jason saw the deep wounds all over my body as Alex treated me with the skin sealer.

"Are you all right, Sam?" Jason asked.

"I can barely move. My joints are incredibly sore," I replied.

"That is something I can help with, Sam. Let's get you into the scanning chamber," Farouk said as he walked over to the control panel to open up the scanning bed that he used the last time I was on this ship.

As I walked over to the medical bed emerging from the wall, I leaned on Erin for support and said to Jason, "Valentino may have known a King Edward at one time, but that story is more than likely a reflection or distortion of the true events that historically took place in another probability."

The bed slid out, Erin helped me up onto it, and I laid down. Once again, I placed my invisihud into deep sleep mode. She stepped back as the medical bed retracted into the wall. I could hear Jason saying to Erin, "So, how long have you known Sam?"

"That breakfast, you saw in the log, was our first one together, so this is day two," Erin replied.

"Wow, that is some good morning," Jason said.

"Tell me about it," Erin said.

I was facing up this time, and the same process occurred as before. There was a series of several light patterns followed by a companion series of sounds that completed the scan of my body. I heard the sliding door retract, and the bed slowly slid out. I could see everyone gathered around Farouk's elevated display reviewing my body scan when Erin returned to the bed to help me sit up.

"I am seeing multiple micro-fractures in your scapula, acromion, acetabulum, and ischium. No wonder it hurts to move," Farouk said.

"Can you do anything for him, Farouk?" Jason asked.

"I believe so. Sam, the last time you were aboard this ship, you left behind what looked like two medical kits. I have been studying the internal operational guides provided with the devices, and I believe I can use the skin sealer to seal those microfractures," Farouk said.

"So, who is experimenting now?" I asked with a grin.

"I am quite confident that I can effect positive healing using the device. Do you consent?" Farouk asked.

"Sure, doc, patch me up," I said with a smile.

Farouk headed over to the partition wall stacked with various books, containers, and what looked like animal cages where he opened a lower drawer, producing a medkit.

"What happens if you don't find a way to calm down this Valentino?" Jason asked.

"I don't know, more attacks, perhaps," I replied. "It was terrifying being suspended and bound by magical tentacles as he raged in anger against me."

"How did you escape, if you don't mind me asking?" Jason asked.

"Some time ago, I placed a biomedical device inside Valentino to track him, so I could detect if he approached my location. I don't think he ever detected I did that. It was the only option that was available to me. I was able to trigger the release of a tranquilizer into his bloodstream, using a remote device, even while bound. Once he passed out, the tentacles released their grip," I said.

Farouk returned with the skin sealer and began treatment on my shoulders, saying, "Hold as still as possible."

"That is some clever forethought on your part, Sam. What caused you to place the device within him in the first place?" Jason asked.

"This isn't the first time Valentino has tried to kill me. The last time was several years ago. When I defeated him and his companions. I placed them all in cryogenic chambers, with a virtual reality feed applied to their brains. It kept them sedated and immobile for years. I recently released them from their virtual prison, but before doing so, I implanted the medical device as a tracker and a failsafe, in case I needed to knock them out at a moment's notice," I replied.

"Why did you release him?" Erin asked, and Jason gave me the same questioning look, presumably he was going to ask the same thing.

"In my future memories, there were serious consequences suffered by my friends because I did not release Valentino from his virtual prison. I tried to avoid that scenario by preemptively releasing him, this time around," I said.

"So, the tentacle attack never occurred in your other future memories?" Jason asked.

"That's right, and I am starting to feel like I am temporally robbing Peter to pay Paul. It seems time itself has a way of exacting a toll upon me no matter what action I take," I said.

Farouk finished up with the skin sealer on my right shoulder and said, "How does that feel?"

I moved my right arm around, and it did feel better, less acute pain, more of an ache. "It feels better," I said.

Farouk moved over to my left arm and started repeating the treatment using the skin sealer.

"I did not know the skin sealer could reach below the skin," I said to Farouk.

"It's all there in the user's guide. Quite a remarkable device, all of them. The medjector has become my go-to instrument for treating mild injuries. It supports quite a few species. I was pleasantly surprised at the wealth of additional Ursonian knowledge I was able to obtain just by reading the manuals," Farouk said as he worked.

"I apologize if my unethical approaches have offended you, Farouk," I said. "I am open to any other options you might have to offer."

"Each species approaches solutions in their own way. I understand, all too well, the desperate measures one might take when fighting for one's life. During the Mirandian war, I was forced to make life and death decisions on the battlefield," Farouk said, stopping treatment, for a moment to look at me, "and I felt shame and guilt over some of those decisions."

Erin spoke up, "My blood. I have micro machines in my blood. Could we reprogram those to search for heavy elements inside a body?"

Farouk paused treatment again and looked over at Erin, "I don't know enough about your species to assess that at this time, but if the technology could be modified, perhaps."

Jason looked at Erin and said, "Sam told us, the first time we met, that you are part cybernetic, constructed by androids."

"That's right, my species is called Melog," Erin said.

"Please lie down now, Sam," Farouk said, and I laid down on the scanning bed so Farouk could apply regeneration to my pelvic area. I unzipped and pulled down my pants.

"Do you know how to reprogram the micro machines in your blood?" Jason asked.

"We weren't built that way. My line of Melog was designed to be as human as possible. We were built to infiltrate. Remaining human, even ignorant of our own construction, was part of the deception the androids planned against their human creators," Erin said.

"So, your android creators did not look human, like you do?" Jason asked.

"No, they are metallic and more robotic," Erin said. "I guess it's ironic. The humans built the robotic machines, and the machines built enhanced cloned humans."

"That is extraordinary," Farouk said to Erin, then to me, "Please turn over and lie on your stomach."

I turned over and put my face in the hole provided by the bed design.

"It didn't feel extraordinary, more like nightmarish. Some of my production line were programmed to lie, deceive friends, and cause havoc throughout the Imperial fleet," Erin said.

"I'm sorry to hear that," Jason said.

"Me too. I still feel the guilt of what others in my production line did," Erin said.

"So, you are no longer at war with the Imperial fleet?" Jason asked.

"That's right. We nearly exterminated one another. The Melog attack against the humans was so effective that it reduced a population of billions down to a mere seventy thousand. In the conflict, we suffered greatly. We are effectively on the brink of extinction unless we can figure out how to procreate. If it weren't for *Journey* and Sam finding us a planet, we might all be dead by now," Erin said.

"I'm sorry to pry. My own human heritage is riddled with wars and senseless loss of life," Jason said.

"Mine too," Farouk said while continuing to apply the skin sealer to my hip, "Ursa has had its share of wars. It seems no matter what species we are, we all find a way to kill one another."

"That's okay. I feel like my life has taken a turn for the better since I met this guy," Erin said, rubbing the hair on the back of my head.

"I know what you mean. I don't know if Sam told you, but he saved my life and the ship when we were under Rulkan attack," Jason said.

Farouk made a few more passes with the skin sealer and said, "That's it, Sam. That is about all I can do with this device."

I flipped over on the bed and pulled my pants on. I was able to sit up on my own and get down from the bed without assistance. Stepping over to him, I gave Farouk a quick hug saying, "Thank you, Farouk. My joints feel a lot better," forgetting that Ursonian's don't like to be touched.

"Now, now. No need for that," Farouk said as he put the skin sealer to the medkit.

Jason asked, "Would you like your medkits returned to you?"

"Oh, no, that is not necessary. I can replicate as many as I like. You keep them. It seems Farouk has an affinity for leveraging them to their maximum potential. I'm going to have to brush up a bit more on their usage," I replied.

"They are very useful. Thank you, Sam," Farouk said as he returned the medkit to the drawer.

"As far as the original matter we were discussing, I can do a little research into possible mechanisms to dislodge heavy elements embedded in the body, but I can't promise if I'll achieve anything soon," Farouk said.

"I understand. If you do come up with something, you can contact me using the card I gave Jason," I said, then turning to Jason. "Did the card survive the attack?"

"It did. We found it during cleanup after you left," Jason said.

"I guess we are off to other pastures then. Until we meet again," I said to them both.

They both looked at me with an expression of, "Well, how are you leaving?"

"Erin, do you have that vignette in your back pocket?" I asked.

"Oh, yeah," she said, and she pulled it out, handing it to me.

"No, you should try to operate it. Look at it and pretend that the location is real," I said.

"All right," she said as she held the card before her, concentrating on it.

It took a few seconds before she said, "Oh, wow, I see what you mean."

Jason stood close by. He looked over her shoulder from afar and said, "I don't see any change."

I put my hand around Erin's waist, and we stepped through the vignette into the tech hallway of Xanadu.

CHAPTER 42

Micro Machines

"N ow I see what you mean about vignette travel being more organic than transporters," Erin said, looking up at me and returning the vignette to her back pocket.

I turned around and said, "Follow me."

We headed down the corridor away from the tech door where we appeared. I guided us to an exit of the Xanadu building. Concrete steps led down to a lawn, and across the lawn were the stables that housed my small collection of horses. It was a nice sunny day, and I took a seat on the top step and motioned for Erin to sit down beside me.

She could sense something was up and sat down next to me, asking, "What is it?"

"Because I have future memories of our relationship, there are some things I know about you that you don't know about me. I know that makes it unfair, from your point of view. Also, it does not mean that everything will work out the same way it did," I said.

"All right," Erin said slowly as she pulled her hair behind her ear.

"What scares me the most about yesterday's tentacle attack is that if Valentino chose you instead of me, you may not have survived. Not because you couldn't endure the trip through the inter-dimensional corridor, but because once you shifted through echo, the micro machines in your blood might distort and fail to operate," I said.

Erin listened intently and felt uneasy.

"I was aware of your blood-based micro machines as soon as I acquired my future memories those long months ago. When I moved the *Pentacraft* into the new probability, I transported the remaining Melogs to the surface of Zenith. This transport left a memory buffer imprint of all the Melog revisions. I forwarded the revision nine blood-based micro machine design to this facility so the doctors could study them and produce replicated copies that can withstand the stress of traveling through echo. In my future memories, I arrogantly shifted you through echo without considering this. It left you sick and dying and nearly broke my heart to see you that way," I said with tears welling up in my eyes.

"Sam," Erin said.

"Fortunately, the team at this facility was able to replicate new echo sturdy versions of these micro machines, and your life was saved. But I can't help wonder if Farouk is right about my undisciplined methods. I don't want to be reckless with your life and assume you would want to undergo such a transfusion. I know I just met you two days ago, and already I worry about you becoming a target of my enemies. With the transfusion, you would at least be able to survive an echo shift if that ever happens. I don't know what," I said.

Erin interrupted me and said, "I want to, Sam. I want the transfusion. I can see how worried you are about this, and I trust your wisdom in these echo matters. After seeing the devastation that Valentino can wreak upon our lives, just using his mind, I know my life has already been forever altered. I don't want to be a liability in a critical situation. If this transfusion can help me survive an echo shift, I most certainly want it."

I heaved a sigh and said, "All right, let's head inside and see what progress has been made with the replication of these micro machines."

We got up and walked into the Xanadu building. Erin put her arm around my waist and slipped her hand into my back pocket as we walked down the hallway. We headed up the step and reached the tech door arrival points for the vignette. It opened automatically when we approached. This door led us into the room that Candy brought me to when I received treatment after subduing the dragon.

A middle-aged Blinn woman approached and said, "Welcome to Xanadu. I am DaLaHaLaMaNaSa. What can I do for you?"

"Hello, I am Erin," Erin said and extended her hand.

"We're here to check on the progress of a project I submitted remotely. Is it all right to call you DaLa?" I asked.

"Of course, many do. What is the nature of this project?" she asked as she led us into the room and over to the console that HorEl used the last time I was here.

"I supplied a transporter subject cache with instructions to try and replicate the micro machines found in the bloodstream of the transportee. In this case, it was a Melog female clone that looks just like Erin," I replied.

DaLa brought up a series of auragraphic displays, some spherical and others were rectangular. She swiped certain information from one auragraphic display to another, gathering information onto one display dismissing others before saying, "Here it is. It looks like replication is ninety-two percent possible from the subject cache, but an actual sample of blood from the source would increase the accuracy of the replication."

Erin and I gathered around DaLa and looked at the final merged display of information. There was an outline view of Erin's body along with a circle showing a small cylindrical tube object with tech depressions along its surface. The micromachine blood cell slowly rotated within the display.

"I can provide some actual blood cells now," Erin said.

"Wonderful," DaLa said, and she bent down to open a cabinet door built into the workstation where she stood. It took her a minute or so, but she finally produced a small pen device similar in size to the medjector found in the standard medkit.

"Hold out your finger. You might feel a small prick," DaLa said, positioning the tip of the pen device at the end of one of Erin's fingers then pressing a button.

It only took a second, and Dala said to Erin, "Just use direct pressure to stop any blood flow. It should stop bleeding in a few minutes."

DaLa tapped and swiped on a few of the virtual auragraphic displays, and a small physical compartment opened on the console she worked. She opened the pen device and removed an inner tube that held a very small quantity of Erin's blood. She placed the tube into the small compartment, tapped, and gestured a few times, causing the compartment to descend into the console, seamlessly leaving no trace it was ever there.

A new auragraphic display popped up, containing an image of the micro machine. We watched as the previous micro machine candidate revised with more detail retrieved from the blood sample. The result appeared as a slightly blurry image coming into focus. A small percentage bar moved up, and DaLa said, "It looks like we have a ninety-seven point eight percent match for replication."

"That looks pretty good. On the Melog *Pentacraft* we rarely produced predictive results so close to expected outcomes," Erin said.

"What do you think DaLa?" I asked, "This is a life-supporting function that we are considering."

DaLa made a few more gestures and said, "Let me run a few comparisons on the two data sets."

We watched as DaLa scrolled through data. She generated and dismissed selection sets, dropped entire selection sets into algorithms, and overall ran the numbers through the digital wringer before replying, "Even within the blood sample I just took, I am seeing a zero point seven percent deviation. The new replicated models should be more accurate than the originals."

"I guess it's up to you, Erin. Is there anything special about the micro machines you know about or want to convey to DaLa?" I asked.

Erin thought about it for a moment and said, "We were never really involved in our own construction, but my model line did review information about the internal micro machines. I don't recall any special exceptions. How accurate is the code match on the replicated models?"

DaLa replied, "The code match is one hundred percent. The minor deviations are mainly surface-related and should not interfere with normal operations."

"All right. Let's do it," Erin said with forced enthusiasm.

"DaLa, we need to replicate these new replacements from the same source that the cloaked scanners and invisihuds are constructed from. Also, I would like to store and preserve the originals," I said.

"Understood. Erin, the process is simple for you. You need to lie as still as possible on the biobed over there. The process will take a few minutes as the system scans your body for all micro machines. Each micro machine will be tracked. Once a solid lock is obtained, the new micro machine will be trans-placed with the replicated version. Do you understand these instructions?" DaLa asked with a professional tone.

Erin shook her head and said, "I understand."

Dala continued, "At any time during the process, if you feel something is wrong or out of place, please alert me or Sam, and we will halt the process. Although this has never been done before, you may experience the feeling of butterflies in your stomach or experience an itchy sensation. Try not to move."

Erin took a deep breath and said, "Got it," while giving an affirmative head nod.

"Please disrobe and lie down on the biobed over there," Dala said.

Erin and I walked over to the biobed where she took off her clothes and sat down on the biobed.

"It feels warm, like skin. Reminds me of an alcove on the *Pentacraft*," Erin said.

"I thought the same thing the last time I was lying down here," I said, holding her hand as she lie down on the biobed naked.

I could see her blow out another heavy breath like she was mustering up her courage. I thought about kissing her, but I did not want her to think I was kissing her goodbye. I smiled as best as I could, letting go of her hand as I stepped back from the stairs leading up to the biobed. DaLa activated the process, and the rings around the bed retracted into the wall as the biobed mechanisms spun into action.

I knew this was risky, but I also knew it worked in the two other time loops. It's really hard to feel so helpless as your loved one undergoes a life-changing procedure. The process was different compared to what I experienced. Erin wasn't lowered into the bed, and there was no fluidic element involved in her treatment. A series of small blinking lights hovered and randomly danced around her, leaving the impression that the entire bed was covered in fireflies emitting blue light. The lights softly glowed for a moment, then quickly faded. At one point during the procedure, I noticed Erin glance over at me, and I gave her a slight smile as I watched intently for signs that something was going wrong. It was one of those processes that seemed to take forever but was probably only six to eight minutes. As the process continued, the volume of glowing lights dramatically reduced until there was just an occasional one here and there. The metal hoops descended from their docking locations in the ceiling to take up their support locations at either end of the bed as it returned to its resting position by the steps.

DaLa said from the control station, "The transfusion of replicated micro machines is complete. I am seeing a one hundred percent replacement of all detected micro machines. How do you feel?"

Erin sat up as I took her hand, and she said, "I feel okay. You were right about the internal butterflies, DaLa."

Erin revealed a big smile of relief as she stepped down to the second step, hugged me for a moment, then kissed me passionately. I felt so relieved and picked her up as she wrapped her legs around my waist, giving me a full-body naked hug. I felt a little twinge in my hips and shoulder, but I didn't mind. My lover survived.

DaLa interjected, while still maintaining her professional voice, "It's best if you spend a complete day in observation so we can monitor you for any side effects."

Erin replied over my shoulder to DaLa, "Yes, of course."

DaLa said, "You can go ahead and get dressed, and I'll show you to the observation lounge."

I slightly shook my head no, and a sly smile crossed Erin's face as she picked up her clothes but didn't put them on. We followed DaLa out of the medical procedure room and down the hall, one door, to the observation area. It was basically an efficiency apartment with a large window revealing a scene of beautiful rolling hills. DaLa showed us a panel by the door with a large red button and said, "If you need anything, press the button," then she left.

"How do you feel about putting these new micro machines to the test?" I asked.

"You read my mind, darling," Erin said, and we headed into the bedroom and went at it.

The cruel content editor came in to remove a long-winded, detailed description of lovemaking, leaving a single line reading, "Faen, that was good."

"I love you, baby," I said.

We both lay on our backs for a few minutes, not saying anything before she moved over to put her arm across my chest and lay her head on my shoulder, saying, "I love you deeply, Sam. I know it's just words, but you have changed me so much, stirring something up inside me."

"I feel it too, Erin. You're a part of me now," I said.

We lie together, with her absent-mindedly touching my chest for quite some time, neither of us saying anything. Erin broke the silence by asking, "In your future memories, did I ever betray you?"

"Erin," I said softly.

"I want to know," she said, raising up slightly to look at me.

"Erin, don't do this. Don't second guess yourself. I know you feel guilt from the memories you acquired from Skimmer and Hebe. But that's not you. It doesn't have to be you. Even though Sandra tricked Craig, that doesn't mean you are going to trick me," I said.

"So, did I? Did I betray you?" she asked again.

I paused, remained silent, and she shook me, "I want to know. I need to know, Sam," she pleaded.

"It wasn't betrayal. Every relationship has its ups and downs. You know that, right?" I asked.

Erin shook her head, yes.

"The wisdom of the Ursonian marriage allows for the addition of new relationships. That's why each wife can have three husbands of her own. In the first loop, we hit a rough patch. You found someone else to comfort you. I was emotionally hurt at the time, but I did not feel betrayed. You are allowed to love other people, Erin," I said.

"Who was it?" she asked.

I squirmed away from her and sat on the edge of the bed with my back to her, and said, "Now, you're just making me mad."

"I want to know?" Erin said.

"What do you want me to say? It's John Doe on planet X. Go fuck him now?" I said a bit too harshly.

"No, no, I'm sorry, don't leave me, Sam," Erin said as she climbed over and wrapped her arms around my chest from behind.

I touched her hands as I spoke, "These future memories are a gift as well as a burden, Erin. I don't want them to tear us apart. Some truly horrifying terrible things happened to me in both time loops, and none of it was your fault. But you have to trust me to choose the right ones. Overall the second loop was better than the first, and I want to make this loop even better than that one. But I am not pretending that I can recreate only good parts and dodge the bad things. New bad things have already happened."

She repositioned herself to sit behind me, wrapping her arms around me even tighter, saying, "I'm sorry, Sam. I do trust you. Doesn't the transfusion prove that?"

I turned my head to look at her and said, "You don't have to prove anything to me, Erin. If we reach a point in our relationship where you are attracted to another person, that is your right. I don't own you. It's not something I give you, like permission. It's something you have always had, the right to choose who you want to be with."

I unlocked her hands from my chest, got up, and headed into the bathroom to take a shower. She followed me in as I ran the hot water and asked, "I'm faening up, aren't I?"

"You're not faening up, all right," I said, trying to get into the shower.

She followed me into the shower and started to cry, saying, "I just want to be what you want."

"Erin, you are what I want. Why don't you believe me?" I asked.

"I don't even know who I am anymore, what I am. You're changing me. I'm on a planet in gods who knows where and I'm messing up. I don't want to be like this," Erin said in an all-out cry.

"What do you want to be like?" I asked.

"I don't know. I don't like feeling like this," she pouted.

I rubbed my face and said, "Here, trade me places. You look like you're getting cold."

We swapped places in the small shower, and the warm water poured over her hair as she looked down.

"Don't you think I get to feeling like that sometimes too? We all do. Wondering if I'm doing the right thing, asking myself if I deserve this or that. Who am I to take a woman's heart and drink so thoroughly from it that I use her up?"

Erin looked up with water dripping across her face.

"The fact that you ask these questions about yourself means you're a considerate person, deserving of love. And I do love you. But our love starts and ends here with ourselves and how we treat each other. I'm sorry for getting angry at you for asking a question, but I need you in my life. You're changing me, making me grow, giving me something to hold on to, to look forward to. When you're asking for the name of another lover while we're still lying together in bed, I'm hurt, and I don't like feeling like that either," I said.

"I'm sorry, I didn't mean it like that. It's not like I was just going to toss you aside and run off. I wonder what kind of person I become?" Erin asked.

"You become the kind of person you want to be. Think about what you want to become, don't ask me to provide you a reference to emulate. You're more than that now. You're a beautiful person deserving to achieve your own goals," I said, starting to get a little cold in the shower.

She looked up at me with red eyes and said, "You seem so confident, Sam. You always know what you want and how to get it. I want to feel that same way."

"Well, if I come off that way, I guess that is just good acting. Honestly, I feel like I have been barely hanging on, at the end of my rope, being swung around from event to event, trying to find you. And now that you are here, it's like I can breathe again. You give me hope that the future will be more than just trying to scramble to install the next item from the future memories," I said.

"I love you, Sam," she said, crying a bit more and trying to smile. "Come here. You're starting to shiver."

"Baby, you'll find your confidence, and it won't be something that I give you. You'll find it within yourself," I said, hugging her and getting under the warm water.

I adjusted the showerhead for a wider spray and asked, "Can I wash your hair?"

She looked up at me, gathering her composure, offering a gentle smile, and said, "Yeah, I'd like that."

I kissed her and located the shampoo and conditioner.

We finished showering and settled in for the remainder of a domestic evening together. I ordered us some Thai food. Erin really liked the Shrimp Phad Tai. We spent some time going over how to leverage Ohm in many situations. Erin began to realize that Ohm was much more than just a kiosk that fulfilled food and clothing requests. I helped her come up with some basic outfits containing pockets to hold the Xanadu vignette and any others she might acquire along the way. I showed her my three, and she practiced activating them but not stepping through. I told her about the cloaked scanners I kept hidden in the heels of my boots, and we integrated them into some of her daily footwear. We drank some ales and smoked part of a joint after eating. This smoking and drinking led me to replicate a classical guitar, and I played a few tunes I could remember learning during my virtual prison life. She seemed to like hearing the guitar.

In the morning, we lay together in the bed, and while we did not have sex, we held each other for a long time, not really talking about anything. I put on my basic outfit, with the green shirt, and I mentioned to Erin that we would be traveling outside today and she should dress accordingly. I put together a small breakfast of coffee and breakfast croissants. While we finished up, a melodic tone came from the door. I opened the door, and it was DaLa.

"Come in," I said.

I offered DaLa some food, but she declined and took a seat across from us, asking Erin, "How are you feeling today?"

"I feel fine, DaLa," Erin replied.

"Our monitoring showed some ups and down in your emotional profile. I just wanted to check with you to make sure there were no problems with the newly replicated micro machines," DaLa said.

Erin looked over at me, then to DaLa, and said, "It was an emotional night last night, but I don't think it had anything to do with the new micro machines you replaced."

"Okay, do you mind if I take a localized scan? We can do it here?" DaLa asked.

"Sure," Erin said.

DaLa opened up a folding device she retrieved from her belt and asked Erin, "Please stand up."

Erin got up and moved over near DaLa, who tapped a few times on the device then moved the device from head to toe as she walked around Erin four times. After that, she tapped the device a few more times before proclaiming, "Everything looks great here. You are one hundred percent healthy as far as I can tell."

"That's good news. Thank you, DaLa," Erin said, returning to her seat.

"Well, the observation period is over, so there is no need to remain on-site unless you want to. Is there anything else I can help you with?" DaLa asked.

Erin shook her head no, but I said, "There is a new project I would like to get underway. Can I relate the basics to you now?"

"Certainly, I'll record your request now, and we can get the project started. What do you need?" DaLa asked.

"I need a way to remove accumulated heavy elements from a patient, but the patient won't submit to treatment, so bringing him to this facility is out of the question at this time. I talked with another doctor that mentioned it might be possible to program something like Erin's micro machines to gather the heavy elements and deposit them into the urinary or digestive tract for natural removal," I said.

"I'll have the appropriate teams assembled. What might help in this project would be test subjects that already have heavy elements embedded in their systems," DaLa replied.

"I believe I can provide a location with multiple subjects that you can sample from. I'll send you an update soon," I said.

"Well, enjoy the rest of your day, and I'll let myself out," DaLa said, returning the folding device to her belt and leaving the room.

I looked over at Erin and said, "Are you ready to put the new micro machines to the final test?" I asked.

"What did you have in mind?" Erin asked.

I pulled out the vignettes from my pocket and showed her the Light House of Flynn vignette saying, "This location is very close to the kingdom where Splendorites originate from. Most standard technology does not work at this location. The newly replicated micro machines, inside you, are constructed from echo sturdy materials. In theory, if you can survive there, you can survive in most any other echo you might find yourself in," I said.

I could see her tense up a bit, "Another day, another big decision," Erin said and hesitated before asking, "This is why we did it, right?"

"I'll be there with you and have the return vignette to Xanadu ready in case anything goes wrong. If you fall ill, we can return immediately," I said.

"All right," Erin said.

We both used the bathroom and brushed our teeth.

"I need to make a quick stop, first to get Dala what she needs to for the heavy elements project," I said.

"Okay," Erin said.

I took out the vignettes and located the catwalk vignette. I held it up before me and took Erin's hand. As the vignette came to life, I stepped forward into it, and Erin stepped with me. At the end of the catwalk stood the easel with the painting resting on it and the cloth covering it.

We walked down the catwalk, and I noticed some drops of blood along the floor, reminding me of the last time I was here, right after the tentacle attack. As we approached the painting, I said, "You may be wondering why the painting is covered."

"It crossed my mind. What is this place?" Erin asked.

"This is the starship *Deceptive*. The ship's computer is named Ari. And that painting is like a psychic vignette. It reads your mind and constructs a vignette to the location you have in mind," I said.

"Whoa, that is wild, Sam. Where did you get such a thing?" Erin asked.

"I made it many years ago, before *Tiger Mountain* or this ship ever existed," I said.

"How did you make it?" Erin asked, then took her question back. "Never mind."

"Ari, this is Erin. Recognize her for access when onboard," I said out loud.

"Hello, Sam, and hello, Erin. You are now recognized for access aboard this ship. Welcome aboard the *Deceptive*," Ari replied.

"Thank you, Ari," Erin said, looking around.

"You are welcome, Erin," Ari replied.

"Ari, can I get my spilled blood removed from the catwalk and below if any fell onto the floor?" I asked.

"Certainly, it will be removed by the next time you arrive," Ari replied.

I turned to Erin and said, "There is a side effect with using this painting. When it is left all alone, and there is no one around for it to psychically sense, it tends to construct terrifying and revolting images. When I bring a guest along, I always ask them to look away until the painting reads my mind. There is no real danger if you do see the image other than it might give you nightmares later on.

At least that is what has happened to other people who have not averted their gaze when I remove the cloth."

"That is really weird, Sam," Erin said.

"It's your choice. I just wanted to warn you. It works basically like a vignette. Only you don't hold it,]. You just stand in front of it and concentrate." I said.

"All right," Erin said.

"Ohm, deploy a cloaked scanner to this location. I am going to send it through the painting," I said.

A sparkle appeared in the air and then vanished. I targeted the cloaked scanner in my invisihud and looked over at Erin, saying, "Okay, close your eyes or look away."

Erin closed her eyes, and I removed the cloth covering the *Vision* painting. The canvas presented a scene of a dead zombie wolf leaning over to groom itself, only instead of licking its fur, it was eating its own bowels. The bowels were old and rotten, with maggots crawling and squirming. It seemed to take notice of me and looked up from its grooming to stare at me with a snarl forming around its matted dog lips. One of its eyes fell out and started to roll away. As the wolf got up, its insides remained on the floor. It looked like it sought its own fallen eye, then it turned and snapped at the canvas. I forgot to put together my thought before I revealed the painting, and I struggled to impress my will upon the painting.

Erin said, "Oh my gods."

I brought forth the image of a seaside mining port and imagined the wooden sailing vessels, both docked and in the bay. The canvas changed, revealing the shanty-style houses dotting the cliffside riddled with mines and obvious runoff from heavy elements. I imagined a strong legacy of mining lead, mercury, cadmium, beryllium, and cobalt, finally sealing the intent with an aging fishing population dying from heavy element poisoning.

"Ohm, transfer the cloaked scanner into the scene," I said before picking up the cloth and covering the painting.

I looked over at Erin and said, "I warned you."

"I know, but my gods, that was awful," Erin replied with a disgusted face.

I located the cloaked scanner and set it to map and evade.

"Ohm, can you forward a link to the deployed cloaked scanner to the Xanadu research team. Submit the link to DaLa."

"Forwarding link," Ohm replied.

"Okay, now that we're finished with the painting, let's try something more enjoyable," I said while pulling the vignettes out of my pocket.

CHAPTER 43

Splendor

I handed the Light House of Flynn vignette to Erin, and I held onto the Xanadu vignette. Taking Erin's hand, I said, "I'm ready. Concentrate on the lighthouse and step through."

Erin held the vignette before her. I noticed her face change as the scene in the vignette became more real to her. Her expression changed to a smile, and she said, "Let's step, Mister," and we both stepped forward as the dark scene of the *Deceptive* catwalk brightened into a lovely day by the sea.

"Oh, wow. This place is so vivid," Erin said. "This world is so much richer."

Erin was stunned, looking around slowly, taking it all in as I said, "Now you know why we call the other probabilities echoes. They are muted reflections of this true world, the original world."

I pointed along the coastline to her left where a large flat jutting mountain held an impressive castle several kilometers away and said, "That is the castle of Splendor, the official center of the probable multi-verse."

"Oh, Sam, it's so beautiful. I can't believe the world can be so much more real. It's like a veil was lifted," Erin said.

"How do you feel?" I asked, still holding the emergency escape vignette in my hand.

"I feel wonderful, Sam. You did all this for me?" Erin asked.

"Well, this place existed long before you or I did, so I can't take credit for constructing this world. It's the other way around. This place constructs all the other worlds that exist. But I wanted you to be echo mobile so I could share places like this with you," I said before taking the vignette from her hand and tucking it and the Xanadu vignette into the inner pocket of my shirt.

The vignette to the Lighthouse of Flynn leaves you on a knoll near the lighthouse from which the image on the vignette was framed. We headed down the slope toward the beach, where we could hear the sounds of seals barking. Seabirds flew around, and others who landed ran fast then stopped, leaving footprints in the sand, which were washed away by the next swelling of waves to come ashore. I kept my eyes on Erin and wondered if I should have brought along a medical inspectrograph to verify the micro machines in her blood were holding their shape.

The shore was filled with life forms. Everywhere we looked there were birds, starfish, crabs, and ground animals. Seals barked at us as we passed them by from a distance, with a few of them returning to the water just to be safe. The afternoon clouds had that Maxfield Parrish look to them only with the volumetrics turned way up. In the distance, toward the castle, several sailing ships of various sizes could be seen upon the water.

We walked along the beach, holding hands, and I said, "It feels good to be outside of closed spaces. I have not returned here since before my future memories arrived."

Erin stopped walking and turned to me, putting her hands around my chest, and hugged me, not saying anything. I returned her speechless hug, and it felt good. Being near Splendor has an intoxicating effect, especially for new arrivals, but even I felt it this time. This place was my home. Or was supposed to be. Being an outlaw in your own land sucks.

I thought about that day when I arrived here in Splendor with *Tiger Mountain*. A beautiful glass teardrop shape hovering over the ocean, off the coast where the castle sits. I thought it would bring joy and make people feel safe that the forces of chaos had nothing on the ingenuity of the Lords of Splendor, but I was greeted with fear and even Osric, the King, felt it was best if I take my invention and go. I took my time, however. I submerged *Tiger Mountain* into the sea and spent several months mapping the contours of the ocean bed surrounding Splendor. I presented the maps later to the Splendor library. It was the only compliment that I recall Garret ever giving me. He was impressed with the maps. That was all so long ago.

"I feel like I'm in a dream, Sam. A dream I don't want to wake up from," Erin said as she released her hug.

"Well, don't get too dopey on me. I am considered an outlaw in these lands, and any of my companions would surely be treated the same way. There are dangerous plants and animals here, too," I said.

Erin looked up at me, and we kissed again. It was all so storybook. I knew it might not be a good idea to linger, exposed on the beach like this, so I asked, "Do you want to see the cottage where I conducted a lot of my preliminary research into the morphability of base elements between dimensions?"

"With a line like that, how can a girl say no," Erin said with a smile.

"Ohm, can you replicate an anti-gravity platform?" I asked.

A sparkle appeared in front of us, and when it faded, a slate grey platform remained. I held out my hand to Erin, who took it, and we stepped onto the platform together. Tapping twice on the floor with my boot caused a small auragraphic display to float up from the floor. I activated the virtual railings for the unit, which shimmered in a ring around us.

"If you feel unbalanced, you can hang on to the rails," I said, and Erin held on as I touched the virtual display to set us in motion.

We began to rise, and I started assigning targets for the anti-gravity platform to seek. Before reaching the target, I chose another one, off in the distance to guide us to a new location while heading for the nearby woods.

"The controls are similar to a shuttlecraft, and this unit does auto-balance itself, so you can't issue a command that will dump you off. Give it a try. Pick a target on the map, then touch this re-target icon," I said.

Erin picked a new location on the map within the auragraphic display then touched the re-target icon. The anti-gravity platform started heading off in that direction.

"The anti-gravity platform acts as a sphere as far as collision detection is concerned. So, even if you pick a target location, and there are obstacles in the way, it will go around those obstacles and then return to seeking its current target," I said.

"I have to say this is pretty damn cool, Sam," Erin said.

"Hang on. I'm going to speed us up a bit," I said as I increased our cruising speed while continuously managing new targets.

While the anti-gravity platform is not incredibly fast, at our new speed, we traveled as fast as a horse running at a full gallop. I guided us through the trees of this old-growth forest, hovering over a few footpaths and trails with clear passages. I held onto the virtual rails, which were soft as a balloon. It offered some resistance, but if you squeezed too hard, it would collapse. We eventually entered a more dense part of the forest, requiring me to slow down the anti-gravity platform. Just when the forest seemed to get too dense to travel through, the tree line gave way to a clearing. This clearing was a long wide strip that acted as a divider between what was considered Splendor proper and the edge of echo from which we arrived. The forest picked up a few hundred meters away, where the Forest of Rayleaf officially began. A short distance ahead was a small cottage made of stone with a slate roof. I targeted that area for approach, and we landed near the front door.

Once we landed, I targeted the anti-gravity platform and recycled it. Ivy grew on one side of the cottage walls, and there was moss on some of the slate roof tiles. A few of the leaded glass windows were broken out, and the door was out of alignment. I pushed hard to open it for entry. As we walked in, I called out, "Hello? Mr. Peterson here to check the pipes?"

There was no answer, so we headed inside. It was not a large house. There was an upstairs with a couple of bedrooms, but the lower floor was where I spent most of my time those hundreds of years ago. The thing about Splendor is that it is timeless. In this probability, it was not unreasonable that a structure built in Splendor over six hundred years ago would still be standing. It looked like a few past animals made their homes here, but overall, the place was intact. You could, with a little elbow grease, fix this place up in a week or two for basic human living.

I got lost in nostalgia as I looked over some of the samples I fetched from echo that were still present in a few of the unbroken glass cases. It was nothing special, mainly raw ore samples, the occasional complex object like a crystal radio, and a musket that I could never get to fire. I knew Grayson constructed a working gun in Splendor, but he never shared the recipe for his gun powder. After several attempts, I wasn't able to reproduce that. I wondered how he would feel now that I had brought forth teleportation devices and laser weapons? Erin rummaged around and located an old journal I left behind. Because most of my experiments never produced any meaningful results, I kept my work on site. She was leafing through one of the journals and asked, "What language is this?"

I took a look and said, "That is the language of Splendor. Its nearest modern counterpart you might encounter in our Starnet echo would be that of the Solex Mal, or the solar tongue as it is called now," I replied.

"I find it interesting to see your origins. Thank you for sharing this with me," Erin said, walking over to me. "Thank you for sharing everything, Sam. You are changing who I am and my concept of what the universe is while making me come all over the place at the same time."

I couldn't help but smile, and I returned her kiss. We kept at it for a short time, kissing and holding each other. I touched and smelt her hair. I couldn't help but pull her to me once again and finally moved my hand to her hips as we stopped kissing and just stood close to one another.

"Talk about cumming. I can't believe how hot you make me. Fuck, you're gorgeous, and not just on the outside. You're beautiful all the way through, Erin. I love your soul as well as your body," I said.

"While I have the memories of the other revision-nines that have had relationships with men until I met you, I have only had intercourse with other male Melogs. I love having access to the male equipment. And while I do have memory references of the other males, I really like your shape and size. You turn me on, Sam, all the way through. And you turn on my soul the same way with the way you treat me," Erin said.

She touched me the entire time she talked, slowly moving her hand over my chest and then along my shoulders, but I could sense that we weren't about to jump each other's bones and do it there on the dusty table. I gave her one more long hug and asked, "Are you hungry? Are you ready for lunch?"

"Actually, yeah, now that you mention it. What do you want to have?" Erin asked.

"How about Earth Middle Eastern?" I replied.

"I'm not sure what that means, but I trust your taste," she said.

"Ohm, can we get a large red and white checkered table cloth, some napkins, and silverware? Transport in some Middle Eastern grilled chicken, along with pita bread, salad, hummus, and tabouli. Oh, and, a couple of pistachio baklava with chai tea for two."

A few moments later, a stack of food wrapped in foil appeared on top of the folded table cloth. Erin picked up the foil containers, and I spread out the table cloth over the end of one of the work tables. We pulled up a couple of stools that were still sturdy and functional, sat down across from one another, and started unwrapping the food. It was warm, steamy, and smelled really good. I cut some of the pita bread in half, opened the pocket, and said, "Just stuff what you want into the bread, and it's a portable sandwich."

I demonstrated by putting some hummus in the bottom of my pita, placing chicken inside, and topping it off with tabouli. She got the idea and started making her own pocket pita sandwich, and soon we enjoyed our lunch together.

"I like this drink. What is it called?" Erin asked.

"That is called chai, and there are multiple flavors. If you were to visit local communities, everyone would make it a little bit differently. It's tea with milk and spices. Oh yeah, careful with the olives there, don't bite down too hard on them. They have pits inside. You spit that part out," I said.

We took our time eating, and Erin leafed through one of the journals she found, asking, "Are these your drawings?"

I took a look and said, "Yeah, I used to spend a lot of time drawing, but now I don't do that anymore. I don't even write. I wonder what that says about me?"

"You should give it a try again. I like your style. It's sketchy, but you have a nice way of representing the basic form," Erin said, complimenting me.

"I guess, once I got into playing music, that became my preferred outlet for artistic creativity," I said.

We finished with the baklava, and Erin ordered some more chai from Ohm. It was nice to see her becoming more comfortable interacting with Ohm. We finished our lunch. Outside, we heard the sound of approaching horses. Taking to the sides of the windows, we peered out discreetly to see who arrived. I was glad to see Erin using basic military smarts. She took up a concealed position to observe without me having to direct her at all.

We saw three horses, and one of the riders dismounted, heading to the door of the house.

"I can extend my shield to protect you if you stand close. If things turn ugly, ask Ohm to transport you back to San Francisco. We'll meet up there, got it?" I asked her while looking at her directly in the eye.

"Got it. I'll stay close for now," Erin replied, and she moved over to stand beside me.

Someone forced the door to the cottage open, and stepped inside. I called out, "We're in here."

A young man dressed in light leather armor with a leather armor cap stepped in, looked at us, and said, "Lord Joshua wishes to speak with you at once."

"Very well," I replied, and we walked past the armored soldier who refused to turn his back on us.

He followed us out and shoved Erin to make us move faster as I got stuck trying to move through the messed-up front door. I recognized the emblem on the armor this guard wore. Joshua's crest depicted a rider on a horse surrounded by hounds. He was the man who cut off my finger and handed it over to Valentino on that horrible day when I ended up destroying the Spectre Vorticle. He was considered the Lord of Rayleaf, this forest. If Osric were the King of Splendor, then Joshua was the King of the Forest of Rayleaf.

I dove into my invisihud, which already provided these men as targets. Once we exited the cottage, I stopped, for a moment, to review the scene while Erin stood beside me. It was Joshua all right, and he sat atop Charnelgrim, as he always did. Charnelgrim was to Joshua what *Tiger Mountain* was to me. It was the largest horse I have ever seen. It easily stood two to three hands taller than the other two horses on either side. It was not just that Charnelgrim was large. It was also part mechanical, like a blending of organic and tech. Charnelgrim's coat was a dull silver-grey. While a typical horse might be described as having gentle eyes, Charnelgrim presented the eyes of a trapped soul who knew it could never escape. Along the forearm and gaskin of the legs, hints of pistons moved under the skin. A technical profile defined the barrel of its chest. Where the pastern connected to the hoof, there were mechanical hinges.

The young soldier didn't like the fact we stopped and shoved me hard from behind. I took the opportunity to fall to the ground, and Erin reached down to help, saying, "Leave him alone."

He drew his short sword and yelled, "Keep moving!"

"All right, all right, you don't have to shove. I'm moving," I said, getting up slowly as Erin offered her hand to help me up.

I was basically stalling. I assumed Joshua kept reinforcements hidden among the tree line. The cloaked scanners finally located them and presented nine more targets hidden from my view. I chose the sleep icon, activated it, and proceeded to walk over to stand in front of Charnelgrim, whom I feared more than Joshua.

"Kneel before your Lord!" the soldier demanded with his sword in his hand.

"Watch your tongue, young boy. You are speaking to a Lord of Splendor," I replied to the youth.

He raised his sword to intimidate me as I targeted him with the invisihud and activated the drunken sailor icon. He tipped over backward, losing his balance, and fell to the ground. The older soldier on the other horse next to Joshua dismounted and approached. His armor was even more elaborate but still carried the emblem of Joshua upon his chest. He was a bit older than the youth and said to me as he approached, "The crown no longer recognizes your claim of Lordship. You are trespassing on the King's grounds."

I targeted him with my invisihud and used the drunken sailor icon upon him. He stumbled and fell to the ground. I said, "It is not for you to decide the validity of my claim of Lordship. You are nothing but a drunken fool."

These words caused Joshua to dismount Charnelgrim. He walked over and knelt down to check on the older soldier. He cradled his head in his hand to check for a pulse along his neck when it finally hit me that Joshua was probably gay, and this might be his lover.

Erin interrupted the moment and said, "Your horse is beautiful. May I?"

Joshua did not say a thing to her, but I knew it was highly dangerous to approach Charnelgrim. Even among Joshua's own men, only a few caretakers were granted permission to touch the beast. Permission was not necessarily given by Joshua but by Charnelgrim.

Erin said, "Hello, I am Erin. My, you are a powerful creature."

Charnelgrim whinnied and stomped its front hoof on the ground as Erin continued. "I understand what you are. I am like you."

She reached out and touched the silver coat near the lower chest area. Her size seemed small compared to Charnelgrim's massive frame. I targeted Charnelgrim with my invisihud as Joshua asked, "Why are you here, Sam?"

"Research. I was granted the right to conduct research in this small cottage at the edge of Rayleaf," I said.

"That was well over seven hundred years ago," Joshua replied.

"I don't recall there being any expiration date on the grant from the King," I said while I nervously watched Erin slowly pet Charnelgrim.

"What have you done to my men?" Joshua asked.

"What have I done? You should be asking yourself what they have done to themselves. It seems like there is a lack of discipline within your ranks for these men to report to duty falling down drunk," I replied.

"Let me slay him, my lord," the younger soldier said, trying to stand up but falling back over.

I located the antidote icon in the menu associated with blood-based attacks. Targeting the older soldier, I activated it. If this was Joshua's lover, I did not want to injure him too much, but bruising his pride was certainly on the table as far as I was concerned. I gave Erin a "What the fuck are you doing?" look that she seemed to get it. She stepped away from Charnelgrim to return to my side.

The older soldier regained his composure and rose to his feet with Joshua at his side.

"I might ask you the same thing. Why are you here, Joshua? Do you expect me to believe you just happen to be strolling by at the same time I am visiting my cottage?" I asked.

"I routinely tour my grounds," Joshua replied.

"Well, there you have it. We live in a world of coincidence. Now, if you'll excuse me, I'd like to return to my research," I said merrily.

"I can't allow that," Joshua said, "I want you off my grounds now."

I located the icon for transport in place and used it on Charnelgrim. This feature runs the target through *Tiger Mountain*'s transport memory buffer to remove any weapons before returning the subject to the same spot. By using it on Charnelgrim, I could analyze its biological makeup later if I survived this encounter.

The drunken soldier on the ground said, "My lord, Charnelgrim luminesced."

Joshua stood with Charnelgrim to his back, so I don't think he saw the transport sparkle the drunken soldier reported. He shifted his eyes in a quick dart to his man on the ground before returning his fixed gaze back to me.

"I won't be bullied by you, Joshua. These are not your grounds. They are the King's grounds to be enjoyed by all family members whose royal blood flows through their veins, and that includes me," I said, meeting his gaze.

He turned his back to me, returning to Charnelgrim, and mounted his massive horse. The older soldier helped the younger drunken one to his steed and steadied him on the saddle enough so he could remain mounted.

"Know this, Sam. If you are caught trespassing within the realm of Rayleaf, my men will show no mercy upon you or your companions," Joshua said as the older soldier returned to his steed and mounted it.

"And you know this. If any of your men hurt me, or my traveling companions, they will receive the same back. Make sure you send out your expendables on such missions and not your favorites," I said.

Joshua pulled on the reigns, turning Charnelgrim around twice before saying, "This is not over, Sam," and he rode off with his men.

Erin and I stood there, watching them ride off before she asked, "Isn't that the exact same thing that Valentino said to you?"

"Yeah, I think you are right. What an asshole. Come on, let's head back inside. I need to find something," I said.

We headed into the cottage, and I started rummaging around through drawers and some of the stacks of notes. Erin asked, "What are you looking for?"

"I am looking for the grant of permission given to me by King Osric, those long years ago. In the distant past, Joshua and his men would harass me, often daily, while I conducted my research here. They would enter the house, trash my lab, overturn tables, break chairs, eat my food, and even take a shit on the floor. A real quality bunch that Joshua associates himself with," I said while searching around.

"What does it look like?" Erin asked.

"I had to present it several times to the raiding parties and eventually placed it in a frame. It was the only thing about this place they seemed to respect because it held the King's seal," I said before heading up the stairs.

Erin followed me upstairs and headed into one bedroom while I searched the other one. This cottage was a nice place to live, at one time, if you could look past the harassment. I heard her call out from the other room, "What about this, Sam?"

I headed into the other room, and Erin was in the corner, dusting off a golden picture frame, damaged on one side. The glass was broken, but a few larger shards remained in place over the wax seal.

"That's it, baby. You found it," I said with a smile.

"What does it say?" Erin asked, handing the broken frame to me.

"On this day marked in Aprilis twenty, in the year of the owl, four hundred and fifty-two years after the dawn of the second age, I, King Osric of Splendor, hereby grant Sam Richards full permission to occupy a residence, and conduct research along the outer border of the forest of Rayleaf provided the results of such research are submitted to the master librarian in the city of Splendor," I read to her. "This is it. This grant is the ticket to entering the city."

"I don't get it. What do you mean?" Erin asked.

"I never presented my research. Now I have a document signed by the King, granting me the right to present my research to the royal librarian. The royal library is contained within the castle walls," I said.

"Do you plan on visiting the castle in Splendor?" Erin asked.

"Not yet, but if I do, this might come in handy. Let's head back downstairs."

We headed to the room where we ate our lunch, and I placed the golden frame on the table and said, "Ohm, I would like to replace the frame around this important document. The new frame should have a tracker, give it a flat black finish, and hermetically seal the document inside. Replace the glass with transparent beryllium."

There was a sparkle, and the golden broken frame disappeared, leaving a black streamlined modern frame in its place.

"Ohm, place this framed document in the vault, please," I said.

The revised frame sparkled, and when the sparkles faded, the frame was gone.

"Ohm, scan this residence for a replication imprint. Deploy a Blinn terraforming module to this location. When night falls, begin the reconstruction of this residence. Restore it to its original state. Please preserve all the documents found in this current residence. I would also like to expand it. Add a bathroom, indoor plumbing, a replicated water supply, modern kitchen appliances, and a flagstone patio off of the sunroom. In addition, I want to establish a monitored perimeter in a quarter kilometer radius around this residence. If any of Joshua's men approach, put them into a short, light sleep. Joshua, himself, should be excluded from such processing," I said.

"Queuing request for processing at the appropriate time," Ohm replied.

"I think it's time to get out of here, Erin. What do you say?" I asked.

"Sure, where to now?" Erin asked.

"Ohm, transport Erin and me to Candy's kitchen in Enki's Dale," I said.

The afternoon illumination along the dusty walls of this broken house collapsed my vision inward, returning me to the dark place. How did Joshua know I arrived at the cottage? It was like he said, seven hundred years have passed. Surely he did not keep a vigil on the place for that long? I wondered if he kept some type of scrying device around or knew a telepath who warned him ahead of time? He may have visited Luceat Tou Meer and obtained a vision himself. Either way, this did not change a damn thing. Until the King himself confronts me and commands me to do what Joshua says, I was going to remain defiant to the end. The dim lights of Candy's kitchen drifted in from the sides of my vision as we materialized again.

CHAPTER 44

Magician Attack

"Wow, it's nighttime here, but it was afternoon where we just left," Erin said as she looked around the kitchen.

"Each echo has its own temporal offset. I use Splendor as the baseline. In this echo, time runs one point six-eight times faster than Splendor. In Xanadu, time runs eight times faster than Splendor. This offset means the day we spent there was not really even a full day here," I replied.

"How do you keep track of all that stuff, Sam?" Erin asked.

"I have Ohm. Thank you, Ohm," I said.

"You are welcome, Sam," Ohm replied.

I called out, "Candy, are you home?"

There was no reply. I headed over to the counter drawers to look over any confiscated wands. Ohm had a programmed rule to place them in this drawer. I was about to pull out the possible candidates when I heard someone enter from the living room. It was not Candy. It was a man in dark robes who already held a wand. There was only a moment to shout, "Duck!" before he pointed the wand at us and said, "*Insipida!*"

His spell sent the contents of the kitchen counter flying. Erin was on the other side of the counter and took the full force of his spell. As I heard him advancing upon my position, I managed to dive to the floor using the entire end of the counter as cover and shouted, "Ohm, knock him out!"

There was a thud, then another thud. I looked over, and Erin collapsed on the floor. She was breathing, so I pulled up my detect enemies icon in the invisi-hud and waited for a moment. It reported no other targets, and I was torn about what to do next. I went over to the hooded figure and revealed his face. I did not recognize him. He was flat on his back with his arms extended outward. His wand was on the floor beside his left arm. I jammed my heel down hard on his wand wrist and almost slipped and lost my balance as his arm rolled against my foot stomp. I did it again and again until I heard something snap.

"Ohm, remove this man's clothes and jewelry before transporting him naked to the Eden prison world. Place a tracker inside him and give him a single dagger and a canteen of water," I said before returning to Erin. "Ohm, replicate a medkit."

The medkit appeared a few moments later. I opened it up and quickly fetched the medical inspectrograph. The medical inspectrograph reported no serious injuries, but Erin suffered a mild concussion from falling to the floor. The device recommended an injection of acetaminophen. I clicked the recommended button on the medical inspectrograph and picked up the medjector. The two devices were aware of one another. When I picked the medjector up, the medical inspectrograph had already set it for acetaminophen.

I gave Erin the recommended dose and lifted her unconscious form, holding her in my arms while we both sat on the floor. I was steaming mad, unhinged with rage at being attacked by some two-bit magician. All I could think about was Valentino or Reziko. If that were the case, the magician whose arm I just jacked up, might have been *Praecepited*, himself, and a witless pawn in whoever planned this attack. How could this happen, two seemingly coincidental encounters in two different echoes in one day? Someone was really rattling my cage, and because it spanned multiple echoes, it had to be a Lord of Splendor or an agent of chaos.

Erin finally stirred and awoke, sobbing, "What the hell happened?"

I held her and said, "A magician attacked us. I knocked him out. He is gone now."

"Ow, my head hurts," she said, lifting her arm up to touch the spot on her head.

"Are you all right? Can you sit on the stool at the counter?" I asked.

"Yeah, it's just a bump on the head, but it hurts," Erin said, getting up, holding her head, and taking a seat back at the wrecked kitchen counter.

"I gave you a bit of acetaminophen to help with the pain. Let me see if Candy has some ice in the freezer," I said, and I located a tray of ice before placing a few cubes in the center of a dishtowel.

I handed the bundle to Erin and said, "Try holding this over the bump to prevent swelling."

"Thanks," she said, depressed while holding the ice over the bump on her head.

Searching through Candy's baking drawer for any wand, I walked over to the pile of robes where the attacker's wand lay on the floor. I pointed my wand at the attacker's wand and said, "*Exilium*."

The wand jumped a little. I tried the same thing with the robe pile, and a slight bit of electricity circled around the robes, hopefully neutralizing any residual magic that might have been left behind as a booby trap.

With the wand from the floor in hand, I returned to the kitchen to place both of them on the counter. Some other wands were in the drawer. I put them on the counter and rolled them on the countertop, looking for the one that was the least bent. There were a few straight candidates, including the one I picked up from the floor, but I chose the one the magician attacked us with because of the dark wood color and the red gemstone inlay. I never saw anything like that before. I tucked that wand into the zippered wand pocket along my shirt sleeve, returned the other wands to the drawer, and headed back over to the robes on the floor. After shaking them out, I heard a couple of things clatter to the floor. They stunk like an obese person who sweats into their clothes too much. I patted the robes down and felt something inside one of the pockets. The card I discovered looked an awful lot like a vignette. I placed that card in another pocket along my pants leg. I did not want it close to my standard vignettes. The two items that clinked on the floor looked like a ring and a stiletto. Heading Madison's warning about handling a magician's ring, I targeted the two items on the floor and said, "Ohm, place these two items in the vault, away from other items."

They sparkled on the floor and disappeared.

Erin walked over, still holding the ice to her head, watching as I performed my search of the magician's garment, and asked, "Can we go now?"

"Yes, sorry about all this. How could I know?" I replied.

"I'm not blaming you, Sam. I just want to lie down," Erin said.

I held out my hand and said, "Ohm, create a passage card to the hallway outside of the San Francisco apartment."

My hand sparkled as a new vignette appeared in my hand. I focused on it until the hallway seemed real before I took Erin's hand and stepped through the vignette. We found ourselves in the hallway of the twenty-third floor of the black glass building. I tucked the new vignette inside one of Erin's pockets, right next to the Xanadu vignette I gave her earlier.

"Now you have two vignettes. You can always return here when you need to," I said.

She shook her head in thanks, and we walked slowly toward the first doorway leading to my apartment, which I guess was now our apartment. I heard a door open down the hall, and Candy stepped out. It must be nighttime here, too, because Candy was only wearing a short silk robe that was partially open, revealing her blue panties. She must have noticed my gaze because she pulled her robe closed and tied it shut with the silk sash around her waist as she approached barefoot.

"Where have you been?" Candy started and noticed Erin's head, "Oh my god, she's hurt. How could you let this happen?"

We reached the door to the apartment and headed inside while Candy went on, "How come every time you take this girl out she comes back damaged? What the hell is wrong with you, Sam?"

Candy helped Erin lie down on the white sofa, and Erin said, "Thanks, Candy."

"It's not my fault. A dark magician ambushed us in your kitchen in Enki's Dale," I said, trying to defend myself.

"What? In my kitchen? What were you doing there?" Candy asked.

"The tentacle attack snapped my last wand in three places. We were just popping into your place to pick up a new wand from the bakery drawer when we were attacked. It was like he knew we were going to be there and was just waiting," I said.

Candy started speaking to the air, "Alex. Sam and Erin were just attacked by a magician in Enki's Dale. Can you check on Madison, Nick, Olivia, and the kids?"

We could only hear one side of the conversation.

"Yeah, in my kitchen.

I don't know.

Just now," Candy uttered, looking over to me asking, "Alex wants to know what spell they used?"

"It was only *Insipida*," I replied.

"*Insipida*. Uh-huh. Yeah, let me know," Candy said, ending her conversation with Alex before turning to us. "Alex is gonna check it out."

"How are you feeling?" I asked Erin.

"It's just a bump on the head. I guess it's been a full day," Erin replied, setting the wet dishtowel containing the melted ice on the coffee table next to the sofa. "I've got to use the head."

I walked over to the glass window doors leading to the balcony. It was nighttime here. I returned to the sofa and took a seat. Candy took a seat on the companion sofa across from me and asked, "What's going on?"

I sat there thinking, stroking the stubble of my beard, heaved a sigh, and said quietly, "I'm bad news, Candy."

Candy gave me that "Don't even go there" look and replied, "You're not bad news. I admit, things seem to happen around you, but it's like you said, it's not your fault."

"Not my fault? It's all my fault. Everything is my fault," I said, getting emotional.

"How can everything be your fault? You're not God, Sam, as much as you believe you are sometimes. You're just making the best out of the situations that come your way," Candy encouraged.

"But there is always a new crisis, another problem. Will it ever end?" I asked.

"I don't know, Sam. You play rough, and some of the people you piss off play even rougher," Candy pointed out.

"But there is no forgiveness to be found, even when I try. There is only spite, malice, and revenge. How long can I scramble from scenario to scenario, hoping to not make a mistake, all the while, everyone I have pissed off is just waiting in the wings for me to slip up so they can exact their pound of flesh?" I lamented.

Erin returned, sat down next to me, and said, "What are you talking about?"

"Sam thinks everything is his fault," Candy blurted out.

"Baby, it's not your fault. I'm fine. It's just a bump on the head. When I heard you yell duck, I thought 'what does he mean, duck?' That was just me being stupid," Erin said.

"We got lucky, again? That magician could have used a death spell instead of a confuse spell," I said.

"But he didn't, and everything's fine," Candy reminded me.

"I know I'm new to this, Sam, but I'll get better at traveling with you. I'm sorry," Erin said.

"Sugar, it's not your fault either, and it does take a little while to figure out this crazy way of living with this man. Lord knows I was in over my head once I made the leap to traveling with Sam," Candy said to Erin.

"The problem is that you have to think like a paranoid cold-blooded murderous killer every time you make a move, and then set it aside and pretend that everything is going to be okay to exact any kind of enjoyment out of life," I said morosely.

"No, you don't. But you do have to be aware of your surroundings at all times, especially when moving through echo or arriving at a new location," Candy said.

"I know, and I didn't do that this time. When I forget, people get hurt," I snapped.

"Sam, don't beat yourself up over this, please," Erin implored.

"Ohm, show me the display from Alex's cloaked scanner," I said, and the familiar orange glowing sphere appeared, hanging over the coffee table between Candy and me.

It was like dropping into the middle of an action movie. Alex moved so fast that she was almost a blur. There were red and blue spells flying all around her. I would guess she faced at least three magicians on her own. Through the display, which tracked Alex's movement, I caught a glimpse of Nick, who was knocked out on the floor. I yelled, "Ohm, target all the unknown magicians in the Baker's and the Foster residence and put them to sleep."

Candy didn't hesitate. She stood up and said, "Ohm, transport me to Olivia's house, the front porch."

Even before Candy transported, I could see she activated her cloak and faded from our view. A person-sized sparkle appeared and faded, indicating that a transport took place.

"Ohm, place Candy's cloaked scanner in a new display," I said.

"Holy shit, what is going on tonight?" Erin asked as she moved Alex's display off to the side while Candy's appeared hovering above the coffee table.

"Ohm, wake Lucas and supply Alex's feed to him," I said.

The spells stopped inside of Alex's display, and when I panned around the room, I saw Madison was already rushing over to Nick. Alex dragged the bodies of the three knocked-out magicians across the living room, gathering them up in one location, near the doors leading to the patio. Inside Candy's display, we saw she located the children and dropped her cloak.

"Ohm, scan the countryside. Map out human targets. Use one thousand cloaked scanners. Materialize their starting location inside Alex and Lucas' house to minimize the sparkle detection. Combine their locations inside a new single display," I said.

A new display appeared, and I stood up to drag it away from the other two displays, moving it away from the sofa area. As I waited for the large amount of cloaked scanners to become active and begin their patrols, Erin said, "It looks like Nick is waking up. He's coming around."

I returned to Candy's display and panned around counting the downed magicians, three. It looked like Candy found Olivia. She was unconscious.

"Ohm, transport Ethan Foster from *Journey* to his home in Enki's Dale," I said.

Erin said, "I see that Lucas has arrived now."

I got up and headed over to the larger display, where many of the cloaked scanners reported. They were assuming a grid pattern and conducting a standard sweep. I gestured and relocated them to more logical locations dumping quite a few onto the nearby village of Enki's Dale. The Baker and Foster residents were actually on the outskirts of town.

"Another person has entered the house where Candy is at," Erin said.

I glanced over and took a step toward the display on the coffee table and said, "That is Ethan, Olivia's husband."

"It looks like he is wearing a Starnet uniform," Erin said.

"He probably is. He is serving aboard *Journey* in the Gar sector," I replied.

My attention was drawn to the larger display where a single vector was detected, moving away from the village. It headed toward the Somber Woods, across the wide grassy plain separating it from the village. I also saw a few other stragglers heading out from the village, toward the forest tree line. They seemed to be leading many of the villagers across the plain.

"They're recruiting slaves," I said out loud.

Erin got up from the couch, walked over behind me, and took a look at my larger display.

"Ohm, place all detected evil magicians inside suspended animation chambers on one of the asteroid facilities. Remove all their clothes and place their wands, rings, and other devices inside the vault. Make a catalog of their faces, including the one from Candy's kitchen. Let the one heading into the woods go, for now, but track him. I want to see where he leads us," I said.

"Processing detainees," Ohm replied, and the targeted magicians on the larger display started disappearing.

"Ohm, redirect deployed cloaked scanners to focus on the Somber Woods," I said.

I located the group communication icon inside my invisihud. Selecting Alex, Lucas, and Candy to receive the message, I said, "I have detected several other magicians in the area. It looks like they were raiding the village to capture people for god knows what purpose. I have immobilized and restrained seventeen magicians, but there is a sizable group of confused villagers heading to the forest line. They are probably under the influence of a *Praecepit* bane, please advise," I said.

Erin moved over to the two other displays on the coffee table and said, "It looks like the woman is coming around."

"That's good news. My guess is they attack their victim with an *Insipida* spell. Once they are stunned, they use the *Praecepit* bane upon them," I replied.

Erin looked over at me and asked, "What is the *Praecepit* bane?"

"It's considered one of the deplorable banes that a magician is never supposed to use. It gives you control over another person. You can cast it upon a victim, ask them to go rob a bank and bring you the money. If they get caught, who cares? You can cast the spell on another victim. Evil magicians use the spell to create slaves to do manual labor, sex, or suicide missions," I said.

"What are the other banes?" Erin asked.

"Murder and pain. The evil magician can cast a spell that can instantly kill you. Or cast a spell that causes incredible pain without killing you. For this reason, they are called 'deplorable.' Once you use them, you are heading down the path to becoming an evil magician," I said.

"Hitting you back, Sam. Madison has an idea on how to help the *Praecepited* villagers. Can you send me their location?" Alex asked.

"Ohm, transfer the contents of the large display to Alex's invisihud," I said.

"Transferring display," Ohm said.

"Got it," Alex replied.

"Why do you think this is happening?" Erin asked.

"It could be because of my confrontation with Joshua this afternoon. Rayleaf is the first forest. All other forests, including the Somber Woods in Enki's Dale, are echoes of Rayleaf. He may have been upset enough about our meeting today to have deployed his men to destroy the cottage on the outskirts. His actions may have caused a ripple effect through echo taking the form of a magician raid in Enki's Dale. It depends upon how infuriated he became after we parted ways. I defied him, in front of his men, and got away with it. He won't soon forget that. And you touched his horse which is an extreme no-no."

"I didn't know it was forbidden to do that?" Erin confessed.

"You literally crossed the line during a tense situation. You knew I couldn't protect you unless you stood close to me, but you moved away from me, crossing over past him to touch his magical beast. I was freaking out when you did that," I said with stress.

"I'm sorry. I was drawn to it, Sam. That horse is a Melog," Erin said.

"Charnelgrim is a Melog?" I asked.

"I sensed it. Surely you noticed the biomechanical aspects," Erin said.

"Of course, how could I not. Joshua is way older than me, and as far back as records go, his horse, Charnelgrim is associated with him. He is never far from it, which has led many to speculate that his soul is somehow bound up with that creature. Also, I am still the baby of the bunch. There may be things about manipulating echo that I have not discovered, but Joshua has. That's the thing about my family. No one is very forthcoming with discoveries they may have made about echo manipulation because they may need to use them for leverage at some later date to bargain for their lives or escape another's grasp," I said.

"What do we do now?" Erin asked.

"Defend what we have, stay true to ourselves and our friends. I don't know. What do you think we should do?" I asked Erin.

She laughed to herself and said, "Fight 'em until we can't. That's what the

Imperial fighter pilots said about the Melogs. I used to say that about my own people while I pretended to be one of the Imperials, but even those were not my real memories, they were installed from another revision nine's life. At the time. All of us revision nines thought we were expanding ourselves by incorporating the other nine's memories into ourselves. Instead, we were diluting ourselves by denying our own unique life experiences."

"I like that. Fight 'em until we can't. I guess that's all life has become recently, a fight," I said.

On the display, the single vector target heading into the Somber Woods came to a halt, and other targets started to populate around the original. It looked like the magician returned to his friends. Using my invisihud, I dove into one of the cloaked scanners to get a better look at the area. In the first memory loop, terrible things happened in the Somber Woods to Candy and Alex that also involved a large group of dark magicians. I believe this night's encounter is probably a variation on that theme from the first memory loop. In the first loop, I found many more magicians, including the leader, deep underground, inside caves. As I looked around, through the sensor feed of the cloaked scanner, I was able to locate a tunnel leading down, so I guided the cloaked scanner into the dark hole setting it to seek mode. I used my invisihud to transfer the view from the cloaked scanner to the larger display so Erin could see.

"What just happened to you Sam? Your face looked different?" Erin asked.

"I am part Cybernetic. I have an interface connected to my brain that lets me communicate with Ohm directly, so I don't have to use verbal commands. When I use it, my facial muscles take on an unnatural look, similar to the face of a guitar player performing a solo. I guided the cloaked scanner into the hole to look for more magicians," I explained.

Erin said, "Oh, sorry for prying."

"It's a secret, okay? If any of my family finds out, they will seek ways to disable it," I disclosed seriously.

"Sure, I get it," Erin assured me.

The cloaked scanner I directed into the hole finally reached a large cavern with at least ten more magicians. There were no more passages for it to explore, so I asked, "Ohm, place the newly targeted magicians into the suspended animation chambers on the asteroid facilities with the others."

We watched as the targets on the map slowly disappeared.

"Ohm, how many magicians were transferred to the asteroid holding facility tonight?" I asked.

"Thirty-seven magicians were placed in suspended animation at the asteroid holding facility," Ohm replied.

"Ohm, recover the cloaked scanners but leave ten behind to monitor the area for a few days. Profile newly detected magicians against the makeup of the dark magicians placed in suspended animation. If there are new matches, transfer them to the holding facility and make a note in the weekly report," I said.

"Recovering cloaked scanners. New profiling rules are in place," Ohm replied.

I headed over to the bar in the corner and set about the business of making a Manhattan, asking Erin, "Would you like a drink?"

She walked over to the bar with me and took a seat on the stool before saying, "Sure."

I prepared the drinks and poured them out, placing a few cherries on toothpicks that I leaned against the edge of each glass.

Erin looked at me and said, seriously, "I won't, you know. I won't betray you, Sam."

I looked into her brown eyes and said, "I know," then offered a toast with a whisper, "To secrets."

She smiled, and we sipped our drinks.

I walked around the bar, and Erin stood up. We hugged for a long time, not saying anything before we parted, and I said, "I'm sorry this introduction into my life has led to so much drama."

We headed over to the sofa with our drinks and took in the displays from Candy and Alex's cloaked scanners. Alex was with Madison, and we could see them surrounded by a group of people, making their way back to the village. Candy's display showed a more calm scene with Olivia, Ethan, and the kids all gathered around a table having a snack with tea. I got up and headed over to the larger display and re-targeted the magician camp for more detail. There were still a few people, who Ohm did not target as magicians, milling around the place.

"Ohm, target the remaining people in this magician camp," I said, and new targets appeared on the display.

"What are you thinking?" Erin asked from the sofa.

"These people are probably the slaves of the magicians and need to be released from the *Praecepit* bane," I said to her.

I sent out another group message, saying, "I located a magician camp, not too far from the edge of the Somber Woods. I have subdued thirty-seven magicians and placed them in suspended animation. There are some survivors here, probably under the influence of some spell. Alex, can I send them to your location?" I asked.

While I waited for a reply, I zoomed into the display even further. Erin got up from the sofa to stand behind me again, watching my manipulation gestures of the display. These people were dirty and basically dressed in rags, many of them just standing in one place in a confused state.

Alex replied, "We're approaching the town center with the others. Can you send them here?"

"Hey, can you bring me Alex's display over there?" I asked Erin.

She walked over to the coffee table and grabbed the orange glowing sphere to drag it over to where I stood in front of the larger display. Looking through the lens of Alex's cloaked scanner, I located the town center she mentioned. I marked it with a target and said, "Ohm, transfer the people targeted in the magician camp to the town center. During transport, remove as much surface dirt as possible, give them new clothes appropriate for this echo and a shoulder bag filled with bread, cheese, dried meat, fruit, and wine."

I sent out another group message saying, "Transport underway, expect eighteen refugees at the town center."

Erin and I watched as the targets disappeared from the large display and people showed up at the town center, visible inside Alex's display. I took hold of the glowing orange sphere containing Alex's invisihud feed and tossed it onto the larger display so we could see an expanded view of what happened through Alex's cloaked scanner.

Madison moved over to the group of the new arrivals, which appeared with a sparkle, and used her wand in a very large gesture. She whirled it around, above her head, several times, leaving a blue-glowing streak hovering in the air above her. With each swirl of the wand, the area of the glowing line expanded until she brought it all down and pushed it forward onto the people before her as if she conducted some invisible orchestra. The expressions on their faces changed, and some of them dropped the bags they arrived with. In a surprise to me, some of the other villagers rushed up to greet the new arrivals. Apparently, these were people who were missing.

Bright light flooded the room from the balcony glass windows, and a megaphone voice called out, "You there. You are wanted for questioning. Proceed to the ground floor immediately."

"Ohm, discontinue displays," I said.

Turning to Erin, I said as calmly as possible, "Please remain inside, away from the windows."

"Who are they? What do they want?" Erin asked.

I used the invisihud to activate my shield and jetpack and brought up one of the sub-menus for special actions. I headed over to the glass doors, slid them open, and stepped out on the balcony, with Erin saying, "No, Sam, don't," as I closed the glass doors with her on the other side.

"Ohm, wake up K-Mac and Byrone. Set me to broadcast live," I said.

Hovering just off the edge of my balcony was a compact armored surveillance vehicle. I could see the co-pilot casting a spotlight on me, amplifying his voice and saying, "You there, on the balcony. Make no further moves. Report to ground level immediately."

I located the ice pick claws from the special actions menu and short tapering columns of red lasers emitted from each of my knuckles, wrapping my wrist and palm with a localized force field to support the laser extension. With my shield active, the ice pick claws were stabilized more, acting as extensions to my hands. The spotlight shining on me from above obscured the hovering craft. I used the invisihud to target the vehicle with my jetpack and started running for the edge of the balcony.

The voice from the vehicle called out, "Stop what you're doing. Stop and report to ground level immediately."

When I reached the wall at the edge of the balcony, I took a step up onto it and leaped into the air letting the jetpack guide me to my target, which was already making a retreating maneuver. The height was dizzying, and I felt fear wash over me as I slammed into the side of the vehicle. My shield crackled all around me as I started sliding down the side of the vehicle's smooth curved surface. In a panic, I jammed my red laser claws into the vehicle's metallic surface, puncturing it, before pulling myself up the side. I managed to wrap my legs around one of the features of the hull as the pilot tried to shake me off while recklessly maneuvering the craft. He barely avoided hitting the building as the compact vehicle began a rapid descent.

Working my way up to the top of the craft, I ripped into some of the engine's works with the laser claws, which caused the vehicle to spiral as we descended. Smoke trails emitted from one of the puncture points I inflicted upon the outer hull. I held on as our descent slowed while the pilot guided us to an open field in a nearby park.

The engines screamed with a high-pitched sound as they struggled against gravity to bring the compact vehicle to a non-crash landing. We landed with a thud, and the compact vehicle immediately rolled over on its side. I slid down the opposing side, looking into the cockpit of the crashed vehicle at the stunned pilots who survived the crash while smoke billowed from the rear.

I only stood on the well-kept lawn of the park for a moment before I was transported to another location. When I materialized, I was in a wide corridor with windows to my left revealing stars, and the wall to my right curved as the hallway advanced. The bend of the hallway indicated that I might be aboard some spaceship or station with a curved hull design. In front of me was a Logican in robes, his folded arms interlocked with the sleeves of the robes hiding his hands. To my left and right were large Lerpas in Starnet uniforms holding laser rifles pointed at me ready to fire. The Logican spoke, asking, "If you're done destroying things, would you please follow me?"

Lerpas were bipedal in form but larger than humans. It was not uncommon for them to reach two to three meters. Generally ugly with their oversized incisors, they were known for their short tempers and great strength. For a Lerpa to wear a Starnet uniform meant they were more than likely from the elite ruling Lerpa class who were a cut above the regular brawling type.

I dropped the ice pick claws and jetpack and said, "No, I won't follow you."

This reply prompted immediate laser rifle jabs into my sides from the Lerpas, causing my shield to crackle around me.

The Logican instructed the Lerpas, "Bring him," while turning his back to me and beginning his walk down the hallway. I refused to move, so the Lerpas slung their rifles over their shoulders, grabbed me under my armpits, and dragged me down the hallway. I went limp, trying to leverage passive protest with my shield crackling against the floor as I dragged my feet. As we moved down the hallway, I reached into echo and pulled up the *Motif*, focusing it on the carpeting of the floor. I entertained the idea that this floor I was being dragged down was not the space station floor. Instead, it was the floor of the shopping mall I saw in an advertisement. The shopping mall was not too far from Fisherman's Wharf in San Francisco. Using the *Motif*, I rippled the floor with my mind, and the Lerpas came to a halt. But I did not want them to halt, and I reached even further into echo to manipulate the feeble minds of the Lerpas into carrying on as the hallway emptied into a larger area where I was dragged to an escalator heading up. Reaching into echo, I altered the uniforms of my abductors, so they no longer matched Starnet design, and I altered their communicators and weapons. All around me were shoppers who were aghast at the treatment I received from these Starnet security officers.

I called out, "Help, someone. I have done nothing wrong. Please, help, I am being abducted," as we rode the escalator up.

When we reached the top, They dragged me away from the departure points of the escalator. High-resolution auraprojections of K-Mac and Byrone approached while stunned shoppers watched in awe. I turned off my shield, which caused me to slip out of the Lerpas grip, and I fell to the floor.

"Yo dawg, what's up with dragging citizens through the mall?" K-Mac asked.

"That's right, transporting people without their permission is a crime, even for Starnet," Byrone said.

"This doesn't concern you," one of the Lerpas replied.

"I'm afraid it does, dawg. Sam here is our friend," K-Mac said, standing in the way of the Lerpas advancing any further.

"And even if he wasn't our friend, we'd still have to ask what's going on here. Do you think the public is going to let you walk all over the law of the land?" Byrone asked.

I took this time to set my shield to automatic mode, and I located a song from my library, Stevie Wonder's, I Wish.

The Logican finally spoke, saying, "This man is the target of an ongoing investigation. You're interfering with a Starnet operation."

"We're not interfering with an investigation. We're just shopping at the mall," Byrone spit back at him.

"That's right, pointy dawg, We just headin' over to the escalator and see old school brutality going down," K-Mac said, slapping Byrone's hand, which he put out behind his back.

I got up and started clapping as the music kicked in really loud. Stevie started singing, "Looking back on when I was a nappy-headed little boy."

Rising to my feet, I burst out, "I've got happy feet!" and started dancing in place.

The Logican said, "Stop that."

One of the Lerpas cold-clocked me in the side of the head, knocking me to the floor. Even though my shield was on auto, I could feel the force of the punch, thinking, "Yeah, that's gonna leave a mark."

Mall security arrived at this time, asking, "What's going on here? You can't attack people in this mall."

The Logican started, saying, "This is none," but K-Mac cut him off, saying, "These impostors is posin' as Starnet personnel, and abducting honest shoppers is what is going on, dawg."

"That's right. I don't even think these people are Starnet. I mean, look at their uniforms," Byrone said.

Using the invisihud, I set the music to a slow fade out while wondering if getting punched in the side of the face was really worth it?

The Logican tapped the communicator on his chest, and nothing happened. The Lerpas did the same thing and received a similar response from their communicator brooches.

"What, fake communicators too?" K-Mac exclaimed.

"The real criminals are right in front of you," Byrone said to the Mall Cops.

"That's right, impersonating Starnet personnel, abducting citizens in broad daylight is a serious crime, not to mention those Logican robes really need to be washed. I mean, you need some Old Spice or Brut up in that, dawg," K-Mac said.

One of the Mall Cops reached out a hand to me and helped me up, asking, "Are you alright?"

The side of my face glowed red from the punch, so it wasn't too hard to produce some tears saying, "No, I'm not all right. These men threatened me, attacked me, and I think they tried to extort money from me because I am a high profile personality."

A crowd gathered around the scene, and the Mall Cops asked aloud, "Did anybody here see what happened?"

"I did. I saw those men dragging him up the escalator as he cried for help," One woman reported.

"I'm a member of Starnet, and those are not our uniforms," another man corroborated.

The Mall Cops heard enough. They pulled out their weapons, pointed them at the Starnet group, and said, "Drop the weapons!"

"Holy shit, let's get out of here!" K-Mac yelled, sending the crowd into a panic as everyone spread out, trying to get away from the security force show-down playing out.

I took the opportunity to run, myself, heading off around a pillar to some large potted indoor plants. There was a bench here, and I took a seat. I held out my hand and said, "Ohm, cut the live feed and create a passage card to the control room inside of Black Glass Studios?"

There was a sparkle, and a new vignette appeared in my hand. I stood up, focused on the image of the studio, and stepped through as more people ran, screaming away from the frantic scene I helped create.

Placing the new vignette into one of my pockets, I headed into the broadcast area where K-Mac and Byrone hung out. We slapped hands and bumped fist, Meadowland style as K-Mac said, "Dang, dawg, he got you good, didn't he?"

"Are you all right? What was all that about?" Byrone asked.

"First off, thank you guys for coming to my rescue. You pulled off a stellar performance. I mean that," I said.

"You know we got your back, dawg," K-Mac said, holding up his hand and slapping mine.

"Did you guys see the mid-air leap from my balcony onto the flying cop car?" I asked.

"No, when we got here, you were already on top, ripping it to shreds while it was crash landing into the park," Byrone said.

"Can we check it out? This shit has to be in the movie," I said.

"Damn straight, we can check it out," K-Mac said, and we headed into the broadcast room while K-Mac brought up a large floating display and located tonight's clip.

K-Mac pulled up the start of the recording, and they both high-fived me after watching me leap from the balcony to the compact hovering security vehicle.

"That's some bold shit, Sam. I don't know If I could do that with an entire stunt team behind me, but you just free-styled it on the fly," Byrone said.

"I don't like cops shining lights into my house," I declared.

"I don't blame you, dawg, five-oh all up your house grill," K-Mac said.

"We're still being harassed when we leave the building. Even the new park location is being watched," Byrone said.

"Ohm, relocate the Yerba Buena Gardens transport site to Sydney G. Walton Square," I requested.

"Transport site relocated," Ohm replied.

"You'll show up in a new park now, perhaps, that will throw off their surveillance for a while," I said.

"Thanks, dawg. It sucks being hassled every time we leave our crib," K-Mac said.

"I know. I'm workin' on it. If you guys can keep pluggin' the angle of the citizens versus the man, I'll do what I can to get laws changed to prevent this kind of treatment. I'm about fed up," I said.

"You got it, man. We're on it. It's not hard to do because we are the people," Byrone said.

"Damn straight, Byrone," K-Mac said, slapping Byrone's hand.

"Hold up, go back there. I want to see that again," I said to K-Mac.

K-Mac stopped the log playback at the point just after the Lerpa punched me in the face. I stepped up to the display and scrubbed back a bit, reframing the angle, so I was on the left, and the Lerpa was on the right when his fist crossed the foreground. In the background stood the Logican, with his folded hands in his robes, obviously smiling at the event taking place.

"This is it. This image is the angle to pursue," I said.

"I don't get it, dawg. What am I missing?" K-Mac asked?

"The Logican is smiling," I said.

"You're right. That's an emotion. Logicans are not supposed to show emotions," Byrone explained.

"Damn, dawg, I didn't know that. I just thought they were uptight religious types," K-Mac said.

"No, for a Logican to show an expression of joy at violence being applied to another living creature is a serious character flaw. Serious enough that he will be removed from his office in shame," I said.

"We on it. We'll hit the world up with this knowledge drop," K-Mac said.

"Give it a day or two. Right now they are discredited, but that will soon be rectified once their DNA is scanned and their Starnet membership is verified.

As soon as they are exonerated, hit the world with this knowledge drop. If you have some time, look into the Logican's past record. A Logican doesn't just lapse into an emotional state. It may have taken years to accumulate, but there must be a trail of evidence of other lapses that might be on the record," I said.

"We got it. Wait for the beat, then drop the mic," Byrone said.

"I've got to head back downstairs, my baby is waiting for me, and she's not going to be happy about this," I said, pointing to my face.

"We on it, Sam. You better have that face looked at too," K-Mac said as I headed out of the studio.

I headed down the hall and pushed the button for the elevator. While I waited for it to arrive, I gathered up the *Motif* around me. When the doors opened, I entered and pushed the button for floor twenty-three. On the way down, I let the *Motif* trail above me as the elevator dropped. I extended it out to the perimeter of the building, reinforcing my right to defend the airspace around my building. I reached into the laws of this land, making it illegal for Starnet to conduct unrequested searches and inspections, even with probable cause. I made the laws retroactive, so they were on the books for years, clearly placing tonight's actions by Starnet in the wrong. I rippled the *Motif* through the building as I descended, enforcing my intent to live a peaceful, non-invaded life. Extending it out across the city, the state, I reached out to make this world, my world with my influence, dominating over any other echo influence that might be present.

The elevator came to a stop, and I gathered the *Motif* back up, using it to heal the side of my face as much as possible before drawing it back inside of me. The side of my head started to hurt something fierce as the elevator doors opened, and I headed down the hall to the door of the apartment.

Walking into my home, it was a full house. Candy, Alex, Lucas, and Erin were all here. Erin rushed up to me with an angry look on her face, "What the faen were you thinking leaping off the balcony like that?"

"This harassment has got to stop. We can't continue to live like this. They've become too bold terrorizing us in our own homes," I said while heading into the living area and sitting on the sofa.

"I think what you did tonight has shaken things up, Sam. It's all over the news channels across the galaxy. It paints a picture of a Starnet that has grown too bold and dominating," Lucas reported.

"Usually, I'm all about standing by my girlfriends, but you kicked ass tonight. I don't know if I could have done that any better, myself," Alex said with a smile.

The white sofa rested in the sunken part of the living room, allowing Erin to come up from behind me and drop her hands over the back of the sofa and across my chest, saying, "Sam, I don't want to lose you. I just found you."

"I'm with her, Sam. You can't be acting all reckless and crazy like that. Look at your face," Candy said.

"Look, I had on my shield and the jetpack, so I knew I wasn't going to fall. I've been looking for a reason to try out those laser claws for a while," I said, trying to defend myself.

"I thought those were pretty cool, Sam," Alex said, "I might have to give them a try myself."

"What happened in Enki's Dale? Is Nick okay? What about the others?" I asked the group.

Alex spoke up, "Believe it or not there were no casualties. Those final eighteen you transported in were a few of the villagers that went missing a short while ago."

"What about the kids?" I asked, looking at Candy.

"They shook up, for sure, but you transporting Ethan into the scene helped reassure them a lot. That was a nice gesture," Candy said.

I reached for the drink I left on the table and took a big gulp. The ice had melted, but I didn't care.

"I've got happy feet?" Lucas asked with a smile.

"I thought dancing might diffuse the situation," I replied with a smile that kind of hurt.

Erin walked around and took a seat on the sofa beside me.

"Those goofs upstairs actually did a good job tonight," Alex said.

"Yeah, they do seem to have a way of throwing a curveball at these future types," Lucas added.

"While we're all together, I just wanted to let you know that I shifted this building into a new echo where it is illegal for Starnet, or any organization, to search our building or occupy our airspace. I changed the laws retroactively. That should place us in the right and them in the wrong," I said.

Erin looked up and said, "You can do that, change laws?"

"Laws, orders, paperwork, those kinds of things are pretty malleable and easy to change for a probability traveler," I replied.

"Thank god. I was out on a date with Clarashel, and security forces up and handcuffed me right there in the restaurant, treating me like I was some kind of criminal. I was able to Transfast out later, but she hasn't spoken to me since," Candy said.

"Me too. I was apprehended after teaching a class down at the center. I just let them do it because I didn't want to cause a scene, but it has been getting worse," Alex said.

"Me as well," Lucas affirmed, "I took a walk in the park, and the next thing I know, I'm in handcuffs."

"Well, it stops tonight. We're not gonna live like second-class citizens anymore," I decreed.

Erin put her hand up to touch the side of my face saying, "I don't like solutions like this, Sam. Solutions where you have to take one for the team. It's not right."

"I'm sorry, baby, but when I get backed into a corner with magicians attacking my woman, cops harassing my friends, and Starnet shining a fucking spotlight into my house, I have to say enough is enough. I just lose it and realize I have to reshape my world, our world for the better," I said.

Lucas got up and put his arm around Alex and said, "I think we'd better let these two get some rest," as they headed out of the room to the door.

"Wait up, boo, I'm comin' witcha," Candy said, and she headed for the door, calling back, "You did good tonight, Sam. You kept people from becoming slaves."

Erin looked over and asked, "Do you want to lie down?"

"Yeah, I think that's a good idea," I said, and we headed into the bedroom.

We took off our clothes and laid down together as I said, "I'm sorry our day ended up so crazy. I just wanted to share with you where I come from. By the end of the day, it all turned into a shit show."

"It was nice this morning, Sam. Even though I experienced Splendor first hand, now that I'm not there, I can't quite describe what is really missing from this reality. But something is missing. I guess I see your point that these places are just a reflection or an echo cast from a richer, denser source," Erin said quietly as we lay in each other's arms.

"I do think things are going to turn around to our favor in this local echo, but I still worry about retaliation from family members. Why did Joshua have to be such a dick today?" I asked rhetorically.

"Seeing how you worked together with your friends is illuminating, Sam. They are more than your neighbors, aren't they?" Erin asked.

"They are. Remember when I granted you the title of Squire?" I asked.

"Yeah, I do," Erin replied.

"Those three have the title of 'Guardian.' Which means they have pledged to defend *Tiger Mountain*. In payment for their pledge, they have full access to *Tiger Mountain*'s offerings through the same bio implant that I have. They are also cybernetic."

"Which is a secret," Erin repeated.

"That secret helps keep everyone safe. You never know where you'll find a friend that will change your life. I met Alex and Lucas in a bar in Seattle. I had a drink in a booth behind them and overheard their conversation about Alex not being able to touch Lucas because her DNA produced an allergic reaction on his skin. When I mentioned I might be able to help, Alex was ready to kick my ass for eavesdropping. Once I transported them to a starship, her tune changed. Later, Alex introduced me to Candy. They all helped me out during a tough time, and we have been friends ever since," I said.

"I feel like I'll never really know you, Sam. That what you present to me is an outer layer hiding something else underneath," Erin said.

"You are right. My outer layer is who I am now, who I want to be. But I am not trying to hide anything from you. It just takes time, Erin. How can I relate over eight hundred years of experience to you?" I replied.

"I guess so. I feel emotionally mixed up and melancholy at the same time like I am missing some critical perception," Erin said.

"Well, I can relate to that. I feel like I am constantly asking myself that same question. What am I missing? What have I forgotten?" I said.

"How did you know to activate Alex's cloaked scanner earlier this evening?" Erin asked.

"I don't know. I guess I was just trying to divert the conversation. Checking in on her progress was a way to do that. It was a way to stop thinking about how I messed up today. The emotions I am having for you are overflowing my ability to handle them, Erin. My love for you, the love you give is changing me. You make me believe I can have happiness, which causes me to drop my guard. As soon as that happens, enemies creep in, and friends get hurt," I said.

"I will get better at this, Sam. I was created to deceive and lie, but I was also constructed to fight and defend. That is what I am going to do. I won't just be a liability in this relationship," Erin said.

"I don't think of you as a liability, Erin. You are expanding me, and expansion often brings new options," I replied before difting off to sleep.

CHAPTER 45

Can't Talk Anymore

~~~

W hen I awoke, I was by myself and slept on the side of my face receiving the punch. It hurt a lot more, and I could barely move my mouth. Reaching into my mouth, I tested the stability of my teeth on the side that took the punch. They seemed okay, so I at least had that going for me. I couldn't speak clearly, so I was glad to have the invisihud as a fallback.

I selected some new clothing and set about the business of transferring my items from the old set of clothing, which smelled of smoke and engine fuel. I chose orange for the color of my shirt and slate grey for the color of my pants. I headed into the shower and saw my face in the mirror. It swelled up overnight, and there was bruising along the side of my face that also reached around, causing discoloration to my periorbital region. The hot shower felt good, and I lingered, letting the pulsing spray comfort my aching joints. During last night's balcony jump, I experienced pain in a few of my joints as I clung to the compact vehicle for dear life. I needed a break, but I was not sure I was going to get one.

I toweled off, got dressed, and fixed my hair with my hands. Heading into the living area, I could hear voices. It was Candy and Erin talking.

"...and there were caves riddled through a massive column that shot up from...," Candy trailed off, looked over, and said, "You look like hell, Sam."

Erin approached me smiling, which infected me with hope after last night's ordeal, saying, "Oh, how could I love a face like that?"

She placed her hand gently along the side of my bruised face and kissed me just as gently on the lips. She stared into my eyes for a moment with an examining look and asked, "Do you want some coffee?"

I shook my head yes, and took a seat along the kitchen counter next to Candy as Erin poured me a cup. I tried to say, "At least my teeth are okay," but it came out more of a mumble "Resse my teef otay."

"What was that? You can't even talk, Sam. You need to see a doctor," Candy said.

I shook my head no and took a sip from the coffee cup. I swirled the hot liquid around my teeth to see if they were sensitive, but I did not feel any tooth pain, making me feel a lot better. I tried again, saying slowly, "At reast my teef otay."

Candy had a little fun repeating, "A sheep for the day," as Erin came over and sat next to me.

Erin put her arm around my shoulder and said, "Candy told me about the time you two visited dragon land."

I shook my head, yes, and Candy kept up with the joking, "I weep for the hay," prompting me to give her the finger.

"Ah, I am shocked at such vulgar behavior at the kitchen table," Candy laughed.

"I understand you, baby. Your teeth are okay," Erin said, and she kissed me again.

Erin was certainly in a very good mood, and I wondered why, but I didn't want to experience any more ribbing from Candy by giving her the satisfaction of making fun of more of my speech as Candy said, "Wha cha going to do then?"

I located, and, yes, I know this says a lot about my priorities and character, the quick joint icon inside my invisihud, and activated it. There was a small sparkle on the kitchen counter that faded away revealing the marijuana joint left behind.

Candy looked at me, with her head tilted to the side and a "you've got to be kidding" expression on her face as she said, "Why not? You're pretty banged up, to begin with."

I fished around in my pocket for the lighter when the front door opened, and Lucas and Alex burst in with Lucas, saying, "Hey, Sam, get up. Oh, there you are."

"Wow, that is some shiner," Alex said.

"There is a large group of people gathered out front, at street level. I think they want to talk to you," Lucas said.

I put the joint back on the kitchen counter, stuffed the lighter back into my pocket, and gestured with my hands, "Lead on."

We all headed out of the apartment and got into the elevator, which we packed full, and I said, "I don't think I can talk," which sounded more like "I ron't rink I can rok."

"He can't talk. I don't know what good this will do," Candy said.

"Don't worry, I'll do the talking for you," Lucas said, "We just need to get a picture of that," he paused for a moment, then continued, "face of yours out there for everyone to see."

I shook my head, yes, and Erin held onto the side of my arm. I didn't understand why she was so happy. The elevator doors opened and dumped us into the lobby. Lucas was right, there was a large crowd out front, reporters, cameras, and onlookers with signs saying, "Freedom From Oppression," "Scan Me No More," and "My Life, My Right," to name a few.

Before I walked out, I disengaged Erin's arm from mine, and Candy said, "Hang back, boo," while Lucas and I walked through the front door.

I activated my invisihud and set it to scan for weapons. This gathering was an ideal setting for someone to take a shot at me or my friends. A few security guards popped up, and I targeted them just in case things went sideways during this press conference. Candy, Alex, and Erin followed us through the doors and fell behind us. In the photos being snapped, Lucas and I were in the foreground with three beautiful women behind us.

In my travels through echo, I never sought the spotlight on purpose. It just complicates things. I was a bit unprepared for the barrage of questions and the number of cameras in my face. I wanted to erect a force field to keep them back, but I knew better than that. A lot of the photographers focused on my face and my depressed look. I knew this would be shown all across the galaxy, and I hated it.

"Please, please stand back," Lucas said, trying to direct the crowd, "I can answer some questions. My client can not talk after last night's brutal attack by the security forces of Starnet."

"Are you going to press charges?" a voice shouted from the crowd.

"We're considering it," Lucas replied.

"Is Sam all right?" another cried out.

"Sam will recover. The attack has left him temporarily unable to speak," Lucas replied.

"What are you going to do about it?" another reporter asked.

"Now that's a good question, and it's not just a question for Sam or me. It's a question for all of us. What are we going to do to hold Starnet accountable? Who is going to enforce the laws that Starnet is supposed to abide by? We rely on them for our security, and when that mechanism breaks down, we are all at risk. Today it is Sam, tomorrow it might be you or your children. I personally have experienced Starnet's lack of adherence to its own laws while walking in a park. We have seen cases where profiling is rampant and obvious. If you wear the Starnet uniform, you are part of the Starnet family. But beware the citizen who does not sign up or conform to Starnet norms," Lucas lectured as the crowd calmed down and began to listen.

"But isn't this the action of one rogue Lerpa?" one of the reporters in the front of the group asked.

"Perhaps. I have no doubt that the majority of Starnet personnel have good intentions and only wish to serve and follow the regulations put before them. We, as citizens, are the ones who permit Starnet to serve on our behalf," Lucas pointed out.

"Some say Sam got what he deserves. After all, he did attack and destroy a Starnet surveillance vehicle while terrorizing the pilots in the process," another reporter stated.

"I would like to point out that neither of the pilots was hurt. What is terror? A blinding light in the night shining through your home window with voices commanding you to surrender. The surveillance vehicle was in clear violation of airspace laws. The pilot endangered not only the occupants of this building but also anyone at the street level who may have been injured if the vehicle collided with the building. If a Lerpa can pass through the Starnet training program and still not know how to control himself in a public setting, who is to say that the pilots may have been passed through the training program? At what point do we as citizens say enough is enough?" Lucas fired back.

That same reporter went on, "And who gets to decide," but Lucas cut him off, saying, "We get to decide. I get to decide."

All the while, I gathered up the *Motif*, letting it flow around me as I slowly leaned back and forth. When Lucas said, "I get to decide," I stomped the ground, sending the *Motif* into the crowd while lifting my left hand into the air, making a fist. Behind me, Alex shouted, "We Decide, I Decide!" as Candy and Erin joined in, too. The crowd soon joined in, and all further questions were ignored as the crowd repeated the chant. That was the photo I wanted to be shown all over the galaxy, my left fist raised high in the air, featuring the bruised right side of my face. Lucas stepped back as I showboated for a minute or two, allowing photographers to get the best shot from various angles. I turned around, and we all walked back into the black glass building as the chanting continued.

"Well, that went pretty good, don't you think?" Lucas asked as we all got into the elevator.

"You did good, honey," Alex said.

Erin said, "Yeah, I feel all riled up like I want to break something."

I shook my head, yes, as Lucas pressed the twenty-three button on the panel, and the elevator began its upward motion. I reached over and touched the top floor button for Black Glass Studios. I made a drumming motion with my hands and then followed it up with a smoking a joint motion which caused Lucas and Alex to shake their heads.

"Is that all you think about, Sam?" Candy asked.

I kind of shrugged. The elevator stopped on the twenty-third floor, and Alex, Lucas, and Candy got out. Candy turned around and said, "Later, boo," to Erin, which was kind of flirty, making me wonder?

Erin was very flirty, stroking my package through my pants and touching my chest. Any other time I might have just fucked her there in the elevator, but I still felt the pain from last night and was not really in the mood. Besides, I couldn't even kiss her.

"What's wrong, Sam? Don't you want to?" Erin said.

I asked her, "Why are you so happy?" coming out "Ry uh you so rappy?"

She understood and said, with a smile, "Because I'm in love and surrounded by friends."

I hugged her, and she wrapped her hands around my shoulder before kissing the side of my mouth that was not hurt. My hands eventually moved down to her waist, which I pulled up against what she stirred up. She started a slow grind against me, and I let her do her thing as the elevator dinged and the doors opened. We hung out in the elevator for a couple of minutes as she rubbed against me. Once she realized I was not going to go any further, she backed off and asked, "What's wrong?"

I kind of shrugged and said, "I rant ralk," then pointed at my face with a pissed off look and walked out of the elevator, heading toward the studio doors.

She came up beside me and said, "I want to hang out with you, okay? I want to spend the day your way."

I shook my head, yes, and made my way through the main doors to the lobby and up the wide stairway to the lounge area. The place was a mess, but it was not trashed. I guess the cleanup routine I set in place helps. I headed over to the kitchen area, which was also a bit messy for my tastes, and located a couple of glasses and took them back over to the lounge area. There were some liquor bottles here in various states of fullness. I wanted some bourbon. In this case, all I could find was Rye, so I poured a little less than half a glass for me and gave Erin a little less.

"Sam, you just got up," Erin said.

I mumbled, "Rym ra ralkrolric, ro ray," and took a sip, swishing it around inside my mouth, leaving it there as I tilted my head to the side, so it touched the side where I was hit. I used my hand to touch the sensitive outside and worked my jaw open and closed a bit. I closed my eyes and just held it there a short while before finally swallowing the liquor.

"You're hurt, Sam. Let's go to Xanadu. They can fix you up. What's wrong?" Erin said.

I shook my head, no, and rummaged around and found half of a joint on the table. I lit up the joint and took a puff, and offered it to her. She declined.

Her happy mood started to vanish, and I felt like shit for killing her joy. I said, "Ris is ra ry ram."

"What, so I'm supposed to watch you get faened up?" Erin asked.

"Ry rot ru ranted ru rang rout?" I asked, picking up my drink and carrying the joint across the room to the mini-stage.

I took another puff, sat down my drink, and located the sound-dampening force field I put in place at the balcony party. I positioned it around the drum set and assigned the reduction rate to one hundred percent of the sound produced by the stage area.

"What am I supposed to do?" Erin asked.

I led her over to Byrone's DJ area and showed her the keyboards. I turned them on and showed her how to select patches and adjust the volume. Her happy mood was entirely gone, and she looked unhappy at my suggestion that she should play music. I offered the joint to her one more time, and she took it, inhaled a puff, and coughed. I took the joint back and patted her on the back as I headed over to the drum set. I cued up some songs from my playlist and started off with some simple beats from Fleetwood Mac. I thought she might like some of those songs. I put out the roach, took a sip of booze, and started playing along with the music.

As I played, I thought about my current situation. Not being able to talk certainly inhibited quite a few *Tiger Mountain* functions that I was used to leveraging during my daily life. I also thought about Valentino's attempt to blind me and knew if I were blind and mute, I would basically be helpless. I wondered if there was a way to construct a better interface so I could still access functions if I ever ended up in that state? I knew it was morose to plan for such a situation, which also brought me around to another thought that was kicking around in my head since my confrontation with Joshua, faking my own death. I wondered if Xanadu could make a dead clone of my body that I could transport into place to convince Valentino to leave me alone? I still needed to figure out how to block direct vignette communication, however. That was the true test to see if a Splendorite was dead. If the subject could no longer be reached by vignette, they were considered dead. This was the state of Grayson's vignette, although no one ever found his body or claimed to have murdered him. Even though we Splendorites were immortal, we were not invulnerable as I pondered the aching punch I received to the side of my face.

Erin plunked around on the keyboard a few times, gave up, and walked away from the stage. As she got to the wide stairway leading down, I could see she held her face in her hands, probably crying. The good boyfriend in me wanted to chase after her and tell her I was sorry, but I couldn't even do that in my current state. I used my invisihud to target her before she walked out of view. I wanted to know where she was going.

After the song finished, I checked on her location. She returned to Candy's apartment. I felt like shit emotionally and pissed at Erin for making me feel this way. I was also mad at myself for not being nicer to her. She says she wants to hang out, but when she sees what I want to do, it's not good enough for her? What's her deal about feeling so happy anyway? What did Candy tell her? Did she just expect me to live in lala land with her?

I appreciated her trying to improve my mood, but it seemed so shallow and hollow to pretend like nothing has happened and everything is fine. I took another swig of booze and wondered why I didn't just return to Xanadu. She was right about that. They probably could fix me up. I realized I felt sorry for myself. I put all this effort into locating her, and now that I found her, I was being unreasonable, forcing her away. I felt trapped, fucked up, stupid, and hurt.

In the past, I played the drums to clear my head. Now that there was emotional baggage weighing me down, I couldn't get into the happier, party-time songs I selected from my playlist. I flipped through the list, trying to find something that might take my mind off my current situation when an alert popped up in my invisihud. It was from the cloaked scanner I set to monitor Jorrie. It reported that the ship she was on was taking heavy damage, predicting that destruction might be imminent.

I wanted to say what I wanted to do to Ohm, but I knew my speech would be garbled. I activated the shield spacesuit mode, the jetpack, and anti-gravity boots icons. I fumbled around in the invisihud menu, trying to find a way to use the location of Jorrie's cloaked scanner to project a target point outside of the ship she was aboard. There were some complex math sub-menus allowing for such computations, but I panicked and did not feel there was enough time to fuss around with learning new tools. I chose the Transfast icon and located a sub-menu with cardinal point directions, and repeatedly selected the up icon to move the transport target out of the ship and into space. Once I was sure I was not going to transport into a bulkhead, I stepped away from the drums and activated the transport.

The sides of the Black Glass Studio collapsed as I disassembled, once again. I felt like I held my breath as I waited to materialize. Perhaps the transport happened as I exhaled? The suffocation was real to me, however. I knew I did not have a body, but It seemed like I could not breathe. It added to the overall state of panic I felt prior to transport. The darkness of space faded in as I materialized, with white streaks of stars zooming in from the sides. I floated, disoriented in space, struggling to breathe.

I acquired a target on Jorrie's ship, the *Contender*, and set my jetpack to the fastest speed possible. Three Hatiss Myxolo attack ships engaged the *Contender*, which issued evasive maneuvers making it difficult to track its location. The jetpack kept up its function to track the ship, and I got visibly closer. I started hyperventilating as the psychological suffocation I experienced during the transport was now made real in my spacesuit environment. Breathing became difficult as the lack of gravity often compounded that situation. With my focus on the invisihud menu system, I plunged through space toward the *Contender*, getting ever closer as it maneuvered through the combat situation. I switched my anti-gravity boots to magnet mode with the hope of locking onto the hull of the *Contender*.

The *Contender* took another hit, and its motion took on that of a ship drifting in space. My jetpack tried to compensate for the sudden, unpredicted new course and crashed into the hull, sending sparks flying as my shield struggled to maintain the enclosure around my body. At some point in the tumbling, the anti-gravity boots locked onto the hull, and I was thrown forward in a lurching motion. I realized I probably would have thrown up at that time if I had eaten any breakfast.

Looking around, I saw the three Hatiss ships circling. I wasn't sure if they were going to finish the *Contender* off or board it to take prisoners. I didn't wait to find out. Reaching deep inside, I pulled up the *Motif* and tried my best to form the correct syllables crying out, "Homsoon!"

I gestured in the direction of the circling ships as purple clouds formed in space, quickly breaking apart, pushed by a brisk wind blowing behind them. Emerging from the cloud front were multiple dragons that immediately sought out the Hatiss warships, their claws ripping at the hulls. They were so swift and terrifying that I worried they might attack the *Contender*. I took steps along the ship's outer hull, lifting the anti-gravity boots up and down, forcing myself forward, directing the *Motif* to wrap its form around the *Contender*, hopefully identifying it as a non-target to the dragons.

Homsoon was the first dragon to emerge from one of the purple clouds. She wasted no time and immediately attacked the green reactor glow on the underside of the Hatiss warship. Several more dragons appeared, and each one seemed to be drawn to the reactor chamber of the ships. There were three large dragons on the scene, with Homsoon being the largest. A swarm of smaller dragons emerged from the purple clouds. These smaller dragons attached themselves to outer struts and nacelle implementations of the Hatiss warship designs. I cried out, "Homsoon mok kil way," translating it to enjoy your energy feast.

The attack was fast and fierce, with bulkheads buckling, decompression blasts, and all-out explosions occurring as the ships were ripped apart by the dragon horde emerging from the purple clouds. The Hatiss starships fired a few laser shots, but they missed the dragons and caused them to immediately tear apart the weapons array.

I felt the *Contender* drifting back, under thruster control only, trying to put some distance between itself and the chaotic frenzied dragon attack. Debris chunks were flying off in all directions, and those became my new main concern. I located the auto-target menu and chose the relocate icon from the submenu. A few of the pieces approached too close and were transported to a new location by Ohm. I couldn't imagine there was much more of the ships left when a sudden flash of bright light flooded the scene. The flash framed Homsoon's silhouette in the center of the brightness, her wings outstretched, screeching her call into the emptiness of space, which could not carry the sound. Another flash and another as the reactors of all three Hatiss warships went critical, each one illuminating a dragon, basking in its glory and consuming the energy released. The smaller dragons were the first to retreat into the purple clouds. Some of them carried pieces of the ships in their claws as they disappeared into the swirling purple fog.

I cried out once more, "Homsoon pak nak tay!" translating as revealed energy consumed.

The remaining dragons fled the scene. They disappeared into the purple clouds with Homsoon flapping her giant wings. Her neck moved in an up and down motion with each new stride taken, leaving behind a scene of drifting debris as the purple clouds slowly dissipated.

Targeting the bridge of the *Contender*, I used Transfast to place myself on the bridge in front of the viewscreen. The transport activated, placing me in the void I had only recently emerged from. It was silent, reminding me of my labored breathing, which was temporarily suspended because I had no body. When I subdued and recruited Homsoon, I wondered if it was worth the effort and back pain I received in the process. But seeing the dragons deployed today shocked me. Even I was in awe of their mighty power to rip apart a starship. They were way more effective than I imagined. The sound of a code one alert reached my ears and low lighting crept in from the sides of my perception as I materialized on the bridge of the *Contender*.

A laser weapon impacted me on the left, and my shield redirected the energy around me. A familiar voice cried out, "Hold your fire!" It was Jorrie's.

The bridge was a wreck and immediately reminded me of the scene I experienced on the *Explorer EX-01* during the Rulkan attack. As I surveyed the scene, I saw that Warren Turner slumped over in the Captain's chair. Soot and cuts covered Jorrie's face. To my right was a collapsed console station, and a crew member was underneath with blood leaking out staining the carpeting. Off to my right and further back was an officer I had not met in this time loop, but I knew very well in other future memories. His name was Ernie Nestor, and he was busy at the console issuing damage reports to the room. On my left at a console was Mia Nasal, pointing a laser weapon at me. She was the one who fired the shot.

"Sam," Jorrie said.

I dropped my shield, jetpack, and anti-gravity boots before heading over to the fallen crewman. I used the medkit icon in my invisihud. The floor sparkled, faded, and left behind a white box with a red cross. I kicked it across the floor toward Jorrie, who bent down and picked it up as I replicated another one. I pulled the broken console from the fallen crewman. The display had shattered into large pieces of glass, with one of them puncturing the skin where the waist meets the hips. It was Brent Stevens, and a large shard impaled his right love handle. As I cleared away the debris, all I could think about was how the highway patrol in the nineteen fifties petitioned the auto industry to make a better windshield. There were too many accidents involving victims killed by large pieces of glass piercing their bodies. This change led to the development of the newer glass windshields that crumbled into tiny pieces instead of breaking into large shards. Here I am, hundreds of years into the future, and it seems Starnet has lost that common sense approach to console glass formulation, which could have prevented the current injury I needed to treat.

Ernie abandoned his console and rushed over to help me remove Brent from the debris as Brent screamed out in agony when the glass shard changed position. He lost a lot of blood. I opened the medkit, located the scissors, and started cutting away the uniform around the gash. Inside one of the invisihud sub-menus was the medical shield. I targeted the glass shard followed by the recycle icon. The large piece of glass disappeared, and his blood started flowing freely.

I could hear Jorrie saying, "Easy, Warren."

Ernie questioned me, asking, "Do you know what you're doing?"

I shook my head, yes, and mumbled, "ess."

Under the medical menu of the invisihud, was a medical shield icon. This feature used the force fields of a cloaked scanner to establish a blue hemispherical force field around the wound. At first, it did not stop the bleeding, and the blood pooled up on one side of the force field. The back pressure finally kicked in and stopped the wound from leaking. I ripped the uniform open more as Brent looked at me wide-eyed with terror. Using the icon for the beta version of the cellepulator, Ohm replicated the device, and it sparkled into existence on the floor next to the medkit.

Picking it up, I sat on my knees, assuming the tripod position to keep the unit stable as I focused the device on Brent's wound. Once it obtained a lock on the wound, I pressed the button to activate the orgamorphic gel depositing process. The red light shot out of the device, passed through the medical shielding, and into the wound on Brent's side. This ray transported a matching volume of orgamorphic gel into his wound. I tossed the device aside as it burnt out, with a quick poof causing Ernie to say, "Holy mackerel."

When I discontinued the medical shielding, the remaining blood dripped down Brent's side and fell to the floor. Brent fell back in relief, and Ernie held his head. With the medical inspectrograph in hand, I ran it along the length of his body. The scanner detected Brent's low blood condition and offered a recommended blood booster. I located the medjector and double-checked that it matched the recommended injection supplied by the medical inspectrograph before applying it to his neck.

"How is he?" Warren asked from his command chair with a dry voice.

"Well, I don't know, sir. The bleeding has stopped," Ernie replied.

I leaned back on the remaining support of the broken console, dropping my arms to my side, and sat there stunned with tears welling up in my eyes. I felt like I had reached my limit of responding to this emergency.

Ernie called out, "I think he's coming around."

Brent tried sitting up on one elbow and looked down at his wound, touching it. I shook my head, no, and mumbled, "Gel."

"Orgamorphic gel? You used the invention you mentioned on me?" Brent asked.

I mumbled, "Yeah."

Brent picked up the medical inspectrograph and pulled himself closer to me to begin scanning my face saying, "That's some hematoma you have there."

He put down the medical inspectrograph and located the skin sealer from the medkit, made some adjustments, and started passing it over the side of my face.

"Chief, what is our status?" Warren called out, assuming command.

"Right away, sir," replied Ernie as he left Brent's side to return to his console.

"Short-range scanners report no immediate ships in the area, but long-range scanners are down," Jorrie called out from her navigator's position.

"Flux drive is down. Shields are down. Communications are down," Ernie began, but Warren interrupted him by asking, "What systems are operational?"

"We have life support, short-range scanners, and weapons," Ernie reported again.

"Head down to engineering and see what you can do," Warren said.

"I'll help you, Chief," Jorrie said, and she left with Ernie to head down to engineering.

At first, it seemed like Brent's application of the skin sealer had no effect, then all of a sudden, I felt my jaw loosen up, and I could open my mouth again.

"Hold still. I am almost finished," Brent said.

He passed the skin sealer over the side of my face a couple more times before setting the device aside and saying, "That is about the best I can do under these circumstances."

"Thank you, Brent. I can talk again," I said.

"Take it easy, Doctor. You were hurt pretty bad," Warren said.

Mia came forward to take up the helm position after Jorrie left. She looked over at me and said, "Sorry for firing on you. I thought we were being boarded."

"A logical assumption," I said to Mia, returning to my feet and helping Brent up from the floor, saying, "Move slowly. I have not perfected the outer coating yet. It needs to set up before you become more active."

"That's an order, Doctor. Take a seat," Warren said to Brent as he turned his head and addressed me. "I presume those were your dragons who tore apart the attacking ships?"

"They are," I replied shortly.

"I still don't know what to think of you, Sam. How did you know we were under attack?" Warren asked.

"I have been monitoring the traffic passing through the radionic tile for some time. I placed a tracker on the *Contender* as it passed by. When the ship started taking structural damage, I was alerted," I said.

Warren shifted in his chair, folding his arms as he calculated how to exploit all the holes in my story, finally asking, "How did you gather a flock of dragons and convince them to do your bidding on a moment's notice?"

"My species are long-lived, allowing me to experience what you might consider multiple lives. In one of my lives, I lived and worked with dragons, becoming a dragon lord. I have a pact with them that requires them to come to my aid," I replied.

"You're the Squire of the Pharaoh, aren't you?" Mia asked.

"That's what some kids called me on Vasco, and the media ran with it," I said, trying to deflect her question.

"Thank you for coming to our rescue, Sam," Warren finally said.

"I can help with repairs if you like. I can swap this heavily damaged ship with one from a nearby probability that took less damage," I offered.

"By all means, that would be wonderful," Warren said with his poker face smile.

"The ship needs to be in motion, and crewmen should be standing clear of damaged areas. Forward thrusters should be enough motion to effect the change," I said.

"Attention, all hands. Sam is going to swap our damaged ship with a less damaged one. Please assume a standing position and help anyone who is injured stand as well. Step away from debris and damaged areas and assume a position in a clear area," Warren said into the intercom system.

"Major, forward thrusters, away from the debris field."

Mia engaged the thrusters to move the ship forward. I stood facing the viewscreen and watched as the debris field from the attack moved off to the left, leaving us looking at open space. Reaching out with the *Motif*, I started pacing back and forth in front of the viewscreen. I cast it out from me and up onto the walls. I recalled the *Motif* I previously cast around the ship during the attack. I knew there were nearby echoes of the *Contender* who experienced a similar attack, and I drew upon those variations as I rippled the hull of this ship to take on the probable nature of a nearby, less damaged version, of the *Contender*. The interior of the starship creaked and groaned as sounds of stressing metal reverberated throughout the corridors. Unbreaking glass rung in the air as the collapsed supports on the bridge rippled and faded. I made a final push to restore systems and drew a thick darkness into this reality before quickly pushing it away. During this mental gesture, I sent as much damage as possible into the void while keeping the concept of what makes the *Contender* intact.

"That's as far as I dare go," I said, feeling a little fatigued.

Warren got up from his commander's chair, walked over to me, put his hand on my shoulder, and said, "You've done good, my Squire."

"Systems are coming back online," Mia belted out.

Brent took a seat at his previously destroyed console, reporting, "I am seeing it too. Long-range communications are restored."

Ernie's voice came over the communications speaker, "I don't know what he did, but we have chemstream, and the flux drive is not that bad off. I should have it online within the hour, sir."

"Good news, Chief. Keep me updated," Warren replied over his communications brooch.

"You look tired. Does changing things wear you out?" Mia asked me.

"Sometimes, it depends on how significant the change is," I said.

Warren took his seat at the commander's chair and said, "Doctor, why don't you offer our guest some quarters. You could probably use some rest too. We're in a lot better shape than before. Take a break."

Brent gestured toward the back of the bridge and said, "This way, Sam."

We entered the magnalift, and Brent said, "Deck three."

The *Contender* was not a large starship like *Journey* or *Explorer*. It was smaller, like a beefed-up cargo vessel with overpowered engines and weapons. It was one of the few Starnet starships with an optical cloak. As we waited for the magnalift to reach its destination, Brent said, "Thank you for saving my life back there, Sam. I thought I was going to bleed out there on the floor of the bridge."

"You're welcome, Brent. I wish I could figure out how to get the orgamorphic gel delivery device to not burn out after a single use," I replied.

"I guess I am beginning to finally understand what you have been trying to tell me all along about being a probability traveler," Brent said.

"I'm sorry I did not get a chance to talk to you at the party that night," I said.

"That's right, Jorrie was in a mood that evening. I really had my eye on visiting that buffet," Brent replied with a smile.

The magnalift came to a stop, and the doors opened up into a hallway leading only one way. We headed down the hall with evenly spaced doors on the left. Brent finally decided on a door and said, "I think this one is unoccupied. If you get hungry, the galley is just down the hall."

"Thanks for fixing my face, Brent. I started to feel like a caveman, not being able to talk," I said.

"Happy to," he said, pressing a button to open the door to the crew quarters.

I stepped inside, and the door closed behind me, leaving me in a room that was only a little larger than a prison cell. There wasn't even a bathroom in these quarters, only bunk beds and a desk. I lay down on the lower bunk. I felt a bit overwhelmed with the amount of action occupying my last two days. I couldn't help but feel like shit about how Erin and I parted. I thought about requesting some booze but lay there listening to the sound of the engines instead.

A person-sized sparkle appeared, leaving Erin standing before me.

"I hope it's okay to drop in on you like this," Erin said, pulling up the chair from the desk and taking a seat.

"I'm sorry for being such a dick this morning. I was incredibly frustrated with not being able to speak. I should have followed your advice and returned to Xanadu," I said.

"Good thing you didn't, huh? You might not have been available to help out this crew. Candy and I watched the whole thing through your cloaked scanner. Dragons eating starships, the medical treatment of your friend. I still feel overwhelmed just saying it. I can't imagine how you felt having to actually do it," Erin said.

"I feel overwhelmed too like I have reached my limit of over the top things to do in one day," I said.

"I still want to know you, Sam, but I could tell today that I was not fitting in that well," Erin said.

"Baby, I get grouchy sometimes. I'm sorry I took it out on you, but I am a pot-smoking alcoholic. I don't try to hide that. And not being able to communicate with you caused me to reach out to those things first. I'm still getting used to being in a relationship, getting used to not just thinking about myself first. But if you want, I can offer you an apartment like Candy has. You know, a place to call your own, to get away to," I said.

Erin got up from the chair to sit next to me on the bunk and said, "I don't want to live down the hall from you, Sam. I want to be part of your life."

"That's the way I want it, too. Can we try again?" I asked.

She looked at me with an up and down glance and said, "Yeah, I'd like that."

The mood was ripe for a kiss, but a chime sounded from the door, and I said, "Come in."

The door slid open, and Jorrie stood there. She removed the soot from her face but still had a few scratches. The scene took her by surprise as she said, "Sam, oh."

Erin stood up and immediately offered her hand, saying, "You're Jorrie, right? I'm Erin."

I could tell Jorrie was blindsided, not expecting this at all, as she seemed to move in slow motion, shaking Erin's hand saying, "I'm intruding. I'm sorry."

"You're not intruding. We were just sitting here talking. Come in and have a seat," I said, sitting up and offering her the rolly chair that Erin abandoned.

"This feels incredibly awkward, Sam. I wanted to apologize to you on more than one occasion, and I used the vignette you gave me, but you were never home," Jorrie started out.

"It took me a while to get over that, Jorrie, but I have. I needed to put my emotional self back together, and I think it did me some good. I feel like I am in a better place now," I said.

"Your designs are beautiful. Are they tattoos?" Erin asked.

"No, they are part of my species. All Vosips have some design. We call them, 'appeal,'" Jorrie said.

Erin smiled and said, "I like that, 'appeal.'"

"I had to put myself back together, Sam. I damn near resigned my commission over that mission. If it weren't for Warren talking me out of it, I probably would have. It made me reevaluate my ethics in following orders," Jorrie said.

"I've been there. My creators programmed me to sabotage the ship I served on and even attempted to murder my commanding officer, all against my will. The programming suppressed my consciousness as I performed these horrible acts, only to become aware again, holding the gun or the detonator. It was a nightmare," Erin revealed.

I could tell Jorrie was torn between replying to me or responding to Erin. She spoke to me first, "That night we spent together was real, Sam. I wasn't pretending or trying to trick you. That's why I felt so much inner loathing for myself afterward. I took your heart and broke it. I could see it breaking on your face when you discovered the recording device and deduced my mission. I'm sorry, Sam."

She turned to Erin and replied, "Sam told me about you from the beginning. His future memories of us living together."

"He told me the same thing. I was furious, at first, thinking, how can I be a second wife? But now I realize that some of that anger," and Erin looked at me, then back at Jorrie indicating she talked to us both, "was from reacting as an Imperial. Reacting to the memories installed into my mind, instead of as my Melog self."

"I have memories from other lives, my Limax Tusk helps manage them, but I still find myself reacting to a situation as if I were a personality from another life. I know that sounds strange, but it's true," Jorrie said.

"No, I get it. Now that I no longer live among the Imperials, I can see how often their belief systems shaped my way of thinking," Erin said.

"Thank you for coming to my rescue today, Sam. Thank you for saving my ship and my friends. It means a lot to me," Jorrie said with tears welling up in her eyes.

"Don't cry, Jorrie. It's only going to get better from here," Erin reassured her.

Jorrie stood up, wiping tears from her cheek, and said, "I had better go. I just wanted to stop in and hopefully clear the air."

Erin stood up and hugged her briefly, saying, "It's so nice to meet you, Jorrie," and Jorrie left the room.

Erin sat down on the bunk next to me and said, "I like her, Sam. I like her a lot. I didn't think I would, but I do."

"I do too, baby. Even though we had a rocky start, I don't hold bad feelings for her," I said.

Erin took my hand and asked, "Do you want to remain here?"

I shook my head, no, and asked, "Can I ask you something?"

"Sure, what," she said with a smile.

"How should I introduce you? Are you my girlfriend, my lover, my main squeeze, my traveling companion, my old lady?" I asked.

"Ugh, old lady, is that really a thing people say?" Erin asked with a frown.

"Yeah, in other times and places," I replied.

"Until I become your wife, I would like to be introduced as your friend. And thank you for asking," Erin said.

I tried it out loud, saying to her, "This is my friend Erin Gallo."

"Very nice. I think that will do," Erin said.

I stood up and said, "Give me a second," as I walked over to the communications panel on the wall.

I pushed the button and said, "Sam to Warren Turner."

It took a moment, and I heard a reply through the speaker in the wall, "Turner here. What is it, Sam?"

"I'm taking leave of your ship, 'Balance In All Things,'" I said into the communications panel.

"Thank you for your help today. Safe journey. Turner out," Warren replied.

"You ready?" Erin asked.

I shook my head, yes, and Erin said, "Ohm, transport us back to our home in San Francisco."

The room collapsed inward, escorting the darkness back for another audition. At least I didn't feel suffocated this time. It felt peaceful. I didn't know if I would ever end up married to Erin and Jorrie, but I felt this first meeting went better than I could have ever planned. I dreaded that moment, thinking of it as a confrontation to avoid. But in reality, for this to work, Jorrie and Erin had to become friends. The evening light of the San Francisco bay flooded in from the sides of my perception as I materialized in my home again.

CHAPTER 46

Loose Ends

⌒∾⌒

The next couple of weeks were ideal. It was sex in the morning, breakfast, getting high, lounging, taking walks in the park, evening drinks, and good food with friends. Early on, I set out on a mission to locate where Clarashel worked, and I revealed my plan to Erin about finding a nearby probability where Clarashel and Candy would meet up by accident. It seemed to work out because I noticed Candy and Clarashel ended up back together. Who knew how long it would last, but everyone deserves to get laid.

I managed to get in some more drum practice regularly. Frogs would stop by, and we started working on a shortlist of songs that rocked out. He was pretty good on the guitar with a sense for arrangements that many musicians don't have. Erin rarely hung out in the Black Glass Studios, preferring to hang out with Candy or Alex and Lucas while I had my music time. Occasionally the twenty-third-floor crew would pop up and catch us finishing up a set before we headed out for the evening. Lucas, Alex, and Candy all reported that the harassment stopped, and so did K-Mac and Byrone. I finally figured out Erin's period cycle taking a weight off my mind that I might have knocked her up.

On the methodical front, the Flexanite detection program was steadily producing detainees at a rate of about three every two months. I gave up on the teddy bear interface and just threw them all into a single cell, rotating them out to Eden after they spent a couple of weeks in prison. My covert inspection of ships coming through the radionic tile from the Ussu sector did boost the rate slightly. It was confirmed that the Flexanites were stowing away in some of the starships passing through the radionic tile. Now that the Myxolo attacked a Starnet vessel, I considered it open season on them. I used my new cloaked swarm ships to destroy any detected Myxolo ships without hesitation. I ramped up replication for that model, sending them deeper into the Ussu sector, seeking out any Myxolo ships, and attacking them on sight.

The cloaked swarm ships were far more effective than I expected. Being cloaked, they were not detected until the attack was underway. The attacks were quick. It only took a few minutes until one of the swarm ships delivered its nuclear payload into the enemy flux reactor. I redirected the cloaked optical probes from the Gar sector into the Ussu sector with hopes of detecting the Flexanite homeworld. I knew they maintained shipyards somewhere, and I wanted to locate and destroy those.

On the family front, it only took about three weeks before Valentino recovered his ring from the vault. I was never able to figure out how he did it. Ohm reported it was missing one day. When I checked Valentino's cloaked scanner, I discovered he wore it upon his finger once again. I instructed Ohm, to make a duplicate of the ring, and swap it with the original ring while Valentino slept. Deciding to disintegrate the original ring, I requested Ohm to transport it into space. After reviewing a few logs, Valentino has not noticed the duplicate ring, as far as I could tell.

The cottage on the edge of Rayleaf attacked the very next day. Joshua's men did fall asleep when they approached the cottage, so all they could do was fire flaming arrows at the place. The terraforming module immediately repaired any damage done. Joshua was forced to enter the area to pull his sleeping men out of range of the field that introduced the sleeping agent. I eventually relaxed the logic on the sleep field so other men could fetch their fallen comrades, assuming they proceeded no further than the recovery point. I did review a log entry where Joshua entered the house and walked around examining some of the papers and appliances. He smashed a few things, but after he left, the terraforming module repaired them.

On the Blinn front, there was progress on the cellepulator. It was still a one-shot device, but it no longer overloaded and burnt out after one use. Cartridges were introduced so they could be reloaded after a single-use. I modified the basic medkit to include one of these along with two extra orgamorphic gel cartridges. Research into heavy metal removal was still ongoing, so there was no news on that front. I instructed the Blinn to lay down the groundwork for a new shipyard replication center that would be dedicated to the construction of the *Kataru*. I gathered up and forwarded all relevant information about the various species of the Starnet Union. The goal was to construct a ship that could maintain life support for all Starnet species. The hope was that all the various gas breathers would be able to openly interact in a shared environment. The more extreme species, such as the aquatic types and the Gilliux were the most challenging. I presented several sketches of the original *Kataru* that I recalled from the first time loop. The sketches outlined how the Gilliux environment was the central core of the ship which was wrapped in the transparent fluidic environment shared by the aquatic species. The overall design was the classic cruiser-style ship with bulbous fluidic cavities, reminiscent of some of the existing aquatic designs.

On the cloaked scanners across the galaxy front, one of my cloaked scanners eventually found its way to the Zitali slave markets. I decided to hit them where it hurts the most. I boldly transported all slaves from the slave market floor to various space stations, where I established a cloaked scanner presence. I set up algorithms to try to detect groups of like species or crewmates so they would be transported together and removed any locking collars applied to the victims. To provide them with some immediate relief, I deposited a care package containing a strip of diamond stamped quaybit, a supply of species-related food, and a change of clothes. It was my way of saying fuck you to the orange slave-driving bastards. After a month passed, the open slave-trading markets were no longer viable to maintain, which drove slave-trading into secret places. I dedicated a few hundred cloaked scanners to the Zitali homeworld, trying to seek out new trading markets. I found a few, but more than likely, slave trading was now taking place discreetly in open space, between consenting vessels. My new initiative was to get a cloaked scanner on as many Zitali vessels as possible as well as the ships of the slave buyers.

CHAPTER 47

Mist Door Operations

❧

Erin and I spent most of our days together, but there were times when she was off doing things on her own or with friends. She seemed to have an interest in going to the library and discovering the history of this new planet that was now her home. While we talked about revisiting Zenith, we never really got around to doing it, and it seemed less important to her as time went on. We visited many of the natural wonders of Earth, including The Grand Canyon, Iguazu Falls, The Great Pyramids of Egypt, Jeju Island, The Great Barrier Reef, and Kilimanjaro to name a few. The transporter made day trips very easy. But the allure of tourism grew old quickly as we settled into the act of trying to figure out what each of us wanted to do. I noticed a sudden change in Erin after about six weeks of living with her. Somewhere along the way, she became more of a roommate instead of a lover, and the act of making love dropped off quite a bit.

Then it finally happened. She just didn't come home one night. I was worried at first, and I checked her life signs via the cloaked scanner. They checked out fine, so I didn't pry any further. I knew I could review all the log activity recorded by the cloaked scanner following her around, but I did not want to become that guy who spied on his girlfriend, so I left it alone.

In the first time loop, I obsessively monitored and reviewed cloaked scanner data on Valentino and Lexi eventually adding Hugo into the monitoring mix leading to disastrous results. The more I knew what they were doing, the more I was sucked into their lives. In the second time loop, I cut way back on the monitoring of other people and I felt like it was a better approach to living. That is why, I did not immediately investigate where Erin was going and what she was doing when she was not with me. The next day, she didn't come home until late in the evening, and when she did, I didn't know what to say.

"Aren't you going to ask where I've been?" Erin asked while rummaging through the refrigerator in the kitchen.

"Sure, where have you been?" I asked while sitting on the white sofa.

"I hung out with some friends, and it got late. I spent the night at their place, so we could pick up where we left off the next morning," she said.

"Oh, that's nice. Did you have fun?" I asked.

"Yeah, I did," she said while eating a bowl of cereal at the kitchen counter.

I felt like a dad instead of a boyfriend. I didn't know what I was to her anymore. It made me feel like shit though. She started looking through some glowing screen device, and I headed into the bedroom to sleep. She joined me, about forty minutes later, climbing into the other side of the bed. She didn't say anything to me, and we both just lay there in silence until I finally fell asleep.

An invisihud alarm woke me. I looked over next to me, and Erin was fast asleep. Grabbing my boots and clothes, I headed into the living room to get dressed. This alarm was serious. The entire MD-Alpha team dropped off the map. Ohm could no longer communicate with them. I replayed the most recent log from Robin's cloaked scanner revealing her captured and bound, with someone dragging her into a ring of stones with energy passing through them. That's when the log went dead. After constructing echo sturdy devices, I have never encountered a situation where my gear just quit working. Even if my Guardians were dead, I should still receive a feed from the cloaked scanners near their location.

I pulled out the vignette to the catwalk on the *Deceptive* and stepped through. As it typically was, the cloth covered the painting at the end of the catwalk. I headed to the end and thought hard about what I needed to do. If the team entered a location where my technology no longer works, my gear would cease to function once I step through the painting. I asked Ohm for a medkit and a combat dagger that I strapped to my left leg. I moved the wand from my lower leg pocket to my right arm pocket for quicker access. Looking through my invisihud under the combat accessories menu, I chose a pair of clear protective eye goggles, a lightweight armored vest, and a nine-millimeter handgun with a full clip.

I was ready to remove the cloth and focus on the team when a series of bright sparkles appeared at the end of the catwalk.

"What do you think you're doing?" Candy asked.

"I'm going to do what I can to help them," I replied.

"We want to help too," Lucas said.

"There is no tech there. You might become targets I could not defend," I said frankly.

"I don't need tech to kick ass," Alex said with sass as they all walked down the catwalk to approach the painting.

"Alex can come, but it's best if you two remain behind and keep the painting focused on our location. We might need an emergency exit," I said.

"We can't just sit back and watch you two go it alone," Lucas said.

"Objects maintain their velocity when they are cast through the painting. One of you can locate targets, and the other can shoot," I said to Candy and Lucas.

I handed Alex the handgun, and she said, "I don't do guns, you know that," while refusing to accept it.

I pulled the combat dagger from the side of my leg, handing it to her, saying, "If you can, free them. Give Jim the gun. He's a good shot."

Alex reluctantly accepted them both, and before anyone could say anything, I removed the cloth from the painting. We all faced a dire scene of brutality, revealing a Minoutar type creature eating from the chest of a fallen knight whose armor was ripped wide open. In a shocking first, the screams of the knight reached through the painting, filling and reverberating off the walls of the *Deceptive*. I focused on David, trying to locate him with the painting and the scene misted over. When the mist cleared, I saw David lying, unconscious, on a large flat stone platform surrounded by rock. I could see Malik was down. Robin and Jim sat up but looked like they were in pretty rough shape. Glancing over at Alex, I touched her on the shoulder, and we stepped through the painting together.

It was nighttime here, with the colors of a nearby nebula broken up by the debris of a shattered moon that hung ominously above. The sky was modulated and distorted by an energy field rippling above us. The field seemed to be stabilized by stacks of energy lines running through stone archways evenly spaced in an elliptical layout around the flat stone platform we arrived upon. The ellipse of staggered stones occupied at least two hundred meters in length and was approximately one hundred meters wide.

At one end, I saw an extra-large Mist Door with all segments of the pillars fully illuminated. The keystone pulsed, which I had never seen happen before. The pillars on each side of the Mist Door cast lines of energy outward. A band of energy emitted from each of the segments, guided by stone archways defining the perimeter of this place. The mist hung suspended between the pillars was a blood-red color instead of the calming teal I observed in other past Mist Door activations.

Opposite the Mist Door, at the far end of the elliptical arena was a circular ring collecting energy and redirecting it at another smaller Mist Door, which appeared to be in operation. Scattered about the interior of the elliptical area were various rubble patches. They may have been stones that fell out of place from some grand design that was no longer valid. A low hum filled the air along with a high-pitched eek that was reminiscent of fingers on a blackboard.

Alex immediately set to work freeing Jim's bindings with the knife, saying, "We're here to get you out."

Jim looked at me, with his dirt-covered face, and screamed, "Look out!"

At the same time, Robin also yelled out, "It's a trap!"

I immediately hit the deck with a diving roll, finally putting some of that *Explorer* aurastage training to good use. In the process, I dropped the medkit and rolled too far, continuing to roll down the wide, stone steps leading up to the platform we arrived upon. The sound of an energy blast flew by me as I thump, thumped down the stairway trying to protect my head. I could finally see what Robin referred to. There was at least a full platoon of Ralla positioned around the perimeter, aiming for our position.

My prediction was correct. The invisihud was down. I felt panic set in as a squad of Ralla advanced upon my position, firing, as I ran for cover behind a piece of the large stone rubble. With Ralla all around, the cover was fleeting. I needed to keep moving between piles of rubble as the energy blasts got closer to hitting me. I summoned the *Motif* and started manipulating echo as I moved between the stones. I could only think of one way to survive this battle. I needed to become large. I continued moving between stones, slowly increasing my height. I pulled out my wand and managed to hit a few of the advancing Ralla with the *Insipida* confusion spell. It seemed to work. They stood there stunned. The platoon positioned along the outer edge began to move in on me. I picked a direction where I noticed a gap in their line and all-out barreled toward them, increasing my size as I advanced. My growing form offered an element of surprise as the Ralla couldn't believe their eyes. They hesitated for a moment, and that was all I needed to crash into their line and knock several of them down. I kept moving along their line, knocking them down as I continued to grow in size. I was easily ten to twelve meters tall now and had knocked down half of the platoon. The disadvantage of this tactic was that I offered the Ralla on the other side of the elliptical arena a larger target. I took a few energy hits as I dodged and performed another diving roll while trying to advance upon their position.

My larger size helped reduce the damage I took from the energy weapons fired at me. The armored vest also seemed to block a couple of hits, but my back was smoldering and my leg burned. Reaching into echo, even more, I stomped the ground as I came out of the roll, standing taller than before. I used the *Motif* to destabilize the ground around me, and my stomp caused it to ripple across the field in all directions, knocking down the Ralla closest to me.

The ground ripple continued out to the perimeter of the elliptical field, causing some of the archways to fall out of alignment. This misalignment created an explosive effect as the energy lines previously traveling through the archways collided against the stone structures, blasting them apart. Fragments of stone went flying as redirected energy shot off in all directions. The energy field, overhead, flickered and collapsed as the circular ring at the other end flashed three times and quit glowing. Its supply of energy was cut off.

Amidst the devastation I wrought, I bellowed, "Flee mortals or perish!"

I charged the remaining members of the platoon at the far end of the elliptical field, thinking I might as well push the theatrics for all they were worth. I heard a couple of gunshots firing off as I approached, and the remaining Ralla turned tail and ran. There must have been some sort of energy buildup in the larger Mist Door, probably due to the flow being interrupted. The charged glowing pillar segments had nowhere to discharge their energy, and the red mist filled with crackling electricity. This build-up looked bad, so I turned around and started running back to the central platform where Alex and I arrived. The low hum I noticed earlier started rising in pitch, and after a few strides, I heard a loud boom as segments of the large Mist Door pillars went flying out in all directions. The keystone crumbled, causing the entire structure to fall in and collapse upon itself.

I discovered David and Malik unconscious as I approached the flat stone platform. The devastation all around caused some of the fallen Ralla to get back up, grab their weapons, and run off in all directions.

Alex was the first to approach, asking with great concern and a little fear, "Are you all right, big fella?"

"I'm hit. Let's get out of here," I replied with a low voice.

Jim and Robin also made their way back to the flat stone platform, staring at me in disbelief.

"Robin, can you activate that smaller Mist Door?" I asked, gesturing to the last remaining part of the arena that stood.

"I don't know. Let's give it a try," Robin said.

"Alex, grab the medkit, and I'll get David and Malik," I bellowed.

Tucking my wand, that grew and become oversized with me, into my sleeve pocket, I gently lifted David and Malik, one in each hand. I took off at a brisk pace, reaching the remaining Mist Door ahead of the other three. I sat David and Malik down on the ground. They both stirred slightly as I placed them on the ground, offering me a bit of relief, indicating they were still alive. With some quick pacing back and forth in front of the Mist Door, I used the *Motif* to bring my size closer to normal. When I turned around to reverse my pace, a dark-cloaked individual sprang out from behind one of the pieces of rubble. It hovered slightly. There was a silvery milky shifting substance where the face should be. The fiend caught me off guard and projected something from its outstretched hand. A ray of modulating light struck my head, bringing me to my knees. It felt like a battle of wills was taking place as I fought back against it. My brain was stabbed with pain. As I resisted the attack, I slowly reached for my wand. Even though the creature did not have a face, it noticed my action, doubling its effort sending even more pain to my head. In a sudden act of desperation, I quickly whipped the wand forward, pointing it at the creature, shouting, "*Tantalis!*"

The resulting spell that sprang from my wand reminded me of the tentacle attack that Valentino used on me, only this one was smaller and more localized. Grey strands of varying length cables lept from the wand tip and encircled the cloaked creature. I poured all that was left into the wand, feeling myself passing out as I caught a final glimpse of the cables wrapping around the cloaked individual and pinning him to the ground. Even while the cloaked individual was on the ground, the cables continued to tighten and compact, smaller and smaller reducing the cloak to nothing before finally disappearing by burrowing into the ground.

CHAPTER 48

Iawoke in a hospital bed inside of Mist Door Operations. I was here many times before and recognized the room and decor. An overwhelming sadness overcame me, and I began to cry. It seemed like the bed was too small for me, but then I remembered I was not able to fully reduce my size back to normal. I felt like I lost my friends in the process of saving them. I couldn't help but recall the looks on Jim, Robin, and even Alex's face when they saw my enlarged form. I wondered if they would ever see me any other way again? And the final kicker was that the spell I used on the cloaked creature was an evil magician spell. I have become an evil magician.

Marsha Bradley approached my bedside with a clipboard saying, "The depression is a side effect of the pain killers, Sam," while adjusting a flow rate valve on the bag of fluid hanging beside my bed, "How are you feeling?" she asked.

"Sad," was all I could say, "Are David and Malik?"

"I'm right here, Sam, and Malik is one bed down. You did it. You rescued us. Thank you," David said.

"Can I get you anything?" Marsha asked.

I shook my head no.

"There are a few people who would like to visit with you. Are you up for that?" Marsha asked.

I shook my head, yes, slowly.

Marsha left the room and in walked Lucas, Candy, Alex, Robin, and Jim.

"How are you feeling, big guy?" Alex asked.

"Don't call me that," I snapped back.

"Sorry, I didn't mean to," Alex said

I interrupted her, saying, "Look at me. I'm a freak," as tears rolled down my face.

"You don't have anything on me, Sam. I was born a freak," Alex replied defensively.

"What was that place?" Candy asked.

"It was a weapon that Akan designed to attack other worlds through the Mist Door. That creature that you killed was his current incarnation," Robin answered.

"I used an evil spell to do it. I'm an evil magician now," I said while continuing to cry.

"You're not an evil magician, Sam," Candy said.

"Ask Madison," I replied.

"Look, every one of us has done things we are not proud of in dire moments. You defended yourself," Jim said.

"Then why do I feel like I have lost everything," I said.

"It's the side effects of the drugs, Sam," Lucas answered.

"He's right, Sam. Give it some time. You've been through a lot," David added.

"The bottom line is we owe you big for that one, Sam. You took on an entire platoon of Ralla without a weapon and kicked em' to the curb while destroying an evil madman's weapon of mass destruction. Dare I say you, 'put your foot down,'" Jim said with a grin.

The pun made me smile as I stopped the tears, taking a few breaths trying to regain my composure.

"There you go, on the mend already," Jim added.

"Our invisihuds are still knocked out," Robin stated.

I tried mine, and it was in the same state, "Mine too. I guess we'll have to revisit Xanadu and see if they can reboot them."

I put my head in my hand and looked down at the bed. I couldn't help but wonder why Erin was not here? I guess it was best that she did not see me in this condition.

"Why don't we let you get some rest. We can talk later," Jim said, and the group headed out.

Candy remained behind and took a seat on my bed, saying, "Scoot over a bit," and I made some room for her.

She took her hand and straightened out my hair, saying, "You are not an evil magician, Sam."

"Genuine Candy speaks the truth, Sam. I have seen true evil, and you are far from it," Malik said from one bed down.

"I don't mean to eavesdrop, but I have to agree with Malik," David said.

"I have lost Erin. We've grown farther apart over the last few weeks, and the night before last she didn't even come home," I said to Candy.

"Did you ask her about it?" Candy asked.

"I did, and she just lied and said she was with friends and decided to spend the night with them," I replied.

"Well, maybe that is what happened," Candy said, taking Erin's side.

"She doesn't even touch me anymore. Most of the time she is gone by the time I get up. And now, when I need her, she's not even here," I said.

"I'm sure there is some reason for it," Candy said.

"Yeah, the oldest reason. She has found someone else," I said.

"You don't know that. She is the only Melog in the Dili sector, you know. Maybe she is just trying to make new friends," Candy defended her.

"I guess that is what I get for being a freak. She never even introduced me to her new friends. I don't know their names or anything. She is ashamed of knowing me," I said.

"I'm not going to do this, Sam. Feed your negativity," Candy replied.

"Does your invisihud still work?" I asked.

"Yeah, whacha need?" Candy asked.

"I need you and Lucas to defend *Tiger Mountain*. Keep an eye on things. This blunder is the perfect time for one of the relatives to attack," I said.

"Got it, anything else?" Candy asked.

"David, do you know what happened to my clothes?" I asked.

"Uhm, I think they might be in the drawer of the end table, next to the bed," David replied.

I leaned over to look and felt a slight twinge along the backside of my shoulder. But I did notice my boots were on the floor, sitting next to the bed.

"Can you ask Ohm to scan those boots and produce a new pair from my wardrobe?" I asked.

"Sure, but what's wrong with those?" Candy asked.

"Their extended features were disabled when Alex and I traveled into the dampening field," I replied.

"Ohm, did you hear what Sam asked for? New boots please, the same size as on the floor, his style," Candy said.

There was a sparkle replacing the old boots with new shiny boots.

"God, I feel awful for snapping at Alex. I'm just so messed up right now," I said, lying back down as the pain in my back flared up.

Candy noticed it and said, "You just get some rest," putting her normal-sized hand in my overly large hand. "I'm going to talk to Lucas about what we need to do to keep everyone safe."

"Before you go, can I have my boots?" I asked.

"Here you go," Candy said, placing the pair of new boots on my belly before leaving the room.

I fussed around with the heel of each boot until I finally located the button that opened up the secret compartment containing the spare cloaked scanners. I tipped them sideways, trying to dump out the contents, but because the scanners were cloaked, I couldn't see a thing. They typically activated automatically, taking up locations that would place them out of sight, even if they were visible, such as corners of rooms, under tables, etc.

"What are you doing there?" David asked.

"I sent out a memo to all Guardians, a while back about integrating spare cloaked scanners into the heels of footwear. It seemed like a discreet way to keep them with you in case something ever went wrong with *Tiger Mountain*. You would still be able to use them locally for personal shielding and other features.

By placing two in each heel of your footwear, you had the bare minimum number of cloaked scanners that could combine to form a basic replication aperture. It's just survivalist stuff, but you would be able to replicate food, water, medicine, and other small items," I replied.

"Interesting, I must have missed that one," David said.

I set the boots on the floor, removed the I.V. line attached to my arm, and said, "Maintenance dock," while holding out both of my hands.

The four small cloaked scanners dropped their cloak and came to rest in my hands. I showed them to David, who was also sitting up in his bed.

"Resume operation," I said, and the four small cloaked scanners rose up, taking flight before vanishing from sight.

"Ohm, are you there?" I asked.

The sound of Ohm's soft modulating voice near my ear lifted my mood considerably as I heard, "Yes, Sam, I am here."

"Ohm, I would like to construct an interface, similar to the invisihud. It should be ring-shaped and adjust its size to the finger of the person wearing it. Once adorned, it should cloak itself. Make it voice-activated with the hud representation taking the form of a floating auragraphic display," I said.

"Working on the design," Ohm replied.

I slowly got up out of bed and reached around to untie the small hospital gown I wore. Opening the drawer next to my bed, I found my shot-up, large, dirty clothes. I stood up, removed the gown, and proceeded to get dressed, pants first, then eased the shirt with burn holes over my shoulder as I winced at the sensitive nature of the energy weapon wound. After slipping on my boots, I was ready to go. After rummaging around in the drawers of the hospital nightstand, I double-checked, but I could not locate my wand. I guess it was not that important. I took that wand from the evil magician that attacked Erin and me in Candy's kitchen. Maybe it was bad luck?

"Design is complete. The ring will function as a wearable cloaked scanner," Ohm replied.

"Ohm, replicate six copies of the new ring. Place five of them in small jewelry boxes. The sixth one is for me and does not need a box. Create them from the same replication source that cloaked scanners are made from," I said.

A series of sparkles appeared on the bed, leaving behind the rings I requested. I picked up the ring that was not in a box and put it on my left hand, the ring finger where a wedding band would go. It adjusted to fit the size of my larger finger, but it did not feel tight. A moment or two after placing it on my finger, it faded from view, but I could still feel that it was in place.

I stacked up the boxes, picked them up, and walked over between the two beds where Malik and David lay. I set the boxes on David's bed and said, "These rings can work as substitute invisihuds until I figure out how to reactivate them. They cloak, once placed on your finger."

I demonstrated the cloaking feature by removing mine and then putting it back on before continuing, "When you take them off, they become visible again. The ring is voice-activated, and the hud feature appears as a floating auragraphic display. They are less discreet, but at least you'll have access to the Mountain."

I handed one of the boxes to Malik and left the remaining four boxes on David's bed.

"Give these to Jim and Robin. You can give one of these rings to Eli. I think his character shows great merit. Can you instruct him on its use?" I asked.

David pushed up his glasses, sitting up in his bed slightly, saying, "I will, and I agree with you on Eli's character."

David offered his hand, but I leaned in for a bro hug, and he ended up tapping me on the back instead, saying, "Thank you again, Sam."

I moved over to Malik's bed and shook his arm in Ralla fashion, saying "Win su row, Malik. Until we meet again."

"Win su row, Sam. I look forward to our next meeting. Thank you for saving my life and the lives of my friends. You are not evil," Malik said.

From behind me, I heard the voice of General Wagner saying, "Are you sure you should be up, son?"

I turned around with a smile at his colloquialism of calling me, son. Looking down at him, I replied, "Probably not Sherman, but I can't remain in this ridiculous size any longer. Give my regards to Marsha for patching me up."

"Of course. I just stopped by to personally say thank you for not only rescuing MD-Alpha but helping secure the safety of the entire planet. We are in your debt," the General said.

"Well then, you can buy the beer at the next party," I replied.

"You've got it," he said with a smile and left the room.

"He's right, you know. What you did, was significant, Sam," David said from his bed. "Akan was targeting Earth with the energy weapon when you destroyed it. With him gone, the safety of Earth is in a much better place than a week ago."

"I'm glad I could help, but I have to take care of this now," I said, gesturing up and down my form with my large hand, "We'll talk soon."

I reached into my shirt pocket, pulled out the vignette set, and located the one for Xanadu. I focused on the tech door, stooped down, and stepped through.

CHAPTER 49

Xanadu

T he hallway was tall enough for me to stand up in, but I did have to duck to fit through the door. I walked into the main treatment area where a new technician I never met approached with a concerned look on his face.

"Hello, I am MaRaDaNaHuTaLo. How can I help you?" he said.

"Nice to meet you. May I call you Mar?" I asked.

"MaRa, if you please," he replied.

"Certainly, sorry," I said, "MaRa, I have a couple of burn wounds caused by an energy weapon, and I was mentally attacked by some form of bright energy ray that caused great pain in my head. Can you help me?"

"I can. If you will disrobe and take a seat on the biobed, I'll determine the best course of treatment," MaRa replied.

I removed my boots and clothes and sat naked on the flesh-like biobed as MaRa scanned me with a handheld device, asking, "Do you know what type of weapon caused the wounds?"

"Yes, the Ralla wrist weapon," I replied.

"And this bright energy ray, do you know where it originated from?" MaRa asked.

"Not really. It was an unknown creature that attacked me," I said.

"I see, and the gigantism, do you know what caused that?" MaRa asked, continuing with the interview.

"I did that to myself. I will return to my normal size on my own. I don't need treatment for that," I explained.

"Very well, I believe I have enough information to construct a treatment regimen. If you will lie down on the biobed, I will program the fluidic repair sequence," MaRa said, heading over to a console that controlled the biobed.

I lie down on the bed that felt like warm flesh, and it reminded me I had not had sex with Erin in quite some time. Not a kiss or even a hug. There was a slight movement of the bed as the anti-gravity kicked in, causing the bed to float. The circular support rings unlocked and retreated into the ceiling as they did before.

I sank into the bed as the fluid rushed in to cover me. It seemed a little more oily this time. I was unconsciously holding my breath until I couldn't any longer. I gasped out bubbles and felt the suffocating feeling overwhelm me as I jerked and heaved before finally taking a breath of the fluid. After a minute or two, I felt more relaxed. I don't know what MaRa put into the fluid this time, but it knocked me out, and all I could think about was betrayal by my own people as I slipped from consciousness.

I awoke on the biobed, lying on my side, while MaRa patted my back as I coughed out the last of the oily fluid. It tasted somewhat like MTC coconut oil.

"How do you feel, Sam?" MaRa asked.

I reached around and touched my back, where the wound was, and felt nothing but soft skin. I looked down at my leg, and the injury was healed. The overall pain in my head was gone too.

"I feel good, thank you, MaRa," I said.

"Do you require any other service at this time?" MaRa asked.

"No, that will be all," I said, and MaRa headed over to the biobed control console.

Using the towels to dry off, I rummaged through the pockets of my clothes, locating the three vignettes and my lighter.

"Ohm, can I get a new set of clothes for my larger body. A green shirt and grey pants," I said.

The old clothes sparkled, disappeared, and a new folded set appeared next to me, on the biobed. I got dressed, put on my boots, and headed to the Xanadu cafeteria. I thought about asking Marsha for food when she asked me if I needed anything, but I was too sad to eat at that time. I didn't like the side effects of her drugs at all. The cafeteria was down the hall from the entrance door where the vignette deposits you when you arrive using that mode of travel. I ducked my head when I entered, and a few Blinn technicians sat at tables talking and eating. They gave me stunned looks, which reinforced my intention that I needed to get back to my normal size sooner than later. But for now, I just wanted something to eat.

I said to the replimat food wall, "Turkey, mashed potatoes, and gravy with stuffing. A large cranberry juice with ice."

There was a sparkle, and a plate of food along with a large glass of juice appeared in the receiving area. It looked small to me. I located a roll of silverware from the basket next to the replimat wall and stuffed it into my pocket. I picked up the plate of food, juice glass, and headed over to one of the benches running along the wall. It seemed like the best place to sit. The chairs at the tables seemed too small for me to consider. I sat the food on the table and moved it out slightly, taking a seat on the bench running along the length of the wall. There was salt and pepper on the table, so I added pepper to my mashed potatoes and dug in. The food was really good, and I finished off my plate a little too quickly. I thought about getting some more, but I knew I was going to be running, so I skipped seconds and headed out of the cafeteria while dropping my plate and glass in the recycle bin.

I walked down the hallway toward the vignette arrival area and took the door on the right, leading outside. This porch is where Erin and I sat on the stairs the first time we were here. I could see the stables off in the distance, and I wanted to use a horse, but I couldn't bring myself to burden a beast with my oversized frame. Instead, I pulled the vignettes out of my pocket, located the Lighthouse of Flynn vignette, and focused on it until it came to life. A few moments later, I stood on the hill looking at the lighthouse, which was a short distance away.

CHAPTER 50

A Horse Of Course

⌒◦⌒

I took in the fresh sea air and basked in the glory of being near Splendor again. It was early afternoon, and the day was bright and sunny, with puffy clouds hanging low in the sky. I headed off in the opposite direction, compared to the last time I was here with Erin. Starting off with a brisk jog, I located the path leading away from the lighthouse. This path eventually took me to a narrow road where I turned left, leaving Splendor behind me. It was harder to shift echo while you were close to Splendor because there were not that many echoes to choose from. Numerically speaking, Splendor is the equivalent of zero, while chaos could be thought of as infinity. While close to zero, small numbers generally produce similar results. The ease of echo manipulation increases as your distance from Splendor increases, somewhat like a logarithmic scale. I was in no real hurry, so I took my time and enjoyed the run. I was never really into running that much and only did it when it was necessary, which was often when running away from something or someone. I think drumming has actually done me some good as far as running was concerned. I did not feel as fatigued as I usually did. My large size may have contributed to my performance as well.

I started testing my ability to alter the reality around me by adding a curve to the road or a rock outcropping just over the next hill. After about thirty minutes, I finally felt like I put enough distance between myself and Splendor to start picking and choosing elements in the scenescape I traveled through. I started using the *Motif* to reduce my size, slowly at first, then finally shifting down to a normal height. I cheated a little bit at the end and kept some of the upper body strength and leg muscle. After that, there was only one intention in mind, to find a horse.

I chose the simplest way, which was considerably gruesome. As I jogged over the next hill, I descended upon a scene of disaster. A horse was in distress, still attached to an overturned cart that spilled its contents along the roadway. Off in a field, to the side of the road, lay a dead body with a bloody stain on its chest. I approached the horse slowly, saying, "Whoa, whoa," while using the *Motif* to calm it down. It was a mare with a shiny pure black coat.

I spoke softly to the horse, touching her side, as I explained to her that she was mine now and we would be leaving the life of cart pulling behind. Inside the back of the cart, I found a saddle and some saddlebags. Inside the saddlebag, there was a waterskin, some apples, carrots, and a small bag of oats. After placing the saddle on the ground next to the horse, I fetched the saddle cloth from the back of the wagon.

"Ohm, can you replicate a combat dagger?" I asked.

There was a sparkle on the ground, and a combat dagger appeared, like the one I replicated before stepping through the painting. I strapped it to my leg, pulled it out of the sheath, and sliced up a couple of apples, removing the core. I fed some to the horse, eating a couple of slices myself, and said, "I think I'll call you Belle."

She whinnied in reply, and I proceeded to place the saddle cloth over her back and the saddle with the bags. With her all saddled up, I removed the tack binding her to the cart and walked her way from the gruesome scene, leading her back to the road. Climbing up on Belle, I put my feet into the stirrups, gathering up the reigns, and gently prodded her, cueing her with my knees to move forward.

It wasn't long until we trotted down the road. Where I was heading was not that far in echo terms. I just needed to shift things around until it all fell into place. I cued Belle to move a little faster and started shifting the world around me to lead into a more magical realm. Belle sensed this change and whinnied a sound of protest whenever I would switch something too drastically. Riding a horse through echo was not the same as driving a vehicle. There was a give and take that occurs. It's not just with horses either. Most mounts, even magical ones, will sometimes rebel against leaving the echo they were born into. It often comes down to the temperament of the beast. Belle seemed to have a decent attitude toward the echo shifts I made.

We made good progress. After riding for more than an hour, I came upon a small stream. I slowed Belle down and dismounted as she headed over to take a drink. Even though there was a water skin in the saddlebag, I asked Ohm for a water bottle, which I knew was clean, and took a drink and a piss, just like Belle.

After she drank, I led her across the stream into a grassy field where she wandered and nibbled at the various field offerings. I kept an eye on the surroundings enjoying this slower-paced lifestyle. After about twenty minutes, I approached Belle, remounted her, and drew the reigns up to continue our journey. She seemed refreshed and was eager to explore these rolling hills without a road. Eventually, a larger forest grew up around us as I pushed slowly into echo. The day darkened, and a bright moon rose in the sky as I shifted us more quickly through echo. Around us, I could feel the presence of eyes. I felt the eyes of animals, the eyes of birds, the eyes of creatures of all kinds. We passed through a shallow bog where the sounds of insects chirped all around, silencing themselves as we passed, with the sound resuming as we left the area. Several colors of glowing insects floated in the air and off into the distant deep woods, which seemed to go on forever on all sides.

We rode for several hours, and the Sun rose as we descended into a wide ravine. The tall trees all around us cast enough shadow that the ground was barren of most underbrush, and only small ferns grew here as ground cover. Once we reached the center of this depression, the sound of many galloping feet surrounded us. A small gathering of magnificent creatures quickly descended upon us. They were part horse and part man, centaurs, easily standing sixteen to twenty hands in height. Sporting Amish style beards with bags slung over their shoulders, they lowered large spears while encircling Belle and me as we came to a halt.

One spoke in a deep guttural tongue, using the language of centaurs, which I was able to understand because of my echo abilities saying, "You have trespassed on lands claimed by the Tallisee. There is but one penalty for such action, death."

"Ohm, target the centaurs, except the speaker, and put them to sleep," I said.

The leader lifted his spear, adjusting it in his massive hand, trying to find the best balance before throwing it. His companions started collapsing around him, and he hesitated, looking over at them as he watched them fall.

I spoke in his tongue, "They are not dead, merely sleeping, but they could be dead if I had chosen. I am a Lord of Splendor, and I request permission to pass through your lands."

He considered the situation, lowered the spear, kneeling and touching the neck of one of his sleeping comrades to verify that they were indeed still alive.

As he did this, I continued, "I recognize these are your lands and that a toll may be required for passage through them. What can I offer you to allow such passage?"

He rose to his feet, looking down upon me, and said, "The Tallisee need nothing from the lands of men. We do not value objects as you do."

"Some values all creatures hold. You value your rank, loyalty, and companionship. You hold a spear as men do. I can give you a better spear with a stronger tip and a shaft that is straighter and lighter. You will be able to throw farther and hit your target with greater accuracy," I replied.

"I see no spears. The word of man is known for lies. If I let you pass, you will only brag amongst your fellow men that you tricked the Tallisee with words," the centaur criticized.

"Ohm, scan the centaur's spear and produce twenty copies of a superior spear. Make the shaft out of a lightweight composite material and the tip out of cold carbon steel," I said.

"What spells do you speak?" the centaur countered as he cantered in place.

The ground sparkled, and a collection of twenty spears appeared. The shafts looked like black oxide aluminum, coated with nylon and the overall design conveyed a tech look that was unusual and somehow fierce at the same time. The shafts were ribbed at certain points along the length for a better grip, and the blunt end was notched so it could be thrown from some oversized bow or launching mechanism.

"I am not a man. I am a Lord of Splendor, and I would never spread lies about the Tallisee. I give you my word that passage through your lands will remain between us. I give you my toll as proof that my word has meaning," I said.

The centaur looked at me with his large yellow eyes and knelt to pick up one of the spears. I could tell by the look on his face that he was surprised at the lighter weight of the spear. He stood the new spear up, side by side, to compare it to the one he held. The length was an exact match as well as the thickness of the shaft.

"They are stronger, lighter, and less likely to break when they hit their target. The tip is easily sharpened," I said, trying to seal the deal on this passage through his lands.

He glanced at his sleeping comrades, and I said, "They will awake within the hour whether you accept my toll or not."

In a single swift motion, he cocked back his arm and threw the new spear at a nearby tree. There was a thunk and a muted tone as the aluminum shaft vibrated after coming to a halt, sinking deep inside the center of the trunk. He trotted over and tried pulling the spear out, eventually dropping his original spear and tugging with both hands until the new spear finally released its hold on the tree.

He returned to me and inspected the spear. It seemed no worse for the wear. He extended his arm to me, and I shook his massive hand, in a long arm handshake, similar to the style of the Ralla as he said, "Wake them now, and I will accept your toll for passage."

"Very well, but if you betray me, the penalty is death," I said quite seriously.

"Ohm, wake the sleeping centaurs," I said while gathering up my reigns.

The sleeping centaurs awoke and slowly returned to their feet. They seemed a little groggy as they rose, taking in the scene. Several of them noticed the stock of spears on the ground.

The lead centaur spoke loudly, saying, "This one may pass," then added, "this time."

I took my win and walked Belle to the outer ring of the centaurs that parted and let me by. I immediately cued Belle to a gallop, and we sped through this magical forest as the Sun rose higher to a bright morning. I shifted echo one last time to make this forest, the Somber Woods, outside of Enki's Dale. I emerged from the edge of this forest and could see the Baker's house, in the distance, perched upon the steep cliffside rising from the wide-open grassland between Enki's Dale and the Somber Woods. I galloped toward the town where I knew I could gain access to the road leading to houses where my friends lived.

I located the path leading up to the village of Enki's Dale. The villagers were out and about, tending to their daily chores. Several of them greeted me with friendly waves and hellos. The village was quite small and quaint, with the center of the town built around the well. Cobblestone was laid around the well and worked its way outward, defining the few streets that were there. I took one of the streets out of town, and it eventually turned into a dirt road with a few grooves dug into it by cart traffic. I passed the small cliff, where Candy's house sat upon, and continued a little farther down the road until I came to the Baker's Tudor style home. I dismounted Belle and patted her.

Stepping back from the horse, I said, "Ohm, transport Belle to the stables at Xanadu. Inform the groom of her name."

There was a large sparkle, and Belle disappeared.

CHAPTER 51

The Guest House

I approached the front door of the house and wondered if my height matched my original size? The door knocker seemed slightly lower than the last time I visited, but I didn't sweat it too much. I figured I was measuring in a little under two meters, which was fine by me. I was about ready to knock on the dark green door when I heard voices around back. Taking the stone path along the side of the house, I announced myself at the white picket gate separating the front yard from the back yard.

"Hello," I said, waving to Madison, who sat at one of the tables on the patio I repaired. She waved for me to come into the yard, and I opened the gate and closed it, making sure it latched in place before approaching the patio.

Nick rounded the corner of the house and said, "Sam, whoa, have you been working out?"

"A little bit, you know, to get better at drumming," I replied as I shook his hand.

Nick shook his head with an all right type of expression and said, "Come on back, we're just puttering around the yard."

"Well, Nick is puttering. I am just lounging," Madison said. "Please, have a seat."

I took a seat on the patio that offered a pleasant view looking over the flat grassland I recently rode Belle across.

"We do appreciate the repair you have done on this patio. I wasn't feeling safe out here before, let alone having Nick's niece or nephew over," Madison said. "But now it's really nice the way you have fixed it up."

"I'm glad you're getting some use out of it. This seating does offer a nice view," I noted.

"So, what brings you around to our neck of the woods?" Nick asked.

"Oh, you know, I am seeking some advice about magic and thought of you two," I said.

"What kind of advice?" Madison asked.

"Did you guys happen to meet or talk to the Mist Door people when you were at my balcony party?" I asked.

"I did. That tough guy, what was his name? Melon or something," Nick said.

"Malik," I corrected him.

"Yeah, Malik. He was some serious wicked dude, but still full of respect. Kind of awesome, though," Nick said.

"I talked with David and Robin. They were both very nice," Madison said.

"Well, the other night, I received an alert they were in trouble. They live in another probability, you know. They travel between worlds fighting an evil enemy known as the Gorgon. It seems one of them got the upper hand and captured the entire team," I said.

"Oh, no, how dreadful," Madison replied.

"I went to their aid and managed to free them, but right as we made our escape, the evil Gorgon who orchestrated the entire affair attacked me with his mind control device," I said.

"No way," Nick gasped as his jaw hung open for a moment.

"Go on," Madison said.

"It hurt a lot. I would describe it as a ray of light that causes extreme headaches. It shot forth from his hand, using some device known in that probability. In a last-ditch effort, I pulled out my wand and shouted a spell I never heard or practiced before. It just came to my mind in that desperate moment. The result was that snake-like cables lept from the end of my wand, wrapped around the ghoulish creature, compressed him into vacuity, finally digging into the ground, leaving nothing behind. I knew in an instant that it was an evil spell," I confessed.

"Oh, my," Madison said. "What was the spell?"

"*Tantalis*," I said, which caused both Madison and Nick to look at each other. Presumably, they knew about that spell and were frightened at the mere mention of it.

"The spell that Hector the Horrible used to slay Lorenzo the Brave. The one from the fairy tale?" Nick asked.

"He probably doesn't know about that fairy tale Nick," Madison said, "'Grimley's Grimoire of Fantastic Tales of the Bold and Pitiful' tells us there was an evil magician who slew an honorable knight using a spell called *Tantalis*. In the story, they are deep in the woods where the vines surrounded Lorenzo, crushing him to death before retreating into the earth."

"How could I know a spell that I have never heard of?" I asked.

"It's called sympathetic magic, and it is probably related to your other ability to travel through probability," Madison stated.

"It felt wrong. The moment I uttered the word, I felt remorse about casting it. I don't want to become an evil magician. That's why I came here today. Is there any way to avoid the path of evil once you have cast an evil spell?" I asked.

"Sam, you're not evil," Nick remarked.

"I agree with Nick. You're not evil, but it is written that evil tends to bend toward evil, and good tends to bend toward good. That is why the deplorable banes must be avoided. Once you start to use them, you start to bend toward evil," Madison stated.

I finished her sentence by saying, "and if you bend too far, you pass the point of no return."

"Precisely," Madison said.

"Is there a way to bend back toward good?" I asked.

"Many ways. There are several fables in that same grimoire that are tales of redemption and salvation. You mustn't cast it again, however. Once it becomes familiar, or you fall back upon it, the journey back to good becomes that much more difficult," Madison said.

"Besides, you have already done good," Nick chimed in. "That night when the dark magicians came to attack our village, you helped save us and the town's people."

"Nick's right. I think you have a bit of a surplus at this time to allow a single transgression. Whatever happened to those magicians?" Madison asked.

"Wow, now that you mention it, I completely forgot about them. I placed them in suspended animation, in a holding facility on an asteroid in space."

"Wicked," Nick said with a smile.

"I don't know what to do with them, do you?" I asked.

"You could submit them to the magician prison for processing," Madison suggested.

"Is that really an effective system for reform?" I asked, thinking about the time, from the first loop, when I was placed in the magician prison by the Magnus Overseer for forging false gold coins. It was detainment, and I fell through the cracks serving more time than my sentence length. In the end, I was forced to bust out, and I freed a lot of evil magicians in the process.

"Why can't you just leave them there?" Nick asked.

"What, leave them in suspended animation until they die? How is that any different than killing them now with a weapon or a spell?" I asked.

"I guess I see your point," Nick conceded.

"It's a tricky situation. I agree, Sam," Madison said.

"I do have a planet, in another probability, where I have been placing other detainees. I am worried that a magician could *Exspiravit*, through probability, to return here and seek revenge on you or the townspeople?" I asked.

"Hmm, that is something no magician has tried to do, as far as I know. I don't know of any tale or story where such a thing has happened," Madison said thoughtfully.

"She's right. You can't *Exspiravit*, through time either," Nick added.

"Well, maybe that is an option for those evil sods. I do worry about throwing so many evil terrible people in one place, though," I said.

"Is it a terrible place?" Nick asked.

"No, I sought it out as a paradise world. It's beautiful. I have named it 'Eden,'" I replied.

"A beautiful planet full of terrible people, how ironic," Madison mused.

"Thank you both for talking with me. I feel a lot better than I did a couple of days ago," I said to them both.

"I always enjoy talking with you, Sam. You seem to encounter fascinating dilemmas. Glad we could help," Madison said.

"What were you puttering around with?" I asked Nick.

"Oh, that. I tried to put together a tool shed out back," he answered.

"Do you want some help?" I asked.

Nick beamed and said, "Sure, it's over here."

We got up from the table and headed over from the side of the house to the back yard. There was already an extension of the stone patio here, and I noticed Nick's pathetic attempt at trying to build some type of shed. He was basically at the start of the project, having cut a few boards on a couple of saw horses. There was a bag of nails and what looked like a page ripped out of a magazine with plans on how to do it yourself.

Nick sensed my immediate evaluation of his progress and said, "I'm just getting started."

"What do you say to thinking a little bit bigger?" I asked.

"How much bigger?" Nick asked in return.

"I have a virtual environment designer where we can layout the proposed plan, and a replication system will do all the hard work and construct it for us," I said.

He shrugged his shoulders and said, "I'm willing if it makes it easier."

"Ohm, bring up a display with the environment designer synchronized to this location," I said.

"You're talking to your spaceship, right, not me?" Nick asked.

"Yep," I said, and a floating orange sphere appeared before us.

"Nice, what is that?" Nick asked.

"It's a virtual interface to your back yard," I said as I reached into the display, twisting it around and locating the unroll icon.

The sphere unrolled to a flat plane about the size of a large screen TV.

"Madison, come over here and take a look at this," Nick called to her.

"Ohm, prepare a couple of options for a small guest house, with two bedrooms, a downstairs living room, a full balcony, and an attached garage. Reference the current Baker's house and match the proposed options to the Tudor style," I said.

Madison walked over and said, "What have you there?"

"This is a new invention I came up with. I call it the environment designer. It scans the current location and allows you to layout a virtual plan for new construction once the plan is approved. It's nice for projects like this," I answered.

"It looks highly technical, Sam," Madison replied.

I moved the rectangular display so we were between the house and the empty space that eventually led to the drop-off into the grasslands below. I grabbed some of the options blinking along the side of the display and dropped them into place. The display acted a lot like a window so Nick and Madison could see what the new construction looked like before it was built.

"You mean to tell me that this device will construct buildings in our back yard?" Madison asked.

"Yes, if you want them. This current design shows a small guest house with an attached garage. You could use that for tool storage instead of building a shed," I suggested.

"I like it," Nick said while shaking his head yes.

I located some of the yard options and dropped in a stone walkway leading from the main house up to the proposed new construction. I placed flower beds on either side.

"That is unbelievable, Sam," Madison said.

"As unbelievable as magic is to space-faring tech species," I replied.

I drew a selection around the current guest house, moving it off to a section of the screen intended for saving layouts. I dropped in one of the other options, and this one provided two floors.

"What do you think?" I asked.

"Blimey, that looks bigger than our main house," Nick replied.

"I think Nick is right. The first design seems more appropriate for a guest house," Madison observed.

I removed the larger option and dragged the saved layout back into position as I moved the display to a new place in the back yard, saying, "I can put the house where ever you like."

I stepped away from the display and said, "Just think of it as a real picture frame and move it around until you find the location you like the best," I said.

Nick and Madison walked around the back yard, dragging the environment designer display with them. They took their time and finally settled upon a location. I walked over and agreed that it was a better spot than I originally picked out. Their choice was off to the left, at an angle, and back a little more than my direct alignment with the main house.

"Is there any way we can have the garage on the other side?" Madison asked.

"Certainly," I replied, and I reached into the display to shake the garage loose from the right side of the guest house and dragged it across the display, letting it snap into position on the left side of the house.

"That makes more sense," I said. "It places your tools closer to the garden."

"That is so cool," Nick said as he watched me perform the virtual adjustment.

"Okay, so now what?" Madison asked.

"If you're happy with this design, I can set the replication in motion, and it will be built in a few minutes," I said.

"A few minutes?" Nick expressed in disbelief.

"What do you think, Nick? Are you happy with this layout? Do you want to give it a try?" Madison asked her husband.

"Sure, love, it looks way better than that toolshed I tried to build. Let's do it," Nick exclaimed.

"Ohm, take the current design and replicate it in place," I said.

The construction phase was like a fireworks display in the daytime, only without any loud booming sounds. Sparkles appeared all over the target area, laying the foundation, and the supporting framing for the house transplaced into position. It took about eighteen minutes before the sparkles finally calmed down, leaving a new guest house with an attached garage and a path leading to the main house. I dismissed the environment designer display, and we headed down the stone walkway to enter the new home.

"Whoa, this is nice," Nick said, walking around the place.

Madison walked in and spun around in the main entrance room, taking it all in, and said, "This is more than nice, Sam. This place is overboard wonderful."

She gave me a quick hug, looked up, and said, "Thank you."

"You're welcome, both of you. It means a lot to have you as friends. I know I don't stop by enough, and when I do, it's usually with a problem. This house is my way of saying thank you for putting up with me," I said.

"Check this out Madison. There's a balcony off the bedroom," Nick called from the back room.

We all walked around and took the tour. It was furnished with furniture, plumbing, appliances, and electric lights. There were one and a half bathrooms, with the half bath located in the downstairs recreation room that was essentially a finished basement. The attached garage was large enough for two cars, but it offered a basic woodworkers bench with a table saw and a drill press along one wall. On the way out of the door, I located the keys. There were two sets. Handing one set to each of them, I said, "It's all yours. If you decide you want to change something or don't like the furniture just let me know. We can revise it as easily as we built it."

I took a short walk into the garden, and they followed. Turning around to look at the new addition, I said, "It seems okay. My initial impression is that it matches the original house."

"It does look nice," Madison said. "The colors are matched."

"I'm glad you stopped by today, Sam. It saved me the trouble of fussing with that shed," Nick added.

"I'm going to head out, back to San Francisco. Enjoy the new place, and I hope to see you soon," I said as they walked back to their guest house and went inside.

"Ohm, transport me to my apartment in San Francisco," I said, and the bright afternoon sun shot in from the sides, placing me in the holding cell of darkness.

CHAPTER 52

While it was just before noon in the probability I left, it was evening here when I materialized in the apartment. There was no one around, so I headed into the bedroom only to find it empty. I removed my clothes, which I knew smelled like a horse, removing the vignettes and lighter before recycling the garments. The showerhead confirmed I was indeed a little taller. I needed to stoop down to wash my hair. After shaving and brushing my teeth, I returned to the bedroom, where I requested new clothes and got dressed. Denim jeans for my pants and a black shirt. I placed vignettes in their special pocket and the lighter in my pants pocket.

"Ohm, are Alex and Lucas home?" I asked.

"Alex and Lucas are in their San Francisco apartment, down the hall," Ohm replied.

"Are they in intimate contact?" I asked, prying a little.

"No, they are not," Ohm replied.

"Great, can you locate a historical vehicle called the Kursaki Ronin 650? It was a motorcycle," I asked.

"I have located the design specifications for the vehicle," Ohm replied.

"Let's go ahead and replicate a black Ronin 650. Place it on the first floor of this building near the ramp of the loading dock. It requires gasoline for fuel, so give it a full tank and replicate an extra five gallons in a closed container that you can place beside the vehicle. Add a motorcycle helmet to the request, sized for Alex's head. Place the keys in my hand," I said while opening my right hand to receive them.

There was a small sparkle, and a set of motorcycle keys appeared in my hand. I placed them in my other pants pocket.

"Ohm, can you replicate another invisihud style ring in a box?" I asked.

Another sparkle occurred, and a small black box appeared on the bed. I picked it up, straightened out my wet hair, and headed down the hall to knock on their door. It took a moment for someone to come to the door, and it was Lucas.

"Sam," Lucas said, pausing in shock while he took in my new appearance, "come in, come in."

"Thanks," I said and walked in behind him.

"Alex, Sam is here," Lucas called out as we headed into the living area and took a seat on the sofa.

Their apartment was very similar to mine, with a living area, a kitchen, two bedrooms, and a deep balcony.

Alex hid her shock at my new size a little better than Lucas, saying, "You look good. Tough but good. How are you feeling?"

"A lot better. I know I didn't get the size quite right, but it will have to do, for now," I said.

"Lucas, I don't want you to take this the wrong way, but I have a ring for your woman," I said.

"Oh really?" Lucas said.

I handed the black box to Alex, and she was all aglow with a smile, accepting it and opening it up.

"I have not figured out how to reactivate our broken invisihuds yet, so I made a less intrusive version of the interface in the form of a self-adjusting ring. It provides a verbal interface to *Tiger Mountain*, but there is not a hud. You can ask for an auragraphic display, but it's less covert than the invisihud," I explained.

I pulled my ring off and placed it on the coffee table as the cloak disengaged, revealing the ring. I picked it back up and put it on my finger, and we all watched it fade from view.

"That is pretty cool, Sam," Lucas said.

Alex tried hers on and said, "Ohm, are you there?"

"Yes, I am, Alex. It is good to hear your voice again," Ohm replied to her.

"Just trying out this new ring dealio. Catch ya later," she said to the room.

I reached into my pocket and pulled out the keys to the Ronin 650, and said, "I'm very sorry for snapping at you back at Mist Door Operations. I guess I never really understood how you felt about your condition until I was in it. I'm still in it, but I'm getting used to being a freak. Anyway, I hope you accept this gift of a Kurasaki Ronin 650 for my apology," I said, dropping the keys into her hand.

The biggest smile came across her face as she tilted her head a little, asking, "How did you know?"

"I know it sounds far-fetched, but do you remember the day we all met in that bar?" I asked.

"Yeah, Smash," Lucas said.

"I sat in the next booth over from you two, and I heard Alex complaining to you about the cops smashing out the headlight of her Ronin 650 and then citing her for it. She said it was the closest representation of her soul that a physical object could take. That was the line that made me eavesdrop further, where I overheard your allergic condition," I said.

"That's remarkable you remember that," Lucas said.

"I think it's pretty cool. Where is it?" Alex asked.

"I replicated it on the first floor of this building, near the ramp by the loading dock," I replied.

"I'm going for a ride, honey," Alex said, walking over to Lucas and kissing him, "and I accept your apology, Sam."

After Alex left the room, Lucas said, "I'd like to apologize too, Sam. When Candy and I saw what was going down, we didn't know what to do. I froze up. I couldn't think of a single thing to replicate and send through the painting to help you out. I felt like I let you both down."

"Don't sweat it. We all got lucky that night. I'm just glad that no one died," I said seriously.

"Me too," Lucas said.

"I was in the same boat as you before you guys appeared on the catwalk. I was racking my brain thinking I have all this technology, but I couldn't come up with anything that would fit through the painting to help out," I expounded.

"That's how I felt. I could think of some things, but fitting them through the painting was the challenge, and when it's just going down, there is no time to figure any of that out," Lucas agreed.

"What does Erin think about all of this?" Lucas asked. "You haven't seen her yet, have you?"

"I don't know what's going on with Erin and me anymore. She seems to have lost interest in our relationship and didn't come home one night," I confessed.

"Uh oh, that is never a good sign," Lucas said.

"I know, but in the first time loop, we experienced some problems. I just hope things can get back on track. I felt like I just spent the last several months trying to achieve a goal, and when I finally accomplish part of it, she slips through my fingers. How do you and Alex do it? You always look so happy?" I asked.

"Well, it's nice of you to say so, but it is not that easy. Knowing Alex is very hard because of her physical makeup because she is a freak. We keep at it though, and try to respect each other's space," Lucas offered.

"I guess that is good advice. I'm not giving up. I just wish it were better," I said.

"I can relate to that," Lucas said.

"I think I am going to head back home and try to get some sleep. I'm feeling a little jet-lagged after traveling through a couple of different echoes. I'll talk to you later," I said.

"All right. Get some sleep, and we'll talk soon," Lucas said.

I let myself out and headed down the hall to my apartment.

CHAPTER 53

The Threesome

I opened the door to the apartment and walked in. Erin turned, looked at me with concern, and asked, "What happened to you?"

"Oh, it's a long story," I said, closing the door and walking over to her.

That's when I noticed Jorrie in the living room with her.

Jorrie was not in a Starnet uniform. She wore a combination of yellow contrasting with her light skin and dark hair. The last time I saw her, she was in uniform aboard the *Contender*, covered in soot and cuts. This time she was a radiant beauty, similar to when she attended my party.

"You're taller now," Jorrie said.

"I need a hug," I said while looking at Erin.

She opened her arms, and we embraced. I had to bend over a little to get the full effect of holding her. We parted, and I said while looking at Jorrie, "From both of you."

She glanced over at Erin first then walked over to where I entered the room. I stepped up to meet her, and we put our arms around each other. Her hair smelled wonderful, and I held on far too long. She didn't let go, though, and as we started to part, I looked into her eyes and kissed her soft lips. It felt a little weird kissing Jorrie in front of Erin, but I didn't care. I put my hands on either side of her head, and we kissed again, this time with more passion as she pressed into me, her hands moving along my shoulders, finally sliding down my arms as she stepped away, taking a breath.

"I need one of those too," Erin pouted.

We embraced again, but this time I picked Erin up. She wrapped her legs around me as I held her in place, feeling her waist. She looked down on me with a devilish grin and went in for a slow hot kiss like Jorrie gave me. This first kiss turned into another and another as she pressed into the arousal Jorrie encouraged with her embrace. We parted as I let go, dropping to the floor.

"Woo, thank you, both," I said, "I really needed that."

"I want to hear the story. Why your form has changed?" Erin asked.

"I'm curious too," Jorrie said.

"Okay, I'll explain what happened, but first, I think I'll join you in a drink,"

I said, heading over to the bar to locate a wine glass.

Jorrie took a seat on the sofa, but Erin followed me over to the bar and said, "It was Jorrie that I was with. I got to know her, Sam."

"Oh, all right, good to know," I said still feeling a bit awkward around her.

We returned to the sofa, and I sat down next to Jorrie with Erin on my other side. Erin poured me a half glass of red wine before she said, "I want to make a toast. To getting to know one another."

Jorrie and I repeated it, and we all took a sip. It was quite tasty, and I picked up the bottle to read the label, saying, "Ah, a blend of reds, this is nice."

"I don't even know what day it is here, but it happened just after the last time you came home, Erin. I went to bed earlier than you. I was awoken in the night by Ohm, an alarm sounded. Ohm lost contact with the entire Guardian team from Mist Door Operations. After checking the last log entry, it revealed Robin, tied up, and the team being dragged into some massive energy conductor. The machine disabled their invisihuds which is what triggered the alarm."

Jorrie interrupted, asking, "What are invisihuds, again?"

"Those are the internal implants that each Guardian has, which allows them to communicate with Ohm," I said.

"And Ohm is the computer that processes the requests," she said, answering her own question.

"Yes. I only had one way to reach them, and that was the painting on the catwalk. I used the vignette to head there immediately," I said, noticing Jorrie probably wanted to ask more about the painting and the catwalk but did not want to keep stopping the story.

"I replicated a gun, a knife, and a medkit. I was ready to step through the painting when Alex, Lucas, and Candy showed up. They wanted to help. I expected my invisihud would probably deactivate once I stepped through the painting, so I knew I could not defend Lucas and Candy if they came along. Alex is a trained soldier, and she insisted upon joining me, so we passed through the painting together," I said, pausing to take another drink of wine.

"Alex didn't tell me about being a soldier," Jorrie said.

"It was a trap, and our tech was disabled. We were immediately attacked, and I fled into the open while Alex, being much smarter, remained near the captives, still trying to free them. The machine was a mix of high and low tech. There was energy flowing through a massive stone works, all powered by the Mist Door device that the MD-Alpha team uses to travel across the galaxy. The machine design was an oval shape, spread out across the field. There were enemy soldiers along the border, all targeting my position," I said.

"That sounds faened," Erin said, concerned.

"Tell me about it. I managed to dodge a few of the shots. They used Ralla wrist weapons to attack my position. I hid amidst the rubble, but they were closing in on me. I panicked, realizing that using the *Motif* was the only way out. Calling out to the cosmic cable, I made myself grow larger, and I charged their line, knocking them down with my massive size. At my largest size, I was probably ten to twelve meters tall. With my mind still connected to the *Motif*, I used it to destabilize the ground, and it rippled as I stomped. I took a few hits from their energy weapons. Being a much larger target now, the wounds were smaller than if I were hit at my normal size. The ground ripple knocked the stones conveying the energy out of alignment, causing the entire system to overload and explode. It was total chaos with debris flying everywhere," I said.

"Is this growing ability part of your species?" Jorrie asked.

"Growing and shrinking are the last remnants of our demonic chaotic heritage. Our lineage goes back to my great, great grandfather, who came from the Vectorless Vale. The beings of the Vectorless Vale can freely change their shape, but because Splendorites rarely practice that, the shape change ability has faded with each new generation," I said.

"Go on," Jorrie said.

"With the machine destroyed and the Ralla ranks shattered, they fled in all directions. I picked up David and Malik and headed over to the undamaged Mist Door to see if we could travel back to their world. In my large form, my strides carried me to the Mist Door ahead of the others. As I waited for Jim, Robin, and Alex to catch up, I paced back and forth, using the *Motif* to reduce my size. Before I could return to my final size a suspicious figure, with no face, lept out and attacked me. It was a hovering faceless being that shot a ray of light at me, causing me to fall unconscious. Before I passed out, I managed to cast one magic spell from my wand. A series of tentacles lept out, wrapped around the creature, and crushed it to death."

"Oh my gods," Erin said.

"The tentacles dragged any evidence the figure ever existed, into the ground, as they burrowed out of sight," I said, pausing to finish off my glass of wine.

"You cast magic spells too?" Jorrie asked.

"I awoke inside the hospital of Mist Door Operations. Their intentions were good, but their methods are still crude, compared to Starnet medicine. I was wounded, drugged, and in an oversized body that was at least three meters tall. My appendages hung over the sides of the bed frame," I said.

"I don't know what to think," Erin said as she sipped her wine.

"David and Malik survived, so we didn't lose anyone that night. David told me the figure attacking me was the ancient god Akan. That is, historically speaking, but in actuality, it was a Gorgon," I said.

Erin and Jorrie both asked at the same time, "What's a Gorgon?"

I thought about saying, "jinx," but then I had had to explain it to them. Instead, I said, "A Gorgon is a starfish based parasitic organism that invades host bodies and takes control of them, overriding the host consciousness."

"Then they are like the Limax," Jorrie said.

"They are the truest form of evil that I have ever encountered. Living for hundreds and hundreds of years, they have adapted their physiology to accommodate a unique technology that only works for them. The Gorgon genetically mutated their slave scpecies to become incubators for their young, which they often eat so they can remain in power and not be challenged by their offspring. They control vast areas of space through slavery and oppression. The Ralla are the incubator species that the Gorgon created."

"You mean, Malik is one of them?" Erin asked.

"You killed a god?" Jorrie asked.

"They are only considered gods because they call themselves that. In reality, they have no principal order or morals at all. When they encounter a lower species, they dominate it and enslave them to extract the resources from their planet. If they detect a species rising in technology, they will often attack and destroy their world. This destruction ensures they remain the dominant species," I said, leaning back into the sofa.

"I want to know more about the Gorgon," Jorrie said. "Not now, but the Zoologist inside me is quite curious."

"I walked through echo to reduce my size back to normal, but I did not get it quite right. I'm sorry if I appear too freakish to you both," I lamented.

"I don't think you look too freakish," Jorrie said. "You're just taller and a bit more muscular."

"Yeah, I'm sorry, it was just a shock to me at first. I think you look great," Erin said, pausing before asking, "is everything, you know, bigger?"

"I guess you'll have to tell me," I said, looking at Erin, then at Jorrie, who pursed her lips.

"Erin and I have been seeing each other, Sam. We have been getting to know one another better," Jorrie said.

"Well, I'm glad it's you rather than some other guy," I replied.

"I wanted to tell you, but you got so serious with me, and I felt cramped and a little trapped. When I started talking with Jorrie, we both discovered we liked each other," Erin said, pausing. "I still like you, Sam. I love you, and I'm not sure how to work this out, having two lovers."

"I'm drawn to you, Sam. Something about those wide shoulders and green eyes goes right to my heart. I knew it that day when I saw you sitting with Brent in Lepton's," Jorrie said.

"I don't know how all this works either, but I am willing to give it a try," I said to both of them before turning to Erin. "If I'm trapping you just let me know. It feels so good to be in love with you that I might have drunk too deeply from your heart. I'm sorry."

"Now you have two wells to drink from," Erin said slyly as she kissed me, placing her hand on my lap.

Jorrie started moving her hand over my chest, and once Erin moved back from kissing me, Jorrie came closer and kissed me instead. I guess it was on.

The cruel content editor came in and removed the explicitly detailed sex scene between the characters, leaving a single line, reading, "Things got hot."

I turned my head to kiss Erin, then turned my head and kissed Jorrie, finally saying, "I hope this doesn't ruin the mood, but I love you both."

"I love you too," Erin said, kissing me again.

"With a fuck like that, I am starting to lean toward love as well, Sam," Jorrie said as she idly moved her hands across my chest.

We lay there a while, and I guess I drifted off to sleep.

CHAPTER 54

No Means No

I left the bedroom and called out to see if anyone else was home. It looked like I was alone this morning. I went ahead and jumped into the shower and washed off, brushed my teeth, and got dressed for the day. Heading out to the kitchen, I made a half pot of coffee and ate a bagel with cream cheese, sliced cucumber, and smoked turkey for my breakfast.

While waiting for the coffee to brew, I asked, "Ohm, where is Jorrie?"

"Jorrie is at one of the command stations aboard *Oasis Seven*," Ohm replied.

"And where is Erin?" I asked.

"Erin is in one of the administrative buildings on the campus of Starnet," Ohm stated.

"Ohm, can you replicate a small projection tablet, the size of a vignette. Transfer the invisihud features to it, please," I said.

A sparkle appeared and disappeared, leaving a small rectangular object behind. The surface was shiny, much like glass on one side, while the other side looked like brushed metal. It was about the size of an old school smartphone and was dubbed a "shingle" by the Blinn development team. I activated the projection feature producing an auragraphic display I could interact with. I was interested in my financial holdings within this echo.

My portfolio was fairly diverse, with holdings on several planets in production, replication, mining, and real estate. I checked the deployment of my cloaked scanners and confirmed they, indeed, reached Bragoria. That was my next goal.

Using the shingle, I connected to the cloaked scanner on Bragoria and scanned the capital city, looking for a piece of real estate I might be able to purchase. After locating a large section of abandoned factories and slums on the outskirts of one of the more populated neighborhoods, I decided to focus on that area.

"Ohm, can you transport me to the location on Bragoria I selected on the shingle?" I asked, discontinuing the display and tucking the shingle into one of my shirt pockets.

The room collapsed inward as I braced for another round in the dark space.

I hoped to at least talk to one of the women I made love to last night, but I guess they had their jobs and or other tasks that needed to get done. I knew there was more to relationships than just having sex, but last night was incredible. I thought about what gesture I needed to make next. Each woman required a different one, and I drew a blank. It needed to be thoughtful enough to show that I cared but was not too extravagant or demanding, indicating I wanted to control them or the relationship. Before I could consider any options, bright lights streamed in from the sides, materializing me on Bragoria.

The gravity was stronger here, and I felt a bit heavier. That makes sense why the Bragorians are more muscular. I chose an alley a few blocks away from my intended target for my arrival point because I needed to adjust echo to make this deal happen. I started walking immediately but noticed a couple of street people probably saw me appear. This society recently converted from a military dictatorship to a Republicanistic way of life. There were still strong ties to the military, but divisions of power were conceded by the military to open up trade and commerce with other worlds.

Taking out my shingle containing the route, I mapped from where I was to where I needed to go. The streets were moderately populated, and I walked by several small markets and street food vendors as I pulled up the *Motif* around me. I drew lots of stares, but no one approached me. Using the *Motif*, I shifted echo here and there, lightly influencing this probability, so I was meeting a registered land holdings broker at the map waypoint. I also adjusted probability, so my portfolio recorded a bonus discovery of azuronite in one of the asteroid mines I owned. I checked my holdings with the shingle and verified an increase of several million credits to my account.

The target on the map grew closer, and I put the shingle away, noticing a couple of Bragorians at the target location, looking around very impatiently.

"Hello," I said as I approached and adjusted my language to theirs.

"It's about time. We were getting ready to leave. I hope your intention to purchase this land parcel is serious," one of the Bragorians said.

"I apologize for being late. This visit is my first time to Bragoria," I said.

"Well, next time, perhaps, you will become better acquainted with your surroundings before imposing your tardiness upon dutiful electorates of the state. I am Soter Manak, and this is recorder Justel. Are you ready to conclude this transaction?" Manak asked.

"Of course," I said.

Recorder Justel pulled out a baseball-sized dodecahedron and pressed two sides at once, causing one of the sides to light up. I could see a few streams of characters move across one of the facets of the device, then he said, "Recording transaction seven hundred and sixty-four on the lunar calendar Nices during the first reign of Hartar."

"Very well," Manak said. "I presume you have a way of providing the funds for this property?"

"Oh, yeah," I said, absentmindedly while reaching into my pocket and pulling out the shingle.

I tapped a few times and brought up the funds section I reviewed earlier, and asked Justel, "How do I make the transfer to your device?"

"One moment," Justel replied. "I see your device, and I am sending you an encrypted requisition package."

I waited, and eventually, a dodecahedron icon showed up on my screen. I moved over to Justel and showed him my screen. He shook his head, yes, indicating I should open it. Manak seemed incredibly irritated about my lack of knowledge of Bragorian transactions and merely, "Humphed."

I tapped the screen, and the Bragorian icon took over to display contract after contract that I was required to agree with and accept. This process took about five minutes for me to wade through all the legal work prompting Manak to ask, irritated, "Didn't you review the contract before arriving to make the final payment?"

"I wanted to, but I had a date last night, you know," I said.

"Well, perhaps you should choose your priorities better next time. I have other appointments to make today, and we're on the verge of being late," Manak stressed.

The Bragorian agreement software closed up and restored my screen, leaving two new icons in its place. One was in the shape of the dodecahedron, and the other was in the shape of a stack of diamond-stamped quaybit. I paused for a moment and asked, "Wow, five point six million credits for this slum?"

"What is it now? You have agreed to the purchase. Your time to haggle has passed," Manak replied smugly.

"This is legal, right? You're not going to renege on the deal after I transfer the funds, correct?" I asked.

"The deal is binding and recorded in the Bragorian database. That is why recorder Justel is here," Manak replied even more irritated than before.

"You mean, if there is a military coup tomorrow, the new ruling party will still honor this real estate sale?" I asked.

"This parcel is of no military value. Regime changes have come and gone while land parcels remain stable. That is why this is such a great investment for you," Manak said, slightly changing his tone to try a different approach to get me to pay.

"Whew, thank you for the clarification. I would hate to have to explain to the board of directors if anything went wrong with the transaction today," I replied before dragging the icon of the diamond-stamped quaybit onto the icon of the dodecahedron, which consumed it, and erased it from my screen.

I leaned over to look at Justel's screen, and it seemed to be processing something rapidly, then finally chimed with a pleasant ding.

"Sale complete. This transfer ends the current transaction between the Bragorian government and Sam Richards," Justel said before tapping the dodecahedron, which went dim. He placed it into a small carrying bag he slung over his shoulder.

"About time. Come Justel. We might be able to make our next appointment if we hurry," Manak said.

Without a thank you or a handshake, they walked off briskly down the street.

"Ohm, remove all structures within the area I purchased here on Bragoria. If there are any living creatures within the area, transport them to a city at least four hundred kilometers away," I said.

"Replicating new cloaked scanners to facilitate the long-distance transport," Ohm replied.

"Ohm, activate an auragraphic display with the environment designer, please," I asked.

The familiar orange sphere appeared. When I unrolled it, I noticed the previous design of the Baker's guest house was still in place. I dragged that off to the save area and started to look into the parks and garden section of the environment designer to get some ideas.

"Ohm, can you add the total area I have purchased to the environment designer? I want to use a Blinn terraforming module to make this area self-replicating to maintain the intended design even if someone alters it or tries to destroy it. In the case of destruction, delay self-repair for twelve hours," I said.

The environment designer updated, and I started dropping in items to populate this park. At the center, I knew I wanted the monument. It was a giant sculpture made up of Vascon symbols reading, "No Means No." Instead of using the word "means," I used the math symbol for equals which turned the sculpture into an equation. Following the Bragorian building code, I kept the size of the monument slightly shorter than the tallest nearby building. The lighting for the monument I took from a preset I found in the sub-menu. The surface of the monument was constructed from a shiny material to reflect the surroundings, ground, and sky. I placed a Vascon visitor center near the base of the monument, similar to the facilities at the Selene amphitheater. For the grounds, I chose gently sloping hills and a playground for kids. I also arranged the flower gardens in the shape of the icon used to represent the Squire of the Pharaoh, but overall it was just an open green space in the middle of an ugly city.

It took a few minutes for Ohm to relocate a cloaked scanner to relay the detected lifeforms to their new location. I assumed there were squatters and or animal life inside this slum, but it was of such wretched quality that I didn't worry for a second that I was disrupting anyone's life for the worse. Bragorians were socialistic by nature, and any squatters I relocated should be able to find equal or better services in the other city.

The sparkle parade began as Ohm started removing people and structures. There was a lot to do, so I didn't feel like I needed to stay here and oversee it. I would check in later once the structure was built, I thought.

"Ohm, transport me to the capital city on the Vosip homeworld, preferably somewhere near a flower shop," I said.

I watched the sparkles fizzle and crash in from my peripheral vision as I returned to the black space. I figured the Bragorians would be very upset with a monument to Vasco constructed in their capital city, but they needed to learn the lesson that no does mean no, and the days of invading worlds and taking their resources is over. I want them to wake up every day and see the reminder that those times are gone and won't be returning anytime soon. A fading afternoon light rushed in as I materialized on a sidewalk in the city of Prelond on the planet Vosip.

I must have looked confused as a Vosip citizen asked me, "Are you lost, my friend?"

"No, not lost. I just arrived. I am looking for a florist. Do you happen to know where I could locate one?" I asked in reply.

"Welcome, traveler. I am Herjamay, and I believe you are not that far off. I recall seeing a florist shop down the street and to your right, at the intersection," Herjamay gestured.

"Well met, Herjamay. Thank you for the directions. I hope you have a pleasant evening," I said, and I walked off in the direction he pointed.

It was interesting to see more Vosip people. Not all Vosips were mingled Vosips, like Jorrie, and in my future memories, we only visited her home a couple of times. Being a mingled Vosip was a bit of an honor and a curse. Even though families recognized the honor, they also knew once their relative mingled, a significant personality alteration could occur. This psychological change often caused a separation in the family if the family could not accept the newly mingled person. This change was the case with Jorrie. Because her Limax was older, it altered the host more significantly than a younger Limax who may be venturing into its first or second mingle experience. The one time I met her parents, the dinner was a nightmare, and her brother, who was somewhat of a grifter, was grilling me and being an asshole. There was still a technology gap between some of the Union worlds, and Vosip was one of them. The general population lived less advanced than the citizens of Earth. I thought about all this as I brought up the *Motif*, shifting echo a little to put a couple of strips of diamond stamped quaybit in my pants pocket.

I walked by the shop, did a double-take, and turned back. The sign read, "Vi Stember." I tried the door, and it seemed like the shop was open, so I went inside. A soft bell rang as the door closed, and I was hit with the wonderful floral smell of many blooming plants at once. There were not a lot of offerings in the cramped storefront, but a doorway behind the counter opened into a much larger back room, probably where they processed orders. An older gentleman appeared through the doorway and asked, "Hello, what can I do for you today?"

"Hello, to you. I am looking for a specific plant and wondered if you might have it. It's a blooming Psylo Furigate?" I asked.

"Ah, the flower of romance. Of course, we have those. How many would you like?" he asked.

"Do you happen to have it potted instead of cut?" I continued with my questioning.

"I do, but they are not presently in bloom. Are you still interested in them," he asked.

"Yes, I would like one, please," I said.

"Our pots are traditional, based upon the decrees of Sugestria. Are you familiar with their meanings?" he asked.

In my future memories, Jorrie and I did discuss the mythic role of Sugestria and how her decrees still wound their ways through everyday lives. It was basic symbology representing fortune or misfortune in luck, business, love, family, success, similar to some of the Earth-based cultures that built up symbolism based upon mystic beliefs.

"I am loosely familiar with the concepts, and I think I need the orange bird, but I am not sure," I said.

"I don't mean to pry, but who is this gift for, and what relation is this person to you?" he asked.

"I appreciate the guidance. I just met this woman, and we shared a wonderful time together. I want to know her better. Does that help?" I asked.

"I think you are right about the bird, but sea green would be better in this case because you just met. If you were family, then orange would be more appropriate," he replied.

"Thank you for pointing out the distinction. A sea-green bird would be great. I have quaybit and Union credit. Can I purchase with that, or do I need to visit a money changer?" I asked.

"Of course, we take Union credit. I'll prepare your order. It will only take a few moments," he said, and he returned to the back room, where I heard him call out to someone else behind the wall.

Looking around the shop, I browsed through a display of cards. I settled on a simple one with a filigree design on the front in some henna ink color. When you opened it, the card read, "thinking of you..." I took the card over to the counter as he returned with a beautiful plant that reminded me of a mix between an orchid and a trumpeting amaryllis. The flower buds were sheath-like and reminiscent of a certain part of Jorrie's anatomy.

"Can you add this card to the bill?" I asked.

"Certainly. You can expect the flowers to emerge in three to seven days. There is a small card in the back here with basic care instructions," he said as he used a handheld device and announced, "that will be seventy-eight credits, please."

I pulled out my shingle, located the money app, and said, "I'm not sure how to get the credits to you, and showed him my device."

He took a look and then said, "Ah, I think I know. Let me try again."

Sure enough, a small icon appeared on my screen, and I said, "Got it."

I dropped one hundred credits onto his icon and said, "That's a tip for being such a wonderful florist. I will certainly recommend this place. May I borrow your writing stylus?"

"Thank you, certainly," he said while handing me a pen.

I wrote inside the card, "I hope to see you soon, Sam."

There was a wooden raised stem with a slot to hold the card. I put my card in place, picked up the plant, and headed out the door, saying thank you, once again, to the shop owner. Out on the street, I set the plant down on the step and said, "Ohm, target the plant and place it on the table in Jorrie's quarters on *Oasis Seven*."

The plant sparkled and disappeared. It was time for me to do the same.

"Ohm, transport me back to my apartment in San Francisco," I said, and the world collapsed in from the sides. I waited in darkness, wondering what gift I should get for Erin. Even though I married her twice and lived with her for years, I couldn't think of a single thing that would delight her. She appreciated experiences over material items. One thing that did come to mind was the first trip into echo that I took with Jorrie and Erin. That was when I discovered echo travel does mess with the balance between the Limax and the host. For Jorrie, it was not as serious a side effect as it was with Erin's micro machines deforming, who almost died, but the trip did help solidify our relationship as a family. I don't think we are that far along, however. Finally, the afternoon light zoomed in from the side of my eyes as I materialized, looking out the glass doors at the bay scene.

"Hey, baby, where have you been?" Erin asked from behind me.

I turned around, and she stood at the kitchen counter with a drink in her hand.

"Sorry about conking out last night. I think I was up for about three days," I replied.

She drank the contents of the glass, leaving it on the counter, and walked around to greet me, saying, "I have some great news to tell you."

"What?" I asked curiously with a smile.

"I have been accepted into Starnet Academy. I'm going to become a cadet!" she said excitedly.

"That's wonderful, baby," I said, but not believing it was wonderful at all while using it as an excuse to hug her, pick her up, and swing her around once.

"Yeah, I can't wait," she said.

"When do you start?" I asked.

"In three weeks, I head out for two weeks of basic training, then back here to San Francisco for daily study and classes. I'm psyched," she said with enthusiasm.

In both time loops, Erin did the same thing when I brought her to the Dili sector. She joined Starnet. Having been born on a starship and programmed to serve a hierarchy in both the Melog hive and the Imperial fleet, it was no surprise when she sought out the same thing here with Starnet. Part of me hoped she might make a different choice this time around, which caused me to wonder if breaking the time loop was even possible?

"I'm happy for you. Does this mean I might have to salute you at some point in the future?" I ribbed her.

"Damn right it does, mister," she said, draping her arms over my shoulders and giving me a light kiss.

"I spent my morning purchasing property on Bragoria," I said.

"Bragoria, why there?" she asked, seemingly puzzled.

"I want them to get a little taste of what it is like to have their homeworld invaded by outsiders," I said.

"Sam, why do you always have to stir up trouble?" Erin asked disapprovingly.

"I guess, to annoy them. They are so damn arrogant. I purchased a large dilapidated slum and set up a terraforming module to turn the area into a park. I placed an excessively large monument in the center," I replied.

"What kind of monument, dare I ask?" Erin continued, frowning.

"Nothing too offensive. The monument is large Vascon symbols that spell out, 'no equals no,'" I told her.

"But aren't things getting better in that region? Couldn't a move like this hurt relations?" Erin pointed out.

"Maybe, but one might argue that it could improve relations. Now Vascon tourists, and other species, will have a reason to travel to Bragoria," I argued.

"To see the monument," Erin said.

"To see the monument. I also built a visitors center," I said.

"I don't know, Sam. It seems kind of iffy," Erin said.

"I was shocked that such an aggressive and technologically advanced species suffers such poverty on their own world. Their commerce could certainly use a boost," I replied.

"Changing the subject, when we woke up this morning, Jorrie and I burst out laughing at your snoring. We thought for sure our laughter would wake you up, but when you didn't, we continued with getting our days started," Erin said in better spirits.

"Well, I'm glad I can amuse you while I sleep," I said.

She gave me a long hug and said, "Oh, yeah. You amuse me and care for me, Sam. I really don't know what I would be doing right now if I was back on Zenith," Erin said with a hint of sadness.

"Do you ever think of them, your fellow Melogs?" I asked.

"I do, and sometimes I feel like shit for enjoying my life while leaving them behind. But each time I think about visiting them, I talk myself out of it by asking myself, 'why?'" Erin said.

"You're right to claim your own life and live it the way you see fit," I said, trying not to go too far down the rabbit hole of feeling sorry for yourself because you have succeeded.

"Thank you for saying that. I guess that is what you are doing with building your monument, huh?" Erin asked.

"Maybe. It's been on my mind for a while now. Ever since I started repairing the structures on Vasco. I saw the greatness of the civilization was still there, standing in partial rubble with people living in the rubble. And why were they standing in the rubble? Because some space-faring assholes decided they wanted the ore from a mine. It's because Bragorians are bullies, and I wanted to bully them back so they could get a taste of their own medicine," I said, getting worked up about the defense of my new construction.

"So, I'm meeting up with Jorrie later, on *Oasis Seven*, after her shift is over. Do you want to come?" Erin asked.

"Of course, I want to come. But I don't want to get in the way of your relationship with her. I guess I feel like the third wheel. Besides, the security guy on the station doesn't like me," I said.

"Who, Mod?" Erin asked.

"Yes, Mod. In one of my future memories, he nearly killed me. He smashed out my teeth while form altering a pseudopod down my throat and solidifying it. It still messes with my head when I see him. I just had my head messed with by that Gorgon device, and now I'm being a dick to the entire Bragorian planet. Perhaps I do stir up trouble more often than I should," I said.

We sat down together on the white sofa, and Erin asked, "Are you feeling better? Candy stopped by after you went to sleep last night. Jorrie and I hung out together. She showed us some of the log from the night you and Alex rescued the MD-Alpha team. It was hard to watch, Sam. How could you take on all those people? You got shot, over and over. Then she showed us that creepy faceless monster sucking the energy out of your head."

"Candy shouldn't have shown you that," I said.

"It was Jorrie that was most interested. She asked Candy to stop the log to view it from various angles. There were some dropouts and completely blank portions because it was recorded through that magic painting. But she really wanted to see the face of that ghoul. I don't know why," Erin said.

"I think she wanted to know what a god looks like," I replied.

"Maybe you're right, but she also wanted to see the magic wand you used to destroy the thing. It gave me shivers to see those tentacles fly out of the wand. I couldn't help but think of our first day on Vasco when you were attacked by those things," Erin said.

"As I said, Candy shouldn't have shown you that. The good news is that Xanadu was able to fix me up as good as new, so I don't feel impaired by the recent attack, but my invisihud is still down," I said, trying to lighten the mood.

"Isn't that important?" Erin asked.

"Yeah, it is to me, but I was more concerned about my soul than remaining in Xanadu for an extended brain session. I headed immediately to Madison's house to ask her about that spell," I said.

"Candy said you feared you became evil. Is that true?" Erin asked with concern.

"I did fear it. When I uttered that spell, I knew it was evil even though I never heard of it or used it before," I said.

"How can you cast a spell that you have never heard of or practiced?" Erin asked.

"I wondered the same thing, and Madison told me it was called sympathetic magic. She told me the spell I used was evil, but I was not. She said I should never cast the spell again, or my soul may start to bend toward becoming evil," I told her.

"Faen, Sam," Erin said softly.

"I'm sorry for bringing you down. You came to me with good news and we end up talking about my morbid life," I said.

"It's our life, Sam, and your well-being is important to me. I'm sorry I was not around for support when you needed me. I know I have been elusive recently as I got to know Jorrie, and that was not fair to you," Erin said.

"Baby, you don't have to," I said.

Erin cut me off, saying, "I do. I could tell you knew something was up, and I didn't come clean. It made me feel like shit inside, but I did it anyway. I started feeling like a lying programmed Melog again," Erin said seriously.

"Thank you for finally telling me and inviting me into your relationship with Jorrie. Sexually, you both blew my mind last night, but personally, I felt loved, and I need that. I guess I'm addicted to you. Without you, I feel like I am missing something," I said with my eyes welling up with a couple of tears.

"I know that feeling, too. You do it for me, Sam, and I don't know if or when Jorrie will tell you, but I know she digs you too. Are you sure you won't come and hang out with us on *Oasis Seven*?" Erin asked one more time.

"OK, you talked me into it. I'd love to join you," I said.

"Great, we're leaving here in a couple of hours," Erin said, getting up and saying, "I've got to find something to wear."

CHAPTER 55

The Little Black Dress

❧

Erin finally settled on the little black dress that could. She looked amazing wearing it, and I managed to put on something a little more formal than my standard pockets shirt. Oh, the pockets were there, but they were well hidden. I also came up with a new dress shoe containing my cloaked scanners in the heel. When we were finally ready to depart, Erin said, "You look good."

"Thank you, my lady," I said, offering my arm to her.

She took my arms and said, "We're meeting Jorrie at one of the new Vascon restaurants on the concourse. Ohm, transport Sam and I to *Oasis Seven*, preferably a location near the concourse where no one is presently located."

The light of the room streamed inward from the side, and my consciousness became a component in the black box of eternity. I still felt uncertain about my role or place in Jorrie's life. I guess I was intimidated by her intelligence, and I was also in awe of her beauty. Those two together left me feeling unsure of myself when I was around her. Maybe if I could get some alone time with her, I might be able to reach a more comfortable situation. Until then, I guess I'll try to "wing it" until I succeed or I am kicked out of the relationship. A series of blinking lights became apparent as Erin and I materialized aboard *Oasis Seven*.

We looked across the concourse at some flashing signs. A quick glance around, and we both started walking together. It seemed like Erin did this often enough that she knew it was best to start moving immediately after an illegal transport to avoid becoming a spectacle. Once we made our way out to the concourse, we took a more leisurely pace. We nearly walked the full circle around the concourse until we came to a restaurant with a sign reading "Fusion" in Vascon letters. Erin said, "This is it."

We went inside, and Erin gave our names to the hostess, who informed us that Jorrie had not arrived yet. We headed over to the bar for a drink. I asked if they served Earth drinks? The bartender said they did, so I ordered a Margarita on the rocks, and Erin decided to have the same thing.

Smiling at me, Erin asked, "It's nice to get out, don't you think?"

There were other people, Vascon, Starnet, and other species scattered around the establishment, but I could not take my eyes off of Erin. Her hair was more formal, and she wore earrings that sparkled along with a necklace of small pearls. I felt special just being in her company, and I said, "Yeah, this place is way better than Lepton's."

Her friendly smile broke as she said, "That's not hard to do. I don't know why Jorrie likes to go there so much."

The bartender returned with our drinks, and we picked them up together. I offered a toast, "To getting out."

We clinked our glasses together and took a small sip of our drinks before setting them back down on the bar. It was not bad. It tasted like top-shelf tequila in my drink, along with real lime.

"Do you think it's too risky to kiss in public?" I asked

She squeezed the lime wedge into her drink and flashed her eyes at me, saying, "Only if it's light-hearted and fun. You know, totally making out is a bit lower class, but a playful kiss can be kind of nice. Are you thinking about it?"

"I am, thinking about it. I just wondered how you felt about that prospect," I replied.

She took a sip of her Margarita, held her drink off to the side, and leaned into me a bit. I tilted my head, leaned into her, and tasted her soft sour lips, lingering before pulling back and considering my drink.

"That's nice. Not too long, but it lets me know that I have your attention," Erin said.

"Oh, yeah, you have my attention. I can't take my eyes off of you," I said.

This reply caused her to smile, and she said, "Careful. If you use up all those one-liners on me, what will you say to Jorrie?"

Speak of the devil. I noticed Jorrie walked in at the entrance to the restaurant, and the hostess directed her over toward us. She seemed a little upset as she approached while still wearing her uniform.

"Sorry, I'm late. I didn't even have time to change, but you two look nice," she said as she leaned in for a quick hug from each of us.

"What's up? Is there something wrong?" Erin asked her.

"Oh, it's just that something happened on Bragoria today, and one of the military commanders kept on grilling us about it. It went on forever. You know how Bragorians are with their speech," Jorrie said.

At the mention of Bragoria, Erin and I looked at each other, which Jorrie picked up on immediately, asking, "You know something about this?"

"Well, I did purchase property on Bragoria today. I installed a terraforming module to create a park and a monument," I said.

"Apparently, one of their ships was destroyed in an unusual way. It has them very upset," Jorrie said.

"Bragorians are always upset," I said, handing my drink to Jorrie, who took a sip.

"I hate to ask, but would you return to operations with me and talk to the Bragorian commander?" Jorrie asked.

"You're off duty, correct?" I asked.

She shook her head, yes.

"You and Erin get a table, and I'll be back as soon as possible. Where is he?"

I asked.

"He's in Warren's office. Do you know where that is located?" she asked.

I shook my head yes, and offered my seat at the bar to Jorrie, who said, "Thank you," with a hint of future reciprocation revealed in her eyes.

I headed out of the restaurant and made my way to the lift to the upper level. From there, I wound my way through the circular maze, making my way to the central shaft. There was another lift here taking me to the top floor, where the operations center for the space station was located. When I exited the lift, I drew a few looks from the personnel. One of them was Ernie Nestor, who was aboard the *Contender* during the dragon attack.

"I was told to report to Warren's office," I said to Ernie.

He pointed to a raised platform with a wide metal stairway leading up to double doors.

"Ah, thanks," I said, and headed up the stairway to knock before entering Warren's office.

Warren's office was fairly sparse. There was a wide wooden desk placed in front of an oval-shaped window revealing a view of space and several of the docking rings. Warren sat behind the desk, leaning back in his chair. Standing in the room was a Bragorian in full battle armor, who looked over at me and said, "If you'll excuse us. This is a private meeting."

"Come in, Sam. This is Kop Lacroth," Warren said as he contained his apparent surprise at my altered appearance compared to the last time we met. "What brings you into my office on this fine day?"

"I met Jorrie below, and she said there was some kind of confusion about the land I purchased on Bragoria today," I said.

"Your land? You mean you are responsible for this," Kop Lacroth said before standing up.

"Responsible for what?" I asked.

"A new weapon appeared in our capital city. When we went to investigate, one of our ships was destroyed. You have committed a serious crime against Bragoria," Kop Lacroth said.

I pulled out the shingle from my inner pocket, which caused Kop Lacroth to take a step back, readying himself for physical combat with me as I said, "Chill out, Dude. Let's take a look at the log."

I located the cloaked scanner, which was monitoring the land parcel I purchased and set the shingle into auragraphic display mode so we could all view the recording. I scanned through the day's events until I saw the Bragorian ship approach and fire upon the monument I constructed. It landed in the park, which triggered the terraforming module to consume the ship into the ground.

"There, our ship was destroyed. Even your log records it," Kop Lacroth said.

"Oh, I see the misunderstanding. You did not follow the rules of entering my property," I said as I panned and tilted the log around to reveal the sign at the entrance of the park reading, "No Weapons or Vehicles Allowed."

"There is a sign that clearly states vehicles are not permitted in the park. I should be suing you for destroying my monument," I said to his face.

"The military has full jurisdiction in all matters and may enter any premises at any time," Kop Lacroth stated.

I fussed around with the shingle until I finally located the lengthy contract I signed earlier that day. It took me a few minutes to locate it, but I finally pulled up the passage that clearly said that a thirty-two-hour notice was required before military inspections.

"I haven't even owned the land for thirty-two hours, and I have not received any notice. You should really review the contracts you sign before overreacting. I was guaranteed, by Soter Manak, that my parcel purchase would be honored by the emerging republic and the established military," I said.

"That only applies in civil matters," Lacroth said.

"Face it, Lacroth, you're in the wrong. My contract says I can build anything I want on my land as long as it does not exceed the height of surrounding structures or compete commercially with neighboring Bragorian businesses. I have built a park, a visitor center, and a monument. None of those violate the contract," I said.

"The destruction of Bragorian military vessel can not be overlooked," Lacroth insisted.

"If you followed the rules, it would not have been destroyed. My park is self-maintaining. When it finds garbage or junk lying on the surface, it is recycled. That is what happened to your ship. It was considered garbage," I said.

"Garbage? That was a class A military peacekeeping vessel!" Lacroth blared.

"The solution is simple, don't land your ships in my park," I said.

My tone riled this guy up. He paced and gestured all around Warren's office, eventually saying, "No one tells the Bragorian military what they can or can not do."

"I beg to differ. The republic does have jurisdiction over the military now. Bragoria is moving into a new era where it can finally be respected for fairness. This new stance opens up new opportunities for trade and commerce. If you kill this deal now, who is going to believe that Bragoria will honor any trade deal?" I asked.

"He has a point Kop Lacroth," Warren weighed in. "You can't have it both ways. If you want to open up trade, the military has to act in accordance with the laws of the republic, otherwise, your new government position will be seen as a mockery."

Lacroth glanced quickly over at Warren before returning his gaze to me, saying, "This is not over. Oh, believe me, this is far from over."

I turned off the display emitted from the shingle and returned it to my inner pocket, saying, "As your new neighbor, I have some simple advice. Stay off my lawn."

"And as your superior military neighbor, I will make sure your site is inspected every day," Lacroth replied.

"It is a park. Anyone can visit any time they like," I said, then looking over at Warren, "Nice to see you again, Warren."

I took my leave of the office, heading down the wide stairway and returning to the lift. Ernie gave me another raised eyebrow look as I passed by. The lift took me down to the upper level. As I wandered through the corridors on my way back to the concourse, I pulled up the *Motif* and started altering echo at a larger generic scale. I changed the contract I signed so the parcel of land I purchased was twice as large.

"Ohm, I would like to extend the park on Bragoria to double its size. Reclaim the land on the side that meets up with the nearest, busiest street. Relocate any residents, as before. Recenter the visitor's center and monument within the new space. I would also like to add shelter houses along the outer edge, with picnic tables and grills. Make them typical open-walled structures where visitors can get some relief from the weather if needed."

"Revising the park on Bragoria," Ohm replied.

"Ohm, also, if Military officers enter the park with weapons, go ahead and recycle their weapons."

I made my way down to the concourse level and located the Fusion restaurant. It looked like Erin and Jorrie moved from the bar to a table, and the hostess pointed them out to me. I headed over and took a seat with them.

"Well, what happened?" Jorrie asked.

"I reviewed my contract with Kop Lacroth, which states I am allowed to build on the land parcel and that his military is in the wrong for attacking my monument. He was, of course, unhappy about the result of the meeting and vowed to make my life hell. That means it was a typical encounter with the Bragorian military," I said, eying some of the food on the table.

"We went ahead and ordered. It's family-style, so help yourself," Erin said.

The dishes on the table looked wonderful. I hadn't eaten Vascon food since the first concert I performed with the boys a while back. There were some spicy dishes and some bland dishes. When I looked at the food on both Erin and Jorrie's' plates, I could see that Erin preferred the spicy food, and Jorrie, like many Vosip, preferred the bland food. I knew this from my future memories, but I realized this was our first meal together. I tried a little of everything as I poured myself a glass of water. There were a couple of fried options with dipping sauces, and this food seemed to be an exception for Jorrie. She liked one of the fried planks and applied a generous amount of sweet brown sauce to it.

"What does that mean?" Erin asked.

"I think it means business as usual. Bragorians aren't happy unless they are complaining or gloating," I said.

"They claimed their ship was attacked. How was that resolved?" Jorrie asked.

"It wasn't attacked. I installed a terraforming module on my land parcel. The function of the module is to maintain a programmed appearance, in this case, a park. When they landed the ship in the park, which is not allowed, the terraforming module commenced to recycle it. All of the crew were transported to safety, but the ship was consumed by the module to restore its programmed appearance," I replied.

"You make interesting devices, Sam," Jorrie said as she took another bite of the bland Lima bean-like dish.

"I mostly strive to make practical things. The terraforming module was one of the first items I created during the Blinn reconstruction period. My Blinn people, and their world, suffered greatly while I was imprisoned. I guess Vasco reminds me of that, in a way. The Blinn people reverted to tribalism and lived in the rubble of a once-great civilization during my forty-year imprisonment," I said.

"Forty years," Erin gasped, "Why did they let you out?"

"I don't know if this is appropriate dinner conversation," I replied.

"Maybe not, but I am curious if it's not too upsetting for you to talk about," Jorrie said.

I spooned a little more of a quinoa-type dish onto my plate and covered it with some of the golden, spicy stew. Taking a bite and trying to talk between chewing, I said, "They didn't let me out. They left me to die, imprisoned in a virtual reality cryogenic chamber while I wasted away slowly from malnutrition. They attacked Ohm with a computer virus, which locked up those maintenance operations, leaving me with no tech support at all. Eventually, the hardware broke because Ohm was not there to maintain it. Ohm was locked in a computational stalemate battle against an invading artificial intelligence. When I awoke, Ohm gave up part of its virtual ground to the invader to perform a site-to-site transport of my weakened body to the Blinn homeworld. From there, I rebuilt the civilization and returned to *Tiger Mountain* to free Ohm."

"That sounds awful, Sam," Erin said.

"I don't mean to pry, but who are they?" Jorrie asked.

I took a drink of water as she took another bite of food, finally saying, "It was Teela, Lexi, and Valentino."

"They are Splendorite's, like you, right?" Erin asked.

"Yes, Valentino was the one who attacked me with the tentacles. Lexi is his aunt, and Teela was my first wife, although she is not technically a Splendorite," I replied.

"What do they have against you?" Jorrie asked, finally trying something from the dessert plate that looked a lot like flan.

"Teela was the first Guardian of *Tiger Mountain*. She used her access to plant the computer virus Valentino created. She is Lexi's protege. Once we began living in Splendor, Lexi attempted to manipulate and drive a wedge between our relationship. I can't explain why people are evil, Jorrie. They just are," I said, then looking at each of them, "If you ever meet them. Don't trust them for a second. They are nice and intelligent people, but all they really want from you is information. I was imprisoned because the woman I loved betrayed me."

This caused silence to fall across the table, with them both feeling guilty to some degree of betrayal. Erin because of her past programmed Melog behavior and Jorrie for the deception she pulled at the balcony party.

Jorrie spoke first, saying, "Thank you for explaining that to me, to us. I'm sorry for asking so many questions, Sam. You're one of the most mysterious people I have ever met across multiple lifetimes. I'm just trying to get to know you."

"If I come across mysterious, it's not because I'm trying to hide who I am from you. It is because I have a lot of junk in my closet that I would rather forget about. Talking about it reminds me how much those events still shape my approach to life, even today," I said, reaching for a slice of dessert.

The waitress came over and asked if we would like anything else, and we all said no, so she presented the bill. Erin pulled a small card from an inner pocket of her black dress to pay for us all, which caused me to smile.

"What?" she asked as she placed the card on the tray and signed for the gratuity.

"You took my advice. It makes me happy," I said.

"What advice?" Jorrie asked.

Erin answered for me instead, "Sam told me that I should create special pockets in my clothing to carry the cards he gave me."

"You never know when you might be transported against your will. It is always nice to have an escape option on your body at all times," I added.

We left the restaurant together and headed over to the lift, taking it up to the residency level where Jorrie's quarters. Once we arrived, Jorrie said, "Make yourself at home. I'm going to change out of my uniform."

The last time I was here, I only remained in the entranceway. This time, I headed into her quarters and took a look around. It was big, much nicer than that room I briefly acquired the first time I visited *Oasis Seven*. This place was fairly spacious, and some of the elegance found on the upper deck of the concourse was evident in this room as well as in a couple of the oversized viewports. Erin and I walked over and took a look. She put her arm around me and tilted her head on my shoulder, similar to the move I made with Candy at Ethan's party those long months ago. I can't believe how far I have come since then.

"What's this?" I heard Jorrie remark as she entered the room wearing more casual clothes.

I turned around, and she discovered the Psylo Furigate that Ohm deposited earlier this day. She read the card and said, "Thank you, Sam. I thought of you too. Where did you find it?"

"After I purchased the land parcel on Bragoria, I transported to Vosip and located a florist. I'm sorry it is not blooming now, but the florist assured me it should blossom in a few days. There's a card in the back with general care instructions," I said.

Jorrie walked over to me and said, "I love it," kissing me. "You were on Bragoria and Vosip, all in one day?"

Erin walked over to inspect the plant and read the card saying, "I can smell a slight floral scent, even though the blooms are not open yet."

"Yes, then back to Earth, and now we're here," I replied.

Jorrie tweaked her neck, trying to relieve some tension, and Erin noticed, saying, "Why don't you let me give you a neck massage?"

"Okay, you talked me into it," Jorrie said with a smile as they headed over to a couch along one wall.

Erin sat at one end of the couch, and Jorrie laid down lengthwise, relaxing back into Erin's arms as she began a series of massaging motions with her hands. I took a seat at the end of the couch and started working on her feet, the left one first.

"Oh, now this is overly indulgent. If you keep this up, I might just have to marry you both," Jorrie said with a smile.

Erin stopped for a moment, and Jorrie looked up at her. They kissed, and Jorrie adjusted her whole body to get into a more comfortable position. They kept at it, and I switched over to massaging Jorrie's right foot. I preferred massaging feet to shoulders. I guess it seemed easier because I could hold them in my hands. With the shoulders, my hands tend to cramp up pretty quickly.

I finished up her right foot, and she sat up, kissing me, saying, "I have something I want to show you."

Jorrie headed off to a dresser and brought back a Starnet tablet. She pulled up an image that was all too familiar on her display. It was the image of the cloud forming around the tentacles. I guessed this probably came from the log of the attack that occurred in the villa on Vasco.

"Your neighbor, Lucas, contacted me after you experienced the tentacle attack and wondered if I might have some time to analyze the sensor readings. I finally took some time to look into it, and I think the recorded phenomena is essentially an atmospheric-based radionic tile couched in a potential well, stabilized through a stream of exotic matter ejected at the destination point. The rainbow effect is essentially gravimetric lensing," Jorrie said.

"So, it might be possible to scan the ejected exotic matter and create a counter spin antithesis using a protonic ray directed at the event horizon," I concluded.

"I thought the same thing. If you can throw off the emission flow, it just might collapse," Jorrie replied.

"Ohm, can you research the practicality of emitting proton or neutrons using the cloaked scanners?" I asked.

"Certainly, I'll research practical emission methods," Ohm replied.

"Wow, a technological defense against magical tentacles. How would we ever test it?" Erin asked.

"I do have the same ability to manipulate the *Vechnost* as Valentino does. I just don't practice using it. I should be able to generate some tentacles for a test, however," I said.

"Wait a second. I thought Madison said you would bend toward evil if you used the tentacle spell again?" Erin asked.

"They are similar, but the *Tantalis* spell coming out of the wand is not the same as the *Vechnost*. I think Madison's main point is using magic to kill someone leads you down an evil path. And that spell has no other use. The *Vechnost* is simply chaos' version of the *Motif*. The *Vechnost* can be used constructive as well as destructive, like an instrument," I said.

"That is interesting. Do all Splendorites have the ability to manipulate the *Motif* and the *Vechnost*?" Jorrie asked.

"Not that I know of. As far as I know, Valentino and I are the only ones to carry both marks within ourselves, but even if I asked other family members, they might not tell me the truth anyway," I replied.

"How did you acquire, what did you call it, the mark?" Erin asked.

"Ironically, it was Valentino that introduced me to the *Vechnost*. In proper terms, you engage the *Motif*, but you mediate the *Vechnost*. Valentino was born in the Vectorless Vale, so he mediated the *Vechnost* first and then engaged the *Motif*. It was the opposite for me," I said.

"What caused your falling out with Valentino? How did the relations end up so bad between you two?" Jorrie asked.

"With him being much older than me, I looked up to him and even admired him at first. He was smart, clever, and possessed an understanding of magic that I still don't fully comprehend. Because he was raised in the Vectorless Vale, he lacked empathy for living things. He only saw them as the result of the interaction of the *Motif* with chaos. I also differ with some of my Splendorite contemporaries on the age-old argument of do we create the realities we inhabit or do we discover them? I guess because I was born in echo, I am in the camp of we discover them, and they are not necessarily our playthings," I replied.

"Do any of the Splendorites hold values similar to yours?" Erin asked.

"It's been so long that I really don't know. I like to think that King Osric keeps an open mind. I think that is why the Re'em picked him to be our ruler. But they are all so proud and set in their ways that I think they might feel a bit ashamed at the way they treated me when we last gathered together."

"What happened?" Jorrie asked.

"At the time, they were under the influence of the chaos strands. They don't want to admit that they could be coerced or taken over by an invisible magical force that only I could detect. That is why I warned you about them. They won't perceive you as people. At best, you might be treated as well as a pet or used as a temporary diversion," I said.

"The King of all probable universes was chosen by a Re'em?" Jorrie asked incredulously.

"What's a Re'em?" Erin asked.

"The Re'em is a shaggy quadruped with a single long horn growing out of its forehead. It is rumored to be incredibly fast and impossible to tame or ride. The Splendorite creation myth goes something like this. One fine day, before any *Motif* existed, an artist sat near the Pit of Eternity, which still exists in the Vectorless Vale. Out of the pit leaped the Re'em, which bowed before the artists, touching its long horn to the ground. A magical ankh necklace slid off the tip of the Re'em's horn, and the artist picked it up. The artist discovered he could draw in the air with the ankh and leave permanent marks, which was unheard of in chaos, after all, chaos is ever-changing. Soon the artist created a master design that became known as the *Motif*. The lords of chaos were furious at the artist for creating something unchanging, but it was too late. The artist escaped into the echoes produced by the interaction of the *Motif* with chaos. The rest of the story is a little grey, but somehow the artist mated with the Re'em and brought forth a child, which was the first king of Splendor. Henceforth, all Splendorites carry the blood of the Re'em in some degree or another,"

I said, thinking I needed a drink.

"You're the offspring of a Re'em?" Jorrie scoffed.

"I am actually the farthest removed, in the bloodline, of all Splendorites to successfully engage the *Motif*. My grandfather's grandfather was the artist who extruded the *Motif*," I remarked.

"Maybe that is why you are different? I mean, in regards to your belief that echo creatures are discovered and not created," Erin said.

"Do you have any booze, Jorrie? I'm thinking of having a drink?" I asked.

"Sure, at that news, I think I need one, too," Jorrie said, and we headed over to a console between the two oversized viewports.

"Maybe that's why you fuck like a stallion," Erin said as she slapped my ass, following us over to the console.

Jorrie rummaged around in the lower cabinet setting a few bottles on top and saying, "I'm afraid this is all I have right now."

"Ooh, blue. Adnexian brandy. I think I'll try a little of that," I said.

Jorrie put three glasses on top and asked Erin, "Do you want to try some of that sweet wine from the other night?"

"Sure, I liked that. It tasted like flowers," she replied.

I poured a taster of the Adnexo brandy, and Jorrie poured her and Erin half cups before returning to the couch.

"Jorrie, I don't know if Erin told you, but I made her a Squire of *Tiger Mountain*. We also replaced the micro machines in her blood with echo sturdy versions, so their normal operations will not be affected if she finds herself relocated to a distant echo," I said.

"Yes, she did tell me, and I was a little concerned that you experimented on her," Jorrie said.

"There was a ninety-eight point seven percent match predicted," Erin said.

"It worked twice, in my future memories. But, I was concerned too," I said.

Jorrie sipped her wine, and I went on, "I was torn over it, but I thought it was the lesser of two evils. Now that Erin knows me, she may become a target of my enemies. If they were to abduct her and transfer her through echo, she might get sick and possibly die. With the transfusion, she at least won't be immediately disabled by the transfer if it ever occurs."

"I get it, Sam. It seems a little cavalier to experiment so quickly," Jorrie said.

"It was not cavalier. There were months of research by some of the smartest medical personnel I have ever met. I guess I am leading up to the fact that you are now in the same boat as her. There is a possible side effect for Vosips if you travel to certain echoes. And as we are getting to know each other better, you may become a target of my enemies," I said, taking a sip of the Adnexian brandy.

"What kind of side effect?" Jorrie asked.

"It's not as drastic as Erin's, but a slight chemical imbalance can occur between the host and the Limax resulting in uncontrolled laughter," I tried to say with a straight face.

Erin smiled and asked, "What, she just giggles?"

"You're joking, right?" Jorrie asked.

"No," I said, looking her directly in the eye.

"So, did you find a cure?" Jorrie asked.

"I haven't tried. It required scanning you while under the influence. It would mean we all would need to take a trip through echo," I said.

"Yes, let's do it, lover," Erin said to Jorrie.

"I don't know," Jorrie said a little sheepishly.

"In my future memories, after we discovered the anomaly, we invited Brent Stevens along to monitor your condition. He was the one who discovered the imbalance and developed a regimen to correct it. Do you trust him enough to see you in a giggly state?" I asked.

"I do. I'll have to think about it, all right?" Jorrie asked.

"Of course. Your condition is less severe than Erin's, but I would like to offer you the same title I gave her, Squire of *Tiger Mountain*," I said.

"What does that do to me, Sam?" Jorrie asked.

"It does not do anything to you. It just lets you communicate with the same voice-activated computer that Sam uses," Erin told her.

"How does it work?" Jorrie asked.

"A dedicated cloaked scanner follows you around all the time and processes your request," I said.

"You were already doing that anyway, weren't you?" Jorrie asked.

"Yes, once Valentino attacked me, I feared for your safety and used one to follow you around without your consent. That is how I was notified the *Contender* was under attack," I said.

"I guess if you are following me around anyway, I might as well have the benefit of making requests when I need them," Jorrie concluded.

"Great, Ohm, recognize Jorrie Tusk for Squire level access to all *Tiger Mountain* offerings."

"Welcome to the *Tiger Mountain* Squire program, Jorrie. I am Ohm. If there is anything you need, don't hesitate to ask," Ohm said in the low pressurized air modulation voice targeted near Jorrie's ear.

Jorrie smiled and said, "I hear a voice. That's the voice of your computer interface, isn't it?" Jorrie asked.

"Yes, and I can hear it too," Erin said.

I headed back over to the console and poured another half glass of Adnexian brandy. I wanted to smoke some weed too, but I didn't feel right just lighting up inside Jorrie's home.

"What can I do with this access?" Jorrie asked as I returned to the couch and took a seat.

"The permissions are managed automatically, so you can't do anything that will damage the system. There is an introduction to *Tiger Mountain* that takes the form of an aurastage presentation. But basically, you use verbal commands prefixed by the word 'Ohm,' which is the name of the computer processing the requests," I said.

Erin jumped in and said, "You can get clothing, food, credits, medicine, booze, transport between planets...what else Sam?"

"You can conduct research and construct virtual displays, replicate designs and send messages," I added.

"Ohm, what is the current temperature in the city of Prelond on the planet Vosip?" Jorrie asked.

"The temperature is thirteen degrees Celsius in the city of Prelond on the planet Vosip," Ohm replied.

"You can alter the units reported," I said.

Jorrie asked, "So, how does the credit system work? Where does the money come from?"

"In this echo, I have the credit cards hooked up to my personal account holdings. I own various business and mining operations that generate income. So, it's not illegal. You could replicate strips of diamond-stamped quaybit, but then you're dealing with a more grey area. The quaybit is real, but it might not be registered with the financial institutions," I replied.

"But Lepton may never know, hmmm," Jorrie said with a smile.

We talked through the remainder of the evening, and it came time to go to sleep. Jorrie used her *Tiger Mountain* access to replace her standard bed with a triple-wide version, which I was happy to see. We all ended up fooling around before falling asleep, and we made love again. I took the outside position on the bed, and so did Jorrie, with Erin in between us. I awoke in the middle of the night and headed into the bathroom to relieve myself. I was just about to return to the bed when all of a sudden, I was transported out of Jorrie's quarters.

This transporter worked differently than mine, the dissolve phase was different. I was placed into the darkness and waited. It took much longer than my transport system. I was finally materialized naked in the back of a metal room with Bragorian guards on either side. In walked Kop Lacroth, with the most devious of smiles.

I felt the ship jump to flux, and before Lacroth could speak, I shouted, "Ohm, knock them all out!"

Lacroth was in the process of raising his hand as his knees gave out under him, and he dropped to the floor along with the other two guards in this room.

"Ohm, use cloaked scanners to locate and transport all personnel aboard this ship to the Eden prison world. Transport them naked and give them each a dagger and a canteen of water," I said.

"Scanning the ship and relocating personnel," Ohm replied.

"Ohm, can you transport me back to the bathroom in Jorrie's quarters."

I watched the grey metallic walls turn into flecks and zoom in from the side, conveying myself into darkness once more. What an asshole. Lacroth represented the exact reason why the no means no monument needs to exist. It's like the Bragorian military sees, hears, and reads but then ignores all input and just does whatever they want. The walls of the dimly lit bathroom expanded, and I was back on *Oasis Seven*. I crept into the bedroom and crawled into bed, pulling some of the blankets over me before drifting off to sleep next to my two new friends.

CHAPTER 56

Eli Finch

∽

I awoke in Jorrie's bedroom, laying next to Erin, but Jorrie was gone, probably reporting to her next duty shift. Erin stirred and woke up at the same time. We snuggled for a few minutes in bed, having a good morning hug before getting up. Erin headed off to the bathroom, and I got up and got dressed.

I made my way into the living area of Jorrie's quarters and took in the view of space through one of the large portals. I could see some small ship traffic and observed the docking of a larger starship taking place. I found it odd living aboard a space station or starship. Even when the lighting was controlled and used to emulate day and night cycles, my body never really seemed convinced. I was left in a perpetual twilight, which I was experiencing at this time.

Erin came up from behind and asked, "What is the plan for today?"

She chose a more casual outfit, compared to the black dress she wore last night. I could see no jewelry in her outfit of dark pants, boots, and a light maroon jacket over a cream-colored top. While fussing with her still wet hair, I said, "I was thinking of heading down to the villa on Vasco. I know the tentacle attack happened there, but I like that place too much to let one incident ruin it for me."

"I'm okay with revisiting it. I did like that world when we arrived. I have learned a little more about it from Jorrie and her friend Mia, who is actually from that planet," Erin said.

"Great, do you have everything you need here? Maybe we should clean up a bit," I suggested.

"Yeah, I think that might be a good idea," Erin agreed, and she headed into the bedroom to make the bed.

I tended to the liquor console and moved the booze bottles from the top back to the bottom storage area.

"Ohm, can you give me a variety of Earth booze that I like and a couple of bottles of red wine?" I asked.

A few sparkles appeared on the floor, and I placed the new selection of booze into the console. There was bourbon, scotch, tequila, and a few cordials for mixing as well as a couple of bottles of red wine. I figured if I was going to spend some time here, I might as well have some of the things I liked in her apartment. Heading over to the couch, I noticed our glasses from last night on the table. I wanted to target them and recycle them. I started to miss my invisi-hud.

"Ohm, can you recycle the glasses on the table and then replicate new replacements for them? Place the new glasses inside the liquor console?" I asked.

The glasses sparkled and disappeared. I looked around the room and saw a few other areas that could probably use straightening up, but they were like that when I arrived, so I walked over to the table with the plant on it. Erin emerged from the bedroom and said, "I'm ready if you are."

There was a sound from the main door area, I assumed it was a doorbell, but I was not sure. Erin and I both looked at each other and started walking over. I touched her on the shoulder, indicating she should wait for a moment, and I asked, "Ohm, who is on the other side of this door?"

"Eli Finch is on the other side of the door," Ohm replied.

"Who is Eli Finch?" Erin asked.

I approached the door and fussed with the buttons, trying to get it to open. Eventually, Erin walked over and located the button that immediately opened the door. The doors slid open from the center, revealing Eli Finch standing before us. Eli was one of the humans from the Mist Door probability. The MD-Alpha team met him on one of their missions, and he ended up living on base with them after helping their cause.

"Hell,o Eli, please come in. This is my friend, Erin," I said, introducing the two.

"Hello, nice to meet you," he said, stepping inside the foyer with the doors closing behind him. "I hope it's all right to stop by? I wanted to thank you, Sam, for inviting me into the Squire program for *Tiger Mountain*. David gave me the ring."

"Oh, great. Is it making sense to you?" I asked.

"Oh yes, it is amazing. I have spent several days on *Tiger Mountain* reviewing the massive amount of resources you have available there. It's all so staggering, the functionality you have developed."

"I'm a Squire too," Erin said while offering her hand to Eli, "but I did not get a ring."

"The rings are new," I said. "I developed them after I lost my invisihud. They are basically a wearable cloaked scanner."

"Are there other Squires in the program?" Eli asked.

"A total of five, with you two included. The others are Jorrie, K-Mack, and Byrone. They were all at the party. You might have met them," I replied.

"Oh, yes, I remember all of them," he said.

"Listen, we were about to head to the planet's surface. I have a small villa down there. You are welcome to join us if you would like?" I asked.

"Most definitely, if I'm not intruding," he replied, glancing at Erin.

"You're not. It should be fun," Erin said.

"Ohm, transport us all to the back yard of the villa on Vasco," I said.

The dimly lit foyer area collapsed inward, returning me to the place of darkness. After experiencing the Bragorian transport system, I was happy to hang out in my own dark closet again. It pleased me that Eli seemed to be doing more than shopping with his Squireship. I thought I heard the chirps of birds and the smell of blossoms in the air as bright blue streaks crept in from the side, zooming the scene together before materializing us in the back yard of the villa on Vasco.

"Wow, this place is beautiful," Eli said, walking around the backyard and examining the blossoms on one of the small flowering trees growing up next to the high wall.

"It is nice to breathe fresh air. I know the air on *Oasis Seven* is filtered and acceptable, but there is just something in planetary atmospheres that can't be duplicated in a controlled environment," Erin said.

"I agree," I said, touching my ring to bring up the glowing orange sphere.

I tapped and unrolled the sphere, locating the scan and review icon along the left side menu. I targeted the interior of the house, and it came up clean.

Eli asked, "Are you looking for something?"

"Just looking. The last time Erin and I were here, an evil magician from another dimension attacked us, so the place holds a little bit of anxiety for me. I want to double-check that everything seems all right before I step inside," I told him.

"Wow, an evil magician. That does not sound good," Eli stated the obvious.

"Yeah, it happened the very first morning I spent with Sam. That was a hell of an initiation," Erin said.

"That's for sure, which is why I am double-checking the house," I said. "Eli, you might as well know this now. There can be a downside to being a Squire, such as what Erin experienced. I do have enemies that can travel between probabilities. Some of them are not nice and are even downright murderous. I don't know if David mentioned that when he presented the ring to you?"

"David did not go into specifics, but he mentioned that it carries responsibilities as well as benefits. That is not new to me. Traveling through the Mist Door has similar consequences. I reviewed a lot of the history available at my permission level while on *Tiger Mountain*. I am familiar with your family member's names and the family tree. I have memorized their faces."

"That's good to know. If you see them, it's best to retreat and report, okay?" I asked.

"Sounds like something Jim might say to me," Eli replied.

"Reporting helps the team. With *Tiger Mountain*, it is often easier to deal with a bad situation remotely than in the thick of a battle or a combat situation," I added.

"What do you mean by memorize them?" Erin asked.

"It's one of my gifts, I guess. I have a photographic memory. I think that is what Robin called it," Eli replied.

"It's easier to walk away now than later. I just wanted you to know that. If you ever become identified as one of my companions by one of my enemies, they may target you, instead of me. After they know who you are, walking away won't be that easy," I explained.

"All the more reason to want to stay in the program. At least if I am a Squire, I will have resources available to help defend myself," Eli replied.

"That's the way I look at it too," Erin said, "besides, I'm in love with this guy, and I couldn't leave him if I tried."

I dismissed the display and said, "It looks clear. Let's head inside."

Ohm restored the villa after the destruction, so it was not an unexpected mess. Everything looked normal as we walked through the back door.

"Everything is repaired," Erin remarked as she looked around.

"Yes, any structure that I designate as 'home,' Ohm will attempt to maintain and repair if any damage is detected. As a Squire, you can invoke the same maintenance or cleanup plan for your designated homes," I replied.

"This is a nice place. It has a practical feel to the layout," Eli said as he looked out the windows running along one side of the breakfast nook.

I headed into the music room and located a silver box holding a few joints.

Erin followed me in and said, "Oh, now I see why you wanted to come down to the surface."

"Why? What is it?" Eli asked as he entered the room.

"Just so you know, I am an alcoholic and a drug addict. I like to smoke weed, and I have not been high in a few days. Would either of you care to join me?" I asked them both.

"I just got up, baby. That will just put me to sleep," Erin said.

"I did enjoy it at the party," Eli said, "but I think I want to keep my wits around me while visiting an alien world for the first time."

"I understand," I said to Eli.

"It's comically called, 'Wake and Bake,'" I said before turning to Erin and lighting up the joint.

I tapped the ring on my finger to bring up the auragraphic display and located the music section. I put together a short playlist with the first four songs from the band named Goats. I played a song called "Wake and Bake" and started to sing along.

"I'm gonna look around outside. Do you want to join me, Eli?" Erin asked.

"Sure," he replied, and they headed out of the music den, leaving me alone with my drug problem.

I didn't find it to be a problem at all. I wondered why I hung around with so many non-music-loving squares to begin with? I guess that is one redeeming quality about the boys from upstairs. They didn't have any problem spending a morning or an afternoon getting high and listening to music. I only smoked a small portion of the joint before I was high enough to put it out and place it in my joint pocket. With those two out of the room, I turned the music up louder and sang along with the parts of the song I could remember. It really did make me happy to listen to music while I was high, but I guess I was being a bit anti-social.

I eventually jumped on the drum kit and played for about forty minutes. It felt good to finally get some practice in. I had not played in a while. A lot of the times when I worked with Frogs or the other boys, there ended up being a lot more talking and explaining rather than continuous playing from song to song. This left me with a runner's high on top of a weed high, and I decided to take a break.

I used the ring to bring up the auragraphic display to locate Eli and Erin. They took a walk down the street past Aberithes'. There was a park, at the bottom of the hill. That was the spot where Erin and I transported in, the first time we visited Vasco. It looked like they were hanging out there.

"Ohm, I would like to start a vegetable garden on Zenith. I want to grow tomatoes, a few varieties, the large heirloom, the smaller round style, and the more oblong Roma versions. I want some hot peppers, bell peppers, and tomatillos. For herbs let's plant some basil, cilantro, peppermint, spearmint, and parsley. I would also like some spinach, cabbage, broccoli, and lettuce. If you could add a card to my weekly report that contains the availability of each vegetable, that would be nice."

"What size would you like the garden to be?" Ohm asked.

"Not too large. How about a quarter of a kilometer. Spread out the plants as you see fit and place them in raised beds with a walkway through the garden for easy harvesting," I replied.

"Commencing garden construction, look for updates about production availability in your weekly report. I'll mark the card green, so it stands out," Ohm said.

"That sounds great. Can you transfer the wands recovered from the Enki's Dale magician's attack to this location?" I asked.

A series of sparkles appeared as wands materialized on the table where the silver box sat. A few began to roll to the edges, and I stopped them from falling off. There were thirty-seven wands on the table, made of various woods with varying magical inlays.

I picked up one of the traditional-looking wands and pointed it at the stack, saying, "*Exilium.*"

The stack jumped, and a few of the wands flew off the table. I gathered them up and started reviewing them. About half of them were too crooked and bent to fit in my pockets, so I set them aside. There was one with the wildest inlay I ever saw embedded in a wand. It zig-zagged down the wands' length, hinting at some lightning bolt dagger design. I set it aside. I began my stick rolling test and narrowed it down to six extremely straight candidates with reasonable inlays. I chose one because it was made of dark rosewood and placed it in the zippered pocket along my pants leg. The other one I chose was a blonde oak wand with a series of lotus flowers and ivy for the band wrapping around it. I tried it out by flicking the wand and saying, "*Meridiem.*"

The wand worked, producing a small glowing light that I dismissed. I placed that wand in the zippered pocket along the sleeve of my right arm. I guess I was a lefty as far as magic was concerned. I had to remember and ask Madison about that the next time I see her?

"Ohm, place these remaining wands in the vault. I would also like to release the captured magicians. Scatter them across the equatorial region of the Eden prison world. Place them there naked with a canteen and a combat dagger. Let's call that the typical deployment from now on," I said.

"Releasing magician prisoners using the typical deployment and returning the wands to the vault," Ohm replied while a series of sparkles danced across the table, removing the wands from this location.

I headed out of the room and left the house using the front door, taking the sidewalk down to the street leading to the park. It was a nice day, and I soon reached the bottom of the hill where a large embossed relief stood. Across from it, there was a natural green space which was the park where I previously located Erin and Eli. I saw them off in the distance, slowly walking and talking together. It looked like Eli picked apart some stick and idly tossed parts of it to the ground.

"Greetings, friends," I said from behind as I approached.

They stopped and turned around with Erin asking, "Are you finally done destroying brain cells?"

"I guess, for the time being," I said.

"What do you want to do now?" Erin asked.

"I don't know. I did not have anything else in mind after getting high," I said with a smile.

"Well, I'm starving, and so is Eli. Can we get some food somewhere?" Erin asked.

"Sure, but I think I have had my fill of Vascon food for a while. Do you want to have a picnic brunch here in the park? If we head to a restaurant, we will have to wait for the food to be prepared," I said.

"Okay, what do you think, Eli?" Erin asked.

"That's fine with me," Eli replied.

We were under some trees, and I noticed a clearing at the bottom of the hill and said, "Let's set up down in that clearing."

We all walked down to the clearing, and I said, "To be fair, I think we should each request some of our favorite food, you know, to get to know each other better."

"I like that idea," Eli said.

"Me too, otherwise, we might be stuck eating popcorn and doughnuts if Sam picks," Erin ribbed.

We reached the clearing, and I said, "Ohm, can you replicate a standard picnic table in this clearing? Make it out of waterproof material and place a red and white table cloth over the top."

After the picnic table appeared, I gestured for everyone to sit down. Eli sat across the table from Erin and me.

Erin said, "I'll go first. Ohm, we are sharing food. Can I get some of that chicken curry salad I ate with Candy? The one with celery, apples, and walnuts? Also a fresh garden salad with raspberry dressing."

"Ohm, I would like some fried chicken strips with dipping sauce," Eli requested.

"Ohm, I would like four strombolis, two meat, two spinach, along with six bottles of soda, two ginger ale, two root beer, and two orange pop. Oh, and also some napkins, plates, and cups for us all," I said.

The table came alive with multiple sparkles appearing in front of us. It was so bright that I leaned back as did the others. After it all settled down, a small food feast covered the table. We each got to work opening up the packages as I handed out plates, opened up the soda, and started pouring us drinks. I cut the strombolis in half and then half again to make sampler size pieces to share. We all tried a little food from each other's request, and we all agreed that the salad with the raspberry dressing was a hit. Overall, we liked each other's food choices. After eating, I lit up the joint again, and Erin said, "What the heck," before she took a hit. Eli tasted it, with a much smaller cough, this time.

"Smoking after eating is one of the joys of life, and getting high in a park is just ideal," I said.

"Will you listen to those birds," Erin said.

"I don't know if it is just me or what, but does it seem like the green on this planet is greener than the green of Earth?" Eli asked.

We all burst out laughing, and I said, "I think you're right. The green here is greener."

Nature eventually called, and we headed back to the villa to use the facilities. I recycled the leftover food items but kept the table cloth. I shook it out, folded it up, took it back to the villa to place it in one of the drawers in the kitchen.

Eli returned from freshening up and said, "I think I am going to head back to *Tiger Mountain*. After getting high, I have some more ideas I want to explore. Is there anything in particular that you think I should focus on?" he asked me.

"One thing that is always useful is medical training. Get familiar with the devices available in the Starnet medical kit. There is no worse feeling than seeing a friend hurt and being paralyzed at the moment, not knowing what to do to help them," I replied.

"Thank you. I will look into learning more about those devices. And thank you again for this opportunity," Eli said.

"Nice meeting you, Eli. As a fellow Squire, I'm sure we will meet again," Erin said.

"Likewise. Ohm, transport me back to *Tiger Mountain*," Eli said, and he disappeared in a sparkle.

"I like him," Erin said, turning to me. "He has a good quality about him."

"Yes, I have to agree," I said.

"Now that we're alone and high, can I interest you in some naked time?" Erin asked.

"Oh my, how forward," I said, picking her up and carrying her up the stairs.

"Yeah, forward and backward," she said, kissing me while hanging on with her arms around my shoulders.

I plopped her down on the bed and proceeded to remove my clothes. She did the same, and soon we made one another feel good again, wrapped in each other's arms.

CHAPTER 57

Getting To Know You

~❧~

Our next couple of weeks together were wonderful. I started feeling like I was finally getting to know Jorrie better. Erin was mostly to blame for this. She acted as the glue for the entire relationship keeping us on track and making sure we spent as much free time together as possible. Once Jorrie learned she could transport to *Tiger Mountain*, she and Erin spent more time there instead of on *Oasis Seven*. We still ended our days in Jorrie's quarters on *Oasis Seven*, which I took up residence, and occasionally spent the night in the villa on Vasco. In a way, this was as good as I remembered in my future memories. I knew there was a lot more time involved in finally reaching the state I sought when I first awoke in my bed on *Tiger Mountain* over a year ago.

I found myself alone more and more. I started to get lost in my thoughts and used the time that Jorrie and Erin spent on *Tiger Mountain*, reviewing cloaked scanner feeds and paying closer attention to what was going on with the Flexanite invasion and the Zitali slave trade. The Flexanite detection initiative produced nine more candidates, which were placed in the holding cell before being rotated out to Eden. There was no mention of or fallout from the Lacroth incident, so I didn't worry about that. My "No means No," monument was destroyed five times in two weeks, only to be rebuilt the next day. The Bragorians lost two more ships when they landed them on the park grounds, and Ohm recycled fifty-three weapons from various Bragorian soldiers who entered the park on patrol. I remained concerned about the possibility of the evil magicians "*Exspiravit*ing" out of my prison world, but so far, none of them have managed to accomplish that, and the group that attacked Enki's Dale was still detected upon the surface of Eden. The only person I kept in contact with was Lucas. We established semi-daily conversations about all the above-mentioned items of concern, and I was grateful he showed an interest in them. I kept a low profile and was not approached by any security officers or noticed any official filings posted against me by the Bragorian or any government.

At the end of the second week, there was a mixer for the new cadets who began the Starnet Academy program, which Erin attended on her own. It was the first time Jorrie and I shared a moment together without Erin. I sat on the couch reviewing data, having a drink when Jorrie came home after her shift. She changed out of her uniform and came over to join me in an obviously bad mood.

"How was your day?" I reluctantly asked.

"Ugh, I don't want to talk about it, if that is okay?" she replied.

"Can I get you something?" I asked.

"Not now. I just want to lay back and forget everything," she said.

She lay back on the couch, and I took to massaging her feet which caused her to say, "Oh, thank you."

"I lost my cool today. I felt very unprofessional," she began as she started to talk about what she didn't want to talk about.

"I don't know what it is about Mercanites that infuriate me so much," she said, gesturing with her hands from her laid-back position.

"It's like they have to argue about everything. Every little detail is a fight," she said, continuing with her gestures.

"I completely lost it and told the little toad, and those were the words I actually used, that if he didn't like the process to go dock his little ship somewhere else," she exasperated.

I moved my massaging to her other foot, and she continued, "He'll probably file a report that will show up on my record," Jorrie fretted.

"Well, you do have a boyfriend who is a probability traveler. Do you want me to go rough him up a bit? You know, give him the ole one-two?" I asked.

"No, I appreciate the offer. You're nice," Jorrie said with a smile.

"That's what I like to see, my baby smiling," I said.

"That's what you call Erin. I think you're going to have to come up with a unique nickname for me. Otherwise, I'll just think you call all the women you meet, baby, after having your way with them," Jorrie said playfully.

"What about honey, darling or beloved? Do you like any of those?" I asked.

"I'm not really drawn toward any of those pet names," she replied.

"Oh, I know, my treasure," I said boldly.

"Definitely not. I am not your treasure," she said emphatically.

"Yes, you're my treasure," I said, quickly reaching up to her side and attempting to tickle her.

"No, stop it," she said, smiling while trying to squirm out of my grasp.

Her squirming stopped. I moved myself up to kiss her, and she met my lips, saying softly to me, "Oh, Sam, I don't know what this is, but it feels so good."

"So, what are we?" I asked, letting my mood slip a bit.

"I didn't mean it that way. I know what we are," she offered.

"What are we then?" I asked her seriously.

"It's complicated because we are many things to one another, but in the end, I think we are becoming family. What am I to you?" she asked, turning it around on me.

"You're my lover and my friend. You're the person that I am afraid of losing and afraid of asking to become more. I sense the becoming you mention, and I want to rush ahead, but I recognize there is wisdom in proceeding at a slower pace. I sometimes feel left out of the relationship when I see you and Erin enjoying each other so freely, and I'm not just talking about sex. I feel like I am on the outside sometimes, and then you both let me in, and I feel your overflowing love followed by shame at being jealous of your relationship with her," I dumped on her.

"I think you hit on some of the complications I could not put into words. I, too, have felt jealousy and shame when I see how you interact with Erin. Even the fact you have that nickname for her makes me feel less important sometimes. And I know it's not something you do intentionally," she said.

"You're not less important to me, Jorrie. You're just less available. Sometimes our window of opportunity together is only a couple of hours. It is hard to decompress in such a short span and become someone else when you know you have to reassemble yourself and report to duty in a short time," I replied.

"I get that, and I know what you mean about unwinding and then rewinding. I guess that is why I was open to having sex with you and Erin upfront. It's like presenting the final dish in a meal first because you know there is not enough time for any of the other courses. But when sex is all there is, the relationship can start to come up short. I feel like that is where we might be heading," she said.

"I love the way you give yourself to me and our time with Erin, but I still want to know you better. Even in my future memories, we needed to work at this and not get caught up in defeating ourselves because of the situations we currently find ourselves in," I said, trying to reposition myself on the couch to lay beside her.

She wrapped her arms around me and kissed me, saying, "I like giving myself to you. I feel your appreciation, too, in the way you give back to me. In my other Vosip lives, I sought this kind of relationship to have two lovers. I cheated on my wife when I was a man, and I cheated on my husband when I was a woman. In my previous life, I moved from relationship to relationship, enjoying the exciting beginning only to be lured away by the prospect of another fancy female catching my eye just to experience the start of a relationship again. Now that we have passed the exciting beginning, all that is left is everyday living, which I might not be that good at, Sam."

"I don't know if I can say anything that will make you want to stay with me. I do love you, Jorrie, and I love putting myself inside you to let you know. If my being here when you get home is cramping your style, please let me know. I don't want you to feel obligated to have to entertain me all the time," I said.

"I know a lot of it is me, Sam. I want both. That's the problem. I want you there when I want you and not there when I don't. And if you can't read my mind and know when I need you, I get mad or grumpy. I know that makes me sound like a terrible person, doesn't it?" she asked.

"Uh oh, I think you just gave yourself a nickname, grumpy," I joked.

"No, no," she said with a smile and started playfully shoving my shoulders, "You're not allowed to call me grumpy."

"Kiss me, beautiful," I said while looking into her eyes.

She leaned into me, and our mouths touched slowly. A short one at first, then another longer one as we touched and felt each other on the couch.

"This is how we did it, Jorrie, how I remember us doing it. We kept trying to understand one another and didn't give up. I know I got used to receiving your love. It was one of the driving forces making me seek you out when I awoke with my future memories. It was something as simple as this, us laying together, holding each other, kissing in each other's arms. I like this a lot," I said to her softly.

"Me too. I'm willing to keep kissing and having you in my bed. I think I have already passed the point of no return for living without love. I'm hooked on this relationship that you and Erin have presented to me. It is like juggling, however, and Erin and I have talked about it too. How do we keep this going and not drop the pieces or become consumed in jealousy, gravitating too far toward one individual?" Jorrie asked.

"I know what you mean. Do we always have to have sex as a group? The other day, Erin and I made love in the afternoon at the villa on Vasco," I said.

Jorrie interrupted angrily, "What? You fucked her, and I was not there?" before breaking into a smile.

"Yep, and hopefully, I can fuck you tonight without her being here," I said.

"That is pretty presumptuous of yourself, don't you think?" Jorrie asked.

"Oh, yeah, very much so, but I'm not sure if I can talk you to orgasm yet," I said with a smile.

"Oh, those words. Say them again, my love," Jorrie playfully stated.

"Sometimes I sense that you'd rather be somewhere else instead of waiting for Erin or me to return so you can make us dinner or listen to our day," Jorrie continued.

"If I were not involved with you two, I probably would be conducting my life a bit differently," I said.

"While I appreciate your attentiveness at times, other times, it can feel somewhat excessive," Jorrie replied.

"I know. I guess when I awoke with my future memories in my mind, I awoke still married to you both. And even though we are not married and may never be married, I still feel that strong commitment from those alternate time loops. I try to dial it back, but it still shapes how I interact with you both," I confessed, sitting up, breaking our cuddle pose.

"Tell me one thing you are considering doing, but holding back on?" Jorrie asked.

"On the night of the magician attack, in Enki's Dale, the magician that stunned Erin carried a vignette on him. I want to travel through the vignette and try to find out who he obtained it from," I told her.

"Why don't you?" Jorrie asked.

"A vignette is a clear sign that a Splendorite is involved in that attack, a direct attack on someone I love. The magician with the vignette, who carried out the attack, is more than likely a pawn of the true attacker. Because that pawn is dispensable, he could be a lure for a trap. And even if it is not a trap, I could be delayed from returning. How long will you wait for me? How long will Erin wait? Is it right for me to ask you to wait for my return, knowing it might be years or decades for you but only a week for me?" I said.

"Time differentials between probable realities. I was discussing that with Eli on *Tiger Mountain* the other day. Is that what you're worried about?" Jorrie asked.

"Partially. An unknown vignette has an unknown time differential. But more importantly, if I discover evidence within that probability, it may lead me to another probability with an even greater time differential. I could be gone for days, weeks, maybe even years," I said.

"This happened in one of your future memories, didn't it, Sam?" Jorrie asked.

"Not this particular vignette. The magician attack in Enki's Dale unfolded in a very different way," I said.

"But, you did experience a time differential, and it impacted our relationship, didn't it?" Jorrie pressed me.

I picked up my glass and finished the remainder of the drink before replying, "Yeah, it happened a couple of times."

"What was the differential?" she asked.

"It was three years for me for one of the episodes. I configured a shuttlecraft with the known time travel formulas, traveled backward in time, and managed to cut that down to seven months, experienced by you. When approaching a destination point in time, braking is still an issue," I said.

She stood up and paced for a moment, reminding me of Erin's habit when she was upset, then asked, "What about the other episode? What was that time differential like?"

I heaved a sigh and said, "I don't even want to say," I replied.

"How long?" Jorrie insisted.

"A long time for me, but I managed to reduce the differential to seventeen months for you. This episode happened after the first one, and you took an interest in refining the braking algorithms for the shuttle. I tried it several times, and seventeen months was as close as I could get," I said.

"Why won't you tell me the length of time you experienced?" Jorrie asked.

"I guess because it's something I would rather forget. The future memories don't just contain my love for you and Erin, they contain all the other things, sometimes terrible things that happened. It was a complex set of events leading to my delay in time. Fortunately, I see no evidence of those events in this time loop," I said.

"Not yet, you mean," Jorrie replied, heading over to the liquor console.

I followed her over to the console with my glass in hand and asked, "What do you want me to say?"

"What do I want you to say," she said, flipping her head around so her hair flew back, "I want you to tell me how long you were 'delayed' in time," pouring herself a small glass of the Adnexian brandy.

"All right," I said, pouring myself another half glass of scotch, "let's sit down, and I'll tell you."

"It happened in the first time loop. You and Erin and I were still together, but we had some relationship problems. We decided to try and spend some extended, uninterrupted time together by hanging out in Xanadu. If you don't know, the time differential between Splendor and Xanadu is eight to one. The time differential between here and Xanadu is approximately seven to one. Basically, we could spend a week together, and you two would only have to take a day off of work.

In that first time loop, I spent much more time keeping watch on Lexi and Valentino. Lexi's brother Hugo was more involved in that time loop, and Valentino was less of an issue. What I discovered by observing them was shocking. As Splendorites, there is only one law that we must obey the law put in place by the first king. It states that no Splendorite can have children with another Splendorite. No brothers impregnating sisters was allowed.

This was the shocking discovery I uncovered through my observation of Lexi and Hugo. Omer married several wives throughout his reign, so not all Splendorites have the same mother. Lexi and Hugo do, however. They mated and produced a demon-like offspring, a female child. This child grew up quickly in a fast echo and became a powerful witch in her own right. Her name was Helgamite. When I discovered this shocking news, I gathered up my evidence and presented it to King Osric. I thought surely, he would know what to do, but he simply accepted the evidence and did nothing. The law was clear, they must die for their crime, but he held no desire to issue a death proclamation upon his older siblings.

There was only one other sibling slain for going against the King's commandment, and that was Timason. He was born before all other known Splendorites, Omer's first son. I began to research as much as I could about Timason, but there was not a lot written about him or his crime. In the end, I sought out Nicolas, who is currently the oldest of the Splendorites. I managed to glean enough information out of him to conclude that Timason's crime was related to breeding. He was put to death for it.

"In an attempt to make our week together a little more exciting, I shifted us through echo. It was near enough to Xanadu to be in the same time differential but far enough away so we didn't feel like we were spending our time next to a hospital. Erin became unhappy with me and was fooling around with a Lama on Vasco. He exposed her to the Tempus Filament, which produced an unexpected result on her Melog physiology. She was transposed in time, by forty years, with her future self but hid that knowledge from you and me," I said.

Jorrie interrupted, asking, "Wouldn't we notice if Erin was forty years older?"

"You'd think so, but it looks like her Melog heritage grants her a life that might be longer than she expects," I replied.

"Fascinating," Jorrie said, "Do go on."

"We were hanging out in this nearby Xanadu probability, in a small cabin in the woods, when Erin broke the news to me that she was done with our relationship and wanted to move on. You had taken a shower and approached the couch we sat upon. While you were still drying your hair with a towel, the roof was ripped from the cabin. I was struck with a magical spell that instantly transported me away from the scene. It was Helgamite, and she brought with her two giants to rip the roof off of that tiny cabin.

"I found myself in the grip of a giant's hand, inside some cave. He flung me to the floor, and I hit hard. My invisihud was down, so there was no tech support. In the first time loop, I never bothered to investigate how to use a wand so I couldn't leverage magic. All that was left was a promise I made to the Re'em, taking the form of an available sword in times of need. This sword was once Grayson's blade. It was named Lazarus. What no one knew, myself included, was that Lazarus was not just a weapon, it was a promise to the Re'em to defend the *Motif*. In one of my adventures, I found myself confronting the Re'em, and it presented the sword to me, making me the new guardian of the *Motif*. From that point on, I could summon the sword in times of need.

"I brought forth the sword and eventually used it to slay Helgamite in that cavernous chamber. I ascended a stone pathway carved into the walls, trying to shift echo to escape, but it wasn't working. This limitation meant I was either near Splendor or in the Vectorless Vale. When you are near Splendor, the number of echoes is close to zero so there is no probability other than Splendor. When you are in the Vectorless Vale you experience something similar because there is no *Motif* to define echoes for you to shift into.

"I made my way to the top of the path and out of the cavern entrance to discover I was indeed in the Vectorless Vale, and my enemies approached on all sides. I had no vignettes to escape with, and I was already injured from the battle with Helgamite. I knew I could not fight them all off and hope to win. My only option was the *Vechnost*. I brought forth the tangle of twisting lines and leaped into them, disappearing from my enemies.

"While I escaped my current crisis, I did not know how to exit the *Vechnost*. I wandered for years inside the *Vechnost*, forgetting who I was, becoming more animal-like all the while. My physical form adapted to that environment as I hunted the ground prey for food. The only thing reminding me I was once human was the sword I carried at my side. My previous life with you and Erin seemed like some faraway fairy tale or a faded dream.

"Then, one day, I was hulking beside a large rock, stalking some prey in the hopes of obtaining a meal, when a glimmer of color flashed off the sword in my hand. It was novel and new to me, the concept of color. I didn't realize it, but the interior of the *Vechnost* drained the color from my perception, or was it that my eyes were changed? The *Vechnost* did that to you. It made you unsure if reality was real. Am I conscious, or is this some kind of a trick?

"I glanced in the direction of the reflection and noticed a break in one of the rock formations. There was a small crevice between two rocks that I forced my way through, dragging the sword behind me. The site presented was full of ever-changing colors. The illumination of the sky was not a gradient. It was a constantly unfolding fractal pattern. The clouds that hung in the sky and sometimes fell out of it were made up of evolving colorized gas as if churned by some Perlin noise. The ground was just as colorful and unsteady. The shape of the rocks was uncertain and changing. I looked at the scene through the mirage haze of a hot desert day, with the objects in the distance constantly morphing and changing shape. Wind freely blew the rocks around this wide-open plane. From the cracks in the ground emerged flying creatures that seemed to ride the wind, burst into flames, and rain down their ash upon the ground, which absorbed them only to emit more creatures at random intervals. Across the plane, I could see a set of rolling hills, which defied the constantly changing nature of the scene. I knew, in a second, that was my destination.

"Scrambling down the rocks I emerged from, I made my way on foot across that chaotic landscape. I doubled back a few times as obstacles appeared in my way, then I realized that the place was alive and trying to stop me from reaching my goal. I traveled more than halfway across the plain before coming to this conclusion, and the obstacles were becoming more frequent. In a desperately frustrated motion, I took the sword at my side and stabbed the ground fiercely with the intent to have my way cleared. The entire landscape reacted to my attack as if it never experienced such a thing. In the aftershock, obstacles retreated, and I took my moment of advantage to run as fast as I could to the unchanging hills. Behind me, the rolling rocks set off in pursuit. They frantically crashed into each other, reducing one another to smaller rubble and dust. The sky turned to flame, and soot rained down from above as the clouds dropped their smoldering gases upon me. I screamed as I burned, fending off some of the approaching stones with the sword, fracturing them with well-placed swings, sending pieces flying in all directions. I made one final dash and came to the base of the unchanging hills. Climbing as fast as I could, fewer and fewer stones tried to pursue me. I realized the clouds and the stones could go no further. They remained within that ever-changing colorful plane I left behind.

"Wandering through the mist, I came upon a shallow pool. I bent down to drink. When I saw my reflection, I burst into tears. During my time inside the *Vechnost*, I became a monster. I looked like one of those evil demon lords, the ones who lived and ruled in the Vectorless Vale. I was even more hideous than Lexi and Hugo's demon child. I raged in anger at what this unfair life did to me, what Helgamite did to me with a single transportation spell. I hated myself for not escaping the *Vechnost* sooner before such a drastic change occurred. In a fit of determination, I grabbed one of the horns growing out of my head and began sawing away at it with Lazarus in one hand while I held on to the horn with the other. I screamed in agony as I mutilated myself, blood spilling into the pool, removing my horrific reflection.

"I finally passed out from the pain, and when I awoke, Lazarus was gone. With one goal in mind, I started shifting myself through echo, trying to put as much distance between myself and the Vectorless Vale. As I shifted echo, I was able to completely discard my tail and hooves and greatly reduced the size of the horns protruding from my forehead.

"I headed for an echo where I placed an emergency cache of vignettes and medical supplies. In that time loop, I constructed a special time travel shuttle that I stored on the dark side of the moon of Splendor. This emergency cache provided a vignette to that moon base, and I proceeded to use the shuttle to return to the proper time frame, as close to the time after Helgamite's attack as possible. After several time travel attempts, I managed to narrow it down to seventeen months.

"Even though I looked more or less human, there were still slight bumps on my forehead that I was unable to get rid of. I still remember the look of shock on your face when you saw my revised form for the first time. I was trapped for one hundred and ninety-four years within the tentacles of the *Vechnost*," I said, putting my empty glass on the table, with tears welling up in my eyes.

"Oh, Sam," Jorrie said, "I'm sorry I made you drag those memories back up."

She put her arms around me and hugged me, saying softly, "I'm sorry. I'm sorry."

CHAPTER 58

Croftsarrow

It was the day of the initiation ceremony for Erin. We gathered across the bay at Starnet headquarters as the new cadets raised their hands and took their oaths. We held a small send-off party on the balcony of the San Francisco apartment before attending this final pledge leading to their departure. Erin seemed so happy to be in uniform again. I knew from the future memories there was something programmed into her, making her want to serve and obey.

In the first two time loops, I encouraged her and even helped her sign up for Starnet. In this loop, I did not and was quite disappointed when she gave me the news she signed up for Starnet on her own. It wasn't that being a member of Starnet was bad. There were a lot of good reasons to serve, but I was being selfish because I wanted her to myself. By pledging her loyalty to Starnet, she was committing herself to a life of service, which meant she would not be able to travel freely through echo with me. After spending so much effort in researching and developing her echo sturdy micro machines, it seemed like such a waste to have to hang out in the same probability all the time. I guess the same could be said for Jorrie. If I did not love them, I probably wouldn't have invested so much time and energy in this echo.

Alex, Candy, Lucas, Eli, Jorrie, and even Warren Turner attended the party and the swearing-in ceremony. After the departure, the crowd broke up, and we were all left standing around wondering what to do.

"I think it was nice," Jorrie said.

"Makes me realize how old I am getting, seeing those young people starting out," Warren said.

"I just know I'm gonna miss that girl. She kind of grows on you," Candy said.

"Well, it's only three weeks. After that, she'll have some local classes, and I'm sure she will be stopping by for breakfast before you know it," I said.

"Let's hope so. Oh, boo, what time is it?" Candy asked Alex.

"It's just past four-twenty," Alex replied.

"We've got to head down to the center then," Candy said.

"Ah, you're right. Lucas, are you still coming with us?" Alex asked.

"Yes, I am," Lucas said to Alex. "It was nice to see you again, Warren, but as Alex might say, we have to bounce."

"Nice to see you all, again," Warren replied before Lucas, Alex, and Candy disappeared in a large sparkle.

"We need to head back too, Sam. Stop by later, if you like," Jorrie said, leaning in to kiss me on the cheek.

"Ohm, transport Warren and myself to Warren's office aboard *Oasis Seven*," Jorrie said, and those two disappeared in a sparkle.

"I guess that just leaves us," Eli said.

"Indeed," I said, doing my best to imitate Malik

"That's pretty good," Eli said with a smile.

"What do you say to taking a trip into the unknown? It could be dangerous?" I asked.

Eli smiled and said, "I'm ready."

"Okay, but you have to stay close and try to do what I say," I said while pulling out the vignette I acquired from the evil magician that attacked Erin and me in Candy's kitchen.

"Got it, basic teamwork. I can handle that," Eli replied.

"This is a form of travel that is not transportation. It is the native mode of travel for Splendorites. The process is you hold the picture before you, pretend it is real, and it will become possible to step forward into the depicted scene," I instructed.

"I did review what vignettes were and how they work. At least as much information as available to a Squire on *Tiger Mountain*," Eli said.

"Ohm, replicate a shingle and link it to Eli's ring," I said.

I held out my hand, and a sparkle materialized the device, which I handed to Eli, who asked, 'What's this for?"

"The floating auragraphic displays are nice, but they are a bit conspicuous. This device acts as a smaller display that draws less attention. Take a look," I said as I handed it to him.

"I see. Basic target types are identified around us," Eli said, tapping and swiping on the screen.

"The case is made of stainless steel with a transparent aluminum screen surface, so it is pretty tough and water-resistant. Keep it in your pocket for now. Try to use it as your display rather than the auragraphic display on this mission," I said.

"Got it," Eli said before tucking it into his jacket's inner pocket.

"Great, then let's go," I said.

The vignette depicted a small town off in the distance. It did not look like a modern city. In the foreground, silhouettes of trees defined our arrival point. In the distance between the hill and the town, a bridge crossed a small river.

I held the vignette before me and concentrated on the scene until I felt it come to life. Touching Eli on the shoulder, I pulled him through as we stepped into the vignette. We arrived on the hillside amid a stand of trees. Returning the vignette to my pocket, I knelt as I pulled out my shingle.

"Check for targets," I asked Eli, and he pulled his shingle out and started messing around with it.

I pulled up the about icon, which was always at the top of the left-hand menu of Blinn-based interfaces. I checked the reported time differential and noticed it held steady at two point three.

"The first thing I typically check when I arrive at a new location, especially if it is a new echo, is the time differential. It's located at the top of the menu. It gives basic statistics about where you are and how *Tiger Mountain* relates to where you are. This place is running at two point three times Splendor time. The place we left is running at one point seven three times Splendor. Right now, we are aging faster than Candy, Alex, and Lucas," I explained to him as I showed him the display on my shingle.

"Good to know," he said, then showed me the display on his shingle reporting. "I don't see any immediate targets or enemies. There are various life forms reported, which I would expect in a forest environment like this."

"One of the nice features of the shingle over the ring is that you can set up a quick slot for activation. Let's go ahead and set up the cloaked shield in our quick slot," and I showed Eli how to locate and assign menu items to the quick slot.

"Now, you can just let Ohm know you want to activate the quick slot instead of having to bring up the display and locate the item each time you want to use it. You can set up several quick slots and request them verbally as needed," I said.

"I can see how that is very convenient," Eli replied.

We arrived in this echo near the end of the day, and I set off walking toward the town. Eli tucked his shingle away and followed along.

"I'm going to shift us into this probability a little bit more, don't be alarmed. I am mainly altering our clothes and adding a bedroll," I said as I brought up the *Motif* and adjusted our clothing to match the clothes typical in this echo.

"I added a short sword to each of our side belts, a small dagger, and a few gold coins to our pockets," I said, remarking. "It would be odd for grown men to walk around without some type of weapon in this echo."

"Wow, that is strange and convenient, so that is part of your probability abilities?" Eli asked.

"Yes. I have also adjusted the language so we should be able to hear and speak with them, however, we will sound and appear to them as foreigners. I have assumed the role of a cartographer many times. It is a convenient cover story and gives us a plausible reason for being in their territory. We are cartographers for the East Empire trading company, mapping new possible trade routes," I said.

"I see. I'll do my best not to stand out," Eli replied.

"Good, we will stand out anyway, but if anyone asks you about specifics, just refer to the lands across the sea and mention this is your first time traveling abroad for the company," I said.

The walk to the bridge took about twenty minutes, and we crossed without any trolls or tolls restricting our passage. Another twenty minutes along a dirt road led us to approach the gate of a walled hamlet. As we approached the hamlet, we passed a couple of travelers along the road, and they responded to simple hand waves and nods, passing us by without a word. Before making our final approach, I asked, "Ohm, can I get a leather canister with an overhead map of the area roughly inked in. Make the map out of paper and provide ink that might be common in this region. Place a quill and an inkwell in the tube."

A sparkle appeared, and I picked up the tube by the convenient strap before slinging it over my shoulder. I noticed the front gate of the city where two guards stood outside. There were at least two more visible guards up above, high on the wall. I walked up and asked one of them, "Could I trouble you for the name of this hamlet?"

The two guards, who stood in light leather armor with swords at their side, looked at each other, and one asked, "Who are you? And what business do you have in Croftsarrow?"

I spoke for us both, saying, "I am Michael, and this is my squire, Lancelot. We are cartographers from the East Empire trading company mapping out new trade routes. Did you say this hamlet is named Croftsarrow?"

"Never heard of your trading company, have you, Mokdale?" he replied, asking his companion for some type of confirmation.

"No, I have never heard of such a company," he replied to his friend.

I took the cap off the end of the leather canister and pulled out the map that I asked Ohm to create for this area. It was a bit more detailed than I needed, but all the major markers were there, the forest, the road, the bridge, and the walled city. I said to Eli, "Lancelot, bend over slightly. I need to borrow your back."

He looked over at me, then caught on to the ruse and bent his back slightly. I dumped out the quill and the ink from the tube and carefully opened the ink. After dipping the quill into the inkwell, I unrolled the map along Eli's back, writing the word "Croftsarrow" on the map over the portion of the city that Ohm provided.

The guards watched as this scene unfolded before them. I waved my hand over the newly drawn ink, blowing on it slightly to accelerate the drying process before removing it from Eli's back and saying, "Thank you, Lancelot. Can you hold this for a moment while the ink dries?"

Eli held the map before him, and I bent down to put the stopper back in the inkwell. I wiped the quill off at the cuff of my pants and said, "Can you roll that up for me, son?"

Eli blew on the map a bit before rolling up the scroll of paper and handing it back to me. I stuffed the map into the canister, dropped the inkwell in, and finally, the quill, closing the lid to the canister before slinging it over my shoulder.

"We seek trade agreements with shop owners. May we enter?" I asked the guard who spoke first.

He replied, "The gates are locked at sundown so no one can enter or leave during the night. If you enter now, you will have to seek lodging inside."

"Not a problem. Can you recommend an inn?" I asked.

"The Elder Orb Inn has fine rooms, and the Nasty Spider has more common accommodations," he said as he walked over to the large wooden gates and knocked a rhythm sequence out with a few short taps.

It took a few moments. We heard the sound of wood on wood sliding, and eventually, the door creaked open enough to let us pass into the interior of the walled hamlet. This one, like most hamlets, was no larger than twenty to thirty buildings, with the largest building being the church, of course. Once we passed through the gate, there was a large open area with a small marketplace. Because this was late in the day, only a few stalls were occupied.

We walked around the small hamlet, noticing a few shops. I pulled out the map several times to review where we were and to mark the names of the shops on the map.

"What are we looking for?" Eli asked.

"I don't know, just looking," I replied as we walked.

"Why is there a vignette to this location? It seems like an insignificant place to me," Eli said.

"I agree. Perhaps this hamlet was not the destination for the user of this vignette. It could be that there is some other secret location nearby, outside of the hamlet," I speculated.

After about an hour, we managed to survey the entire hamlet. The buildings were constructed of large cut wooden logs and stacked stones, with the majority of the upper wall made up of wattle and daub. It was quaint, with craftsmanship evident in some of the larger buildings. The population was small, with only a few people walking around, with most of them carrying some type of load. There was a larger house with guards that was probably the home of the vassal of this area. It was obvious to me we were being watched. I managed to catch a glimpse of a few people staring from the sides of the windows as we passed through the streets and updated our map.

The Nasty Spider was the most run-down-looking building in town. It probably was the place I needed to be if I wanted to uncover more about the evil magician underworld. I decided The Elder Orb offered a better base of operations. After all, I possessed cloaked scanners and could spy on the Nasty Spider from there.

Eli and I took the wide plank stairway up to the front entrance of The Elder Orb, which displayed a hand-painted carved wooden relief sign with the name of the establishment. There was a large glass globe hanging from the sign with an oil lamp inside waiting to be lit for the evening. The multi-faceted globe was made of leaded framing with panels of stained glass defining the outer surface. It seemed silly to knock at the door of an inn, so I opened it up and walked right in.

We entered a small foyer with a wooden counter and a doorway heading back into what looked like a common room. An older woman emerged from the doorway and took her place behind the counter, saying, "I am Gretchen. Welcome to The Elder Orb. Will you be spending the night?"

"Hello Gretchen, I am Michael, and this is my squire, Lancelot. If you have a vacancy, we would like a meal and a room with two beds for the evening," I replied.

She reached under the counter and pulled out a ledger, a quill, and an ink-well before flipping through the pages until she finally decided upon the correct one and asked, "Can you sign the ledger?"

"May I ask what the rate is? We are on a limited budget?" I asked.

She looked us up and down, trying to determine our wealth before finally stating, "Two royal draughts. That comes with a meal and breakfast. You can stay until midday tomorrow."

I glanced over at Eli, who shrugged and shook his head, yes, and I proceeded to sign the ledger. Turning the ledger around, I presented it to Gretchen, who looked at my sloppy writing and made a couple of marks next to my entry, presumably today's date, but I wasn't sure. I put two gold coins on the counter. She picked them up, eying them suspiciously, then placed one in her mouth and gave it a delicate chomp. She shook her head yes before placing the gold coins in her skirt pocket, saying, "Go ahead and take a seat in the common room. I'll have a meal brought out while we prepare your room."

"Thank you, Gretchen," I said, heading through the doorway.

"Thank you, Gretchen, Eli said, which produced a smile from Gretchen to Eli.

This space was indeed a common room with several tables and bench-style seating. At one end of the room was a large hearth with a small fire burning in it. Near the fire were a few stuffed leather chairs with a couple of smaller coffee tables in front of them. On the opposite end were a few commoners occupying the bench seating, which I assumed were staff, based upon their attire, but an older fellow sat in one of the leather chairs near the fire, smoking a pipe. I motioned to Eli that the leather chairs is where I wanted to sit, and we made our way over to a couple of unoccupied seats by the fire.

Eli said, "Hello," to the older smoking man as we both took our seats across from him, with him nodding in acknowledgment but not saying anything.

The room was large enough that I didn't feel like we were intruding upon him, but he could certainly observe our actions without any problem. I removed my traveling jacket and bedroll that appeared when I shifted echo on our approach to the city and placed the cylinder and bedroll beside the chair while draping my jacket over the back.

I walked over to the fire, warming my hands, saying, "Well, what do you think, my squire? After several days of sleeping on the ground, we find ourselves in a comfortable inn with a hot meal on its way."

"A favorable position indeed, my Lord. Excellent planning," Eli said, removing his gear and taking a seat in the chair before propping his feet on the nearby ottoman.

"My name is, Lancelot, and this is my lord, Michael," Eli said to the smoking man.

"Name's Delby. I own this inn. Gretchen is my daughter," Delby finally spoke.

"Thank you for letting us stay at your inn. It is very spacious and welcoming," Eli replied.

"Truly," I added, taking my seat, leaning back, and resting my eyes.

"All are welcome if they got the coin and don't make trouble," Delby replied.

"The name, The Elder Orb, is a bit unusual. How did it come about?" Eli asked.

"Oh, this place has always been called The Elder Orb. It's been in the family for several generations. I inherited this place from my father," Delby said.

The conversation was interrupted by the arrival of two young women carrying trays with food. One of them asked, "Would you like your food here or at one of the tables?"

I looked over at Eli, then at one of the young women, and said, "Let's eat over at the table. I don't want to make a mess here."

They headed over to the closest table and started taking items from the trays and placing them on the table before us while we took our seats on opposite sides of the long picnic-style table. There was not a lot of food, a bowl of stew, some bread, cheese, and a couple of sliced apples on a common plate for both of us to share. We each got a mug of ale too.

"Thank you, lass," I said to the young woman as she nodded and took her leave of us.

Eli looked at the food suspiciously, and I motioned to him to lean in, saying in a whisper, "Ohm routinely scans food to detect poisons. I am getting no warning, so this food is probably all right."

Leaning back, I picked up the mug of ale and said, "To the East Empire trading company," knocking cups with Eli and taking a drink.

Eli and I both looked at each other in agreement. This drink was probably some of the best tasting ale I ever encountered. It was a bit coarse, with small particles floating in it, but the flavor was delicious, and the foam was creamy.

"Your ale is delicious," Eli called across the room to Delby.

"Glad you like it," he called back.

The stew was nothing special. It was a bit gamy for my taste. I ate the vegetables and left the meat in the bowl. The bread was very coarse and dark with a hint of rye. The cheese and apples were pretty good, and we finished the plate off. Soon after we finished our meal, another young woman arrived to clear the dishes, asking us if we wanted more. I spoke for us both and said we had enough. A few more visitors arrived, a couple of them calling out to Delby, who barely acknowledged them as Eli and I made our way over to the leather chairs. Gretchen approached and said our room was ready and invited us to follow her upstairs.

We gathered up our gear and headed to the other end of the large common room to the staircase. We received a couple of sideways glances from the newly arrived patrons, but no one said anything to us. The stairway was wide enough for two people to walk abreast. We took the short rise to the landing then the wide staircase up to the second floor. Gretchen walked us down to the end of the hall, where she pulled out a large ring of skeleton keys from under her skirt. She located the one for our door and proceeded to unlock it.

She opened the door, walked inside the room, saying, "This is it. You can lock the door from the inside. If you need anything, you can find me or one of the young women downstairs."

She left and closed the door behind us, leaving Eli and me in the room. I locked the door and placed my gear on one of the beds as Eli did the same. Our room was a corner room, which was great. It allowed a good view of half of the hamlet.

"What now?" Eli asked.

I opened one of the windows and said, "Ohm, materialize a series of cloaked scanners in this room and have them leave via the open window. Map out the town and the interior of the buildings. As you proceed, create a paper version of the maps of the buildings and place them on the table in this room."

There was a series of sparkles as ten to twenty cloaked scanners appeared, faded from view, and exited through the open window.

"I guess we sit back and wait for a while," I said.

Eli kicked off his boots, stretched out on his bed, and got out his shingle, saying, "Sure, I can follow their progress on my shingle."

I got out my shingle and used it to transport in some more ale and a large apple pie.

"Care for some dessert?" I asked.

Eli smiled and said, "Yeah."

We sat around eating, drinking, and I eventually lit up a joint to get high.

"Aren't you concerned about being high if something starts to go down?" Eli asked.

"Just remember, there is nothing mission-critical here. This mission is only reconnaissance. If anything goes sideways, save yourself and transport back to the mountain. That's the plan," I said, handing the joint to Eli.

We smoked together and reviewed our shingles until the paper maps started appearing. Dusk fell into the early evening. We reviewed each of the twenty-four main buildings in the hamlet, including The Elder Orb inn where we were staying. It looked like there were small secret passages between each of the rooms in this inn, presumably so guests could be spied upon. I pointed at the map and then to the wall, and Eli raised his eyebrow a bit. It appeared there was an underground tunnel from the Nasty Spider running under the wall of the hamlet. It looked like the miscreants could travel in and out of the city whenever they liked, assuming they were associated with the Nasty Spider. But what was the most revealing was the map of the church basement. Buried in this basement were the honored dead. It appeared there was a secret passage down here descending farther than the cloaked scanner could initially probe.

I was both high and a little bit tipsy. I thought it might be the perfect time to inspect the basement of the church. Pulling up the local target menu on my shingle, sure enough, I discovered someone lurked behind the wall of our room. I showed Eli my shingle, then brought up a map to select a target. I issued a transport of the person lurking behind the wall to the bridge just outside of town. I figured even at a dead run, it would take at least ten to fifteen minutes to reach the gate.

I downed my beer, stood up, and steadied myself by putting my hand on the table before opening up another bottle and saying to Eli, "Are you ready to go muck around in a deep dark crypt?"

"Yeah, let me get my boots on," he said as he headed over to the bed, retrieving his footwear.

I tucked the remainder of the joint into my joint pocket and said, "Ohm, recover all cloaked scanners deployed tonight and recycle these maps."

Navigating the map of the hamlet on my shingle, I panned and zoomed around the display until I located the basement. I chose a corner behind the steps descending into the basement, hoping our sparkle transport would go undetected. I brought up the cloak and the shield icon, showing my shingle to Eli, and we activated them together, dropping out of each other's optical view. I issued the transport to the church basement, and our room inside The Elder Orb inn collapsed inward, leaving me in darkness.

I wasn't sure why, but I felt like I started to get the spins, but there was nothing to grab on to. I wanted to blow out with my breath, but I had no body. The spins intensified for a moment as I materialized in near darkness. The dizziness followed me, and I nearly fell over. Eli caught me, and I put my back against the wall to try and recover my sense of balance.

I held the shingle in one hand and the bottle of ale in another. I tucked my shingle into my inner shirt pocket. We waited and listened for a moment to see if our arrival signaled an alarm. Good thing, too. A minute later, we heard voices descending the stone staircase heading to our level. Eli gave me the universal "keep quiet" signal by placing a single finger up to his lips. I shook my head yes as we waited to see what would happen.

It was two men dressed in robes, and they spoke in a language that was not native to this echo, or I would have been able to understand them. Eli looked over at me with a questioning look, and I made the universal signal of "I don't understand" by moving my hand near my ear and shaking my head no. He acknowledged with a head nod, and we crept forward while kneeling, using the stone stairway the two descended as cover even though we were cloaked.

They stopped over at a wall near a sconce and briefly looked around the room before taking their next action. I took a swig of my ale and watched as one of the robed men twisted the wall sconce ninety degrees to the right, and the other man pushed on the wall revealing the revolving secret door. They walked through the revolving door as the wall section rotated one hundred and eighty degrees. When it locked into place, the sconce snapped back to its upright position, and I heard the faint sound of a latch flipping along with the twang of a spring inside the stone wall.

Eli and I stood and looked up the stairway to make sure no one else descended before heading over to the wall. We waited a couple of minutes before performing the same motions as the robed figures. I turned the sconce sideways while Eli pushed on the wall section. The wall gave way and started to spin. We walked through together and found ourselves inside a cavernous passage sloping downward. Eli finished pushing the revolving wall section back into its concealed position, and we heard the snap of the latch again. On this side of the secret door, however, there was no sconce but an obvious lever embedded inside the wall for opening it from this side.

"Ohm, auto-activate the quick slot to sleep all targets if things go wrong," I whispered.

"Quick slot set," Ohm replied, and I noticed Eli heard the reply too.

Creeping down a dark secret passageway, following presumably evil magicians, was probably not the smartest thing to do, but I took another swig of ale, and we proceeded down the passage until we hit a three-way fork. Eli reviewed his shingle the entire time and motioned us down one of the side passages as the walls took on a wet slimy seeping look with moss growing near the floor. The passage narrowed, so we could only walk single-file.

I took the lead while taking another swig from my bottle. I could hear the sound of water flowing ahead, and there was a glow at the end of this passage as it widened and split into a ramp heading down while the original path turned into a ledge overlooking a large cavern. I motioned for us to stay on the ledge so we could remain above the scene but still observe. The ledge was more than wide enough for Eli and me, and we took up a crouched position, taking in the scene.

A blue-white glow emanated from a large orb hanging inside a cage attached to the ceiling of the cave. The orb was softly raining small glowing specks from its bottom. The likeness of this orb to The Elder Orb Inn's sign was unmistakable. Below the orb was a circular pit silently collecting the points of light. Once the lights passed into the pit, a strong localized gravity pulled them rapidly downward, leaving streaks of light behind. Twenty robed figures stood around the pit. From their builds, I guessed they were all male, but I was not sure because their hoods covered their heads and faces. I pulled out my shingle and targeted the orb assembly at the top of the cave, placing it in a quick slot. Eli used his shingle to observe the area, but I didn't know what menu options he leveraged.

From behind us, a sparkle appeared and left Jorrie in its place. I whispered, "Ohm, cloak and shield, Jorrie."

Eli grabbed Jorrie by the hand, pulling her down as her cloak engaged. Because we were so close, she could see us. I gestured with my hand, still holding the bottle, indicating we might have been spotted. Several robed figures looked up at the ledge, but we retreated enough that I don't think they could see us. A few of the ones along the side took a serious interest and headed toward the ledge for further inspection.

At this time, Jorrie started laughing. At first, it was a giggle, then it was a chuckle, and finally, uncontrollable laughter as she bent over in obvious amusement at the situation but was unable to stop laughing. I knew the jig was up, so I tucked the shingle into my pocket and said, "Ohm, give me my loud voice."

I threw my ale bottle from the ledge as hard as I could. It shattered on the cavern floor below while I called out with my loud voice saying, "What the hell do you think you're doing?"

All the magicians looked up at the ledge, and I saw them reach into their robes. I called out, "Quickslot sleep," and the robed men started to fall over. I was not finished yet, and called out, "Quick slot orb," which caused an explosion at the top of the cavern damaging the brackets holding the orb in place over the pit. It crashed to the floor, cracking open, spilling its contents of glowing specks. Many of the specks fell immediately into the pit, which caused an enormous brightness as the pit accelerated them to who knows where? The remaining specks started dissolving the cavern floor, causing plumes of gas to be released upon contact.

"Ohm, discontinue large voice and transport a standard yield magnacite missile into the pit with a one-minute detonation delay. Transport us to Jorrie's quarters on *Oasis Seven*."

The brightness of the cavern raced inward from the sides of my vision, chased by a blackness leaving me nowhere. I thought I could still smell the odor of the released gas even though I had no nose. I hoped to learn a little more about what was going on in Croftsarrow, but I saw enough to realize that place may be acting as a hub for distributing magical attacks throughout echo. At least now, any agents with a return vignette to Croftsarrow were effectively stranded in that echo until their master returns to find out what went wrong. The soft grey-blue lights of *Oasis Seven* zoomed in from the side as all three of us materialized in Jorrie's quarters.

CHAPTER 59

Jorrie laughed, no longer able to stand, so I took a seat next to her on the floor. The past several hours of drinking and smoking left me feeling a bit wasted.

Eli asked, "Is she all right?"

"I don't know? Are you all right, honey?" I asked with a slur before bursting into laughter myself.

"Yes, yes, I am," Jorrie said, shaking her head, "I don't know what came over me. I just couldn't stop laughing."

"It's the side effect," I said.

"I thought you were joking about that," Jorrie replied, managing to regain some form of composure.

"What side effect?" Eli asked.

"Traveling through echo can cause a chemical imbalance to occur for the mingled Vosip," I said, slurring the syllable sip. "I was aware of it, but I have not researched what causes it exactly or how to limit the side effect."

"And the side effect is laughter?" Eli asked with a smile.

"It seems so. I'm sorry for crashing your mission. What were you investigating?" Jorrie asked after finally ridding herself of the giggles.

"Eli accompanied me to investigate where that mystery vignette led. It was the place we just left, Croftsarrow," I informed her.

"What did you learn?" Jorrie asked, standing up and offering me her hand.

"I'm not sure," Eli replied. "It seemed like a normal enough hamlet, but then there was this secret room under the church with an energy orb depositing something into a type of gravity well."

I recovered my footing and patted Jorrie on the shoulder, saying, "Yep, that sounds about right."

"How drunk are you?" Jorrie asked me.

"Oh, I don't know. There was the ale at the inn, then more ale in the room, and I was chugging it pretty fast as we explored the secret passage. And we also got really high," I said to her with my slurred speech and red glazed eyes.

"I liked your outburst, Sam, 'What the hell do you think you're doing?' It really caught their attention," Eli remarked.

"Yeah, fuck em'. They got what they deserved, attacking me and my woman while lurking in the dark," I slurred out while having a difficult time standing.

"Help me get him to the couch," Jorrie said to Eli.

"Where's my ale? I think I dropped it," I mumbled as those two maneuvered to plop me down on the couch.

"Ohm, can you materialize one Starnet medical kit on the table?" Jorrie asked.

Eli shook his head, yes, saying, "Good idea."

There was a sparkle that faded, leaving behind a standard Starnet medical kit. Jorrie opened it up, located the medical inspectrograph, and started moving it along my body, finally saying, "Damn, Sam, you are very drunk."

"How are you feeling, Eli?" Jorrie asked, returning the medical inspectrograph to the kit and retrieving the medjector.

"I'm okay. I noticed Sam drank a few more ales than me," Eli said.

"I'm hurt, Eli. As my squire, you are not supposed to point out my flaws. You are supposed to sing songs of my great deeds and make them sound more exciting than they really were," I replied, gesturing wide with my arms making it difficult for Jorrie to administer the hangover antidote.

"Sorry, my Lord. I will endeavor to take up an instrument so that I might celebrate your accomplishments in song," Eli replied, keeping up the spirit.

"Thank you, my squire," I said to Eli, then turned to Jorrie. "And thank you, my Lady, for tending to me."

"Oh, jeez. It should take effect soon, Sam," Jorrie replied.

"Did you get any useful readings while you were there?" Jorrie asked Eli.

"I'm not sure how useful they are," reaching into his pocket to fetch the shingle, "but I did manage to conduct a few scans."

"Can I review them?" Jorrie asked, and Eli handed his shingle to her.

Jorrie tapped around on the shingle and said, "It looks like the orb was emitting some type of precipitate before depositing it into a gravitized singularity. That is incredibly fascinating. These types of phenomena are rarely if ever encountered in space. Yet here it is in the basement of a church."

"Is the streaking simply extreme acceleration?" Eli asked.

"Perhaps, but there may be some temporal element at work, helping to produce the visual phenomena observed," Jorrie replied.

I felt the medjector antidote start to take effect, and I sat up on the couch, running my hands through my hair, saying, "Whew, I guess I had one too many."

"One?" Jorrie remarked with a disapproving look.

"I have seen them before," I said. "Magicians call them 'A Well of Souls.' It's typically a place of sacrifice, and the power extracted from them is proportional to the amount of magical understanding the smartest magician has."

"What type of power is extracted?" Jorrie asked.

"Most of the time, elemental. The magician might be able to infuse a weapon or armor with characteristics of the element, causing the user of the item to obtain an affinity for the element. Such as the classic flaming sword or lightning arrows. But some have been known to bring forth entire elemental beings to do their biddings for the construction of large projects or to use them as weapons against an enemy," I said.

"But we didn't see anything like that taking place," Eli said.

"No, something else was going on there. I would guess messaging or transportation, but we may never know because I blew it up," I said.

"Maybe not the best solution," Jorrie said with a frown.

"Whatever was good for them was probably bad for us. It produced at least one evil magician who attacked Erin and me, so I have no problem with shutting that down," I said.

"Sounds like something Jim would do, though," Eli said.

"More scans of the phenomena might have been useful, however," Jorrie added.

"If you want to explore echo looking for fascinating phenomena, we can do that, but we will have to address the Limax chemical imbalance to make that happen," I replied.

"We might have to make that happen. I think tonight may have stirred up a taste for adventure that I had not dreamed possible," Jorrie said, returning the medjector to the medkit and closing it up.

"That's the spirit. I like the sound of that. Ice cream cone mountains and chocolate rivers with sweet butterflies you can eat," I said with my fading drunken gusto.

"Let me get a scan of that. Egad, it looks like the life form's bloodstream is made up entirely of caramel sauce," Eli added playfully.

"Ha, ha, very funny. Maybe I should give you an anti-alcohol injection too," Jorrie threatened lightheartedly.

"That won't be necessary, just kidding," Eli said.

"So, what time is it here, Jorrie? The echo that Eli and I were in ran in an alternate time differential, compared to here?" I asked.

"It's just after my shift ended. I thought I might hear from you, but when I didn't, I wondered what you were up to, so I popped in," Jorrie said.

"That makes sense. We were aging faster than you in that echo," I said.

"Could that be what throws off the balance with the Limax?" Eli asked.

"Hmm, interesting hypothesis, perhaps there is a connection between the Limax and host that is temporal," Jorrie mused.

"Or, the Limax is still providing chemical regulation at the previous temporal rate, which causes the imbalance," I added.

"Another possibility. I guess we won't know until we conduct some controlled test," Jorrie replied.

"Well, do you think Brent might be up for some adventure this evening?" I asked Jorrie.

A clever smile crossed Jorrie's face as she said, "I'm up for it. Let's go find him and see if he wants to help."

"Are you okay to travel, my Lord?" Eli asked with a grin.

I stood up and felt much more balanced than before, replying, "I think I am."

Jorrie tapped her communications brooch and asked, "Computer, where is the location of Brent Stevens?"

A tinny reply came through the communications brooch, "Brent Stevens is in Lepton's, on the concourse."

"Let's head down there," Jorrie said with a smile.

Grabbing the medical kit, Eli and I followed Jorrie out of her quarters and down the hall. We took the lift down to the concourse level and made our way past shops until we saw the sign for Lepton's and went inside. Jorrie seemed to know her way around the place, leading us to the back of the first floor, where we found Ernie and Brent having a drink while playing a friendly game of darts.

In a gesture reminiscent of Alex's posing skill, Jorrie asked, "Brent, can I ask a big favor?"

"Hello, Sam," Brent said to me, then turned to Jorrie and replied, "I'm not sure I like where this is heading."

"I'm Ernie," Ernie offered his hand to Eli, who shook it, saying, "I'm Eli. Nice to meet you."

"It's probably best if we discuss it somewhere other than here. Can we head over to your office?" Jorrie asked, applying the pretty eyes routine fairly thick.

"I don't know, Jorrie. Ernie and I are in the middle of the all-time galactic championship dart-throwing contest. I'd have to forfeit the game," Brent complained as he took his turn and threw another set of darts.

"That's right, Commander. If Brent walks away, I become the all-time galactic champion dart thrower," Ernie beamed.

"I think I'm going to go get a drink," I said.

This remark drew a quick response from Jorrie, who said, "No, you're not."

"Of water, I'm getting a drink of water," I replied, finishing my sentence.

I headed over to the bar, and I could hear Jorrie trying to convince Brent while Ernie and Eli struck up a conversation now that the dart-throwing match was interrupted.

Lepton approached and said, "There you are. I saw you get punched in the face on the news. Are you okay?"

"Yeah, it hurt like hell, but I am better now. Can I get a glass of ice water?" I asked.

"Just water, not scotch?" Lepton asked, double-checking he heard me correctly.

"Yeah, water, please," I said.

"You know I tried your opening act suggestion with the Vascons, but it didn't work out as well as expected," Lepton said while handing me a tall glass of ice water.

"Entertainment is a finicky business. I have been working on a one-man show, practicing my instrument, but I have not had a chance to perform anywhere recently," I said.

"Well, if you are ever interested, Thursdays, at eight p.m. is available. Consider it an open stage," Lepton said.

"Thanks, I may take you up on that," I replied, and Lepton headed off to serve other patrons farther down the bar.

I felt a tap on my shoulder, and I turned around to see Brent, Ernie, and Eli standing there as Jorrie said, "The galactic championship dart-throwing contest is willing to accept a temporary time out if Ernie can join us on our expedition."

I took a large drink from the water, set the glass on the bar, and said, "That's fine with me. We should probably depart from some inconspicuous location, however."

"Let's use your office, Brent," Jorrie said.

"Very well, this way, but this delay better be worth it," Brent said, and we all filed out of Lepton's, heading across the concourse to Brent's office.

We walked into the waiting room for medical services. This room was the same place where I first met Brent. He led us through a door, past the frosted glass wall where the receptionist typically sat, but no one was on duty at this time. We passed a couple of technicians on duty in the medical services area, which is where most treatment takes place aboard *Oasis Seven*. Off to the right was a small room with a desk, Brent's private office. I was the last one to file in and located a button on the wall to close the door.

I placed the medical kit I carried on Brent's desk and asked Brent, "Can you use these tools to monitor Jorrie during this trip?"

Brent opened up the kit and took out the medical inspectrograph, and said, "Yes, I think I can. These are a little bit non-standard, but I think I can use them. What is so special about them?"

"They have been constructed out of materials designed to withstand the stresses of probability travel. Your tools may not function or function incorrectly if we took them where we are heading," I replied.

"Where are we heading?" Ernie asked.

"It is a probability that lies approximately halfway between Splendor, which is my home probability, and chaos, which is the absence of any probability," I said, which did not register too well based on Ernie's expression.

"Is this dangerous?" Ernie asked.

"This is as dangerous as a remote task to a planet you have never been to before. There is oxygen and gravity, but we may encounter other life forms. This place is a type of Mecca for magicians and other species that can naturally travel through probability. Rely on your Starnet training, and you'll do fine," I said.

"Magicians," Ernie said and then noticed our expressions and asked no more questions.

"Brent, can you take a detailed reference scan of Jorrie using the medical inspectrograph?" I asked.

We all shuffled around in the small room, so Jorrie stood in front of Brent, and he walked around her twice, moving the medical inspectrograph from head to toe, recording a baseline set of readings for later comparison.

"Got it. I have Jorrie's data saved in this device," Brent said.

"Eli, can you be responsible for Ernie while we are there? If anything goes wrong, bring him back here," I said.

"Will do," Eli replied.

"There is a two-step process to get there. Our first leg of the journey will be to the catwalk of my ship, the *Deceptive*. To do this, we must all hold hands," I said as I pulled out the vignettes from my pocket and located the catwalk vignette.

We all gathered in front of Brent's desk, holding hands as I looked into the vignette with the image of the catwalk. It shifted for a moment, and the concept that it was a destination became real. I tugged on the group and said, "Step forward, now," as I stepped into the vignette depositing us on the dark catwalk of the *Deceptive*.

"Now that's somethin' new," Ernie said as he looked around the *Deceptive*'s interior.

"This is incredible, Sam," Brent exclaimed as the group spread out on the catwalk.

"This way," I said and headed down the catwalk to the covered painting.

We all filed down to the end of the catwalk and gathered around the painting, where I said, "This is the second step of the journey. We arrived here by looking at the vignette. We will arrive at our final destination by stepping through the image that will appear on the canvas underneath this covering cloth."

"We're going to step through a painting?" Ernie asked.

"Yes, and because you are professionals, you are all aware of safety protocols within your given fields of study. Brent, you wouldn't hold uranium in your hand, would you? Ernie, you wouldn't attempt welding without protective eye gear, would you?

"The image that initially lies underneath this cloth is psychologically like uranium or blinding light. If you see it, nothing physical will happen to you, but you may experience nightmares, perhaps, for the rest of your life. I am just warning you, in case you decide to 'peek,'" I said.

"What about you, Sam?" Jorrie asked, "How can you look at it?"

"I can look at it because I created it," I said. "Please turn around, now, and I'll let you know when it is safe to look at the painting."

The group turned around, and I thought about the place I wanted to visit. I was there in my future memories, but also in my distant past. It was a place that I'm sure every Splendorite eventually visits. It goes by many names, but the one we always used was Equarius. It is the halfway point between Splendor and chaos. Because of its proximity, Equarius is a place of continuous massive energy exchanges. I thought about the ground, I thought about the sky, I thought about the atmospheric layers that lie in between, and I thought of the monuments. That was our destination, one of the observation decks of one of the monuments located in Equarius.

With all this in mind, I removed the cloth covering *Vision* and tossed it to the floor. A ghostly figure stood before me wearing robes that reminded me of the Croftsarrow magicians. This one pressed hard against the canvas with its red glowing ruby eyes. Its bony hands, extending from the robes made of swimming mealy worms, clawed at the canvas, ripping off its fingernails and breaking whatever tendon connections were left between the bone and dried paper skin as black fluid drained out of its gaping mouth. I forced my thoughts of Equarius onto the canvas and mentally pushed against the hovering shade as he was yanked quickly back into the distance, pulled by an invisble rope. The morbid scene faded away to be replaced by a shimmering light showcasing some of the features of the Equarian landscape.

"Okay, you can turn around," I said as I kept the painting focused.

Each one of my traveling companions uttered vocal awe at the scene depicted in the painting, but Ernie's statement stood out the most when he said, "It's a window into another world."

"I have to keep the window open with my mind, but we must all hold hands and step forward together. Brent, when we arrive, you will be tempted to take in the scenery. Please focus on the medical scanning device. The initial changes may be of the most importance," I said while holding the scene in my mind.

"Understood," Brent affirmed.

I felt Jorrie take my left hand and Eli take my right as I said, "On the count of three. One, two, three, step."

A rush of wind accompanied the step forward as we arrived on a white marble terrace with hints of Greco-Roman architecture. If ever there was a balcony for the gods in Olympus, this just might be it. The marble terrace was part of a large carved relief of a complex scene depicting a battle on one side and victory on the other. We arrived in this scene on the victorious, decorative rampart. This relief was embossed into the mountain by what one must imagine was the hand of an artisan giant or perhaps one of the elemental golems I mentioned to Jorrie earlier this evening when describing what a magician might summon from A Well of Souls.

My crew gasped in awe at the wondrous scene presented before their eyes. Even I couldn't help but admire the spectacle that was Equarius. Looking out from this raised balcony was a sharp drop off as we stood suspended on an outcrop on the side of a mountain. Looking across the wide valley revealed a great river flowing through a low flat plain. On either side of the plain rose mountains, that our embossed balcony was a part of. The mountains held various monuments carved into them. There were large statues of heroes, screaming faces, spiral towers, and magical symbols, all carved out of the stone making up the surrounding mountains. A collection of connecting bridges and stairways could be seen, offering possible exterior passages between the monuments. The river did not just wind through the flat landscape of the valley floor, it was guided and directed by large canals that formed a design with a circular shape forcing the river to exit at cardinal points. Along the valley floor, in large numbers, grazed the Zildacast, who looked like large shaggy dinosaurs feeding on the abundance of the Linowaith trees that were reminiscent of the Baobabs trees found in Madagascar.

Soaring through the air were magnificent Gryphons that seemed to rejoice in the air currents rising up from the valley floor, mounted by riders as often as not. Countless numbers of small black, red, and gold birds took flight around the Linowaith as the Zildacast disturbed them in the treetops while they grazed.

The birds rose into the air in great flocks, forming magical symbols for a moment only to be drawn back down to the treetops where they would settle until disturbed again. Floating upon the waters were ships of various sizes with the largest sporting golden or black sails with their figureheads ranging from the beautiful maiden to the foulest demon. Many of the ship designs were unconventional, and it was not surprising to see one take flight from or land in the water. The circular design offered a maze for the watercraft to negotiate with a pulsating energy plume rising into the sky from the center. The plume would shoot out in regular intervals, indicating a recharge needed to occur before emitting another discharge.

Gossamer strands hung in the air and gently drifted. They were so close to your face that you were sure that you breathed them in. They prevented you from seeing clearly, causing distortions along their edges as if looking through glass or water. High above the mountains and the target of the plume that ascended from the center of the canal river design was a free-form energy layer spanning kilometers. It occupied the area traditional clouds might have taken up if this were anywhere else. It luminesced through all the known colors and even presented colors that challenged one's imagination to produce a name. Emerging from and darting back into the energy layer were all manner of dragons and other winged fantasy creatures. They seemed to bask in the energy as a lizard might bask in the glow of the sun on a hot rock.

Between the energy layer and the valley floor was another visual oddity that could only be described as hovering magical writing. This writing was called the Symbacord. It hung in the air, constructed of symbols, many familiar like triangles, circles, and squares. There were glyphs from the zodiac and other magical texts. They were tightly woven into each other so a large shape might contain medium shapes and within the medium ones were even smaller glyphs. They formed an ever-changing brilliant design casting a shadow of themselves upon the creatures and the valley floor below, giving the impression that everything living on the valley floor was marked and branded by the Symbacord layer above.

The sound of the medical inspectrograph off to my left broke the suspended state of our arrival moment. The scene revealed was through a cubist vision as I watched Brent scan Jorrie through gossamer strands distorting my vision. I stared at Jorrie, who seemed to be in a state of suspended orgasm, watching her eyes jump around on her face, her mouth turning sideways for a moment, as my vision continued to be distorted by the atmospheric disturbances of this place. I looked over to my right and saw a similar portrait painted with Eli and Ernie. They each held different distorted features on their faces, sometimes the ear, other times the eyes, or an enlarged hand.

It seemed like our arrival did not go unnoticed. I could see a group of robed figures heading up the long marble staircase toward our balcony vantage point. They, too, were distorted and not just in their features, in their actions. They were far away, then closer than before, only to appear farther away again.

"Ohm, prepare to transport us back to sickbay on *Oasis Seven*," I said out loud.

"Standing by," I heard Ohm reply, which was a relief. I have not visited here in hundreds of years, and I couldn't remember how well my technology worked in this echo.

I heard Jorrie break into laughter. Glancing over, I saw her covered in visible sweat. The gossamer strands seemed to cling to her. I looked over to my right, and the approaching robed figures were closer than I imagined they would be, which probably meant they were closer than I thought.

"Ohm engage transport," I said, and the world collapsed inward, rolling with a cubist style, tricking me for a second before depositing me in the black void of the transporter. I realized, now, that this was probably a bit more dangerous than I remembered. The last time I did this, in my future memories, we arrived at a lower level along the steps. I don't remember the gossamer strands being present. Perhaps they were some form of weather that I missed the last time I was here, or maybe they were only present on this terrace where we arrived? Cool white lights zoomed inward forming the sickbay of *Oasis Seven* as we materialized. We all stood there for a moment, then dropped to our knees, drained by the experience.

CHAPTER 60

About Religion

S orry about that, everyone. I have never experienced those types of distortions when visiting Equarius before," I said to the group as two sickbay
technicians came to help us up.

"Are you all right?" one of the technicians asked Brent, who shook his head
yes as they helped him up.

The distortions of Equarius were quickly fading, and there seemed to be no
permanent damage as far as I could tell. But I wondered if any of these people
would ever follow me into echo again? I helped Jorrie regain her footing, and
Brent motioned for me to bring her over to one of the examination beds. She
seemed the slowest out of the group to recover, and I worried for a moment
until she reached out to me and spoke slowly, saying, "That was overwhelmingly beautiful, Sam."

"I don't know exactly what I saw, but it was breathtaking," Ernie added.

"How are you feeling, Jorrie?" Brent asked as he continued with the medical
inspectrograph.

"I have been to many worlds, but that place is definitely the wildest sight I
have ever seen," Eli said.

"I'm returning to normal," Jorrie said, looking at Brent with her lovely eyes,
offering him at least her gaze as some form of physical reciprocation for his
attentiveness.

Brent accepted her gift wistfully, then looked down and folded up the medical inspectrograph proclaiming, "I think she is all right."

"Doctor, what happened? Where did you arrive from?" one of the Vascon
medics asked Brent.

"A strange place indeed, Doctor Cresh. Thank you for your attendance, but
I think we are all right now. I'll fill you both in later," Brent replied, and the two
Vascon aids returned to some consoles along the wall to continue their work.

"Ohm, transfer the information stored in Brent Stevens' medical inspectrograph, to the Blinn research team," I said.

"Who are you talking to?" Ernie asked.

"It's a voice-activated computer," I replied.

"I like the name, Ohm. It's like a chant and a measurement. It makes sense," Ernie replied, trying to reach out in a friendly manner.

Eli was the first to depart as he announced, "Thank you all for an interesting adventure. It was nice to meet you, Ernie, and I hope to see you all again sometime."

"Likewise," Ernie said, and Brent offered a nod.

"Ohm, transport me back to *Tiger Mountain*," Eli said, and he disappeared in a sparkle.

"Where is *Tiger Mountain*?" Ernie asked, turning to look at me.

"It's a space station in another dimension. Perhaps you can visit sometime? I guarantee that it will not be a harsh experience such as what you all experienced here tonight," I offered.

"That might be nice. What do you think, Brent? Are you up for continuing our tournament?" Ernie asked.

"I don't know. I wouldn't mind going at it again after a good night's sleep," Brent said.

Before Brent could finish his sentence, Jorrie, who looked over the medical inspectrograph log, interrupted, saying, "Wait a second, this can't be right. Three hours of station time have elapsed since we left. We couldn't have been gone that long?"

"Let me see that?" Brent asked, and Jorrie handed the medical inspectrograph back to him.

"I had guessed we were gone maybe twenty minutes at best and only at the window world for five to ten minutes at the most," Ernie said.

"There are varying time differentials between probabilities. Equarius, time runs faster than Starnet Union time. We could have been gone for three hours," I said.

"You mean if we stayed there a day, several might pass here?" Ernie asked.

"Yes, and I think that might be what causes the Vosip disorientation. Some temporal offset that evolution never imagined it had to deal with," I said.

"I think I'm hooked on researching this phenomenon, Jorrie. I will look into these readings as soon as I get a chance, but if three hours have gone by, I might just call it a night and head back for some rest," Brent said.

"Me too. See you later," Ernie said.

"Thank you, Brent, Chief," Jorrie said as Ernie and Brent headed out of sickbay, talking among themselves.

I took Jorrie's hand, helped her down from the medical bed, and asked, "How about you? Are you ready to call it a night?"

"Actually, I'm starving. That was my original thought when I crashed your mission with Eli. I was going to see if you wanted to get something to eat," Jorrie answered.

"Do you have a place in mind, or should we order in from your quarters?" I asked.

"I feel a little grungy after our experience, so I don't want to go out, but would you care to join me in the food court? We can get something from the replicators there," she said.

"Sure, lead on," I said, and we both headed out of the medical exam area.

When we got to the hallway, out of the sight of others, Jorrie said, "Hold on a second."

"What is it?" I asked.

She moved up close to me and said, "Tonight, taking me, us there, thank you. I know it was a bit extreme and out of control, but I wanted you to know that this journeying with you means a lot to me."

"No problem," I said and started to head down the hall.

Jorrie blocked my path and continued, "This thing, we have."

I interrupted her, asking, "You mean our love?"

"Yes, our love," she conceded while looking me in the eye. "It is changing me, Sam."

"It's changing me too," I said, placing my hands on her hips and leaning in for a kiss.

"That's nice," she said as we parted lips. "I just wanted you to know how I feel."

A growl rumbled out of her stomach, and we laughed as I said, "I guess we better get you some food."

We made our way over to the food court, and each took our turn obtaining food at the replicators. We took our trays over to a two-top table and took seats as we enjoyed our replicated dinner. Jorrie ordered some bland-looking steamed white beans and a clear broth soup while I tried the salmon and broccoli. My food was fairly flavorless even though the replicator got the colors right. The broccoli was a nice bright green, and the salmon a rich pink. Jorrie began recalling her day's events from work, as women often do, and as a man, I thought about something else while nodding and eating. One thing that came to my mind was the promise I made to Erin and Jorrie on our wedding day. It was a promise to stay together, to be together as much as possible. Even though this was just us eating at the Replimat, I was glad to be in Jorrie's company, but I could not help but wonder how Erin got along on her first day? This type of situation with her out on her own made me nervous. Her separation would be the exact setting that one of my enemies might look for. A chance to exact some form of revenge.

All the while, Jorrie talked and finally asked, "Do you think I gave her the right advice?"

It was like my mind played catch up, processing the one-sided information dump Jorrie presented, and just as her face turned sour, sensing I might have tuned her out, I said, "It's hard to judge how deeply someone takes their religion? When you give advice that suggests they discard it or defy it, the advice may not be the best."

"Oh, maybe I went too far? I guess I thought I knew Mia well enough to offer that suggestion," Jorrie said with a pondering expression.

"What about you? Are you a religious woman?" I asked.

She smiled, putting the fork in her mouth and pulling it out slowly, looking down at her plate then back up at me, saying, "When I was young, and obviously before I was a mingled Vosip, I was infatuated with myth and religion. My family was not very religious, but they indulged my interests, and we visited temples and attended services. That was when I took an interest in Sugestria and some of the other iconic figures of Vosip mythology."

"So you are," I said.

"The Vosip people are at a spiritual crossroads, where the concept of believing in old religions is starting to seem more and more childlike. As we embrace technology and venture out to the stars, our religions are a little bit like the blanky of a young person. We still want them from time to time to cuddle up with when we are feeling insecure."

"And Vasco is, 'coming of age,' in a sense. But their religion has a real, tangible connection to the non-temporal aliens inside the radionic tile," I said.

"Exactly, with most worlds, religion is mostly a thing of the past, used to organize and offer structure to developing societies. With Vasco, religion is still alive and changing because their gods are aliens that still exist," Jorrie said.

"It is a fascinating one, that's for sure," I said, drinking the last of my water.

"What about you? Are you religious?" Jorrie asked.

"Once you have engaged the *Motif*, there is no other religion. The truth of reality is bound within you. But even Splendorites don't know what happens when you die. I never really spend any time wondering or fretting over it," I said.

"Are you ready to head up to the quarters?" Jorrie asked.

"Sure," I said, and we headed over to the recycle bins and dropped off our plates while placing our trays on the recycle stack.

As we walked along the concourse, I asked Jorrie, "I hope this isn't too morbid of a question, but what was it like? Does Tusk retain any information about the dying process? The last thoughts from the dying host?"

She looked over a little serious, then looked ahead, talking while walking, saying, "With traumatic death, there is not a lot remembered, mostly sorrow and regret. With natural death, I experienced at least three similar scenarios where the host consciousness was drawn toward a shining light before my memories ceased."

"Damn, that is wild," I said as we headed to the residency loop.

"So, in all your long years, you never went through a near-death experience or some type of out-of-body experience that brought you insight?" Jorrie asked.

"I have been close to death several times, and I also remember some terrible near-death experiences from the other time loops. In this time loop, however, none of that has happened yet. It's similar to what you said. When close to death, I experienced sorrow and regret along with fear. When you engage the *Motif*, your body is integrated into the multi-verse. You are literally drained of your blood, and it is combined with the *Motif* so the multi-verse can recognize you. Your identity is challenged in the process, and there is a real sense you could lose your identity if you do not conform to the *Motif*. I see it everywhere. See the curve of that handrail in this lift? That small section reminds me of one of the curves of the *Motif*. It's always there. It could be that a Splendorite's life is nothing more than a dying delusion as the *Motif* destroys us," I replied.

We exited the lift and headed down to our quarters as Jorrie said, "Now that sounds wild too, Sam."

It was late enough to consider getting ready for bed, and Jorrie headed off to the shower. I headed over to the liquor console and poured a quarter rocks glass of scotch. It was the first thing I thought of when I came in the door. I plan on drinking this before Jorrie finishes her shower, and I probably won't tell her about it. I guess I am an alcoholic.

As I sat there drinking, I asked, "Ohm, what are Erin's life signs?"

"Erin is alive and well in a non-stress environment," Ohm replied.

"Ohm, while Erin is on her own, it's up to you to keep her safe.," I said.

"Adjustments to monitoring rules are in place," Ohm replied.

I tipped back my glass, finished it off, and returned it to the console. Heading into the bedroom, I passed Jorrie, who smiled, wrapped in two towels, one around her body and the other around her hair. I jumped in the shower to rinse off quickly before brushing my teeth and climbing in bed with her.

"This is nice," Jorrie said. "The large bed does make me miss her, though."

"Yeah, me too," I said as I cuddled up next to her and fell asleep.

We became very domestic, and the next week was an everyday sex fest for Jorrie and me. Sometimes it was in the morning and sometimes after her shift. There was one time when we did it on her lunch break. We did it everywhere in her quarters, in every possible position, and became much closer. I felt a deep connection to her form, and for the first time since I awoke with my future memories, I finally felt like I was living my life again. The content of the future memories seemed less important, at least at the relationship level. There were still some inviting prospects worth mining from the future memories, but I mainly focused on managing *Tiger Mountain* and processing my backlog of weekly reports.

When the first crop of vegetables came in from the Zenith gardens, we ate dinner in San Francisco with Lucas, Alex, and Candy. We brought the salad. I gave them and the other Guardians a Transfast icon to the Zenith garden. Candy brought a date, which was nice to see, so it ended up as a couples dinner, with a game of dominoes to finish off the evening.

CHAPTER 61

It was morning. Jorrie and I headed into week two without Erin when a sparkle appeared in our quarters, leaving behind Robin Cooper. She was dressed in full military gear and said, "Sorry to interrupt, Sam, but I need your help. My dad is in trouble."

Jorrie and I parted from our embrace. I asked, "What is wrong?"

"I can fill you in on the way. We're kind of on a time limit, and actors are in motion," she said with a concerned look.

I patted my pockets and felt the vignettes and my wand, then said to Jorrie, "I'm going to see what I can do to help. I'll talk to you later."

"Be careful, Sam," Jorrie said with a concerned look.

I walked over next to Robin and said, "I am ready."

"Ohm, return Sam and me to the Gorgon cargo ship with the rest of the team," Robin said, and I watched my vision collapse inward, Jorrie along with it. The darkness overtook me, and I had a bad feeling about this. I don't know why but I felt like I might not see Jorrie again for a very long time.

My ears reassembled first. I heard the screeching of a panel overloading as I fell to the floor of the Gorgon cargo shuttle upon materialization. The ship was in a combat situation, and the tumbling was the result of evasive maneuvers. I saw Robin stumble forward to the cockpit area, issuing some order to Ohm as we took another hit.

One of the panels in this back area was emitting smoke. I approached and pushed in on the panel to release the spring mechanism causing it to slide out from the wall. More smoke billowed into the cargo hold, and I coughed. Several of the crystals providing power for this circuit were burnt out and shattered.

I pulled out my wand and said, *"Meliorum,"* targeting each broken crystal with a new spell vocalization as I coughed in between. I watched as the shards from the burnt, broken crystal reformed from their shattered locations, restoring each crystal to its unbroken shape. I pushed on the panel, and it retracted into the wall. Once it settled into place, the ship lurched. I heard a high-pitched energy sound resonating behind the repaired panel. The whining calmed down, giving the impression that the repair held.

I heard the familiar voice of David Scott say, "Ohm, remove the smoke from this area and replace it with fresh air."

The cargo bay filled with a subtle sparkle. Ohm removed the smoke, and the air became easier to breathe as I said, "Thank you, David."

"What did you do?" David asked as he looked at my wand.

"I used a repair spell on the crystals. I think they are holding," I answered.

"I didn't know you could do that," David remarked, pushing his glasses up.

"Well, it was the first thing that came to mind," I said.

We headed to the cockpit area where Robin and Malik piloted this Gorgon cargo shuttle. It looked like we were in some tunnel space, reminding me of flux, but the star streaks were almost completely solid. Time appeared completely stopped outside of this interstellar tunnel we moved through.

"Sam used a magic spell to fix the broken crystals," David reported.

"How convenient," Robin said, "and not a moment too soon. If we didn't jump to tunnel space, our goose might have been cooked."

"It is good to see you again, Sam," Malik said, "I feel our odds have significantly increased with your presence."

"It's good to see you, Malik. What is going on?" I asked.

"It's the fallout from our last encounter. The destruction of Akan has left a power vacuum filled by a lower Gorgon. My father and a few other Gorfar were already deployed in the service of Akan when things started to fall apart. The Gorfar reported to us that he was captured and sent to a planetoid prison. Jim, and MD-Beta, are in another Gorgon cargo ship attempting to extract the remaining Gorfar operatives before they are discovered," Robin reported.

"The quickest way to rescue him is to use the painting. Because I have never met him, however, I can't be the one to activate it. You'll have to do it," I said to Robin.

"I thought you were the only one who could activate that artifact?" David asked.

"Anyone can activate it, but whoever does must face the frightful images that first appear," I replied.

"You mean the images of madness that you instructed me to look away from?" David asked.

"Yes, they don't hurt you, but they can remain with you psychologically," I said.

"It might be a better plan than we have. You two could redirect to Jim's coordinates and offer support while Sam and I rescue my father," Robin said.

"I'm more worried about your sanity, Robin," David said.

"How do you do it, Sam? How do you live with the images of madness?" Robin asked.

"It's unpleasant but not unbearable. In my travels through echo I have seen so many terrible things that adding one more to the list doesn't feel like that heavy of a weight to carry," I replied.

"I'm willing to try," Robin said.

"Wait, wait, wait, don't we have a say in this too?" David asked.

"The longer it takes to reach my father, the slimmer the chances are that we'll find him alive," Robin said to David.

"Major Cooper is correct. The prison world is known to be severely dangerous, and many do not survive," Malik said.

"I'll send you a message through the *Tiger Mountain* rings once we arrive, so you'll know we made it, all right?" Robin offered as a compromise.

"I guess I don't have a choice," David said, defeated.

Robin gathered her military gear next to the wall, put it on, and said, "I'm ready."

I pulled the vignette to the catwalk out of my pocket and said, "Take my hand."

Holding up the vignette, I focused on it and stepped through. We arrived on board the *Deceptive*, and I said, "This way."

We walked to the end of the catwalk, where the covered painting sat on the easel, and I instructed, "Just think of it as a scary movie. It can't hurt you. The way I do it is to prepare the image of my goal in my mind before removing the cloth covering. Don't be drawn into the initial image presented. Think of your father and your goal, and push that thought forward into the painting. It will try to bully you, so be determined with your thoughts."

Robin shook her head yes as she took in my instructions but still looked a little unsure. Finally, she blew out a breath and said, "Here goes."

She removed the cloth revealing a large, hellish face of a devil covering the entire canvas, staring her down. She stepped back, startled, bumping into me as the devil's face grinned.

I took the cover cloth from her hand and dropped it to the floor, saying, "Push back."

Robin stepped up to the painting, and it looked like she was in some psychic combat with the painting as the devil raged and continued to challenge her right to command the canvas. This struggle went on longer than it usually took me to produce an image, and I said, "Think of your father, not the image." This instruction seemed to help as the face of the devil morphed into a human face, presumably Robin's father. There was a slight recognition, for a moment, as he saw his daughter before the scene drifted back, and we could see the room. I touched Robin on the shoulder, and we took a step through.

I pulled out my shingle to review the immediate area and map out targets. We arrived at the bottom of a rock slide. Noxious gas filled the air. A short distance away, a ramp led up to a metal gate blocking the exit. There was a large doorway leading farther into the prison compound, but there were no cells or gates to contain other prisoners. The shingle mapped out a few distant targets from us. Other than that, we were alone with Robin's father, who sat slumped upon a rock pile. He looked like he was in pretty bad shape.

"Dad, I brought some help," Robin said.

"You shouldn't have come, kiddo," her father said.

"Sam, this is my father, Walter," Robin said.

"Ohm, transport all three of us back to the Gorgon cargo ship," I said.

The dim lighting collapsed inward from the side of my vision, and I returned to the dark place. I knew Walter was a Gorfar which was physically identical to a Gorgon. Having the same physical makeup, the difference between the Gorfar and the Gorgon was purely psychological. The Gorfar believed in sharing the host body, while the Gorgon believed in dominating it. With the Vosip, the Limax was much more passive, acting as a memory sponge between lives producing a truly blended consciousness. With the Gorfar or Gorgon, they could take control of the host at any time leading me to believe they were more of a parasite rather than symbiotic. As the probability traveler, I realized they were varied echoes of each other. But I did fear the Gorgon, because I knew it was possible for one to take over a Splendorite. This all passed through my mind as the lighting zoomed in from the sides, materializing us inside the Gorgon cargo ship.

The materialization left Walter in an unsupported position. As he started to fall backward, he screamed out in pain. Robin caught him before he hit the floor and supported him.

"Ohm, I need a medkit," I said, and a sparkle soon appeared, leaving behind a white box with a red cross.

"Sorry about that, Walter. I thought it would be better to treat you here where the air is cleaner," I said as I opened the medkit and located the medical inspectrograph. He looked beaten up pretty badly, with cuts and bruises on his face and hands. The medical inspectrograph revealed two cracked ribs on his left side, but there was also a wound on his back from an energy blast weapon. The medical inspectrograph detected the Gorfar inside him and reported it was under stress, probably because it was trying to repair such extreme damage to the host.

"Hang in there, Dad," Robin said, holding him up from behind with a tear rolling down her cheek.

I did a little more studying of the medical gear after Farouk leveraged some of the additional features of the skin sealer. I think I knew how he activated the additional features. The medical inspectrograph could offer a recommended dose to the medjector. It could also transfer recommended setting to the skin sealer. This transfer is what I used for the cracked ribs. I turned on the skin sealer. The medical inspectrogrpah transferred the recommendation for deep bone mending. Remembering my bedside manner, I said, "I'm going to repair your ribs first, then we can roll you over, and I'll take care of that burn wound on your back."

The small screen of the skin sealer showed the area of focus transferred to the device from the medical inspectrograph. The operation was similar to surface wound repair. I moved the device back and forth over the targeted area, and a ray of light conveyed material to the bone surface, building up a repair, filling in the cracks so the bone would become one piece again. This transfer acted as a temporary outer cast. Eventually, the interior of the bone would heal on its own. It took about ten minutes to repair the ribs. The medical inspectrograph detected two major breaks, but as I viewed the targeted area with the skin sealer screen, I noticed a couple of hairline fractures on neighboring ribs which I tended to as well.

"I think that's it for the ribs. Let's lay you down on your stomach, and I'll get to work on your back wound," I said as I helped Robin lay her father down on the floor of the cargo ship. While the move produced a grimace on Walter's face, he didn't cry out in agony as he did when we first arrived.

David observed my treatment of Walter and said, "We have redirected this ship to converge with Jim. I filled him in on the revised plan. How is it going?"

"I have completed one of three major operations. I'm tending to the burn wound now," I said as I fetched a pair of scissors from the medkit. It looked like a wrist weapon wound. I cut Walter's clothes away from the burned area as gently and quickly as possible, but he called out in pain a couple of times as I did so. Some of his clothing fused into the outer ring of the burned skin.

I located the cellepulator, which I added to the standard medkit, and loaded one of the orgamorphic gel cartridges into the unit. Because Walter lay flat on the floor, I stood over him and focused the device on the wound, saying, "This will feel a little cool and gooey. It takes a few moments to set up, so try to relax."

Robin and David watched as I targeted Walter's wound, obtained a lock, and fired the device at the wound. A red light shot out of the device and deposited the gel upon the surface. It was transparent on first contact but bubbled and started taking on the color of the nearby skin as the conversion process took place.

"What is that device?" Robin asked.

"I call it the cellepulator. It's a medical gel depositing tool. The gel is initially molecularly neutral. When it comes in contact with cells, it morphs into new skin cells, repairing the damage at an accelerated rate," I replied.

"That is truly remarkable," David said.

"It is most useful on burns and deep cuts," I said. "It's part of the standard medkit now. If you summon one using Ohm, you can review its operation. There is a help icon on the small screen, or just talk to Ohm."

"I feel it working," Walter said in a relieved tone.

I put the cellepulator back in the medkit and located the medical inspectrograph again. The Gorfar, like the Gorgon, are small starfish-like creatures that attach themselves to the bottom of the cerebellum near the brainstem. Their proximity to the brain is probably how they take control of the host. The Limax is located much lower in the body and functions more like an organ. I focused my scan on the brain area at the back of the head and was able to locate the Gorfar inside of Walter and asked, "I have detected your Gorfar is under stress. I have never treated your species before, but my device recommends basic dermal regeneration. Would you like me to proceed?"

"I'm willing to try it," Walter said.

I located the skin sealer and verified the medical inspectrograph adjusted the settings for the new recommended treatment before beginning a short series of small motions over the back of Walter's head.

"That helps, thank you," Walter said in a slightly altered voice that creeped me out.

"I'm going to have to get up to speed on some of this medical tech," David said.

"Yeah, me too. I did not realize we had this stuff available," Robin said.

I continued the slow motions across the back of his head until Walter finally said, "I think that is enough." I discontinued the scanning, and he got up on his knees and managed to turn around on his own as he took a seat on the floor. "Thank you," he said to me. "Thank you all for coming to rescue me."

Malik entered the cargo area and said, "I am glad to see you on the mend, Walter Cooper."

Walter said, "I'm glad to be on the mend, Malik," finally standing up with some help from Robin, twisting around to try and see the back wound I repaired.

"It will probably get itchy where the new skin meets the old skin," I stated as I noticed his attempt to inspect the repaired wound.

"How do you feel, Dad?" Robin asked.

"A lot better, that's for sure. I think Kaymos can take care of the rest of it. You done good, kiddo," he said to his daughter. Turning to me, he held out his hand, saying, "Robin has mentioned you before. You're Sam, the probability traveler. I'm Walter Cooper."

I shook his hand and said, "Nice to meet you."

An alarm sounded from beyond the doorway, and Malik turned to attend to it. We all eventually headed out of the cargo hold to the cockpit, where Walter took one of the pilot's seats next to Malik. It looked like we approached an intended destination. The solid appearance of the star tunnel gave way to streaks as we departed from tunnel space, with a slight shift in momentum catching me off balance. Malik operated the controls and consulted a central panel that, I guessed, contained a map of this portion of space.

"What's the plan?" Walter asked.

"Colonel Young is in another Gorgon cargo ship like this one heading for the main complex. He has MD-Beta with him, as well as Reshet. The plan is to extract as many Gorfar operatives as possible and get the hell out as quickly as we can," Robin told her father.

Through the large canopy of the cockpit, I took in the view as we rapidly approached a set of planets. One of them was shattered, locking an asteroid debris field in orbit with its companion planets. From this distance, the smaller debris looked a lot like colored gas. Malik maneuvered the Gorgon cargo ship to approach one of the inner planets with the least amount of traveling through the debris field, but as we got closer to the target planet, there was no way to avoid passing through the asteroid rubble. Walter seemed to know this ship well, and I watched while Walter mapped out a course on the central console and Malik implemented course corrections guiding us through the debris field.

We finally cleared the debris field and made our final approach to the planet. I could hear Malik talking to someone, I assumed was Jim Young, as he dialed in final coordinates on the central console taking the Gorgon cargo ship into the atmosphere. Visible flames briefly flowed over the canopy glass, and we experienced turbulence as the planet's atmosphere knocked this small ship around.

After a couple of minutes, it smoothed out, and we began our final descent to a peninsula on the southern part of this planet.

David asked, "Are we still cloaked?"

"I believe so," Malik replied.

"We'll have to drop it to activate the ascension ladder," Walter said.

"Okay, I'll bite. What is the ascension ladder?" I asked.

Robin said, "That is what the Gorgon call their transportation technology. It does have some ladder-like qualities, in that it relays matter in a series of steps deposited by a ray emitter."

"I'll bet the emitter can't function through the cloak," I deduced.

"Exactly, that is one of the limitations of the technology," Walter added.

We rapidly approached a large building complex sprawled across the ground next to a large river. The river dropped off to a wide waterfall where a good part of the complex was built. This site was clearly a Gorgon facility due to the nature of the design. The number nine could be detected everywhere. Nine major pseudopods extended out of the complex, and nine-sided buildings stood in the center of each pseudopod. Hovering over the river was a Gorgon mothership. There were nine sides to the ship, and it looked a lot like a tipi, although no points rose out of the top. The panels between the nine edges were sunken inward, emulating the physical shape of the Gorgon itself. The entire craft's design looked very organic.

I heard Malik say, "Young, we are nearly in position. Awaiting your signal to drop the ascension ladder."

I headed back into the cargo area and gathered up my supplies, returning them to the medkit and closing it up. As I glanced up at the ceiling, I noticed some glass-like discs with a ripple pattern, and I wondered if they were part of this ascension ladder mechanism.

Robin said from the doorway, "Sam, you'd better step out of the cargo hold before we activate the ladder."

I returned to the cockpit, and from the doorway, Robin called out, "All clear."

I looked through the doorway and watched the glass discs in the ceiling light up, finally seeing why it was called an ascension ladder. Outlines of people were rapidly filled in as the circular discs pulsed and oscillated. At one point, during the transport, it looked like the subject of the transport was only halfway transported, with obvious gaps in their vertical makeup. The gaps quickly filled in as three solid people appeared in the cargo hold. They moved off to the side, indicating that they may have seen or experienced this type of transport before and wanted to make room for new arrivals.

Robin called again, "Clear."

The process repeated seven times before this Gorgon cargo ship became the target of Gorgon wasps emerging from the Gorgon mothership. David called out, "Ohm, disable those attacking ships!"

The other Guardians in this Gorgon cargo ship could hear Ohm's reply, "Please specify a method for disabling the attacking ships."

I said, "Ohm, attach a two hundred kilogram weight to one of the wingtips on each of the attacking ships."

Brief sparkles appeared upon the wings of each of the attacking vessels. This alteration caused them to spin out of control, and many of them fell from the sky, while others seemed to break off their attack as they attempted some type of controlled landing. After processing the Gorgon wasp vessels near us, Ohm extended processing to those still emerging from the Gorgon mothership. This action caused many wasps to slam into the hull and generate explosions upon the mothership's surface.

"How did you do that?" Walter asked.

David said while adjusting his glasses, "Well, I was going to say that next."

"It doesn't matter. Malik, do we have everyone?" I asked.

"I count nineteen new passengers," Robin said.

"Young reports, that is everyone," Malik replied. He dialed in new settings on the central control panel, and the Gorgon cargo ship was set in motion once again. As the Gorgon mothership moved out of the canopy view, I saw smaller explosions taking place upon its surface. Up ahead, another Gorgon cargo ship which was probably the ship that Jim Young was aboard, faded from sight as it enabled its cloak. I noticed Walter activating some similar feature on this ship.

"Ohm, discontinue the previous command," I said.

Walter got up from his pilot's chair, rubbed his back a bit, and slowly made his way back to the cargo area. I could hear him speaking to the crowd in the cargo hold with that same altered voice he addressed me with while I treated Kaymos' wounds. I watched as Malik navigated the ship back through the asteroid debris field. I could hear some of the smaller particles impacting the hull, like rain, as he seemed to take a shortcut through some of the finer debris material. Eventually, we exited the debris field and headed off into deep space. After about ten to fifteen minutes, we cleared the solar system. Malik adjusted the central control panel before engaging the tunnel space drive. The stars zoomed at us for a moment before freezing in space, forming a corridor the Gorgon cargo ship could travel through.

A slight depression overcame me as I realized how much I did not know these people. This is how my Guardians lived. They were more tightly bound to their source echo than Candy, Alex, and Lucas, who already bandoned their echo to come live in mine. It wasn't that I expected the MD-Alpha team to just follow me around, but seeing them perform under pressure made me realize how little of the Guardian offerings they used. I wondered how often vague commands were issued to Ohm, and Ohm just improvised a solution for them. They obviously faced more combat situations than the other Guardians but seemed to have little knowledge of field medicine. Maybe I was being too hard on them in my mind. Who am I to think that people should live one way or the other?

David interrupted my thoughts by asking, "How did you come up with that request for Ohm? Once you said it, it seemed so obvious."

"In any combat situation balance should always be considered. Your own first and then your enemies. It was the first thing that came to mind. To knock them off balance," I said.

"Sam is correct. Balance is one of the first lessons taught in Ralla training," Malik replied.

David shook his head, then moved off through the door, saying, "I'm going to see if I can help out in the cargo hold."

I took the empty pilot's seat next to Malik and stared through the canopy as our ship hurled through the tunnel space.

"You seem very distant, Sam. Is there something bothering you?" Malik asked.

"I guess it is being so close to the Gorfar. You and I have been on many missions, standing side by side fighting the Gorgon, and now that they are in the cargo hold, I am not sure how I feel about that," I replied.

"Young expressed similar feelings at first, unable to distinguish between a Gorgon and a Gorfar. Once Robin Cooper's father became one, he learned to accept that the Gorfar are not the Gorgon," Malik replied.

"Maybe it will come to me with time, but for now I still fear them. I don't hate them, but I do fear them," I said.

"Fear is an important ally to a warrior. When a warrior knows no fear, he becomes reckless," Malik replied.

"How long is our journey in this tunnel space?" I asked.

"We have to remain on this course for a few hours. Our destination is a planet with a Mist Door. From there, the Gorfar will depart, returning to their base of operations," Malik said.

The smell of food wafted to the front of the ship through the cargo hold door, and Malik raised one eyebrow saying, "The ship can remain unattended for a while. I am going to take this time to review the food offerings."

I smiled and shook my head, saying, "I think I'll just sit here. I have never been inside tunnel space before."

Malik headed to the back of the ship, and I asked, "Ohm, can you materialize a half glass of scotch and a joint?"

There was a flat space on the console where a sparkle materialized a rocks glass and a joint. I fetched the lighter from my pocket and lit up the joint. As I blew out the smoke, I said, "Ohm, can you remove the smoke I am emitting from the cabin?"

"Certainly," Ohm replied, and soft sparkles appeared and faded a short distance from wherever I blew smoke. I took a sip of the scotch, savoring the smoky peat flavor before swallowing it. Leaning back in the chair, I blew smoke out again. After a few minutes of smoking and sipping, I heard someone approach. It was Walter. He carried a plate of food.

"I thought I'd watch the helm while Malik takes a break," he said. "Ah, what have you there?"

"Weed and scotch. Would you like some?" I asked.

"Not the weed, but what kind of scotch?" he replied.

"It's Lagavulin 16-year-old single malt," I said.

A big smile crossed his face, and he said, "Oh, yeah. When I lived on Earth,

I tried many a scotch and that one, in particular, was one of my favorites."

"Ohm, another half glass of scotch," I said, and a sparkle came and went, leaving behind a half-filled rocks glass on the console. I handed it to Walter, and he placed his plate of food on the empty console shelf in front of his seat, taking the scotch.

Before taking a sip, he said, "Thank you for saving my life and for being a friend to my daughter. She has told me about your unusual abilities."

I clinked my glass gently to his and said, "You're welcome. Your daughter and the MD-Alpha team helped me out in a bad situation. I don't forget a thing like that."

"Oh, that is good," he said, taking a sip and placing the glass on the console. "I'm going to sip that, however, after I eat."

I put out the joint on my boot heel and tucked it away in my hip joint pocket.

It looked like Walter's plate contained lettuce, potato salad, and some type of meatloaf. In between bites, he asked, "Do you mind if I ask how you accomplished that amazing feat of disabling an entire squadron of attack vessels with a voice command?"

"I am reluctant to reveal how my technology works to people I have just met, but because you are family, I am going to go out on a limb here. I used the same technology to disable the attack vessels as I did to deliver the scotch. A series of scanners targeted the attack vessels in flight, relaying their design specifications to a central processing center residing in another probability. In that probability, there are replication factories that can produce new items in a matter of seconds," I said.

"Replication in another probability, fascinating," Walter said.

"An inverse mold of the wingtip of the attacking vessel was quickly generated, and the two hundred kilogram weight was replicated to match the wing profile. After replication, it was transported into place along the wing, which destabilized the design of the spacecraft. It could no longer function as a flying vehicle," I revealed.

"That is the most incredible series of technology combinations that I have ever heard. So, this scotch, is it replicated?" he asked.

"Oh no, this is the real deal. I have placed a hidden transport locater in one of the Lagavulin aging casks. I just tap it as needed," I said.

He took another sip and shook his head, saying, "This is an amazing life. I thought, for sure, I would be dead by the end of the day, and here I am drinking scotch and making a new friend. It's unbelievable."

Robin walked up to us and said, "Uh oh, what is that smell?"

"I was wondering if I could make a slight modification to this ship? I think we need a blacklight poster of a dolphin right here," I said, pointing to the wall next to my seat.

She smiled and said, "I just spoke with Jim, and I believe we managed to extract all known Gorfar operatives. His count and our count match the deployed total."

"That is good news, Robin. You have indebted yourself to the Gorfar a great deal today. Your actions won't be forgotten," Walter said. "And you too, Sam. If you are ever in trouble, and we can help, I'll make sure it happens."

"Did my dad tell you that he is the oldest and wisest of all the Gorfar?" Robin added with a smile.

"No, he didn't," I said to her. "I accept your offer of future help. You never know when having an extra friend can come in handy."

We clinked our glasses together again and took another sip.

"What, you didn't bring enough for everyone?" Robin ribbed me.

"Here you go, kiddo, take a sip of that," Walter said, handing Robin his glass, "it's one thing Sam and I have in common. A love of delicious scotch."

Robin took a little too big of a sip and said, "Oh, that is smooth," handing the glass back to her father.

I finished my scotch, recycled the glass, and Malik returned from the cargo hold. I gave up my seat to him and took to standing behind the pilot's seats.

A person-sized sparkle appeared in the large front cockpit area, leaving behind Jorrie. She was still in her Starnet uniform. I walked over to her as she said, "Sam, I wondered how things were going?"

David emerged from the cargo hold, saying, "Did you just see, oh, hello."

"Do you remember Jorrie from the balcony party?" I asked David.

"Of course, nice to see you again," he replied.

Robin walked over and said, "Thank you for letting me borrow, Sam, today."

Jorrie smiled, saying, "I take it things went well?"

"Very, we were able to save my father and rescue the others. Dad, come over here for a minute. I want you to meet someone," Robin said.

Walter got up from the pilot's chair, walked up, and stood beside his daughter, looking at us.

"Dad, this is Jorrie. She is a blended person like you, only from another probability," Robin said.

"Pleased to meet you. I'm Walter, Walter Cooper," Walter said.

"Likewise, Jorrie, Jorrie Tusk," Jorrie said.

There was an awkward silence for a moment or two as if the meeting of these different blended people was supposed to produce some incredible exchange of experiences or information. A beeping sounded from the pilot's area, and Walter said, "If you'll excuse me, I have to pilot the ship, or we'll crash into the planet."

"Certainly," Jorrie said, and we took up positions behind the pilot's chairs, taking in the view of tunnel space.

"This ship uses an engine that travels through, what they call tunnel space," I said to Jorrie.

"It looks a lot like the view from inside a glide step spacecraft, only I have never seen such a static pre-wake before," Jorrie said.

"The pre is right, only it's not actually a wake. That is to say, the perceived walls are not the result of field emission. It's more like a folded space approach only no fold occurs, but temporally the time between the entry and the exit point are virtually the same," Robin explained.

"Does that mean when you are inside the tunnel, you age, but those outside do not?" I asked.

"That is correct," Robin said.

"Interesting, so velocity upon entry is maintained throughout the tunnel?" Jorrie asked.

"For the most part. You can accelerate while in the tunnel, but if you slow too much, the tunnel space will collapse, returning you to normal space," Robin clarified.

The view through the canopy changed as the tunnel space slowly started to drift and quickly accelerated into streaks returning the Gorgon cargo ship to normal space. Malik and Walter worked together again, and the stars in the canopy rolled and drifted until a distant planet came into view.

"I think I'll let the others know we are approaching the destination," Robin said, and she headed back to the cargo hold.

"Thanks for helping out today, Sam," David said, "it really made the difference."

"No problem. It's interesting to get a chance to see this Gorgon technology in action," I replied.

"This technology must seem fairly crude compared to what you use in Starnet," David said.

"Not at all. What I have seen today rivals some of the technology that Starnet has. I would love to get a look at how this tunnel space is actually implemented," Jorrie said.

"You'd have to ask Robin about that. All I could really say is crystals," David replied.

"The crystals are dangled before small rodents that run on a wheel. The wheels are hooked to magnets, and well, that's how it works," I joked.

"Ha, ha, very funny," Jorrie said with a pouty face.

The planet grew to a large size, and entry into the atmosphere was very similar. Flames briefly covered the canopy as turbulence buffeted us around. The ride smoothed out, leaving the sound of rushing air surrounding the Gorgon cargo ship. Walter made some adjustments on the central console, and Malik implemented them, guiding the ship to its final destination. As we dropped to the ground, I caught a glimpse of the Mist Door, sitting upon its typical stone riser. The Gorgon cargo ship came to a halt, and the sound of hissing was heard followed by another sound of a door opening.

Walter said, "Well, we're here."

CHAPTER 62

The Mist Door

❧

T his way," David said, and we followed him through the doorway into the cargo hold, which opened to the planet's surface. The door hinged from the bottom, acting as a ramp for us to walk down as we exited the Gorgon cargo ship. We emerged into a grassy field with a blue sky above. It was nice to breathe fresh air again. I walked around the shuttlecraft, trying to get a look at the Mist Door as another Gorgon cargo ship landed a short distance from us.

Jorrie stayed close by me and said, "That structure. That's what I saw in the log when that ghoul attacked you."

"They call it a Mist Door. It creates a transient threshold between two energized doors. The secondary, vertical element is called the totem and is used to configure the Mist Door. Robin explained it to me once. The totem emits signals through a type of subspace, causing nearby Mist Doors to synchronize their pillar segments. A transient threshold is established once the segments match, and you can walk across the threshold to appear at the new location in a matter of seconds," I told Jorrie.

"That sounds reminiscent of the ancient gate builders mentioned in some of the archaeological ruins scattered across many of the Starnet Union worlds," Jorrie replied.

"I thought so too. I often wondered if this probability might be a window into the Union's distant past. Could this be forty-eight hundred years ago?" I asked.

The Gorfar from the newly arrived ship gathered with their counterparts and congregated around the totem near the Mist Door. I could see Jim Young approaching, so we walked in his direction, meeting him halfway. He extended his arm for a handshake saying, "You did good work today. When Malik told me you recovered, Walter, I felt a whole lot better about the rest of the mission. And I take it the downing of all those Gorgon wasps was your work?" Jim asked, beaming.

"Well, David started the disabling process of those Gorgon wasps. I just added weights to the wings to throw them off balance," I replied.

"Hi there. Jim," Jim said to Jorrie while extending his hand to her before saying, "I know we've met before, but I forget your name."

"Jorrie," Jorrie said.

"Yes, Jorrie," Jim said, "I always get a little goofy when everything works out for the best, and I have to tell you when we started out today, I had my doubts."

Malik, David, Robin, and Walter approached with Walter saying, "I just wanted to say thank you again, to you all, before I head out with the others." He shook our hands and hugged Robin before heading over to join the group of Gorfar, who already activated the Mist Door and were passing people through the ancient gateway.

"That is a fascinating device," Jorrie said, indicating the Mist Door.

"That it is, indeed," Malik replied.

"What is next on your list of things to do today?" I asked the MD-Alpha team.

"I think we are going to activate the Mist Door once the Gorfar leave and head back to the base. You're welcome to join us," Jim spoke for the team.

"Are you going to leave the two ships here?" I asked.

"We are kind of far away from Earth. Even if we wanted to fly them back, the distance is so great that it could take months inside the tunnel space corridor to return them to Earth," Robin said.

"You do realize that Ohm can transport them, don't you?" I asked.

David pushed his glasses up and said, "No, we didn't realize that," looking over at Robin for confirmation of his ignorance.

"Sam, how is that possible?" Robin asked.

"You are aware of the cloaked scanners, right?" I asked, and they shook their heads, with Jim looking left and right at the group first before shaking his head in agreement. "I also constructed an array of cloaked scanners that just sit in space. They act like relay conduits for large-scale transports. There are limits, you couldn't fit one of those Gorgon motherships through, but shuttlecraft and medium-size vessels can be transported."

"Well, you learn something new every day," Jim said, "Let's do it. I wouldn't mind having a new ride when I get back home."

"How does it work, Sam?" Robin asked.

"I'll just make the necessary adjustments, and then you can repeat the same steps if you want to extend your transportation range at a later date," I said, and Robin nodded her agreement. "Ohm, locate a cloaked scanner in the Earth-based probability where MD-Alpha resides. Duplicate it and launch it into orbit. Do the same thing for this planet."

"But wait a minute, I thought cloaked scanners couldn't move in outer space?" Robin asked.

The sound of the reverse piano note generated by each Mist Door passenger softly repeated in the background as the Gorfar passed into the mist. I noticed Jorrie was more interested in the Mist Door operation than the conversation about cloaked scanners.

"That is true, but they can reach high altitude before their maneuvering mechanism becomes ineffective. At that point, Ohm will transport them to the desired location using a Transfast. Once they reach high altitude a series of Transfasts are issued to get them to a target location. In this case, we want them hanging out in space, a short distance from the planet," I said.

Robin finished my sentence by adding, "When they reach their final goal, they can act as a target for transportation from the replication facilities, allowing the larger cloaked scanner to be transported into place. This process is a huge game-changer for us, Sam."

"Great, I wouldn't mind poking around inside one of the Gorgon cargo ships to figure out how this tunnel space engine works," I said.

Jorrie returned her attention to our conversation and said, "Me too. I have never experienced that form of travel before."

"Well, you're both welcome at any time to stop by. Cooper will give you the guided tour," Jim said.

"Please excuse the interruption, but the larger cloaked scanners are in place and ready for use," Ohm said to the group.

"Well, are you ready to head off," he said to his team, and then to us, "Are you coming with?"

"I think I would like to stay here and get a closer look at the Mist Door. I'm kind of a closet archaeologist," Jorrie said.

Robin leaned in for a hug and looked at me seriously, saying, "Thank you again for saving my father."

"Win su ro, Sam," Malik replied.

"Call me. We'll do lunch, okay?" David said, and I shook my head yes.

"You're with me, David. Let's try this transporter thing," Jim said, and the four walked off, two heading to each ship.

We heard the sound of the Gorgon cargo ship doors sliding shut, and a short time later, two large sparkles appeared and faded, removing the Gorgon cargo ships from the scenes. The only thing left to indicate they were ever there was an impression left in the grassy field.

"I want to get a closer look at the Mist Door. Do you mind?" Jorrie asked.

"Not at all," I replied, and we headed toward the Mist Door. The Gorfar departed, so all that remained were Jorrie and me. As we approached, the mist inside the door collapsed and fell to the ground while the segments of the pillars spun around to reset themselves.

"You mean it turns itself off?" Jorrie asked as we walked up the wide stairway leading up to the Mist Door.

"Yes, I think Robin told me it has some theoretical limit for how long it can be kept open during a single activation," I replied.

We walked around and through the deactivated Mist Door, inspecting the symbols found upon the pillar segments. Despite the device being incredibly old and made of sliding stone on stone, I could discover no evidence of wear or tear due to the motion of its operation or weather exposure in this outdoor environment. We headed over to the totem, which was more human-sized, and pressed a few of the symbols, but nothing happened. Jorrie did a quick count of the symbols and said, "Probably millions of possible combinations. Do you know how to operate it?"

"I don't. I traveled with MD-Alpha through the Mist Door several times, but it was always David or Robin that activated the totem during our adventures. I think Malik knows a few combinations too," I said.

"It's so fascinating," she said, turning to me and giving me that look. I took the hint and leaned in to kiss her next to this ancient artifact while standing in the green field with the blue sky above. Her response said it all by the way she gave in to the moment, returning a very passionate kiss that turned into a groping caress. We probably would have did it there on the steps in front of the Mist Door, but all of a sudden the sound of sliding stones emitted from the device. It was being activated from another location.

"This is not good," I said, "Stay close to me. I am activating my shield and cloak. Let's see who comes through."

We moved off a short distance from the totem and took a kneeling position in the grass. I pulled out my shingle and located the icon I used for placing subjects in Cryovirts. I also brought up the shared cloaked scanner feed and targeted the members of MD-Alpha, so they could see what happened at the location of my cloaked scanner. The sliding of the pillar segments completed, and the keystone glowed. The teal mist dropped between the pillars, obscuring the view behind them. A moment later, the sound of five reverse piano notes rang out as people emerged from the mist. I knew in a second that this was a Gorgon. There were two Ralla guards in front of him and two behind. Not only was this classic Gorgon deployment, but the central figure wore the gaudy, tasteless colors the Gorgon seemed to prefer.

"Who do you think that is?" Jorrie asked softly as the central figure stepped forward, looking over the area from the raised platform.

"I think it is a Gorgon and his Ralla guard," I said quietly, knowing that the cloak could also mute sounds.

"Why are they here?" Jorrie asked.

"I think it might be obvious. They expected the ships to still be here," I said as the central figure barked orders at his Ralla guard, ordering them to descend the staircase and explore the grassy field.

"How would the Gorgon know that?" Jorrie asked.

"There must be a spy in the Gorfar ranks. The Gorgon and the Gorfar are physically identical. The only thing that makes them appear to be different is how they conduct themselves," I said.

"Which means one of those people rescued today informed the Gorgon," Jorrie said.

"Yep, that is a problem. It means Walter and the others are still in danger," I said.

One of the Ralla guards called out. It seemed he discovered the impression in the grass left behind by the two ships that landed. The remaining guards joined their companion, and the central Gorgon figure descended the stairway to examine the discovery himself. The host of this Gorgon appeared to be a young male, I would guess in his mid-twenties. He passed within eight meters of us, and Jorrie gripped my bicep as he walked by. After passing us, he somehow sensed we were there and performed a quick turn to face our position while shouting, "Ralla Aten!"

I said, "Ohm, place the targets in the Cryovirt holding facility on one of the asteroids. Keep this group together."

As the Gorgon figure advanced upon our position a startled expression crossed his face when he and his companions sparkled out of existence.

I tucked my shingle away, took Jorrie's hand, standing up, saying, "Come on, let's pass through the Mist Door before it closes."

We ran while holding hands, which was a little clumsy, but I did not want to drop my cloak and shield, and I also did not want Jorrie to be exposed. We reached the stairs quickly and ascended them, slowly approaching the Mist Door, preparing to walk through. The transient threshold generated by the Mist Door was a two-way street, so it was possible to move through the Mist Door, look around and head back before the mist expired.

"We'll step through and find ourselves emerging from another Mist Door on the other side. We are still cloaked, but anyone who observes us will hear the arrival tone. We'll move quickly and try to find some cover," I said.

"Got it. Let's go," Jorrie said, and we stepped forward into the teal mist. Traveling across the transient threshold only takes a few steps. The mist obscures your vision, and you take two or three steps only to find yourself emerging from the mist at the new location. What happens somewhere in the middle of the mist is a type of transport I have never been able to identify. It's like stepping off a ledge to a rising platform that catches you on the other side before you fall. This ledge transfer seems to be what causes the tone to emit for each candidate passing through. This tone also happens if cargo is pushed through the mist.

We arrived inside a large hall with an overall ornate appearance. There were statues of animals carved out of dark wood, large potted palm trees, and tapestries hung on the walls, attached to rods mounted near the tall ceiling as two braziers burned at the top of either side of the stairway leading down from the Mist Door. Not far from the bottom of the stairway was an open doorway to a stone walkway leading to an outside environment. A Ralla guard wearing a wrist weapon stood on either side of the doorway.

We executed the plan and quickly moved off to our left as we entered this room. The reverse tone emitted from the Mist Door and alerted the guards. Even though they saw no one appear, the velocity of our movement out of the mist gave away the direction we traveled, and one called out, "See moo ee."

I knew the jig was up, so I said, "Ohm, put those two guards to sleep."

A moment or two later, the approaching guards dropped to their knees and passed out on the stairway. I said, "Ohm drop the cloak, but keep a shield on Jorrie and me."

We moved down the stairway, and these two guards looked very similar to the ones accompanying the central figure on the other side of the Mist Door. Grabbing the arms of one of the guards, I dragged him out of the immediate view of the stairway and hid him behind one of the potted plants. Jorrie caught on to what I was doing and did the same thing with the other guard.

"You can tell it's going to be a good adventure when you start off hiding bodies behind potted plants," I said.

Jorrie cracked a slight smile and tilted her head in the direction of the doorway, asking, "Do you want to explore?"

"Sure, but let's put a cloak on each of us. That way, if we are separated, you will still be protected and hidden. "Ohm, place a cloak around Jorrie and me," I said.

The physical world dimmed slightly as Jorrie and I entered cloak mode. We could still see each other, and I tested this by asking her, "Can you still see me? I can see you."

"Yes, it's working. Your voice is coming through as communication at my ear," Jorrie said.

"That is to be expected. This way we can communicate while still cloaked and shielded," I informed her.

We turned our attention to the doorway and took a step onto the walkway leading left or right. From this vantage point, I guessed we emerged from some sort of ziggurat structure, about halfway up from ground level. The place was incredibly beautiful, with carefully tended flower gardens running along the walkways. At the foot or top of the stairways were animal sculptures, mostly of jaguars in a stalking pose, but other creatures were depicted as well. The stonework was top-notch with intricate marble inlays appearing in the walls and floors, mixed in with cut sandstone and limestone. We wandered down a few of the wide stairways, noticing Ralla guards at various intersections but very few people or citizens. We took our time and quietly walked by the Ralla guards and passed unnoticed. The citizens we did see were poorly dressed laborers.

Jorrie motioned me over to a white marble bench in a nook next to the last stairway we descended and said, "I'm not sure what we're looking for."

"I'm not either. I think we may have pressed our luck far enough. Do you want to keep exploring?" I asked.

She looked at me through the muted energy field, which fritzed for a second, distorting my image, and said, "No, I've seen enough. Thank you for indulging the explorer in me."

"Ohm, discontinue transmission to the MD-Alpha team and transport Jorrie and me back to *Oasis Seven*," I said.

The bright terrace light dove in from the sides of my peripheral vision, leaving nothing behind but darkness. I forgot how upsetting it was to be around Gorgon. The fact they can take over your body scared the shit out of me. That was one reason why I quit hanging out in that probability. Once I met Alex, Lucas, and Candy, I spent more and more time with them in a less dangerous place. But I still felt a strong connection to my Guardians in the Mist Door universe, and the unique technology options certainly merited further exploration. I just didn't want curiosity to kill the cat in this case. It seemed like too many things were on my mind at once, and the dark space only took a moment before we reassembled in our quarters on *Oasis Seven*.

"Ohm, drop our cloaks and shield," I said.

Jorrie paced the room and said, "Damn, that was exhilarating, Sam. To be on one planet and then a moment later to be on another. To walk through a mist only to arrive at an unknown location. Maybe I am revealing too much to you, but that really turned me on, Sam. That kind of adventure is something you only read about, but to actually experience it has put me in a heightened state."

"Ohm, can I have one medical inspectrograph?" I asked.

A sparkle appeared on the table and left behind a medical inspectrograph. I walked over, turned it on, and Jorrie looked at me with a cross face saying, "I don't want to be scanned. Is it wrong to feel something, to feel so alive in a moment that you want to burst?"

"It was risky to travel to an unknown probability. We still don't fully understand what all the side effects are for a Vosip," I said.

"I did check the time differential before I transported into your location, it's one point seven three here, and it was one point six eight there. I thought a zero point five differential was a reasonable risk. Besides, how can we understand the side effect if we don't conduct experiments?" Jorrie asked me.

"Is that what it was, an experiment? You'd think if it were truly an experiment that you would not object to me taking readings after the fact. Maybe not all side effects are giggles and laughs. There might be an even more dangerous side to this than we realize," I argued.

"There's nothing wrong with me. I feel great," Jorrie screamed at me with her arms outstretched. "I want to do it again, Sam. I want to feel something."

"What do you mean?" I asked.

"This place, this life, is that all there is? Am I supposed to just keep showing up at work and punching buttons while pretending I like my job? Ever since Equarius, I keep thinking about how can I get back there? How can I feel like that again?" Jorrie confessed to me.

I leaned my head over and ran my hand through my hair before, saying, "I don't know what to say to that."

"Why don't you have another drink, Sam? Isn't it about that time? Do you think I don't know why you drink so much? It's because you have to stay here, in this probability, pretending to be normal when you know you want to be so much more," Jorrie continued to lay into me.

"So, what, we just run wild through probability, on a bender, until one of us is broken or dead? Is that what you want?" I said, raising my voice.

"What I want is to feel like I am alive somehow," Jorrie said, putting her hands behind her head for a moment, still pacing around our quarters.

"Then let's do it, but not there, not the Gorgon probability," I conceded.

"Why not? I want to explore the Mist Door further?" Jorrie asked.

"Why not? Because the Gorgon live there. In case you haven't noticed, I am very afraid of them," I said.

"I find it hard to believe that you are afraid of them, Sam. There has to be something more. What are you not telling me?" Jorrie kept on fishing.

"They are truly evil, Jorrie, and I could lose my identity to them. I'm not willing to entertain that concept for the sake of a joy ride through echo," I said, wishing I did have a drink in my hand.

"They didn't seem that evil to me. If they are so evil, why did you save one today?" Jorrie asked.

"Those weren't the Gorgon, those were the Gorfar, and the only reason I saved that one today was that he was Robin's father. Even Walter didn't have a choice. It was either blend with the parasite or die," I said, regretting it as soon as it came out of my mouth.

"Well, if that's how you feel about blended species, what the fuck are we doing?" Jorrie yelled.

"We're trying to make a life together. At least that's what I thought we were doing," I said, trying to bring the conversation back from left field.

"Well, maybe you thought wrong. It's clear that the thought of a blended species terrifies you. Am I some kind of thrill ride for you?" Jorrie asked, getting closer to me.

"No, I don't see you that way, but the Gorgon and the Gorfar are not truly blended. They are parasitic. Did you notice how strange Walter's voice sounded when Robin introduced the two of you?" I asked.

"No, I didn't," Jorrie said, calming down a bit.

"That's my point. Walter's parasite opted not to speak to you even though Robin was clearly trying to introduce you to the parasite that shares her father's body. He did the same thing to me, spoke to me as a human. When he addressed his fellow Gorfar, he became another person with a distinctly different voice. That isn't a blend. That is a switch. Yes, I fear the switch I can't turn off that robs me of my life, my voice, and my decision-making," I said defending myself.

Jorrie said nothing but continued to pace and brood around the room.

"You are blended, Jorrie. In my interactions with you, even this fight included, I have never once thought I was talking to two different people in one body," I said.

"I have said too much, Sam. I think I need to be alone. Can you sleep somewhere else tonight?" Jorrie asked while looking at the floor.

"Of course. I'll talk to you later," I said and headed out the doors of her quarters.

CHAPTER 63

A Burst Of Insight

~⌐

I stepped into the hallway and turned to my right, bumping into David Scott.

"Sorry, Sam, I wasn't eavesdropping, but I kind of heard the entire fight you just had. I think this whole section might have heard it," David said.

I sat down there in the hallway and said, "Ohm, remove Jorrie's transport privileges between echoes. You can still fulfill transportation requests to locations within this echo, however."

"New rule in place," Ohm replied.

"I know you are upset right now, but that might not be the wisest thing to do to her," David said, taking a seat on the floor beside me.

"There are side effects for the Vosip when it relocates to a new echo. It just surfaced a few days ago, but I knew about it from the future memories. Something about the temporal offset between echoes causes a chemical imbalance between the Limax and the host," I told David.

"Oh, I did not know that," David said, pushing his glasses up.

"The only way to get data on the side effect is to place Jorrie in an echo and measure the effects, but that should be done under controlled conditions. Today was not a controlled condition, and I feel like this outburst is the result of that. I don't want to use Jorrie as a guinea pig, or worse, have her use herself as a guinea pig to obtain faster results," I said.

"The reason I showed up outside your door in the first place was that follow up on the feed you sent us. We agree with your assessment that there might be a spy in the Gorfar ranks, but we still don't know how to contact them or warn them," David said.

"Okay, why not," I said, getting back up on my feet as David stood up with me.

I pulled out the vignette to the catwalk and said, "Back to the images of madness."

Focusing on the scene, I transferred David and me to the *Deceptive*. As I walked down the catwalk, I said, "Ohm, prepare a cloaked scanner to send through the painting."

"Cloaked scanner ready for deployment," Ohm replied.

"Time to look away, David," I said.

"Sorry, Sam," David said, looking away.

I removed the cloth from the *Vision* painting and tossed it to the floor. A grey misty scene danced on the canvas. On the right side of the composition was a leafless tree with a strong branch extending to the left, a little past the middle of the canvas. Hanging from the branch was a rope and a body slowly swung as the mist stirred. In my mind, I thought it was beautiful, and I wondered if I may have crossed the limit of madness where I might not be able to tell the difference anymore? I focused on Walter's face, and it appeared before me. He seemed to look right at me. I noticed he was in some type of purple cave, and I focused on the background, which broke the immediate connection between us. While holding the connection to the cave open, I said, "Ohm, send the cloaked scanner through."

A small rainbow circle appeared, briefly, on the surface of the painting as the cloaked scanner passed through the canvas. A moment later, Ohm reported, "Cloaked scanner is on-site and functioning."

I broke the connection with the painting and picked up the cloth from the floor, covering the painting once again before stating, "It's in place, David. You have a cloaked scanner now, so you guys can send messages or transport in. Whatever you need to do."

"Thank you, again," David said, "I seem to be saying that a lot."

"Ohm, place the newly deployed scanner in map and evade mode. Add the scanner to the MD-Alpha Guardian group display. Once a full map is generated of the Gorfar base, conduct detailed medical scans of all Gorfar when they sleep. Look for any discrepancies between the parasites that inhabit the hosts," I said.

"Are you going to be all right?" David asked.

"Yeah, you know, time heals all wounds. Maybe Jorrie is right, and we do need some space between us," I said.

"If you need anything, please don't hesitate to drop by or whatever," David offered.

I shook my head, yes, and David said, "Ohm, transport me to my office at Mist Door Operations."

David disappeared in a sparkle, leaving me standing alone on the catwalk in a dark starship next to the painting that generates the images of madness. In a sudden burst of insight, I knew exactly what I needed to do, and I needed time to do it.

"Ohm, transport me to the development lab on Xanadu," I said. The dimly lit space of the *Deceptive* collapsing inward was barely noticeable. Recent tests on the replicated *Falcon* produced a workable FSL drive, and that was what I needed for my new ship design. But to design a new ship took time, and that was one thing Xanadu had an abundance of. A stinging white light rushed in from the side as I materialized into my new surroundings.

CHAPTER 64

I took up residency in the Xanadu development lab, asking Ohm only to relay emergency communications. With the help of Ohm and the technicians, I managed to map out a basic design for the new ship. I created this ship in both of the other time loops, so I felt like it was a goal worth pursuing. The name of this ship is the *Shutterfly*. In the previous time loops, there was a slow progression through various designs, with a few different test models created before I came up with this final concept for the *Shutterfly*. I felt like I was on a time crunch, so I took everything I remembered from those time loops and dropped it into what I hoped would be a single iteration final design.

In the previous time loops, Erin and I spent a lot more time hanging out together before she joined up with Starnet, and I built a few Starnet based ships containing Imperial flight controls that she was more familiar with. It was during this time that I was introduced to the Imperial folded space link or the FSL drive. The computers the Imperials used to generate the coordinates, which were the heart of the targeting system, were vastly slower compared to Starnet technology. I got it into my head to use the Starnet computers to calculate the jump coordinates for the Imperial FSL drive. I was able to quickly calculate jump coordinates. Using this approach. I was able to improve the arrival accuracy, which translated into previously unachievable combat moves. A series of jumps could be quickly plotted, transporting the ship into close quarters of a larger enemy. Several shots could be fired as the ship jumped along the plot sequence. The ship could jump away before the enemy even knew what hit them. This flexibility is what I wanted in the cloaked attack ships, but the blank probability canvas was a much slower technology.

Even with upgraded modifications to some of the components making up the Imperial FSL, I was never able to really achieve the kind of performance that I knew I needed for a special mission I wanted to undertake. Then it finally hit me. Use two FSL drives, one in the front and one in the back. While one FSL is recharging, the second one can be discharging. The plot coordinates were interleaved between the two drives, and the *Shutterfly* concept was born.

Using a Starnet science-based shuttlecraft, I added a cargo hold to the front and back of the ship. The two new cargo holds are where the Imperial FSL drives were located. This design caused the shuttlecraft to take on the appearance of a large dog bone from the outside. I kept the flux and chemstream drives from the original Starnet design, so the ship offered three engine types. I added the cloaking technology from the cloaked scanners because it was fairly compact. It just needed a series of emitters placed along the hull. Maneuverability was not its strong suit, but the wide, thick profile was easy to shield, and armor plating covered the hull. There was a modest cargo compartment with a single retractable medical biobed. The ship included a two-person transporter, long and short-range sensors, standard gleam gun weapons, and a complement of two programmable yield magnacite missiles.

At the end of the first week, this was the ship I proposed to the Blinn. This design was the starship I tasked my people with building. I took to directing many teams, simultaneously developing all parts at once. Most of the parts used in the design I presented were already available and were fully tested in other ship concepts. The bottlenecks were mainly in the connecting portions where different technologies needed to hook together. I guided the FSL team to work on testing the dual FSL concept with the already working *Falcon*. They were able to retrofit a physical prototype by mirroring the existing *Falcon* design, front to back. It was, indeed, an ugly duckling, but it enabled the team to focus on getting the interleave to work correctly, while developing the console controls necessary to plan and deploy jump sequences.

Over the next couple of weeks, I reviewed many models of the various systems, including a one-sixteenth scale version of the entire ship. I requested the Blinn technicians to meet and work as much as possible in the Xanadu time frame, although the final replication was to take place in Blinn space. I stressed that the part count was important to me, although I never revealed to them why. I was constantly asking the team leaders to reduce the part count. The reason for this was that I needed to infuse every part with the presence of the *Vechnost*. Where I was taking this ship, there was no *Motif*.

One thing I never told anyone was that Xanadu was more than a fast echo healing center. It was also the storage area for the raw elements I used when replicating echo sturdy devices. There were large container bins in subterranean vaults containing raw elements I infused with the *Motif*. One of the first things I did at Xanadu when I started the *Shutterfly* project was to set up a Blinn terraforming module to mirror the existing *Motif* infused element bins located far below the Xanadu complex. I stocked these bins with matching raw elements found in the *Motif*-based bins. The goal was to create a supply of raw elements I could replicate *Vechnost* sturdy devices from. In the evenings, I spent time in the subterranean vaults bringing forth the *Vechnost* and infusing the raw elements inside each bin with the essence of the *Vechnost*. In the end, all the parts making up this ship would need to be replicated from these supply bins.

On the surface of this planet, outside of the Xanadu complex, I dropped another Blinn terraforming module to construct a launch platform for the *Shutterfly*. The platform supported retractable doors so the ship could emerge from underground. I connected tunnels from the underground platform to the design lab where I made my quarters. By week six, the Blinn constructed a working prototype of the *Shutterfly* that functioned to specifications in their probability.

The next step was to replicate all the pieces from the *Vechnost* element bins and perform the infusion of the *Vechnost* into each part before final assembly. Even with the teams doing their best to control part count, the part count was extraordinary. This is why I wanted to construct the parts from the *Vechnost* infused base elements. I wanted a backup if I missed something at the final *Vechnost* part-infusing step. It ended up taking two more weeks of all day long *Vechnost* infusing sessions to prepare the parts for final assembly. Upfront, I infused a lot of the small fiddly bits just to get the feel of working with the *Vechnost* in this manner. By day three, I felt more confident and focused on the system's critical parts, including the engine and the hull. As I approached the end of the two-week *Vechnost* part infusing stage, the *Shutterfly* stood assembled on the Xanadu underground platform and was ready for launch.

I entered the *Shutterfly* and took the pilot's seat on the left. The basic cockpit of the ship was similar to the *Zanna* only the *Shutterfly* was a little larger with more interior space. In the cargo hold, I placed two Cryovirt units and a Blinn terraforming module. I constructed these items from the *Vechnost* element supply bins and infused their parts with the impression of the *Vechnost*.

After testing some of the ship's technology, everything seemed to be working here in the Xanadu probability. So far, all systems worked to their specifications, and these systems carried no trace of the *Motif* within them. I felt good about proceeding with the launch and spoke to the system's computer, which the Blinn technicians named "Eve."

The *Shutterfly* launchpad rose to the surface, and I ran through a series of ground-based engine tests designed to verify if the craft was capable of flight. There were a couple of overloads during the first test, but the thermal protectors kicked in to shut everything down. After inspection and some fussing with cabling, I tried the tests again and received green lights across the board before saying, "Eve, take us up and out of the atmosphere."

The ascension from the planet's surface to outer space was much rougher than proven crafts such as the *Zanna* or even the Gorgon cargo ship. I was shaken all over the place but managed to stay in my seat. I located the control window for the velocity isolators and started playing with the offset slider. At first, I moved it in the wrong direction and the ride became extremely bumpy. Sliding it the other way calmed things down, and the ride smoothed out as we broke through the atmosphere, heading into space.

"Eve, if the ride becomes too bumpy, I may not be able to adjust the velocity isolators. Can you use the current setting as a baseline and auto-adjust this setting if we experience turbulence?" I asked.

"Using current settings for velocity isolators as the new baseline," Eve replied in a synthetic female voice.

"Feel free to auto adapt other settings that make sense. This is a new ship, so it will require some tuning to get this running smoothly," I said, not knowing how well Eve could process such a request.

"Placing request in the queue. I will attempt auto-adapting settings to maintain smooth operations as needed," Eve replied.

"Thank you," I said.

Using the console, I brought up the control window for the flux engines and set a course away from the Xanadu planet. I never bothered to name the planet because I never left the surface. I located it by traveling through echo. Setting the engines to flux one, I saw the familiar star streak through the canopy window. Once again, there was a bit of turbulence as I tested out this new system. It soon smoothed out, and Eve reported, "Auto adapting velocity isolators to compensate for flux turbulence."

Opening a new control window, I set its display type to the cooling system and reviewed the engine temperature. It all looked good, so I nudged the speed up to flux two. I reviewed the crystal regeneration display, and it looked like no excessive wear was taking place during this maiden voyage. This starship was a flux-five ship, but I did not feel any need to push the flux engines any further.

"Ohm, can you fetch the vignette of Zanna from the vault?" I asked.

A sparkle appeared, and a vignette was left behind on the console. It was the vignette for Zanna. Zanna was a dead Lord of Splendor. She was slain by her brother Fabio during the last great uprising that produced the extension to the *Motif*, Grayson's *Motif*. Fabio tried to erase Darwin's *Motif* so he might extrude a new one, installing his version of what reality was supposed to be. But this failed and left the *Motif* vandalized. He was insane, like his son Reziko.

It was Omer who used the Ankh of Extrusion to repair the damage to the *Motif* caused by his son Fabio. The repair process was essentially a retrace of Darwin's *Motif* involving an erase followed by an extrusion. With the *Motif* removed, chaos ruled once again, and all of echo ceased to exist. The only problem with re-extruding the *Motif* was that performing an erase and an extrude at the same time used up all of your blood in the process. The *Motif* could not return it to you once you reached the center. As Omer's last dying act, he used the gift at the center to convey the Ankh, by aurora borealis, through the Obscurio to the hands of his son. Grayson didn't know if his father succeeded in repairing the *Motif*. He used the Ankh to extrude a new *Motif*, so there would at least be one in place to reestablish the existence of echo. This act of determination is how we ended up with two *Motifs* stabilizing echo.

My first shuttlecraft, the *Zanna*, was originally created with the intent of traveling back in time to rescue Grayson's sister Zanna from her brother Fabio's final vengeance at the Pit of Eternity. But as I learned more about the last great uprising, I feared my shuttlecraft could not endure the Obscurio that rushed in when the *Motif* was erased. In the *Zanna*, I relied on the *Motif* to maintain the ship's parts integrity. If the *Motif* did not exist, I feared that the ship would fall apart. After mediating the *Vechnost* and obtaining that "mark" within me, I considered building a ship to attempt the crossing through the Obscurio, but after thinking about it, I was not convinced I could stay on course after entering the Obscurio. It wasn't until I was exposed to the mathematical process of FSL that the possibility of maintaining a course inside the Obscurio began to dance around my mind again. That is why I built the *Shutterfly*. It worked in both time loops, so I at least had that going for me.

Before departure, I created a few cloaked scanners infused with the *Vechnost* along with a new *Vechnost* based control ring that I wore. I didn't want any *Motif* sourced technology on my person. I replaced the *Motif*-based cloaked scanners in my boots with the *Vechnost* infused ones, but I also brought along four additional ones in the cockpit for my final journey. This bring-along was my attempt to try to have a portable Ohm. Once I pass back in time, far enough, *Tiger Mountain* will cease to exist.

I delayed long enough and set my course toward Splendor. There is an axiom in the library of Splendor. It hangs on the wall between two of the many bookcases, an embroidered tapestry reading, "All roads lead to Splendor."

The same could be true for ships. All courses lead to Splendor. It did not matter what my heading was because I planned to shift through echo, putting the *Shutterfly* to the final test. Would a *Vechnost* based ship hold together so close to the source of the *Motif?*

Long ago, when I took *Tiger Mountain* on that original epic journey, I obtained star charts of the sector surrounding Splendor. Ohm programmed Eve with all known star charts in Blinm, Starnet, and other echo space systems I traveled in. After bringing up Splendor's stars on my navigator's console, I projected them as an overlay across the *Shutterfly* canopy. I believe I was the only Splendorite to actually explore the space surrounding the planet where Splendor is located. While there are no other habitable planets within that solar system, there is a human habitable planet approximately four point three lightyears from the Splendor solar system. I named it Seron, which loosely translated as the bountiful basket. It was fertile and green with a thriving animal population, but no civilized species with language resided there. In the first time loop, I placed a Blinn replication module on the surface, but in this time loop, it did not seem that important. This planet was my goal.

Reaching into echo, I began the first shift of this new ship into the probable universe, which was my destination. The stars blurred and shifted. I heard the sound of the hull stress as we passed out of the temporal oddity of the Xanadu universe, returning to normal time, Splendor time.

"Eve, continuously scan the stars outside the ship and compare them to the star charts I have currently displayed. Highlight matches on the canopy when you detect them," I said.

I was not sure how effective this method would be, but having a computer verify my gut feeling about locations couldn't hurt. I made course adjustments multiple times trying to wring probability shifts out of the *Motif* as I continued my trek through the stars. These adjustments went on for at least an hour or more before the canopy hud highlighted one of the displayed stars. I locked in on that one and made a course adjustment along that heading. More stars began to fill in, and I finally accumulated enough reference points to plot a course for Seron.

Increasing to flux three, I heard the engines groan and settle down. I set the *Motif* aside, focusing on the system consoles. The coolant ran a little hot, so I backed the flux down to two point two, and it fell into a safer temperature range. The slower speed meant there was more time to investigate the problem. I tracked it down to a faulty coolant regulator and placed it on Eve's maintenance list. There was not a lot that could be done while the ship traveled at flux, but a basic flush and cycling of the regulator might free it up. I felt like I made great progress by locating the planet and setting a course, so I ordered some comfort food from the San Francisco offerings. After eating, I took a nap in the mini quarters I borrowed from the basic dual bunk bed design aboard the *Contender.*

I slept longer than I intended and was woke by Eve, informing me we were approaching the planet. I placed the *Shutterfly* in orbit around Seron and issued a set of Starnet operations considered standard procedure when you first encounter a new planet. It was mainly surface scans, geological surveys, and atmospheric modeling. I took this time to instruct Eve to run a series of diagnostics on the ship and apply any maintenance plans that seemed appropriate.

While the maintenance tasks ran and the standard operations took place, I took the time to bring up the control window for the temporal operations. This control window was taken directly from the shuttlecraft *Zanna* and was probably one of the crudest of all the systems. It was based on the work of an Opturi scientist who proposed that just as flux fields could push a ship through space, flux fields could also push a starship through time. She made a basic comparison to the way an electromagnet works. When you apply an electric charge to the copper windings, the permanent magnet is propelled away from the field. In her proof, the flux fields took the place of wrapped copper, and the ship took on the role of the permanent magnet. The electric charge driving the system became graviton waves that could be found in abundance near the surface of stars or black holes.

I went over the plan in my head. The plan is to closely orbit the surface of Splendor's sun while maintaining the flux field profile to propel the ship backward in time. At some point, I will travel far enough back in time that the *Motif* will cease to exist. That is when I'll encounter the Obscurio. Because I will be in orbit around a sun that will suddenly cease to exist, I face the possibility of being randomly hurled throughout the Obscurio. This moment is when the interleaved FSL drive will be used. When it becomes apparent I am about to be consumed by the Obscurio, I will initiate an FSL jump sequence in a straight line from the last known point. The goal is to arrive on the other side of the Obscurio before Omer makes the repair attempt on Darwin's *Motif.* The limitation of the system is braking. The reversal of the chemstream engines acts as my temporal brake, but I could not stop exactly at a specific time. I will have to start braking as soon as the Obscurio collapses and I am on the other side. At that point, I will be hurtling farther back in time until I can reverse the field.

The maintenance cycles completed, and I broke orbit from Seron. I obtained a star coordinate for Splendor and headed there at flux speed. I nudged the flux drive up to three and checked the cooling display, relieved to see it running much cooler than before. Deciding to chance it, I increased to flux four and felt a little ship shutter which settled down quickly as Eve auto-adjusted the velocity isolators. The ship ran to spec. I pushed the flux drive up to four point two and did the math. It took about five days to travel one lightyear at this speed, so it took around twenty-four days to reach the planet of Splendor from Seron. This long wait is why I placed the Cryovirts in the cargo hold to eliminate the monotony of space travel. I hung around for another hour, keeping an eye on the systems and all consoles reported stable readings. I asked Eve to wake me in case of an emergency or arrival at the destination. I set my shield to space suit mode with a one-hour delay. After I was in suspended animation for an hour, my cloaked scanners kicked in and surround me with the shield. If the ship did blow up while I was asleep, I might have a few seconds to use an escape vignette. At least those were my last thoughts as the gas of the Cryovirt clouded my vision, and I fell into a deep sleep.

I awoke from the Cryovirt, dehydrated and stiff, hesitantly emerging from my chamber, wishing I thought to remember to place some water nearby. I dropped the shield and stumbled to the replicator panel, and rasped out a command for water which I guzzled down before requesting more. I think the next time I do this, I'll try to have a medjector in the chamber set to rehydrate. It took me about twenty minutes or so to fully recover from the cryogenic sleep and get to my feet. I sat there chugging water then visiting the bathroom after that. This process was definitely not my preferred mode of travel.

The good news was that I was there, or at least approaching the solar system where the planet of Splendor resided in physical space. "Eve, take up a position between the fourth planet and its moon," I said.

"Adjusting course to new heading, arrival time thirteen minutes and seventeen seconds," Eve replied.

I felt good enough to eat some food, but I didn't want to chance it too much, so I asked Ohm for some soup Du jour from one of the San Francisco markets. The cream of broccoli was very delicious, with a hint of bacon. I finished a glass of cranberry juice and finally felt fully hydrated again. We came to a full stop between the planet of Splendor and Splendor's moon. I instructed Ohm to drop one of the large ship transport spheres at this location. I wanted a way to transport a ship to this location at some future date.

Having reached the final point where I could still back out of this insane plan, I checked my courage one more time. I counted on making up the lost time with family and friends on the return trip. I had an idea I wanted to try out for final braking. Setting aside all thoughts of regret, I brought up the console containing the flux field modifications for time travel. I set a course for The Sun with the intent to achieve orbit.

"Ohm, this may be my last transmission for a while. If I don't return, protect the mountain as we previously discussed. If the Guardians or Squires ask about my whereabouts, you can let them know I am on a temporal mission with no predicted return date but offer no more information," I said.

"Understood," Ohm replied, adding, "good luck," which lifted my spirits.

The *Shutterfly* dove into the outer corona of The Sun as I brought up the shields to fend off the heat. I routed the power from the cloaking system to reinforce the shielding. I would not need the cloak during this phase. Sensors detected a wide graviton belt, and I altered the orbit to drop into the stream. After activating the flux field modifications, a low "whoom" was heard from the rear section of the ship. I calculated the FSL course to lead the ship out of The Sun's corona against the orbital plane of the planets in this solar system. Because I could emerge from the Obscurio at any possible time, I wanted to avoid the possibility of slamming into a planet, a moon, or amy other celestial body.

Keeping an eye on the sensors, I thought I noticed the stars start to drift in reverse. I kept a series of displays open on the console and focused on them all.

The outer hull temperature rose, but the additional power routed to shields held the temperature at bay. The orbit speed was irrelevant. It was more about surfing the graviton wave, trying to stay in an energized particle state while maintaining as full immersion as possible inside the graviton field.

The increased flux energy produced a more visible effect, and I noticed the star drift on the console pick up at a more rapid pace. All I looked for was about a twelve hundred year regression. That was my best guess at when the last *Motif* extrusion occurred. The flux temperature coolant rose, and the hull temperature rose despite the shields and the reinforced energy. I used some new formula on the hull plating that was supposed to offer more resistance to high temperatures. I guess this mission would be the literal "trial by fire" for these components. The flux drive held steady, consuming the equivalent energy of traveling at the flux three speed. I bumped it up to three point six, and the low "whoom" from the back began to howl at a higher frequency, in an oscillating fashion, as the ship started shaking. I was tempted to slow the engine down, but I held off for a moment, and the shaking subsided as Eve compensated with adjustments to the velocity isolators. While checking the cooling system, I saw she ran at about ninety percent hot, which worried me. I knew sustained high temps could damage the system, and there was the return trip to think about. The higher flux energy, however, caused the star drift recorded by the sensors to increase at an accelerated rate. I focused on the navigation control window and maneuvered the ship to a slightly stronger graviton wave. That's when it happened.

The Sun disappeared, and a series of screeching groans rippled through the ship as the absence of the large gravity-generating device stressed the structural integrity. I dropped to half flux, afraid to cut off the engine so quickly when under such high temperatures, and engaged the FSL. The groaning sounds from the back of the ship stopped, and the back and forth clickety-clack of the dual FSL system resonated throughout the ship. The view through the canopy was of a dull grey, producing a slight headache. At first, it seemed like a rolling mist, but it quickly settled down to a uniform nothing. I was in the void between the existence of everything and the existence of total chaos.

I activated the four *Vechnost* infused cloaked scanners and used the control ring to bring up the auragraphic display to select the space suit shield. I was not sure what good it would actually do. Even if the ship fell apart inside this grey void, escape vignettes would be of no use. I resumed my inspection of the ship's systems and was happy to see that the flux drive cooling dropped down into the safe zone. Nudging the power down even further to one-quarter flux produced no visible change through the cockpit viewport. The scanners recorded nothing, which was not surprising.

I decided to try and guide my destination using the *Vechnost*. Working with the *Vechnost* these past few weeks gave me more confidence in using it. I still did not feel as comfortable with it as I did with the *Motif*, but at least I no longer feared it. Reaching out through the front of the ship, I imagined the tentacles of the *Vechnost* snaking out, pulling the shuttlecraft in the right direction, guiding it through this void to the destination I had in mind. That destination was the safe arrival on the other side of the Obscurio.

Pacing the ship, I felt my headache get worse. I wondered if this was it?

Maybe this was my fate, to exist for an eternity in the Obscurio that lies between what is and what was. I continued the seeking, with my mind, extending ever farther from the ship with the tentacles, looking for something to wrap around, to grab on to, to reel myself in. And then, slowly, the mist started rolling again, and streaks of color flowed past the *Shutterfly* shooting forward only to be gobbled up by the mist.

I took my seat at the console, focusing on the flux field modifications panels. The Obscurio started churning more and more and finally gave way to a blackness that quickly filled with blinking stars. I made it through. I was on the other side of the Obscurio. I cut the FSL drives and started up the chemstream engines to begin braking. There was a slight lurch when the flux powered down as the three engine systems switched roles. While keeping an eye on the speed of the solar drift, I threw the engines in full reverse, trying to stop the ship before I went too far back in time.

It took a minute or two, but the ship finally came to a full stop. My headache lessened a bit but was still nagging me. The basic concept worked. The FSL vectored the *Shutterfly* at a right angle to the planetary orbital planes giving me plenty of open space to brake within. I checked the damage report, and there were a few minor systems out, including the long-range sensors, and the replication system. It looked like Eve was able to compensate for the other down systems. I don't know if it was just temporal jet lag or what. but I felt completely wiped out with a strong need to lay down. I didn't have the mental capacity to figure out how much time I needed to wait before the event I returned for happened again. I could tell there were at least several days, and I was about five hours away from the planet. I set course for Splendor, instructing Eve to place the ship into orbit when we arrived. I headed back to my bunk, asking Eve to wake me when we arrived at the planet.

CHAPTER 65

No Good Scoundrel

I awoke to a hangover headache, which I felt was unfair because I haven't had a drink in weeks. This impairment was an unexpected side effect that I didn't anticipate, being incapacitated in the past. I checked the date, compared to passing through the Obscurio, and guessed there were about nine days, Splendor time before the Obscurio returned. Setting a course for the planet's surface, I intended to fly the ship through echo, traversing the entire range from Splendor to the Vectorless Vale.

I needed to locate Zanna, find an echo double of her, make the switch, and place her in the Cryovirt, all while avoiding detection. In Grayson's recounting of the tale, he mentioned the Obscurio broke apart and traveled no farther as he observed it while standing in the Vectorless Vale. This would be my plan as well, fetch Zanna, head for the Vectorless Vale, and wait this thing out.

The descent into the atmosphere was a little rough, but I raised the shields before atmospheric entry, and the ship took no damage. I piloted the *Shutterfly* to the continent, near the equator, where the castle of Splendor stood. Activating the cloak as I neared the area, I performed a flyby over the forest of Rayleaf, leaving behind a sonic boom as a gift for Joshua.

It was a straight course south from there, and I thought of the *Motif*. Grayson's *Motif* didn't exist yet, so I brought up the image of Darwin's *Motif* in my mind and started reaching for the farthest echoes. I shifted echo, and the *Shutterfly* groaned. The effects of quickly traversing probability rippled across the hull as I recklessly manipulated echo. I reached deeper, traveling faster than I ever have before, as I rocketed toward the Vectorless Vale.

Mountains rose and fell. I crossed seas and deserts. Forests grew and burned only to grow again as I passed through every landscape imaginable, even fantastical landscapes. Along the way, various flying creatures briefly joined me. A flock of flying horses kept pace for a time until I passed into a cloud front to emerge in another echo. Hippogryphs rose to meet the ship, twirled and zoomed, then fell back. A large dragon descended from above, attempting to force me from the sky, only to have its claws rebuffed by the shielding that sparked and tweaked from the physical contact. I passed through a sky filled with fantastic machines driven by steam power and propellers. There were creatures from dreams flowing through the sky on gossamer wings, only to be rattled and tossed aside in the disturbance of the *Shutterfly*'s wake. The landscape changed from organic to geometric as mechanical snakes lept out of hexagon holes, trying to make my ship their lunch.

After traveling deep into echo, I pulled out the vignette for Zanna and focused on her image. Even from this classic miniature painting, crafted by Darwin so long ago, her beauty was evident. If I had to nail down one single attribute of her beauty, it was the symmetrical nature of her face. Her facial proportions were nearly identical on each side. I tried to activate her vignette in the past, which was now the future from my current point of view, and it never worked. But this time, I felt something, and the portrait of Zanna that remained static for so long came to life. Her face was dirty, her hair was a mess, and there was a look of fear and distrust in her eyes as she met my gaze, not knowing who I was or how I obtained her vignette. She was chained to a wall so I couldn't pull her through at this time.

"My name's Sam. I'm coming to rescue you. Take this token. It will act as a beacon so I can find you," I said to Zanna as I held up a cloaked scanner in a non-cloaked state.

She shook her head yes and managed to pull one of her chained arms close enough to her head so it became visible through the vignette communication. Reaching in slightly, I placed the cloaked scanner in her hand, saying, "You don't have to hold on to it. The token will hide itself. Don't despair."

I already set the cloaked scanner to hide and evade mode while mapping, but I also activated the beacon feature. I was still not sure how to locate the cloaked scanner, but at least there was a signal emitting somewhere. I knew, from the future memories, that Zanna was kept in a ruined keep near the Vectorless Vale. I returned my attention to piloting the *Shutterfly*, with one goal in mind, to reach the Vectorless Vale.

Approaching the Vectorless Vale is a lot like approaching Splendor. As you draw nearer, your options become limited. This limit was a good thing for me because it meant there was less probable area to cover while searching for the signal from the cloaked scanner.

After reaching the badlands, which were the gateway to the Vectorless Vale, I began a standard Starnet grid search pattern hoping something would turn up. I also launched the remaining three cloaked scanners to conduct a free-form atmospheric search with their search patterns set to fractal algorithms splitting the difference against my ship-based grid approach. While the *Shutterfly* was on autopilot, I headed back to the cargo area and set up the Cryovirt to receive Zanna. I gathered up the supplies I would need when I finally headed out of the ship. I put on a pair of climbing gloves and placed a medjector and a standard Starnet gleam gun in my pants pockets. Returning to the cockpit, I checked on the scanning process, and there was still no signal for me to home in on. The replicators were still down, so I located some water and a food pack from the emergency rations locker. I ate what could be my last meal in silence.

I thought about the grisly task ahead of me. I didn't need to wait for the signal to be found to locate the echo of Zanna. A variation of her had to be nearby. I located a craggy knoll with a fairly flat top and set the ship down, instructing Eve to keep the engines in a low power idle state so we could take off in a hurry. I lowered the ramp, walked outside of the *Shutterfly*, and activated the cloaked scanners hidden within my boot heels.

"Eve, can you hear me?" I asked.

"Yes, Sam, I can hear you," Eve replied.

"Close the entry ramp and remain on standby," I said.

"Standing by," Eve replied as I watched the ramp retract into its locked position, sealing the cloak and rendering the ship invisible.

I didn't have time to reproduce a *Vechnost* sturdy shingle, so I used the ring to bring up an auragraphic display. I unrolled the display and shrunk it down considerably, keeping it inside the shield. I should appear cloaked, but there was no way to verify that.

After activating the jetpack icon, I headed off in a vector across the landscape. Reaching into echo, I held one intention in mind, to find the nearby version of Zanna. I imagined her echo self was in a similar situation, trapped by an echo Fabio. I needed to be careful. I sought a mist bank and passed into it. I quickly brought up a strong wind to blow the mist away. In the distance, I saw the profile of a ruined keep. Making a beeline with the jetpack, I brought up the targeting option on the auragraphic display. One of my cloaked scanners reviewed the area to make a map. It revealed multiple targets stationed throughout the decaying keep. What I needed was a distraction. I wish I had the forethought to bring along some explosives, but I didn't put much thought into the minutia of performing these final acts. At least seventy to eighty percent of the features of this makeshift invisihud were no longer available. There was a shield, a cloak, and some repulsion features such as the jetpack and the anti-gravity boots.

Then it hit me. I brought a wand. I didn't know if the few magic spells I could recall would work in this distant echo, but I thought it was worth a try. I reviewed the map and thought I knew where the echo version of Zanna was located. There was a lone figure right next to a wall in a lower section. I needed to create a large enough distraction to draw enough guards away from the keep so I could sneak in and steal the body. And that is what I thought of her. I knew she was a living person I condemned to death, but she would die anyway when the Obscurio rolled in, erasing this echo. This moment was no time for a philosophical debate. I was a no-good scoundrel with a no-good task to do before I ran out of time. I was on the side of the keep farthest from the room where my quarry resided. As I took up my position, I sought the mist I dismissed earlier. I forced it forward, rolling and breaking against the stone walls of the keep as I pulled out my wand and shouted, "*Minima!*"

I targeted the front gate and supporting walls to the left and right of the gate, as well as a far turret. The multiple spells took effect in delayed stages, and the effects were staggering and loud. The wooden gates shattered and splintered as the spell caused the objects to shrink in size. The walls came down as stones holding them up were no longer of the appropriate size, and the structure could not support itself. Tucking my wand into the sleeve pocket, I used the jetpack to propel my cloaked self around to the side of the keep, up and over the wall.

For the most part, it worked. Many of the guards rush forward to see what the ruckus was about. Taking out the gleam gun, I set it to kill. I entered the keep from one of the upper levels. As soon as I opened the first door, I faced two guards who climbed the steps, presumably to head out and see what was going on. These were not men, per se. They were bipedal creatures of echo dressed in light armor, carrying forged metal weapons at their side. Firing my weapon, I struck them with the green gleam gun ray. It looked like one shot was all it took to disable them. I did not bother to check if they actually died. I treated this as if it were one of the aurastage programs I trained with when I stowaway aboard the *Explorer SSH-801*. If I encountered a lone or a couple of guards, I shot them dead while winding my way down the stairways revealed to me by the auragraphic display. At the bottom of the steps were two more guards standing in front of a wooden door. They detected me somehow, but it was too late. I fired upon them, and they fell to the floor. I tried the door and it was locked. After checking the guards, I found one of them carried a small ring of keys. It took me the third try before I found the one that opened this door. I headed inside, and there, chained to the wall, was Zanna's echo self. She looked around the room in a panicked state, but could not see me. Dropping the keyring, I fetched the medjector. I dialed up a mild dose of anesthesia and quickly applied it to her neck. She cried out a bit frightful before passing out, hanging from chains attached to the wall. I put away the medjector and pulled out my wand, targeting the shackles at her wrist, saying, "*Patentibus.*"

The shackles binding her wrist clicked, and I forced the rusty hinge open to free one of her wrists. I moved to the other side and did the same thing. Tucking my wand away in the sleeve pocket, I located the radius control on the auragraphic display. I extended the shield and cloak radius to encompass her. With her body free from the bindings, I proceeded to pick her up, carrying her in front of me as a groom might carry his bride. She was limp as a fish and heavier than she looked. I had to stop and put her on the ground to use the ring to activate the jetpack again. Once it activated, I picked up Zanna's echo self and lumbered back up the series of hallways and steps I used when descending to the cell. It was easy to know which way to go. All I had to do was follow the path of dead bodies. I made it back to the upper-level entrance and fled the area. Soon I was jetting away from the ruined keep, which was even more ruined now that it met me.

I tried to retrace my physical path as much as possible and returned to the flat plane where I started vectoring from before beginning this morbid task. It was hard enough to see in this dark and dismal echo, let alone try to find a cloaked ship within it. I started shifting echo back to the place where I left the *Shutterfly*. My arms were tired, which aggravated my headache even more.

Looking around the bleak landscape, I decided to take a short break. I set the body of echo Zanna on the ground, and I located the medjector. I changed the setting to a mild analgesic and gave myself a shot. I went ahead and returned the medjector to the anesthesia offering and returned it to my pocket. The next time I needed it, the medjector would be set and ready for use. I set the communications icon on the auragraphic display to open communication. This way, I could talk to Eve without fussing with the controls in the display. I picked up the limp body of Zanna once again and made my way across the landscape using the jetpack. With the short respite, I felt a renewed determination to find the *Shutterfly* and get on with this gruesome duty. I brought forth the *Motif* and made the slightest changes to this echo, seeking that which I needed so desperately. I called out, "Sam to Eve, come in. *Shutterfly*, please respond."

After several attempts and meandering around the flat plane where I presumed the *Shutterfly* to be, I finally heard a reply, "Sam, this is Eve."

"Open the hatch, Eve. I am returning to the ship," I said.

I looked around the landscape in all directions before I finally saw it. There was a light coming out of nowhere. I vectored across the plane, thankful for the jetpack mode. I don't think I could have done this if I needed to accomplish these tasks on foot.

Making my way up the ramp, I stepped into the *Shutterfly*. I asked Eve to close the ramp and take the ship to a hovering altitude of three hundred meters. I placed echo Zanna on the transporter pad and collapsed on the floor next to her. I searched around for the rest of the bottle of water I drank from earlier and finished it off. Damn, I was out of shape. Everything just hurt. I dragged myself to the front of the ship and took the pilot's seat on the left. The *Shutterfly* reached the altitude I requested, and I used the navigational controls to move the *Shutterfly* forward, setting a course in the direction where I located echo Zanna. Trying the same thing I did on the landscape below, I used the slightest shifts in echo with my intent to locate Zanna as the most important aspect of the echo I sought. I was sure the ship traveled past the location of the alternate ruined keep, and I felt a little despair. An icon flashed on the targeting display. The sensors picked up a reading from the cloaked scanner I sent through the vignette to Zanna, and I said, "Eve, recall the other three cloaked scanners and set a course for the detected beacon."

Focusing the short-range scanners on the beacon, I located a ruined fort. Luck seemed to have favored me this time. It was much more ruined, and I only detected a few life signs. Yes, one of them was in a basement section, near a wall. I increased altitude, placing the ship above the ruined fort. I was going to transport directly into the lower chamber. I headed back to the transporter pad, picked up the slumped form of echo Zanna, and held her in my arms. "Eve, transport us directly into the lower chamber. Keep a lock on me," I said.

The transporter pad energized, and the brightly lit ship interior collapsed in from the top and bottom of my eyes. It freaked me out, I hadn't traveled through a transporter stabilized by the *Vechnost* before, and I was surprised at the immediate difference. Instead of a dark place, it was a scary place. There was nothing peaceful about it, and all I could think about was how can I get out of here? Muted screams surrounded me in the dark. I felt like something was right next to me, waiting to pounce or get me. Then the reverse happened. I materialized in the dark cell, holding echo Zanna.

Looking around, I saw the real Zanna chained to the wall. But they both were real. That is what I was having a problem with. Glancing across the room from her, I noticed the door to this cell was closed. Even if I was detected, I had a few seconds before they could get it open. I propped the body of echo Zanna against the wall and reached into my pocket for the medjector. It took the real Zanna a moment before noticing the copy of herself lying on the floor, and she cried out softly to herself. With a press of the medjector to her neck, I sedated Zanna.

After returning the medjector to my pants pocket, I pulled out my wand. Once again, I used the *Patentibus* spell to open the shackles on Zanna's wrist before lowering her to the ground. I held back tears as I lifted up the echo Zanna and clamped each arm into the wrist shackles, locking them in place. It was harder than you think to do that, to hold up a limp body while trying to shackle her wrists in place. I felt like I lost part of my soul performing that action, and I wasn't sure how I was going to live with myself after this? With echo Zanna in place, I looked at them both. Anyone would be hard-pressed to tell them apart. Setting my grief aside, I picked up the real Zanna and held her close to me, and said, "Eve, two to transport."

The vertical collapse of the *Vechnost* infused transporter happened again. It wasn't just a fluke. I found myself in the cauldron of lost souls. The moans and whispers were everywhere. I could feel them centimeters away from my non-existent body. I tried to tell myself this was just my imagination, that it was this journey. But I knew I was lying to myself. Something was terrifying about the dark space the *Vechnost* based transporter placed you in. When I reached the point of nearly giving up hope, the bright lights of the interior of the *Shutterfly* rushed in as my eyes and the rest of my body materialized with me holding Zanna. I didn't waste a moment and dragged her limp form back to the cargo hold. I leaned her against the wall and opened up the Cryovirt I prepared for her. Placing her in the Cryovirt was difficult, and I strained my back in the process. I activated the controls, and the mist rolled over her as the sealing sound of hissing faded to nothing. I hobbled back to the front of the *Shutterfly*, taking my seat at the controls. I recovered the cloaked scanner I used as a beacon and set a course for the only direction left to go, deeper into echo, toward the Vectorless Vale.

It wasn't long before there was no more echo to traverse, and I came upon the ever-shifting terrain of the flat plane at the end of the rolling hills. This ridge marked the spot where all echo ended, and the Vectorless Vale began. This ridge was the plane I told Jorrie about when she pressed me about revealing how long I was trapped in time before returning to her and Erin. The time I morphed into a monster, trapped inside the tentacles of the *Vechnost*. I took some time, slowly maneuvering in and about the hills and jutting rock that formed the line between reality and chaos, before finally settling on a small plateau. Using the short-range sensors, I conducted a brief stability test before landing. It looked like the ground was stable enough to hold the ship's weight. After landing the *Shutterfly*, I launched a single cloaked scanner. The premise was to try and detect when the Obscurio approached, so I had some warning. I stared in a stupor at the ever-shifting plane that was the ground of the Vectorless Vale. Clouds in the sky formed, danced around, and burst into flame, sending soot down as rain touched the ever-changing ground bringing forth life that burst into flight only to burn up, casting the remains of their bodies down as ash to fertilize more of the same. In the hazy distance stood enormous jagged mountains with a hint of Equarius in their majesty. But they did not act like mountains as you or I might know them. They acted like creatures and freely moved around and collided with their neighboring mountains giving the impression they were wrestling each other for some preferred momentary spot that kept changing location. The sky was constantly changing. It was never a true blue, always a dark gradient of muted colors that did not form any hint of a horizon. It was more like a fractal algorithm whose translational offset was randomly animated to produce a new pattern every moment. Sometimes, you could see normal stars through the empty gaps in the fractal pattern, giving you hope there might be some galaxy beyond this place of madness, then the translational offset shifted again, and the next time you saw the stars, they were wildly dancing as if standing still was the silliest thing you could imagine.

I needed this rest, and I felt the burden of my recent activity weigh heavy on my physical frame. The headache let up, and I took the time to locate more water and a salty snack. It felt like waiting for the inevitable to occur was worse than the physical trials I went through. I wasn't sure what would happen if I fell asleep in this place, but I did not want to take that chance. I set the medjector to a mild stimulant and sat with it in my hand. I had a feeling it would flare up my headache, so I wanted to wait until the last possible moment before I dosed myself again.

The replicator was still down, and I didn't think about bringing any weed or alcohol. Jorrie's words in our last fight rang true when she called out my drinking problem. I wish we hadn't parted on such bad terms. I wondered what Erin thought when she finished her three-week training only to find that I disappeared? Would she care? Why did I really do this?

In my future memories, I remember telling Jorrie and Erin that it was my way to try to achieve some type of forgiveness from my Splendor peers. But as I sat here on the edge of reality, waiting for death or creation to come rolling in, I knew I would never be forgiven by my Splendor counterparts. Even if they sincerely welcomed me, I would always be suspicious, wondering if it was yet, another ruse to trick me or steal my technology. I was indeed cursed, and it wasn't something a demon of chaos or a Lord of Splendor enforced. It was a curse of my own making.

I could never trust any of them. Because if I did, that would mean sharing the technology I developed with them. I was already duped once, and I was sure they would do it again. There is no escape. My curse is to be alone forever, living forever, watching friends and lovers grow old and die until I finally go mad and take my own life or recklessly throw it away. Perhaps that is what I am doing here? Did I really think I could pull this off?

On paper, I'm sure it looked a lot like a suicide mission. But in my heart, I knew what this was about. I felt it the first time I read Grayson's tale of this event that I was now a part of. I was infuriated when Fabio dragged Zanna to her death along with himself. A part of me cried out, "No!" as I read the lines in the Splendor library. This mission was my way to say, "Fuck you," to Fabio and his crazy-ass notions of rewriting reality. You can't have Zanna too.

I must have drifted off because I awoke to an alarm sound. The cloaked scanner detected the approach of the Obscurio. I asked Eve to recover the cloaked scanner, but it was too late, and it disappeared into the approaching void. "Eve, get us into the air. We have to avoid that approaching cloud," I said.

The medjector was still in my hand, so I stuffed it into my pants pocket. The sleep did my headache some good. It was still there but not a raging bull anymore. We gained some altitude, and I moved the ship from the mountainous cliff area over the ever-changing terrain. I tried to stay as close to the line of reality as possible. I had no idea what type of turbulence existed beyond, and I doubted that Eve was prepared to navigate a randomly changing environment. The ship might fail to work if I took it out farther. The short-range scanners were going wild with their reported readings. They were not sure if it was solid ground below or not. Sometimes the ever-changing terrain appeared to be energy, and other times it registered as matter. I watched the approach of the cloud, but then below, a large hole appeared, and I knew in a second that it was the Pit of Eternity. This hole was the same pit I rode the fire horse out of so long ago. At least it seemed long ago, but in reality, I'm sure it might have only been a few years back when Candy and I traveled together. The appearance of the Pit of Eternity seemed to stabilize the flat terrain. The sensors read solid ground. I always wondered why the ground around the Pit of Eternity crumbled when that lord of chaos lept up to attack me. I guess even the inhabitants of this place could not reliably predict when the ground would be solid. Multiple life form readings appeared, two of them were dangerously close to the edge. Then I realized this was the point in Grayson's story where Isaac slays Fabio with an arrow. I tried directing the basic optical sensors in that direction and zoomed in on the scene. It was Fabio, and he held echo Zanna close to him. I watched in horror as an arrow tagged him in the right shoulder, knocking him off balance. The wild look on his face when he knew there was nowhere to step back to, nowhere to regain his footing. He grabbed wildly at echo Zanna, and she screamed her last breath before they both tumbled into the Pit of Eternity. Even though I read about this story, to see it unfold before my eyes shocked me to my core.

I didn't have time to think about that, though, proximity alarms were going off, and I raised the shields. It seemed the Obscurio didn't stop at the edge of the ridgeline as Grayson reported in his tale. The *Shutterfly* was buffeted and pushed farther out onto the ever-changing chaotic terrain. I tried gaining altitude, and this seemed to be working. The Obscurio did have a height, and from that vantage point, I could see the cloud was being drawn into the Pit of Eternity. I just had to wait it out. I set up my escape vector and used the thrusters to try to stay as close to the last known location of the ridgeline. As I expected, the air was much more turbulent, farther away from the solid ground of reality, and the ship dropped suddenly, only to rapidly gain height again. I feared being slammed into the ground and sought more altitude. This ascent might have been a mistake as I encountered a strong current pushing me farther away from the line of reality. From this new distance, I could see the end of the Obscurio approaching. I just needed to hang in there for another minute or two. The problem is that if I drifted any more, I feared I might not be able to return. I was like a swimmer being pulled farther and farther out to sea. I decided I could wait no longer and set the ship into motion. The *Shutterfly* struggled at first until I dropped to a lower height. It seemed to pick up some traction and hurled us forward toward the last known ridgeline and into the Obscurio cloud bank. I did not bother engaging the FSL drives. I thought of the *Vechnost* and imagined tentacles reaching out from my ship, parting the weakened Obscurio, and soon I burst through to the other side. This side was my reality, the reality of two *Motifs*. I dismissed the *Vechnost* and reached out with the image of Grayson's *Motif*, and I felt it alive and fresh. I sought the fastest imaginable passageway back to Splendor. The entire terrain bent and wrapped around me, leaving the *Shutterfly* traveling through an unobstructed tube. I increased speed and checked the temperature on the chemstream drive, finding it well within operational norms. This stability emboldened me to increase the speed, even more as I spun the tube I was in, twisting it and navigating along the bending pathways. I reached out with blue. I reached out with green. I sought the colors of a pleasant Splendor sky. When I felt the tube was sufficiently saturated, I unwrapped it all to find myself flying over a forest landscape. I was close and headed out over the nearby sea. Reaching out one more time, I pulled this starship into the echo that was Splendor. The hull rippled and groaned as I saw it shining on the horizon. The golden roofs of the marble spires glinted in The Sun as the castle sat upon the high jutting rock overlooking the sea. I couldn't help but do a flyby before setting a course for the upper atmosphere and outer space. I headed toward the moon. There was one last task to perform before returning to my time and, hopefully, my friends and family.

I chose a spot near the dark side of the moon, a nice, flat, level crater. I dragged the two large pieces making up this Blinn terraforming module from the cargo hold and transported them, one at a time, down to the moon's surface. I already preprogrammed them to make a docking base for the *Shutterfly*, similar to the one I constructed on Xanadu, for the launch. With the module in place and activated, I headed for the corona of The Sun and brought up the time travel control panel. To move forward in time, I needed to reverse the field and travel in the opposite direction against the graviton streams located within the surface of The Sun. I felt my headache flare up as I made my final orbital approach. Dropping the cloak, I routed all additional energy to the shields and used the short-range scanners to locate the graviton streams. Starting at flux one and increasing the flux field in point two five increments, I reached the equivalent of flux three point five. This speed was a little below what I used when traveling to the past, but I decided to set my exit point a little early. I continued the orbit of The Sun as I watched the stellar drift start to approach my targeted time for an exit. It was still a manual process, however, temporal braking. I never figured it out completely in any of the time loops. As I approached my targeted date, I dropped back on the flux field emission in the same manner as I increased them, in point two five increments, eventually disengaging the flux drive completely before altering course out of The Sun's corona. I activated an immediate full reverse from the chemstream engines and brought the ship to a full stop. While reversing course back to the moon of Splendor, I checked the star charts. I set my targeted date to three months before I left. In my future memories, I was always overshooting reentry by three months or more, so I thought I'd try and undershoot, this time, to see if I could dial it in better. I was nine days past the end of Erin's three-week boot camp. Whew, I felt like this was the closest I've ever been to hitting my return date, and I wasn't going to fuss over that. I scanned the location where I dropped the Blinn terraforming modules in the past, and there it was, a mini base on Splendor's moon. I set Eve to auto dock and watched as I descended to the moon's surface, and the ceiling closed over-head. I set the ship to power down mode and asked, "Ohm, are you there?"

"Yes, Sam, I am here. What do you need?" Ohm replied.

"I need a passage card to the black glass building," I said.

A sparkle appeared on the console, leaving behind a passage card to the hallway outside my apartment. I picked it up and headed back to the cargo hold.

Opening one of the small drawers in the Cryovirt unit, I pulled out a small box. It contained vignettes that I wanted to give to Zanna. The question now was, how would she react to all this?

"Ohm, start the revival process for the subject in the Cryovirt," I said.

I watched the mist fill the chamber, and I stood back as the sidewall dropped down and the glass lid retracted. She sat up, and I said, "Don't be alarmed. You are safe here."

Her time in the unit was not that long, so she did not suffer the full dehy-drating effects of long-term suspended animation. She looked over at me as she climbed out of the Cryovirt and said, "You're the man from the vignette."

"My name's Sam," I said, stepping forward to shake her hand.

She took it and looked me over before letting go of my hand. Even in her dirty wounded state, she was strikingly beautiful. I told her, "I am Grayson's grandson."

"Thank you for getting me out of that prison. I lost all hope," she said look-ing down, afraid to show me the despair in her eyes.

I handed her the small box I fetched from the Cryovirt drawer and said, "This is a small set of vignettes to get you started. But I do have some startling news to tell you."

She opened the box, briefly looked through the vignettes, then closed the box and slipped it into a pocket of her pants before asking, "What, what has happened?"

"A lot has happened. History recorded your death at the Pit of Eternity by the hands of your brother Fabio. Your father died repairing the *Motif*. Osric is now the King. The starship you are standing in is a time travel ship. I have brought you approximately twelve hundred years into the future to save your life. I located your echo self and chained her up in your cell. She died in your place. To preserve the timeline, I brought you forward so history would remain the same," I said.

She moved her head left and right and said, "You've got to be kidding?"

My headache started to flare up, and I said, "It will take time to process all this, I know. I am injured, and I have to get some help. You can come with me or leave via the vignettes. Talk to Isaac first," I said as I pulled out the vignette to floor twenty-three of the black glass building.

"All right. I'll go with you for now," she said.

I stood beside her, and I lifted up the vignette. I noticed she took in the style of the vignette I held in my hand. Once the image came to life, I put my hand on her shoulder, and we stepped through together. I motioned for her to follow me as I made my way to the first door along the hall. The apartment was empty, and I told her, "Feel free to make yourself at home. There's a bar over there, food in the kitchen, and a bathroom over there. She didn't consider any of my suggestions. Instead, she headed over to the glass windows and took in the view. I stumbled over to the white sofa and took a seat, putting my head in my hand.

When the headache started after entering the Obscurio, I thought, "How could I have been such a fool?" I spent all that time constructing *Vechnost* sturdy parts, but I forgot about the part that was still in my head. The broken invisihud was made of *Motif* sturdy parts. I wondered how much it morphed out of shape inside my brain?

The door to the apartment burst open, and in walked Candy asking, "Where the hell have you been?"

"Selling my soul to the devil," I replied as she walked into the apartment, finally noticing Zanna.

"Who are you?" Candy asked.

"I am Zanna," Zanna replied.

Candy looked at me and said, "Like the ship, *Zanna*?"

"Yep, the one and only," I said, falling over and laying my head down.

"What do you mean like the ship?" Zanna asked Candy.

"Holy shit, Sam, you're bleeding from your ears. What happened to him?" Candy asked Zanna, and that was the last thing I remember.

Made in United States
North Haven, CT
27 October 2022

26002045R00361